TRANSFINITE

THE ESSENTIAL A. E. VAN VOGT

A. E. VAN VOGT

Edited by Joe Rico and Rick Katze

NESFA
PRESS

P. O. Box 809
Framingham, MA 01701
www.nesfapress.org

FIRST EDITION
Third Printing
January 2019

ISBN: 978-1-886778-34-4

NESFA Press is an imprint of the
New England Science Fiction Association, Inc.

NESFA® is a registered trademark of the
New England Science Fiction Association, Inc.

dedicated to Bruce Pelz,
friend

CONTENTS

TRANSFINITE

THE MAN IN THE LABYRINTH

A s I was working on this volume, I wondered if there was any unifying theme of the stories collected within it. Certainly they are all gems of Science Fiction and testaments to the mastery of A. E. van Vogt. They range from the super-science background of "Recruiting Station" and "The Search" to the mundane setting of "The Ghost." They span eons of time as in "The Harmonizer," or one evening as in "The Sound." But no matter what the setting, every story is one of discovery of secrets—and the most important secret for a van Vogt character to discover is that of self.

Powerful figures learn they are pawns and pawns become major players. Victims become heroes in the blink of an eye, and bring invincible villains low. The world of every man is constantly recreated in a new image with every turn in the labyrinth of life.

My own labyrinth of life changed as I attempted to produce this book. My mundane workload increased to the point that I had no time to finish it. Fortunately my friends took up the load. I like to thank them, particularly Rick Katze, Priscilla and Mark Olson, and Tony Lewis. The scanning and OCR of "Black Destroyer" and "Discord in Scarlet" were done by Bill Shawcross of Rotten Apple Press, from microfiche.

It is always better to find your way with the help of friends.

Joe Rico

ALFRED E. VAN VOGT

A little over six decades ago, when I was a teenager between the freshman and sophomore college years, "Black Destroyer" caught my eye on a Harvard Square magazine stall. I did not at first realize that the author had accomplished the feat of making the *Astounding* cover with his first sale. It was the cover that caught my eye, but I would have bought the magazine anyway. I had been introduced to Jules Verne by my father more than a decade earlier, had discovered the magazines only a few years after that, and was by then an *Astounding* regular. Verne sold me on technology based adventure story, and Neil R. Jones and his Professor Jameson on weird-alien type space opera. The cover suggested the latter, so I was tempted to cut my next couple of classes (no, I didn't yield; I had started maturing by then).

I had also, by then, developed enough scientific education and critical power to realize why at least some stories in those genres were improbable, but I had already formed, perhaps unfortunately, the reflex-level distaste which I still have for the word "impossible."

The Black Destroyer, Coeurl (I may be spelling this wrongly; the editor should feel free to call attention to such slips, but please do it with a "sic" or a footnote. Readers have a right to data on the reliability of my memory; I have not reread any of the stories mentioned in this introduction at all recently), was the last survivor of a basically immortal species which had nevertheless never mastered interstellar travel.

The author justified this adequately. The sun had only one planet, the planet had no satellites, and the nearest other star was nine hundred light years away. All but the top rungs of the ladder to star flight were missing.

11

Even at that age, though, I was a little dubious about the ecology. That word had not yet come into general public consciousness, but water cycles and carbon cycles and nitrogen cycles were all, familiar to elementary science students. Coeurl's essential nutrient was phosphorus, which is an element and should not have disappeared from a world's biological cycle unless its nuclear structure was altered in the native's metabolism, presumably to obtain energy. Even then a life form reversing the reaction using stellar or some other energy source was conceivable. I couldn't help wondering, just in passing, where the phosphorus had gone.

Embarrassingly, I was less critical of another point which remained in my mind as background "knowledge" for something like sixty years. One of the biologists in the exploring human-staffed spacecraft was startled to find that Coeurl, dweller an a planet whose atmosphere was twenty eight percent chlorine, was not bothered by the presence of oxygen or lack of chlorine in the air of the. visiting ship. This caused the biologist to make the disastrous mistake of recommending that Coeurl be allowed aboard for study …

Well, most dangerous adventures can be traced back to mistakes, can't they? One of my biggest plotting problems is explaining why the character could have been so silly, or at least so ignorant.

Nothing was said or implied about the planet's being waterless, and I offer no excuse for failing to notice while reading "Black Destroyer" that any world with a chlorine-rich atmosphere and liquid water is also going to have a respectable amount of free oxygen. I had already taken high school chemistry, after all.

I raise this and some later points not to belittle Mr. van Vogt's science, which some people have done, but to remind readers that nothing used as background or inspiration by any science fiction writer, including me, should be taken as written on stone. A Hal Clement or an A. E. van Vogt fundamentalist is as ridiculous as any other kind, be it Homeric, Biblical, or Freudian. Read critically, always. Just be a little tolerant, please; the errors (I prefer the word "inconsistencies" myself) which you spot *may* have been essential to the plot, and it hurts to waste a promising story idea. Also, it may turn out that the mistake is on you. I have at least two stories to my (dis)credit in which Mercury has the same hemisphere always facing the sun. This not an exclusive club.

In any case, "Black Destroyer" and, a couple of months later in the same magazine, "Discord in Scarlet" made me a firm van Vogt fan. *Slan*, a full length novel serialized there in the next year or so, helped.

His tendency later on to base story ideas on more controversial aspects of science, such as the Bates eye-exercise fad and the non-Aristotelian aspect of "general semantics," sometimes made me a little unhappy, but did little if any real harm to the stories themselves. This, it seems to me, was because van Vogt had mastered, or possibly was born with, the most basic technique essential to science fiction and fantasy writers. He could work in the key details of a non standard background situation without slowing the pace of his story. After all, even John Campbell, the editor who bought his tales then and for years afterward, displayed the same tendency to use dianetics, psionics, and similar aberrations to a sometimes annoying (my own tastes show here) degree. I commonly use faster than light situations myself, and have been accused in consequence by at least one purist of being a fantasy and *not* a science fiction writer.

Van Vogt frequently re-used stories and story ideas already published as parts of longer and more complex ones, so it is a little hard to make a bibliography of his work. Again, I don't blame him; he provides interesting exercises for fledgling writers. Read "The Rull" and "The Sound" together from this book, and try to decide how you would combine them; then, if you can find copies—I don't think they are were included in here—read "Cooperate or Else" and "The Second Solution." Finally, again if you can find a copy, read the novel *The War Against the Rull.*

The first two stories I mentioned above, "Black Destroyer" and "Discord in Scarlet," were similarly used as part of the novel-length *Voyage of the (Space Ship) Beagle.* (I'm pretty sure the parenthesized words were in the title, but they may have been edited in by my memory to help me distinguish the book from Darwin's. It's a nuisance to have the neural network's insulation fraying with age, but I suppose it would be worse not to know it.)

Like many of his colleagues and competitors, again including myself, van Vogt took shots at the Fermi Paradox (if those aliens are really out there, shouldn't they visited us by now?) The one of his I liked best was "Asylum," which does appear here. Another I remember was "Not Only Dead Men," which does not. In the first of these I was struck not so much by the Fermi aspect as by an extremely good paragraph about the reaction of a supposed vastly superhuman intelligence to a work (a garden) of only slightly superhuman art. See whether you can spot it. If you really must base an author's standing on a single paragraph of his writings—unwise, in my opinion—I'd nominate that one for van Vogt.

To sum up a lot of the foregoing, he was an explorer of ideas, to whatever extent that one central idea can make a story. He did not, as far as I can judge, have much interest in developing characters to the extent now considered politically correct for "real literature" I don't blame him. In *The Art of Writing Science Fiction*, published by Fantasy Press in, as I recall, the 1950s, he claimed to use rules about such things as the word count of a scene which suggested strongly that he was much more interested in the action—the, pace—of his story. The rules certainly worked for him.

Some people nowadays tend to criticize a. story on the basis of its movie prospects.

"Black Destroyer" and "Discord in Scarlet" are straight space opera action which could probably be handled by present-day special effects techniques, and I'd very much like to see someone try them. For straightforward meaningful action, however, the Fermi-solution stories, "Asylum" and "Not Only Dead Men," would be my vote. The fact that, as the stories stand now, the viewers would have to think, really shouldn't make a competent screen writer hesitate.

You don't have to agree with me, of course. I've never had a chance to write a script.

Some of his stories I liked less than others, probably because of my personal taste in "reliable" science; but I don't recall anything by Alfred. E. van Vogt that did not meet the qualifications of a *story*.

Hal Clement
Milton, MA
December, 2002

BLACK DESTROYER

On and on Coeurl prowled! The black, moonless, almost starless night yielded reluctantly before a grim reddish dawn that crept up from his left. A vague, dull light, it was, that gave no sense of approaching warmth, no comfort, nothing but a cold, diffuse lightness, slowly revealing a nightmare landscape.

Black, jagged rock and black, unliving plain took form around him, as a pale-red sun peered at last above the grotesque horizon. It was then Coeurl recognized suddenly that he was on familiar ground.

He stopped short. Tenseness flamed along his nerves. His muscles pressed with sudden, unrelenting strength against his bones. His great forelegs—twice as long as his hindlegs—twitched with a shuddering movement that arched every razor-sharp claw. The thick tentacles that sprouted from his shoulders ceased their weaving undulation, and grew taut with anxious alertness.

Utterly appalled, he twisted his great cat head from side to side, while the little hairline tendrils that formed each ear vibrated frantically, testing every vagrant breeze, every throb in the ether.

But there was no response, no swift tingling along his intricate nervous system, not the faintest suggestion anywhere of the presence of the all-necessary id. Hopelessly, Coeurl crouched, an enormous catlike figure silhouetted against the dim reddish skyline, like a distorted etching of a black tiger resting on a black rock in a shadow world.

He had known this day would come. Through all the centuries of restless search, this day had loomed ever nearer, blacker, more frightening—this inevitable hour when he must return to the point where he began his systematic hunt in a world almost depleted of id-creatures.

The truth struck in waves like an endless, rhythmic ache at the seat of his ego. When he had started, there had been a few id-creatures in every hundred square miles, to be mercilessly rooted out. Only too well Coeurl knew in this ultimate hour that he had missed none. There were no id-creatures left to eat. In all the hundreds of thousands of square miles that he had made his own by right of ruthless conquest—until no neighboring coeurl dared to question his sovereignty—there was no id to feed the otherwise immortal engine that was his body.

Square foot by square foot he had gone over it. And now—he recognized the knoll of rock just ahead, and the black rock bridge that formed a queer, curling tunnel to his right. It was in that tunnel he had lain for days, waiting for the simple-minded, snakelike id-creature to come forth from its hole in the rock to bask in the sun—his first kill after he had realized the absolute necessity of organized extermination.

He licked his lips in brief gloating memory of the moment his slavering jaws tore the victim into precious toothsome bits. But the dark fear of an idless universe swept the sweet remembrance from his consciousness, leaving only certainty of death.

He snarled audibly, a defiant, devilish sound that quavered on the air, echoed and re-echoed among the rocks, and shuddered back along his nerves—instinctive and hellish expression of his will to live.

And then—abruptly—it came.

He saw it emerge out of the distance on a long downward slant, a tiny glowing spot that grew enormously into a metal ball. The great shining globe hissed by above Coeurl, slowing visibly in quick deceleration. It sped over a black line of hills to the right, hovered almost motionless for a second, then sank down out of sight.

Coeurl exploded from his startled immobility. With tiger speed, he flowed down among the rocks. His round, black eyes burned with the horrible desire that was an agony within him. His ear tendrils vibrated a message of id in such tremendous quantities that his body felt sick with the pangs of his abnormal hunger.

The little red sun was a crimson ball in the purple-black heavens when he crept up from behind a mass of rock and gazed from its shadows at the crumbling, gigantic ruins of the city that sprawled below him. The silvery globe, in spite of its great size, looked strangely inconspicuous against that vast, fairy-like reach of ruins. Yet about it was a leashed aliveness, a dynamic quiescence that, after a moment, made it stand out, dominating the foreground. A massive, rock-crushing thing of metal, it rested on a cradle made by its own weight in the harsh, resisting plain which began abruptly at the outskirts of the dead metropolis.

Coeurl gazed at the strange, two-legged creatures who stood in little groups near the brilliantly lighted opening that yawned at the base of the ship. His throat thickened with the immediacy of his need; and his brain grew dark with the first wild impulse to burst forth in furious charge and smash these flimsy, helpless-looking creatures whose bodies emitted the id-vibrations.

Mists of memory stopped that mad rush when it was still only electricity surging through his muscles. Memory that brought fear in an acid stream of weakness, pouring along his nerves, poisoning the reservoirs of his strength. He had time to see that the creatures wore things over their real bodies, shimmering transparent material that glittered in strange, burning flashes in the rays of the sun.

Other memories came suddenly. Of dim days when the city that spread below was the living, breathing heart of an age of glory that dissolved in a single century before flaming guns whose wielders knew only that for the survivors there would be an ever-narrowing supply of id.

It was the remembrance of those guns that held him there, cringing in a wave of terror that blurred his reason. He saw himself smashed by balls of metal and burned by searing flame.

Came cunning—understanding of the presence of these creatures. This, Coeurl reasoned for the first time, was a scientific expedition from another star. In the olden days, the coeurls had thought of space travel, but disaster came too swiftly for it ever to be more than a thought.

Scientists meant investigation, not destruction. Scientists in their way were fools. Bold with his knowledge, he emerged into the open. He saw the creatures become aware of him. They turned and stared. One, the smallest of the group, detached a shining metal rod from a sheath, and held it casually in one hand. Coeurl loped on, shaken to his core by the action; but it was too late to turn back.

Commander Hal Morton heard little Gregory Kent, the chemist, laugh with the embarrassed half gurgle with which he invariably announced inner uncertainty. He saw Kent fingering the spindly metalite weapon.

Kent said: "I'll take no chances with anything as big as that."

Commander Morton allowed his own deep chuckle to echo along the communicators. "That," he grunted finally, "is one of the reasons why you're on this expedition, Kent—because you never leave anything to chance."

His chuckle trailed off into silence. Instinctively, as he watched the monster approach them across that black rock plain, he moved forward until he stood a little in advance of the others, his huge form bulking the transparent metalite suit. The comments of the men pattered through the radio communicator into his ears:

"I'd hate to meet that baby on a dark night in an alley."

"Don't be silly. This is obviously an intelligent creature. Probably a member of the ruling race."

"It looks like nothing else than a big cat, if you forget those tentacles sticking out from its shoulders, and make allowances for those monster forelegs."

"Its physical development," said a voice, which Morton recognized as that of Siedel, the psychologist, "presupposes an animal-like adaptation to surroundings, not an intellectual one. On the other hand, its coming to us like this is not the act of an animal but of a creature possessing a mental awareness of our possible identity. You will notice that its movements are stiff, denoting caution, which suggests fear and consciousness of our weapons. I'd like to get a good look at the end of its tentacles. If they taper into handlike appendages that can really grip objects, then the conclusion would be inescapable that it is a descendant of the inhabitants of this city. It would be a great help if we could establish communication with it, even though appearances indicate that it has degenerated into a historyless primitive."

Coeurl stopped when he was still ten feet from the foremost creature. The sense of id was so overwhelming that his brain drifted to the ultimate verge of chaos. He felt as if his limbs were bathed in molten liquid his very vision was not quite clear, as the sheer sensuality of his desire thundered through his being.

The men—all except the little one with the shining metal rod in his fingers—came closer. Coeurl saw that they were frankly and curiously examining him. Their lips were moving, and their voices beat in a monotonous, meaningless rhythm on his ear tendrils. At the same time he had the sense of waves of a much higher frequency—his own communication level—only it was a machinelike clicking that jarred his brain. With a distinct effort to appear friendly, he broadcast his name from his ear tendrils, at the time pointing at himself with one curving tentacle.

Gourlay, chief of communications, drawled: "I got a sort of static in my radio when he wiggled those hairs, Morton. Do you think—"

"Looks very much like it," the leader answered the unfinished question. "That means a job for you, Gourlay. If it speaks by means of radio waves, it might not be altogether impossible that you can create some sort of television picture of its vibrations, or teach him the Morse code."

"Ah," said Siedel, "I was right. The tentacles each develop into seven strong fingers. Provided the nervous system is complicated enough, those fingers could, with training, operate any machine."

Morton said: "I think we'd better go in and have some lunch. Afterward, we've got to get busy. The material men can set up their machines and start gathering data on the planet's metal possibilities, and so on. The others can do a little careful exploring. I'd like some notes on architecture and on the scientific development of this race, and particularly what happened to wreck the civilization. On earth civilization after civilization crumbled, but always a new one sprang up in its dust. Why didn't that happen here? Any questions?"

"Yes. What about pussy? Look, he wants to come in with us."

Commander Morton frowned, an action that emphasized the deep-space pallor of his face. "I wish there was some way we could take it in with us, without forcibly capturing it. Kent, what do you think?"

"I think we should first decide whether it's an it or a him, and call it one or the other. I'm in favor of him. As for taking him in with us—" The little chemist shook his head decisively. "Impossible. This atmosphere is twenty-eight percent chlorine. Our oxygen would be pure dynamite to his lungs."

The commander chuckled. "He doesn't believe that, apparently." He watched the catlike monster follow the first two men through the great door. The men kept an anxious distance from him, then glanced at Morton questioningly. Morton waved his hand. "O.K. Open the second lock and let him get a whiff of the oxygen. That'll cure him."

A moment later, he cursed his amazement. "By Heaven, he doesn't even notice the difference! That means he hasn't any lungs, or else the chlorine is not what his lungs use. Let him in! You bet he can go in! Smith, here's a treasure house for a biologist—harmless enough if we're careful. We can always handle him. But what a metabolism!"

Smith, a tall, thin, bony chap with a long, mournful face, said in an oddly forceful voice: "In all our travels, we've found only two higher forms of life. Those dependent on chlorine, and those who need oxygen— the two elements that support combustion. I'm prepared to stake my reputation that no complicated organism could ever adapt itself to both gases in a natural way. At first thought I should say here is an extremely advanced form of life. This race long ago discovered truths of biology that we are just beginning to suspect. Morton, we mustn't let this creature get away if we can help it."

"If his anxiety to get inside is any criterion," Commander Morton laughed, "then our difficulty will be to get rid of him."

He moved into the lock with Coeurl and the two men. The automatic machinery hummed; and in a few minutes they were standing at the bottom of a series of elevators that led up to the living quarters.

"Does that go up?" One of the men flicked a thumb in the direction of the monster.

"Better send him up alone, if he'll go in."

Coeurl offered no objection, until he heard the door slam behind him; and the closed cage shot upward. He whirled with a savage snarl, his reason swirling into chaos. With one leap, he pounced at the door. The metal bent under his plunge, and the desperate pain maddened him. Now, he was all trapped animal. He smashed at the metal with his paws, bending it like so much tin. He tore great bars loose with his thick tentacles. The machinery screeched; there were horrible jerks as the limitless power pulled the cage along in spite of projecting pieces of metal that scraped the outside walls. And then the cage stopped, and he snatched off the rest of the door and hurtled into the corridor.

He waited there until Morton and the men came up with drawn weapons. "We're fools," Morton said. "We should have shown him how it works. He thought we'd double-crossed him."

He motioned to the monster, and saw the savage glow fade from the coal-black eyes as he opened and closed the door with elaborate gestures to show the operation.

Coeurl ended the lesson by trotting into the large room to his right. He lay down on the rugged floor, and fought down the electric tautness of his nerves and muscles. A very fury of rage against himself for his fright consumed him. It seemed to his burning brain that he had lost the advantage of appearing a mild and harmless creature. His strength must have startled and dismayed them.

It meant greater danger in the task which he now knew he must accomplish: To kill everything in the ship, and take the machine back to their world in search of unlimited id.

With unwinking eyes, Coeurl lay and watched the two men clearing away the loose rubble from the metal doorway of the huge old building. His whole body ached with the hunger of his cells for id. The craving tore through his palpitant muscles, and throbbed like a living thing in his brain. His every nerve quivered to be off after the men who had wandered into the city. One of them, he knew, had gone—alone.

The dragging minutes fled; and still he restrained himself, still he lay there watching, aware that the men knew he watched. They floated a metal machine from the ship to the rock mass that blocked the great half-open door, under the direction of a third man. No flicker of their fingers escaped his fierce stare, and slowly, as the simplicity of the machinery became apparent to him, contempt grew upon him.

He knew what to expect finally, when the flame flared in incandescent violence and ate ravenously at the hard rock beneath. But in spite of his preknowledge, he deliberately jumped and snarled as if in fear, as that white heat burst forth. His ear tendrils caught the laughter of the men, their curious pleasure at his simulated dismay.

The door was released, and Morton came over and went inside with the third man. The latter shook his head.

"It's a shambles. You can catch the drift of the stuff. Obviously, they used atomic energy, but ... but it's in wheel form. That's a peculiar development. In our science, atomic energy brought in the nonwheel machine. It's possible that here they've progressed *further* to a new type of wheel mechanics. I hope their libraries are better preserved than this, or we'll never know. What could have happened to a civilization to make it vanish like this?"

A third voice broke through the communicators: "This is Siedel. I heard your question, Pennons. Psychologically and sociologically speaking, the only reason why a territory becomes uninhabited is lack of food."

"But they're so advanced scientifically, why didn't they develop space flying and go elsewhere for their food?"

"Ask Gunlie Lester," interjected Morton. "I heard him expounding some theory even before we landed."

The astronomer answered the first call. "I've still got to verify all my facts, but this desolate world is the only planet revolving around that miserable red sun. There's nothing else. No moon, not even a planetoid. And the nearest star system is *nine hundred light-years* away.

"So tremendous would have been the problem of the ruling race of this world, that in one jump they would not only have had to solve interplanetary but interstellar space traveling. When you consider how slow our own development was—first the moon, then Venus—each success leading to the next, and after centuries to the nearest stars; and last of all to the anti-accelerators that permitted galactic travel. Considering all this, I maintain it would be impossible for any race to create such machines without practical experience. And with the nearest star so far away, they had no incentive for the space adventuring that makes for experience."

Coeurl was trotting briskly over to another group. But now, in the driving appetite that consumed him, and in the frenzy of his high scorn, he paid no attention to what they were doing. Memories of past knowledge, jarred into activity by what he had seen, flowed into his consciousness in an ever developing and more vivid stream.

From group to group he sped, a nervous dynamo—jumpy, sick with his awful hunger. A little car rolled up, stopping in front of him, and a formidable camera whirred as it took a picture of him. Over on a mound of rock, a gigantic telescope was rearing up toward the sky. Nearby, a disintegrating machine drilled its searing fire into an ever-deepening hole, down and down, straight down.

Coeurl's mind became a blur of things he watched with half attention. And ever more imminent grew the moment when he knew he could no longer carry on the torture of acting. His brain strained with an irresistible impatience; his body burned with the fury of his eagerness to be off after the man who had gone alone into the city.

He could stand it no longer. A green foam misted his mouth, maddening him. He saw that, for the bare moment, nobody was looking.

Like a shot from a gun he was off. He floated along in great, gliding leaps, a shadow among the shadows of the rocks. In a minute, the harsh terrain hid the spaceship and the two-legged beings.

Coeurl forgot the ship, forgot everything but his purpose, as if his brain had been wiped clear by a magic, memory-erasing brush. He circled widely, then raced into the city, along deserted streets, taking short cuts with the ease of familiarity, through gaping holes in time-weakened walls, through long corridors of moldering buildings. He slowed to a crouching lope as his ear tendrils caught the id vibrations.

Suddenly, he stopped and peered from a scatter of fallen rock. The man was standing at what must once have been a window, sending the glaring rays of his flashlight into the gloomy interior. The flashlight clicked off. The man, a heavy-set, powerful fellow, walked off with quick, alert steps. Coeurl didn't like that alertness. It presaged trouble; it meant lightning reaction to danger.

Coeurl waited till the human being had vanished around a corner, then he padded into the open. He was running now, tremendously faster than a man could walk, because his plan was clear in his brain. Like a wraith, he slipped down the next street, past a long block of buildings. He turned the first corner at top speed; and then, with dragging belly, crept into the half-darkness between the building and a huge chunk of debris. The street ahead was barred by a solid line of loose rubble that made it like a valley, ending in a narrow, bottlelike neck. The neck had its outlet just below Coeurl.

His ear tendrils caught the low-frequency waves of whistling. The sound throbbed through his being; and suddenly terror caught with icy fingers at his brain. The man would have a gun. Suppose he leveled one burst of atomic energy—*one burst*—before his own muscles could whip out in murder fury.

A little shower of rocks streamed past. And then the man was beneath him. Coeurl reached out and struck a single crushing blow at the shimmering transparent headpiece of the spacesuit. There was a tearing sound of metal and a gushing of blood. The man doubled up as if part of him had been telescoped. For a moment, his bones and legs and muscles combined miraculously to keep him standing. Then he crumpled with a metallic clank of his space armor.

Fear completely evaporated, Coeurl leaped out of hiding. With ravenous speed, he smashed the metal and the body within it to bits. Great chunks of metal, torn piecemeal from the suit, sprayed the ground. Bones cracked. Flesh crunched.

It was simple to tune in on the vibrations of the id, and to create the violent chemical disorganization that freed it from the crushed bone. The id was, Coeurl discovered, mostly in the bone.

He felt revived, almost reborn. Here was more food than he had had in the whole past year.

Three minutes, and it was over, and Coeurl was off like a thing fleeing dire danger. Cautiously, he approached the glistening globe from the opposite side to that by which he had left. The men were all busy at their tasks. Gliding noiselessly, Coeurl slipped unnoticed up to a group of men.

Morton stared down at the horror of tattered flesh, metal and blood on the rock at his feet, and felt a tightening in his throat that prevented speech. He heard Kent say:

"He *would* go alone, damn him!" The little chemist's voice held a sob imprisoned; and Morton remembered that Kent and Jarvey had chummed together for years in the way only two men can.

"The worst part of it is," shuddered one of the men, "it looks like a senseless murder. His body is spread out like little lumps of flattened jelly, but it seems to be all there. I'd almost wager that if we weighed everything here, there'd still be one hundred and seventy-five pounds by earth gravity. That'd be about one hundred and seventy pounds here."

Smith broke in, his mournful face lined with gloom: "The killer attacked Jarvey, and then discovered his flesh was alien—uneatable. Just like our big cat. Wouldn't eat anything we set before him—" His words died out in sudden, queer silence. Then he said slowly: "Say, what about that creature? He's big enough and strong enough to have done this with his own little paws."

Morton frowned. "It's a thought. After all, he's the only living thing we've seen. We can't just execute him on suspicion, of course—"

"Besides," said one of the men, "he was never out of my sight."

Before Morton could speak, Siedel, the psychologist, snapped, "Positive about that?"

The man hesitated. "Maybe he was for a few minutes. He was wandering around so much, looking at everything."

"Exactly," said Siedel with satisfaction. He turned to Morton. "You see, commander, I, too, had the impression that he was always around; and yet, thinking back over it, I find gaps. There were moments—probably long minutes—when he was completely out of sight."

Morton's face was dark with thought, as Kent broke in fiercely: "I say, take no chances. Kill the brute on suspicion before he does any more damage."

Morton said slowly: "Korita, you've been wandering around with Cranessy and Van Horne. Do you think pussy is a descendant of the ruling class of this planet?"

The tall Japanese archaeologist stared at the sky as if collecting his mind. "Commander Morton," he said finally, respectfully, "there is a mystery here. Take a look, all of you, at that majestic skyline. Notice the almost Gothic outline of the architecture. In spite of the megalopolis which they created, these people were close to the soil. The buildings are not simply ornamented. They are ornamental in themselves. Here is the equivalent of the Doric column, the Egyptian pyramid, the Gothic cathedral, growing out of the ground, earnest, big with destiny. If this lonely, desolate world can be regarded as a mother earth, then the land had a warm, a spiritual place in the hearts of the race.

"The effect is emphasized by the winding streets. Their machines prove they were mathematicians, but they were artists first; and so they did not create the geometrically designed cities of the ultra-sophisticated world metropolis. There is a genuine artistic abandon, a deep joyous emotion written in the curving and unmathematical arrangements of houses, buildings and avenues; a sense of intensity, of divine belief in an inner certainty. This is not a decadent, hoary-with-age civilization, but a young and vigorous culture, confident, strong with purpose.

"There it ended. Abruptly, as if at this point culture had its Battle of Tours, and began to collapse like the ancient Mohammedan civilization. Or as if in one leap it spanned the centuries and entered the period of contending states. In the Chinese civilization that period occupied 480–230 B.C. at the end of which the State of Tsin saw the beginning of the Chinese Empire. This phase Egypt experienced between 1780–1580 B.C., of which the last century was the 'Hyksos'—unmentionable— time. The classical experienced it from Chæronea—338—and at the pitch of horror, from the Gracchi—133—to Actium—31 B.C. The West European Americans were devastated by it in the nineteenth and twentieth centuries, and modern historians agree that, nominally, we entered the same phase fifty years ago; though, of course, we have solved the problem.

"You may ask, commander, what has all this to do with your question? My answer is: there is no record of a culture entering abruptly into the period of contending states. It is always a slow development; and the first step is a merciless questioning of all that was once held sacred. Inner certainties cease to exist, are dissolved before the ruthless probings of scientific and analytic minds. The skeptic becomes the highest type of being.

"I say that this culture ended abruptly in its most flourishing age. The sociological effects of such a catastrophe would be a sudden vanishing of morals, a reversion to almost bestial criminality, unleavened by any sense of ideal, a callous indifference to death. If this ... this pussy is a descendant of such a race, then he will be a cunning creature, a thief in the night, a cold-blooded murderer, who would cut his own brother's throat for gain."

"That's enough!, It was Kent's clipped voice. "Commander, I'm willing to act the role of executioner."

Smith interrupted sharply: "Listen, Morton, you're not going to kill that cat yet, even if he is guilty. He's a biological treasure house."

Kent and Smith were glaring angrily at each other. Morton frowned at them thoughtfully, then said: "Korita, I'm inclined to accept your theory as a working basis. But one question: Pussy comes from a period earlier than our own? That is, we are entering the highly civilized era of our culture, while he became suddenly historyless in the most vigorous period of his. *But* it is possible that his culture is a later one on this planet than ours is in the galactic-wide system we have civilized?"

"Exactly. His may be the middle of the tenth civilization of his world; while ours is the end of the eighth sprung from earth, each of the ten, of course, having been built on the ruins of the one before it."

"In that case, pussy would not know anything about the skepticism that made it possible for us to find him out so positively as a criminal and murderer?"

"No; it would be literally magic to him."

Morton was smiling grimly. "Then I think you'll get your wish, Smith. We'll let pussy live; and if there are any fatalities, now that we know him, it will be due to rank carelessness. There's just the chance, of course, that we're wrong. Like Siedel, I also have the impression that he was always around. But now—we can't leave poor Jarvey here like this. We'll put him in a coffin and bury him."

"No, we won't!" Kent barked. He flushed. "I beg your pardon, commander. I didn't mean it that way. I maintain pussy wanted something from that body. It looks to be all there, but something must be missing. I'm going to find out what and pin this murder on him so that you'll have to believe it beyond the shadow of a doubt."

It was late night when Morton looked up from a book and saw Kent emerge through the door that led from the laboratories below.

Kent carried a large, flat bowl in his hands; his tired eyes flashed across at Morton, and he said in a weary, yet harsh, voice: "Now watch!"

He started toward Coeurl, who lay sprawled on the great rug, pretending to be asleep.

Morton stopped him. "Wait a minute, Kent. Any other time, I wouldn't question your actions, but you look ill; you're overwrought. What have you got there?"

Kent turned, and Morton saw that his first impression had been but a flashing glimpse of the truth. There were dark pouches under the little chemist's gray eyes—eyes that gazed feverishly from sunken cheeks in an ascetic face.

"I've found the missing element," Kent said. "It's phosphorus. There wasn't so much as a square millimeter of phosphorus left in Jarvey's bones. Every bit of it had been drained out—by what superchemistry I don't know. There are ways of getting phosphorus out of the human body. For instance, a quick way was what happened to the workman who helped build this ship. Remember, he fell into fifteen tons of molten metalite—at least, so his relatives claimed—but the company wouldn't pay compensation until the metalite, on analysis, was found to contain a high percentage of phosphorus—"

"What about the bowl of food?" somebody interrupted. Men were putting away magazines and books, looking up with interest.

"It's got organic phosphorus in it. He'll get the scent, or whatever it is that he uses instead of scent—"

"I think he gets the vibrations of things." Gourlay interjected lazily. "Sometimes, when he wiggles those tendrils, I get a distinct static on the radio. And then, again, there's no reaction, just as if he's moved higher or lower on the wave scale. He seems to control the vibrations at will."

Kent waited with obvious impatience until Gourlay's last word, then abruptly went on: "All right, then, when he gets the vibration of the phosphorus and reacts to it like an animal, then—well, we can decide what we've proved by his reaction. Can I go ahead, Morton?"

"There are three things wrong with your plan," Morton said. "In the first place, you seem to assume that he is only animal; you seem to have forgotten he may not be hungry after Jarvey; you seem to think that he will not be suspicious. But set the bowl down. His reaction may tell us something."

Coeurl stared with unblinking black eyes as the man set the bowl before him. His ear tendrils instantly caught the id-vibrations from the contents of the bowl—and he gave it not even a second glance. He recognized this two-legged being as the one who had held the weapon that morning. Danger! With a snarl, he floated to his feet. He caught the bowl with the fingerlike appendages at the end of one looping tentacle, and emptied its contents into the face of Kent, who shrank back with a yell.

Explosively, Coeurl flung the bowl aside and snapped a hawser-thick tentacle around the cursing man's waist. He didn't bother with the gun that hung from Kent's belt. It was only a vibration gun, he sensed—atomic powered, but not an atomic disintegrator. He tossed the kicking Kent onto the nearest couch—and realized with a hiss of dismay that he should have disarmed the man.

Not that the gun was dangerous—but, as the man furiously wiped the gruel from his face with one hand, he reached with the other for his weapon. Coeurl crouched back as the gun was raised slowly and a white beam of flame was discharged at his massive head.

His ear tendrils hummed as they canceled the efforts of the vibration gun. His round, black eyes narrowed as he caught the movement of men reaching for their metalite guns. Morton's voice lashed across the silence. "Stop!"

Kent clicked off his weapon; and Coeurl crouched down, quivering with fury at this man who had forced him to reveal something of his power.

"Kent," said Morton coldly, "you're not the type to lose your head. You deliberately tried to kill pussy, knowing that the majority of us are in favor of keeping him alive. You know what our rule is: If anyone objects to my decisions, he must say so *at the time*. If the majority object, my decisions are overruled. In this case, no one but you objected, and, therefore, your action in taking the law into your own hands is most reprehensible, and automatically debars you from voting for a year."

Kent stared grimly at the circle of faces. "Korita was right when he said ours was a highly civilized age. It's decadent." Passion flamed harshly in his voice. "My God, isn't there a man here who can the horror of the situation? Jarvey dead only a few hours, and this creature, whom we all know to be guilty, lying there unchained, planning his next murder; and the victim is right here in this room. What kind of men are we—fools, cynics, ghouls—or is it that our civilization is so steeped in reason that we can contemplate a murderer sympathetically?"

He fixed brooding eyes on Coeurl. "You were right, Morton, that's no animal. That's a devil from the deepest hell of this forgotten planet, whirling its solitary way around a dying sun."

"Don't go melodramatic on us," Morton said. "Your analysis is all wrong, so far as I am concerned. We're not ghouls or cynics; we're simply scientists, and pussy here is going to be studied. Now that we suspect him, we doubt his ability to trap any of us. One against a hundred hasn't a chance." He glanced around. "Do I speak for all of us?"

"Not for me, commander!" It was Smith who spoke, and, as Morton stared in amazement, he continued: "In the excitement and momentary confusion, no one seems to have noticed that when Kent fired his vibration gun, the beam hit this creature on his cat head—and didn't hurt him."

Morton's amazed glance went from Smith to Coeurl, and back to Smith again. "Are you certain it hit him? As you say, it all happened so swiftly— when pussy wasn't hurt I simply assumed that Kent had missed him."

"He hit him in the face," Smith said positively. "A vibration gun, of course, can't even kill a man right away—but it can injure him. There's no sign of injury on pussy, though, not even a singed hair."

"Perhaps his skin is a good insulation against heat of any kind."

"Perhaps. But in view of our uncertainty, I think we should lock him up in the cage."

While Morton frowned darkly in thought, Kent spoke up. "Now you're talking sense, Smith."

"Morton asked: "Then you would be satisfied , Kent, if we put him in the cage?"

Kent considered, finally: "Yes. If four inches of micro-steel can't hold him, we'd better give him the ship."

Coeurl followed the men as they went out into the corridor. He trotted docilely along as Morton unmistakably motioned him through a door he had not hitherto seen. He found himself in a square, solid metal room. The door clanged mechanically behind him; he felt the flow of power as the electric lock clicked home.

His lips parted in a grimace of hate, as he realized the trap, but he gave no other outward reaction. It occurred to him that he had progressed a long way from the sunk-into-primitiveness creature who, a few hours before, had gone incoherent with fear in an elevator cage. Now, a thousand memories of his powers were reawakened in his brain; ten thousand cunnings were, after ages of disuse, once again part of his very being.

He sat quite still for a moment on the short, heavy haunches into which his body tapered, his ear tendrils examining his surroundings. Finally, he lay down, his eyes glowing with contemptuous fire. The fools! The poor fools!

It was about an hour later when he heard the man—Smith—fumbling overhead. Vibrations poured upon him, and for just an instant he was startled. He leaped to his feet in pure terror—and then realized that the vibrations were vibrations, not atomic explosions. Somebody was taking pictures of the inside of his body.

He crouched down again, but his ear tendrils vibrated, and he thought contemptuously: the silly fool would be surprised when he tried to develop those pictures.

After a while the man went away, and for a long time there were noises of men doing things far away. That, too, died away slowly.

Coeurl lay waiting, as he felt the silence creep over the ship. In the long ago, before the dawn of immortality, the coeurls, too, had slept at night; and the memory of it had been revived the day before when he saw some of the men dozing. At last, the vibration of two pairs of feet, pacing, pacing endlessly, was the only human-made frequency that throbbed on his ear tendrils.

Tensely, he listened to the two watchmen. The first one walked slowly past the cage door. Then about thirty feet behind him came the second. Coeurl sensed the alertness of these men; knew that he could never surprise either while they walked separately. It meant—he must be doubly careful!

Fifteen minutes, and they came again. The moment they were past, he switched his senses from their vibrations to a vastly higher range. The pulsating violence of the atomic engines stammered its soft story to his brain. The electric dynamos hummed their muffled song of pure power. He felt the whisper of that flow through the wires in the walls of his cage, and through the electric lock of his door. He forced his quivering body into straining immobility, his senses seeking, searching, to tune in on that sibilant tempest of energy. Suddenly, his ear tendrils vibrated in harmony—he caught the surging change into shrillness of that rippling force wave.

There was a sharp click of metal on metal. With a gentle touch of one tentacle, Coeurl pushed open the door, and glided out into the dully gleaming corridor. For just a moment, he felt contempt, a glow of superiority, as he thought of the stupid creatures who dared to match their wit against a coeurl. And in that moment, he suddenly thought of other coeurls. A queer, exultant sense of race pounded through his being; the driving hate of centuries of ruthless competition yielded reluctantly before pride of kinship with the future rulers of all space.

Suddenly, he felt weighed down by his limitations, his need for other coeurls, his aloneness—one against a hundred, with the stake all eternity; the starry universe itself beckoned his rapacious, vaulting ambition. If he failed, there would never be a second chance—no time to revive long-rotted machinery, and attempt to solve the secret of space travel.

He padded along on tensed paws—through the salon—into the next corridor—and came to the first bedroom door. It stood half open. One swift flow of synchronized muscles, one swiftly lashing tentacle that caught the unresisting throat of the sleeping man, crushing it; and the lifeless head rolled crazily, the body twitched once.

Seven bedrooms, seven dead men. It was the seventh taste of murder that brought a sudden return of lust, a pure, unbounded desire to kill, return of a millennium-old habit of destroying everything containing the precious id.

As the twelfth man slipped convulsively into death, Coeurl emerged abruptly from the sensuous joy of the kill to the sound of footsteps.

They were not near—that was what brought wave after wave of fright swirling into the chaos that suddenly became his brain.

The watchmen were coming slowly along the corridor toward the door of the cage where he had been imprisoned. In a moment, the first man would see the open door—and sound the alarm.

Coeurl caught at the vanishing remnants of his reason. With frantic speed, careless now of accidental sounds, he raced—along the corridor with its bedroom doors—through the salon. He emerged into the next corridor, cringing in awful anticipation of the atomic flame he expected would stab into his face.

The two men were together, standing side by side. For one single instant, Coeurl could scarcely believe his tremendous good luck. Like a fool the second had come running when he saw the other stop before the open door. They looked up, paralyzed, before the nightmare of claws and tentacles, the ferocious cat head and hate-filled eyes.

The first man went for his gun, but the second, physically frozen before the doom he saw, uttered a shriek, a shrill cry of horror that floated along the corridors—and ended in a curious gurgle, as Coeurl flung the two corpses with one irresistible motion the full length of the corridor. He didn't want the dead bodies found near the cage. That was his one hope.

Shaking in every nerve and muscle, conscious of the terrible error he had made, unable to think coherently, he plunged into the cage. The door clicked softly shut behind him. Power flowed once more through the electric lock.

He crouched tensely, simulating sleep, as he heard the rush of many feet, caught the vibration of excited voices. He knew when somebody actuated the cage audioscope and looked in. A few moments now, and the other bodies would be discovered.

"Siedel, gone!" Morton said numbly. "What are we going to do without Siedel? And Breckenridge! And Coulter and— Horrible!"

He covered his face with his hands, but only for an instant. He looked up grimly, his heavy chin outthrust as he stared into the stern faces that surrounded him. "If anybody's got so much as a germ of an idea, bring it out."

"Space madness!"

"I've thought of that. But there hasn't been a case of a man going mad for fifty years. Dr. Eggert will test everybody, of course, and right now he's looking at the bodies with that possibility in mind."

As he finished, he saw the doctor coming through the door. Men crowded aside to make way for him.

"I heard you, commander," Dr. Eggert said, "and I think I can say right now that the space-madness theory is out. The throats of these men have been squeezed to a jelly. No human being could have exerted such enormous strength without using a machine."

Morton saw that the doctor's eyes kept looking down the corridor, and he shook his head and groaned:

"It's no use suspecting pussy, doctor. He's in his cage, pacing up and down. Obviously heard the racket and— Man alive! You can't suspect him. That cage was built to hold literally *anything*—four inches of micro-steel—and there's not a scratch on the door. Kent, even you won't say, 'Kill him on suspicion,' because there can't be any suspicion, unless there's a new science here, beyond anything we can imagine—"

"On the contrary," said Smith flatly, "we have all the evidence we need. I used the telefluor on him—you know the arrangement we have on top of the cage—and tried to take some pictures. They just blurred. Pussy jumped when the telefluor was turned on, as if he felt the vibrations.

"You all know what Gourlay said before? This beast can apparently receive and send vibrations of any lengths. The way he dominated the power of Kent's gun is final proof of his special ability to interfere with energy."

"What in the name of all the hells have we got here?" One of the men groaned. "Why, if he can control that power, and send it out in any vibrations, there's nothing to stop him killing all of us."

"Which proves," snapped Morton, "that he isn't invincible, or he would have done it long ago."

Very deliberately, he walked over to the mechanism that controlled the prison cage.

"You're not going to open the door!" Kent gasped, reaching for his gun.

"No, but if I pull this switch, electricity will flow through the floor, and electrocute whatever's inside. We've never had to use this before, so you had probably forgotten about it."

He jerked the switch hard over. Blue fire flashed from the metal, and a bank of fuses above his head exploded with a single bang.

Morton frowned. "That's funny. Those fuses shouldn't have blown! Well, we can't even look in, now. That wrecked the audios, too."

Smith said: "If he could interfere with the electric lock, enough to open the door, then he probably probed every possible danger and was ready to interfere when you threw that switch."

"At least, it proves he's vulnerable to our energies!" Morton smiled grimly. "Because he rendered them harmless. The important thing is, we've got him behind four inches of the toughest of metal. At the worst we can open the door and ray him to death. But first I think we'll try to use the telefluor power cable—"

A commotion from inside the cage interrupted his words. A heavy body crashed against a wall, followed by a dull thump.

"He knows what we were trying to do!" Smith grunted to Morton. "And I'll bet it's a very sick pussy in there. What a fool he was to go back into that cage and does he realize it!"

The tension was relaxing; men were smiling nervously, and there was even a ripple of humorless laughter at the picture Smith drew of the monster's discomfiture.

"What I'd like to know," said Pennons, the engineer, "is why did the telefluor meter dial jump and waver at full power when pussy made that noise? It's right under my nose here, and the dial jumped like a house afire!"

There was silence both without and within the cage, then Morton said: "It may mean he's coming out. Back, everybody, and keep your guns ready. Pussy was a fool to think he could conquer a hundred men, but he's by far the most formidable creature in the galactic system. He may come out of that door, rather than die like a rat in a trap. And he's just tough enough to take some of us with him—if we're not careful."

The men backed slowly in a solid body; and somebody said: "That's funny. I thought I heard the elevator."

"Elevator!" Morton echoed. "Are you sure, man?"

"Just for a moment I was!" The man, a member of the crew, hesitated. "We were all shuffling our feet—"

"Take somebody with you, and go look. Bring whoever dared to run off back here—"

There was a jar, a horrible jerk, as the whole gigantic body of the ship careened under them. Morton was flung to the floor with a violence that stunned him. He fought back to consciousness, aware of the other men lying all around him. He shouted: "Who the devil started those engines!"

The agonizing acceleration continued; his feet dragged with awful exertion, as he fumbled with the nearest audioscope, and punched the engine-room number. The picture that flooded onto the screen brought a deep bellow to his lips:

"It's pussy! He's in the engine room—and we're heading straight out into space."

The screen went black even as he spoke, and he could see no more.

It was Morton who first staggered across the salon floor to the supply room where the spacesuits were kept. After fumbling almost blindly into his own suit, he cut the effects of the body-torturing acceleration, and brought suits to the semiconscious men on the floor. In a few moments, other men were assisting him; and then it was only a matter of minutes before everybody was clad in metalite, with anti-acceleration motors running at half power.

It was Morton then who, after first looking into the cage, opened the door and stood, silent as the others crowded about him, to stare at the gaping hole in the rear wall. The hole was a frightening thing of jagged edges and horribly bent metal, and it opened upon another corridor.

"I'll swear," whispered Pennons, "that it's impossible. The ten-ton hammer in the machine shops couldn't more than dent four inches of micro with one blow—and we only heard one. It would take at least a minute for an atomic disintegrator to do the job. Morton, this is a super-being."

Morton saw that Smith was examining the break in the wall. The biologist looked up. "If only Breckenridge weren't dead! We need a metallurgist to explain this. Look!"

He touched the broken edge of the metal. A piece crumbled in his fingers and slithered away in a fine shower of dust to the floor. Morton noticed for the first time that there was a little pile of metallic debris and dust.

"You've hit it," Morton nodded. "No miracle of strength here. The monster merely used his special powers to interfere with the electronic tensions holding the metal together. That would account, too, for the drain on the telefluor power cable that Pennons noticed. The thing used the power with his body as a transforming medium, smashed through the wall, ran down the corridor to the elevator shaft, and so down to the engine room."

"In the meantime, commander," Kent said quietly, "we are faced with a super-being in control of the ship, completely dominating the engine room, and its almost unlimited power, and in possession of the best part of the machine shops."

Morton felt the silence, while the men pondered the chemist's words. Their anxiety was a tangible thing that lay heavily upon their faces; in every expression was the growing realization that here was the ultimate situation in their lives; their very existence was at stake, and perhaps much more. Morton voiced the thought in everybody's mind:

"Suppose he wins. He's utterly ruthless, and he probably sees galactic power within his grasp."

"Kent is wrong," barked the chief navigator. "The thing doesn't dominate the engine room. We've still got the control room, and that gives us *first* control of all the machines. You fellows may not know the mechanical set-up we have; but, though he can eventually disconnect us, we can cut off all the switches in the engine room *now*. Commander, why didn't you just shut off the power instead of putting us into spacesuits? At the very least you could have adjusted the ship to the acceleration."

"For two reasons." Morton answered. "Individually, we're safer within the force fields of our spacesuits. And we can't afford to give up our advantages in panicky moves."

"Advantages. What other advantages have we got?"

"We know things about him," Morton replied. "And right now, we're going to make a test. Pennons, detail five men to each of the four approaches to the engine room. Take atomic disintegrators to blast through the big doors. They're all shut, I noticed. He's locked himself in.

"Selenski, you go up to the control room and shut off everything except the drive engines. Gear them to the master switch, and shut them off all at once. One thing, though—leave the acceleration on full blast. No anti-acceleration must be applied to the ship. Understand?"

"Aye, sir!" The pilot saluted.

"And report to me through the communicators if any of the machines start to run again." He faced the men. "I'm going to lead the main approach. Kent, you take No. 2; Smith, No. 3, and Pennons, No. 4. We're going to find out right now if we're dealing with unlimited science, or a creature limited like the rest of us. I'll bet on the last possibility."

Morton had an empty sense of walking endlessly as he moved, a giant of a man in his transparent space armor, along the glistening metal tube that was the main corridor of the engine-room floor. Reason told him the creature had already shown feet of clay, yet the feeling that here was an invincible being persisted.

He spoke into the communicator: "It's no use trying to sneak up on him. He can probably hear a pin drop. So just wheel up your units. He hasn't been in that engine room long enough to do anything.

"As I've said, this is largely a test attack. In the first place, we could never forgive ourselves if we didn't try to conquer him now, before he's had time to prepare against us. But, aside from the possibility that we can destroy him immediately, I have a theory.

"The idea goes something like this: Those doors are built to withstand accidental atomic explosions, and it will take fifteen minutes for the atomic disintegrators to smash them. During that period the monster will have no power. True, the drive will be on, but that's straight atomic explosion. My theory is, he can't touch stuff like that; and in a few minutes you'll see what I mean—I hope."

His voice was suddenly crisp: "Ready, Selenski?"

"Aye, ready."

"Then cut the master switch."

The corridor—the whole ship, Morton knew—was abruptly plunged into darkness. Morton clicked on the dazzling light of his spacesuit; the other men did the same, their faces pale and drawn.

"Blast!" Morton barked into his communicator.

The mobile units throbbed; and then pure atomic flame ravened out and poured upon the hard metal of the door. The first molten droplet rolled reluctantly, not down, but up the door. The second was more normal. It followed a shaky downward course. The third rolled sideways—for this was pure force, not subject to gravitation. Other drops followed until a dozen streams trickled sedately yet unevenly in every direction—streams of hellish, sparkling fire, bright as fairy gems, alive with the coruscating fury of atoms suddenly tortured, and running blindly, crazy with pain.

The minutes ate at time like a slow acid. At last Morton asked huskily: "Selenski?"

"Nothing yet, commander."

Morton half whispered: "But he must be doing something. He can't be just waiting in there like a cornered rat. Selenski?"

"Nothing, commander."

Seven minutes, eight minutes, then twelve.

"Commander!" It was Selenski's voice, taut. "He's got the electric dynamo running."

Morton drew a deep breath, and heard one of his men say:

"That's funny. We can't get any deeper. Boss, take a look at this."

Morton looked. The little scintillating streams had frozen rigid. The ferocity of the disintegrators vented in vain against metal grown suddenly invulnerable.

Morton sighed. "Our test is over. Leave two men guarding every corridor. The others come up to the control room."

He seated himself a few minutes later before the massive control keyboard. "So far as I'm concerned the test was a success. We know that of all the machines in the engine room, the most important to the monster was the electric dynamo. He must have worked in a frenzy of terror while we were at the doors."

"Of course, it's easy to see what he did," Pennons said. "Once he had the power he increased the electronic tensions of the door to their ultimate."

"The main thing is this," Smith chimed in. "He works with vibrations only so far as his special powers are concerned, and the energy must come from outside himself. Atomic energy in its pure form, not being vibration, he can't handle any differently than we can."

Kent said glumly: "The main point in my opinion is that he stopped us cold. What's the good of knowing that his control over vibrations did it? If we can't break through those doors with our atomic disintegrators, we're finished."

Morton shook his head. "Not finished—but we'll have to do some planning. First, though, I'll start these engines. It'll be harder for him to get control of them when they're running."

He pulled the master switch back into place with a jerk. There was a hum, as scores of machines leaped into violent life in the engine room a hundred feet below. The noises sank to a steady vibration of throbbing power.

Three hours later, Morton paced up and down before the men gathered in the salon. His dark hair was uncombed; the space pallor of his strong face emphasized rather than detracted from the outthrust aggressiveness of his jaw. When he spoke, his deep voice was crisp to the point of sharpness:

"To make sure that our plans are fully co-ordinated, I'm going to ask each expert in turn to outline his part in the overpowering of this creature. Pennons first!"

Pennons stood up briskly. He was not a big man, Morton thought, yet he looked big, perhaps because of his air of authority. This man knew engines, and the history of engines. Morton had heard him trace a machine through its evolution from a simple toy to the highly complicated modern instrument. He had studied machine development on a hundred planets; and there was literally nothing fundamental that he didn't know about mechanics. It was almost weird to hear Pennons, who could have spoken for a thousand hours and still only have touched upon his subject, say with absurd brevity:

"We've set up a relay in the control room to start and stop every engine rhythmically. The trip lever will work a hundred times a second, and the effect will be to create vibrations of every description. There is just a possibility that one or more of the machines will burst, on the principle of soldiers crossing a bridge in step—you've heard that old story, no doubt—but in my opinion there is no real danger of a break of that tough metal. The main purpose is simply to interfere with the interference of the creature, and smash through the doors."

"Gourlay next!" barked Morton.

Gourlay climbed lazily to his feet. He looked sleepy, as if he was somewhat bored by the whole proceedings, yet Morton knew he loved people to think him lazy, a good-for-nothing slouch, who spent his days in slumber and his nights catching forty winks. His title was chief communication engineer, but his knowledge extended to every vibration field; and he was probably, with the possible exception of Kent, the fastest thinker on the ship. His voice drawled out, and—Morton noted—the very deliberate assurance of it had a soothing effect on the men—anxious faces relaxed, bodies leaned back more restfully:

"Once inside," Gourlay said, "we've rigged up vibration screens of pure force that should stop nearly everything he's got on the ball. They work on the principle of reflection, so that everything he sends will be reflected back to him. In addition, we've got plenty of spare electric energy that we'll just feed him from mobile copper cups. There must be a limit to his capacity for handling power with those insulated nerves of his."

"Selenski!" called Morton.

The chief pilot was already standing, as if he had anticipated Morton's call. And that, Morton reflected, was the man. His nerves had that rocklike steadiness which is the first requirement of the master controller of a great ship's movements; yet that very steadiness seemed to rest on dynamite ready to explode at its owner's volition. He was not a man of great learning, but he "reacted" to stimuli so fast that he always seemed to be anticipating.

"The impression I've received of the plan is that it must be cumulative. Just when the creature thinks that he can't stand any more, another thing happens to add to his trouble and confusion. When the uproar's at its height, I'm supposed to cut in the anti-accelerators. The commander thinks with Gunlie Lester that these creatures will know nothing about anti-acceleration. It's a development, pure and simple, of the science of interstellar flight, and couldn't have been developed in any other way. We think when the creature feels the first effects of the anti-acceleration— you all remember the caved-in feeling you had the first month— it won't know what to think or do."

"Korita next."

"I can only offer you encouragement," said the archaeologist, "on the basis of my theory that the monster has all the characteristics of a criminal of the early ages of any civilization, complicated by an apparent reversion to primitiveness. The suggestion has been made by Smith that his knowledge of science is puzzling, and could only mean that we are dealing with an actual inhabitant, not a descendant of the inhabitants of the dead city we visited. This would ascribe a virtual immortality to our enemy, a possibility which is borne out by his ability to breathe both oxygen and chlorine—or neither—but even that makes no difference. He comes from a certain age in his civilization, and he has sunk so low that his ideas are mostly memories of that age.

"In spite of all the powers of his body, he lost his head in the elevator the first morning, until he remembered. He placed himself in such a position that he was forced to reveal his special powers against vibrations. He bungled the mass murders a few hours ago. In fact, his whole record is one of the low cunning of the primitive, egotistical mind which has little or no conception of the vast organization with which it is confronted.

"He is like the ancient German soldier who felt superior to the elderly Roman scholar, yet the latter was part of a mighty civilization of which the Germans of that day stood in awe.

"You may suggest that the sack of Rome by the Germans in later years defeats my argument; however, modern historians agree that the 'sack' was an historical accident, and not history in the true sense of the word. The movement of the 'Sea-peoples' which set in against the Egyptian civilization from 1400 B.C. succeeded only as regards the Cretan island-realm—their mighty expeditions against the Libyan and Phœnician coasts, with the accompaniment of Viking fleets, failed as those of the Huns failed against the Chinese Empire. Rome would have been abandoned in any event. Ancient, glorious Samarra was desolate by the tenth century; Pataliputra, Asoka's great capital, was an immense and completely uninhabited waste of houses when the Chinese traveler Hsinan-tang visited it about A.D. 635.

"We have, then, a primitive, and that primitive is now far out in space, completely outside of his natural habitat. I say, let's go in and win."

One of the men grumbled, as Korita finished: "You can talk about the sack of Rome being an accident, and about this fellow being a primitive, but the facts are facts. It looks to me as if Rome is about to fall again; and it won't be no primitive that did it, either. This guy's got plenty of what it takes."

Morton smiled grimly at the man, a member of the crew. "We'll see about that—right now!"

In the blazing brilliance of the gigantic machine shop, Coeurl slaved. The forty-foot, cigar-shaped spaceship was nearly finished. With a grunt of effort, he completed the laborious installation of the drive engines, and paused to survey his craft.

Its interior, visible through the one aperture in the outer wall, was pitifully small. There was literally room for nothing but the engines—and a narrow space for himself.

He plunged frantically back to work as he heard the approach of the men, and the sudden change in the tempest-like thunder of the engines—a rhythmical off-and-on hum, shriller in tone, sharper, more nerve-racking than the deep-throated, steady throb that had preceded it. Suddenly, there were the atomic disintegrators again at the massive outer doors.

He fought them off, but never wavered from his task. Every mighty muscle of his powerful body strained as he carried great loads of tools, machines and instruments, and dumped them into the bottom of his makeshift ship. There was no time to fit anything into place, no time for anything—no time—no time.

The thought pounded at his reason. He felt strangely weary for the first time in his long and vigorous existence. With a last, tortured heave, he jerked the gigantic sheet of metal into the gaping aperture of the ship—and stood there for a terrible minute, balancing it precariously.

He knew the doors were going down. Half a dozen disintegrators concentrating on one point were irresistibly, though slowly, eating away the remaining inches. With a gasp, he released his mind from the doors and concentrated every ounce of his mind on the yard-thick outer wall, toward which the blunt nose of his ship was pointing.

His body cringed from the surging power that flowed from the electric dynamo through his ear tendrils into that resisting wall. The whole inside of him felt on fire, and he knew that he was dangerously close to carrying his ultimate load.

And still he stood there, shuddering with the awful pain, holding the unfastened metal plate with hard-clenched tentacles. His massive head pointed as in dread fascination at that bitterly hard wall.

He heard one of the engine-room doors crash inward. Men shouted; disintegrators rolled forward, their raging power unchecked. Coeurl heard the floor of the engine room hiss in protest, as those beams of atomic energy tore everything in their path to bits. The machines rolled closer; cautious footsteps sounded behind them. In a minute they would be at the flimsy doors separating the engine room from the machine shop.

Suddenly, Coeurl was satisfied. With a snarl of hate, a vindictive glow of feral eyes, he ducked into his little craft, and pulled the metal plate down into place as if it was a hatchway.

His ear tendrils hummed, as he softened the edges of the surrounding metal. In an instant, the plate was more than welded—it was part of his ship, a seamless, rivetless part of a whole that was solid opaque metal except for two transparent areas, one in the front, one in the rear.

His tentacle embraced the power drive with almost sensuous tenderness. There was a forward surge of his fragile machine, straight at the great outer wall of the machine shops. The nose of the forty-foot craft touched—and the wall dissolved in a glittering shower of dust.

Coeurl felt the barest retarding movement; and then he kicked the nose of the machine out into the cold of space, twisted it about, and headed back in the direction from which the big ship had been coming all these hours.

Men in space armor stood in the jagged hole that yawned in the lower reaches of the gigantic globe. The men and the great ship grew smaller. Then the men were gone; and there was only the ship with its blaze of a thousand blurring portholes. The ball shrank incredibly, too small now for individual portholes to be visible.

Almost straight ahead, Coeurl saw a tiny, dim, reddish ball—his own sun, he realized. He headed toward it at full speed. There were caves where he could hide and with other coeurls build secretly a spaceship in which they could reach other planets safely—now that he knew how.

His body ached from the agony of acceleration, yet he dared not let up for a single instant. He glanced back, half in terror. The globe was still there, a tiny dot of light in the immense blackness of space. Suddenly it twinkled and was gone.

For a brief moment, he had the empty, frightened impression that, just before it disappeared, it moved. But he could see nothing. He could not escape the belief that they had shut off all their lights, and were sneaking up on him in the darkness. Worried and uncertain, he looked through the forward transparent plate.

A tremor of dismay shot through him. The dim red sun toward which he was heading was not growing larger. *It was becoming smaller* by the instant. And it grew visibly tinier during the next five minutes, became a pale-red dot in the sky—and vanished like the ship.

Fear came then, a blinding surge of it, that swept through his being and left him chilled with the sense of the unknown. For minutes, he stared frantically into the space ahead, searching for some landmark. But only the remote stars glimmered there, unwinking points against a velvet background of unfathomable distance.

Wait! One of the points was growing larger. With every muscle and nerve tensed, Coeurl watched the point becoming a dot, a round ball of light—red light. Bigger, bigger, it grew. Suddenly, the red light shimmered and turned white—and there, before him, was the great globe of the spaceship, lights glaring from every porthole, the very ship which a few minutes before he had watched vanish behind him.

Something happened to Coeurl in that moment. His brain was spinning like a flywheel, faster, faster, more incoherently. Suddenly, the wheel flew apart into a million aching fragments. His eyes almost started from their sockets as, like a maddened animal, he raged in his small quarters.

His tentacles clutched at precious instruments and flung them insensately; his paws smashed in fury at the very walls of his ship. Finally, in a brief flash of sanity, he knew that he couldn't face the inevitable fire of atomic disintegrators.

It was a simple thing to create the violent disorganization that freed every drop of id from his vital organs.

They found him lying dead in a little pool of phosphorus.

"Poor pussy," said Morton. "I wonder what he thought when he saw us appear ahead of him, after his own sun disappeared. Knowing nothing of anti-accelerators, he couldn't know that we could stop short in space, whereas it would take him more than three hours to decelerate; and in the meantime he'd be drawing farther and farther away from where he wanted to go. He couldn't know that by stopping, we flashed past him at millions of miles a second. Of course, he didn't have a chance once he left our ship. The whole world must have seemed topsy-turvy."

"Never mind the sympathy," he heard Kent say behind him. "We've got a job—to kill every cat in that miserable world."

Korita murmured softly: "That should be simple. They are but primitives; and we have merely to sit down, and they will come to us, cunningly expecting to delude us."

Smith snapped: "You fellows make me sick! Pussy was the toughest nut we ever had to crack. He had everything he needed to defeat us—"

Morton smiled as Korita interrupted blandly: "Exactly, my dear Smith, except that he reacted according to the biological impulses of his type. His defeat was already foreshadowed when we unerringly analyzed him as a criminal from a certain era of his civilization.

"It was history, honorable Mr. Smith, our knowledge of history that defeated him." said the Japanese archaeologist, reverting to the ancient politeness of his race.

THE MONSTER

The great ship poised a quarter of a mile above one of the cities. Below was a cosmic desolation. As he floated down in his energy bubble, Enash saw that the buildings were crumbling with age.

"No sign of war damage!" The bodiless voice touched his ears momentarily. Enash tuned it out.

On the ground he collapsed his bubble. He found himself in a walled enclosure overgrown with weeds. Several skeletons lay in the tall grass besides the rakish building. They were of long, two-legged, two-armed beings with the skulls in each case mounted at the end of a thin spine. The skeletons, all of adults, seemed in excellent preservation, but when he bent down and touched one, a whole section of it crumbled into a fine powder. As he straightened, he saw that Yoal was floating down nearby. Enash waited until the historian had stepped out of his bubble, then he said:

"Do you think we ought to use our method of reviving the long dead?"

Yoal was thoughtful. "I have been asking questions of the various people who have landed, and there is something wrong here. This planet has no surviving life, not even insect life. We'll have to find out what happened before we risk any colonization."

Enash said nothing. A soft wind was blowing. It rustled through a clump of trees nearby. He motioned toward the trees. Yoal nodded and said, "Yes, the plant life has not been harmed, but plants after all are not affected in the same way as the active life forms."

There was an interruption. A voice spoke from Yoal's receiver: "A museum has been found at approximately the center of the city. A red light has been fixed on the roof."

Enash said, "I'll go with you, Yoal. There might be skeletons of animals and of the intelligent being in various stages of his evolution. You didn't answer my question. Are you going to revive these beings?"

Yoal said slowly. "I intend to discuss the matter with the council, but I think there is no doubt. We must know the cause of this disaster." He waved one sucker vaguely to take in half the compass. He added as an afterthought, "We shall proceed cautiously, of course, beginning with an obviously early development. The absence of the skeletons of children indicates that the race had developed personal immortality."

The council came to look at the exhibits. It was, Enash knew, a formal preliminary only. The decision was made. There would be revivals. It was more than that. They were curious. Space was vast, the journeys through it long and lonely, landing always a stimulating experience, with its prospect of new life forms to be seen and studied.

The museum looked ordinary. High-domed ceilings, vast rooms, plastic models of strange beasts, many artifacts—too many to see and comprehend in so short a time. The life span of a race was imprisoned here in a progressive array of relics. Enash looked with the others, and was glad when they came to the line of skeletons and preserved bodies. He seated himself behind the energy screen, and watched the biological experts take a preserved body out of a stone sarcophagus. It was wrapped in windings of cloth, many of them. The experts did not bother to unravel the rotted material. Their forceps reached through, pinched a piece of skull—that was the accepted procedure. Any part of the skeleton could be used, but the most perfect revivals, the most complete reconstructions resulted when a certain section of the skull was used.

Hamar, the chief biologist, explained the choice of body. "The chemicals used to preserve this mummy show a sketchy knowledge of chemistry. The carvings on the sarcophagus indicate a crude and unmechanical culture. In such a civilization there would not be much development of the potentialities of the nervous system. Our speech experts have been analyzing the recorded voice mechanism which is a part of each exhibit, and though many languages are involved—evidence that the ancient language spoken at the time the body was alive has been reproduced—they found no difficulty in translating the meanings. They have now adapted our universal speech machine, so that anyone who wishes to need only speak into his communicator, and so will have his words translated into the language of the revived person. The reverse, naturally, is also true. Ah, I see we are ready for the first body."

Enash watched intently with the others as the lid was clamped down on the plastic reconstructor, and the growth processes were started. He could feel himself becoming tense. For there was nothing haphazard about what was happening. In a few minutes a full-grown ancient inhabitant of this planet would sit up and stare at them. The science involved was simple and always fully effective.

... Out of the shadows of smallness, life grows. The level of beginning and ending, of life and—not life; in that dim region matter oscillates easily between old and new habits. The habit of organic, or the habit of inorganic. Electrons do not have life and un-life values. Atoms know nothing of inanimateness. But when atoms form into molecules, there is a step in the process, one tiny step, that is of life—if life begins at all. One step, and then darkness. Or aliveness.

A stone or a living cell. A grain of gold or a blade of grass, the sands of the sea or the equally numerous animalcules inhabiting the endless fishy waters—the difference is there in the twilight zone of matter. Each living cell has in it the whole form. The crab grows a new leg when the old one is torn from its flesh. Both ends of the planarian worm elongate, and soon there are two worms, two identities, two digestive systems each as greedy as the original, each a whole, unwounded, unharmed by its experience. Each cell can be the whole. Each cell remembers in a detail so intricate that no totality of words could ever describe the completeness achieved.

But—paradox—memory is not organic. An ordinary wax record remembers sounds. A wire recorder easily gives up a duplicate of the voice that spoke into it years before. Memory is a physiological impression, a mark on matter, a change in the shape of a molecule, so that when a reaction is desired the *shape* emits the same rhythm of response.

Out of the mummy's skull had come the multi-quadrillion memory shapes from which a response was now being evoked. As ever, the memory held true.

A man blinked, and opened his eyes.

"It is true, then," he said aloud, and the words were translated into the Ganae tongue as he spoke them. "Death is merely an opening into another life—but where are my attendants?" At the end, his voice took on a complaining tone.

He sat up, and climbed out of the case, which had automatically opened as he came to life. He saw his captors. He froze, but only for a moment. He had a pride and a very special arrogant courage, which served him now. Reluctantly, he sank to his knees and made obeisance, but doubt must have been strong in him. "Am I in the presence of the gods of Egyptus?" He climbed to his feet. "What nonsense is this? I do not bow to nameless demons."

Captain Gorsid said, "Kill him!"

The two-legged monster dissolved, writhing, in the beam of a ray gun.

The second revived man stood up, pale, and trembled with fear. "My God, I swear I won't touch the stuff again. Talk about pink elephants—"

Yoal was curious. "To what *stuff* do you refer, revived one?"

"The old hooch, the poison in the hip pocket flask, the juice they gave me at that speak ... my lordie!"

Captain Gorsid looked questioningly at Yoal, "Need we linger?"

Yoal hesitated. "I am curious." He addressed the man. "If I were to tell you that we were visitors from another star, what would be your reaction?"

The man stared at him. He was obviously puzzled, but the fear was stronger. "Now, look," he said, "I was driving along, minding my own business. I admit I'd had a shot or two too many, but it's the liquor they serve these days. I swear I didn't see the other car—and if this is some new idea of punishing people who drink and drive, well, you've won. I won't touch another drop as long as I live, so help me."

Yoal said. "He drives a 'car' and thinks nothing of it. Yet we saw no cars. They didn't even bother to preserve them in the museums."

Enash noticed that everyone waited for everyone else to comment. He stirred as he realized the circle of silence would be complete unless he spoke. He said, "Ask him to describe the car. How does it work?"

"Now, you're talking." said the man. "Bring on your line of chalk, and I'll walk it. And ask any questions you please. I may be so tight that I can't see straight, but I can always drive. How does it work? You just put her in gear, and step on the gas."

"Gas." said engineering officer Veed. "The internal combustion engine. That places him."

Captain Gorsid motioned to the guard with the ray gun.

The third man sat up, and looked at them thoughtfully. "From the stars?" he said finally. "Have you a system, or was it blind chance?"

The Ganae councilors in that domed room stirred uneasily in their curved chairs. Enash caught Yoal's eye on him. The shock in the historian's eyes alarmed the meteorologist. He thought: "The two-legged one's adjustment to a new situation, his grasp of realities, was unnormally rapid. No Ganae could have equaled the swiftness of the reaction."

Hamar. the chief biologist, said, "Speed of thought is not necessarily a sign of superiority. The slow, careful thinker has his place in the hierarchy of intellect."

But Enash found himself thinking, it was not the speed; it was the accuracy of the response. He tried to imagine himself being revived from the dead, and understanding instantly the meaning of the presence of aliens from the stars. He couldn't have done it.

He forgot his thought, for the man was out of the case. As Enash watched with the others, he walked briskly over to the window and looked out. One glance, and then he turned back.

"Is it all like this?" he asked.

Once again, the speed of his understanding caused a sensation. It was Yoal who finally replied.

"Yes. Desolation. Death. Ruin. Have you any idea as to what happened?"

The man came back and stood in front of the energy screen that guarded the Ganae. "May I look over the museum? I have to estimate what age I am in. We had certain possibilities of destruction when I was last alive, but which one was realized depends on the time elapsed."

The councilors looked at Captain Gorsid, who hesitated; then, "Watch him," he said to the guard with the ray gun. He faced the man. "We understand your aspirations fully. You would like to seize control of this situation and insure your own safety. Let me reassure you. Make no false moves, and all will be well."

Whether or not the man believed the lie, he gave no sign. Nor did he show by a glance or a movement that he had seen the scarred floor where the ray gun had burned his two predecessors into nothingness. He walked curiously to the nearest doorway, studied the other guard who waited there for him, and then, gingerly, stepped through. The first guard followed him, then came the mobile energy screen, and finally, trailing one another, the councilors.

Enash was the third to pass through the doorway. The room contained skeletons and plastic models of animals. The room beyond that was what, for want of a better term, Enash called a culture room. It contained the artifacts from a single period of civilization. It looked very advanced. He had examined some of the machines when they first passed through it, and had thought: Atomic energy. He was not alone in his recognition. From behind him, Captain Gorsid said to the man:

"You are forbidden to touch anything. A false move will be the signal for the guards to fire."

The man stood at ease in the center of the room. In spite of a curious anxiety, Enash had to admire his calmness. He must have known what his fate would be, but he stood there thoughtfully, and said finally, deliberately, "I do not need to go any farther. Perhaps you will be able to judge better than I of the time that has elapsed since I was born and these machines were built. I see over there an instrument which, according to the sign above it, counts atoms when they explode. As soon as the proper number have exploded it shuts off the power automatically, and for just the right length of time to prevent a chain explosion. In my time we had a thousand crude devices for limiting the size of an atomic reaction, but it required two thousand years to develop those devices from the early beginnings of atomic energy. Can you make a comparison?"

The councilors glanced at Veed. The engineering officer hesitated. At last, reluctantly, he said, "Nine thousand years ago we had a thousand methods of limiting atomic explosions." He paused, then even more slowly, "I have never heard of an instrument that counts out atoms for such a purpose."

"And yet," murmured Shuri, the astronomer, breathlessly, "the race was destroyed."

There was silence. It ended as Gorsid said to the nearest guard, "Kill the monster!"

But it was the guard who went down, bursting into flame. Not just one guard, but the guards! Simultaneously down, burning with a blue flame. The flame licked at the screen, recoiled, and licked more furiously, recoiled and burned brighter. Through a haze of fire, Enash saw that the man had retreated to the far door, and that the machine that counted atoms was glowing with a blue intensity.

Captain Gorsid shouted into his communicator, "Guard all exits with ray guns. Spaceships stand by to kill alien with heavy guns."

Somebody said, "Mental control. Some kind of mental control. What have we run into?"

They were retreating. The blue flame was at the ceiling, struggling to break through the screen. Enash had a last glimpse of the machine. It must still be counting atoms, for it was a hellish blue. Enash raced with the others to the room where the man had been resurrected. There, another energy screen crashed to their rescue. Safe now, they retreated into their separate bubbles and whisked through outer doors and up to the ship. As the great ship soared, an atomic bomb hurtled down from it. The mushroom of flame blotted out the museum and the city below.

"But we still don't know why the race died," Yoal whispered into Enash's ear, after the thunder had died from the heavens behind them.

The pale yellow sun crept over the horizon on the third morning after the bomb was dropped, the eighth day since the landing. Enash floated with the others down on a new city. He had come to argue against any further revival.

"As a meteorologist," he said, "I pronounce this planet safe for Ganae colonization. I cannot see the need for taking any risks. This race has discovered the secrets of its nervous system, and we cannot afford—"

He was interrupted. Hamar, the biologist, said dryly, "If they knew so much why didn't they migrate to other star systems and save themselves?"

"I will concede," said Enash, "that very possibly they had not discovered our system of locating stars with planetary families." He looked earnestly around the circle of his friends. "We have agreed that was a unique accidental discovery. We were lucky, not clever."

He saw by the expressions on their faces that they were mentally refuting his arguments. He felt a helpless sense of imminent catastrophe. For he could see that picture of a great race facing death. It must have come swiftly, but not so swiftly that they didn't know about it. There were too many skeletons in the open, lying in the gardens of magnificent homes, as if each man and his wife had come out to wait for the doom of his kind. He tried to picture it for the council, that last day long, long ago, when a race had calmly met its ending. But his visualization failed somehow, for the others shifted impatiently in the seats that had been set up behind the series of energy screens, and Captain Gorsid said, "Exactly what aroused this intense emotional reaction in you, Enash?"

The question gave Enash pause. He hadn't thought of it as emotional. He hadn't realized the nature of his obsession, so subtly had it stolen upon him. Abruptly now, he realized.

"It was the third one," he said, slowly. "I saw him through the haze of energy fire, and he was standing there in the distant doorway watching us curiously, just before we turned to run. His bravery, his calm, the skillful way he had duped us—it all added up."

"Added up to his death!" said Hamar. And everybody laughed.

"Come now, Enash," said Vice-captain Mavad good-humoredly, "you're not going to pretend that this race is braver than our own, or that, with all the precautions we have now taken, we need fear one man?"

Enash was silent, feeling foolish. The discovery that he had had an emotional obsession abashed him. He did not want to appear unreasonable. He made a final protest, "I merely wish to point out," he said doggedly, "that this desire to discover what happened to a dead race does not seem absolutely essential to me."

Captain Gorsid waved at the biologist, "Proceed," he said, "with the revival."

To Enash, he said, "Do we dare return to Gana, and recommend mass migrations—and then admit that we did not actually complete our investigations here? It's impossible, my friend."

It was the old argument, but reluctantly now Enash admitted there was something to be said for that point of view. He forgot that, for the fourth man was stirring.

The man sat up. And vanished.

There was a blank, startled, horrified silence. Then Captain Gorsid said harshly, "He can't get out of there. We know that. He's in there somewhere."

All around Enash, the Ganae were out of their chairs, peering into the energy shell. The guards stood with ray guns held limply in their suckers. Out of the corner of his eye, he saw one of the protective screen technicians beckon to Veed, who went over. He came back grim. He said, "I'm told the needles jumped ten points when he first disappeared. That's on the nucleonic level."

"By ancient Ganael," Shuri whispered. "We've run into what we've always feared."

Gorsid was shouting into the communicator. "Destroy all the locators on the ship. Destroy them, do you hear!"

He turned with glaring eyes. "Shuri," he bellowed, "They don't seem to understand. Tell those subordinates of yours to act. All locators and reconstructors must be destroyed."

"Hurry, hurry!" said Shuri weakly.

When that was done they breathed more easily. There were grim smiles and a tensed satisfaction. "At least," said Vice-captain Mayad, "he cannot now ever discover Gana. Our great system of locating suns with planets remains our secret. There can be no retaliation for—" He stopped, said slowly, "What am I talking about? We haven't done anything. We're not responsible for the disaster that has befallen the inhabitants of this planet."

But Enash knew what he had meant. The guilt feelings came to the surface at such moments as this—the ghosts of all the races destroyed by the Ganae, the remorseless will that had been in them, when they first landed, to annihilate whatever was here. The dark abyss of voiceless hate and terror that lay behind them; the days on end when they had mercilessly poured poisonous radiation down upon the unsuspecting inhabitants of peaceful planets—all that had been in Mayad's words.

"I still refuse to believe he has escaped." That was Captain Gorsid. "He's in there. He's waiting for us to take down our screens, so he can escape. Well, we won't do it."

There was silence again as they stared expectantly into the emptiness of the energy shell. The reconstructor rested on its metal supports, a glittering affair. But there was nothing else. Not a flicker of unnatural light or shade. The yellow rays of the sun bathed the open spaces with a brilliance that left no room for concealment.

"Guards," said Gorsid, "destroy the reconstructor. I thought he might come back to examine it, but we can't take a chance on that."

It burned with a white fury. And Enash, who had hoped somehow that the deadly energy would force the two-legged thing into the open, felt his hopes sag within him.

"But where can he have gone?" Yoal whispered.

Enash turned to discuss the matter. In the act of swinging around, he saw that the monster was standing under a tree a score of feet to one side, watching them. He must have arrived at *that* moment, for there was a collective gasp from the councilors. Everybody drew back. One of the screen technicians, using great presence of mind, jerked up an energy screen between the Ganae and the monster. The creature came forward slowly. He was slim of build, he held his head well back. His eyes shone as from an inner fire.

He stopped as he came to the screen, reached out and touched it with his fingers. It flared, blurred with changing colors. The colors grew brighter, and extended in an intricate pattern all the way from his head to the ground. The blur cleared. The pattern faded into invisibility. The man was through the screen.

He laughed, a soft curious sound: then sobered. "When I first awakened," he said, "I was curious about the situation. The question was, what should I do with you?"

The words had a fateful ring to Enash on the still morning air of that planet of the dead. A voice broke the silence, a voice so strained and unnatural that a moment passed before he recognized it as belonging to Captain Gorsid.

"Kill him!"

When the blasters ceased their effort, the unkillable thing remained standing. He walked slowly forward until he was only a half a dozen feet from the nearest Ganae. Enash had a position well to the rear. The man said slowly:

"Two courses suggest themselves, one based on gratitude for reviving me, the other based on reality. I know you for what you are. Yes, *know* you—and that is unfortunate. It is hard to feel merciful. To begin with," he went on, "let us suppose you surrender the secret of the locator. Naturally, now that a system exists, we shall never again be caught as we were."

Enash had been intent, his mind so alive with the potentialities of the disaster that was here that it seemed impossible that he could think of anything else. And yet, a part of his attention was stirred now. "What did happen?" he asked.

The man changed color. The emotions of that far day thickened his voice. "A nucleonic storm. It swept in from outer space. It brushed this edge of our galaxy. It was about ninety light-years in diameter, beyond the farthest limit of our power. There was no escape from it. We had dispensed with spaceships, and had no time to construct any. Castor, the only star with planets ever discovered by us, was also in the path of the storm." He stopped. "The secret?" he said.

Around Enash, the councilors were breathing easier. The fear of race destruction that had come to them was lifting. Enash saw with pride that the first shock was over, and they were not even afraid for themselves.

"Ah," said Yoal softly, "you don't know the secret. In spite of all your great development, we alone can conquer the galaxy." He looked at the others, smiling confidently. "Gentlemen," he said, "our pride in a great Ganae achievement is justified. I suggest we return to our ship. We have no further business on this planet."

There was a confused moment while their bubbles formed, when Enash wondered if the two-legged one would try to stop their departure. But when he looked back, he saw that the man was walking in a leisurely fashion along a street.

That was the memory Enash carried with him, as the ship began to move. That and the fact that the three atomic bombs they dropped, one after the other, failed to explode.

"We will not," said Captain Gorsid, "give up a planet as easily as that. I propose another interview with the creature."

They were floating down again into the city, Enash and Yoal and Veed and the commander. Captain Gorsid's voice tuned in once more:

"… As I visualize it"—through the mist Enash could see the transparent glint of the other three bubbles around him—"we jumped to conclusions about this creature, not justified by the evidence. For instance, when he awakened, he vanished. Why? Because he was afraid, of course. He wanted to size up the situation. He didn't believe he was omnipotent."

It was sound logic. Enash found himself taking heart from it. Suddenly, he was astonished that he had become panicky so easily. He began to see the danger in a new light. Only one man alive on a new planet. If they were determined enough, colonists could be moved in as if he did not exist. It had been done before, he recalled. On several planets, small groups of the original populations had survived the destroying radiation, and taken refuge in remote areas. In almost every case, the new colonists gradually hunted them down. In two instances, however, that Enash remembered, native races were still holding small sections of their planets. In each case, it had been found impractical to destroy them because it would have endangered the Ganae on the planet. So the survivors were tolerated. One man would not take up very much room.

When they found him, he was busily sweeping out the lower floor of a small bungalow. He put the broom aside and stepped onto the terrace outside. He had put on sandals, and he wore a loose-fitting robe made of very shiny material. He eyed them indolently but he said nothing.

It was Captain Gorsid who made the proposition. Enash had to admire the story he told into the language machine. The commander was very frank. That approach had been decided on. He pointed out that the Ganae could not be expected to revive the dead of this planet. Such altruism would be unnatural considering that the ever-growing Ganae hordes had a continual need for new worlds. Each vast new population increment was a problem that could be solved by one method only. In this instance, the colonists would gladly respect the rights of the sole survivor of this world.

It was at that point that the man interrupted. "But what is the purpose of this endless expansion?" He seemed genuinely curious. "What will happen when you finally occupy every planet in this galaxy?"

Captain Gorsid's puzzled eyes met Yoal's, then flashed to Veed, then Enash. Enash shrugged his torso negatively, and felt pity for the creature. The man didn't understand, possibly never could understand. It was the old story of two different viewpoints, the virile and the decadent, the race that aspired to the stars and the race that declined the call of destiny.

"Why not," urged the man, "control the breeding chambers?"

"And have the government overthrown!" said Yoal.

He spoke tolerantly, and Enash saw that the others were smiling at the man's naiveté. He felt the intellectual gulf between them widening. The creature had no comprehension of the natural life forces that were at work. The man spoke again:

"Well, if you don't control them, we will control them for you."

There was silence.

They began to stiffen. Enash felt it in himself, saw the signs of it in the others. His gaze flicked from face to face, then back to the creature in the doorway. Not for the first time, Enash had the thought that their enemy seemed helpless. "Why," he decided, "I could put my suckers around him and crush him."

He wondered if mental control of nucleonic, nuclear, and gravitonic energies included the ability to defend oneself from a macrocosmic attack. He had an idea it did. The exhibition of power two hours before might have had limitations, but if so, it was not apparent. Strength or weakness could make no difference. The threat of threats had been made: "If you don't control—we will."

The words echoed in Enash's brain, and, as the meaning penetrated deeper, his aloofness faded. He had always regarded himself as a spectator. Even when, earlier, he had argued against the revival, he had been aware of a detached part of himself watching the scene rather than being a part of it. He saw with a sharp clarity that that was why he had finally yielded to the conviction of the others. Going back beyond that to remoter days, he saw that he had never quite considered himself a participant in the seizure of the planets of other races. He was the one who looked on, and thought of reality, and speculated on a life that seemed to have no meaning. It was meaningless no longer. He was caught by a tide of irresistible emotion, and swept along. He felt himself sinking, merging with the Ganae mass being. All the strength and all the will of the race surged up in his veins.

He snarled, "Creature, if you have any hopes of reviving your dead race, abandon them now."

The man looked at him, but said nothing. Enash rushed on, "If you could destroy us, you would have done so already. But the truth is that you operate within limitations. Our ship is so built that no conceivable chain reaction could be started in it. For every plate of potential unstable material in it there is a counteracting plate, which prevents the development of a critical pile. You might be able to set off explosions in our engines, but they, too, would be limited, and would merely start the process for which they are intended—confined in their proper space."

He was aware of Yoal touching his arm. "Careful." warned the historian. "Do not in your just anger give away vital information."

Enash shook off the restraining sucker. "Let us not be unrealistic," he said harshly. "This thing has divined most of our racial secrets, apparently merely by looking at our bodies. We would be acting childishly if we assumed that he has not already realized the possibilities of the situation."

"*Enash!*" Captain Gorsid's voice was imperative.

As swiftly as it had come, Enash's rage subsided. He stepped back. "Yes, commander."

"I think I know what you intended to say," said Captain Gorsid. "I assure you I am in full accord, but I believe also that I, as the top Ganae official, should deliver the ultimatum."

He turned. His horny body towered above the man. "You have made the unforgivable threat. You have told us, in effect, that you will attempt to restrict the vaulting Ganae spirit."

"Not the spirit," said the man. He laughed softly. "No, not the spirit."

The commander ignored the interruption. "Accordingly, we have no alternative. We are assuming that, given time to locate the materials and develop the tools, you might be able to build a reconstructor. In our opinion it will be at least two years before you can complete it, *even if you know how*. It is an immensely intricate machine, not easily assembled by the lone survivor of a race that gave up its machines millennia before disaster struck."

"You did not have time to build a spaceship. We won't give you time to build a reconstructor.

"Within a few minutes our ship will start dropping bombs. It is possible you will be able to prevent explosions in your vicinity. We will start, accordingly, on the other side of the planet. If you stop us there, then we will assume we need help. In six months of traveling at top acceleration, we can reach a point where the nearest Ganae planet would hear our messages. They will send a fleet so vast that all your powers of resistance will be overcome. By dropping a hundred or a thousand bombs every minute, we will succeed in devastating every city so that not a grain of dust will remain of the skeletons of your people.

"That is our plan. So it shall be. Now, do your worst to us who are at your mercy."

The man shook his head. "I shall do nothing—now!" he said. He paused, then thoughtfully, "Your reasoning is fairly accurate. Fairly. Naturally, I am not all-powerful, but it seems to me you have forgotten one little point. I won't tell you what it is. And now," he said, "good day to you. Get back to your ship, and be on your way. I have much to do."

Enash had been standing quietly, aware of the fury building up in him again. Now, with a hiss, he sprang forward, suckers outstretched. They were almost touching the smooth flesh—when something snatched at him.

He was back on the ship.

He had no memory of movement, no sense of being dazed or harmed. He was aware of Veed and Yoal and Captain Gorsid standing near him as astonished as he himself. Enash remained very still, thinking of what the man had said: "... *Forgotten one little point.*" Forgotten? That meant they knew. What could it be? He was still pondering about it when Yoal said:

"We can be reasonably certain our bombs alone will not work."

They didn't.

Forty light-years out from Earth, Enash was summoned to the council chambers. Yoal greeted him wanly, "The monster is aboard."

The thunder of that poured through Enash, and with it came a sudden comprehension. "That was what he meant we had forgotten," he said finally, aloud and wonderingly. "That he can travel through space at will within a limit—what was the figure he once used—of ninety light-years."

He sighed. He was not surprised that the Ganae, who had to use ships, would not have thought immediately of such a possibility. Slowly, he began so retreat from the reality. Now that the shock had come, he felt old and weary, a sense of his mind withdrawing again to its earlier state of aloofness. It required a few minutes to get the story. A physicist's assistant, on his way to the storeroom, had caught a glimpse of a man in a lower corridor. In such a heavily manned ship, the wonder was that the intruder had escaped earlier observation. Enash had a thought.

"But after all we are not going all the way to one of our planets. How does he expect to make use of us to locate it if we only use the video—" he stopped. That was it of course. Directional video beams would have to be used, and the man would travel in the right direction the instant contact was made.

Enash saw the decision in the eyes of his companions, the only possible decision under the circumstances. And yet, it seemed to him they were missing some vital point. He walked slowly to the great video plate at one end of the chamber. There was a picture on it, so sharp, so vivid, so majestic that the unaccustomed mind would have reeled as from a stunning blow. Even to him, who knew the scene, there came a constriction, a sense of unthinkable vastness. It was a video view of a section of the milky way. Four hundred *million* stars as seen through telescopes that could pick up the light of a red dwarf at thirty thousand light-years.

The video plate was twenty-five yards in diameter—a scene that had no parallel elsewhere in the plenum. Other galaxies simply did not have that many stars.

Only one in two hundred thousand of those glowing suns had planets.

That was the colossal fact that compelled them now to an irrevocable act. Wearily, Enash looked around him.

"The monster has been very clever," he said quietly. "If we go ahead, he goes with us, obtains a reconstructor and returns by his method to his planet. If we use the directional beam, he flashes along it, obtains a reconstructor, and again reaches his planet first. In either event, by the time our fleets arrived back here, he would have revived enough of his kind to thwart any attack we could mount."

He shook his torso. The picture was accurate, he felt sure, but it still seemed incomplete. He said slowly, "We have one advantage now. Whatever decision we make, there is no language machine to enable him to learn what it is. We can carry out our plans without his knowing what they will be. He knows that neither he nor we can blow up the ship. That leaves us one real alternative."

It was Captain Gorsid who broke the silence that followed. "Well, gentlemen, I see we know our minds. We will set the engines, blow up the controls, and take him with us."

They looked at each other, race pride in their eyes. Enash touched suckers with each in turn.

An hour later, when the heat was already considerable, Enash had the thought that sent him staggering to the communicator, to call Shuri, the astronomer. "Shuri," he yelled, "when the monster first awakened—

remember Captain Gorsid had difficulty getting your subordinates to destroy the locators. We never thought to ask them what the delay was. Ask them ... ask them—"

There was a pause, then Shuri's voice came weakly over the roar of the static, "They ... couldn't ... get ... into the ... room. The door was locked."

Enash sagged to the floor. They had missed more than one point, he realized. The man had awakened, realized the situation; and, when he vanished, he had gone to the ship, and there discovered the secret of the locator and possibly the secret of the reconstructor—if he didn't know it previously. By the time he reappeared, he already had from them what he wanted. All the rest must have been designed to lead them to this act of desperation.

In a few moments, now, *he* would be leaving the ship, secure in the knowledge that shortly no alien mind would know his planet existed. Knowing, too, that his race would live again, and this time never die.

Enash staggered to his feet, clawed at the roaring communicator, and shouted his new understanding into it. There was no answer. It clattered with the static of uncontrollable and inconceivable energy. The heat was peeling his armored hide as he struggled to the matter transmitter. It flashed at him with purple flame. Back to the communicator he ran shouting and screaming.

He was still whimpering into it a few minutes later when the mighty ship plunged into the heart of a blue-white sun.

FILM LIBRARY

The hundred delegates to the electronic manufacturers' convention, who had attended the showing, were drifting towards the doors. Several wives had been present, and their voices mingled with the deeper tones of the men. The sounds faded swiftly into the distance of the hotel, but Señor Pedro del Corteya, looking up suddenly from what he was doing, saw that he was still not alone.

He continued rewinding the reel, then he put it back into its can, and began to pack away the projector. Out of the corner of his eyes he watched the other with the curious, speculative intentness of the Latin. At last, his job completed, he turned.

"Is it me you wish to speak to, señor?"

The big man hesitated, then he came forward. He was a tall, chunky, fortyish individual with brown eyes and skimpy hair.

"Odd picture you showed us here tonight."

Corteya smiled his personal acceptance of the compliment. "You were amused, señor?"

Again that hesitation; then, "Where did you get it?"

Corteya shrugged. These direct Americans. Did the man expect him to hand over his trade secrets? He said as much.

"Do you think I am a fool, señor? Perhaps you are planning to start up in opposition to my business. You have plenty of money, maybe, and I go broke when you undercut my prices."

The stranger laughed. But he drew out a card and handed it over. Corteya read:

WALTER DORMAN
President
ELECTRONIC COMPANY OF AMERICA

59

Corteya looked at it, then handed it back. He saw that Dorman was staring at him hard. The man said finally, with a tiny note of incredulity in his voice, "You still don't believe I'm not after your hide."

Corteya shrugged. "What is it you wish to know, señor?"

"That film?"

Corteya raised his hands in a gesture of deprecation. "A ten-minute novelty."

"Very smoothly done, if you ask me."

"All the world, señor, knows that Hollywood is wonderful."

"Hollywood never made a picture as good as that."

Corteya smiled his if-you-say-so-it-must-be-so smile. For the first time, then, he let his mind go back over the picture he had shown. He couldn't remember it very clearly. It was his custom to watch the audience, not the film. Nevertheless, he recollected that it had been about an automatic electric stove that merely had to be supplied with the appropriate ingredients, and it would mix them, and serve up the finished meal piping hot at any desired time. He had shown the same film two weeks earlier at a local dieticians' meeting, and the audience had laughed heartily at the non-existent device.

Corteya said, "Señor, I obtain my films from several film libraries. Where they secure them, I do not know. They compete for my business. All I do is look over their catalogues and order films when I need them." He lifted his shoulders. "It is so simple as that."

"Have you had any other novelties like the one tonight?"

"A few. I cannot remember."

"Do they all come from the same film library?"

Dorman's persistence was beginning to wear. "I really cannot remember, señor. To me it is all ordinary business."

"Have you any similar films on hand right now?"

"You mean here? No!"

"I mean at your office."

Corteya looked unhappy. He was a simple, honest man, who could lie as well as the next man, but only if he had started out with a lie, and had to carry on. Having started with the truth, he could not stop.

"At the Aero Club dinner tomorrow," he said gloomily, "I am showing a film about a trip to one of the planets. The catalogue says it is very amusing."

Dorman said, "I know this is a lot to ask, but will you drive over to your office, and show me that picture now?"

"Señor, my wife, she is waiting for me at home."

Dorman said nothing. He took out his pocketbook and peeled off a twenty-dollar bill. As he expected, the other's slim hand reached forth delicately but without diffidence, and accepted the money.

It took only eight minutes to get to Corteya's place of business, and a few minutes after that the young man's projector was set up and purring. A seascape broke the shadows of a cloudy but brilliantly bright horizon. The sea was flat, a tideless expanse of water. Suddenly, in those murky depths, there was a stirring. A creature charged into view. It burst the surface and leaped up, twenty, fifty, a hundred feet. Its enormous, bulbous head and vast, yawning mouth seemed almost to touch the camera. And then it began to fall, still struggling, still furiously determined to grasp the prey at which it had leaped.

It failed. It fell. It hit the water with a splash so gigantic that Dorman was startled. He had been admiring the illusion of stark reality that had been produced with what must be an artificial monster-being mechanically activated in some indoor imitation sea. But those splashes looked *real*. A moment later, the narrator said:

"That was a Venusian squid. These creatures, which frequent the depths of the warm seas of Venus, come to the surface only after food. Our camera artist acted as bait, and so enticed the squid to attack him. He was not, however, in danger. Electronic devices protected him at all times."

Dorman smiled twistedly. First an electric stove that prepared meals, now a trip to Venus. Both slick jobs of photography, and, in this case, it was especially clever to suggest there had been no danger. So many of these travelogues about places that actually existed faked suspense and excitement to the point of nausea. He climbed to his feet, his interest close to the vanishing point. He felt very tolerant of himself. Just for a moment, while watching the stove go through its motions, he had had the wild thought that the picture was an advertising stunt for a competitor. The Venusian film put the whole affair into its proper perspective. He saw that Corteya had stopped the machine. The overhead light clicked on.

"Have you learned what you desire?"

"Practically."

The younger man continued to rewind the reel. While he waited, Dorman glanced around the small room. It had a counter at the front. The projector rested on it near the wall. Behind the counter was a single chair and a small set of shelves. That was all the furniture. The white calcimined walls of the office were decorated with still pictures from one-reel and two-reel films. Printed on each of the pictures was a caption giving the subject and the cost of showing. It was obviously a selling business. No one would come into a place like this without having been previously canvassed or told about it in some way.

"What else, señor?"

Dorman turned. The film was in its can, the projector in its case. "I'd like you to check to see if the two films came from the same film library."

"They did, señor." Corteya had not moved. He was smiling in his deprecating fashion. "I looked in the can," he explained, "when I came in."

Dorman made no move to leave. There was nothing else, really, but he hated to leave unfinished anything he had started. Check on everything, then recheck. That was his method, and he had no intention of changing now. He took out his pocketbook and removed a ten-dollar bill.

"The catalogue of this particular library. I'd like to have a look at it."

Corteya accepted the bill and reached under the counter. He came up with several folders. "They send one of these to me every month. These are for the last four months."

Only the final two contained lists of the novelty films. Dorman ran his gaze down the column, the smile on his lips broadening. There were several travelogues. Venus, a journey through a Martian desert, a spaceship voyage to the moon, an aerial trip over mountainous Europa, one of the moons of Jupiter, a camera examination of the rings of Saturn, a boat trip down a river of liquid oxygen on the far planet, Pluto, and, finally, the size of the Sun as seen from each one of its ten planets.

Dorman glanced swiftly at the remaining score or so films given under the novelty heading. He found the one he wanted instantly. The caption was, "Amusing account of an automatic stove that does EVERYTHING." He closed the folder, and paused to look at the address. Arlay Film Library, Sunset Boulevard, Hollywood, California.

"Thanks," said Dorman.

He went out into the street and climbed into his car. It was getting cooler, so he turned up the window, and sat for a minute lighting a cigarette. He drove unhurriedly back to the hotel. In the lobby, a man hailed him:

"Hey, Wally, come into the bar and have a drink. The boys have been looking for you. Where you been?"

As he settled into a booth a minute later, Dorman said, "I've been wild goose chasing." He explained briefly. One of the other men looked at him.

"Wally," he said, "you're a smart man." He gulped down a drink. "I mean that more than you think. One of the reasons I attended this convention was to find a man who could be the new chairman of the board for our firm. You'd have to buy about a thousand shares, but you'll see what a deal it is when I show you the statements tomorrow. What we're mainly interested in is a good man who doesn't miss any bets. Your action tonight is pure genius, so far as I am concerned, and you're in."

"Waiter," said Dorman, "more drinks."

The ever happy music swelled around them. The voices rose and fell in gyrations of sound. The night dragged on.

Ten weeks before, Mr. Lester Arlay, of the Arlay Film Library, had read the first complaint with a faint frown creasing his already lined forehead. The letter had been shoved inside the can of film, and it began:

"Dear Mr. Arley—"

Mr. Arlay started to scowl right there. He did not approve of his name being misspelled. He read on, grimly:

Dear Mr. Arley:
The sound film, "Food Magic," which you sent me, is entirely different from what I expected. Neither the audience nor I could make head or tail of it. Certainly, it has nothing to do with food. My program for the retailers' convention here was ruined.

The letter was signed by one of his best customers; and Mr. Arlay, who remembered the two-reeler, "Food Magic," perfectly, was dismayed. It was an educational feature turned out by one of the big food distributors. And it was a really dandy job, one of those films which small film libraries could borrow for nothing, and then rent out at a small but profitable rate. It was a film definitely suitable for a grocery retailers' convention.

Frowning, Mr. Arlay shoved the letter back into the can of film and put the can on the "To Be Examined" shelf. He began to open the other ten cans of film that had been returned that morning. Of the ten, four borrowers complained that "This is not the film we asked for." "I cannot understand your sending a film so different from what we ordered." "This is visual gibberish." "Your joke ruined our show."

For several moments, Mr. Arlay stared palely at the letters, and then, with a sudden burst of activity, he examined one of the criticized films. Presently, he slid the reel onto the projector, made the necessary adjustments, switched off the light, and stared with a blank expectancy at the screen.

There was a faraway rustle of music. The music drew closer, but the nearer it came the more uncertainty there was in it. Singing violins played a sweet melody, but swiftly a harsher theme intruded, a trill of doubt. The doubt grew and grew until finally the happy strains were completely dominated. Darkly, almost discordantly, the music played—and retreated into distance.

The screen itself came to life. Color flared over it, an intricate weaving movement of color that never quite formed a recognizable pattern. And the rich, vivid colors grew darker and darker until finally the screen was almost black.

Out of the darkness walked a young woman. She came from the shadows into the light with a casual grace, an agreeable ease, that marked her immediately as one of those marvelous photogenic types. Mr. Arlay had never seen her before, but she quirked her lips into a smile, made a movement with her fingers; and she was a personality.

The trouble was, she had barely appeared when, abruptly, she vanished in a gyrating puff of dark colors. She came on again, and this time she walked along an intense blue hallway into a living room, where a young man sat reading beside a vast window. Mr. Arlay had a flashing glimpse of a city beyond that window; and then the camera angle shifted to the girl.

She was standing behind the man, hesitant. As she stood, the human details of her flesh merged into the dark thematic colors; and it was these colors in human form that moved forward and very obviously kissed the young man on the lips. It was a long kiss, and at the end of it the young man, too, was a color pattern.

The mingled colors began to twist and spin. The screen was a chromatic splendor of gyrating light. It was just beginning to stir with returning music as Mr. Arlay emerged from his puzzlement and held the letter he had received about this particular film in the blazing beam of the projector.

He read: "This is visual gibberish!"

So that was the one! He laid the letter down, and held up the can cover with the title on it: "How to Operate a Chicken Farm."

On the screen, the young woman was walking uncertainly along a street, looking back at the man who was coming along slightly behind her. Mr. Arlay clicked it off, re-wound the reels, then took another film out of its can. It was the one about which the complainant had said: "Your joke ruined our show."

He threaded the reel into place, and presently a picture of a machine came onto the screen. It was a very bright, clear picture, without any non-sense about it, but the machine was not one that Mr. Lester Arlay remembered having seen before. The fact did not disturb him immediately. The world was full of machines that he had never seen; and, what was more, that he never wanted to see. He waited; and a quiet baritone said:

"No spaceman should have any difficulty repairing this new space drive."

Mr. Arlay sighed, and lifted the can cover into the light. The title on it was: "How to Operate the American Cogshill Diesel Engine."

What had happened was clear enough, it seemed to Mr. Arlay. Some-body had returned a whole series of wrong films to him; and he had sent them out in their original cans. The fantastically bad-luck angle of the affair was that no less than five wrong films had gone out all at once.

On the screen, the baritone voice was saying, "Now, raise the drive case itself. Since the standard weight of the case is eight tons, care must be taken when near a planetary body to balance the antigravity needles at a similitude of ninety-nine gravitons. Unwringing them becomes a matter of one good shove—"

Mr. Arlay shut the film off, and he was packing it into a can when the thought came: "What did he say? *What* did he say?"

He stood owlishly blinking his realization that something was very wrong.

There was an interruption. The outer door opened, and a young woman came in. She wore a mink coat, and heavily jeweled rings flashed on her fingers. "'Lo, honey," she said in a husky voice.

Mr. Arlay, all extraneous thoughts flying from his mind, came around the counter. His wife skillfully evaded the kiss he attempted to plant on her lips.

"Have you any money?" she asked. "I'm going shopping."

Mr. Arlay said, "Careful, Tania. We're almost at rock bottom."

He said it affectionately. He tried to kiss her again, and this time managed to brush her cheek. His words made her shake her slim body impatiently.

"That's all I ever hear from you," she said darkly. "Why don't you make money like some of the people in this town?"

Mr. Arlay almost pointed out that he did. He refrained. He had no illusions about his hold on this young woman. His business netted him between three and five hundred dollars a week. It was not a terrific amount of money, but it rivaled the salaries of featured movie players. They might make a little more per week, but few of them made it fifty-two weeks a year. It was that income which had enabled him, three years before, to marry a small-part player who was a far more attractive person physically than he could have hoped to marry without money. Mentally—that was another matter. She was a survival type in a sense that would have startled Darwin. Regardless of the variation in his income, she managed to spend it all, month in, month out. Her adaptability sometimes amazed even that defeatist Mr. Arlay.

What he did not realize, and certainly she neither knew nor would she have cared if she had known, was the profound influence she had had on him. All the imaginative qualities that had built his business had been replaced by a complete dependence on experience. He regarded himself as a practical man, and he had no inkling that his habit of thinking of himself as "Mr." was but one compensation for the psychic disaster he had suffered when she entered his life.

Not that he would necessarily have suspected anyway that he had come into possession of films that had been made more than fifty years in the future.

Now that she had come into the office, he strove to keep her there. "Got something here that might interest you," he said eagerly. "Somebody sent me a film of some other library by mistake, and it's quite an odd affair, a sort of a visual freak."

"Now, darling, I'm in a hurry, and—"

Her narrowed eyes saw that this was no moment to refuse him. He needed an occasional crumb, and he was so *completely* unsuspicious. After all, she'd be a nut to let this soft touch walk out on her.

"All right, honey," she crooned. "If you want me to."

He showed her the film with the man and the girl and the swirling colors—and realized the moment the girl appeared on the screen that he had made a mistake. His wife stiffened as that superb actress came into view.

"Hm-m-m-m," she said bitingly. "What kind of ham are you serving up now?"

Mr. Arlay let the film run its course without another comment. He had momentarily forgotten that his wife did not admire other actresses, particularly stars. Watching the film, he noticed absently that the reason for the dark tones of music and color seemed to be that the girl was unhappily married, and the twisting colors were designed to show her changing emotions, the doubts that came, and the thoughts that welled up in her mind.

"Interesting," he thought. "I wonder who made it."

As the reel ended, Tania jumped to her feet. "Well, got to be running. I'll cash a check for five hundred dollars O.K.?"

"Three!" said Mr. Arlay.

"Four," said his wife in a tone of friendly give and take.

Four hundred it was. When she had gone, Mr. Arlay began a check-up to see who had sent him the unusual films. The card index for the film, "How to Operate a Chicken Farm," gave a list of men and schools and institutions that had rented the item. The second last renter would obviously be the one. His gaze flashed down to it.

"Tichenor Collegiate," he read.

Mr. Arlay frowned at the name, and mentally changed the wording in the letter he had intended to write. Tichenor Collegiate was easily one of his best customers. And, what was more, the operator in charge, Peter Caxton, a science teacher, was a thoroughly experienced man. It seemed scarcely possible that Caxton could be guilty.

Quickly, Mr. Arlay examined the card for another of the eccentric films. The second last borrower was Tichenor Collegiate. The same name came up for each of the three other returned films, which didn't belong to his library. Mr. Arlay sat down at his typewriter and, bearing in mind that customers were seldom offended by the facts of the case, wrote:

Dear Mr. Claxton:
A number of films which you have returned to us were not the ones which we originally sent you. Altogether five films—

He paused there. Five? How did he know there were only five? Mr. Arlay made a beeline for the Tichenor Collegiate's personal file card. It was a thick one, additions having been glued to it from time to time.

He skipped down to the fifteenth name on the card. That would take it back just a little over two weeks. The title was "Pruning Fruit Trees." The film itself was a fantastic concoction in which a curiously shaped ship seemed to leave the Earth's surface and go to the Moon. The illusions were very realistic, and the photography had a Hollywood slickness.

Mr. Arlay shut it off finally, thinking for the first time that whoever was making those pictures would be well worth representing.

Meanwhile, there was a job to do. One by one, he screened the last nineteen films that had been borrowed by Tichenor. That is, he screened the sixteen that were in. Three had been re-rented, and in due course, no doubt, he would hear from them.

Of the sixteen, seven were travelogues. Travelogues: Unique, incredible creations, filmed by a madman. But mad or not, he was a genius, and he had designed some of the most life-like backgrounds ever conceived for fantasia. Among the first few that Mr. Arlay screened was the one about Venus which, ten weeks later, Pedro del Corteya showed to electronics manufacturer Walter Dorman. Mr. Arlay watched it and the other reels about the solar system with an appraising eye. There was, it seemed to him, much to be said for a skillful motion-picture presentation of what science believed about the various planetary bodies.

Seven travelogues and eight how-to-operate or how-to-repair films— of the eight, one dealt with the operation of a meaningless engine. At least, it seemed meaningless to Mr. Arlay. It had a single extrusion in a strong boxing. There were little chambers in the boxing, and when they were filled with a fine metallic powder, the extrusion could be made to turn with a velocity that did not slow when it was connected to a large machine of intricate construction. Another machine dealt with the repair of what was called an atomic gun. Here, too, the fine metallic powder was tamped into tiny chambers, but there was a transformation tunnel, the purpose of which was not clear. When fired at the end, the gun, a hand weapon, blew a four-hundred-foot-high hill into dust.

Mr. Arlay became impatient as the eight films unreeled onto the screen. This was going a little too far. The travelogues had a certain scientific value, but these operation and repair films, with their pretense to details, strained all credulity. An atomic engine and an atomic gun. How to repair a space drive. Care and operation of the Fly-O, an individual flyer—a combination of straps and a metallic tube that lifted the man in the film off the ground and transported him through the air like Buck Rogers. A radio that was simply a bracelet made of what was called "sensitive metal." The crystalline structure of the sensitivity was shown, and also the radio waves were shown, transformed into sound by ultra-thin bubbles in the metal. There were three rather amusing films about household devices. There was a light that focused wherever desired out of thin air; rugs and furniture that couldn't get dirty; and finally the automatic electric stove that was later to rouse Walter Dorman's competitive instincts. Long before the showing was finished, it had struck Mr. Arlay that there was a type of audience that would be interested in such novelties. It would be important, however, to stress the novelty angle, so that the people would be prepared to laugh.

His best bet, of course, would be to locate their source, and stock a few himself. He phoned Tichenor Collegiate, and asked for Caxton. Caxton said:

"My dear Mr. Arlay, it cannot possibly be we who are at fault. To prevent confusion in bookkeeping, I have long adopted a policy of renting from only one library at a time. For the past two months we have secured our material from you, and returned it promptly. Perhaps you had better re-examine your files."

His tone was faintly patronizing, and there was just enough suggestion in it of an affronted customer to make Mr. Arlay back down permanently.

"Yes, yes, of course. I'll have a look at them myself. My helper must have ... uh—"

Mr. Arlay hung up, saw that it was nearly one o'clock, and went out to lunch. He drove all the way up to Vine Street for a bowl of tomato soup. The fever in him died slowly, and he realized that it was not actually a difficult situation. He had lost nineteen films, but if he wrote careful letters to the firms that had supplied them to him they would probably send him new ones immediately. And as a sort of compensation for the wear and tear on his nerves, he had sixteen, possibly nineteen, novelty films which might go over rather well.

They did. At least once a week the novelties went out into the mails, and returned again. And by the time they came back there were orders waiting for most of them for the following week. Mr. Arlay did not worry about what the real owner of the films would think when he discovered what was happening. No single library film was worth very much. The owner would probably demand the wholesaler's percentage, and this Mr. Arlay was prepared to pay.

And just in case audience reaction would be required, Mr. Arlay sent printed forms for comments. They came back properly filled out. The size of the audience: 100, 200, 75, 150. The nature of the audience: Retailers' dinner, university astronomy class, the society of physicists, high school students. The reaction of the audience—comments most often made—"Amusing," "Interesting," "Good photography put it over." One common criticism was, "it seems to me the dialogue could be more humorous, befitting the nature of the subject matter."

The situation did not remain static. At the end of the second month, Mr. Arlay had thirty-one more novelty films, and every one of them had been sent him by Peter Caxton of Tichenor Collegiate.

After ten weeks, just about the time that Pedro del Corteya was due to show the stove picture to the electronic manufacturers' convention, two things happened approximately simultaneously. Mr. Arlay raised the rental rate of the novelties fifty percent, and Caxton sent him a letter, which read in part:

"I have noticed in your folders a reference to some novelty films. I would like one dealing with a planet for next Wednesday."

"Now," thought Mr. Arlay, "now, we shall see."

The can came back on Thursday. The film inside was also a novelty type. But it was not the same one he had sent out.

On his way to Tichenor Collegiate for the afternoon classes, Peter Caxton stopped in the corner drugstore and bought a pack of cigarettes. There was a full-length mirror just in front of the door. And, as he emerged, he paused briefly to survey himself in it.

The picture he saw pleased him. His tall form was well dressed, his face clean but not too youthful, and his eyes were a smiling gray. The well-groomed effect was accentuated by a neat, gray hat. He walked on, content. Caxton had no illusions about life. Life was what you made it. And so far as he could see, if he worked things right, he ought to be principal of Tichenor in another two years. The time limit was unavoidable. Old Varnish was not due for retirement until then, and Caxton could see no way by which the process could be speeded up.

Tichenor was no super-school, nor did it have the fancy money behind it that some neighboring communities raised every year for education. The smoking-room for the men and women was a joint affair. Caxton settled into one of the chairs and puffed quickly at his cigarette. He was about halfway through when Miss Gregg came in.

She smiled warmly: "'Lo, Peter," she said. Her gaze flashed significantly to the closed doors of the men's and women's dressing rooms, then back to him.

Caxton said, "Nobody in the men's."

She opened the door to the women's, glanced in, then came over in a gliding motion and planted a kiss on his lips.

"Careful," said Peter Caxton.

"Tonight," she said in a low tone, "at the end of the park."

Caxton could not suppress a faint look of irritation. "I'll try," he said, "but my wife—"

She whispered fondly, "I'll expect you."

The door closed softly behind her. Caxton sat frowning, disturbed. At first it had been pleasant, his conquest of Miss Gregg's heart. But after six months of ever more frequent rendezvous, the affair was beginning to be a little wearing. She had reached the stage where she half anticipated that he would somehow manage to get a divorce, and that somehow it would not hurt his career, and that everything would come out all right. Caxton shared neither her anxiety for such a culmination, nor her vague conviction that there would be no repercussions.

Miss Gregg, he realized too late, was an emotional fool. For a month he had known that he must break off with her, but so far only one method had occurred to him. She must be eased out of the school. How? The answer to that, too, had come easily. A whispering campaign against her and Dorrit. That way he could kill two birds with one stone. Ancil Dorrit was his only serious rival for the principalship, and what was worse, he and Old Varnish got along very well.

It shouldn't be very hard. Everybody except Miss Gregg knew that Dorrit was nuts about her, and Dorrit didn't seem to suspect that his secret was known. The situation amused Caxton. He, a married man, had walked off with Dorrit's dream girl. There was no reason why he shouldn't also snatch the principalship from under Dorrit's nose, so to speak. He'd have to think a little more about the moves, and proceed with the utmost caution.

Caxton rubbed his cigarette into an ashtray with a speculative thoughtfulness, then he headed for the auditorium. His first class was to have a film showing—a nuisance, those things. In the beginning, he had been quite interested, but there were too many poor films. Besides, the dopes never learned anything anyway. He had once questioned some of the brighter students about what they had learned from a film, and it was pitiful. Proponents, however, maintained that the effect was cumulative, the kids preferred it to other methods of teaching, and last week the school board had ordered that Grade Ten, as well as Grade Eleven, was to be shown each film.

That meant that once in the morning, once in the afternoon, he had to handle a swarm of fifteen- to seventeen-year-olds in the darkness of an auditorium. At least, this was the last showing for today. The film had been running for about a minute when Caxton took his first real look at the screen. He stared for a moment blankly, then shut off the projector, turned on the lights, and came down from the projection room.

"Who's responsible for this silly trick?" he asked angrily.

No one answered. The girls looked a little scared, the boys stiffened, except for a few teachers' pets, who turned pale.

"Somebody," Caxton shouted, "has switched films on me over the lunch hour."

He stopped. His own words jarred him. He had charged out of the projection booth without pausing to assess the implications of what had happened. Now, suddenly, he realized. For the first time in his four years at Tichenor he had been the victim of a student's prank, and he was taking it badly. After a moment of further thought, he made an even greater mental adjustment, and the situation was saved.

Caxton swallowed hard. A wan smile lighted his tense face. He looked around coolly. "Well," he said, "if this is what you want, you'll get it."

The second day his smile was grimmer, and it became a matter of discipline. "If this," he said, "happens again, I shall have to report to Old Varn—" He stopped. He had been about to say "Old Varnish." He finished instead, properly—"report to Mr. Varney."

It was a shaken and somewhat mystified Caxton who went into the principal's office the following day. "But where do they obtain the replacement films?" the old man asked helplessly. "After all, they cost money."

The question was not his final word. On Thursday, the film again being different, he trotted dutifully to each of the two classes, and pointed out the unfairness of their action. He also indicated that, since the lost films would have to be paid for, the affair was beginning to take on a decidedly criminal aspect.

The fifth day was Friday, and it was evident that the students had talked things over, for the president of each of the two classes made a brief denial of the suspicions of the faculty. "As you probably know," said one, "the students are usually aware of what is going on among themselves. But this class as a whole is unaware of the identity of the guilty party. Whoever is changing the films is playing a lone hand, and we herewith denounce him, and withdraw any support or sympathy we might normally give to a student who has gotten in wrong."

The words should have quieted Caxton's nerves. But they had the reverse effect. His first conviction, that he was being made game of by the students, had already partly yielded to a wilder thought, and the speeches merely enlivened the newer feeling. That afternoon at recess, without proper forethought, he made the mistake of voicing the suspicion to the principal.

"If the students are not to blame, then one of the teachers must be. And the only one I know who dislikes me intensely is Dorrit." He added grimly. "If I were you, I would also investigate the relationship between Miss Gregg and Dorrit."

Varney showed a surprising amount of initiative. The truth was, the old man was easily tired, and he was already worn out by the affair. He called both Miss Gregg and Dorrit and, to Caxton's dismay, repeated the accusations. Miss Gregg flashed one amazed look at the stunned Caxton, and then sat rigid throughout the rest of the meeting. Dorrit looked angry for a moment, then he laughed.

"This week," he said, "has been an eye opener for most of us here. We have seen Caxton wilt under the conviction that the student body didn't like him. I always thought he was a highly developed neurotic, and now in five days he has shown that he is worse than anything I imagined. Like all true neurotics of the more advanced kind, he failed to make even the most elementary investigations before launching his accusations. For instance, his first charge—I can prove that, for at least two days this week, I could not possibly have been near the projection room."

He proceeded to do so. He had been sick at his boarding house on Tuesday and Wednesday.

"As for the second and more unforgivable accusation, I only wish it were true, though in a different sense than Caxton has implied. I am one of those shy individuals where women are concerned, but under the circumstances I can say that I have long been an admirer of Miss Gregg from a distance."

The young woman showed her first vague interest at that point. From the corner of her eyes, she glanced at Dorrit, as if she were seeing him in a new light. The glance lasted only a moment, then she returned to her tensed contemplation of the wall straight in front of her. Dorrit was continuing:

"It is difficult, of course, to disprove anything so vague as the charge Mr. Caxton has leveled but—"

Old Varnish cut him off. "It is quite unnecessary to say anything further. I do not for one moment believe a word of it, and I cannot understand what Mr. Caxton's purpose could have been, to introduce such an ill-considered accusation into this wretched affair of the lost films. If the film situation does not rectify, I will report to the school board at their meeting next week, and we shall have an investigation. That is all. Good day, gentlemen. Good day, Miss Gregg."

Caxton spent a confused weekend. He was pretty sure that the principal had derived satisfaction from the situation. but there was nothing to do about that except curse himself for having provided the man with an opportunity to get rid of an unwanted heir to his own position. The worst confusion, however, had nothing to do with Varney. Caxton had the sinking feeling that things were happening behind his back. It was a feeling that turned out to be correct.

On Monday morning all the women teachers snubbed him, and most of the men were distinctly unfriendly. One of the men walked over and said in a low tone, "How did you happen to make such a charge against Gregg and Dorrit?"

"I was beside myself with worry," Caxton said miserably. "I was not in my right senses."

"You sure weren't," said the other. "Gregg's told all the women."

Caxton thought grimly, "A woman scorned."

The other man finished, "I'll try to do what I can but—"

It was too late. At lunchtime, the women teachers entered the principal's office in a body, and announced that they would refuse to work in the same school with a male teacher capable of such an untrue story about one of themselves. Caxton, who had already permitted himself flashing thoughts on the possibility of resignation, was now confronted by the necessity of an actual decision. He resigned at intermission, the separation to take effect at the end of the month, the following weekend.

His action cleared the air. The male teachers were friendlier, and his own mind slowly and painfully straightened out. By Tuesday he was thinking savagely but with clarity, "Those films! If it hadn't been for that mix-up, I wouldn't have lost my head. If I could find out who was responsible—"

It seemed to him that the resulting satisfaction would almost compensate him for the loss of his job. He did not go home for lunch. He only pretended to start out. Swiftly, he doubled back to the rear entrance, and, hurrying to the projection room, concealed himself behind a substitute screen that stood against one wall.

He waited during the entire lunch period. Nothing happened. Nobody tampered with the locked doors of the auditorium. No one came near the door of the projection room. And then, after lunch, when he started the projector, the film was different.

In the morning, it had been an ordinary film, concerned with dairy farming. The afternoon film was about the development and use of chemicals to thin or thicken the human blood, and so enable human beings to fit themselves overnight for extreme changes of temperature.

It was the first time that Caxton had closely examined one of the strange novelty films, of which he had ordered several about two weeks before. Examined it, that is, with his mind as well as his eyes. He thought, amazed, "Who is making those pictures? Why, they're wonderful; so full of ideas that—"

He returned to the projection room after school for another look. And received the shock of his life. It was a different film. Different from the one in the morning. Different from the one after lunch. It was a third film, its subject the inside of the sun. With trembling fingers, Caxton rewound the reel—and ran it through again. The perspiration came out on his face as an entirely different, a fourth film, unwound on the screen. The wild impulse came to rush down to the office to phone up Varney. That ended with the realization that the man would refuse. The principal had implied at least twice that the film tangle would probably rectify the moment Caxton left. The burden of weariness that he wore would make him cling to that conviction. "Tomorrow," he would say. "I'll have a look at the projector tomorrow."

It couldn't wait till tomorrow, so it seemed to Caxton. For the first time, he remembered the phone call he had received more than two months before from Mr. Arlay of the Arlay Film Library. The memory cooled him off. His second impulse within minutes—this time to call Arlay—faded before a recollection of what he had said to the owner of the film library. He had been rather snooty. He'd phone Arlay later.

Caxton began swiftly to dismantle the projector. What, exactly, he was looking for he didn't know, and he didn't find it. The machine was in first-class shape, everything as normal as it should be.

He reassembled it slowly, and, shoving it back into position, he once more re-ran the reel, this time there was no switch. It was the same film. He ran it over again, and again there was no change.

Caxton sank heavily into a chair. He had, he realized, made a mistake. Something fantastic had happened—just what, his mind was not quite prepared to consider—but whatever it was, his action in dismantling the projector had nullified the process. Now he couldn't even mention what he had discovered.

He grew angry. Why should he worry about lost films when he was leaving the school shortly? Still angry, he climbed to his feet and strode out of the school, home.

The year was 2011 A.D., and though the automatic projector at Tichenor Collegiate was aware in an electronic sense that something was wrong, it continued functioning. The film distribution machine that operated from Los Angeles was aware that something was wrong, but the disturbance was not great enough to set alarm relays into action. Not at first. Not for about three months. And by then—but here is what happened from the very first moment.

An order came through from Tichenor by the usual electronic channels. The order was of human origin. First, the number of the film was punched, then the assigned number of the school. Usually, when the film was in its place in the library, no other human agency was required. However, if the film and all its duplicates were out on loan, a red light flashed in the projection room at Tichenor, and then it was up to the would-be-renter to order a substitute film.

On this occasion a copy of the film was available. The electronic imprint of the number of the school was stamped onto the container's sensitives, and onto a series of bookkeeping plates. The bookkeeping plates moved through a machine which took information from them, as a result of which money was collected from Tichenor in due time. The film flashed out of its shelf into a tube.

Its speed at the beginning was not great. Instant by instant other film containers clicked into the tube in front of it or behind it, and constant automatic readjustments of speed were necessary to prevent collisions. The number of the film's destination, Tichenor Collegiate, was 9-7-43-6-2 Zone 9, Main Tube 7, Suburban Tube 43, Distribution 6, School 2.

The cut-off at Zone 9 opened in its automatic fashion as the forces from the film container actuated the mechanism. A moment later, the film was in main mail channel number 7. It was the channel of small packages, and they were strung out in an endless train, each in its electronically controlled container. The train never stopped, but it slowed and speeded as new containers were precipitated into the tube, or old ones darted off into cut-offs to their separate destinations.

… 43—6—2.With a click, the film arrived in the receptor. Automatic devices slipped it into position on the projector, and at a set time—in this case about an hour later—the projector's seeing eye attachment opened and surveyed the auditorium. Several students were still in the aisles. It clanged a warning alarm, waited half a minute, then locked the auditorium doors, and once more slid the cover from its "eye." This time a single student remained in one aisle.

The projector clanged its final alarm for the students. The next warning would be a light flash in the principal's office, together with a television picture of the auditorium, which would clearly show the recalcitrant student. This final action proved unnecessary. The youth ceased his capering, and tumbled into a seat. The showing began.

It was not within the capacity of the electronic devices of the projector to realize what happened then. The proper film showed on the screen, but the film that was subsequently put into the container and returned to the film library was an obsolete creation called "Food Magic," loaned to Tichenor by the Arlay Film Library in 1946.

The container likewise was not equipped to discover such errors. By pure chance, neither it nor any other container which subsequently acquired a 1946 film went out on call for nearly three months. When one finally clicked onto a projector in Santa Monica it was already too late. Caxton had dismantled the 1946 projector, and the sequential process of time connection had been broken.

Time is the great unvariant, but the unvariance is no simple relation. Time is here where you are. It is never the same elsewhere. A starbeam penetrates the atmosphere. It brings a picture from seven hundred thousand years in the past. An electron makes a path of light across a photographic plate. It brings a picture from fifty. a hundred years in the future—or a hundred thousand years. The stars, the world of the infinitely large, are always in the past. The world of the infinitely small is always in the future.

This is a rigor of the universe. This is the secret of time. And for one second of eternity two motion-picture projectors in two separate space-time periods lost some of their aspects of separateness, and there was a limited liaison.

It ended, and was never more.

Señor Pedro del Corteya packed away his projector. He was vaguely unhappy. Poor audience response always affected him that way. It was late when he got outside, but he stood for a moment beside his car looking thoughtfully up at the star-filled night. Blue was that sky above, alive with the mystery of the immense universe. Corteya scarcely noticed. He was thinking:

"It is those novelty films that bored them. I have shown too many in this town. No more."

He began to feel better, as if a weight had lifted from his soul. He climbed into his car, and drove home.

THE ENCHANTED VILLAGE

"Explorers of a new frontier" they had been called before they
left for Mars.

For a while, after the ship crashed into a Martian desert,
killing all on board except—miraculously—this one man, Bill Jenner spat
the words occasionally into the constant, sand-laden wind. He despised
himself for the pride he had felt when he first heard them.

His fury faded with each mile that he walked, and his black grief for
his friends became a gray ache. Slowly he realized that he had made a
ruinous misjudgment.

He had underestimated the speed at which the rocketship had been
traveling. He'd guessed that he would have to walk three hundred miles to
reach the shallow, polar sea he and the others had observed as they glided
in from outer space. Actually, the ship must have flashed an immensely
greater distance before it hurtled down out of control.

The days stretched behind him, seemingly as numberless as the hot,
red, alien sand that scorched through his tattered clothes. A huge scarecrow of a man, he kept moving across the endless, arid waste—he would
not give up.

By the time he came to the mountain, his food had long been gone.
Of his four water bags, only one remained, and that was so close to being
empty that he merely wet his cracked lips and swollen tongue whenever
his thirst became unbearable.

Jenner climbed high before he realized that it was not just another
dune that had barred his way. He paused, and as he gazed up at the
mountain that towered above him, he cringed a little. For an instant he
felt the hopelessness of this mad race he was making to nowhere—but he

77

reached the top. He saw that below him was a depression surrounded by hills as high as, or higher than, the one on which he stood. Nestled in the valley they made was a village.

He could see trees and the marble floor of a courtyard. A score of buildings was clustered around what seemed to be a central square. They were mostly low-constructed, but there were four towers pointing gracefully into the sky. They shone in the sunlight with a marble luster.

Faintly, there came to Jenner's ears a thin, high-pitched whistling sound. It rose, fell, faded completely, then came up again clearly and unpleasantly. Even as Jenner ran toward it, the noise grated on his ears, eerie and unnatural.

He kept slipping on smooth rock, and bruised himself when he fell. He rolled halfway down into the valley. The buildings remained new and bright when seen from nearby. Their walls flashed with reflections. On every side was vegetation—reddish-green shrubbery, yellow-green trees laden with purple and red fruit.

With ravenous intent, Jenner headed for the nearest fruit tree. Close up, the tree looked dry and brittle. The large red fruit he tore from the lowest branch, however, was plump and juicy.

As he lifted it to his mouth, he remembered that he had been warned during his training period to taste nothing on Mars until it had been chemically examined. But that was meaningless advice to a man whose only chemical equipment was in his own body.

Nevertheless, the possibility of danger made him cautious. He took his first bite gingerly. It was bitter to his tongue, and he spat it out hastily. Some of the juice which remained in his mouth seared his gums. He felt the fire on it, and he reeled from nausea. His muscles began to jerk, and he lay down on the marble to keep himself from falling. After what seemed like hours to Jenner, the awful trembling finally went out of his body and he could see again. He looked up despisingly at the tree.

The pain finally left him, and slowly he relaxed. A soft breeze rustled the dry leaves. Nearby trees took up that gentle clamor, and it struck Jenner that the wind here in the valley was only a whisper of what it had been on the flat desert beyond the mountain.

There was no other sound now. Jenner abruptly remembered the high-pitched, ever-changing whistle he had heard. He lay very still, listening intently, but there was only the rustling of the leaves. The noisy shrilling had stopped. He wondered if it had been an alarm, to warn the villagers of his approach.

Anxiously he climbed to his feet and fumbled for his gun. A sense of disaster shocked through him. It wasn't there. His mind was a blank, and then he vaguely recalled that he had first missed the weapon more than a week before. He looked around him uneasily, but there was not a sign of creature life. He braced himself. He couldn't leave, as there was nowhere to go. If necessary, he would fight to the death to remain in the village.

Carefully Jenner took a sip from his water bag, moistening his cracked lips and his swollen tongue. Then he replaced the cap and started through a double line of trees toward the nearest building. He made a wide circle to observe it from several vantage points. On one side a low, broad archway opened into the interior. Through it, he could dimly make out the polished gleam of a marble floor.

Jenner explored the buildings from the outside, always keeping a respectful distance between him and any of the entrances. He saw no sign of animal life. He reached the far side of the marble platform on which the village was built, and turned back decisively. It was time to explore interiors.

He chose one of the four tower buildings. As he came within a dozen feet of it, he saw that he would have to stoop low to get inside.

Momentarily, the implications of that stopped him. These buildings had been constructed for a life form that must be very different from human beings.

He went forward again, bent down, and entered reluctantly, every muscle tensed.

He found himself in a room without furniture. However, there were several low marble fences projecting from one marble wall. They formed what looked like a group of four wide, low stalls. Each stall had an open trough carved out of the floor.

The second chamber was fitted with four inclined planes of marble, each of which slanted up to a dais. Altogether there were four rooms on the lower floor. From one of them a circular ramp mounted up, apparently to a tower room.

Jenner didn't investigate the upstairs. The earlier fear that he would find alien life was yielding to the deadly conviction that he wouldn't. No life meant no food or chance of getting any. In frantic haste he hurried from building to building, peering into the silent rooms, pausing now and then to shout hoarsely.

Finally there was no doubt. He was alone in a deserted village on a lifeless planet, without food, without water— except for the pitiful supply in his bag—and without hope.

He was in the fourth and smallest room of one of the tower buildings when he realized that he had come to the end of his search. The room had a single stall jutting out from one wall. Jenner lay down wearily in it. He must have fallen asleep instantly.

When he awoke he became aware of two things, one right after the other. The first realization occurred before he opened his eyes—the whistling sound was back; high and shrill, it wavered at the threshold of audibility.

The other was that a fine spray of liquid was being directed down at him from the ceiling. It had an odor, of which technician Jenner took a single whiff. Quickly he scrambled out of the room, coughing, tears in his eyes, his face already burning from chemical reaction.

He snatched his handkerchief and hastily wiped the exposed parts of his body and face.

He reached the outside and there paused, striving to understand what had happened.

The village seemed unchanged.

Leaves trembled in a gentle breeze. The sun was poised on a mountain peak. Jenner guessed from its position that it was morning again and that he had slept at least a dozen hours. The glaring white light suffused the valley. Half hidden by trees and shrubbery, the buildings flashed and shimmered.

He seemed to be in an oasis in a vast desert. It was an oasis, all right, Jenner reflected grimly, but not for a human being. For him, with its poisonous fruit, it was more like a tantalizing mirage.

He went back inside the building and cautiously peered into the room where he had slept. The spray of gas had stopped, not a bit of odor lingered, and the air was fresh and clean.

He edged over the threshold, half inclined to make a test. He had a picture in his mind of a long-dead Martian creature lazing on the floor in the stall while a soothing chemical sprayed down on its body. The fact that the chemical was deadly to human beings merely emphasized how alien to man was the life that had spawned on Mars. But there seemed little doubt of the reason for the gas. The creature was accustomed to taking a morning shower.

Inside the "bathroom," Jenner eased himself feet first into the stall. As his hips came level with the stall entrance, the solid ceiling sprayed a jet of yellowish gas straight down upon his legs. Hastily Jenner pulled himself clear of the stall. The gas stopped as suddenly as it had started.

He tried it again, to make sure it was merely an automatic process. It turned on, then shut off.

Jenner's thirst-puffed lips parted with excitement. He thought, "If there can be one automatic process, there may be others."

Breathing heavily, he raced into the outer room. Carefully he shoved his legs into one of the two stalls. The moment his hips were in, a steaming gruel filled the trough beside the wall.

He stared at the greasy-looking stuff with a horrified fascination—food—and drink. He remembered the poison fruit and felt repelled, but he forced himself to bend down and put his finger into the hot, wet substance. He brought it up, dripping, to his mouth.

It tasted flat and pulpy, like boiled wood fiber. It trickled viscously into his throat. His eyes began to water and his lips drew back convulsively. He realized he was going to be sick, and ran for the outer door—but didn't quite make it.

When he finally got outside, he felt limp and unutterably listless. In that depressed state of mind, he grew aware again of the shrill sound.

He felt amazed that he could have ignored its rasping even for a few minutes. Sharply he glanced about, trying to determine its source, but it seemed to have none. Whenever he approached a point where it appeared to be loudest, then it would fade or shift, perhaps to the far side of the village.

He tried to imagine what an alien culture would want with a mind-shattering noise—although, of course, it would not necessarily have been unpleasant to them.

He stopped and snapped his fingers as a wild but nevertheless plausible notion entered his mind. Could this be music?

He toyed with the idea, trying to visualize the village as it had been long ago. Here a music-loving people had possibly gone about their daily tasks to the accompaniment of what was to them beautiful strains of melody.

The hideous whistling went on and on, waxing and waning. Jenner tried to put buildings between himself and the sound. He sought refuge in various rooms, hoping that at least one would be soundproof. None were. The whistle followed him wherever he went.

He retreated into the desert, and had to climb halfway up one of the slopes before the noise was low enough not to disturb him. Finally, breathless but immeasurably relieved, he sank down on the sand and thought blankly: What now?

The scene that spread before him had in it qualities of both heaven and hell. It was all too familiar now—the red sands, the stony dunes, the small, alien village promising so much and fulfilling so little.

Jenner looked down at it with his feverish eyes and ran his parched tongue over his cracked, dry lips. He knew that he was a dead man unless he could alter the automatic food-making machines that must be hidden somewhere in the walls and under the floors of the buildings.

In ancient days, a remnant of Martian civilization had survived here in this village. The inhabitants had died off, but the village lived on, keeping itself clean of sand, able to provide refuge for any Martian who might come along. But there were no Martians. There was only Bill Jenner, pilot of the first rocketship ever to land on Mars.

He had to make the village turn out food and drink that he could take. Without tools, except his hands, with scarcely any knowledge of chemistry, he must force it to change its habits.

Tensely he hefted his water bag. He took another sip and fought the same grim fight to prevent himself from guzzling it down to the last drop. And, when he had won the battle once more, he stood up and started down the slope.

He could last, he estimated, not more than three days. In that time he must conquer the village.

He was already among the trees when it suddenly struck him that the "music" had stopped. Relieved, he bent over a small shrub, took a good firm hold of it—and pulled.

It came up easily, and there was a slab of marble attached to it. Jenner stared at it, noting with surprise that he had been mistaken in thinking the stalk came up through a hole in the marble. It was merely stuck to the surface. Then he noticed something else—the shrub had no roots. Almost instinctively, Jenner looked down at the spot from which he had torn the slab of marble along with the plant. There was sand there.

He dropped the shrub, slipped to his knees, and plunged his fingers into the sand. Loose sand trickled through them. He reached deep, using all his strength to force his arm and hand down; sand—nothing but sand.

He stood up and frantically tore up another shrub. It also came up easily, bringing with it a slab of marble. It had no roots, and where it had been was sand.

With a kind of mindless disbelief, Jenner rushed over to a fruit tree and shoved at it. There was a momentary resistance, and then the marble on which it stood split and lifted slowly into the air. The tree fell over with a swish and a crackle as its dry branches and leaves broke and crumbled into a thousand pieces. Underneath where it had been was sand.

Sand everywhere. A city built on sand. Mars, planet of sand. That was not completely true, of course. Seasonal vegetation had been observed near the polar icecaps. All but the hardiest of it died with the coming of summer. It had been intended that the rocketship land near one of those shallow, tideless seas.

By coming down out of control, the ship had wrecked more than itself. It had wrecked the chances for life of the only survivor of the voyage.

Jenner came slowly out of his daze. He had a thought then. He picked up one of the shrubs he had already torn loose, braced his foot against the marble to which it was attached, and tugged, gently at first, then with increasing strength.

It came loose finally, but there was no doubt that the two were part of a whole. The shrub was growing out of the marble.

Marble? Jenner knelt beside one of the holes from which he had torn a slab, and bent over an adjoining section. It was quite porous—calciferous rock, most likely, but not true marble at all. As he reached toward it, intending to break off a piece, it changed color. Astounded, Jenner drew back. Around the break, the stone was turning a bright orange-yellow. He studied it uncertainly, then tentatively he touched it.

It was as if he had dipped his fingers into searing acid. There was a sharp, biting, burning pain. With a gasp, Jenner jerked his hand clear.

The continuing anguish made him feel faint. He swayed and moaned, clutching the bruised members to his body. When the agony finally faded and he could look at the injury, he saw that the skin had peeled and that blood blisters had formed already. Grimly Jenner looked down at the break in the stone. The edges remained bright orange-yellow.

The village was alert, ready to defend itself from further attacks.

Suddenly weary, he crawled into the shade of a tree. There was only one possible conclusion to draw from what had happened, and it almost defied common sense. This lonely village was alive.

As he lay there, Jenner tried to imagine a great mass of living substance growing into the shape of buildings, adjusting itself to suit another life form, accepting the role of servant in the widest meaning of the term.

If it would serve one race, why not another? If it could adjust to Martians, why not to human beings?

There would be difficulties, of course. He guessed wearily that essential elements would not be available. The oxygen for water could come from the air … thousands of compounds could be made from sand …. Though it meant death if he failed to find a solution, he fell asleep even as he started to think about what they might be.

When he awoke it was quite dark.

Jenner climbed heavily to his feet. There was a drag to his muscles that alarmed him. He wet his mouth from his water bag and staggered toward the entrance of the nearest building. Except for the scraping of his shoes on the "marble," the silence was intense.

He stopped short, listened, and looked. The wind had died away. He couldn't see the mountains that rimmed the valley, but the buildings were still dimly visible, black shadows in a shadow world.

For the first time, it seemed to him that, in spite of his new hope, it might be better if he died. Even if he survived, what had he to look forward to? Only too well he recalled how hard it had been to rouse interest in the trip and to raise the large amount of money required. He remembered the colossal problems that had had to be solved in building the ship, and some of the men who had solved them were buried somewhere in the Martian desert.

It might be twenty years before another ship from Earth would try to reach the only other planet in the Solar System that had shown signs of being able to support life.

During those uncountable days and nights, those years, he would be here alone. That was the most he could hope for—if he lived. As he fumbled his way to a dais in one of the rooms, Jenner considered another problem: How did one let a living village know that it must alter its processes? In a way, it must already have grasped that it had a new tenant. How could he make it realize he needed food in a different chemical combination than that which it had served in the past; that he liked music, but on a different scale system; and that he could use a shower each morning—of water, not of poison gas?

He dozed fitfully, like a man who is sick rather than sleepy. Twice he wakened, his lips on fire, his eyes burning, his body bathed in perspiration. Several times he was startled into consciousness by the sound of his own harsh voice crying out in anger and fear at the night.

He guessed, then, that he was dying.

He spent the long hours of darkness tossing, turning, twisting, befuddled by waves of heat. As the light of morning came, he was vaguely surprised to realize that he was still alive. Restlessly he climbed off the dais and went to the door.

A bitingly cold wind blew, but it felt good to his hot face. He wondered if there were enough pneumococci in his blood for him to catch pneumonia. He decided not.

In a few moments he was shivering. He retreated back into the house, and for the first time noticed that, despite the doorless doorway, the wind did not come into the building at all. The rooms were cold but not draughty.

That started an association: Where had his terrible body heat come from? He teetered over to the dais where he spent the night. Within seconds he was sweltering in a temperature of about one hundred and thirty.

He climbed off the dais, shaken by his own stupidity. He estimated that he had sweated at least two quarts of moisture out of his dried-up body on that furnace of a bed.

This village was not for human beings. Here even the beds were heated for creatures who needed temperatures far beyond the heat comfortable for men.

Jenner spent most of the day in the shade of a large tree. He felt exhausted, and only occasionally did he even remember that he had a problem. When the whistling started, it bothered him at first, but he was too tired to move away from it. There were long periods when he hardly heard it, so dulled were his senses.

Late in the afternoon he remembered the shrubs and the trees he had torn up the day before and wondered what had happened to them. He wet his swollen tongue with the last few drops of water in his bag, climbed lackadaisically to his feet, and went to look for the dried-up remains.

There weren't any. He couldn't even find the holes where he had torn them out. The living village had absorbed the dead tissue into itself and had repaired the breaks in its "body."

That galvanized Jenner. He began to think again … about mutations, genetic readjustments, life forms adapting to new environments. There'd been lectures on that before the ship left Earth, rather generalized talks designed to acquaint the explorers with the problems men might face on an alien planet. The important principle was quite simple: adjust or die.

The village had to adjust to him. He doubted if he could seriously damage it, but he could try. His own need to survive must be placed on as sharp and hostile a basis as that.

Frantically Jenner began to search his pockets. Before leaving the rocket he had loaded himself with odds and ends of small equipment. A jackknife, a folding metal cup, a printed radio, a tiny superbattery that could be charged by spinning an attached wheel—and for which he had brought along, among other things, a powerful electric fire lighter.

Jenner plugged the lighter into the battery and deliberately scraped the red-hot end along the surface of the "marble." The reaction was swift. The substance turned an angry purple this time. When an entire section of the floor had changed color, Jenner headed for the nearest stall trough, entering far enough to activate it.

There was a noticeable delay. When the food finally flowed into the trough, it was clear that the living village had realized the reason for what he had done. The food was a pale, creamy color; where earlier it had been a murky gray.

Jenner put his finger into it but withdrew it with a yell and wiped his finger. It continued to sting for several moments. The vital question was: Had it deliberately offered him food that would damage him, or was it trying to appease him without knowing what he could eat?

He decided to give it another chance, and entered the adjoining stall. The gritty stuff that flooded up this time was yellower. It didn't burn his finger, but Jenner took one taste and spat it out. He had the feeling that he had been offered a soup made of a greasy mixture of clay and gasoline.

He was thirsty now with a need heightened by the unpleasant taste in his mouth. Desperately he rushed outside and tore open the water bag, seeking the wetness inside. In his fumbling eagerness, he spilled a few precious drops onto the courtyard. Down he went on his face and licked them up.

Half a minute later, he was still licking, and there was still water.

The fact penetrated suddenly. He raised himself and gazed wonderingly at the droplets of water that sparkled on the smooth stone. As he watched, another one squeezed up from the apparently solid surface and shimmered in the light of the sinking sun.

He bent, and with the tip of his tongue sponged up each visible drop. For a long time he lay with his mouth pressed to the "marble," sucking up the tiny bits of water that the village doled out to him.

The glowing white sun disappeared behind a hill. Night fell, like the dropping of a black screen. The air turned cold, then icy. He shivered as the wind keened through his ragged clothes. But what finally stopped him was the collapse of the surface from which he had been drinking.

Jenner lifted himself in surprise, and in the darkness gingerly felt over the stone. It had genuinely crumbled, Evidently the substance had yielded up its available water and had disintegrated in the process. Jenner estimated that he had drunk altogether an ounce of water.

It was a convincing demonstration of the willingness of the village to please him, but there was another, less satisfying, implication. If the village had to destroy a part of itself every time it gave him a drink, then clearly the supply was not unlimited.

Jenner hurried inside the nearest building, climbed onto a dais—and climbed off again hastily, as the heat blazed up at him. He waited, to give the Intelligence a chance to realize he wanted a change, then lay down once more, The heat was as great as ever.

He gave that up because he was too tired to persist and too sleepy to think of a method that might let the village know he needed a different bedroom temperature, He slept on the floor with an uneasy conviction that it could *not* sustain him for long. He woke up many times during the night and thought, "Not enough water. No matter how hard it tries—" Then he would sleep again, only to wake once more, tense and unhappy.

Nevertheless, morning found him briefly alert; and all his steely determination was back—that iron will power that had brought him at least five hundred miles across an unknown desert.

He headed for the nearest trough. This time, after he had activated it, there was a pause of more than a minute; and then about a thimbleful of water made a wet splotch at the bottom.

Jenner licked it dry, then waited hopefully for more. When none came he reflected gloomily that somewhere in the village an entire group of cells had broken down and released their water for him.

Then and there he decided that it was up to the human being, who could move around, to find a new source of water for the village, which could not move.

In the interim, of course, the village would have to keep him alive, until he had investigated the possibilities. That meant, above everything else, he must have some food to sustain him while he looked around.

He began to search his pockets. Toward the end of his food supply, he had carried scraps and pieces wrapped in small bits of cloth. Crumbs had broken off into the pocket, and he had searched for them often during those long days in the desert. Now, by actually ripping the seams, he discovered tiny particles of meat and bread, little bits of grease and other unidentifiable substances.

Carefully he leaned over the adjoining stall and placed the scrapings in the trough there. The village would not be able to offer him more than a reasonable facsimile. If the spilling of a few drops on the courtyard could make it aware of his need for water, then a similar offering might give it the clue it needed as to the chemical nature of the food he could eat.

Jenner waited, then entered the second stall and activated it. About a pint of thick, creamy substance trickled into the bottom of the trough. The smallness of the quantity seemed evidence that perhaps it contained water.

He tasted it. It had a sharp, musty flavor and a stale odor. It was almost as dry as flour—but his stomach did not reject it.

Jenner ate slowly, acutely aware that at such moments as this the village had him at its mercy. He could never be sure that one of the food ingredients was not a slow-acting poison.

When he had finished the meal he went to a food trough in another building. He refused to eat the food that came up, but activated still another trough. This time he received a few drops of water.

He had come purposefully to one of the tower buildings. Now he started up the ramp that led to the upper floor. He paused only briefly in the room he came to, as he had already discovered that they seemed to be additional bedrooms. The familiar dais was there in a group of three.

What interested him was that the circular ramp continued to wind on upward. First to another, smaller room that seemed to have no particular reason for being. Then it wound on up to the top of the tower, some seventy feet above the ground. It was high enough for him to see beyond the rim of all the surrounding hilltops. He had thought it might be, but he had been too weak to make the climb before. Now he looked out to every horizon. Almost immediately the hope that had brought him up faded.

The view was immeasurably desolate. As far as he could see was an arid waste, and every horizon was hidden in a mist of wind-blown sand.

Jenner gazed with a sense of despair. If there were a Martian sea out there somewhere, it was beyond his reach.

Abruptly he clenched his hands in anger against his fate, which seemed inevitable now. At the very worst, he had hoped he would find himself in a mountainous region. Seas and mountains were generally the two main sources of water. He should have known, of course, that there were very few mountains on Mars. It would have been a wild coincidence if he had actually run into a mountain range.

His fury faded because he lacked the strength to sustain any emotion. Numbly he went down the ramp.

His vague plan to help the village ended as swiftly and finally as that.

The days drifted by, but as to how many he had no idea. Each time he went to eat, a smaller amount of water was doled out to him. Jenner kept telling himself that each meal would have to be his last. It was unreasonable for him to expect the village to destroy itself when his fate was certain now.

What was worse, it became increasingly clear that the food was not good for him. He had misled the village as to his needs by giving it stale, perhaps even tainted, samples, and prolonged the agony for himself. At times after he had eaten, Jenner felt dizzy for hours. All too frequently his head ached and his body shivered with fever.

The village was doing what it could. The rest was up to him, and he couldn't even adjust to an approximation of Earth food.

For two days he was too sick to drag himself to one of the troughs. Hour after hour he lay on the floor. Some time during the second night the pain in his body grew so terrible that he finally made up his mind.

"If I can get to a dais," he told himself, "the heat alone will kill me and in absorbing my body, the village will get back some of its lost water."

He spent at least an hour crawling laboriously up the ramp of the nearest dais, and when he finally made it, he lay as one already dead. His last waking thought was: "Beloved friends, I'm coming."

The hallucination was so complete that momentarily he seemed to be back in the control room of the rocketship, and all around him were his former companions.

With a sigh of relief Jenner sank into a dreamless sleep.

He woke to the sound of a violin. It was a sad-sweet music that told of the rise and fall of a race long dead.

Jenner listened for a while and then, with abrupt excitement, realized the truth. This was a substitute for the whistling—the village had adjusted its music to him!

Other sensory phenomena stole in upon him. The dais felt comfortably warm, not hot at all. He had a feeling of wonderful physical well-being.

Eagerly he scrambled down the ramp to the nearest food stall. As he crawled forward, his nose close to the floor, the trough filled with a steamy mixture. The odor was so rich and pleasant that he plunged his face into it and slopped it up greedily. It had the flavor of thick, meaty soup and was warm and soothing to his lips and mouth. When he had eaten it all, for the first time he did not need a drink of water.

"I've won!" thought Jenner. "The village has found a way!"

After a while he remembered something and crawled to the bathroom. Cautiously, watching the ceiling, he eased himself backward into the shower stall. The yellowish spray came down, cool and delightful.

Ecstatically Jenner wriggled his four-foot-tail and lifted his long snout to let the thin streams of liquid wash away the food impurities that clung to his sharp teeth.

Then he waddled out to bask in the sun and listen to the timeless music.

ASYLUM

Indecision was dark in the man's thoughts as he walked across the spaceship control room to the cot where the woman lay so taut and so still. He bent over her. He said in his deep voice:

"We're slowing down, Merla."

No answer, no movement, not a quiver in her delicate, abnormally blanched cheeks. Her fine nostrils dilated ever so slightly with each measured breath. That was all.

The Dreegh lifted her arm, then let it go. It dropped to her lap like a piece of lifeless wood, and her body remained rigid and unnatural. Carefully, he put his fingers to one eye, raised the lid, peered into it. It stared back at him, a clouded, sightless blue. He straightened. As he stood there in the silence of the hurtling ship, he seemed the embodiment of grim, icy calculation. He thought grayly: "If I revived her now, she'd have more time to attack me, and more strength. If I waited, she'd be weaker."

Slowly, he relaxed. Some of the weariness of the years he and this woman had spent together in the dark vastness of space came to shatter his abnormal logic. Bleak sympathy touched him, and he made his decision. He prepared an injection, and fed it into her arm. His gray eyes held a steely brightness as he put his lips near the woman's ear. In a ringing resonant voice he said, "We're near a star system. There'll be blood, Merla! And life!"

The woman stirred. Momentarily, she seemed like a golden-haired doll come alive. No color touched her perfectly formed cheeks, but her eyes grew alert. She stared up at him with a hardening hostility, half questioning.

"I've been chemical," she said. Abruptly, she was no longer doll-like. Her gaze tightened on him, and some of the prettiness vanished from her face. She said, "It's damned funny, Jeel, that you're still O.K. If I thought—"

89

He was cold, watchful. "Forget it," he said curtly. "You're an energy waster, and you know it. Anyway, we're going to land."

The flamelike tenseness of her faded. She sat up painfully, but there was a thoughtful look on her face as she said, "I'm interested in the risks. This is not a Galactic planet, is it?"

"There are no Galactics out here. But there is an Observer. I've been catching the secret *ultra* signals for the last two hours"—a sardonic note entered his voice—"warning all ships to stay clear because the system isn't ready for any kind of contact with Galactic planets."

Some of the diabolic glee that was in his thoughts must have communicated through his tone. The woman stared at him, and slowly her eyes widened. She half whispered, "You mean—"

He shrugged. "The signals ought to be registering full blast now. We'll see what degree system this is. But you can start hoping hard right now."

At the control board, he cautiously manipulated the room into darkness and set the automatics. A picture took form on a screen on the opposite wall. At first there was only a point of light in the middle of a starry sky, then a planet floating brightly in the dark space, continents and oceans plainly visible. A voice came out of the screen:

"This star system contains one inhabited planet, the third from the Sun, called Earth by its dominant race. It was colonized by Galactics about seven thousand years ago in the usual manner. It is now in the third degree of development, having attained a limited form of space travel little more than a hundred years ago."

With a swift movement, the man cut off the picture and turned on the light, then looked across at the woman triumphantly. "Third degree!" he said softly, and there was an almost incredulous note in his voice. "Only third degree. Merla, do you realize what this means? This is the opportunity of the ages. I'm going to call the Dreegh tribe. If we can't get away with several tankers of blood and a whole battery of 'life,' we don't deserve to be immortal."

He turned toward the communicator; and for that exultant moment caution was dim in the back of his mind. From the corner of his eye, he saw the woman leap from the edge of the cot. Too late, he twisted aside. The movement saved him only partially. It was their cheeks not their lips that met.

Blue flame flashed from him to her. The burning energy seared his cheek to instant, bleeding rawness. He half fell to the floor. And then, furious with the intense agony, he fought free. "I'll break your bones!" he raged.

Her laughter, unlovely with her own suppressed fury, floated up at him from the floor where he had flung her, She said, "So you did have a secret supply of 'life' for yourself. You damned double-crosser!"

His mortification yielded to the realization that anger was useless. Tense with the weakness that was already a weight on his muscles, he whirled toward the control board, and began feverishly to make the adjustments that would pull the ship back into normal space and time.

The body urge grew in him swiftly, a dark, remorseless need. Twice, he reeled to the cot in a fit of nausea. But each time he fought back to the control board. He sat there finally at the controls, head drooping, conscious of the numbing tautness that crept deeper, deeper. He drove the ship too fast. It turned a blazing white when at last it struck the atmosphere of the third planet. But those hard metals held their shape; and the terrible speeds yielded to the fury of the reversers and to the pressure of air that thickened with every mile.

It was the woman who helped his faltering form into the tiny lifeboat. He lay there, gathering strength, staring eagerly down at the blazing sea of lights that was the first city he had seen on the night side of this strange world. Dully, he watched as the woman eased the small ship into the darkness behind a shed in a little back alley. And, because succor seemed suddenly near, he was able to walk beside her to the dimly lighted residential street near by.

He would have walked on blankly into the street, but the woman's fingers held him back into the shadows of the alley. "Are you mad?" she whispered. "Lie down. We'll stay here until someone comes."

The concrete was hard beneath his body, but after a moment of the painful rest it brought, he felt a faint surge of energy, and he was able to voice his bitter thought. "If you hadn't stolen most of my carefully saved 'life,' we wouldn't be in this desperate position. You well know that it's more important that I remain at full power."

In the dark beside him, the woman lay quiet for a while. Then her defiant whisper came. "We both need a change of blood, and a new charge of 'life.' Perhaps I did take a little too much out of you, but that was because I had to steal it. You wouldn't have given it to me of your own free will, and you know it."

For a time, the futility of argument held him silent, but as the minutes dragged, that dreadful physical urgency once more tainted his thought. He said heavily:

"You realize, of course, that we've revealed our presence. We should have waited for the others to come. There's no doubt at all that our ship was spotted by the Galactic Observer in this system before we reached the outer planets. They'll have tracers on us wherever we go, and no matter where we bury our machine, they'll know its exact location. It's impossible to hide the interstellar drive energies; and since they wouldn't make the mistake of bringing such energies to a third-degree planet, we can't hope to locate them in that fashion. But we must expect an attack of some kind. I only hope one of the great Galactics doesn't take part in it."

"One of *them!*" Her whisper was a gasp. She controlled herself, and snapped irritably, "Don't try to scare me. You've told me time and again that—"

"All right, all right!" He spoke grudgingly, wearily. "A million years have proven that they consider us beneath their personal attention. And" —in spite of his appalling weakness, scorn came—"let any of the kind of agents they have in these lower category planets try to stop us."

"Hush!" Her whisper was tense. "Footsteps! Quick, get to your feet!"

He was aware of the shadowed form of her rising. Then her hands were tugging at him. Dizzily, he stood up.

"I don't think," he began wanly, "that I can—"

"Jeel!" Her whisper beat at him; her hands shook him. "It's a man and a woman. They're 'life,' Jeel, 'life!' "

Life!

He straightened. A spark of the unquenchable will to live that had brought him across the black miles and the blacker years burst into flame inside him. Lightly, swiftly, he fell into step beside Merla, and strode into the open. He saw the shapes of the man and the woman. In the half-night under the trees of that street, the couple came towards them, drawing aside to let them pass. First the woman came, then the man—and it was as simple as if all his strength had been there in his muscles.

He saw Merla launch herself at the man; and then he was grabbing the woman, his head bending instantly for that abnormal kiss.

Afterwards—after they had taken the blood, too—grimness came to the man, a hard fabric of thought and counter-thought, that slowly formed into purpose. He said, "We'll leave the bodies here."

Her startled whisper rose in objection, but he cut her short, harshly. "Let me handle this. These dead bodies will draw to this city news gatherers, news reporters, or whatever their breed are called on this planet. And we need such a person now. Somewhere in the reservoir of facts possessed by a person of this type must be clues, meaningless to him but by which we can discover the secret base of the Galactic Observer in this system. We must find that base, discover its strength, and destroy it if necessary when the tribe comes."

His voice took on a steely note. "And now, we've got to explore this city, find a much frequented building under which we can bury our ship, learn the language, replenish our own vital supplies, and capture that reporter.

"After I'm through with him"—his tone became silken-smooth— "he will undoubtedly provide you with that physical diversion which you apparently crave when you have been particularly chemical."

He laughed gently, as her fingers gripped his arm in the darkness, a convulsive gesture. She said, "Thank you, Jeel. You do understand, don't you?"

II

Behind Leigh, a door opened. Instantly the clatter of voices in the room faded to a murmur. He turned alertly, tossing his cigarette onto the marble floor and stepping on it, all in one motion.

Overhead, the lights brightened to daylight intensity. In that blaze he saw what the other eyes were already staring at: the two bodies, the man's and the woman's, as they were wheeled in. The dead couple lay side by side on the flat, gleaming top of the carrier. Their bodies were rigid, their eyes closed. They looked as dead as they were, and not at all, Leigh thought, as if they were sleeping.

He caught himself making a mental note of that fact, and felt shocked at himself. The first murders on the North American continent in twenty-seven years. And it was only another job. He was tougher than he'd ever believed.

Around him, the voices had stopped. The only sound was the hoarse breathing of the man nearest him, and the scrape of his own shoes as he went forward. His movement acted like a signal on that tense group of men. There was a general pressing forward. Leigh had a moment of anxiety. And then his bigger, harder muscles brought him where he wanted to be, opposite the two heads. He leaned forward, absorbed. His fingers probed gingerly where the incisions showed on the neck of the woman. He did not look up at the attendant as he said softly:

"This is where the blood was drained?"

"Yes."

Before he could speak again, another reporter interjected, "Any special comment from the police scientists? The murders are more than a day old now. There ought to be something."

Leigh scarcely heard. The woman's body, electrically warmed for embalming, felt eerily lifelike to his touch. It was only after a long moment that he noticed her lips were badly, almost brutally, bruised.

His gaze flicked to the man. And there were the same neck cuts, the same torn lips. He looked up. Questions quivered on his tongue. They remained unspoken as the calm-voiced attendant said:

"Normally, when the electric embalmers are applied, there is resistance from the static electricity of the body. Curiously, that resistance was not present in either body."

Somebody said, "Just what does that mean?"

"This static force is actually a form of life force, which usually trickles out of a corpse over a period of a month. We know of no way to hasten the process, but the bruises on the lips show distinct burns, which are suggestive."

There was a craning of necks, a crowding forward. Leigh allowed himself to be pushed aside. He stopped attentively as the attendant said, "Presumably, a pervert could have kissed with such violence."

"I thought," Leigh said distinctly, "there were no more perverts since Professor Ungarn persuaded the government to institute his brand of mechanical psychology in all schools, thus ending murder, theft, war, and all unsocial perversions."

The black frock-coated attendant hesitated, then said, "A very bad one seems to have been missed." He finished, "That's all, gentlemen. No clues, no promise of an early capture, and only this final fact: We've wirelessed Professor Ungarn and, by great good fortune, we caught him on his way to Earth from his meteor retreat near Jupiter. He'll be landing shortly after dark, in a few hours from now."

The lights dimmed. As Leigh stood frowning, watching the bodies being wheeled out, a phrase floated out of the gathering chorus of voices:

"—The kiss of death—"

"I tell you," another voice said, "the captain of this space liner swears it happened—the spaceship came past him at a million miles an hour, and it was slowing down, get that, slowing down—two days ago."

"—The vampire case! That's what I'm going to call it—"

That's what Leigh called it, too, as he talked briefly into his wrist communicator. He finished, "I'm going to supper now, Jim."

"O.K., Bill." The local editor's voice sounded metallic. "And say, I'm supposed to commend you. Nine thousand papers took the Planetarian Service on this story, as compared with about forty-seven hundred who bought from Universal, who had the second largest coverage. And I think you've got the right angle for today, too. Husband and wife, ordinary young couple, taking an evening walk. Some devil hauls up alongside of them, drains their blood into a tank, their life energy onto a wire or something—people will believe that, I guess. Anyway, you suggest it could happen to anybody; so be careful, folks. And you warn that, in these days of interplanetary speeds, he could be anywhere tonight for his next murder. As I said before, good stuff. That'll keep the yarn alive for tonight. Oh, by the way—"

"Shoot!"

"A kid called half an hour ago to see you. Said you expected him."

"A kid?" Leigh frowned to himself.

"Name of Patrick. High school age, about sixteen. No, come to think of it, that was only my first impression. Eighteen, maybe twenty, very bright, confident, proud."

"I remember now," said Leigh. "College student. Interview for a college paper. Called me up this afternoon. One of those damned persuasive talkers. Before I knew it, I was signed up for supper at Constantine's."

"That's right. I was supposed to remind you. O.K.?"

Leigh shrugged. "I promised," he said.

Actually, as he went out into the blaze of the late afternoon sunlit street, there was not an important thought in his head. Nor a premonition.

Around him, the swarm of humankind began to thicken. Vast buildings discharged the first surge of the five o'clock tidal wave. Twice, Leigh felt the tug at his arm before it struck him that someone was not just bumping into him.

He turned and stared down at a pair of dark, eager eyes set in a brown, wizened face. The little man waved a sheaf of papers at him. Leigh caught a glimpse of writing in longhand on the papers. Then the fellow was babbling, "Mr. Leigh, a hundred dollars for these ... biggest story—"

"Oh," said Leigh. His interest collapsed. He said politely, "Take it up to the Planetarian office. Jim Brian will pay you what the story is worth."

He walked on, a vague conviction in his mind that the matter was settled. Then, abruptly, there was the tugging at his arm again. "Scoop!" the little man said. "Professor Ungarn's log, all about a spaceship that came from the stars. Devils in it who drink blood and kiss people to death!"

"See here!" Leigh began, irritated; then stopped. An ugly chill wind swept through him. He stood, swaying a little from the shock of the thought that was frozen in his brain: *The newspapers with those details of "blood" and "kiss" were not on the street yet, wouldn't be for another five minutes.*

The man said, "Look, it's got Professor Ungarn's name printed in gold on the top of each sheet, and it's all about how he first spotted the ship eighteen light years out, and how it came all that distance in a few hours ... and he knows where it is now and—"

Leigh's reporter's brain, that special, highly developed department, was whirling with a little swarm of thoughts that suddenly straightened into a hard, bright pattern. In that tightly built design, there was no room for any such coincidence as this man coming to him here in this crowded street.

He said, "Let me see those!" and reached as he spoke.

The papers came free from the other's fingers into his hand, but Leigh did not even glance at them, His brain was crystal-clear, his eyes cold. He snapped, "I don't know what your game is. I want to know three things, and make your answers damned fast! One: How did you pick me out, name and job and all, here in this packed street of a city I haven't been in for a year?"

The little man stammered incomprehensible words. Leigh paid no attention. Remorselessly, he pounded on, "Two: Professor Ungarn is arriving from Jupiter in three hours. How do you explain your possession of papers he must have written less than two days ago?"

"Look, boss," the man chattered, "you've got me all wrong—"

"My third question," Leigh said grimly, "is how are you going to explain to the police your pre-knowledge of the details of murder?"

"Huh!" The little man's eyes were glassy, and for the first time pity came to Leigh. He said almost softly, "All right, fellah, start talking."

The words came swiftly, and at first they were simply senseless sounds. Only gradually did coherence come. "—And that's the way it was, boss. I'm standing there, and this kid comes up to me and points you out, and gives me five bucks and those papers you've got, and tells me what I'm supposed to say to you and—"

"Kid!" said Leigh; and the first shock was already in him.

"Yeah, kid about sixteen; no, more like eighteen or twenty ... and he gives me the papers and—"

"This kid," said Leigh, "would you say he was of college age?"

"That's it, boss; you've got it. That's just what he was. You know him, eh? O.K., that leaves me in the clear, and I'll be going—"

"Wait!" Leigh called. But the little man seemed suddenly to realize that he need only run. He vanished around a corner, and was gone forever.

Leigh stood, frowning, and read the thin sheaf of papers. There was nothing beyond what the little man had already conveyed by his incoherent talk. It was a vague series of entries on sheets from a loose-leaf notebook. Written down, the tale about the spaceship and its occupants lacked depth, and seemed more unconvincing each passing second. True, there was the single word "Ungarn" inscribed in gold on the top of each sheet but—

The sense of silly hoax grew so violently that Leigh thought angrily: "If that college kid really pulled a stunt like this, it'll be a short interview." The thought ended. The notion was as senseless as everything else that had happened.

And still there was no real tension in him. He was only going to a restaurant.

He turned into the splendid foyer that was the beginning of the vast and wonderful Constantine's. In the great doorway, he paused to survey the expansive glitter of tables, the hanging garden tearooms. Brilliant Constantine's, famous the world over, but not much changed from his last visit.

Leigh gave his name, and began, "A Mr. Patrick made reservations, I understand."

The girl said, "Oh, yes, Mr. Leigh. Mr. Patrick reserved Private Three. He just now phoned to say he'd be along in a few minutes. Our premier will escort you."

Leigh turned away, puzzled at the way the girl had gushed. Then a thought struck him. He turned back to the girl. "Just a minute," he said, "did you say *Private Three*? Who's paying for this?"

The girl said, "It was paid by phone. Forty-five hundred dollars!"

Leigh stood very still. Even after what had happened on the street, this meeting seemed scarcely more than an irritation to be gotten over with. Now, abruptly, it was become a fantastic, abnormal thing. Forty-five— hundred—dollars! Could it be some fool rich kid determined to make a strong, personal impression?

With cold logic, he rejected that solution. Humanity produced egotists on an elephantine scale, but not one who would order a feast like that to impress a reporter. His eyes narrowed on an idea. "Where's your registered phone?" he asked curtly.

A minute later, he was saying into the mouthpiece: "Is this the Amal-gamated Universities Secretariat? I want to find out if there is a Mr. Pat-rick registered at any of your local colleges, and if there is, whether or not he has been authorized by any college paper to interview William Leigh of the Planetarian News Service. This is Leigh calling."

It took six minutes, and then the answer came, brisk, tremendous, and final: "There are three Mr. Patricks in our seventeen units. All are at present having supper at their various official residences. There are four Miss Patricks, similarly accounted for by our staff of secretaries. None of the seven is in any way connected with a university paper. Do you wish any assistance in dealing with the impostor?"

Leigh hesitated. When he finally spoke, it was with the queer, dark realization that he was committing himself. "No," he said, and hung up.

He came out of the phone booth, shaken by his own thoughts. There was only one reason why he was in this city at this time. Murder! And he knew scarcely a soul. It seemed incredible that any stranger would want to see him for a reason not connected with his own purpose. He waited until the ugly thrill was out of his system. Then he said to the attendant, "To Private Three, please."

Presently, he was examining the luxurious suite. It turned out to be a splendidly furnished apartment with a palace-like dining salon dominating the five rooms. One entire wall of the salon was lined with decorated mirror facings, behind which glittered hundreds of bottles of liquor. The brands were strange to his inexpensive tastes, the bouquet of several that he opened heady but inviting. In the ladies' dressing room was a long showcase display-ing a gleaming array or jewelry. He estimated that there was several hundred thousand dollars' worth, if it were genuine. Leigh was not impressed. For his taste, Constantine's did not supply good value for the money they charged.

"I'm glad you're physically big," said a voice behind him. "So many reporters are thin and small."

The tone was subtly different than it had been over the phone in the early afternoon. Deliberately different. The difference, he noted as he turned, was in the body, too, the difference in the shape of a woman from a boy, skillfully but not perfectly concealed under the well-tailored man's suit.

Actually, of course, she was quite boyish in build, young, finely molded. And, actually, he would never have suspected if she had not allowed her voice to be so purposefully womanish. She echoed his thought coolly.

"Yes, I wanted you to know. But now, there's no use wasting words. You know as much as you need to know. "Here's a gun. The spaceship is buried below this building."

Leigh made no effort to take the weapon, nor did he glance at it. The first shock was over. He seated himself on the silken chair of the vanity dresser, leaned back against the vanity dresser itself, raised his eyebrows, and said, "Consider me a slow-witted newsman who's got to know what it's all about. Why so much preliminary hocus-pocus?"

He thought deliberately: He had never in his adult life allowed himself to be rushed into anything. He was not going to start now.

III

He saw after a moment that the girl was small of build. Which was odd, he decided carefully. Because his first impression had been of considerable height. Or perhaps—he considered the possibility unhurriedly—this second effect was a more considered result of her male disguise.

He dismissed that particular problem as temporarily insoluble. Actually, the girl's size was unimportant. She had long, black lashes and dark eyes that glowed at him from a proud, almost haughty face. And that was it. That was the essence of her personality. There was pride in the way she held her head. And in the poised easiness of every movement, in the natural shift from grace to grace as she walked slowly toward him. It was not a conscious pride, but an awareness of superiority that affected every movement of her muscles, and came vibrantly into her voice, as she said scathingly:

"I picked you because every newspaper I've read today carried your account of the murders, and because it seemed to me that somebody who already was actively working on the case would be reasonably quick at grasping essentials. As for the dramatic preparation, I considered that would be more convincing than explanation. I see I was mistaken." She was quite close to him now. She leaned over, laid her revolver on the vanity beside his arm, and finished almost indifferently, "Here's an effective weapon. It doesn't shoot bullets, but it has a trigger and you aim it like any gun. In the event you develop the beginning of courage, come down the tunnel after me as quickly as possible, but don't blunder in on me and the people I shall be talking to. Stay hidden! Act only if I'm threatened."

Tunnel, Leigh thought stolidly, as she walked with a free, swift stride out of the room. A tunnel here in this apartment, Private Three. Either he was crazy, or she was.

He realized suddenly that he ought to be offended at the way she had spoken. He felt annoyed at her trick of leaving the room, leaving him to develop curiosity. He smiled ruefully. If it wasn't for the fact that he was a reporter, he'd show her that such a second-rate psychology didn't work on him. Still irritated, he climbed to his feet, took the gun, and then paused briefly as the odd, muffled sound of a door reluctantly opening came to his ears.

He found her in the bedroom to the left of the dining salon. He felt only the vaguest surprise when he saw that she had the end of a thick green rug rolled back, and that there was a hole in the floor at her feet. The square of floor that was the tunnel-covering lay back neatly, pinned to position by a complicated-looking hinge.

Leigh's gaze reached beyond the opening to the girl. In that moment, just before she became aware of him, there was a hint of uncertainty in her manner. Her right profile, half turned away from him, showed pursed lips and a strained whiteness. The impression he received was of indecision. He had the subtle sense of observing a young woman who, briefly, had lost her superb confidence. Then she saw him, and her attitude changed.

She didn't seem to stiffen in any way. Paying no attention to him at all, she stepped to the first step of the little stairway that led down into the hole, and began to descend without a quiver of hesitation. Yet his first conviction that she had faltered brought him forward with narrowed eyes. And, suddenly, the certainty of her brief fear made his whole madness real. He plunged forward, down the steep stairway, and pulled up only when he saw that he was actually in a smooth, dimly-lighted tunnel, and that the girl had paused, one finger to her lips.

"Sssssh!" she said. "The door of the ship may be open."

That irritated Leigh, a hard trickle of anger. Now that he had committed himself, he felt automatically the leader of this fantastic expedition. The girl's pretensions, her haughty manner merely made him impatient.

"Don't 'Ssssh!' me!" he whispered sharply. "Just give the facts and I'll do the rest."

He stopped. The meaning of the words she had spoken penetrated. His anger collapsed. "Ship!" he said incredulously. "Are you trying to tell me there's actually a spaceship buried here under Constantine's?"

The girl seemed not to hear. Leigh saw that they were at the end of a short passageway. Metal gleamed dully just ahead. Then the girl was saying, "Here's the door. Now, remember, you act as guard. Stay hidden, ready to shoot. And if I yell 'Shoot,' you shoot!"

She bent forward. There was the tiniest scarlet flash. The door opened, revealing a second door just beyond. Again that minute, intense blaze of red, and then that door also swung open.

It was swiftly done, too swiftly. Before Leigh could more than grasp that the crisis had come, the girl stepped coolly into the brilliantly lighted room beyond the second door.

Leigh poised, undecided, in the shadows, startled by the girl's action. There was deeper shadow against the metal wall toward which he pressed himself in one instinctive move. He froze there. Silently he cursed a stupid young woman who actually walked into a den of enemies of unknown numbers without an organized plan of self-protection. Or did she know how many there were? And who?

The questions disturbed him. Finally, he thought grimly: She wasn't wholly unprotected. At least he was out here with a gun, unnoticed.

He waited tensely. But the door remained open; and there was no apparent movement towards it. Slowly, Leigh let himself relax, and allowed his straining mind to absorb its first considered impressions. The portion of underground room that he could see showed one end of what seemed to be a control board, a metal wall that blinked with tiny lights. He could see the edge of a rather sumptuous cot. The whole was actually so suggestive of a spaceship that Leigh thought, astounded: The girl had not been trying to fool him. Incredibly, here under the ground, actually *under* Constantine's, was a small spaceship.

That thought ended as the silence beyond the open door, the curiously long silence, was broken by a man's cool voice. "I wouldn't even try to raise that gun if I were you. The fact that you have said nothing since entering shows how enormously different we are to what you expected." He laughed gently, an unhurried, deep-throated, derisive laughter that came clearly to Leigh; then he went on, "Merla, what would you say is the psychology behind this young lady's action? You have of course noticed that she is a young lady, and not a boy."

A richly toned woman's voice replied, "She was born here, Jeel. She has none of the normal characteristics of a Klugg, but she is a Galactic, though definitely not the Galactic Observer. Probably, she's not alone. Shall I investigate?"

"No!" The man sounded indifferent. "We don't have to worry about a Klugg's assistant."

Leigh relaxed slowly, but he had a sense of emptiness. For the first time he realized how great a part the calm assurance of the young woman had played in the fabricating of his own confidence. Shattered now! Before the enormous certainties of these two, and in the face of their instant penetration of her male disguise, the effects of the girl's rather wonderful personality seemed a remote pattern, secondary, overwhelmed by a greater power.

He forced the fear from him as the girl spoke. Forced his courage to grow with each word she uttered, feeding on the confidence of her tone. It didn't matter whether she was simulating or not, because they were in this now, he as deep as she. Only the utmost boldness could hope to draw victory from the defeat that threatened them both.

With admiration, he noted the intensity of her voice as she said, "My silence had its origin in the fact that you are the first Dreeghs I have ever seen. Naturally, I studied you with some curiosity. But I can assure you I am not impressed. However, in view of your extraordinary opinions on the matter, I shall come to the point at once: I have been instructed by the Galactic Observer of this system to inform you to be gone by morning. Our sole reason for giving you that much leeway is that we don't wish to bring the truth of all this into the open. But don't count on that. Earth is on the verge of being given fourth-degree rating; and, as you probably know, in emergencies fourths are given Galactic knowledge. That emergency we will consider to have arrived tomorrow at dawn."

"Well, well" —the man was laughing gently, satirically—"a pretty speech, powerfully spoken, but meaningless for us who can analyze its pretensions, however sincere, back to the Klugg origin."

"What do you intend to do with her, Jeel?"

The man was cold, deadly, utterly sure. "There's no reason why she should escape. She has blood, and more than normal life. It will convey to the Observer with clarity our contempt for his ultimatum."

He finished with a slow, surprisingly rich laughter, "We shall now enact a simple drama. The young lady will attempt to jerk up her gun and shoot me with it. Before she can succeed, I shall have my own weapon out, and be firing. The whole thing, as she will discover, is a matter of nervous coordination. And Kluggs are chronically almost as slow-moving as human beings."

His voice stopped. His laughter trickled away. Silence.

In all his alert years, Leigh had never felt more indecisive.

His emotions said—*now*; surely, she'd call now. And even if she didn't, he must act on his own. Rush in! Shoot!

But his mind was cold with an awful dread. There was something about the man's voice, a surging power. Abnormal, savage strength was here. Could this really be a spaceship from the stars? His brain wouldn't follow that terrible thought. He crouched, fingering the gun she had given him, dimly conscious that it felt queer, unlike any revolver he had ever had.

The silence from the spaceship control room continued. It was the same curious silence that had followed the girl's entrance short minutes before. Only this time it was the girl who broke it, her voice faintly breathless but withal cool, vibrant, unafraid, "I'm here to warn, not to force issues. And unless you're charged with the life energy of fifteen men, I wouldn't advise you to try anything. After all, I came knowing what you were."

"What do you think, Merla? Can we be sure she's a Klugg? Could she possibly be of the higher Lennel type?" It was the man, his tone conceding her point, but the derision was still there, the implacable purpose, the high, tremendous confidence.

And yet, in spite of that sense of imminent violence, Leigh felt himself torn from the thought of danger. His reporter's brain twisted irresistibly to the fantastic meaning of what was taking place:

—*Life energy of fifteen men*—

It was all there. In a monstrous way, it all fitted. The two dead bodies he had seen drained of blood and *life energy*, the repeated reference to a Galactic Observer, with whom the girl was connected. He grew aware that the woman was speaking.

"Klugg!" she said positively. "Pay no attention to her protestations, Jeel. You know I'm sensitive when it comes to women. She's lying. She's just a little fool who walked in here expecting us to be frightened of her. Destroy her at your pleasure."

"I'm not given to waiting," said the man. "So—"

There was no delaying now. Leigh leaped for the open doorway. He had a flashing glimpse of a man and woman, dressed in evening clothes, the man standing, the woman seated. He was aware of a gleaming, metallic background. The control board, part of which he had already seen, was now revealed as a massive thing of glowing instruments; and then all that was blotted out as he snapped:

"That will do. Put up your hands."

For a moment he had the impression that his entry was a surprise, and that he dominated the situation. None of the three people in the room was turned toward him. The man, Jeel, and the girl were standing facing each other. The woman, Merla, sat in a deep chair, her fine profile to him, her golden head flung back. It was she who, still without looking at him, spoke the words that ended his brief conviction of triumph. She said to the disguised girl:

"You certainly travel in low company, a stupid human being. Tell him to go away before he's damaged."

The girl said, "Leigh, I'm sorry I brought you into this. Every move you made in entering was heard, observed, and dismissed before you could even adjust your mind to the scene."

"Is his name Leigh?" said the woman sharply. "I thought I recognized him as he entered. He's very like his photograph over his newspaper column." Her voice grew strangely tense: "Jeel, a newspaper reporter!"

"We don't need him now," the man said. "We know who the Galactic Observer is."

"Eh?" said Leigh. His mind fastened hard on those amazing words. "Who? How did you find out? What—"

"The information," said the woman, and it struck him suddenly that the strange quality in her voice was eagerness, "will be of no use to you. Regardless of what happens to the girl, you're staying."

She glanced swiftly at the man, as if seeking his sanction. "Remember, Jeel, you promised."

It seemed so meaningless that Leigh had no sense of personal danger. His mind scarcely more than passed the words. His eyes concentrated tautly on a reality that had, until that moment, escaped his awareness. He said softly, "Just now you used the phrase, 'Regardless of what happens to the girl.' When I came in, you said, 'Tell him to go away before he's damaged.'" Leigh smiled grimly. "I need hardly say this is a far cry from the threat of immediate death that hung over us a few seconds ago. And I have just now noticed the reason.

"A little while ago, I heard our pal, Jeel, dare my little girl friend here to raise her gun. I notice now that *she has it raised.* My entrance did have an effect." He addressed himself to the girl, "Shall we shoot—or withdraw?"

It was the man who answered. "I would advise withdrawal. I could still win, but I am not the heroic type who takes the risk of what might well be a close call." He added, in an aside to the woman: "Merla, we can always catch this man Leigh now that we know who he is."

The girl said, "You first, Mr. Leigh." And Leigh did not stop to argue.

Metal doors clanged behind him as he charged along the tunnel. After a moment, he was aware of the girl running lightly beside him.

The strangely unreal, the unbelievably murderous little drama was over, finished as fantastically as it had begun.

IV

Outside Constantine's a gray light gathered around them. It was a twilight side street, and people hurried past them with the strange, anxious look of the late for supper. Night was falling. Leigh stared at his companion. In the dimness of the deep dusk, she seemed all boy, slightly, lithely built, striding along boldly. He laughed a little, huskily, then more grimly.

"Just what was all that?" he said. "Did we escape by the skin of our teeth? Or did we win? What made you think you could act like God, and give those tough eggs twelve hours to get out of the solar system?"

The girl was silent after he had spoken. She walked just ahead of him, head bent into the gloom. Abruptly, she turned. She said, "I hope you will have enough sense to refrain from telling what you've just seen and heard."

Leigh said, "This is the biggest story since—"

The girl's voice was pitying. "You're not going to print a word of it because in about ten seconds you'll see that no one in the world would believe any of it."

In the darkness, Leigh smiled tightly. "The mechanical psychologist will verify every syllable."

"I came prepared for that, too!" said the vibrant voice. Her hand swung up toward his face. Too late, he jerked back.

Light flared in his eyes, a dazzling, blinding force that exploded into his sensitive optic nerves with all the agonizing power of intolerable brightness. Leigh cursed aloud, wildly, and snatched at his tormentor. His right hand grazed a shoulder. He lashed out violently with his left, and tantalizingly caught only the edge of a sleeve that instantly jerked away.

"You little devil!" he raged. "You've blinded me."

"You'll be all right," came the cool answer. "But you'll find that the mechanical psychologist will analyze anything you say as pure imagination. In view of your threat to publish, I had to do that. Now, give me my gun."

The first glimmer of sight was returning. Leigh could see her body, a dim shape in the night. In spite of the continuing pain, he smiled grimly. His voice was soft as he said, "I've just now remembered you said this gun didn't shoot bullets. Even the *feel* of it suggests that it'll make an interesting proof of anything I say. So—"

His smile faded abruptly. For the girl stepped forward. The metal that jabbed into his ribs was so hardly thrust it made him grunt.

"Give me that gun!"

"Like fun I will," Leigh snapped. "You ungrateful little ruffian, how dare you treat me so shoddily after I saved your life? I ought to knock you one right on the jaw."

He stopped. With staggering suddenness the hard realization struck that she meant it. This was no girl raised in a refined school, who wouldn't dare to shoot, but a cold-blooded young creature who had already proved her determination against a deadlier opponent than he himself.

He had never had any notions about the superiority of man over woman, and he felt none now. Hastily, he handed the weapon over. The girl took it, and said coldly, "You seem to be laboring under the illusion that your entry into the spaceship enabled me to raise my weapon. You're quite mistaken. What you did do was to provide me with the opportunity to let them think that that was the situation, and that they dominated it. But I assure you, that is the extent of your assistance. It was almost valueless."

Leigh laughed out loud, a pitying, ridiculing laugh.

"In my admittedly short life," he said, "I've learned to recognize a quality of personality and magnetism in human beings. You've got it, a lot of it, but not a fraction of what either of those two had, particularly the man. He was terrible. He was the most abnormally magnetic human being I've ever run across. Lady, I can only guess what all this is about, but

I'd advise you"—Leigh paused, then finished slashingly—"you and all the other Kluggs to stay away from that couple. Personally, I'm going to get the police in on this, and there's going to be a raid on Private Three. I didn't like that odd threat that they could capture me at any time. Why me?"

He broke off hastily, "Hey, where are you going? I want to know your name. I want to know what made you think you could order those two around. *Who did you think you were?*"

He said no more. His whole attention was concentrated on running. He could see her for a moment, a hazy, boyish figure against a dim corner light. Then she was around the corner. Leigh thought: "She's my only point of contact with all this. If she gets away—"

Sweating, he rounded the corner; and at first the street seemed dark and empty of life. Then he saw the car. A normal-looking, high-hooded coupé, long, low-built, that began to move forward noiselessly and quite naturally. It became unnatural. It lifted. Amazingly, it lifted from the ground. He had a swift glimpse of white rubber wheels folding out of sight. Streamlined, almost cigar-shaped now, the spaceship that had been a car darted at a steep angle into the sky.

Swiftly, it was gone.

Above Leigh the gathering night towered, a strange, bright blue. In spite of the brilliant lights of the city glaring into the sky, one or two stars showed. He stared up at them, empty inside, thinking: "It was like a dream. Those—Dreeghs—coming out of space—bloodsuckers, vampires."

Suddenly hungry, he bought a chocolate bar from a sidewalk stand and stood munching it. He began to feel better. He walked over to a near-by wall socket, and plugged in his wrist radio.

"Jim," he said, "I've got some stuff, not for publication, but maybe we can get some police action on it. Then I want you to have a mechanical psychologist sent to my hotel room. There must be some memory that can be salvaged from my brain—"

He went on briskly. His sense of inadequacy waned. Reporter Leigh was himself again.

V

The little glistening balls of the mechanical psychologist whirred faster and faster. They became a single, glowing circle in the darkness. And not till then did the first, delicious whiff of psycho-gas touch his nostrils. He felt himself drifting, slipping. A voice began to speak in the dim distance, so far away that not a word came through. There was only the sound, the faint, curious sound, and the feeling, stronger every instant, that he would soon be able to hear the fascinating things it seemed to be saying.

The longing to hear, to become a part of the swelling, murmuring sound tugged at him, in little rhythmical, wavelike surges. And still the promise of meaning was unfulfilled. Private thoughts ended utterly. Only the mindless chant remained and the pleasing gas holding him so close to sleep, its flow nevertheless so delicately adjusted that his mind hovered minute after minute on the ultimate abyss of consciousness. He lay, finally, still partially awake, but even the voice was merging now into blackness. It clung for a while, a gentle, friendly, melodious sound in the remote background of his brain, becoming more remote with each passing instant. He slept, a deep, hypnotic sleep, as the machine purred on.

When Leigh opened his eyes, the bedroom was dark except for the floor lamp beside a corner chair. It illuminated the darkly dressed woman who sat there, all except her face, which was in shadow above the circle of light. He must have moved, for the shadowed head suddenly looked up from some sheets of typewriter-size paper. The voice of Merla, the Dreegh, said:

"The girl did a very good job of erasing your subconscious memories. There's only one possible clue to her identity and—"

Her words went on, but his brain jangled them to senselessness in that first shock of recognition. It was too much, too much fear in too short a time. For a moment, he was like a child, and strange, cunning, intense thoughts of escape came. If he could slide to the side of the bed, away from where she was sitting, and run for the bathroom door—

"Surely, Mr. Leigh," the woman's voice reached toward him, "you know better than to try anything foolish. And, surely, if I had intended to kill you, I would have done it much more easily while you were asleep."

Leigh lay still, gathering his thoughts and licking dry lips. Her words were not reassuring. "What—do—you— want?" he managed finally.

"Information!" Laconically. "What was that girl?"

"I don't know." He stared into the half-gloom, where her face was. His eyes were more accustomed to the light now, and he could catch the faint, golden glint of her hair. "I thought—you knew." He went on more swiftly, "I thought you knew the Galactic Observer; and that implied the girl could be identified any time."

He had the impression she was smiling. She said, "Our statement to that effect was designed to throw both you and the girl off guard, and constituted the partial victory we snatched from what had become an impossible situation."

The body sickness was still upon Leigh. But the desperate fear that had produced it faded before the implications of her confession of weakness. These Dreeghs were not so superhuman as he had thought. Relief was followed by caution. Careful, he warned himself, it wouldn't be wise to underestimate. But he couldn't help saying:

"I'd like to point out that even your so-called snatching of victory from defeat was not so well done. Your husband's statement that you could pick me up any time could easily have spoiled the picking."

The woman's voice was faintly contemptuous. "If you knew anything of psychology, you would realize that the vague phrasing of the threat actually lulled you. Certainly, you failed to take even minimum precautions. And the girl has made no effort to protect you."

The suggestion of deliberately subtle tactics brought to Leigh a twinge of returning alarm. Deep inside him he thought: What ending did the Dreegh woman plan for this strange meeting?

"You realize, of course," the Dreegh said softly, "that you will either be of value to us alive—or dead. There are no easy alternatives. I would advise alertness and sincerity in your cooperation. You are in this affair without any limitations."

So that was the idea. A thin bead of perspiration trickled down Leigh's cheek. His fingers trembled as he reached for a cigarette on the table beside the bed. He was shakily lighting the cigarette when his gaze fastened on the window. That brought a faint shock. For it was raining, a furious rain that hammered soundlessly against the noiseproof glass.

He pictured the bleak, empty streets, their brilliance dulled by the black, rain-filled night. Deserted streets—deserted Leigh. For he was deserted here. All the friends he had, scattered over the great reaches of the earth, couldn't add one ounce of strength, or bring one real ray of hope to him in this darkened room, against this woman who sat so calmly under the light, studying him from shadowed eyes.

With an effort, Leigh steadied himself. He said, "I gather that's my psychograph report you have in your hand. What does it say?"

"Very disappointing." Her voice seemed far away. "There's a warning in it about your diet. It seems your meals are irregular."

She was playing with him. The attempt at humor made her seen more inhuman, not less. For, somehow, the words clashed unbearably with the reality of her; the dark immensity of space across which she had come, the unnatural lusts that had brought her and the man to unprotected Earth. Leigh shivered. Then he thought fiercely, "Damn it, I'm scaring myself. So long as she stays in her chair, she can't pull the vampire on me."

Aloud he said, "If there's nothing in the psychograph, then I'm afraid I can't help you. You might as well leave. Your presence isn't adding to my happiness."

In a dim way, he hoped she'd laugh. But she didn't. She sat there, her eyes glinting dully out of the gloom. At last she said, "We'll go through this report together. I think we can safely omit the references to your health as being irrelevant. But there are a number of factors that I want developed. Who is Professor Ungarn?"

"A scientist." Leigh spoke frankly. "He invented this system of mechanical hypnosis, and he was called in when the dead bodies were found because the killings seemed to have been done by perverts."

"Have you any knowledge of his physical appearance?"

"I've never seen him," Leigh said more slowly. "He never gives interviews and his photograph is not available now. I've heard stories, but—" He hesitated. He was giving her general knowledge only, but even that could be dangerous.

"These stories," the woman said, "do they give the impression that he's a man of inordinate magnetic force, but with lines of mental suffering etched in his face, and a sort of resignation?"

"Resignation to what?" Leigh exclaimed sharply. "I haven't the faintest idea what you're talking about. I've only seen photographs, and they show a fine, rather sensitive, tired face."

She said, "There would be more information in any library?"

"Or in the Planetarian Service morgue," Leigh said, and could have bitten off his tongue for that bit of gratuitous information.

"Morgue?" said the woman.

Leigh explained, but his voice was trembling with self-rage. For seconds now the feeling had been growing on him: Was it possible this devilish woman was on the right track? And getting damaging answers out of him because he dared not stop and organize for lying. He had an incongruous sense of the unfairness of the abnormally swift way she had solved the Observer's identity. Because, damn it, it could be Professor Ungarn.

Ungarn was a mysterious figure, a scientist, great inventor in a dozen highly complicated, widely separated fields. He had a home near one of Jupiter's moons, and he had a daughter named Patricia. Good heavens, Patrick—Patricia!

His shaky stream of thoughts ended as the woman said, "Can you have your office send the information to your recorder here?"

"Y-yes." His reluctance was so obvious that the woman bent into the light. For a moment, her golden hair glittered; her pale blue eyes glowed at him in a strangely humorless, satanic amusement.

"Ah!" she said. "You think so, too?"

She laughed, an odd, musical laugh, odd in that it was at once so curt and so pleasant. The laugh ended abruptly, unnaturally, on a high note. And then—although he had not seen her move—there was a metal thing in her hand, pointing at him. Her voice came at him with a brittle, jarring command, "You will climb out of the bed, operate the recorder, and naturally you will do nothing and say nothing but what is necessary."

Leigh moved slowly to obey the woman's command. As he stood up, the room swayed dizzily. He thought sickly: If only he could faint. But he recognized that that was beyond the power of his tough body. It was dismay that made him so shivery. Annoyingly, he grew steadier even as he walked to the recorder. For the first time in his life, he hated the resilience of his strength. He set the machine, and said:

"This is William Leigh. Give me all the dope you've got on Professor Garret Ungarn."

There was a pause, then a brisk voice said, "You've got it. Sign the form."

Leigh signed, and watched the signature dissolve into the machine. It was then, as he was straightening, that the woman said, "Shall I read it here, Jeel, or shall we take the machine with us?"

Leigh blinked, and whirled; and then, very carefully, he sat down on the bed. The Dreegh, Jeel, was leaning idly against the jamb of the bathroom door, a dark, malignantly handsome man, with a faint, unpleasant smile on his lips. Behind him—incredibly, behind him, through the open bathroom door, was, not the gleaming bath, but another door; and beyond that door still another door, and beyond that the control room of the Dreegh spaceship!

There it was, exactly as he had seen it in the solid ground under Constantine's. He had the same partial view of the sumptuous cot, the imposing section of instrument board, the tastefully padded floor. *In his bathroom!*

Leigh thought insanely: "I keep my spaceship in my bathroom, of course."

It was the Dreegh's voice that drew his brain from its dizzy contemplation. The Dreegh said, "I think we'd better leave, I'm having difficulty holding the ship on the alternation of space-time planes. Bring the man and the machine and—"

Leigh didn't hear the last word. He jerked his mind all the way out of the bathroom, "You're—taking—me?"

"Why, of course." It was the woman who spoke. "You've been promised to me, and besides, we'll need your help in finding Ungarn's meteor."

Leigh sat quiet, and without plans of his own. He saw after a moment that the rain was still beating against the glass, great sparkling drops that washed murkily down the broad panes. And he saw that the night was dark. Dark night, dark rain, dark destiny—they fitted his dark, grim thoughts. With an effort he forced his body and his mind to relax, When at last he faced his alien captors again, Reporter Leigh was cold with acceptance of his fate, and ready to fight for his life.

"I can't think of a single reason," he said, "why I should go with you. And if you think I'm going to help you destroy the Observer, you're crazy."

The woman said matter-of-factly, "There was a passing reference in your psychograph to a Mrs. Henry Leigh, who lives in a village called Relton, on the Pacific coast. We could be there in half an hour, your mother and her home destroyed within a minute after that. Or, perhaps, we could add her blood to our reserves."

"She would be too old," the man said in a chill tone. "We do not want the blood of old people."

It was the icy objection that brought horror to Leigh. He had a mental picture of a silent, immensely swift ship sweeping out of the eastern night, over the peaceful hamlet. The destroying energy would reach down, and the ship would sweep on over the long, dark waters to the west.

The deadly picture faded. The woman was saying, gently, "Jeel and I have evolved an interesting little system of interviewing human beings of the lower order. For some reason, he frightens people merely by his presence. Similarly, people develop an unnatural fear of me when they see me clearly in a strong light. So we have always tried to arrange our meetings with human beings with me sitting in semidarkness and Jeel in the background. It has proved very effective."

She stood up, a tall, lithely built, shadowed figure in a rather tight-fitting skirt and a dark blouse. She finished, "But now, shall we go? You bring the machine, Mr. Leigh."

"I'll take it," said the Dreegh.

Leigh glanced sharply at the lean, sinewed face of the terrible man, startled at the instant, accurate suspicion of his own desperate intention.

The Dreegh loomed over the small machine, where it stood on a corner desk. "How does it work?" he asked.

Leigh stepped forward. There was still a chance that he could manage this without additional danger to anyone. Not that it would be more than a vexation, unless, as their suggestion about finding the Ungarn meteor indicated, they headed straight out to space. If they did that, then he might actually delay them. He said, "Press the key marked 'Titles,' and the machine will type all the main headings."

"That sounds reasonable." The long, grim-faced head nodded. The Dreegh reached forward, pressed the button. The recorder hummed softly, and a section of it lit up, showing typed lines under a transparent covering. There were several headings.

" '—His Meteor Home'," read the Dreegh. "That's what I want. What is the next step?"

"Press the key marked 'Subheads.' "

Leigh was suddenly shaky. He groaned inwardly. Was it possible this creature-man was going to obtain the information he wanted? Certainly, such a tremendous intelligence would not easily be led away from logical sequence. He forced himself to grimness. He'd have to take a chance.

"The subhead I desire," said the Dreegh, "is marked 'Location.' And there is a number, one, in front of it. What next?"

"Press Key No. 1," Leigh said, "then press the key lettered 'General Release'."

The moment he had spoken, he grew taut. If this worked, and there was no reason why it shouldn't, Key No. 1 would impart all the information under that heading. And surely the man would not want more until later. After all, this was only a test. They were in a hurry. And later, when the Dreegh discovered that the "General Release" key had dissolved all the other information, it would be too late.

The thought dimmed. Leigh started. The Dreegh was staring at him bleakly. The man said, "Your voice has been like an organ; each word uttered full of subtle shadings that mean much to the sensitive ear. Accordingly"—a ferocious smile twisted the lean face—"I shall press Key No. 1. But not 'General Release.' And as soon as I've examined the little story on the recorder, I shall attend to you for that attempted trick. The sentence is—death."

"Jeel!"

"Death!" reiterated the man flatly. And the woman was silent.

There was silence, then, except for the subdued humming of the recorder. Leigh's mind was almost without thought. He felt fleshless, and only gradually did he realize that he was waiting here on the brink of a night darker than the black wastes of space from which these monster humans had come.

He felt a kinship with the black rain that poured with such solid, noiseless power against the glinting panes. His aimless gaze returned to the recorder machine, and to the grim man who stood so thoughtfully staring down at the words it was unfolding. His thought quickened. And, suddenly, there was purpose in him.

If death was inescapable, at least he could try again, somehow, to knock down that "General Release" key. He stared at the key, measuring the distance. Three feet, he thought, perhaps four. If he should fling himself toward it, how could even a Dreegh prevent the dead weight of his body and his extended fingers from accomplishing such a simple mission? After all, his sudden action had once before frustrated the Dreeghs by allowing the Ungarn girl—in spite of her denials—to get her gun into position for firing.

He saw that the Dreegh was turning away from the machine. The man pursed his lips, but it was the woman, Merla, who spoke from where she stood in the gloom:

"Well?"

The man frowned. "The exact location is nowhere on record. Apparently, there has been no development of meteors in this system. I suspected as much. After all, space travel has only existed a hundred years; and the new planets and the moons of Jupiter have absorbed all the energies of exploring, exploiting man."

"I could have told you that," said Leigh.

If he could move a little to one side of the recorder, so that the Dreegh would have to do more than simply put his arm out—

The man was saying, "There is, however, a reference to some man who transports food and merchandise from the moon Europa to the Ungarns. We will ... er ... persuade this man to show us the way."

"One of these days," said Leigh, "you're going to discover that all human beings cannot be persuaded. What pressure are you going to put on this chap? Suppose he hasn't got a mother."

"He has—life!" said the woman softly.

"One look at you," Leigh snapped, "and he'd know that he'd lose that, anyway."

As he spoke, he stepped to the left, one short step. He had an impulse to say something, anything to cover the action. But his voice had betrayed him once. And actually, it might already have done so again. The cold face of the man was almost too enigmatic.

"We could," said the woman, "use William Leigh to persuade him."

The words were softly spoken, but they shocked Leigh. For they offered a distorted hope. And that shattered his will to action. His purpose faded into remoteness. He fought to draw that hard determination back into his consciousness. He concentrated his gaze on the recorder machine, but the woman was speaking again; and his mind wouldn't hold anything except the urgent meaning of her words:

"He is too valuable a slave to destroy. We can always take his blood and energy, but now we must send him to Europa, there to find the freighter pilot of the Ungarns, and actually accompany him to the Ungarn meteor. If he could investigate the interior, our attack might conceivably be simplified, and there is just a possibility that there might be new weapons, of which we should be informed. We must not underestimate the science of the great Galactics. Naturally, before we allowed Leigh his freedom, we would do a little tampering with his mind, and so blot out from his conscious mind all that has happened in this hotel room. The identification of Professor Ungarn as the Galactic Observer we would make plausible for Leigh by a little rewriting of his psychograph report; and tomorrow he will awaken in his bed with a new purpose, based on some simple human impulse such as love of the girl."

The very fact that the Dreegh, Jeel, was allowing her to go on, brought the first, faint color to Leigh's cheeks, a thin flush at the enormous series of betrayals she was expecting of him. Nevertheless, so weak was his resistance to the idea of continued life, that he could only snap: "If you think I'm going to fall in love with a dame who's got twice my I.Q., you're—"

The woman cut him off. "Shut up, you fool! Can't you see I've saved your life?"

The man was cold, ice-cold. "Yes, we shall use him, not because he is essential, but because we have time to search for easier victories. The first members of the Dreegh tribe will not arrive for a month and a half, and it will take Mr. Leigh a month of that to get to the moon, Europa, by one of Earth's primitive passenger liners. Fortunately, the nearest Galactic military base is well over three months distant—by Galactic ship speeds.

"Finally"—with a disconcerting, tigerish swiftness the Dreegh whirled full upon Leigh, eyes that were like pools of black fire measured his own startled stare—"as a reminder to your subconscious of the error of trickery, and as complete punishment for past and—intended—offenses, *this!*"

Despairingly, Leigh twisted away from the metal that glowed at him. His muscles tried horribly to carry out the purpose that had been working to a crisis inside him. He lunged for the recorder—but *something* caught his body. Something not physical.

The pain that struck him seemed mortal. There was no visible flame of energy, only that glow at the metal source. But his nerves writhed; enormous forces contorted his throat muscles; froze the scream that quivered there. His whole being welcomed the blackness that mercifully blotted out the hellish pain.

VI

On the third day Europa began to give up some of the sky to the vast mass of Jupiter behind it. The engines that so imperfectly transformed magnetic attraction to a half-hearted repulsion functioned more and more smoothly as the complication of gravitic pull and counterpull yielded to distance. The old, slow, small freighter scurried on into the immense, enveloping night; and the days dragged into weeks, the weeks crawled their drab course toward the full month. On the thirty-seventh day, the sense of slowing up was so distinct that Leigh crept dully out of his bunk, and croaked, "How much farther?"

The stolid-faced space trucker grinned at him. The man's name was Hanardy, and he said now matter-of-factly, "We're just pulling in. See that spot of light over to the left? It's moving this way."

He ended with a rough sympathy. "Been a tough trip, eh? Tougher'n you figured when you offered to write up my little route for your big syndicate."

Leigh scarcely heard. He was clawing at the porthole, straining to penetrate the blackness. At first his eyes kept blinking compulsively, and nothing came. Stars were out there, but it was long seconds before his bleary gaze made out moving lights. He counted them with sluggish puzzlement. "One, two, three—seven—" he counted. "And all traveling together."

"What's that?" Hanardy bent beside him. "Seven?"

There was a brief silence between them as the lights grew visibly dim with distance and winked out.

"Too bad," Leigh ventured, "that Jupiter's behind us. They mightn't fade out like that in silhouette. Which one was Ungarn's meteorite?"

Hanardy stood up, his heavy face dark with frown. He said slowly, "Those were ships. I never saw ships go so fast before. They were out of sight in less than a minute." The frown faded from his stolid face. He shrugged. "Some of those new police ships, I guess. And we must have seen them from a funny angle for them to disappear so fast."

Leigh half sat, half knelt, frozen into immobility. And after that one swift glance at the pilot's rough face, he averted his own. For a moment, the black fear was in him that his wild thoughts would blaze from his eyes.

Dreeghs! Two and a half months had wound their slow course since the murders. More than a month to get from Earth to Europa, and now this miserable, lonely journey with Hanardy, the man who trucked for the Ungarns. Every day of that time he had known with inner certainty that the danger had not basically altered but had assumed a more hidden form. The one fortunate reality in the whole affair was that he had wakened on the morning after the mechanical psychologist test from a dreamless sleep; and there in the psychograph report was the identification of Ungarn as the Observer, and the statement, borne out by an all too familiar emotional tension, that he was in love with the girl.

Now this! His mind flared. Dreeghs in seven ships. That meant the first had been reinforced by many. And perhaps the seven were only a reconnaissance group, withdrawing at Hanardy's approach. Or perhaps those fantastic murderers had already attacked the Observer's base. Perhaps the girl was dead.

He watched uneasily as the Ungarn meteorite made a dark, glinting path in the blackness to one side. The two objects, the ship and the bleak, rough-shaped mass of metallic stone, drew together in the night, the ship slightly behind. A great steel door slid open in the rock. Skillfully, the ship glided into the chasm. There was a noisy clicking. Hanardy came out of the control room, his face dark with puzzlement.

"Those damn ships are out there again," he said. "I've closed the big steel locks, but I'd better tell the professor and—"

Crash! The world jiggled. The floor came up and hit Leigh a violent blow. He lay there, cold in spite of the thoughts that burned at fire heat in his mind. For some reason, the vampires had waited until the freighter was inside. Then instantly, ferociously, attacked. In packs!

"Hanardy!" A vibrant girl's voice blared from one of the loudspeakers.

The pilot sat up shakily on the floor, where he had fallen, near Leigh. "Yes, Miss Patricia."

"You dared to bring a stranger with you!"

"It's only a reporter, miss. He's writing up my route for me."

"You conceited fool! That's William Leigh. He's a hypnotized spy of those devils who are attacking us. Bring him immediately to my apartment. He must be killed at once."

"Huh!" Leigh began, and then stiffened. The pilot was staring at him from narrowing eyes, all the friendliness gone from his rough, heavy face. Leigh laughed curtly. "Don't you be a fool too, Hanardy. I made the mistake once of saving that young lady's life, and she's hated me ever since."

The heavy face scowled at him. "So you knew her before, eh. You didn't tell me that. You'd better come along before I sock you one."

Awkwardly, he drew the gun from his side holster and pointed its ugly snout at Leigh.

"Get along!" he said.

Hanardy reached toward an arrangement of tiny lights beside the paneled door of Patricia Ungarn's apartment—and Leigh made a single leap and struck one blow. He caught the short, heavy body as it fell, grabbed at the sagging gun, lowered the dead weight to the floor of the corridor, and then stood like a great animal, straining for sound.

Silence! He studied the blond panels of the doorway to the apartment, as if by sheer, savage intentness he would penetrate their golden, beautifully grained opaqueness. It was the silence that struck him again, presently, the emptiness of the long, tunnel-like corridors. He thought, amazed: Was it possible father and daughter actually lived here without companions or servants or any human association? And that they had some idea that they could withstand the attack of the mighty and terrible Dreeghs?

They had a lot of power here, of course. The earth-like gravity alone would take stupendous energy to maintain. But now, he'd better be on his way before the girl grew impatient and came out with one of her weapons. What he must do was quite simple, unconnected with any nonsense of spying, hypnotic or otherwise. He must find the combination automobile-spaceship in which—*Mr. Patrick*—had escaped him that night after they left Constantine's. And with that tiny ship, he must try to slip out of Ungarn's meteorite, sneak through the Dreegh line, and so head back for Earth.

What a fool he'd been, a mediocre human being, mixing with such people. The world was full of normal girls of his own general I.Q. level. Why wasn't he safely married to one of them? Still thinking about that, he began laboriously to drag Hanardy along the smooth flooring. Halfway to the nearest corner, the man stirred. Without hesitation, Leigh struck him hard with the revolver butt. This was no time for squeamishness.

The pilot went limp again, and the rest was simple. He deserted the body as soon as he had pulled it out of sight around the corner, and raced along the hallway, trying doors. The first four wouldn't open. The fifth was also locked, but this time Leigh paused to consider.

It seemed unbelievable that the whole place was locked up. Two people in an isolated meteorite wouldn't go around perpetually locking and unlocking doors. Carefully, he examined the door before him. And found its secret. It opened to a slight pressure on a tiny, half-hidden push button that had seemed an integral part of the design of the latch. He stepped through the entrance, then started back with a terrible shock.

The room had no ceiling. Above him was—space. An ice-cold blast of air swept at him. He had a glimpse of gigantic machines in the room, machines that dimly resembled the ultramodern astronomical observatory on the moon that he had visited on opening day two years before. That one, swift look was all Leigh allowed himself. Then he stepped back into the hallway. The door of the observatory closed automatically in his face.

As he hurried to the next door, it struck him that he had made a fool of himself. The existence of the cold air showed that the open effect of the ceiling was only an illusion of invisible glass. But he decided not to go back.

The sixth door opened into a little cubbyhole. A blank moment passed before he recognized what it was. An elevator!

He scrambled in. The farther he got away from the residential floor, the less likelihood of quick discovery. He turned to close the door, and saw that it was shutting automatically. It clicked softly, then immediately started up. Leigh frowned. The elevator was apparently geared to go to some definite point. And that could be very bad. His eyes searched for controls; but nothing was visible. Gun poised, he stood alert as the elevator stopped. The door slid open.

Leigh stared. There was no room. The door opened onto blackness. Not the blackness of space with its stars. Or a dark room, half revealed by the light from the elevator. But blackness! Impenetrable. He put a tentative hand forward, half expecting to feel a solid object. But as his hand entered the black area, it vanished. He jerked it back, and stared at it, dismayed. It shone with a light of its own, all the bones plainly visible.

Swiftly, the light faded, the skin became opaque, but his whole arm pulsed with a pattern of pain. He thought: Fool, fool! He laughed bitterly, braced himself. And then it happened.

There was a flash out of the blackness. Something that sparkled vividly, something material that blazed a brilliant path to his forehead—and drew itself inside his head. And then—

He was no longer in the elevator. On either side of him stretched a long corridor. The stocky Hanardy was just reaching for some tiny lights beside the door of Patricia Ungarn's apartment. The man's fingers touched one of the lights. It dimmed. Softly, the door opened. A young woman with proud, insolent eyes and a queen-like bearing stood there.

"Father wants you down on Level 4," she said to Hanardy. "One of the energy screens has gone down; and he needs some machine work before he can put up another."

She turned to Leigh. Her voice took on metallic overtones as she said, "*Mr. Leigh, you can come in!*"

VII

Leigh entered with scarcely a physical tremor. A cool breeze caressed his cheeks; and there was the liltingly sweet sound of birds singing in the distance. He stopped as he saw the sunlit garden beyond the French windows. After a moment, he thought:

"What happened to me?"

He put his hands to his head, and felt his forehead, then his whole head. But nothing was wrong, not a contusion, not a pain. He saw that the girl was staring at him, and he realized that his actions must seem unutterably queer.

"What's the matter with you?" she asked.

Leigh looked at her suspiciously. He said harshly, "Don't pull that innocent stuff. I've been up in the blackness room, and all I've got to say is, if you're going to kill me, don't skulk behind artificial night and other trickery."

The girl's eyes, he saw, were narrowed, unpleasantly cold. "I don't know what you're trying to pretend," she said icily. "I assure you it will not postpone the death we have to deal you." She hesitated, then finished sharply, "The *what* room?"

Leigh explained, puzzled by her puzzlement, then annoyed by the contemptuous smile that came into her face. She cut him off curtly, "I've never heard a less balanced story. If your intention was to astound me and delay your death with that improbable tale, it has failed. You must be mad. You didn't knock out Hanardy, because when I opened the door, Hanardy was there, and I sent him down to Father."

"See here!" Leigh began. Then he stopped. Because Hanardy *had* been there as she opened the door! And yet earlier—

When?

Doggedly, Leigh pushed the thought on: Earlier, he had attacked Hanardy. And then he—Leigh—had gone up in an elevator; and then, somehow, back. He began to feel unbalanced. With trembling fingers, he felt his head again. And it was absolutely normal. Only, he thought, there was something inside it that sparkled and tingled.

With a start, he saw that the girl was drawing a gun from a pocket of her simple white dress. He stared at the weapon, and he thought, "I've got to delay her some more."

He said urgently, "I'm going to assume you're puzzled by my words. Let's begin at the beginning. There is such a room, is there not?"

"Please," said the girl wearily, "let us not have any of your logic. My I.Q. is 243, yours is 112. So I assure you I am quite capable of reasoning from any beginning you can think of." She went on, her low voice curt, "There is no 'blackness' room, as you call it, no sparkling thing that crawls inside a human head. There is but one fact: The Dreeghs in their visit to your hotel room hypnotized you; and this curious mind illusion can only be a result of that hypnotism—don't argue with me—"

With a savage gesture of her gun, she cut off his attempt to speak. "There's no time. For some reason, the Dreeghs did something to you. Why? What did you see in those rooms?"

As he explained and described, Leigh realized that he would have to attack her, and take all the attendant risk. The purpose was a taut thing in his mind as he obeyed her motion and went ahead of her into the corridor. It was there, an icy determination, as he counted the doors from the corner where he had left the unconscious Hanardy.

"One, two, three, four, *five*. This door!" he said.

"Open it!" the girl said.

He did so; and his lower jaw sagged. He was staring into a fine, cozy room filled with shelf on shelf of beautifully bound books. There were comfortable chairs, a magnificent handwoven rag rug, and a desk.

It was the girl who closed the door firmly and once more motioned him ahead of her. They came to the sixth room.

"And this is your elevator?"

Leigh nodded mutely; and because his whole body was shaking, he was only dimly surprised that there was no elevator, but only a long, empty, silent corridor. The girl was standing with her back partly to him; and if he hit her, it would knock her head against the doorjamb.

The sheer brutality of the thought was what stopped him, held him for an instant. And then it was too late. The girl whirled and looked straight into his eyes.

Her gun came up and pointed steadily. "Not that way," she said quietly. "For a moment I was wishing you would have the nerve to try it. But that would be the weak way for me." Her eyes glowed with pride. "After all, I've killed before through necessity, and hated it. You can see that, because of what the Dreeghs have done to you, it is necessary."

Her voice was curt again. "So back to my rooms. I have a space lock there to get rid of your body. Move!"

It was the emptiness, the silence except for the faint click of their shoes that caught at Leigh's nerves. He felt hopeless as he walked back to the apartment. He was trapped in this meteorite, hurtling darkly through the remote wastes of the solar system. Here in this prison, pursued and attacked by deadly ships from the fixed stars, he was under sentence of death, the executioner to be a girl. That was the devastating part. He couldn't argue with this young woman. Every word would sound like pleading, and that he would not do.

The singing of the birds, as he entered the apartment, brought him out of his mental depression. He walked to the stately French windows, and stared at the glorious summery garden. At least two acres of grass and flowers and trees spread before him. There was a wide, deep pool of green, green water. Everywhere gorgeously colored birds fluttered and trilled, and over all blazed the glory of brilliant sunshine.

It was the sunshine that held Leigh longest. Finally, it seemed to him that he had the solution. He said in a hushed voice, without turning, "The roof—is an arrangement—of magnifying glass. It makes the Sun as big as on Earth. Is that the—"

"You'd better turn around," came the hostile, vibrant voice from behind him. "I don't shoot people in the back. And I want to get this over with."

It was the moralistic smugness of her words that enraged Leigh. He whirled. "You damned little Klugg. You can't shoot me in the back, eh? Oh, no! And you couldn't possibly shoot me while I was attacking you because that would be the weak way. It's all got to be made right with your conscience."

He stopped so short that, if he had been running, instead of talking, he would have stumbled. Figuratively, almost literally, he saw Patricia Ungarn for the first time since his arrival. His mind had been so concentrated, so absorbed by deadly danger—

—For the first time as a woman.

Leigh drew a long breath. Dressed as a man, she had been youthfully handsome. Now, she wore a simple, snow-white sports dress. It was scarcely more than a tunic, and came well above her knees. Her hair shone with a brilliant brownness, and cascaded down to her shoulders. Her bare arms and legs gleamed a deep, healthy tan. Pure white sandals graced her feet. Her face gave the impression of extraordinary beauty. And then, amazed, he saw that her perfect cheeks were flushing vividly.

The girl said, "Don't you dare use that word to me."

She must have been utterly beside herself with rage. Her fury was such an enormous fact that Leigh gasped. Abruptly, he realized his tremendous opportunity.

"Klugg!" he said. "Klugg, Klugg, Klugg! So you realize now that the Dreeghs had you down pat, that all your mighty pretension was simply your Klugg mind demanding pretentious compensation for a dreary, lonely life. You had to think you were somebody, and yet all the time you must have known they'd only ship the tenth-raters to these remote posts. Klugg, not even Lennel; the Dreegh woman wouldn't even grant you Lennel status, whatever that is. And she'd know. Because if you're I.Q. 243, the Dreeghs were 400. You've realized that, too, haven't you?"

"Shut up! Or I'll kill you by inches!" said Patricia Ungarn. And Leigh was amazed to see that she had blanched under the tan. Stronger than before, he realized that he had struck, not only the emotional Achilles' heel of this strange and terrible young woman, but the very vital roots of her mental existence.

"So," he said deliberately, "the high morality is growing dim. Now you can torture me to death without a qualm. And to think that I came here to ask you to marry me because I thought a Klugg and a human being might get along."

"You what?" said the girl. Then she sneered. "So that was the form of their hypnotism. They would use some simple impulse for a simple human mind." She broke off, visibly fighting for calmness. "I think we've had just about enough. I know just the type of thoughts that come to a male human in love. Even knowing you're not responsible makes the idea none the less bearable. I feel sickened, insulted. Know, please, that my future husband is arriving with the reinforcements three weeks from now. He will be trained to take over Father's work—"

"Another Klugg!" said Leigh, and the girl turned shades whiter.

Leigh stood thunderstruck. In all his life, he had never seen anyone so violently affected as was this young girl. The intellectual mask was off, and underneath was a seething mass of emotions bitter beyond the power of words to express. Here was evidence of a life so lonely that it strained his imagination. Her every word showed an incredible pent-up masochism as well as sadism, for she *was* torturing herself as well as him. But he couldn't stop now to feel sorry for her. His life was at stake, and only more words could postpone death—or bring the swift and bearable surcease of a bullet fired in passion. He went on grimly:

"I'd like to ask one question. How did you find out my I.Q. is 112? What special interest made you inquire about that? Is it possible that, all by yourself here, you, too, had a special type of thought, and that, though your intellect rejected such lowly love, its existence is the mainspring behind your determination to kill, rather than cure me? I—"

"That will do," interrupted Patricia Ungarn.

It required a moment for Leigh to realize that in those few short seconds she had pulled herself completely together. He watched her tensely as her gun motioned toward a door he had not noticed before. She said curtly, "I suppose there is a solution other than death. That is, immediate death. And I have decided to accept the resultant loss of my spaceship."

She nodded at the door. "It's there in the air lock. It works very simply. The steering wheel pulls up or down or sideways, and that's the way the ship will go. Just step on the accelerator, and the machine will go forward. The decelerator is the left pedal. The automobile wheels fold in automatically as soon as they lift from the ground. Now, get going. I need hardly tell you that the Dreeghs will probably catch you. But you can't stay here. That's obvious."

"Thanks." That was all Leigh allowed himself to say. He had exploded an emotional powder keg, and he dared not tamper with it further. There was a tremendous psychological mystery here, but it was not for him to solve. Suddenly shaky from the realization of what was still ahead of him, he walked gingerly toward the air lock. And then—

It happened!

He had a sense of awful nausea. There was a wild swaying through blackness.

And then he was standing at the paneled doorway leading from the corridor to Patricia Ungarn's apartment. Hanardy stood beside him. The door opened. The young woman who stood on the other side of the threshold said strangely familiar words to Hanardy about going down to the fourth level to fix an energy screen. Then she turned to Leigh, and in a voice hard and metallic said:

"Mr. Leigh, you can come in."

VIII

The crazy part of it was that he walked in with scarcely a physical tremor. A cool breeze caressed his cheeks. And there was the liltingly sweet sound of birds singing in the distance. Leigh paused uncertainly. By sheer will power he shook the daze out of his mind, and bent mentally into the cyclone path of complete memory. Everything was there suddenly, the way the Dreeghs had come to his hotel apartment and ruthlessly forced him to their will, the way the "blackness" room had affected him, and how the girl had spared his life.

For some reason, the whole scene with the girl had been unsatisfactory to—Jeel; and it was now, fantastically, to be repeated.

That thought ended. The entire, tremendous reality of what had happened yielded to a vastly greater fact: There was—something—inside his head, a physical something. In a queer, horrible, inexperienced way, his mind instinctively fought against it. The result was ghastly confusion. Whatever it was, rested inside his head, unaffected by his brain's feverish contortions, cold, aloof, watching.

Watching.

Madly, then, he realized what it was. Another mind. Leigh shrank from the fact as from destroying fire. He tensed his brain. For a moment, his frenzy was so great that his face twisted with the anguish of his efforts. And everything blurred.

Exhausted finally, he simply stood there. And the thing-mind was still inside his head. Untouched.

What had happened to him?

Shakily, Leigh put his hands up to his forehead. Then he felt his whole head. There was a vague idea in him that if he pressed hard, it would be affected. He jerked his hands down with an unspoken curse. Damnation on damnation, he was even repeating the actions of this scene. He grew aware of the girl staring at him. He heard her say:

"What's the matter with you?"

It was the sound of the words, exactly the same words, that did it. He smiled wryly. His mind drew back from the abyss where it had teetered. He was sane again.

Gloomily, he recognized that he was still far from normal. Sane yes, but dispirited. Clearly, the girl had no memory of the previous scene, or she wouldn't be parroting. That thought ceased, too. A strange thing was happening. The mind inside him stirred, and looked through his eyes. Looked intently.

Intently.

The room and the girl in it changed, not physically, but subjectively, in what he saw, in the details. The details burned at him. Furniture and design that a moment before had seemed a flowing, artistic whole, abruptly showed flaws, errors in taste and arrangement and structure. His gaze flashed to the garden, and in instants tore it to mental shreds. Never in all his existence had he seen or felt criticism on such a high, devastating scale.

Only it wasn't criticism. Actually. The mind was indifferent. It saw things. Automatically, it saw some of the possibilities. By comparison the reality suffered. It was not a matter of anything being hopelessly bad. The wrongness was frequently a subtle thing. Birds not suited, for a dozen reasons, to their environment. Shrubs that added infinitesimal discord, not harmony, to the superb garden.

The mind flashed back from the garden; and this time, for the first time, studied the girl. On all Earth, no woman had ever been so piercingly examined. The structure of her body and her face, to Leigh so finely, proudly shaped, so gloriously patrician—he found low grade now.

An excellent example of low-grade development in isolation.

That was the thought, not contemptuous, nor derogatory, simply an impression by an appallingly direct mind that saw overtones, realities behind realities, a thousand facts where one showed.

There followed crystal-clear awareness of the girl's psychology, objective admiration for the system of isolated upbringing that made Klugg girls such fine breeders; and then—

Purpose!

Instantly carried out. Leigh took three swift steps toward the girl. He was aware of her snatching at the gun in her pocket. There was startled amazement on her face. Then he had her. Her muscles writhed like steel springs. But they were useless against his superstrength, his superspeed. He tied her with some wire he had noticed in a half-opened clothes closet.

Then he stepped back, and to Leigh came the shocked personal thought of the incredible thing that had happened, comprehension that all this, which seemed so normal, was actually so devastatingly superhuman, so swift that—seconds only had passed since he came into the room.

His private thought ended. He grew aware of the mind, contemplating what it had done, and what it must do before the meteorite would be completely under control.

Vampire victory was near.

There was a phase of walking along empty corridors, down several flights of stairs. Leigh thought dully, his own personal thought, that the Dreegh seemed to know thoroughly the interior of the meteorite. Somehow, during the periods of transition, of time manipulated, the creature-mind must have used his captive body to explore the place completely. And now, with simple, deadly purpose, he was heading for the machine shops on the fourth level, where Professor Ungarn and Hanardy labored to put up another energy defense screen.

He found Hanardy alone, working at a lathe that throbbed, and the sound made it easy to sneak up—

The professor was in a vast room, where great engines hummed a strange, deep tune of titanic power. He was a tall man, and his back was turned to the door as Leigh entered. But his reactions were much quicker than Hanardy's, quicker even than the girl's. He sensed danger. He whirled with a catlike agility. And succumbed instantly to muscles that could have torn him limb from limb. It was during the binding of the man's hands that Leigh had time for an impression.

In the photographs that Leigh had seen, as he had told the Dreegh, Merla, in the hotel, the professor's face had been sensitive, tired-looking, withal noble. He was more than that. The man radiated power, as no photograph could show it, *good power* in contrast to the savage, malignant, greater power of the Dreegh.

The sense of a powerful personality faded before the aura of cosmic weariness. It was a lined, an amazingly lined face. In a flash, Leigh remembered what the Dreegh woman had said. It was all there: deep-graven lines of tragedy and untold mental suffering, interlaced with a curious peacefulness. Like resignation. On that night months ago, he had asked the Dreegh woman: Resignation to what? And now, here in this tortured, kindly face was the answer: *Resignation to hell.*

Queerly, an unexpected second answer trickled into his consciousness: Morons, they're Galactic morons. Kluggs. The thought seemed to have no source; but it gathered strength. Professor Ungarn and his daughter were Kluggs, *morons* in the incredible Galactic sense. No wonder the girl had reacted like a crazy person. Obviously born here, she must have guessed the truth only in the last two months.

The I.Q. of human morons wavered between seventy-five and ninety, of Kluggs possibly between two hundred and twenty-five, and, say, two hundred and forty-three. What could be the nature of Galactic civilization if Dreeghs were four hundred, and Kluggs of the lowest I.Q. range were on the highest genius level by Earth standards? Somebody, of course, had to do the dreary, routine work of civilization. Kluggs and Lennels and their kind were obviously elected. No wonder they looked tired with that weight of inferiority to influence their very nerve and muscle structure. No wonder whole planets were kept in ignorance.

Leigh left the professor tied hand and foot, and began to turn off power switches. Some of the great motors were slowing noticeably as he went out of that mighty engine room. The potent hum of power dimmed.

Back in the girl's room, he entered the air lock, climbed into the small automobile spaceship, and launched into the night. Swiftly, the gleaming mass of meteorite receded into the darkness behind him. Suddenly, magnetic force rays caught his tiny craft, and drew it remorselessly toward the hundred-and-fifty-foot, cigar-shaped machine that flashed out of the darkness. He felt the spy rays; and he must have been recognized. For another ship flashed up to claim him. Air locks opened noiselessly, and shut again. Sickly, Leigh stared at the two Dreeghs, the tall man and the tall woman. He explained what he had done. Dimly, hopelessly, he wondered why he should have to explain. Then he heard Jeel say:

"Merla, this is the most astoundingly successful case of hypnotism in our existence. He's done everything. Even the tiniest thoughts we put into his mind have been carried out to the letter. And the proof is, the screens are going down. With the control of this station, we can hold out even after the Galactic warships arrive, and fill our tankers and our energy reservoirs for ten thousand years. Do you hear, *ten thousand years!*"

His excitement died. He smiled with sudden dry understanding as he looked at the woman. Then he said laconically, "My dear, the reward is all yours. We could have broken down those screens in another twelve hours, but it would have meant the destruction of the meteorite. This victory is so much greater. Take your reporter. Satisfy your craving—while the rest of us prepare for the occupation. Meanwhile, I'll tie him up for you."

Leigh thought, a cold, remote thought: The kiss of death. And shivered in appalled realization of what he had done.

IX

He lay on the couch, where Jeel had tied him. He was surprised, after a moment, to notice that, though *the* mind had withdrawn into the background of his brain, it was still there, cold, steely, abnormally conscious.

He wondered: what possible satisfaction could Jeel obtain from experiencing the mortal thrill of death with him? These people must be ultimately sadistic. The wonder died like dry grass under a heat ray as the woman came into the room and glided toward him. She smiled. She sat down on the edge of the couch.

"So here you are," she said.

She was, Leigh thought, like a tigress. There was purpose in every tense muscle of her long body. In surprise he saw that she had changed her dress. She wore a sleek, flimsy, tight-fitting gown that set off in startling fashion her golden hair and starkly white face. He watched her with fascination. He said, "Yes, I'm here."

Silly words. But he didn't feel silly. He stiffened even as he spoke. It was her eyes that did it. For the first time since he had first seen her, her eyes struck him like a blow. Blue eyes, and steady. So steady. Not the steady frankness of honesty. But steady like dead eyes. A chill grew on Leigh, a special, extra chill, adding to the ice that was already there inside him. He had the unholy thought that this was a dead woman, artificially kept alive by the blood and *life* of dead men and women. She smiled, but the bleakness remained in those cold, fish eyes. No smile, no warmth could ever bring light to that chill, beautiful countenance. But she smiled the form of a smile, and she said:

"We Dreeghs live a hard, lonely life. So lonely that sometimes I cannot help thinking our struggle to remain alive is a blind, mad thing. We're what we are through no fault of our own. It happened during an interstellar flight that took place a million years ago—" She stopped, almost hopelessly. "It seems longer. It must be longer. I've really lost track."

She went on, suddenly grim, as if the memory, the very telling, brought a return of horror, "We were among several thousand holidayers who were caught in the gravitational pull of a sun, afterward called the Dreegh Sun. Its rays, immensely dangerous to human life, infected us all. It was discovered that only continuous blood transfusions and the life force of other human beings could save us. For a while we received donations; then the government decided to have us destroyed as hopeless incurables. We were all young, and in love with life, of course. Some hundreds of us had been expecting the sentence, and we still had friends in the beginning. We escaped. We've been fighting ever since to stay alive."

And still he could feel no sympathy. It was odd, for all the thoughts she undoubtedly wanted him to have, came. Picture of a bleak, endless existence in spaceships, staring out into the perpetual night. Life processes circumscribed by the tireless, abnormal needs of bodies gone mad from ravenous disease. It was all there, the emotional pictures. But no emotions came. She was too cold. The years and that devil's hunt had stamped her soul and her eyes and her face.

And besides, her body seemed tenser now, leaning toward him, bending forward closer, closer, till he could hear her slow, measured breathing. Even her eyes suddenly held the vaguest inner light. Her whole being quivered with the chill tensity of her purpose. When she spoke, she almost breathed the words, "I want you to kiss me, and don't be afraid. I shall keep you alive for days, but I must have response, not passivity. You're a bachelor, at least thirty. You won't have any more morals about the matter than I. But you must let your whole body yield."

He didn't believe it. Her face hovered six inches above him. And there was such ferocity of suppressed eagerness in her that it could mean only death. Her lips were pursed, as if to suck, and they quivered with a strange, tense, trembling desire, unnatural, almost obscene. Her nostrils dilated at every breath. Surely no normal who had kissed as often as she must have in all her years could feel like that, if that was all she expected to get.

"Quick!" she said breathlessly. "Yield, yield!"

Leigh scarcely heard. For that other mind that had been lingering in his brain surged forward in its incredible way. He heard himself say, "I'll trust your promise because I can't resist such an appeal. You can kiss your head off. I guess I can stand it—"

There was a blue flash, an agonizing burning sensation that spread in a wave to every nerve of his body.

The anguish became a series of tiny pains, like small needles piercing a thousand bits of his flesh. Tingling, writhing a little, amazed that he was still alive. Leigh opened his eyes.

He felt a wave of purely personal surprise. The woman lay slumped, lips half twisted off of his, body collapsed hard across his chest. And the mind, that blazing mind was there, watching, as the tall figure of the Dreegh man sauntered into the room, stiffened, and then darted forward.

He jerked her limp form into his arms. There was the same kind of blue flash as their lips met, from the man to the woman. She stirred finally, moaning. He shook her brutally. "You wretched fool!" he raged. "How did you let a thing like that happen? You would have been dead in another minute, if I hadn't come along."

"I—don't—know." Her voice was thin and old. She sank down to the floor at his feet, and slumped there like a tired old woman. Her blonde hair straggled and looked curiously faded. "I don't know, Jeel. I tried to get his life force, and he got mine instead. He—"

She stopped. Her blue eyes widened. She staggered to her feet. "Jeel, he must be a spy. No human being could do a thing like that to me. Jeel"—there was sudden terror in her voice—"Jeel, get out of this room. Don't you realize? He's got my energy in him. He's lying there now, and whatever has control of him has my energy to work with—"

"All right, all right." He patted her fingers. "I assure you he's only a human being. And he's got your energy. You made a mistake, and the flow went the wrong way. But it would take much more than that for *anyone* to use a human body successfully against us. So—"

"You don't understand!"

Her voice shook. "Jeel, I've been cheating. I don't know what got into me, but I couldn't get enough life force, Every time I was able, during the four times we stayed on Earth, I sneaked out. I caught men on the street. I don't know exactly how many because I dissolved their bodies after I was through with them. But there were dozens. And he's got all the energy I collected, enough for scores of years, enough for—don't you see?—enough for *them.*"

"My dear!" The Dreegh shook her violently, as a doctor would an hysterical woman. "For a million years, the great ones of Galactic have ignored us and—"

He paused. A black frown twisted his long face. He whirled like the tiger man he was, snatching at his gun as Leigh stood up.

The man Leigh was no longer surprised at anything. At the way the hard cords fell rotted from his wrists and legs. At the way the Dreegh froze rigid after one look into his eyes. For the first shock of the tremendous, the almost cataclysmic truth was already in him.

"There is only one difference," said Leigh in a voice so vibrant that the top of his head shivered from the unaccustomed violence of the sound. "This time there are two hundred and twenty-seven Dreegh ships gathered in one concentrated area. The rest—and our records show only a dozen others—we can safely leave to our police patrols."

The Great Galactic, who had been William Leigh, smiled darkly and walked toward his captives. "It has been a most interesting experiment in deliberate splitting of personality. Three years ago, our time manipulators showed this opportunity of destroying the Dreeghs, who hitherto had escaped by reason of the vastness of our galaxy. And so I came to Earth, and here built up the character of William Leigh, reporter, complete with family and past history. It was necessary to withdraw into a special compartment of the brain some nine-tenths of my mind, and to drain completely an equal percentage of life energy.

"That was the difficulty: How to replace that energy in sufficient degree at the proper time, without playing the role of vampire. I constructed a number of energy caches, but naturally at no time had we been able to see all the future. We could not see the details of what was to transpire aboard this ship, or in my hotel room that night you came, or under Constantine's restaurant. Besides, if I had possessed full energy as I approached this ship, your spy ray would have registered it. And you would instantly have destroyed my small automobile spaceship. My first necessity, accordingly, was to come to the meteorite, and obtain an initial control over my own body through the medium of what my Earth personality called the 'blackness' room.

"That Earth personality offered unexpected difficulties. In three years it had gathered momentum as a personality, and that impetus made it necessary to repeat a scene with Patricia Ungarn, and to appear directly as another conscious mind in order to convince Leigh that he must yield. The rest, of course, was a matter of gaining additional life energy after boarding your ship, which"—he bowed slightly at the muscularly congealed body of the woman—"which she supplied me.

"I have explained all this because of the fact that a mind will accept complete control only if full understanding of defeat is present. I must finally inform you, therefore, that you are to remain alive for the next few days, during which time you will assist me in making personal contact with your friends."

He made a gesture of dismissal. "Return to your normal existence. I have still to coordinate my two personalities and that does not require your presence."

The Dreeghs went out blank-eyed, almost briskly; and the two minds in one body were alone!

For Leigh, the Leigh of Earth, the first desperate shock was past. The room was curiously dim, as if he were staring out through eyes that were no longer—his! He thought, with a horrible effort at self-control: "I've got to fight. Some *thing* is trying to possess my body. All the rest is lie."

A soothing mind-pulsation stole into the shadowed chamber where his—self—was cornered: "No lie, but wondrous truth. You have not seen what the Dreeghs saw and felt, for you are inside this body, and know not that it has come marvelously *alive*, unlike anything that your petty dreams on Earth could begin to conceive. You must accept your high destiny, else the sight of your own body will be a terrible thing to you. Be calm, be braver than you've ever been, and pain will turn to joy."

Calm came not. His mind quivered in its dark corner, abnormally conscious of strange and unnatural pressures that pushed in at it like winds out of unearthly night. For a moment of terrible fear, it funked that pressing night, then forced back to sanity, and had another thought of its own, a grimly cunning thought: The devilish interloper was arguing. Could that mean—his mind rocked with hope—that coordination was impossible without *his* yielding to clever persuasion?

Never would he yield.

"Think," whispered the alien mind, "think of being one valuable facet of a mind with an I.Q. twelve hundred, think of yourself as having played a role. And now you are returning to normalcy, a normalcy of unlimited power. You have been an actor completely absorbed in your role, but the play is over. You are alone in your dressing room removing the grease paint. Your mood of the play is fading, fading, fading—"

"Go to hell!" said William Leigh loudly. "I'm William Leigh, I.Q. one hundred and twelve, satisfied to be just what I am. I don't give a damn whether you built me up from the component elements of your brain, or whether I was born normally. I can see what you're trying to do with that hypnotic suggestion stuff, but it isn't working. I'm here. I'm myself. And I stay myself. Go find yourself another body, if you're so smart."

Silence settled where his voice had been. And the emptiness, the utter lack of sound brought a sharp twinge of fear greater than that which he had had before he spoke.

He was so intent on that inner struggle that he was not aware of outer movement until, with a start, he realized he was staring out of a port window. Night spread there, the living night of space.

A trick, he thought, in an agony of fear; a trick somehow designed to add to the corroding power of hypnotism. A trick! He tried to jerk back. And, terrifyingly, couldn't. His body wouldn't move. Instantly, then, he tried to speak, to crash through that enveloping blanket of unholy silence. But no sound came.

Not a muscle, not a finger stirred; not a single nerve so much as trembled. He was alone.

Cut off in his little corner of brain.

Lost.

Yes, lost, came a strangely pitying sibilation of thought, lost to a cheap, sordid existence, lost to a life whose end is visible from the hour of birth, lost to a civilization that has already had to be saved from itself a thousand times. Even you, I think, can see that all this is lost to you forever.

Leigh thought starkly: The *thing* was trying by a repetition of ideas, by showing evidence of defeat, to lay the foundations of further defeat. It was the oldest trick of simple hypnotism for simple people. He couldn't let it work.

You have, urged the mind inexorably, accepted the fact that you were playing a role; and now you have recognized our oneness, and are giving up the role. The proof of this recognition on your part is that you have yielded control of—our—body.

—Our body, *our* body, OUR body—

The words re-echoed like some Gargantuan sound through his brain, then merged swiftly into that calm, other-mind pulsation:

—concentration. All intellect derives from the capacity to concentrate; and, progressively, the body itself shows *life*, reflects and focuses that gathering, vaulting power.

—One more step remains: You must see—

Amazingly, then, he was staring into a mirror. Where it had come from, he had no memory. It was there in front of him where, an instant before, had been a black porthole—and there was an image in the mirror, shapeless at first to his blurred vision.

Deliberately—he felt the enormous deliberateness—the vision was cleared for him. He saw. And then he didn't.

His brain wouldn't look. It twisted in a mad desperation, like a body buried alive, and briefly, horrendously conscious of its fate. Insanely, it fought away from the blazing thing in the mirror. So awful was the effort, so titanic the fear, that it began to gibber mentally, its consciousness to whirl dizzily, like a wheel spinning faster, faster.

The wheel shattered into ten thousand aching fragments. Darkness came, blacker than Galactic night. And there was—

Oneness!

VAULT OF THE BEAST

The creature crept. It whimpered from fear and pain. Shapeless, formless thing yet changing shape and form with each jerky movement, it crept along the corridor of the space freighter, fighting the terrible urge of its elements to take the shape of its surroundings. A gray blob of disintegrating stuff, it crept and cascaded, it rolled, flowed, and dissolved, every movement an agony of struggle against the abnormal need to become a stable shape. Any shape! The hard chilled-blue metal wall of the Earth-bound freighter, the thick, rubbery floor. The floor was easy to fight. It wasn't like the metal that pulled and pulled. It would be easy to become metal for all eternity.

But something prevented. An implanted purpose. A purpose that drummed from molecule to molecule, vibrated from cell to cell with an unvarying intensity that was like a special pain: Find the greatest mathematical mind in the solar system, and bring it to the vault of the Martian ultimate metal. The Great One must be freed. The prime number time lock must be opened!

That was the purpose that pressed on its elements. That was the thought that had been seared into its fundamental consciousness by the great and evil minds that had created it.

There was movement at the far end of the corridor. A door opened. Footsteps sounded. A man whistling to himself. With a metallic hiss, almost a sigh, the creature dissolved, looking momentarily like diluted mercury. Then it turned brown like the floor. It became the floor, a slightly thicker stretch of dark brown rubber spread out for yards.

It was ecstasy just to lie there and be flat and have shape, and to be so nearly dead that there was no pain. Death was sweet and desirable. And

131

life such an unbearable torment. If only the life that was approaching would pass swiftly. If the life stopped, it would pull it into shape. Life could do that. Life was stronger than metal. The approaching life meant torture, struggle, pain.

The creature tensed its now flat, grotesque body—the body that could develop muscles of steel—and waited for the death struggle.

Spacecraftsman Parelli whistled happily as he strode along the gleaming corridor that led from the engine room. He had just received a wireless from the hospital. His wife was doing well, and it was a boy. Eight pounds, the radiogram had said. He suppressed a desire to whoop and dance. A boy. Life sure was good.

Pain came to the thing on the floor. Primeval pain that sucked through its elements like burning acid. The brown floor shuddered in every molecule as Parelli strode over it. It had a tremendous urge to pull toward him, to take his shape. The thing fought its desire, fought with dread, and more consciously now that it could think with Parelli's brain. A ripple of floor rolled over the man.

Fighting didn't help. The ripple grew into a blob that momentarily seemed to become a human head. Gray nightmare of demoniac shape. The creature hissed metallically in terror, then collapsed palpitating with fear and pain and hate as Parelli strode on rapidly—too rapidly for its creeping pace. The thin sound died. The thing dissolved into brown floor, and lay quiescent yet quivering from its uncontrollable urge to live—live in spite of pain, in spite of terror. To live and fulfill the purpose of its creators.

Thirty feet up the corridor, Parelli stopped. He jerked his mind from its thoughts of child and wife. He spun on his heels, and stared uncertainly along the passageway from the engine room.

"Now what the devil was that?" he pondered aloud.

A queer, faint, yet unmistakably horrid sound was echoing through his consciousness. A shiver ran the length of his spine. That devilish sound.

He stood there, a tall, magnificently muscled man, stripped to the waist, sweating from the heat generated by the rockets that were decelerating the craft after its meteoric flight from Mars. Shuddering, he clenched his fists, and walked slowly back the way he had come.

The creature throbbed with the pull of him, a torment that pierced into every restless, agitated cell. Slowly it became aware of the inevitable, the irresistible need to take the shape of the life.

Parelli stopped uncertainly. The floor moved under him, a visible wave that reared brown and horrible before his incredulous eyes and grew into a bulbous, slobbering, hissing mass. A venomous demon head reared on twisted, half-human shoulders. Gnarled hands on apelike, malformed arms clawed at his face with insensate rage, and changed even as they tore at him.

"Good God!" Parelli bellowed.

The hands, the arms that clutched him grew more normal, more human, brown, muscular. The face assumed familiar lines, sprouted a nose, eyes, a red gash of mouth. The body was suddenly his own, trousers and all, sweat and all.

"—God!" his image echoed; and pawed at him with letching fingers and an impossible strength.

Gasping, Parelli fought free, then launched one crushing blow straight into the distorted face. A scream came from the thing. It turned and ran, dissolving as it ran, fighting dissolution, uttering half-human cries. Parelli chased it, his knees weak and trembling from funk and sheer disbelief. His arm reached out, and plucked at the disintegrating trousers. A piece came away in his hand, a cold, slimy, writhing lump like wet clay.

The feel of it was too much. His gorge rising in disgust, he faltered in his stride. He heard the pilot shouting from ahead: "What's the matter?"

Parelli saw the open door of the storeroom. With a gasp, he dived in, came out a moment later, an ato-gun in his fingers. He saw the pilot, standing with staring brown eyes, white face, and rigid body, facing one of the great windows.

"There it is!" the man cried.

A gray blob was dissolving into the edge of the glass, becoming glass. Parelli rushed forward, ato-gun poised. A ripple went through the glass, darkening it; and then, briefly, he caught a glimpse of a blob emerging on the other side of the glass into the cold of space. The officer came up beside him. The two of them watched the gray, shapeless mass creep out of sight along the side of the rushing freight liner.

Parelli sprang to life. "I got a piece of it!" he gasped. "Flung it down on the floor of the storeroom.

It was Lieutenant Morton who found it. A tiny section of floor reared up, and then grew amazingly large as it tried to expand into human shape. Parelli, with distorted, crazy eyes, scooped it up in a shovel. It hissed. It nearly became a part of the metal shovel, but couldn't because Parelli was so close. Parelli staggered with it behind his superior officer. He was laughing hysterically. "I touched it," he kept saying. "I touched it."

A large blister of metal on the outside of the space freighter stirred into sluggish life, as the ship tore into Earth's atmosphere. The metal walls of the freighter grew red, then white-hot, but the creature, unaffected, continued its slow transformation into gray mass. It realized vaguely that it was time to act.

Suddenly, it was floating free of the ship, falling slowly, heavily, as if somehow the gravitation of Earth had no serious effect upon it. A minute distortion inside its atoms started it falling faster, as in some alien way it suddenly became more subject to gravity. The earth was green below; and in the dim distance a city glittered in the sinking sun. The thing slowed and drifted like a falling leaf in a breeze toward the still-distant surface. It landed in an arroyo beside a bridge at the outskirts of the city.

A man walked over the bridge with quick, nervous steps. He would have been amazed, if he had looked back, to see a replica of himself climb from the ditch to the road, and start walking briskly after him.

Find the—greatest mathematician!

It was an hour later; and the pain of that thought was a continuous ache in the creature's brain, as it walked along the crowded street. There were other pains, too. The pain of fighting the pull of the pushing, hurrying mass of humanity that swarmed by with unseeing eyes. But it was easier to think, easier to hold form now that it had the brain and body of a man.

Find—mathematician!

"Why?" asked the man's brain of the thing. And the whole body shook with shock at such heretical questioning. The brown eyes darted in fright from side to side, as if expecting instant and terrible doom. The face dissolved a little in that brief moment of mental chaos, became successively the man with the hooked nose who swung by, and the tanned face of the tall woman who was looking into the shop window.

The process would have gone on, but the creature pulled its mind back from fear, and fought to readjust its face to that of the smooth-shaven young man who sauntered idly in from a side street. The young man glanced at him, looked away, then glanced back again startled. The creature echoed the thought in the man's brain: "Who the devil is that? Where have I seen that fellow before?"

Half a dozen women in a group approached. The creature shrank aside as they passed. Its brown suit turned the faintest shade of blue, the color of the nearest dress, as it momentarily lost control of its outer cells. Its mind hummed with the chatter of clothes and "My dear, didn't she look dreadful in that awful hat?"

There was a solid cluster of giant buildings ahead. The thing shook its human head consciously. So many buildings meant metal; and the forces that held metal together would pull and pull at its human shape. The creature comprehended the reason for this with the understanding of the slight man in a dark suit who wandered by dully. The slight man was a clerk; the thing caught his thought. He was thinking enviously of his boss, who was Jim Brender, of the financial firm of J. P. Brender & Co.

The overtones of that thought made the creature turn abruptly and follow Lawrence Pearson, bookkeeper. If passers-by had paid attention to him they would have been amazed after a moment to see two Lawrence Pearsons proceeding down the street, one some fifty feet behind the other. The second Lawrence Pearson had learned from the mind of the first that Jim Brender was a Harvard graduate in mathematics, finance, and political economy, the latest of a long line of financial geniuses, thirty years old, and head of the tremendously wealthy J. P. Brender & Co.

"Here I'm thirty, too," Pearson's thoughts echoed in the creature's mind, "and I've got nothing. Brender's got everything—everything while all I've got to look forward to is the same old boardinghouse till the end of time."

It was getting dark as the two crossed the river. The creature quickened its pace, striding forward aggressively. Some glimmering of its terrible purpose communicated itself in that last instant to the victim. The slight man turned, and let out a faint squawk as those steel-muscled fingers jerked at his throat, a single fearful snap. The creature's mind went black and dizzy as the brain of Lawrence Pearson died. Gasping, fighting dissolution, it finally gained control of itself. With one sweeping movement, it caught the dead body and flung it over the concrete railing. There was a splash below, then a sound of gurgling water.

The thing that was now Lawrence Pearson walked on hurriedly, then more slowly till it came to a large, rambling brick house. It looked anxiously at the number, suddenly uncertain if it had remembered rightly. Hesitantly, it opened the door. A streamer of yellow light splashed out, and laughter vibrated in the thing's sensitive ears. There was the same hum of many thoughts and many brains, as there had been in the street. The creature fought against the inflow of thought that threatened to crowd out the mind of Lawrence Pearson. It found itself in a large, bright hall, which looked through a door into a room where a dozen people were sitting around a dining table.

"Oh, it's you, Mr. Pearson," said the landlady from the head of the table. She was a sharp-nosed, thin-mouthed woman at whom the creature stared with brief intentness. From her mind, a thought had come. She had a son who was a mathematics teacher in a high school. The creature shrugged. In one glance it penetrated the truth. This woman's son was as much of an intellectual lightweight as his mother. "You're just in time," she said incuriously. "Sarah, bring Mr. Pearson's plate."

"Thank you, but I'm not feeling hungry," the creature replied; and its human brain vibrated to the first silent, ironic laughter that it had ever known. "I think I'll just lie down."

All night long it lay on the bed of Lawrence Pearson, bright-eyed, alert, becoming more and more aware of itself. It thought: "I'm a machine, without a brain of my own. I use the brains of other people. But somehow my creators made it possible for me to be more than just an echo. I use people's brains to carry out my purpose."

It pondered about these creators, and felt panic sweeping along its alien system, darkening its human mind. There was a vague physiological memory of pain and of tearing chemical action that was frightening.

The creature rose at dawn, and walked the streets till half-past nine. At that hour, it approached the imposing marble entrance of J. P. Brender & Co. Inside, it sank down in the comfortable chair initialed L P., and began painstakingly to work at the books Lawrence Pearson had put away the night before. At ten o'clock, a tall young man in a dark suit entered the arched hallway and walked briskly through the row after row of offices. He smiled with easy confidence to every side. The thing did not need the chorus of "Good Morning, Mr. Brender" to know that its prey had arrived. It rose with a lithe, graceful movement that would have been impossible to the real Lawrence Pearson, and walked briskly to the washroom. A moment later, the image of Jim Brender emerged from the door and walked with easy confidence to the door of the private office which Jim Brender had entered a few minutes before. The thing knocked, walked in—and simultaneously became aware of three things. First, it had found the mind after which it had been sent. Second, its image mind was incapable of imitating the finer subtleties of the razor-sharp brain of the young man who was staring up with startled, dark-gray eyes. And third was the large metal bas-relief that hung on the wall.

With a shock that almost brought chaos, it felt the tug of that metal. And in one flash it knew that this was ultimate metal, product of the fine craft of the ancient Martians, whose metal cities, loaded with treasures of furniture, art and machinery, were slowly being dug up by enterprising human beings from the sands under which they had been buried for thirty or fifty million years. The ultimate metal! The metal that no heat would even warm, that no diamond or other cutting device could scratch, never duplicated by human beings, as mysterious as the ieis force which the Martians made from apparent nothingness.

All these thoughts crowded the creature's brain, as it explored the memory cells of Jim Brender. With an effort, the thing wrenched its mind from the metal, and fastened its gaze on Jim Brender. It caught full the flood of the wonder in his mind as he stood up.

"Good lord," said Jim Brender, "who are you?"

"My name's Jim Brender," said the thing, conscious of grim amusement, conscious, too, that it was progress for it to be able to feel such an emotion.

The real Jim Brender had recovered himself. "Sit down, sit down," he said heartily. "This is the most amazing coincidence I've ever seen."

He went over to the mirror that made one panel of the left wall. He stared, first at himself, then at the creature. "Amazing," he said. "Absolutely amazing."

"Mr. Brender," said the creature, "I saw your picture in the paper, and I thought our astounding resemblance would make you listen, where otherwise you might pay no attention. I have recently returned from Mars, and I am here to persuade you to come back to Mars with me."

"That," said Jim Brender, "is impossible."

"Wait," the creature said, "until I have told you why. Have you ever heard of the Tower of the Beast?"

"The Tower of the Beast!" Jim Brender repeated slowly. He went around his desk and pushed a button.

A voice from an ornamental box said, "Yes, Mr. Brender?"

"Dave, get me all the data on the Tower of the Beast and the legendary city of Li in which it is supposed to exist."

"Don't need to look it up," came the crisp reply. "Most Martian histories refer to it as the beast that fell from the sky when Mars was young— some terrible warning connected with it—the beast was unconscious when found—said to be the result of its falling out of sub-space. Martians read its mind, and were so horrified by its subconscious intentions they tried to kill it, but couldn't. So they built a huge vault, about fifteen hundred feet in diameter and a mile high—and the beast, apparently of these dimensions, was locked in. Several attempts have been made to find the city of Li, but without success. Generally believed to be a myth. That's all, Jim."

"Thank you!" Jim Brender clicked off the connection, and turned to his visitor. "Well?"

"It is not a myth. I know where the Tower of the Beast is, and I also know that the beast is still alive."

"Now, see here," said Brender good-humoredly, "I'm intrigued by your resemblance to me. But don't expect me to believe such a story. The beast, if there is such a thing, fell from the sky when Mars was young. There are some authorities who maintain that the Martian race died out a hundred million years ago, though twenty-five million is the conservative estimate. The only artifacts remaining of their civilization are their constructions of ultimate metal. Fortunately, toward the end they built almost everything from that indestructible metal."

"Let me tell you about the Tower of the Beast," said the thing quietly. "It is a tower of gigantic size, but only a hundred feet or so projected above the sand when I saw it. The whole top is a door, and that door is geared to a time lock, which in turn has been integrated along a line of ieis to the ultimate prime number."

Jim Brender stared; and the thing caught his startled thought, the first uncertainty, and the beginning of belief. "Ultimate," Brender said.

He snatched at a book from the little wall library beside his desk, and rippled through it. "The largest known prime is ah, here it is—is 230584300921393951. Some others, according to this authority, are 77843839397, 182521213001, and 78875944372201."

His frown deepened. "That makes the whole thing ridiculous. The ultimate prime would be an indefinite number." He smiled at the thing. "If there is a beast, and it is locked up in a vault of ultimate metal, the door of which is geared to a time lock, integrated along a line of ieis to the ultimate prime number—then the beast is caught. Nothing in the world can free it."

"To the contrary," said the creature. "I have been assured by the beast that it is within the scope of human mathematics to solve the problem, but that what is required is a born mathematical mind, equipped with all the mathematical training that Earth science can afford. You are that man."

"You expect me to release this evil creature—even if I could perform this miracle of mathematics?"

"Evil nothing!" snapped the thing. "That ridiculous fear of the unknown which made the Martians imprison it has resulted in a very grave wrong. The beast is a scientist from another space, accidentally caught in one of his experiments. I say 'his' when of course I do not know whether this race has a sexual differentiation."

"You actually talked with the beast?"

"It communicated with me by mental telepathy."

"It has been proven that thoughts cannot penetrate ultimate metal."

"What do humans know about telepathy? They cannot even communicate with each other except under special conditions." The creature spoke contemptuously.

"That's right. And if your story is true, then this is a matter for the Council."

"This is a matter for two men, you and me. Have you forgotten that the vault of the beast is the central tower to the great city of Li—billions of dollars' worth of treasure in furniture, art, and machinery? The beast demands release from its prison before it will permit anyone to mine that treasure. You can release it. We can share the treasure."

"Let me ask you a question," said Jim Brender. "What is your real name?"

"P-Pierce Lawrence!" the creature stammered. For the moment, it could think of no greater variation of the name of its first victim than reversing the two words, with a slight change on "Pearson." Its thoughts darkened with confusion as Brender went on.

"On what ship did you come from Mars?"

"O-on F4961," the thing stammered chaotically, fury adding to the confused state of its mind. It fought for control, felt itself slipping, suddenly felt the pull of the ultimate metal that made up the bas-relief on the wall, and knew by that tug that it was dangerously near dissolution.

"That would be a freighter," said Jim Brender. He pressed a button. "Carltons, find out if the F4961 had a passenger or person aboard named Pierce Lawrence. How long will it take?"

"A few minutes, sir."

Jim Brender leaned back. "This is mere formality. If you were on that ship, then I shall be compelled to give serious attention to your statements. You can understand, of course, that I could not possibly go into a thing like this blindly."

The buzzer rang. "Yes?" said Jim Brender.

"Only the crew of two was on the F4961 when it landed yesterday. No such person as Pierce Lawrence was aboard."

"Thank you." Jim Brender stood up. He said coldly, "Goodbye, Mr. Lawrence. I cannot imagine what you hoped to gain by this ridiculous story. However, it has been most intriguing, and the problem you presented was very ingenious indeed."

The buzzer was ringing. "What is it?"

"Mr. Gorson to see you, sir."

"Very well, send him right in."

The thing had greater control of its brain now, and it saw in Brender's mind that Gorson was a financial magnate, whose business ranked with the Brender firm. It saw other things, too; things that made it walk out of the private office, out of the building, and wait patiently until Mr. Gorson emerged from the imposing entrance. A few minutes later, there were two Mr. Gorsons walking down the street. Mr. Gorson was a vigorous man in his early fifties. He had lived a clean, active life; and the hard memories of many climates and several planets were stored away in his brain. The thing caught the alertness of this man on its sensitive elements, followed him warily, respectfully, not quite decided whether it would act. It thought: "I've improved a great deal from the primitive life that couldn't hold its shape. My creators, in designing me, gave to me powers of learning, developing. It is easier to fight dissolution, easier to be human. In handling this man, I must remember that my strength is invincible when properly used."

With minute care, it explored in the mind of its intended victim the exact route of his walk to his office. There was the entrance to a large building clearly etched on his mind. Then a long, marble corridor, into an automobile elevator up to the eighth floor, along a short corridor with two doors. One door led to the private entrance of the man's private office. The other to a storeroom used by the janitor. Gorson had looked into the place on various occasions; and there was in his mind, among other things, the memory of a large chest.

The thing waited in the storeroom till the unsuspecting Gorson was past the door. The door creaked. Gorson turned, his eyes widening. He didn't have a chance. A fist of solid steel smashed his face to a pulp, knocking the bones back into his brain. This time, the creature did not make the mistake of keeping its mind tuned to that of its victim. It caught him as he fell, forcing its steel fist back to a semblance of human flesh. With furious speed, it stuffed the bulky and athletic form into the large chest, and clamped the lid down tight. Alertly, it emerged from the storeroom, entered the private office of Mr. Gorson, and sat down before the gleaming desk of oak. The man who responded to the pressing of a button saw John Gorson sitting there, and heard John Gorson say:

"Crispins, I want you to start selling these stocks through the secret channels right away. Sell until I tell you to stop, even if you think it's crazy. I have information of something big on."

Crispins glanced down the row after row of stock names; and his eyes grew wider and wider. "Good lord, man!" he gasped finally, with that familiarity which is the right of a trusted adviser, "these are all gilt-edged stocks. Your whole fortune can't swing a deal like this."

"I told you I'm not in this alone."

"But it is against the law to break the market," the man protested.

"Crispins, you heard what I said. I'm leaving the office. Don't try to get in touch with me. I'll call you."

The thing that was John Gorson stood up, paying no attention to the bewildered thoughts that flowed from Crispins. It went out of the door by which it had entered. As it emerged from the building, it was thinking: "All I've got to do is kill a half a dozen financial giants, start their stocks selling, and then—"

By one o'clock it was over. The exchange didn't close until three, but at one o'clock the news flashed on the New York tickers. In London, where it was getting dark, the papers brought out an extra. In Hankow and Shanghai, a dazzling new day was breaking as the newsboys ran along the streets in the shadow of skyscrapers, and shouted that J.P. Brender & Company had assigned; and there was to be an investigation—

"We are facing," said the district court judge, in his opening address the following morning, "one of the most astounding coincidences in all history. An ancient and respected firm, with world-wide affiliations and branches, with investments in more than a thousand companies of every description, is struck bankrupt by an unexpected crash in every stock in which the firm was interested. It will require months to take evidence on the responsibility for the short-selling which brought about this disaster. In the meantime, I see no reason, regrettable as the action must be to all the old friends of the late J.P. Brender, and of his son, why the demands of the creditors should not be met, and the properties liquidated through auction sales and other such methods as I may deem proper and legal—"

Commander Hughes of Interplanetary Spaceways entered the office of his employer truculently. He was a small man, but extremely wiry; and the thing that was Louis Dyer gazed at him tensely, conscious of the force and power of this man.

Hughes began: "You have my report on this Brender case?"

The thing twirled the mustache of Louis Dyer nervously, then picked up a small folder, and read out loud:

"Dangerous for psychological reasons ... to employ Brender ... So many blows in succession. Loss of wealth, and position ... No normal man could remain normal under ... circumstances. Take him into office ... befriend him ... give him a sinecure, or position where his undoubted great ability ... but not on a spaceship, where the utmost hardiness, both mental, moral, spiritual, and physical is required—"

Hughes interrupted: "Those are exactly the points which I am stressing. I knew you would see what I meant, Louis."

"Of course I see," said the creature, smiling in grim amusement, for it was feeling very superior these days. Your thoughts, your ideas, your code, and your methods are stamped irrevocably on your brain and"—it added hastily—"you have never left me in doubt as to where you stand. However, in this case, I must insist. Jim Brender will not take an ordinary position offered by his friends. And it is ridiculous to ask him to subordinate himself to men to whom he is in every was superior. He has commanded his own space yacht; he knows more about the mathematical end of the work than our whole staff put together; and that is no reflection on our staff. He knows the hardships connected with space flying, and believes that it is exactly what he needs. I, therefore, command you, for the first time in our long association, Peter, to put him on space freighter F4961 in the place of Spacecraftsman Parelli, who collapsed into a nervous breakdown after that curious affair with the creature from space, as Lieutenant Morton described it— By the way, did you find the ... er ... sample of that creature yet?"

"No, sir. It vanished the day you came in to look at it. We've searched the place high and low—queerest stuff you ever saw. Goes through glass as easy as light; you'd think it was some form of light stuff—scares me, too. A pure sympodial development—actually more adaptable of environment than anything hitherto discovered; and that's putting it mildly. I tell you, sir— But see here, you can't steer me off the Brender case like that."

"Peter, I don't understand your attitude. This is the first time I've interfered with your end of the work and—"

"I'll resign," groaned that sorely beset man.

The thing stifled a smile. "Peter, you've built up the staff of Spaceways. It's your child, your creation; you can't give it up, you know you can't—"

The words hissed softly into alarm; for into Hughes' brain had flashed the first real intention of resigning. Just hearing of his accomplishments and the story of his beloved job brought such a rush of memories, such a realization of how tremendous an outrage was this threatened interference. In one mental leap, the creature saw what this man's resignation would mean: the discontent of the men; the swift perception of the situation by Jim Brender; and his refusal to accept the job. There was only one way out—for Brender to get to the ship without finding out what had happened. Once on it, he must carry through with one trip to Mars, which was all that was needed.

The thing pondered the possibility of imitating Hughes' body. Then agonizingly realized that it was hopeless. Both Louis Dyer and Hughes must be around until the last minute.

"But, Peter, listen!" the creature began chaotically. Then it said, "Damn!" for it was very human in mentality. And the realization that Hughes took its words as a sign of weakness was maddening. Uncertainty descended like a black cloud over its brain.

"I'll tell Brender when he arrives in five minutes how I feel about all this!" Hughes snapped; and the creature knew that the worst had happened. "If you forbid me to tell him, then I resign. I—Good God, man, your face!"

Confusion and horror came to the creature simultaneously. It knew abruptly that its face had dissolved before the threatened ruin of its plans. It fought for control, leaped to its feet, seeing the incredible danger. The large office just beyond the frosted glass door—Hughes' first outcry would bring help. With a half sob, it sought to force its arm into an imitation of a metal fist, but there was no metal in the room to pull it into shape. There was only the solid maple desk. With a harsh cry, the creature leaped completely over the desk, and sought to bury a pointed shaft of stick into Hughes' throat.

Hughes cursed in amazement, and caught at the stick with furious strength. There was sudden commotion in the outer office, raised voices, running feet—

Brender parked his car near the ship. Then stood for a moment. It was not that he had any doubts. He was a desperate man, and therefore a long chance was in order. It wouldn't take very much time to find out if the Martian city of Li had been found. If it had been, then he would recover his fortune. He started to walk swiftly toward the ship.

As he paused beside the runway that led to the open door of F4961—a huge globe of shining metal, three hundred feet in diameter—he saw a man running toward him. He recognized Hughes.

The thing that was Hughes approached, fighting for calmness. The whole world was a flame of cross-pulling forces. It shrank from the thoughts of the people milling about in the office it had just left. Everything had gone wrong. It had never intended to do what it now had to do. It had intended to spend most of the trip to Mars as a blister of metal on the outer shield of the ship. With a tremendous effort, it controlled itself. "We're leaving right away," it said.

Brender looked amazed. "But that means I'll have to figure out a new orbit under the most difficult—"

"Exactly," the creature interrupted. "I've been hearing a lot about your marvelous mathematical ability. It's time the words were proved by deeds."

Jim Brender shrugged. "I have no objection. But how is it that you're coming along?"

"I always go with a new man."

It sounded reasonable. Brender climbed the runway, closely followed by Hughes. The powerful pull of the metal was the first real pain the creature had known for days. For a long month, it would now have to fight the metal, fight to retain the shape of Hughes, and carry on a thousand duties at the same time. That first pain tore along its elements, smashing the confidence that days of being human had built up. And then, as it followed Brender through the door, it heard a shout behind it. It looked back hastily. People were streaming out of several doors, running toward the ship. Brender was several yards along the corridor. With a hiss that was almost a sob, the creature leaped inside, and pulled the lever that clicked the great door shut.

There was an emergency lever that controlled the anti-gravity plates. With one jerk, the creature pulled the heavy lever hard over. Instantly, it experienced a sensation of lightness and a sense of falling. Through the great plate window the creature caught a flashing glimpse of the field below, swarming with people. White faces turning upward, arms waving. Then the scene grew remote, as a thunder of rockets vibrated through the ship.

"I hope," said Brender, as Hughes entered the control room, "you wanted me to start the rockets."

"Yes," the thing replied thickly. "I'm leaving the mathematical end entirely in your hands."

It didn't dare stay so near the heavy metal engines, even with Brender's body there to help it keep its human shape. Hurriedly, it started up the corridor. The best place would be the insulated bedroom.

Abruptly, it stopped in its headlong walk, teetering on tiptoes. From the control room it had just left, a thought was trickling—a thought from Brender's brain. The creature almost dissolved in terror as it realized that Brender was sitting at the radio, answering an insistent call from Earth.

It burst into the control room, and braked to a halt, its eyes widening with humanlike dismay. Brender whirled from before the radio with a single twisting step. In his fingers he held a revolver. In his mind, the creature read a dawning comprehension of the whole truth. Brender cried: "You're the … thing that came to my office, and talked about prime numbers and the vault of the beast."

He took a step to one side to cover an open doorway that led down another corridor. The movement brought the telescreen into the vision of the creature. In the screen was the image of the real Hughes. Simultaneously, Hughes saw the thing.

"Brender," he bellowed, "it's the monster that Morton and Parelli saw on their trip from Mars. It doesn't react to heat or any chemicals, but we never tried bullets. Shoot, quick!" It was too much metal, too much confusion. With a whimpering cry, the creature dissolved. The pull of the metal twisted it horribly into thick half metal. The struggle to be human left it a malignant structure of bulbous head, with one eye half gone and two snakelike arms attached to the half metal of the body. Instinctively, it fought closer to Brender, letting the pull of his body make it more human. The half metal became fleshlike stuff that sought to return to its human shape.

"Listen, Brender!" Hughes' voice was urgent. "The fuel vats in the engine room are made of ultimate metal. One of them is empty. We caught a part of this thing once before, and it couldn't get out of the small jar of ultimate metal. If you could drive it into the vat while it's lost control of itself, as it seems to do very easily—"

"I'll see what lead can do!" Brender rapped in a brittle voice.

Bang! The creature screamed from its half-formed slit of mouth, and retreated, its legs dissolving into gray dough.

"It hurts, doesn't it?" Brender ground out. "Get over into the engine room, you damned thing, into the vat!"

"Go on, go on!" Hughes was shouting from the telescreen.

Brender fired again. The creature made a slobbering sound, and retreated once more. But it was bigger again, more human. And in one caricature hand a caricature of Brender's revolver was growing.

It raised the unfinished, unformed gun. There was an explosion, and a shriek from the thing. The revolver fell, a shapeless, tattered blob, to the floor. The little gray mass of it scrambled frantically toward the parent body, and attached itself like some monstrous canker to the right foot.

And then, for the first time, the mighty and evil brains that had created the thing sought to dominate their robot. Furious, yet conscious that the game must be carefully played, the Controller forced the terrified and utterly beaten thing to its will. Scream after agonized scream rent the air, as the change was forced upon the unstable elements. In an instant, the thing stood in the shape of Brender, but instead of a revolver, there grew from one browned, powerful hand a pencil of shining metal. Mirror bright, it glittered in every facet like some incredible gem. The metal glowed ever so faintly, an unearthly radiance. And where the radio had been, and the screen with Hughes' face on it, there was a gaping hole. Desperately, Brender pumped bullets into the body before him, but though the shape trembled, it stared at him now, unaffected. The shining weapon swung toward him.

"When you are quite finished," it said, "perhaps we can talk."

It spoke so mildly that Brender, tensing to meet death, lowered his gun in amazement. The thing went on: "Do not be alarmed. This which you hear and see is an android, designed by us to cope with your space and number world. Several of us are working here under the most difficult conditions to maintain this connection, so I must be brief.

"We exist in a time world immeasurably more slow than your own. By a system of synchronization, we have geared a number of these spaces in such fashion that, though one of our days is millions of your years, we can communicate. Our purpose is to free Kalorn from the Martian vault. Kalorn was caught accidentally in a time warp of his own making and precipitated onto the planet you know as Mars. The Martians, needlessly fearing his great size, constructed a most diabolical prison, and we need your knowledge of the mathematics peculiar to your space and number world—and to it alone—in order to free him."

The calm voice continued, earnest but not offensively so, insistent but friendly. The speaker regretted that their android had killed human beings. In greater detail, he explained that every space was constructed on different number systems, some all negative, some all positive, some a mixture of the two, the whole an infinite variety, and every mathematics interwoven into the very fabric of the space it ruled.

Ieis force was not really mysterious. It was simply a flow from one space to another, the result of a difference in potential. This flow, however, was one of the universal forces, which only one other force could affect, the one he had used a few minutes before. Ultimate metal was *actually* ultimate. In their space they had a similar metal, built up from negative atoms. He could see from Brender's mind that the Martians had known nothing about minus numbers, so that they must have built it up from ordinary atoms. It could be done that way, too, though not so easily. He finished:

"The problem narrows down to this: Your mathematics must tell us how, with our universal force, we can short-circuit the ultimate prime number—that is, factor it—so that the door will open any time. You may ask how a prime can be factored when it is divisible only by itself and by one. That problem is, for your system, solvable only by your mathematics. Will you do it?"

Brender pocketed his revolver. His nerves were calm as he said, "Everything you have said sounds reasonable and honest. If you were desirous of making trouble, it would be the simplest thing in the world to send as many of your kind as you wished. Of course, the whole affair must be placed before the Council—"

"Then it is hopeless—the Council could not possibly accede—"

"And you expect me to do what you do not believe the highest governmental authority in the System would do?" Brender exclaimed.

"It is inherent in the nature of a democracy that it cannot gamble with the lives of its citizens. We have such a government here; and its members have already informed us that, in a similar condition, they would not consider releasing an unknown beast upon their people. Individuals, however, can gamble where governments must not. You have agreed that our argument is logical. What system do men follow if not that of logic?"

The Controller, through the creature, watched Brender's thoughts alertly. It saw doubt and uncertainty, opposed by a very human desire to help, based upon the logical conviction that it was safe. Probing his mind, it saw swiftly that it was unwise, in dealing with men, to trust too much to logic. It pressed on:

"To an individual we can offer—everything. In a minute, with your permission, we shall transfer this ship to Mars; not in thirty days, but in thirty seconds. The knowledge of how this is done will remain with you. Arrived at Mars you will find yourself the only living person who knows the whereabouts of the ancient city of Li, of which the vault of the beast is the central tower. In this city will be found literally billions of dollars' worth of treasure made of ultimate metal; and according to the laws of Earth, fifty percent will be yours. Your fortune re-established, you will be able to return to Earth this very day."

Brender was white. Malevolently, the thing watched the thoughts sweeping through his brain—the memory of the sudden disaster that had ruined his family. Brender looked up grimly.

"Yes," he said, "I'll do what I can."

A bleak range of mountains fell away into a valley of reddish gray sand. The thin winds of Mars blew a mist of sand against the building. *Such* a building! At a distance, it had looked merely big. A bare hundred feet projected above the desert, a hundred feet of height and *fifteen hundred feet of diameter*. Literally thousands of feet must extend beneath the restless ocean of sand to make the perfect balance of form, the graceful flow, the fairylike beauty which the long-dead Martians demanded of all their constructions, however massive. Brender felt suddenly small and insignificant as the rockets of his spacesuit pounded him along a few feet above the sand toward that incredible building.

At close range the ugliness of sheer size was miraculously lost in the wealth of the decorative. Columns and pilasters assembled in groups and clusters broke up the facades, gathered and dispersed again restlessly. The flat surface of wall and roof melted into a wealth of ornaments and imitation stucco work, vanished and broken into a play of light and shade.

The creature floated beside Brender. Its Controller said, "I see that you have been giving considerable thought to the problem, but this android seems incapable of following abstract thought, so I have no means of knowing the course of your speculations. I see, however, that you seem to be satisfied."

"I think I've got the answer," said Brender, "but first I wish to see the time lock. Let's climb."

They rose into the sky, dipping over the lip of the building. Brender saw a vast flat expanse; and in the center— He caught his breath!

The meager light from the distant sun of Mars shone down on a structure located at what seemed the exact center of the great door. The structure was about fifty feet high, and seemed nothing less than a series of quadrants coming together at the center, which was a metal arrow pointing straight up. The arrow head was not solid metal. Rather, it was as if the metal had divided in two parts, then curved together again. But not quite together. About a foot separated the two sections of metal. But that foot was bridged by a vague, thin, green flame of ieis force.

"The time lock!" Brender nodded. "I thought it would be something like that, though I expected it would be bigger, more substantial."

"Do not be deceived by its fragile appearance," answered the thing. "Theoretically, the strength of ultimate metal is infinite; and the ieis force can only be affected by the universal I have mentioned. Exactly what the effect will be, it is impossible to say as it involves the temporary derangement of the whole number system upon which that particular area of space is built. But now tell us what to do."

"Very well." Brender eased himself onto a bank of sand, and cut off his antigravity plates. He lay on his back, and stared thoughtfully into the blue-black sky. For the time being all doubts, worries and fears were gone from him. He relaxed, and began to explain: "The Martian mathematic, like that of Euclid and Pythagoras, was based on endless magnitude. Minus numbers were beyond their philosophy. On Earth, however, beginning with Descartes, an analytical mathematic was evolved. Magnitude and perceivable dimensions were replaced by that of variable-values between positions in space.

"For the Martians, there was only one number between 1 and 3. Actually, the totality of such numbers is an infinite aggregate. And with the introduction of the idea of the square root of minus one—or i—and the complex numbers, mathematics definitely ceased to be a simple thing of magnitude, perceivable in picture. Only the intellectual step from the infinitely small quantity to the lower limit of every possible finite magnitude brought out the conception of a variable number which oscillated beneath any assignable number that was not zero.

"The prime number, being a conception of pure magnitude, had no reality in real mathematics, but in this case was rigidly bound up with the reality of the ieis force. The Martians knew ieis as a pale-green flow about a foot in length and developing say a thousand horsepower. (It was actually 12.171 inches and 1021.23 horsepower, but that was unimportant.) The power produced never varied, the length never varied, from year end to year end, for tens of thousands of years. The Martians took the length as their basis of measurement, and called it one 'el'; they took the power as their basis of power and called it one 'rb.' And because of the absolute invariability of the flow they decided it was eternal.

"They decided furthermore that nothing could be eternal without becoming prime. Their whole mathematic was based on numbers which could be factored, that is, disintegrated, destroyed, rendered less than they had been; and numbers which could not be factored, disintegrated, or divided into smaller groups.

"Any number which could be factored was incapable of being infinite. Contrariwise, the infinite number must be prime.

"Therefore, they built a lock and integrated it along a line of ieis, to operate when the ieis ceased to flow—which would be at the end of Time, provided it was not interfered with. To prevent interference, they buried the motivating mechanism of the flow in ultimate metal, which could not be destroyed or corroded in any way. According to their mathematic, that settled it."

"But you have the answer," said the voice of the thing eagerly.

"Simply this: The Martians set a value on the flow of one 'rb.' If you interfere with that flow to no matter what small degree, you no longer have an 'rb.' You have something less. The flow, which is a universal, becomes automatically less than a universal, less than infinite. The prime number ceases to be prime. Let us suppose that you interfere with it to the extent of ultimate prime *minus one*. You will then have a number divisible by two. As a matter of fact, the number, like most large numbers, will immediately break into thousands of pieces, i.e., it will be divisible by tens of thousands of smaller numbers. If the present time falls anywhere near one of those breaks, the door would open immediately if you can so interfere with the flow that one of the factors occurs in immediate time."

"That is very clear," said the Controller with satisfaction, and the image of Brender was smiling triumphantly. "We shall now use this android to manufacture a universal; and Kalorn shall be free very shortly." He laughed aloud. "The poor android is protesting violently at the thought of being destroyed, but after all it is only a machine, and not a very good one at that. Besides, it is interfering with my proper reception of your thoughts. Listen to it scream, as I twist it into shape."

The cold-blooded words chilled Brender, pulled him from the heights of his abstract thought. Because of the prolonged intensity of his thinking, he saw with sharp clarity something that had escaped him before.

"Just a minute," he said. "How is it that the robot, introduced from your world, is living at the same time rate as I am, whereas Kalorn continues to live at your time rate?"

"A very good question." The face of the creature was twisted into a triumphant sneer, as the Controller continued. "Because, my dear Brender, you have been duped. It is true that Kalorn is living in our time rate, but that was due to a shortcoming in our machine. The machine which Kalorn built, while large enough to transport him, was not large enough in its adaptive mechanism to adapt him to each new space as he entered it. With the result that he was transported but not adapted. It was possible, of course, for us, his helpers, to transport such a small thing as the android, though we have no more idea of the machine's construction than you have.

"In short, we can use what there is of the machine, but the secret of its construction is locked in the insides of our own particular ultimate metal, and in the brain of Kalorn. Its invention by Kalorn was one of those accidents which, by the law of averages, will not be repeated in millions of our years. Now that you have provided us with the method of bringing Kalorn back, we shall be able to build innumerable interspace machines. Our purpose is to control all spaces, all worlds—particularly those which are inhabited. We intend to be absolute rulers of the entire Universe."

The ironic voice ended, and Brender lay in his prone position the prey of horror. The horror was twofold, partly due to the Controller's monstrous plan, and partly to the thought that was pulsing in his brain. He groaned, as he realized that his warning thought must be ticking away on the automatic receiving brain of the robot. "Wait," his thought was saying, "that adds a new factor. Time—"

There was a scream from the creature as it was forcibly dissolved. The scream choked to a sob, then silence. An intricate machine of shining metal lay there on that great gray-brown expanse of sand and ultimate metal.

The metal glowed; and then the machine was floating in the air. It rose to the top of the arrow, and settled over the green flame of ieis.

Brender jerked on his antigravity screen, and leaped to his feet. The violent action carried him some hundred feet into the air. His rockets sputtered into staccato fire, and he clamped his teeth against the pain of acceleration. Below him, the great door began to turn, to unscrew, faster and faster, till it was like a flywheel. Sand flew in all directions in a miniature storm.

At top acceleration, Brender darted to one side. Just in time. First, the robot machine was flung off that tremendous wheel by sheer centrifugal power. Then the door came off, and, spinning now at an incredible rate, hurtled straight into the air and vanished into space.

A puff of black dust came floating out of the blackness of the vault. Suppressing his horror, yet perspiring from awful relief, he rocketed to where the robot had fallen into the sand. Instead of glistening metal, a time-dulled piece of junk lay there. The dull metal flowed sluggishly and assumed a quasi-human shape. The flesh remained gray and in little rolls as if ready to fall apart from old age. The thing tried to stand up on wrinkled legs, but finally lay still. Its lips moved, mumbled:

"I caught your warning thought, but I didn't let them know. Now, Kalorn is dead. They realized the truth as it was happening. End of Time came—"

It faltered into silence; and Brender went on, "Yes, end of time came when the flow became momentarily less than eternal—came at the factor point which occurred a few minutes ago."

"I was ... only partly ... within its ... influence, Kalorn all the way ... Even if they're lucky ... 'twill be years before ... they invent another machine ... and one of their years is billions ... of yours ... I didn't tell them ... I caught your thought ... and kept it ... from them—"

"But why did you do it— Why?"

"Because they were hurting me. They were going to destroy me. Because ... I liked ... being human. I was ... somebody!"

The flesh dissolved. It flowed slowly into a pool of lava-like gray. The lava crinkled, split into dry, brittle pieces. Brender touched one of the pieces. It crumbled into a fine powder of dust. He gazed out across that grim, deserted valley of sand, and said aloud, pityingly, "Poor Frankenstein."

He turned and flew toward the distant spaceship.

THE GHOST

"Four miles," Kent thought, "four miles from the main-line town of Kempster to the railway-less village of Agan." At least, he remembered that much.

He remembered the hill, too, and the farm at the foot of it. Only it hadn't been deserted when he saw it last.

He stared at the place as the hotel car edged down the long hill. The buildings showed with a curious, stark bleakness. All the visible windows of the farmhouse itself were boarded up. And great planks had been nailed across the barn door.

The yard was a wilderness of weeds and—Kent experienced an odd sense of shock—the tall, dignified old man who emerged abruptly from behind the house, seemed as out of place in that desolate yard as ... as life itself.

Kent was aware of the driver leaning toward him, heard him say above the roar of the ancient engine:

"I was wondering if we'd see the ghost, as we passed; and yep. there he is, taking his morning walk."

"The ghost!" Kent echoed.

It was as if he had spoken a key word. The sun burst brilliantly from behind an array of dark clouds and flooded the valley with warm light. The blaze of it illuminated the drab old buildings—and wrought changes. The over-all grayness of the house showed in that bright illumination as a faded green.

The old man walked slowly toward the gate that led to the main highway. Nearer now, he seemed taller, thinner, a gaunt caricature of a human being; his black frock coat glinted in the sun.

151

Kent found his voice. "Ghost!" he said again. "Why, that's old Mr. Wainwright. He doesn't look a day older than when I left this part of the world fifteen years ago."

The old, square-fronted car ground queasily to a stop before the farm gate. The driver turned. It struck Kent that the man was smugly enjoying the moment.

"See that gate?" the fellow asked. "Not the big one: the little one. It's padlocked, eh?"

Kent nodded. "What about it?"

"Watch!"

The old man stood fumbling at the gate less than ten feet away. It was like gazing at a pantomime, Kent thought; for the man paid no attention to the padlock, but seemed absorbed with some simpler catch.

Abruptly, the patriarch straightened, and pushed at the gate. Kent had no real sense of alienness. Without having given the matter any thought be believed it was the gate that was going to open. and that it was some unusual aspect of the opening that he had been admonished to watch.

The gate didn't. It did not so much as stir; not a creak came from its rusty hinges. It remained solid, held in position by the uncompromising padlock.

The old man walked through it.

Through it! Then he turned, seemed to push at some invisible counterpart of the gate and, once again, stood there, as if manipulating a hidden catch.

Finally, apparently satisfied, he faced the car again; and, for the first time, saw it and its occupants. His long, finely wrinkled face lighted.

"Hello, there!" he said.

Kent hadn't expected speech. The words caught him like a blow. He felt a chill; his mind whirled with a queer, twisting motion that momentarily wrecked the coherence of his thought. He half leaned, half fell back against the seat because his muscles wouldn't support him.

"Ghost," he thought finally, dizzily. Good heavens, what was going on here?

The world began to right itself. The land and the horizon straightened; and there was the house and the barn, an almost colorless, utterly lifeless background to the beanpole of an old, old man and the magic gate through which he had stepped.

"Hello!" Kent said shakily. "Hello!"

The old man came nearer, peered; and an expression of surprise flitted across his face. "Why, it's Mr. Kent. I thought you'd left the Agan Hotel."

"Eh!" Kent began.

Out of the corner of his eyes be saw the driver make a sharp movement with one hand. The man whispered hastily:

"Don't act surprised at anything the ghost says. It confuses him."

Ghost! There it was again. Kent swallowed hard. "Am I mad?" he thought "The last time I saw this old follow was when I was twenty. He didn't know my name then. How—"

The old man was speaking again, in bewilderment: "I distinctly remember Mr. Jenkins, the proprietor, informing me that you had found it necessary to leave at once. He said something about a prophecy coming out exactly to the day, August 17th. People are always talking to me about prophecies. But that was the date he said it was, August 17th."

He looked up, unscrewing the frown from his thin, worn face. "I beg your pardon, young sir, It is very remiss of me to stand here mumbling to myself. May I say that I am glad that the report was untrue, as I have very much enjoyed our several conversations."

He raised his hat. "I would invite you in for tea; but Mrs. Carmody is not in the best of moods this morning. Poor woman! Looking after an old man must be a great trial; and I dare not add to her afflictions. Good morning to you, Mr. Kent. Good morning, Tom."

Kent nodded, unable to speak. He heard the driver say:

"S'long, Mr. Wainwright."

Kent watched, as the tall, frail figure walked slowly across the road behind the car, and moved unhurriedly across the open pasture land to the south. His mind and gaze came back to the car, as the driver, Tom, said:

"Well, Mr. Kent, you're lucky. You know how long you're staying at the Agan Hotel."

"What do you mean?"

"Mr. Jenkins will have your bill ready for you August 17th."

Kent stared at him, uncertain whether he ought to laugh, or—what! "You're not trying to tell me that the ghost also tells the future. Why, today's only July 8th, and I intend to stay till the end of Septem—"

He stopped. The eyes that were staring into his were utterly earnest, humorless: "Mr. Kent, there never was anyone like Mr. Wainwright in the world before. When he tells the future, it happens; it was that way when he was alive, and it's the same now that he's dead.

"The only thing is that he's old. He's over ninety, and weak in the head. He gets confused; he always mixes the future with the past. To him it is the past, and its all equally blurred. But when he says anything as clear as a date, it's so. You wait and see."

There were too many words; and the concreteness of them, the colloquial twang of them on the still air, built an oddly insubstantial picture.

Kent began to feel less startled. He knew these country folk; and the conviction was suddenly strong in him that, in some obscure way, he was being made the victim of a practical joke.

It wouldn't do, of course, to say so. Besides, there was the unaccountable episode of the gate.

"This Mrs. Carmody," he said finally. "I don't recall her. Who is she?"

"She came to look after the farm when her sister-in-law, the old man's granddaughter, died. No blood relation, but—" The driver drew a deep breath, tried hard to look casual, and said: "She's the one, you know, who murdered old Wainwright five years ago. They put her in the crazy house at Peerton for doing it."

"Murdered!" Kent said. "What is this—the local ghost story?" He paused; then: "Just a minute. He talked as if he was still living with her."

"Look, Mr. Kent"—the man was pitying—"let's not go into why the ghost says what he says. People have tried figuring out what's going on, and have ended with their brains twisted into seventeen knots."

"There must be a natural explanation."

The driver shrugged. "Well, then, you find it." He added: "I was the one who drove Mrs. Carmody and her two kids from Kempster to the farm here. Maybe you'd like to hear as much of the story as I can tell you the rest of the way to the hotel."

Kent sat quietly as gears shifted; and the machine moved heavily off. He turned finally to look at the farm. It was just passing out of sight behind a long spread of trees.

That last look showed—desolation, deadness. He shuddered involuntarily, and did not look again. He said: "This story ... what about it?"

The woman saw the farm as the car slowed at the lip of the hill. She was dimly aware that the car was in low gear, with brakes on, slithering down the loose gravel of the steep incline.

The farm, she thought with a greedy intensity that shook her heavy body; safety at long, long last. And only a senile old man and a girl standing between her and possession.

Between her—and the hard, sordid years that stretched behind her. Years of being a widow with two children in a tenement house, with only an occasional job to eke out the income from the relief department.

Years of hell!

And here was heaven for the taking. Her hard blue eyes narrowed; her plump, hard body grew taut—if she couldn't take the treasure of security that was here, she'd better—

The thought faded. Fascinated, she stared at the valley farm below, a green farmhouse, a great red barn and half a dozen outhouses. In the near distance a vast field of wheat spread; tiny wheat, bright green with a mid-spring greenness.

The car came down to the level of the valley; and trees hid the distant, rolling glory of the land. The automobile came to a stop, its shiny front pointed at the gate; and, beside her, the heavily built boy said:

"This it, ma?"

"Yes, Bill!" The woman looked at him anxiously. All her ultimate plans about this farm centered around him. For a moment she was preternaturally aware of his defects, his sullen, heavy, yet not strong face. There was a clumsiness of build in his chunky, sixteen-year-old body that made him something less than attractive.

She threw off that brief pattern of doubt; she ventured "Isn't it wonderful?"

"Naw!" The thick lips twisted. "I'd rather be in the city." He shrugged. "But I guess I know what's good for us."

"That's right." She felt relieved. "In this world it's what you get, not what you want. Remember that, Bill ... what is it, Pearl?"

She spoke impatiently. It was the way her daughter always affected her. What good was a pasty-faced, twelve-year-old, too plump, too plain, and without the faintest promise of ever being pretty. With an even sharper annoyance, the woman repeated:

"What is it?"

"There's a skinny old man coming across the field. Is that Mr. Wainwright, ma?"

Mrs. Carmody turned slowly and stared in the direction Pearl was pointing. And, after a moment, a current of relief surged through her. Until this instant she had felt a sharp edge of worry about the old man. Old, her sister-in-law had written in her occasional letter. But she hadn't imagined he'd be this old. Why, he must be ninety, a hundred; utterly no danger to her at all.

She saw that the driver had opened the gate, and was coming back to drive the car through. With a new confidence she raised her voice at him:

"Wait!" she said, "wait for the old man. He's been out for a walk, and he'll be tired. Give him a lift to the house."

Might as well make a good first impression, she thought. Politeness was the watchword. Iron hands within velvet gloves.

It struck her that the driver was staring at her peculiarly; the man said: "I wouldn't count on him driving with us. He's a queer old duck, Mr. Wainwright is. Sometimes he's deaf and blind, and he don't pay attention to no one. And he does a lot of queer things."

The woman frowned. "For instance?"

The man sighed. "Well, ma'am, it's no use trying to explain. You might as well start learning by experience, now as later. Watch him."

The long, thin figure came at an even, slow pace across the pasture to the south. He crossed the road, passing the car less than three feet from the fenders, seemingly completely blind to its presence. He headed straight for the gate.

Not the open gate, wide enough for the car to go through, but the narrow, solidly constructed wooden gate for human beings. He seemed to fumble at some hidden catch. And then—

The gate did not open, but he stepped through as if it had.

Stepped through the solid wooden gate.

For a long second Mrs. Carmody was aware of a harsh woman's voice screaming. With a terrible shock, she realized it was her own voice.

The effort to choke that wild cry was so horrible that she fell back against the seat, the blood hammering at her temples. She sagged there, sick, cold as ice, her vision blurred, her throat ash dry, every muscle in her body jumping with tiny, painful surges of nervous convulsion; and, for a long moment, her mind wouldn't hold thoughts.

"Just a minute!" Kent interrupted the driver. "I thought you told me the old man was alive at this time. How come he walked through the gate?"

His narrator stared at him strangely: "Mr. Kent, the only reason that old man hasn't made us all crazy these past twelve years is that he's harmless. He walked through gates when he was alive just as he does now. And not only gates. The difference is that we know we buried him. Maybe he's always been a ghost, and killing him don't do no good. All we know is, he's harmless. That's enough, isn't it?"

Kent nodded, but there was a world of doubt in his voice as he said:

"I suppose so; anyway, go on."

The dark blur of fear in the woman's mind yielded to an awareness of tugging at her arm; and then she realized that the driver was speaking:

"It's all right, ma'am, he's just a queer, harmless old man. Nothing to get excited about."

It was not the driver, but the boy beside her, whose words pulled her together; the boy saying rather scornfully:

"Gee, ma, you sure take on. I seen a trick like that on the stage last year, only it was better than that. It don't mean a thing."

The woman began to feel better. Bill was such a solid, practical boy, she thought gratefully. And of course he was right. Some trick, of course, and—what was that stupid little fool of a girl saying. She found herself repeating the question out loud:

"What did you say, Pearl?"

"He sees us, ma—look!" the girl said.

The woman saw that the old man was peering at her over the gate. A thin, long, gentle, wrinkled face it was, bright with gathering interest. He said with an astonishingly crisp voice for one so old:

"You're back from town rather early, Mrs. Carmody. Does that mean an early dinner?"

He paused politely; then: "I have no objection naturally. I am only too happy to fit myself into any routine you desire."

The deadly thought that came to her was that she was being made ridiculous in some way. Her face grew taut, her eyes narrowed, then she mustered an uncertain smile, and tried to force her mind past his words. The fierce whisper of the driver rescued her from that developing confusion:

"Begging your pardon, ma'am," the man said hurriedly, "don't let on you're new here. He's got the gift of seeing, and he's been acting for months as if you were already living here, and, if you contradict him, it only puzzles him. Toward the end, he was actually calling Mrs. Wainwright by your name. He's just a queer old man."

Mrs. Carmody sat very still, her blue eyes brighter, wide with abrupt calculation. The thrill that came was warm along her nerves. Expected!

One of the several things she had feared was this moment of her arrival; but now—expected!

All her careful preparation would go over smoothly. The letter she had forged so painstakingly, in which the dead woman, the old man's grand-daughter, *asked* her to come to look after her daughter, Phyllis—that prize letter would merely be a confirmation of something which had already been accepted as inevitable. Though how—

The woman shook herself firmly. This was no time to worry about the curious actions of an old man. She had a farm to take over; and the quicker that problem was solved, the better.

She smiled again, her thick face smirking a little with the comfortable glow of her inner triumph.

"Won't you ride to the house with us, Mr. Wainwright? You must be tired after your walk"

The old fellow nodded alertly. "Don't mind if I do, madam. I was all the way to Kempster, and I'm a little tired. Saw your sister there, by the way."

He had come through the gate, this time the one that was standing open for the car, and he was heading for the front door of the machine when Mrs. Carmody managed heavily:

"My—sister?"

"*Sssshh!*" hissed the driver. "Pay no attention. He's mixed up in his head. He thinks everyone of us has a living image, and he's always meeting them. He's been like this for years, perfectly harmless."

It was easier to nod this time. The episode of the gate was a vague unreality in her mind, becoming dimmer by the minute. She smiled her smile as the old man politely lifted his hat, watched as he climbed into the front seat beside the driver.

The car puffed along the yard road, rounded the house and drew up before the veranda. A girl in a white dress came to the screen door, and stood there very quietly staring at them.

She was a pretty, fragile thing, Mrs. Carmody noted with a sharp eye to detail, slim, with yellow hair, about fifteen or sixteen, and—the woman's mind tightened—not very friendly.

The woman smiled sweetly. "Hello, Phyllis," she said, "I'm so glad to see you."

"Hello," said Phyllis; and the older woman smiled comfortably at the reluctant greeting. Because—it *had* been a greeting. It was acceptance of a sort.

The woman smiled a thin smile to herself. This simple country girl was going to learn how impossible it was to fight a friendly approach, backed by an iron purpose.

She could see the whole future smoothly fitting in with her wishes. First, to settle down; then to set about throwing Bill and Phyllis together, so that they'd consider marriage a natural and early conclusion to their relationship. And then—

It was night; and she had blown out the lamp in the master bedroom before she thought again of the old man, and the astounding things he had said and done.

She lay in the darkness, nestling into the special comfort of the great bed, frowning. Finally, sleepily, she shrugged. Harmless, the driver had said. Well, he'd better stay that way, the old coot.

Mrs. Carmody wakened the following morning to the sounds of movement downstairs. She dressed hurriedly with a sense of having been outmaneuvered on her first day; and that empty feeling became conviction when she saw the old man and Phyllis eating breakfast.

There were three other plates set with bowls of cereal: and Mrs. Carmody sank down before one of them in a dead silence. She saw that the girl had a notebook open in front of her; and she clutched at the straw of conversation it offered.

"Doing your homework?" she asked in her friendliest voice.

"No!" said the girl, closing the notebook and getting up from the table.

Mrs. Carmody sat very still, fighting the surge of dull color that crept up into her cheeks. No use getting excited, she thought. The thing was, somehow—somehow she had to make friends with this quiet girl.

And besides, there was some information she had to have—about food, about the house, about—money.

Abruptly, breakfast was a meaningless, tasteless act. She got up from her half-finished cereal; in the kitchen she found Phyllis washing the dishes.

"Let me wash," said the woman, "you dry."

She added: "Pretty hands like yours shouldn't be in dish water."

She sent a swift glance at the girl's face, and spoke for the third time: "I'm rather ashamed of myself for getting up so late. I came here to work, not to rest."

"Oh, you'll get used to it," said the girl; and Mrs. Carmody smiled her secret smile. The dangerous silence strike was over. She said:

"What about food? Is there any particular store where you buy it? Your mother didn't mention such details in her letter. I—"

She stopped, startled in spite of herself at that mention of the letter. She stood for a moment, hands rigid in the hot water; then forced on:

"Your poor mother! It was such a tired letter she wrote. I cried when I read it."

From under half-closed eyes she saw that the girl's lips were trembling—and she knew her victory. She had a brief, blazing exultation at the way every word, every mood of this moment was under her control. She said swiftly:

"We can talk about those details later."

The girl said tearfully: "We have a charge account at Graham's General Store in Agan. You can phone up. He delivers this far."

The woman walked hurriedly into the dining room to get the dishes that were still there, and to hide the irrepressible light of triumph in her eyes. A charge account! The problem of obtaining control of the money had actually made her feel sick, the consciousness that legal steps might be necessary, the conviction that she must first establish herself in the household and in the community.

And here was her stepping-stone: a charge account! Now, if this Graham's store would only accept her order—what was the girl saying?

Mrs. Carmody, I want to apologize for not answering your question about my notebook at breakfast. You see, the neighbors always want know what great-grandfather says about them: so at breakfast, when he's strongest, I ask him questions, and take notes. I pretend to him that I'm going to write a book about his life when grow up. I couldn't explain all that in front of him, could I?"

"Of course not," said the woman. She thought sharply: So the neighbors were interested in the old man's words about them. They'd be interested and friendly with anyone who kept them supplied with the latest tidbits of news. She'd have keep her ears open, and perhaps keep a notebook herself.

She grew aware that the girl was speaking again: "I've been wanting to tell you, great-grandpa really has the gift of seeing. You won't believe that yet, but—"

The girl's eyes were bright, eager; and the woman knew better than to let such enthusiasm pass.

"Why, of course, I believe it," she said. "I'm not one of these skeptics who won't face facts. All through history there have been people with strange powers; and besides, didn't I see with my own eyes Mr. Wainwright step through a solid gate. I—"

Her voice faltered; her own words describing that incredible action brought a vivid return of reality, and she could only finish weakly: "Of course, I believe it."

"What I meant, Mrs. Carmody," the girl was saying, "don't be offended if he seems to say something unpleasant. He always thinks he's talking about events that have already happened, and then, of course, there's the way he talks about your sister, if you're a woman, and your brother if you're a man. It's really you he means."

Really you—

The woman's mind spun curiously; and the memory of the words stayed with her after the girl had ridden off to school, even after Graham's accepted her order on behalf of the Wainwright farm with a simple, utterly effective: "Oh, yes, Mrs. Carmody, we know about you."

It was not until nearly noon that she went out onto the porch, where the old man was sitting and asked the question that had been quivering in her mind:

"Mr. Wainwright, yesterday you mentioned you had seen my sister in Kempster. W-what did she have to say?"

She waited with a tenseness that startled her; and there was the queer thought that she was being utterly ridiculous. The old man took his long pipe out of his mouth, thoughtfully. He said:

"She was coming out of the courthouse, and—"

"Courthouse!" said Mrs. Carmody.

The old man was frowning to himself. "She didn't speak to me, so I cannot say what she was doing there." He finished politely: "Some little case, no doubt. We all have them."

Kent was aware of the car slowing. The driver nodded at a two-story wooden building with a veranda, and said:

"That's the hotel. I'll finish that story for you some other time. Or, if I'm too busy, just ask anyone. The whole district knows all about it."

The following morning the sun peered with dazzling force into his hotel room. Kent walked to the window and stared out over the peaceful village.

For a moment there was not a sound audible. The little spread of trees and houses lay almost dreamily under the blue, blue sky.

Kent thought quietly: He had made no mistake in deciding to spend the rest of the summer here, while, in a leisurely fashion, he carried on negotiations for the sale of the farm his parents had left him. Truth was he had been overworking.

He went downstairs and amazed himself by eating two eggs and four slices of bacon in addition to cereal and toast. From the dining room he walked to the veranda—and there was the ghost sitting in one of the wicker chairs.

Kent stopped short. The tiny beginning of a chill formed at the nape of his spine; then the old man saw him and said:

"Good morning. Mr. Kent. I should take it very kindly if you would sit down and talk with me. I need cheering up."

It was spoken with an almost intimate pathos; and yet Kent had a sudden sense of being beyond his depth. Somehow the old man's friendliness of the day before had seemed unreal.

Yet here it was again.

He shook himself. After all, part of the explanation at least was simple. Here was an old man—that ghost part was utterly ridiculous, of course—an old man, then, who could foretell the future. Foretell it in such a fashion that, in the case of Mrs. Carmody, he, the old man, had actually had the impression that she had been around for months before she arrived.

Apparently, he had had the same impression about Kent. Therefore—

"Good morning, Mr. Wainwright!" Kent spoke warmly as he seated himself. "You need cheering up, you say. Who's been depressing you?"

"Oh!" The old man hesitated, his finely line face twisted into a faint frown. He said finally, slowly. "Perhaps it is wrong of me to have mentioned it. It is no one's fault, I suppose, The friction of daily life, in this case. Mrs. Carmody pestering me about what her sister was doing in court."

Kent sat silent, astounded. The reference of the old man to the only part of the story that he, Kent, knew was—shattering. His brain recoiled from the coincidence into a tight, corded layer of thoughts:

Was this—alien—creature a mind reader as well as seer and ghost? An old, worn-out brain that had taken on automaton qualities, and reacted almost entirely to thoughts that trickled in from other minds? Or—

He stopped, almost literally pierced by the thought that came: Or was this reference to Mrs. Carmody, this illusion that Mrs. Carmody was still looking after him, one of those fantastic brain-chilling re-enactments of which the history of haunted houses was so gruesomely replete?

Dead souls, murderess and murdered, doomed through all eternity to live over and over again their lives before and during the crime!

But that was impossible. Mrs. Carmody was still alive; in a madhouse to be sure, but *alive.*

Kent released carefully the breath of air he had held hard in his lungs for nearly a minute. "Why don't you tell her," he said finally, "to ask her sister about what she was doing in court?"

The thin, gray, old face wrinkled into puzzlement, The old man said with a curious dignity:

"It is more complicated than that, Mr. Kent. I have never quite understood the appearance of so many twins in the world during the recent years of my life; and the fact that so many of them are scarcely on speaking terms with each other is additionally puzzling."

He shook his head. "It is all very confusing. For instance, this courtroom appearance of Mrs. Carmody's sister—I seem to remember having heard something else about it, but it must have struck me as unimportant at the time, for I cannot rightly recollect the details. It's not a pleasant situation for a harmless old man to handle."

Harmless! Kent's eyes narrowed involuntarily. That was what people kept saying about—the ghost. First, the driver, Tom; then, according to Tom's story, the girl Phyllis, and now the old man himself.

Harmless, harmless, harmless— Old man, he thought tensely, what about the fact that you drove a woman to murder you? What is your purpose? What—

Kent loosened the tight grip his fingers had taken on the arms of the chair. What was the matter with him, letting a thing like this get on his nerves?

He looked up. The sky was as blue as ever; the summer day peaceful, perfect. All was well with the world of reality.

There was silence, a deep, peaceful quiet during which Kent studied that long, aged face from half-closed eyes. The old man's skin was of a normal grayish texture with many, very many crisscross lines. He had a lean, slightly hawklike nose, and a thin, rather fine mouth.

Handsome old man; only—that explained nothing, and—

He saw that the old man was rising; he stood for a moment very straight, carefully adjusting his hat on his head; then:

"I must be on my way. It is important, in view of our strained relations, that I do not keep Mrs. Carmody waiting for lunch. I shall be seeing you again, Mr. Kent."

Kent stood up, a little, fascinated thought in his mind. He had intended to walk over to the farm that had belonged to his parents and introduce himself to the tenants. But that could wait.

Why not go with the—ghost—to the deserted Wainwright place, and— What?

He considered the question blankly; then his lips tightened. After all, this mysterious business was on his mind. To let it go would be merely to have a distraction at the back of his head, sufficient perhaps to interfere with anything he might attempt. Besides, there was no rush about the business. He was here for a rest and change as much as anything.

He stood there, still not absolutely decided, chilled by a dark miasma of mind stuff that welled up inside him:

Wasn't it perhaps dangerous to accompany a ghost to a hide-out in an isolated, old house?

He pressed the clammy fear out of his system because—it wasn't Mrs. Carmody who had been killed. She was out of her head, yes; but the danger was definitely mental, not physical, and—

His mind grew hard, cool. No sudden panic, no totality of horrendous threats or eerie menaces would actually knock his reason off its base. Therefore—

Kent parted his lips to call after the old man, who was gingerly moving down the wooden walk to the wooden sidewalk. Before he could speak, a deep voice beside him said:

"I noticed you were talking to the ghost, Mr. Kent."

Kent turned and faced a great, gross fat man whom he had previously noticed sitting in a little office behind the hotel desk. Three massive chins quivered as the man said importantly:

"My name is Jenkins, sir, proprietor of the Agan Hotel."

His pale, deep-set eyes peered at Kent.

"Tom was telling me that you met our greatest local character yester-day. A very strange, uncanny case. Very uncanny."

The old man was farther up the street now, Kent saw, an incredibly lean, sedately figure, who vanished abruptly behind a clump of trees. Kent stared after him, his mind still half on the idea of following as soon as he could reasonably break away from this man.

He took another look at the proprietor; and the man said heavily:

"I understand from Tom that he didn't have time to finish the story of what happened at the Wainwright farm. Perhaps I could complete the uncanny tale for you."

It struck Kent that the word "uncanny" must be a favorite with this dark mountain of flesh.

It struck him, too, that he would have to postpone his visit to the ghost farm, or risk offending his host.

Kent frowned and yielded to circumstances. It wasn't actually necessary to trail the old man today. And it might be handy to have all the facts first, before he attempted to solve the mystery. He seated himself after watching the fat man wheeze into a chair. He said:

"Is there any local theory that would explain the"—he hesitated—"uncanny appearance of the ghost. You do insist that he is a ghost, in spite of his substantial appearance."

"Definitely a ghost!" Jenkins grunted weightily. "We buried him, didn't we? And unburied him again a week later to see if he was still there; and he was, dead and cold as stone. Oh. yes, definitely a ghost. What other explanation could there be?"

"I'm not," said Kent carefully, "not exactly—a believer—in ghosts."

The fat man waved the objection aside with flabby hand. "None of us were, sir, none of us. But facts are facts."

Kent sat silent; then: "A ghost that tells the future. What kind of future? Is it all as vague as that statement of his to Mrs. Carmody about her sister coming out of the courthouse?"

Sagging flesh shook as Mr. Jenkins cleared his throat. "Mostly local events of little importance, but which would interest an old man who lived here all his life."

"Has he said anything about the war?"

"He talks as if it's over, and therefore acts as if the least said the better." Mr. Jenkins laughed a great husky, tolerant laugh. "His point about the war is amazement that prices continue to hold up. It confuses him. And it's no use keeping after him, because talking tires him easily, and he gets a persecuted look. He did stay something about American armies landing in northern France, but"—he shrugged—"we all know that's going to happen, anyway."

Kent nodded. "This Mrs. Carmody—she arrived when?"

"In 1933, nearly nine years ago."

"And Mr. Wainwright has been dead five years?"

The fat man settled himself deeper into his chair. "I shall be glad," he said pompously, "to tell you the rest of the story in an orderly fashion. I shall omit the first few months after her arrival, as they contained very little of importance—"

The woman came exultantly out of the Wholesale Marketing Co. She felt a renewal of the glow that had suffused her when she first discovered this firm in Kampster two mouths before.

Four chickens and three dozen eggs—four dollars cash.

Cash!

The glow inside her dimmed. She frowned darkly. It was no use fooling herself; now that the harvesting season was only a week away, this make-shift method of obtaining money out of the farm couldn't go on— Her mind flashed to the bank book she had discovered in the house, with its tremendous information that the Wainwrights had eleven thousand seven hundred thirty-four dollars and fifty-one cents in the Kempster Bank.

An incredible fortune, so close yet so far away—

She stood very still in front of the bank finally, briefly paralyzed by a thought dark as night. If she went in—in minutes she'd know the worst.

This time it wouldn't be an old, old man and a young girl she'd be facing. It would be—

The banker was a dapper little fellow with horn-rimmed glasses, behind which sparkled a large pair of gray eyes.

"Ah, yes, Mrs. Carmody!" The man rubbed his fingers together. "So it finally occurred to you to come and see me."

He chuckled. "Well, well, we can fix everything; don't worry. I think between us we can manage to look after the Wainwright farm to the sat-isfaction of the community and the court, eh?"

Court! The word caught the woman in the middle of a long, ascending surge of triumph. So this was it. This was what the old man had prophe-sied. And it was good, not bad.

She felt a brief, ferocious rage at the old fool for having frightened her so badly—but the banker was speaking again:

"I understand you have a letter from your sister-in-law, asking you to look after Phyllis and the farm. It is possible such letter is not absolutely necessary, as you are the only relative, but in lieu of a will it will constitute a definite authorization on the basis of which the Courts can appoint you executrix."

The woman sat very still, almost frozen by the words. Somehow, while she had always felt that she would in a crisis produce the letter she had forged, now that the terrible moment was here—

She felt herself fumbling in her purse, and there was the sound of her voice mumbling some doubt about the letter still being around. But she knew better.

She brought it out, took it blindly from the blank envelope where she had carefully placed it, handed it toward the smooth, reaching fingers— and waited her doom.

As he read, the man spoke to himself, half to her: "Hm-m-m, she offers you twenty-five dollars a month over and above expenses—"

The woman quivered in every muscle of her thick body. The incredible violent thought came that she must have been mad to put such a thing in the letter. She said hurriedly: "Forget about the money. I'm not here to—"

"I was just going to say," interrupted the banker, "that it seems an inadequate wage. For a farm as large and wealthy as that of the Wainwrights', there is no reason why the manager should not receive fifty dollars, at least, and that is the sum we shall petition the judge for."

He added: "The local magistrate is having a summer sitting this morning just down the street, and if you'll step over there with me we can have this all settled shortly."

He finished: "By the way, he's always interested in the latest predictions of old Mr. Wainwright."

"I know them all!" the woman gulped.

She allowed herself, a little later, to be shepherded onto the sidewalk. A brilliant, late July sun was pouring down on the pavement. Slowly, it warmed the chill out of her veins.

It was three years later, three undisturbed years. The woman stopped short in the task of running the carpet sweeper over the living-room carpet, and stood frowning. Just what had brought the thought into her mind, she couldn't remember, but—

Had she seen the old man, as she came out of the courthouse that July day three years before, when the world had been handed to her without a struggle.

The old man had predicted that moment. That meant, in some way, he must have seen it. Had the picture come in the form of a vision? Or as a result of some contact in his mind across the months? Had he in short been physically present; and the scene had flashed back through some connection across time?

She couldn't remember having seen him. Try as she would, nothing came to her from that moment but a sort of blurred, enormous contentment.

The old man, of course, thought he'd been there. The old fool believed that everything he ever spoke about was a memory of his past. What a dim, senile world that past must be.

It must spread before his mind like a road over which shifting tendrils of fog drifted, now thick and impenetrable, now thin and bright with flashing rays of sunlight—and pictures.

Pictures of events.

Across the room from her she was vaguely aware of the old man stirring in his chair. He spoke:

"Seems like hardly yesterday that Phyllis and that Couzens boy got married. And yet it's—"

He paused; he said politely: "When was that, Pearl? My memory isn't as good as it was, and—"

The words didn't actually penetrate the woman. But her gaze, in its idle turning, fastened on plump Pearl—and stopped. The girl sat rigid on the living-room couch, where she had been sprawling. Her round, baby eyes were wide.

"Ma?" she shrilled. "Did you hear that? Grandpa's talking like Phyllis and Charlie Couzens are married."

There was a thick, muffled sound of somebody half choking. With a gulp the woman realized that it was she who had made the sound. Gasping, she whirled on the old man and loomed over him, a big, tight-lipped creature, with hard blue eyes.

For a moment, her dismay was so all-consuming that words wouldn't come. The immensity of the catastrophe implied by the old man's statement scarcely left room for thought. But—

Marriage!

And she had actually thought smugly that Bill and Phyllis— Why, Bill had told her and—

Marriage!

To the son of the neighboring farmer. Automatic end to her security. She had nearly a thousand dollars, but how long would that last, once the income itself stopped?

Sharp pain of fear released the explosion that, momentarily, had been dammed up by the sheer fury of her thoughts:

"You old fool, you!" she raged. "So you've been sitting here all these years while I've been looking after you, scheming against me and mine. A trick, that's what it is. Think you're clever, eh, using your gift to—"

It was the way the old man was shrinking that brought brief, vivid awareness to the woman of the danger of such an outburst after so many years of smiling friendliness. She heard the old man say:

"I don't understand, Mrs. Carmody. What's the matter?"

"Did you say it?" She couldn't have stopped the words to save her soul.

"Did I say what?"

"About Phyllis and that Couzens boy—"

"Oh, them!" He seemed to forget that she was there above him. A benign smile crept into his face. He said at last quietly: "It seems like hardly yesterday that they were married—"

For a second time he became aware of the dark, forbidding expression of the woman who towered above him.

"Anything wrong?" he gasped. "Has something happened to Phyllis and her husband?"

With a horrible effort the woman caught hold of herself. Her eyes blazed at him with a slate-blue intensity.

"I don't want you to talk about them, do you understand? Not a word. I don't want to hear a word about them."

The old man stirred, his face creasing into a myriad extra lines of bewilderment. "Why, certainly, Mrs. Carmody, if you wish, but my own great-granddaughter—"

He subsided weakly as the woman whipped on Pearl: "If you mention one word of this to Phyllis, I'll ... you know what I'll do to you."

"Oh, sure, ma," Pearl said. "You can trust me, ma."

The woman turned away shaking. For years there had been a dim plan in the back of her mind, to cover just such a possibility as Phyllis wanting to marry someone else.

She twisted her face with distaste and half fear, and brought the ugly thing out of the dark brain corridor where she had kept it hidden.

Her fingers kept trembling as she worked. Once she saw herself in the mirror over the sink—and started back in dismay at the distorted countenance that reflected there.

That steadied her. But the fear stayed, sick surge after sick surge of it. A woman, forty-five, without income, in the depths of the depression. There was Federal relief, of course, but they wouldn't give that to her till the money was gone. There was old-age pension—twenty-five years away.

She drew a deep breath. Actually, those were meaningless things, utter defeats. Actually, there was only her desperate plan—and that required the fullest co-operation from Bill.

She studied Bill when he came in from the field at lunch. There had been a quietness in him this last year or so that had puzzled her. As if, at twenty, he had suddenly grown up.

He looked like a man; he was strongly built, of medium height with lines of dark passion in his rather heavy face.

That was good, that passion; undoubtedly, he had inherited some of her own troubled ambition—and there was the fact that he had been caught stealing just before they left the city, and released with a warning.

She hadn't blamed him then, felt only his bitter fury against a world that lashed out so cruelly against boys ruthlessly deprived by fate of spending money.

That was all over, of course. For two years he had been a steady, quiet worker, pulling his full share with the other hired men. Nevertheless—

To get Phyllis, that earlier, harder training would surely rise up once more—and win for all of them.

Slyly, she watched as, out of the corner of his eyes, he took one of his long, measured glances at Phyllis, where she sat across the table slantwise from him. For more than a year now, the woman had observed him look at Phyllis like that—and besides she had asked him, and—

Surely a young man of twenty would fight to get the girl he loved.

Fight unscrupulously. The only thing was—

How did a mother tell her son the particular grim plan that was in her mind? Did she … she just tell him?

After lunch, while Phyllis and Pearl were washing the dishes, the woman softly followed Bill up to his room. And, actually, it was easier than she had thought.

He lay for a while, after she had finished, staring at the ceiling; his heavy face was quiet almost placid. Finally:

"So the idea is that this evening you take Pearl in to Kempster to a movie; the old man, of course, will sleep like a log. But after Phyllis goes to bed at her usual time, I go into her room—and then she'll have to marry me."

It was so baldly put that the woman shrank, as if a mirror had been held up to her; and the image was an incredibly evil, ravaged thing. The cool voice went on:

"If I do this it means we'll be able to stay on the farm, is that right?"

She nodded, because no words would come. Then, not daring to stay a moment longer, she turned and left the room.

Slowly, the black mood of that interview passed. It was about three o'clock in the afternoon when she came out onto the veranda; and the old man looked up from his chair, and said:

"Terrible thing," he said, "your sister hanged. They told me at the hotel. Hanged. Terrible, terrible; you've been right to have nothing to do with her."

He seemed to forget her, simply sat there staring into space.

The whole thing was utterly unreal, and, after a moment quite unthinkably fantastic. The woman stared at him with a sudden, calm, grim understanding of the faint smile that was creeping back into his face, a serene smile.

So that was his plan, she thought coolly. The mischievous old scoundrel intended that Phyllis should not marry Bill. Therefore, knowing his own reputation for prophecy, he had cleverly told her that Phyllis and Charlie Couzens—

That was his purpose. And now he was trying to scare her into doing nothing about it. Hanging indeed. She smiled, her thick face taut with inward anger.

He was clever—but not clever enough.

In the theater she had a curious sense of chattering voices and flickering lights. Too much meaningless talk, too much light.

Her eyes hurt and, afterward, when they came out onto the pale dimness of Kempster's main street, the difference—the greater darkness—was soothing.

She must have said, "Pearl, let's go in and have a banana split."

She must have said that or agreed to it because after a while they were sitting at a little table; and the ice cream was cold as it went into her mouth; and there was a taste of banana.

Her mind held only a variation of one tense thought: If she and Bill could put this over, the world was won. Nothing thereafter could ever damage them to the same dreadful degree as this could.

"Aw, gee, ma, I'm sleepy. It's half past eleven."

The woman came to reality with a start. She looked at her watch; and it was true. "Goodness gracious!" she exclaimed with artificial amazement. "I didn't realize—"

The moon was shining, and the horse anxious to get home. Coming down the great hill, she could see no light anywhere in the house. The buildings loomed silent in the moonlit darkness, like great semi-formless shapes against the transparent background of the land.

She left Pearl to unhitch the animal and, trembling; went into the house. There was a lamp in the kitchen turned very low. She turned it into brightness, but the light didn't seem to help her feet on the stairs. She kept stumbling, but she reached the top, reached Bill's door. Ever so softly, she knocked.

No answer.

She opened the door. The pale, yellow light of the lamp poured onto the empty bed—and it was only the sound of Pearl coming into the kitchen downstairs that made her close hastily the door of Bill's room. Pearl came up, yawning, and disappeared instantly into her own room.

The fat man stopped abruptly as a distant telephone thrummed. He rolled apologetically out of his seat. "I'll be right back," he said.

One question, Kent asked hastily. "What about that. prophecy of hanging? I thought Mrs. Carmody was in a madhouse, very much alive."

"She is." The vast bulk of the hotel proprietor filled the door. "We figured out that the old man was definitely tying to put something over?"

The minutes dragged. Kent took his notebook and wrote with the elaborate ornateness of vague purpose:

> An old man
> Who can tell the future
> Who caused a woman to murder him
> But still lives
> Who walks through solid objects
> Who reads minds (possibly)

He sat thoughtful, then added to the list:

A senile ghost

For long minutes he stared at the combination. Finally, he laughed ruefully—and simultaneously grew aware of the clicking of pool balls inside.

He stood up, peered through the door—and smiled sardonically as he saw that fat Jenkins was playing a game of snooker with a chunky man of his own age.

Kent shrugged; and, turning, went down the steps. It was obvious that he would have to get the rest of this story piecemeal, here and there over the countryside; obvious, too, that he'd better write Miss Kincaid to send him some books on ghosts and seers, the folklore as well as anything remotely scientific.

He'd need everything he could lay his hands on if he was going to solve the mystery of—the ghost!

The books kept trickling in over a period of four weeks. Miss Kincaid sent ghost stories, compilations of true ghost tales, four books on psychic phenomena, a history of magic, a treatise on astrology and kindred arts, the works of Charles Fort; and, finally, three thin volumes by one J. W. Dunne, on the subject of time.

Kent sat on the veranda in the early morning just after the arrival of the mail that had brought them, and read the three books in one sitting, with an excitement that gathered at every page.

He got up at last, shaky, and half convinced that he had the tremendous answer; and yet—there were things to clear up—

An hour later he was lying in a little wooded dell that overlooked the house and yard, waiting. It was almost time for the—ghost—to come out, if he intended to take his morning walk—

At noon Kent returned to the hotel thinking tensely: The old man must have gone somewhere else today ... somewhere else—

His mind nearly came out of his head from contemplating that somewhere else. The following morning, eight o'clock found him in his little copse, waiting. Again, the old man failed to appear.

The third morning. Kent's luck was better. Dark, threatening clouds rode the sky as he watch the thin, tall figure move from behind the house and slowly approach the gate. The old man came across the field; Kent showed himself in plenty of time striding along out of the bush as if he, too, was out for a walk.

"Hello, there, Mr. Wainwright," he said.

The old man came closer without answering, and Kent saw that the man was peering at him curiously. The old man stopped.

"Do I know you, young sir?" he asked politely.

For the barest moment Kent was thrown mentally off balance; and then—

"Good heavens!" he thought excitedly, "even this fits. It *fits*. There had to be a time when he met me."

Aloud, he explained patiently that he was the son of Angus Kent, and that he had come back to the district for a visit. When he had finished the old man said:

"I shall be glad to come to the hotel and talk about your father. It is a pleasure to have met you."

He walked off. The moment he was out of sight, Kent started toward the gate. The first drops of rain fell as he crawled laboriously under the wire. He stood just inside the gate, hesitant. It was important that he get inside the house before the old man, driven by the rain, returned.

The question was, would he have time?

He hurried toward the buildings, glancing over his shoulders every few seconds, expecting to see that long form come into sight.

The house stood quietly under the soft, glinting rain. The weight of the neglectful years lay heavily on its wooden walls. A burst of rain whipped into Kent's face, and then thudded dully on the wood as he ducked into the shelter of the building.

He stood there waiting for the blast to die down. But, as the seconds passed, and there was no abatement, he peered around the corner and saw the veranda.

He reached the safety it offered; and then, more leisurely, investigated the two boarded windows and the boarded door. They were solid, and, though he had expected it, the reality brought a stab of disappointment.

Getting inside was going to be a tough job.

The rain became a thin splatter; and he went hastily down the steps, and saw that there was an open balcony on the second floor. It was hard work climbing, but the effort proved its worth.

A wide, loose board on one of the two balcony windows came off with a jerk, and made it easy to tear off the rest. Beyond was a window, locked.

Kent did not hesitate. He raised one of the boards and, with a single sharp blow, struck. The glass shattered with a curious, empty tinkling sound.

He was inside. The room was empty, dusty, dark, unfurnished. It led out onto a long, empty hallway, and a line of empty, dark rooms.

Downstairs it was the same; empty rooms, unlived in. The basement was dark, a cemented hole. He fumbled around it hurriedly, lighting matches; and then hurriedly went back to the ground floor. There were some cracks in the boards that covered the downstairs windows and, after locating the likeliest ones, he stationed himself at the one that faced the gate—and waited.

It didn't take long.

The old man came through the gate, toward the house. Kent shifted to a window at the side of the house, then at the back; and each time the old man came into view after a moment.

Kent raced to the crack he had selected in the veranda window, expecting to see the old man come into sight.

Ten minutes passed; and that tall figure had still to come around the back corner of the house. Slowly, Kent went upstairs, and out onto the balcony.

It was simple hammering the boards back into position, not so simply easing down to the ground.

But he had his fact. Somewhere at the rear of the house the ghost vanished. The problem was—how to prevent that disappearance.

How did one trap the kind of—ghost—that the long-dead Mr. Wainwright had become?

It was the next day, nearly noon. Kent lay well into the field south of the farmhouse. Earlier, he had watched the old man emerge from the gate, and go past his hiding place along the valley. Now—

Through his field glasses Kent watched the long, straight form coming toward him, toward the farm.

Kent emerged casually from the wood and walked along as if he had not seen the other. He was wondering just what his verbal approach should be when the old man hailed him:

"Hello there, Mr. Kent. Out for a walk?"

Kent turned and waited for the aged man to come up to him. He said: "I was just going to go in to Mrs. Carmody, and ask for a drink of water, before heading on to the hotel. If you don't mind, I'll walk with you."

"Not at all, sir," said the old man.

They walked along, Kent consciously more erect as he tried to match that superb straightness of body. His mind was seething. What *would* happen at the gate? Somewhere along here the old man's body would become less substantial, but—

He couldn't hold the thought. Besides, he'd better start laying his groundwork. He said tautly:

"The farm looks rather deserted from here, does it not, Mr. Wainwright?"

Amazingly, the old man gulped; he said almost swiftly: "Have you noticed it, too, Mr. Kent? I have long thought it an illusion on my part, and I have felt rather uneasy about my vision. I have found that the peculiar desolated appearance vanishes as soon as I pass through the gate."

So it was the gate where the change began— He jerked his soaring thought back to earth, listened as the old man said in evident relief:

"I am glad that we both share this illusion, Mr. Kent. It has had me worried."

Kent hesitated, and then very carefully took his field glasses out of their case; and handed than to the old man.

"Try a look through these," he said casually. "Perhaps they will help to break the illusion."

The moment he had given the instrument over compunction came, a hard, bright pity for the incredible situation he was forcing.

Compunction passed; pity yielded to an almost desperate curiosity. From narrowed eyes he stared at that lined face as the man's thin, bony hands held the glasses up to his face and slowly adjusted the lens.

There was a harsh gasp; and Kent, who had expected it, leaped forward and caught the glasses as they fell toward the ground.

"Why," the old man was quavering, "it's impossible. Windows boarded up, and"—a wild suspicion leaped into his eyes—"has Mrs. Carmody gone so swiftly?"

"What's wrong, sir?" Kent said, and felt like a villain. But—he *couldn't* let this go now.

The old man was shaking his head. "I must be mad. My eyes ... my mind ... not what they used to be—"

"Let's go over," Kent suggested. "I'll get my drink and we'll see what's wrong."

It was important that the old man retain in his wandering mind that he had a companion. The patriarch straightened, said quietly:

"By all means, you shall have your drink, Mr. Kent."

Kent had a sick feeling as he walked beside that tall form across the road to the gate, the empty feeling that he had meddled in human tragedy.

He watched, almost ill with his victory, as the trembling nonagenarian fumbled futilely with the padlocked gate.

He thought, his mind as tight as a drum: For perhaps the first time since this strange, strange phenomena had started, the old man had failed to walk *through* the gate.

"I don't understand it!" the old man said. "This gate locked—why, this very morning, I—"

Kent had been unwinding the wire that held the large gate. "Let's go in here," he said gently.

The dismay of the old man was so pitiful it was dreadful. He stopped and peered at the weeds. Incredulously, he felt the black old wood that was nailed, board on board of it, over one of the windows. His high shoulders began to sag. A haunted expression crept into his face. Paradoxically, he looked suddenly *old*.

He climbed the faded veranda steps with the weariness of unutterable age. And then—

The flashing, terrible realization of the truth struck at Kent in that last instant, as the old man stepped timidly, almost blindly, toward the nailed door.

"Wait! He shrilled."Wait!"

His piercing voice died. Where the old man had been was—nothingness.

A thin wind howled with brief mournfulness around the house, rattling the eaves.

He stood alone on that faded, long-unused veranda. Alone with the comprehension that had, in one dreadful kaleidoscope of mind picture, suddenly cleared up—everything.

And dominating everything else, was the dreadful fear that he would be too late.

He was running, his breath coming in great gulps. A tiny wind caught the dust that his shoes kicked up from the soft roadbed, and whipped it in little, unpleasant gusts around his nostrils.

The vague thought came that it was lucky he had done so much walking the past month; for the exercise had added just enough strength to bring the long, lone mile and a half to the hotel within his powers—

A tangy, unpleasant taste of salt was in his mouth as he staggered up the steps. Inside, he was blurrily aware of the man, Tom, staring at him across the counter. Kent grasped:

"I'll give you five dollars if you can pack my things and get me to Kempster in time to catch the twelve-o'clock train. And tell me how to get to the insane asylum at Peerton. For Heaven's sake, make it fast."

The man goggled. "I had the maid pack your things right after breakfast, Mr. Kent. Don't you remember, this is August 17th."

Kent glared at him with a blank horror. *That* prophecy came true. Then what about the other, more awful one—

On the way to Kempster he was vaguely aware of the driver speaking, something about Peerton being a large town, and he'd be able to get a taxi at the station—

From the taxi the asylum showed as a series of long, white buildings, a green, tree-filled enclosure, surrounded by a high iron fence. He was led through an endless, quiet corridor; his mind kept straining past the sedate, white-clothed woman ahead of him. Couldn't she realize this was life and death?

The doctor sat in a little, bright cozy room. He stood up politely as Kent entered, but Kent waited only for the woman to close the door as she went out.

"Sir, you have a woman here named Mrs. Carmody." He paused a fraction of a second to let the name sink in, then rushed on "Never mind if you can't remember her name. It's true."

The fine, strong face of the white-haired doctor cleared. "I remember the case."

"Look," said Kent desperately. "I've just found out the truth about that whole affair; and this is what you've got to do—at once:

"Take me to the woman, and I'll assure her, and you assure her, that she has been found innocent, and will be freed. Do you understand?"

"I think," said the doctor quietly, "that you had better begin at the beginning."

Kent had a frantic sense of walls rising up between him and his purpose. "For Heaven's sake, sir, believe me, there's no time. I don't know just how it is supposed to happen, but the prediction that she would be hanged can only come true in—"

"Now, Mr. Kent, I would appreciate—"

"Don't you understand?" Kent yelled. "If that prophecy is not to be fulfilled, you must act. I tell you I have information that will release this woman. And, therefore, *the next few minutes* are the vital ones."

He stopped because the man was frowning at him. The doctor said: "Really, Mr. Kent, you will have to calm down. I am sure everything will be all right."

The strained wonder came to Kent, if all sane, becalmed people seemed as maddening as this quiet-spoken doctor.

He thought shakily: "He'd better be careful or they'd be keeping him in here with the rest of the lunatics."

He began to speak, to tell what he'd heard and seen and done. The man kept interrupting him with incisive questions; and, after a while, it came to Kent, that he would actually have to begin at the beginning to fill in the gaps of this fellow's knowledge.

He stopped, sat shaky for a moment, struggling to clear his brain, and then with a tense quietness, began again.

He found himself, as the minutes dragged, listening to his own voice. Every time his words speeded up or rose in crescendo, he would deliberately slow down and articulate every syllable. He reached the point where the Dunne books came into the story, and—

His mind paused in a wild dismay: Good heavens, would he have to explain the Dunne theory of time with its emphasis on time as a state of mind. The rest was unimportant, but that part—

He grew aware that the doctor was speaking, saying: "I've read several volumes by Mr. Dunne. I'm afraid I cannot accept his theory of multidimensional time. I—"

"Listen," said Kent in a tight voice, "picture an old man in his dotage. It's a queer, incoherent mind-world he lives in; strange, frequently unassociated ideas are the normal condition; memory, particularly memory, is unutterably mixed up. And it is in that confused environment that somehow *once* a variation of the Dunne phenomena operated.

"An old man whose time sense has been distorted by the ravages of senility, an old man who walks as easily into the future as you and I walk into the next room."

"What!"

The doctor was on his feet, pacing the rugged floor. He stared at Kent finally.

"Mr. Kent, this is a most extraordinary idea. But still I fail to see why Mrs. Carmody—"

Kent groaned, then with a terrible effort pulled himself together. "Do you remember the murder scene?"

"Vaguely. A domestic tragedy, I believe."

"Listen. Mrs. Carmody woke up the morning after she thought she'd made everything right for herself and her family, and found a note on her dressing table. It had been lying there all night, and it was from her son, Bill.

"In it, he said he couldn't go through with her plan. Besides, he didn't like the farm, so he was going immediately to the city—and in fact he walked to Kempster and caught the train while she was in the theater.

"Among other things, he said in his note that a few days before the old man had acted surprised at seeing him, Bill, still around. The old man talked as if he thought Bill had gone to the city—"

That was what kept stabbing into the woman's mind. The old man, the interfering old man—

He had, in effect, told Bill that he, Bill, had gone to the city, and so in a crisis Bill had gone.

Gone, gone, gone—and all hope with him. Phyllis would marry Charlie Couzens; and what then? What would become of a poor, miserable woman of forty-five?

The old man, she thought, as she went down the stairs from her room, the old man planned it all. Fiendish old man! First, telling Bill about the city, then suggesting who Phyllis was to marry, then trying to scare *her* with that hanging—

Hanging—

The woman stopped short in the downstairs hallway, her blue eyes stark, a strange, burning sensation in her brain. Why—

If all the rest came true, then—*hanging!*

Her mind whirled madly. She crouched for moment like an animal at bay, cunning in her eyes. They couldn't hang you unless you murdered someone, and—

She'd see that she didn't pull anything so stupid.

She couldn't remember eating breakfast But there was a memory of her voice asking monotonously:

"Where's Mr. Wainwright?"

"He's gone for a walk, ma. Hey, ma, are you ill?"

Ill! Who asked a silly question like that. It was the old man who'd be ill when she got through with him.

There was a memory, too, of washing the dishes, but after that a strange, dark gap, a living, evil night flooding her mind ... gone ... hope ... Bill ... damned old man—

She was standing at the screen door for the hundredth time, peering malignantly at the corner of the house where the old man would come into sight—when it happened.

There was the screen door and the deserted veranda. That was one instant. The next, the old man materialized out of the thin air two feet away. He opened the screen door, and then half fell against the door, and slowly crumbled to the ground, writhing, as the woman screamed at him, meaningless words—

"That was her story," Kent said wearily, "that the old man simply fell dead. But the doctor who came testified that Mr. Wainwright died of choking, and besides, in her hysteria, Mrs. Carmody told everything about herself, and the various facts taken together combined to discredit her story."

Kent paused, then finished in a queer voice: "It is medically recognized, I believe, that very old people can choke themselves to death by swallowing saliva the wrong way, or by a paralysis of the throat produced by shock—"

"Shock!" The doctor sank back into his chair from which he had half risen. "Man!" he gasped, "are you trying to tell me that your interference with the old man that day caused his abrupt appearance before Mrs. Carmody, and that it was the shock of what he had himself gone through that—"

"I'm trying to tell you," said Kent, "that we've got minutes to prevent this woman from hanging herself. It could only happen if she did do it with her own hands; and it could only happen today, for if we can get there in time to tell her, why, she'll have no incentive. Will you come ... for Heaven's sake, man—"

The doctor said: "But the prophecy. If this old man actually had this incredible power, how can we hope to circumvent the inevitable?"

"Look!" said Kent, "I influenced the past by an act from the future. Surely, I can change the future by—*but come along!*"

He couldn't take his eyes off the woman. She sat there in her bright little room, and she was still smiling, as she had been when they first came in, a little more uncertainly now, as the doctor talked.

"You mean," she said finally, "that I am to be freed, that you're going to write my children, and they'll come and get me."

"Absolutely!" Kent spoke heartily, but with just the faintest bit of puzzlement in his voice. "I understand your son, Bill, is working in a machine factory, and that he's married now, and that your daughter is a stenographer for the same company."

"Yes, that's true." She spoke quietly—

Afterward, while the doctor's maid was serving Kent a warmed-up lunch, he said frowningly: "I can't understand it. I ought to feel that everything is cleared up. Her children have small jobs, the girl Phyllis is married to that Couzens chap, and is living in his family home. As for Mrs. Carmody—and this is what gets me—I had no impression that she was in danger of hanging herself. She was cheerful; she had her room fixed with dozens of little fancily sewed things and—"

The doctor said: "The records show that she's been no trouble while she's been here. She's been granted special privileges; she does a lot of sewing— What's the matter?"

Kent wondered grimly if he looked as wild as the thought that had surged into his mind. "Doctor!" he gasped, "there's a psychological angle here that I forgot completely."

He was on his feet. "Doctor, we've got to get to that woman again, tell her she can stay here, tell her—"

There was the sound of a door opening violently, then running footsteps. A man in uniform burst in.

"Doctor, there's a woman just hanged herself, a Mrs. Carmody. She cut her dress into strips and, using the light fixture—"

They had already cut her down when Kent and the doctor arrived. She lay stiff in death, a dark, heavily built woman. A faint smile was fixed on her rigid lips—Kent was aware of the doctor whispering to him:

"No one's to blame, of course. How could we sane people remember that the greatest obsession in her life was security, and that here in this asylum was that security she craved."

Kent scarcely heard. He felt curiously cold; the room seemed remote. In his mind's eye he could see the Wainwright house, empty, nailed-up; and yet for years an old, old man would come out of it and wander over the land before he, too, sank forever into the death that long ago struck him down.

The time would come when the—ghost—would walk no more.

THE RULL

P rofessor Jamieson saw the other space boat out of the corner of one eye. He was sitting in a hollow about a dozen yards from the edge of the precipice, and some score of feet from the doorway of his own lifeboat. He had been intent on his survey book, annotating a comment beside the voice graph to the effect that Laertes III was so close to the invisible dividing line between Earth-controlled and Rull-controlled space that its prior discovery by man was in itself a major victory in the Rull-human war.

It was at that point that he saw the other boat, above and somewhat to his left, approaching the tableland. He glanced up at it—and froze where he was, torn between two opposing purposes.

His first impulse, to run for the lifeboat, yielded to the realization that the movement would be seen instantly by the electronic reflexes of the other ship. For a moment, then, he had the dim hope that if he remained quiet enough, neither he nor his ship would be observed.

Even as he sat there, perspiring with indecision, his tensed eyes noted the Rull markings and the rakish design of the other vessel. His vast knowledge of things Rull enabled him to catalogue it instantly as a survey craft.

A *survey* craft. The Rulls had discovered the Laertes sun.

The terrible potentiality was that behind this small craft might be fleets of battleships, whereas he was alone. His own lifeboat had been dropped by the *Orion* nearly a parsec away while the big ship was proceeding at antigravity speeds. That was to insure that Rull energy traces did not record its passage through this area of space.

The *Orion* was to head for the nearest base, load up with planetary defense equipment, and return. She was due in ten days.

Ten days. Jamieson groaned inwardly, and drew his legs under him and clenched his survey book in the fingers of one hand. But still the possibility that his ship, partially hidden under a clump of trees, might escape notice if he remained quiet, held him there in the open. His head tilted up, his eyes glared at the alien, and his brain willed it to turn aside.

Once more, flashingly, while he waited, the implications of the disaster that could be here struck deep. In all the universe there had never been so dangerous an intelligence as the Rull. At once remorseless and immune to all attempts at establishing communication, Rulls killed human beings on sight. A human-manned warship that ventured into Rull-patrolled space was attacked until it withdrew or was destroyed. Rull ships that entered Earth-controlled space *never* withdrew once they were attacked. In the beginning, man had been reluctant to engage in a death struggle for the galaxy. But the inexorable enemy had forced him finally to match in every respect the tenacious and murderous policies of the Rull.

The thought ended. The Rull ship was a hundred yards away, and showed no signs of changing its course. In seconds, it would cross the clump of trees that half-hid the lifeboat.

In a spasm of a movement, Jamieson launched himself from his chair. Like a shot from a gun, with utter abandon, he dived for the open doorway of his machine. As the door clanged behind him, the boat shook as if it had been struck by a giant. Part of the ceiling sagged; the floor staggered toward him, and the air grew hot and suffocating.

Gasping, Jamieson slid into the control chair and struck at the main emergency switch. The rapid-fire blasters huzzaed into automatic firing positions and let go with a hum and deep-throated *ping*. The refrigerators whined with power; a cold blast of air blew at his body. The relief was so quick that a second passed before Jamieson realized that the atomic engines had failed to respond, and that the lifeboat, which should already have been sliding into the air, was still lying inert in an exposed position.

Tense, he stared into the visiplates. It took a moment to locate the Rull ship. It was at the lower edge of one plate, tumbling slowly out of sight beyond a clump of trees a quarter of a mile away. As he watched, it disappeared; and then the crash of the landing came clear and unmistakable from the sound board in front of him.

The relief that came was weighted with an awful reaction. Jamieson sank back into the cushions of the control chair, weak from the narrowness of his escape. The weakness ended abruptly as a thought struck him. There had been a sedateness about the way the enemy ship fell. *The crash hadn't killed the Rulls aboard.*

He was alone in a damaged lifeboat on an impassable mountain with one or more of the most remorseless creatures ever spawned. For ten days, he must fight in the hope that man would still be able to seize the most valuable planet discovered in a century.

He saw in his visiplate that it was growing darker outside.

Jamieson took another antisleep pill and made a more definitive examination of the atomic motors. It didn't take long to verify his earlier diagnosis. The basic graviton pile had been thoroughly frustrated. Until it could be reactivated on the *Orion*, the motors were useless.

The conclusive examination braced Jamieson. He was committed irrevocably to the battle of the tableland, with all its intricate possibilities. The idea that had been turning over in his mind during the prolonged night took on new meaning. This was the first time in his knowledge that a Rull and a human being had faced each other on a limited field of action, where neither was a prisoner. The great battles in space were ship against ship and fleet against fleet. Survivors either escaped or were picked up by overwhelming forces. Actually, both humans and Rulls, captured or facing capture, were conditioned to kill themselves. Rulls did it by a mental *willing* that had never been circumvented. Men had to use mechanical methods, and in some cases that had proved impossible. The result was that Rulls had had occasional opportunities to experiment on living, conscious men.

Unless he was bested before he could get organized, here was a priceless opportunity to try some tests on Rulls—and without delay. Every moment of daylight must be utilized to the uttermost limit.

By the time the Laertes sun peered palely over the horizon that was the northeast cliff's edge, the assault was under way. The automatic defensors, which he had set up the night before, moved slowly from point to point ahead of the mobile blaster.

Jamieson cautiously saw to it that one of the three defensors also brought up his rear. He augmented that basic protection by crawling from one projecting rock after another. The machines he manipulated from a tiny hand control, which was connected to the visiplates that poked out from his headgear just above his eyes. With tensed eyes he watched the wavering needles that would indicate movement or that the defensor screens were being subjected to energy opposition.

Nothing happened.

As he came within sight of the Rull craft, Jamieson stalled his attack while he seriously pondered the problem of no resistance. He didn't like it. It was possible that all the Rulls aboard *had* been killed, but he doubted

it mightily. Rulls were almost boneless. Except for half a dozen strategi-
cally linked cartilages, they were all muscles.

With bleak eyes, Jamieson studied the wreck through the telescopic
eyes of one of the defensors. It lay in a shallow indentation, its nose
buried in a wall of gravel. Its lower plates were collapsed versions of
the originals. His single-energy blast the evening before, completely
automatic though it had been, had really dealt a smashing blow to the
Rull ship.

The overall effect was of utter lifelessness. If it were a trick, then it
was a very skillful one. Fortunately, there were tests he could make, not
absolutely final but evidential and indicative.

He made them.

The echoless height of the most unique mountain ever discovered
hummed with the fire-sound of the mobile blaster. The noise grew to
a roar as the unit's pile warmed to its task and developed its maximum
kilo-curie activity.

Under that barrage, the hull of the enemy craft trembled a little and
changed color slightly, but that was all. After ten minutes, Jamieson cut
the power and sat baffled and indecisive.

The defensive screens of the Rull ship were full on. Had they gone on
automatically after his first shot of the evening before? Or had they been
put up deliberately to nullify just such an attack as this?

He couldn't be sure. That was the trouble; he had no positive knowledge. The Rulls could be lying inside dead. They could be wounded
and incapable of doing anything against him. They could have spent
the night marking up the tableland with *elled* nerve-control lines—he'd
have to make sure he never looked directly at the ground—or they could
simply be waiting for the arrival of the greater ship that had dropped it
onto the planet.

Jamieson refused to consider the last possibility. That way was death,
without qualification or hope.

Frowningly, he studied the visible damage he had done the ship. All
the hard metals had held together so far as he could see, but the whole
bottom of the ship was dented to a depth that varied from one to four
feet. Some radiation must have got in, and the question was, what would
it have damaged?

He had examined dozens of captured Rull survey craft, and if this one
ran to the pattern, then in the front would be the control center, with a
sealed-off blaster chamber. In the rear the engine room, two storerooms,
one for fuel and equipment, the other for food and—

For food. Jamieson jumped, and then with wide eyes noted how the
food section had suffered greater damage than any other part of the ship.

Surely, surely, some radiation must have got into it, poisoning it, ruining it, and instantly putting the Rull, with his swift digestive system, into a deadly position.

Jamieson sighed with the intensity of his hope, and prepared to retreat. As he turned away, quite accidentally, he glanced at the rock behind which he had shielded himself from possible direct fire.

Glanced at it, and saw the *elled* lines in it. Intricate lines, based on a profound and inhuman study of the human nervous system. Jamieson recognized them, and stiffened in horror. He thought in anguish: *Where, where am I supposed to fall? Which cliff?*

With a desperate will, with all his strength, he fought to retain his senses a moment longer. He strove to see the lines again. He saw, briefly, flashingly, five vertical and above them three lines that pointed east with their wavering ends.

The pressure built up, up, up inside him, but still he fought to keep his thoughts moving. Fought to remember if there were any wide ledges near the top of the east cliff.

There were. He recalled them in a final agony of hope. *There*, he thought. *That one, that one. Let me fall on that one.* He strained to hold the ledge image he wanted, and to repeat, repeat the command that might save his life. His last, dreary thought was that here was the answer to his doubts. The Rull *was* alive.

Blackness came like a curtain of pure essence on night.

Somberly, the Rull glided toward the man's lifeboat. From a safe distance, he examined it. The defense screens were up, but he couldn't be sure they had been put up before the attack of the morning, or had been raised since then, or had come on automatically at his approach.

He couldn't be sure. That was the trouble. Everywhere, on the tableland around him, was a barrenness, a desolation unlike anything else he had ever known. The man could be dead, his smashed body lying at the remote bottom of the mountain. He could be inside the ship badly injured; he had, unfortunately *had* time to get back to the safety of his craft. Or he could be waiting inside, alert, aggressive, and conscious of his enemy's uncertainty, determined to take full advantage of that uncertainty.

The Rull set up a watching device that would apprise him when the door opened. Then he returned to the tunnel that led into his ship, laboriously crawled through it, and settled himself to wait out the emergency.

The hunger in him was an expanding force, hourly taking on a greater urgency. It was time to stop moving around. He would need all his energy for the crisis.

The days passed.

Jamieson stirred in an effluvium of pain. At first it seemed all-enveloping, a mist of anguish that bathed him in sweat from head to toe. Gradually, then, it localized in the region of his lower left leg.

The pulse of the pain made a rhythm in his nerves. The minutes lengthened into an hour, and then he finally thought: *Why, I've got a sprained ankle!* He had more than that, of course. The pressure that had driven him here clung like a gravitonic plate. How long he lay there, partly conscious, was not clear, but when he finally opened his eyes, the sun was still shining on him, though it was almost directly overhead.

He watched it with the mindlessness of a dreamer as it withdrew slowly past the edge of the overhanging precipice. It was not until the shadow of the cliff suddenly plopped across his face that he started to full consciousness with a sudden memory of deadly danger.

It took a while to shake the remnants of the *elled* "take" from his brain. And, even as it was fading, he sized up, to some extent, the difficulties of his position. He saw that he had tumbled over the edge of a cliff to a steep slope. The angle of descent of the slope was a sharp fifty-five degrees, and what had saved him was that his body had been caught in the tangled growth near the edge of the greater precipice beyond.

His foot must have twisted in those roots, and sprained.

As he finally realized the nature of his injuries, Jamieson braced up. He was safe. In spite of having suffered an accidental defeat of major proportions, his intense concentration on this slope, his desperate will to make *this* the place where he must fall, had worked out.

He began to climb. It was easy enough on the slope, steep as it was; the ground was rough, rocky, and scraggly with brush. It was when he came to the ten-foot overhanging cliff that his ankle proved what an obstacle it could be.

Four times he slid back, reluctantly; and then, on the fifth try, his fingers, groping desperately over the top of the cliff, caught an unbreakable root. Triumphantly, he dragged himself to the safety of the tableland.

Now that the sound of his scraping and struggling was gone, only his heavy breathing broke the silence of the emptiness. His anxious eyes studied the uneven terrain. The tableland spread before him with not a sign of a moving figure anywhere.

To one side, he could see his lifeboat. Jamieson began to crawl toward it, taking care to stay on rock as much as possible. What had happened to the Rull he did not know. And since, for several days, his ankle would keep him inside his ship, he might as well keep his enemy guessing during that time.

Professor Jamieson lay in his bunk, thinking. He could hear the beating of his heart. There were the occasional sounds when he dragged himself out of bed. But that was almost all. The radio, when he turned it on, was dead. No static, not even the fading in and out of a wave. At this colossal distance, even subspace radio was impossible.

He listened on all the more active Rull wave lengths. But the silence was there, too. Not that they would be broadcasting if they were in the vicinity.

He was cut off here in this tiny ship on an uninhabited planet, with useless motors.

He tried not to think of it like that. "Here," he told himself, "is the opportunity of a lifetime for an experiment."

He warmed to the idea as a moth to flame. Live Rulls were hard to get hold of. About one a year was captured in the unconscious state, and these were regarded as priceless treasures. But here was an even more ideal situation.

We're prisoners, both of us. That was the way he tried to picture it. Prisoners of an environment, and, therefore, in a curious fashion, prisoners of each other. Only each was free of the conditioned need to kill himself.

There were things a man might discover. The great mysteries—as far as men were concerned—that motivated Rull actions. Why did they want to destroy other races totally? Why did they needlessly sacrifice valuable ships in attacking Earth machines that ventured into their sectors of space when they knew that the intruders would leave in a few weeks anyway? And why did prisoners who could kill themselves at will commit suicide without waiting to find out what fate was intended for them? Sometimes they were merely wanted as messengers.

Was it possible the Rulls were trying to conceal a terrible weakness in their make-up of which man had not yet found an inkling?

The potentialities of this fight of man against Rull on a lonely mountain exhilarated Jamieson as he lay on his bunk, scheming, turning the problem over in his mind.

There were times during those dog days when he crawled over to the control chair and peered for an hour at a stretch into the visiplates. He saw the tableland and the vista of distance beyond it. He saw the sky of Laertes III, bluish pink sky, silent and lifeless.

He saw the prison. Caught here, he thought bleakly. Professor Jamieson, whose appearance on an inhabited planet would bring out unwieldy crowds, whose quiet voice in the council chambers of Earth's galactic empire spoke with final authority—that Jamieson was here, alone, lying in a bunk, waiting for a leg to heal, so that he might conduct an experiment with a Rull.

It seemed incredible. But he grew to believe it as the days passed.

On the third day, he was able to move around sufficiently to handle a few heavy objects. He began work immediately on the mental screen.

On the fifth day it was finished. Then the story had to be recorded. That was easy. Each sequence had been so carefully worked out in bed that it flowed from his mind onto the visiwire.

He set it up about two hundred yards from the lifeboat, behind a screening of trees. He tossed a can of food a dozen feet to one side of the screen.

The rest of the day dragged. It was the sixth day since the arrival of the Rull, the fifth since he had sprained his ankle.

Came the night.

A gliding shadow, undulating under the starlight of Laertes III, the Rull approached the screen the man had set up. How bright it was, shining in the darkness of the tableland, a blob of light in a black universe of uneven ground and dwarf shrubbery.

When he was a hundred feet from the light, he sensed the food—and realized that here was a trap.

For the Rull, six days without food had meant a stupendous loss of energy, visual blackouts on a dozen color levels, a dimness of life-force that fitted with the shadows, not the sun. That inner world of disjointed nervous system was like a run-down battery, with a score of organic "instruments" disconnecting one by one as the energy level fell. The *yeli* recognized dimly, but with a savage anxiety, that only a part of that nervous system would ever be restored to complete usage. And even for that speed was essential. A few more steps downward, and then the old, old conditioning of mandatory self-inflicted death would apply even to the high Aaish of the Yeell.

The worm body grew quiet. The visual center behind each eye accepted light on a narrow band from the screen. From beginning to end, he watched the story as it unfolded, and then watched it again, craving repetition with all the ardor of a primitive.

The picture began in deep space with a man's lifeboat being dropped from a launching lock of a battleship. It showed the battleship going on to a military base, and there taking on supplies and acquiring a vast fleet of reinforcements, and then starting on the return journey. The scene switched to the lifeboat dropping down on Laertes III, showed everything that had subsequently happened, suggested the situation was dangerous to them both—and pointed out the only safe solution.

The final sequence of each showing of the story was of the Rull approaching the can to the left of the screen and opening it. The method was shown in detail, as was the visualization of the Rull busily eating the food inside.

Each time that sequence drew near, a tension came over the Rull, a will to make the story real. But it was not until the seventh showing had run its course that he glided forward, closing the last gap between himself and the can. It was a trap, he knew, perhaps even death—it didn't matter. To live, he had to take the chance. Only by this means, by risking what was in the can, could he hope to remain alive for the necessary time.

How long it would take for the commanders cruising up there in the black of space in their myriad ships—how long it would be before they would decide to supersede his command, he didn't know. But they would come. Even if they waited until the enemy ships arrived before they dared to act against his strict orders, they would come.

At that point they could come down without fear of suffering from his ire.

Until then he would need all the food he could get.

Gingerly, he extended a sucker, and activated the automatic opener of the can.

It was shortly after four in the morning when Professor Jamieson awakened to the sound of an alarm ringing softly. It was still pitch dark outside—the Laertes day was twenty-six sidereal hours long; he had set his clocks the first day to coordinate—and at this season dawn was still three hours away.

Jamieson did not get up at once. The alarm had been activated by the opening of the can of food. It continued to ring for a full fifteen minutes, which was just about perfect. The alarm was tuned to the electronic pattern emitted by the can once it was opened, and so long as any food remained in it. The lapse of time involved fitted with the capacity of one of the Rull's suckers in absorbing three pounds of pork.

For fifteen minutes, accordingly, a member of the Rull race, man's mortal enemy, had been subjected to a pattern of mental vibrations corresponding to its own thoughts. It was a pattern to which the nervous system of other Rulls had responded in laboratory experiments. Unfortunately, those others had killed themselves on awakening, and so no definite results had been proved. But it had been established by the ecphoriometer that the unconscious and not the conscious mind was affected.

Jamieson lay in bed, smiling quietly to himself. He turned over finally to go back to sleep, and then he realized how excited he was.

The greatest moment in the history of Rull-human warfare. Surely, he wasn't going to let it pass unremarked. He climbed out of bed and poured himself a drink.

The attempt of the Rull to attack him through his unconscious mind had emphasized his own possible actions in that direction. Each race had discovered some of the weaknesses of the other.

Rulls used their knowledge to exterminate. Men tried for communication, and hoped for association. Both were ruthless, murderous, pitiless, in their methods. Outsiders sometimes had difficulty distinguishing one from the other.

But the difference in purpose was as great as the difference between black and white, the absence as compared to the presence of light.

There was only one trouble with the immediate situation. Now that the Rull had food, he might develop a few plans of his own.

Jamieson returned to bed, and lay staring into the darkness. He did not underrate the resources of the Rull, but since he had decided to conduct an experiment, no chance must be considered too great.

He turned over finally, and slept the sleep of a man determined that things were working in his favor.

Morning. Jamieson put on his cold-proof clothes and went out into the chilly dawn. Again he savored the silence and the atmosphere of isolated grandeur. A strong wind was blowing from the east, and there was an iciness in it that stung his face. Snow? He wondered.

He forgot that. He had things to do on this morning of mornings. He would do them with his usual caution.

Paced by defensors and the mobile blaster, he headed for the mental screen. It stood in open high ground where it would be visible from a dozen different hiding places, and so far as he could see it was undamaged. He tested the automatic mechanism, and for good measure ran the picture through one showing.

He had already tossed another can of food in the grass near the screen and he was turning away when he thought: *That's odd. The metal framework looks as if it's been polished.*

He studied the phenomena in a de-energizing mirror, and saw that the metal had been varnished with a clear substance. He felt sick as he recognized it.

He decided in agony, *If the cue is not to fire at all, I won't do it. I'll fire even if the blaster turns on me.*

He scraped some of the "varnish" into a receptacle, began his retreat to the lifeboat. He was thinking violently: *Where does he get all this stuff? That isn't part of the equipment of a survey craft.*

The first deadly suspicion was on him that what was happening was not just an accident. He was pondering the vast implications of that, narrow-eyed, when, off to one side, he saw the Rull.

For the first time in his many days on the tableland, he saw the Rull. *What's the cue?*

Memory of purpose came to the Rull shortly after he had eaten. It was dim at first, but it grew stronger.

It was not the only sensation of his returning energy.

His visual centers interpreted more light. The starlit tableland grew brighter—not as bright as it could be for him, by a very large percentage, but the direction was up instead of down. It would never again be normal. Vision was in the mind, and that part of his mind no longer had the power of interpretation.

He felt unutterably fortunate that it was no worse.

He had been gliding along the edge of the precipice. Now, he paused to peer down. Even with his partial night vision, the view was breathtaking. There was distance below and distance afar. From a spaceship, the height was almost minimum. But gazing down that wall of gravel into those depths was a different experience. It emphasized how completely he had been caught by an accident. And it reminded him of what he had been doing before the hunger.

He turned instantly away from the cliff and hurried to where the wreckage of his ship had gathered dust for days. Bent and twisted wreckage, half buried in the hard ground of Laertes III. He glided over the dented plates inside to one in which he had the day before sensed a quiver of antigravity oscillation. Tiny, potent, tremendous minutiae of oscillation, capable of being influenced.

The Rull worked with intensity and purposefulness. The plate was still firmly attached to the frame of the ship. And the first job, the heartbreakingly difficult job, was to tear it completely free. The hours passed.

R-r-i-i-i-pp! The hard plate yielded to the slight rearrangement of its nucleonic structure. The shift was infinitesimal, partly because the directing nervous energy of his body was not at norm, and partly because it had better be infinitesimal. There was such a thing as releasing energy enough to blow up a mountain.

Not, he discovered finally, that there was danger in this plate. He found that out the moment he crawled onto it. The sensation of power that aura-ed out of it was so dim that, briefly, he doubted if it would lift from the ground.

But it did. The test run lasted seven feet, and gave him his measurement of the limited force he had available. Enough for an attack only.

He had no doubts in his mind. The experiment was over. His only purpose must be to kill the man, and the question was, how could he insure that the man did not kill him while he was doing it? The varnish!

He applied it painstakingly, dried it with a drier, and then, picking up the plate again, he carried it on his back to the hiding place he wanted.

When he had buried it and himself under the dead leaves of a clump of brush, he grew calmer. He recognized that the veneer of his civilization was off. It shocked him, but he did not regret it.

In giving him the food, the two-legged being was obviously doing something to him. Something dangerous. The only answer to the entire problem of the experiment of the tableland was to deal death without delay.

He lay tense, ferocious, beyond the power of any vagrant thoughts, waiting for the man to come.

It looked as desperate a venture as Jamieson had seen in Service. Normally, he would have handled it effortlessly. But he was watching intently—*intently*—for the paralysis to strike him, the negation that was of the varnish.

And so, it was the unexpected normal quality that nearly ruined him. The Rull flew out of a clump of trees mounted on an antigravity plate. The surprise of that was so great that it almost succeeded. The plates had been drained of all such energies, according to his tests the first morning. Yet here was one alive again and light again with the special antigravity lightness which Rull scientists had brought to the peak of perfection.

The action of movement through space toward him was, of course, based on the motion of the planet as it turned on its axis. The speed of the attack, starting as it did from zero, did not come near the eight-hundred-mile-an-hour velocity of the spinning planet, but it was swift enough.

The apparition of metal and six-foot worm charged at him through the air. And even as he drew his weapon and fired at it, he had a choice to make, a restraint to exercise: *Do not kill!*

That was hard, oh, hard. The necessity exercised his capacity for integration and imposed so stern a imitation that during the second it took him to adjust the Rull came to within ten feet of him.

What saved him was the pressure of the air on the metal plate. The air tilted it like a wing' of a plane becoming airborne. At the bottom of that metal he fired his irresistible weapon, seared it, burned it, deflected it to a crash landing in a clump of bushes twenty feet to his right.

Jamieson was deliberately slow in following up his success. When he reached the bushes, the Rull was fifty feet beyond it gliding on its multiple suckers over the top of a hillock. It disappeared into a clump of trees.

He did not pursue it or fire a second time. Instead, he gingerly pulled the Rull antigravity plate out of the brush and examined it. The question was, how had the Rull degravitized it without the elaborate machinery necessary? And if it was capable of creating such a "parachute" for itself why hadn't it floated down to the forest land far below where food would be available and where it would be safe from its human enemy?

One question was answered the moment he lifted the plate. It was "normal" weight, its energy apparently exhausted after traveling less than a hundred feet. It had obviously never been capable of making the mile-and-a-half trip to the forest and plain below.

Jamieson took no chances. He dropped the plate over the nearest precipice and watched it fall into distance. He was back in the lifeboat when he remembered the varnish.

Why, there had been no cue, not yet.

He tested the scraping he had brought with him. Chemically, it turned out to be a simple resin, used to make varnishes. Atomically, it was stabilized. Electronically, it transformed light into energy on the vibration level of human thought.

It was alive, all right. But what was the recording?

Jamieson made a graph of every material and energy level, for comparison purposes. As soon as he had established that it had been altered on the electronic level—which had been obvious, but which, still, had to be proved—he recorded the images on a visiwire. The result was a hodgepodge of dreamlike fantasies.

Symbols. He took down his book, "Symbol Interpretations of the Unconscious," and found the cross reference: "Inhibitions, Mental."

On the referred page and line, he read: "Do not kill!"

"Well, I'll be—" Jamieson said aloud into the silence of the lifeboat interior. "That's what happened."

He was relieved, and then not so relieved. It had been his personal intention not to kill at this stage. But the Rull hadn't known that. By working such a subtle inhibition, it had dominated the attack even in defeat.

That was the trouble. So far he had got *out* of situations, but had created no successful ones in retaliation. He had a hope, but that wasn't enough.

He must take no more risks. Even his final experiment must wait until the day the *Orion* was due to arrive.

Human beings were just a little too weak in certain directions. Their very life cells had impulses which could be stirred by the cunning and the remorseless.

He did not doubt that, in the final issue, the Rull would try to stir.

On the ninth night, the day before the *Orion* was due, Jamieson refrained from putting out a can of food. The following morning he spent half an hour at the radio, trying to contact the battleship. He made a point of broadcasting a detailed account of what had happened so far, and he described what his plans were, including his intention of testing the Rull to see if it had suffered any injury from its period of hunger.

Subspace was as silent as death. Not a single pulse of vibration answered his call.

He finally abandoned the attempt to establish contact and went outside. Swiftly, he set up the instruments he would need for his experiment. The tableland had the air of a deserted wilderness. He tested his equipment, then looked at his watch. It showed eleven minutes of noon. Suddenly jittery, he decided not to wait the extra minutes.

He walked over, hesitated, and then pressed a button. From a source near the screen, a rhythm on a very high energy level was being broadcast. It was a variation of the rhythm pattern to which the Rull had been subjected for four nights.

Slowly, Jamieson retreated toward the lifeboat. He wanted to try again to contact the *Orion*. Looking back, he saw the Rull glide into the clearing and head straight for the source of the vibration.

As Jamieson paused involuntarily, fascinated, the main alarm system of the lifeboat went off with a roar. The sound echoed with an alien eeriness on the wings of the icy wind that was blowing, and it acted like a cue. His wrist radio snapped on, synchronizing automatically with the powerful radio in the lifeboat. A voice said urgently:

"Professor Jamieson, this is the battleship *Orion*. We heard your earlier calls but refrained from answering. An entire Rull fleet is cruising in the vicinity of the Laertes sun.

"In approximately five minutes, an attempt will be made to pick you up. Meanwhile—*drop everything.*"

Jamieson dropped. It was a physical movement, not a mental one. Out of the corner of one eye, even as he heard his own radio, he saw a movement in the sky. Two dark blobs that resolved into vast shapes. There was a roar as the Rull super-battleships flashed by overhead. A cyclone followed their passage that nearly tore him from the ground, where he clung desperately to the roots of intertwining brush.

At top speed, obviously traveling under gravitonic power, the enemy warships turned a sharp somersault and came back toward the tableland. Expecting death, and beginning to realize some of the truth of the situation on the tableland, Jamieson quailed. But the fire flashed past him, not at him. The thunder of the shot rolled toward Jamieson, a colossal sound that yet did not blot out his sense awareness of what had happened. His lifeboat. They had fired at his lifeboat.

He groaned as he pictured it destroyed in one burst of intolerable flame. And then, for a moment, there was no time for thought or anguish.

A third warship came into view, but, as Jamieson strained to make out its contours, it turned and fled. His wrist radio clicked on:

"Cannot help you now. Save yourself. Our four accompanying battleships and attendant squadrons will engage the Rull fleet and try to draw them toward our great battle group cruising near the star, Bianca, and then re—"

A flash of vivid fire in the distant sky ended the message. It was a full minute before the cold air of Laertes III echoed to the remote thunder of the broadside. The sound died slowly, reluctantly, as if endless little overtones of it were clinging to each molecule of air.

The silence that settled finally was, strangely, not peaceful, but like the calm before a storm, a fateful quiescent stillness, alive with unmeasurable threat.

Shakily, Jamieson climbed to his feet. It was time to assess the immediate danger that had befallen him. The greatest danger he dared not even think about.

Jamieson headed first for his lifeboat. He didn't have to go all the way. The entire section of the cliff had been sheared away. Of the ship there was no sign.

It pulled him up short. He had expected it, but the shock of the reality was terrific.

He crouched like an animal and stared up into the sky, into the menacing limits of the sky. It was empty of machines. Not a movement was there, not a sound came out of it, except the sound of the east wind. He was alone in a universe between heaven and earth, a mind poised at the edge of an abyss.

Into his mind, tensely waiting, pierced a sharp understanding. The Rull ships had flown once over the mountain to size up the situation on the tableland, and then had tried to destroy him.

Who was the Rull here with him, that super-battleships should roar down to insure that no danger remained for it on the tableland?

Well, they hadn't quite succeeded. Jamieson showed his teeth to the wind. Not quite. But he'd have to hurry. At any moment they might risk one of their destroyers in a rescue landing.

As he ran, he felt himself one with the wind. He knew that feeling, that sense of returning primitiveness during moments of excitement. It was like that in battles, and the important thing was to yield one's whole body and soul to it. There was no such thing as fighting efficiently with half your mind or half your body. All, all, was demanded.

He expected falls, and he had them. Each time he got up, almost unconscious of the pain, and ran on again. He arrived bleeding—but he arrived.

The sky was silent.

From the shelter of a line of brush, he peered at the Rull.

The captive Rull, *his* Rull to do with as he pleased. To watch, to force, to educate—the fastest education in the history of the world. There wasn't any time for a leisurely exchange of information.

From where he lay, he manipulated the controls of the screen.

The Rull had been moving back and forth in front of the screen. Now, it speeded up, then slowed, then speeded up again, according to his will.

Some thousands of years before, in the twentieth century, the classic and timeless investigation had been made of which this was one end result. A man called Pavlov fed a laboratory dog at regular intervals, to the accompaniment of the ringing of a bell. Soon, the dog's digestive system responded as readily to the ringing of the bell without the food as to the food and the bell together.

Pavlov himself never did realize the most important reality behind his conditioning process. But what began on that remote day ended with a science that could control animals and aliens—and men—almost at will. Only the Rulls baffled the master experimenters in the later centuries when it was an exact science. Defeated by the will to death of all Rull captives, the scientists foresaw the doom of Earth's galactic empire unless some beginning could be made in penetrating the minds of Rulls.

It was his desperate bad luck that he had no time for real penetrations.

There was death here for those who lingered.

But even what he had to do, the bare minimum of what he had to do, would take precious time. Back and forth, back and forth; the rhythm of obedience had to be established.

The image of the Rull on the screen was as lifelike as the original. It was three dimensional, and its movements were like an automaton. The challenge was actually irresistible. Basic nerve centers were affected. The Rull could no more help falling into step than it could resist the call of the food impulse.

After it had followed that mindless pattern for fifteen minutes, changing pace at his direction, Jamieson started the Rull and its image climbing trees. Up, then down again, half a dozen times. At that point, Jamieson introduced an image of himself.

Tensely, with one eye on the sky and one on the scene before him, he watched the reactions of the Rull—watched them with narrowed eyes and a sharp understanding of Rull responses to the presence of human beings. Rulls were digestively stimulated by the odor of man. It showed in the way their suckers opened and closed. When, a few minutes later, he substituted himself for his image, he was satisfied that this Rull had temporarily lost its normal automatic hunger when it saw a human being.

And now that he had reached the stage of final control, he hesitated. It was time to make his tests. Could he afford the time?

He realized that he had to. This opportunity might not occur again in a hundred years.

When he finished the tests twenty-five minutes later, he was pale with excitement. He thought: *This is it. We've got it.*

He spent ten precious minutes broadcasting his discovery by means of his wrist radio—hoping that the transmitter on his lifeboat had survived its fall down the mountain, and was picking up the thready message of the smaller instrument and sending it out through subspace.

During the entire ten minutes, there was not a single answer to his call.

Aware that he had done what he could, Jamieson headed for the cliff's edge he had selected as a starting point. He looked down and shuddered, then remembered what the *Orion* had said: "An entire Rull fleet cruising ..."

Hurry!

He lowered the Rull to the first ledge. A moment later he fastened the harness around his own body, and stepped into space. Sedately, with easy strength, the Rull gripped the other end of the rope, and lowered him down to the ledge beside it.

They continued on down and down. It was hard work, although they used a very simple system.

A long plastic rope spanned the spaces for them. A metal climbing rod, used to scale the smooth vastness of a spaceship's side, held position after position while the rope did its work.

On each ledge, Jamieson burned the rod at a downward slant into solid rock. The rope slid through an arrangement of pulleys in the metal as the Rull and he, in turn, lowered each other to ledges farther down.

The moment they were both safely in the clear of one ledge, Jamieson would explode the rod out of the rock, and it would drop down ready for use again.

The day sank towards darkness like a restless man into sleep—slowly, wearily. Jamieson grew hot and tired, and filled with the melancholy of the fatigue that dragged at his muscles.

He could see that the Rull was growing more aware of him. It still cooperated, but it watched him with intent eyes each time it swung him down.

The conditioned state was ending. The Rull was emerging from its trance. The process should be completed before night.

There was a time, then, when Jamieson despaired of ever getting down before the shadows fell. He had chosen the western, sunny side for that fantastic descent down a black-brown cliff the like of which did not exist elsewhere in the known worlds of space. He found himself watching the Rull with quick, nervous glances. When it swung him down onto a ledge beside it, he watched its blue eyes, its staring blue eyes, come closer and closer to him, and then as his legs swung below the level of those strange eyes, they twisted to follow him.

The intent eyes of the other reminded Jamieson of his discovery. He felt a fury at himself that he had never reasoned it out before. For centuries man had known that his own effort to see clearly required a good twenty-five per cent of the energy of his whole body. Human scientists should have guessed that the vast wave compass of Rull eyes was the product of a balancing of glandular activity on a fantastically high energy level. A balancing which, if disturbed, would surely affect the mind itself either temporarily or permanently.

He had discovered that the impairment was permanent.

What would a prolonged period of starvation diet do to such a nervous system?

The possibilities altered the nature of the war. It explained why Rull ships had never attacked human food sources or supply lines; they didn't want to risk retaliation. It explained why Rull ships fought so remorselessly against Earth ships that intruded into their sectors of the galaxy. It explained their ruthless destruction of the other races. They lived in terror that their terrible weakness would be found out.

Jamieson smiled with a savage anticipation. If his message had got through, or if he escaped, Rulls would soon feel the pinch of hunger. Earth ships would concentrate on that basic form of attack in the future. The food supplies of entire planetary groups would be poisoned, convoys would be raided without regard for casualties. Everywhere at once the attack would be pressed without letup and without mercy.

It shouldn't be long before the Rulls began their retreat to their own galaxy. That was the only solution that would be acceptable. The invader must be driven back and back, forced to give up his conquests of a thousand years.

Four P.M. Jamieson had to pause again for a rest. He walked to the side of the ledge away from the Rull and sank down on the rock. The sky was a brassy blue, silent and windless now, a curtain drawn across the black space above, concealing what must already be the greatest Rull-human battle in ten years.

It was a tribute to the five Earth battleships and their escort that no Rull ship had yet attempted to rescue the Rull on the tableland.

Possibly, of course, they didn't want to give away the presence of one of their own kind.

Jamieson gave up the futile speculation. Wearily, he compared the height of the cliff above with the depth that remained below. He estimated they had come two-thirds of the distance. He saw that the Rull was staring out over the valley. Jamieson turned and gazed with it.

The scene which they took in with their different eyes and different brains was fairly drab and very familiar, yet withal strange and wonderful. The forest began a quarter of a mile from the bottom of the cliff, and it almost literally had no end. It rolled up over the hills and down into the shallow valleys. It faltered at the edge of a broad river, then billowed out again and climbed the slopes of mountains that sprawled mistily in the distance.

His watch showed four-fifteen. Time to get going again.

At twenty-five minutes after six, they reached a ledge a hundred and fifty feet above the uneven plain. The distance strained the capacity of the rope, but the initial operation of lowering the Rull to freedom and safety was achieved without incident. Jamieson gazed down curiously at the worm. What would it do now that it was in the clear?

It looked up at him and waited.

That made him grim. Because this was a chance he was not taking. Jamieson waved imperatively at the Rull, and took out his blaster. The Rull backed away, but only into the safety of a gigantic rock. Blood-red, the sun was sinking behind the mountains. Darkness moved over the land. Jamieson ate his dinner. It was as he was finishing it that he saw a movement below.

He watched as the Rull glided along close to the edge of the precipice.

It disappeared beyond an outjut of the cliff.

Jamieson waited briefly, then swung out on the rope. The descent drained his strength, but there was solid ground at the bottom. Three quarters of the way down, he cut his finger on a section of the rope that was unexpectedly rough.

When he reached the ground, he noticed that his finger was turning an odd gray. In the dimness, it looked strange and unhealthy.

As Jamieson stared at it, the color drained from his face. He thought in a bitter anger, *The Rull mast have smeared it on the rope on his way down.*

A pang went through his body. It was knife sharp, and it was followed instantly by a stiffness. With a gasp, he grabbed at his blaster, to kill himself. His hand froze in midair. He fell to the ground. The stiffness held him there, froze him there motionless.

The will to death is in all life. Every organic cell ecphorizes the inherited engrams of its inorganic origin. The pulse of life is a squamous film superimposed on an underlying matter so intricate in its delicate balancing of different energies that life itself is but a brief, vain straining against that balance.

For an instant of eternity, a pattern is attempted. It takes many forms, but these are apparent. The real shape is always a time and not a space shape. And that shape is a curve. Up and then down. Up from the darkness into the light, then down again into the blackness.

The male salmon sprays his mist of milt onto the eggs of the female. And instantly he is seized with a mortal melancholy. The male bee collapses from the embrace of the queen he has won back into that inorganic mold from which he climbed for one single moment of ecstasy. In man, the fateful pattern is repressed into quadrillions of individual cells.

But the pattern is there. Waiting.

Long before, the sharp-minded Rull scientists, probing for chemical substances that would shock man's system into its primitive forms, found the special secret of man's will to death.

The *yeli*, Meeesh, gliding back toward Jamieson, did not think of the process. He had been waiting for the opportunity. It had occurred. He was intent on his own purposes.

Briskly, he removed the man's blaster; then he searched for the key to the lifeboat. And then he carried Jamieson a quarter of a mile around the base of the cliff to where the man's ship had been catapulted by the blast from the Rull warship.

Five minutes later, the powerful radio inside was broadcasting on Rull wave lengths an imperative command to the Rull fleet.

Dimness. Inside and outside his skin. He felt himself at the bottom of a well, peering out of night into twilight. As he lay, a pressure of something swelled around him, lifted him higher and higher and nearer to the mouth of the well.

He struggled the last few feet, a distinct mental effort, and looked over the edge. Consciousness.

He was lying on a raised table inside a room which had several large mouselike openings at the floor level, openings that led to other chambers. Doors, he realized, odd-shaped, alien, unhuman. Jamieson cringed with the stunning shock of recognition.

He was inside a Rull warship.

There was a slithering of movement behind him. He turned his head and rolled his eyes in their sockets.

In the shadows, three Rulls were gliding across the floor toward a bank of instruments that reared up behind and to one side of him. They pirouetted up an inclined plane and poised above him. Their pale eyes, shiny in the dusk of that unnatural chamber, peered down at him.

Jamieson tried to move. His body writhed in the confines of the bonds that held him. That brought a sharp remembrance of the death-will chemical that the Rull had used. Relief came surging. He was not dead. *Not dead.* NOT DEAD. The Rull must have helped him, forced him to move, and so broken the downward curve of his descent to dust.

He was alive—for what?

The thought slowed his joy. His hope snuffed out like a flame. His brain froze into a tensed, terrible mask of anticipation.

As he watched with staring eyes, expecting pain, one of the Rulls pressed a button. Part of the table on which Jamieson was lying lifted. He was raised to a sitting position.

What now?

He couldn't see the Rulls. He tried to turn, but two head shields clamped into the side of his head and held him firmly.

He saw that there was a square of silvery sheen on the wall which he faced. A light sprang onto it, and then a picture. It was a curiously familiar picture, but at first because there was a reversal of position Jamieson couldn't place the familiarity.

Abruptly, he realized.

It was a twisted version of the picture that he had shown the Rull, first when he was feeding it, and then with more weighty arguments after he discovered the vulnerability of man's mortal enemy.

He had shown how the Rull race would be destroyed unless it agreed to peace.

In the picture he was being shown it was the Rull that urged cooperation between the two races. They seemed unaware that he had not yet definitely transmitted his knowledge to other human beings. Or perhaps that fact was blurred by the conditioning he had given to the Rull when he fed it and controlled it.

As he glared at the screen, the picture ended—and then started again. By the time it had finished a second time, there was no doubt. Jamieson collapsed back against the table. They would not show him such a picture unless he was to be used as a messenger.

He would be returned home to carry the message that man had wanted to hear for a thousand years. He would also carry the information that would give meaning to the offer.

The Rull-human war was over.

RECRUITING STATION

She didn't dare! Suddenly, the night was a cold, enveloping thing. The edge of the broad, black river gurgled evilly at her feet as if, now that she had changed her mind—it hungered for her.

Her foot slipped on the wet, sloping ground; and her mind grew blurred with the terrible senseless fear that *things* were reaching out of the night, trying to drown her now against her will.

She fought up the bank—and slumped breathless onto the nearest park bench, coldly furious with her fear. Dully, she watched the gaunt man come along the pathway past the light standard. So sluggish was her brain that she was not aware of surprise when she realized he was coming straight toward her.

The purulent yellowish light made a crazy patch of his shadow across her where she sat. His voice, when he spoke, was vaguely foreign in tone, yet modulated, cultured. He said:

"Are you interested in the Calonian cause?"

Norma stared. There was no quickening in her brain, but suddenly she began to laugh. It was funny, horribly, hysterically *funny* funny. To be sitting here, trying to get up the nerve for another attempt at those deadly waters, and then to have some crackbrain come along and—

"You're deluding yourself, Miss Matheson," the man went on coolly. "You're not the suicide type."

"Nor the pickup type!" she answered automatically. "Beat it before—"

Abruptly, it penetrated that the man had called her by name. She looked up sharply at the dark blank that was his face. His head against the background of distant light nodded as if in reply to the question that quivered in her thought.

"Yes, I know your name. I also know your history and your *fear!*"

"What do you mean?"

"I mean that a young scientist named Garson arrived in the city tonight to deliver a series of lectures. Ten years ago, when you and he graduated from the same university, he asked you to marry him, but it was a career you wanted—and now you've been terrified that, in your extremity, you would go to him for assistance and—"

"Stop!"

The man seemed to watch her as she sat there breathing heavily. He said at last, quietly:

"I think I have proved that I am not simply a casual philanderer."

"What other kind of philanderer is there?" Norma asked, sluggish again. But she made no objection as he sank down on the far end of the bench. His back was still to the light, his features night-enveloped.

"Ah," he said, "you joke; you are bitter. But that *is* an improvement. You feel now, perhaps, that if somebody has taken an interest in you, all is not lost."

Norma said dully: "People who are acquainted with the basic laws of psychology are cursed with the memory of them even when disaster strikes into their lives. All I've done the last ten years is—"

She stopped; then: "You're very clever. Without more than arousing my instinctive suspicions, you've insinuated yourself into the company of a hysterical woman. What's your purpose?"

"I intend to offer you a job."

Norma's laugh sounded so harsh in her own ears that she thought, startled: "I am hysterical!"

Aloud, she said: "An apartment, jewels, a car of my own, I suppose?"

His reply was cool: "No! To put it frankly, you're not pretty enough. Too angular, mentally and physically. That's been one of your troubles the last ten years; a developing introversion of the mind which has influenced the shape of your body unfavorably."

The words shivered through the suddenly stiffened muscles of her body. With an enormous effort, she forced herself to relax. She said: "I had that coming to me. Insults are good for hysteria; so now what?"

"Are you interested in the Calonian cause?"

"There you go again," she complained. "But yes, I'm for it. Birds of a feather, you know."

"I know very well indeed. In fact, in those words you named the reason why I am here tonight, hiring a young woman who is up against it. Calonia, too, is up against it and—" He stopped; in the darkness, he spread his shadow-like hands. "You see: good publicity for our recruiting centers."

Norma nodded. She did see, and, suddenly, she didn't trust herself to speak; her hand trembled as she took the key he held out.

"This key," he said, "will fit the lock of the front door of the recruiting station; it will also fit the lock of the door leading to the apartment above it. The apartment is yours while you have the job. You can go there tonight if you wish, or wait until morning if you fear this is merely a device—now, I must give you a warning."

"Warning?"

"Yes. The work we are doing is illegal. Actually, only the American government can enlist American citizens and operate recruiting stations. We exist on sufferance and sympathy, but at any time someone may lay a charge and the police will have to act."

Norma nodded rapidly. "That's no risk," she said. "No judge would ever—"

"The address is 322 Carlton Street," he cut in smoothly. "And for your information, my name is Dr. Lell."

Norma had the distinct sense of being pushed along too swiftly for caution. She hesitated, her mind on the street address. "Is that near Bessemer?"

It was his turn to hesitate. "I'm afraid," he confessed, "I don't know this city very well, at least not in its twentieth century ... that is," he finished suavely, "I was here many years ago, before the turn of the century."

Norma wondered vaguely why he bothered to explain; she said, half-accusingly: "You're not a Calonian. You sound—French, maybe."

"You're not a Calonian, either!" he said, and stood up abruptly. She watched him walk off into the night, a great gloom-wrapped figure that vanished almost immediately.

She stopped short in the deserted night street. The sound that came was like a whisper touching her brain; a machine whirring somewhere with almost infinite softness. For the barest moment, her mind concentrated on the shadow vibrations; and then, somehow, they seemed to fade like figments of her imagination. Suddenly, there was only the street and the silent night.

The street was dimly lighted; and that brought doubt, sharp and tinged with a faint fear. She strained her eyes and traced the numbers in the shadow of the door: 322! That was it!

The place was dark. She peered at the signs that made up the window display:

FIGHT FOR THE BRAVE CALONIANS
THE CALONIANS ARE FIGHTING FREEDOM'S
FIGHT—YOUR FIGHT!
IF YOU CAN PAY YOUR OWN WAY, IT WOULD BE
APPRECIATED; OTHERWISE WE'LL GET YOU OVER!

There were other signs, but they were essentially the same, all terribly honest and appealing, if you really thought about the desperate things that made up their grim background.

Illegal, of course. But the man had admitted that, too. With sudden end of doubt, she took the key from her purse.

There were two doorways, one on either side of the window. The one to the right led into the recruiting room. The one on the left—

The stairs were dimly lighted, and the apartment at the top was quite empty of human beings. The door had a bolt; she clicked it home, and then, wearily, headed for the bedroom.

And it was as she lay in the bed that she grew aware again of the incredibly faint whirring of a machine. The shadow of a shadow sound; and, queerly, it seemed to reach into her brain: the very last second before she drifted into sleep, the pulse of the vibration, remote as the park bench was a steady beat inside her.

All through the night that indescribably faint whirring was there. Only occasionally did it seem to be in her head; she was aware of turning twisting, curling, straightening and, in the fractional awakedness that accompanied each move, the tiniest vibrational tremors would sweep down along her nerves like infinitesimal currents of energy.

Spears of sunlight piercing brilliantly through the window brought her awake at last. She lay taut and strained for a moment, then relaxed, puzzled. There was not a sound from the maddening machine, only the noises of the raucous, awakening street.

There was food in the refrigerator and in the little pantry. The weariness of the night vanished swiftly before the revivifying power of breakfast. She thought in gathering interest: what did he look like, this strange-voiced man of night?

Relieved surprise flooded her when the key unlocked the door to the recruiting room, for there had been in her mind a little edged fear that this was all quite mad.

She shuddered the queer darkness out of her system. What was the matter with her, anyway? The world was sunlit and cheerful, not the black and gloomy abode of people with angular introversion of the mind.

She flushed at the memory of the words. There was no pleasure in knowing that the man's enormously clever analysis of her was true. Still stinging, she examined the little room. There were four chairs, a bench, a long wooden counter and newspaper clippings of the Calonian War on the otherwise bare walls.

There was a back door to the place. Dimly curious, she tried the knob—once! It was locked, but there was something about the feel of it—

A tingling shock of surprise went through her. The door, in spite of its wooden appearance, was solid metal!

Momentarily, she felt chilled; finally she thought: "None of my business."

And then, before she could turn away, the door opened, and a gaunt man loomed on the threshold. He snapped harshly, almost into her face:

"Oh, yes, it is your business!"

It was not fear that made her back away. The deeps of her mind registered the cold hardness of his voice, so different from the previous night. Vaguely she was aware of the ugly sneer on his face. But there was no real emotion in her brain, nothing but a blurred blankness.

It was not fear; it couldn't be fear because all she had to do was run a few yards, and she'd be out on a busy street. And besides she had never been afraid of Negroes, and she wasn't now.

That first impression was so sharp, so immensely surprising that the fast-following second impression seemed like a trick of her eyes. For the man wasn't actually a Negro; he was—

She shook her head, trying to shake that trickiness out of her vision. But the picture wouldn't change. He wasn't a Negro, he wasn't white, he wasn't—anything!

Slowly her brain adjusted itself to his alienness. She saw that he had slant eyes like a Chinaman, his skin, though dark in texture, was dry with a white man's dryness. The nose was sheer chiseled beauty, the most handsome, most normal part of his face; his mouth was thin-lipped, commanding; his chin bold and giving strength and power to the insolence of his steel-gray eyes. His sneer deepened as her eyes grew wider and wider.

"Oh, no," he said softly, "you're not afraid of me, are you? Let me inform you that my purpose is to *make* you afraid. Last night I had the purpose of bringing you here. That required tact, understanding. My new purpose requires, among other things, the realization on your part that you are in my power beyond the control of your will or wish.

"I could have allowed you to discover gradually that this is not a Calonian recruiting station. But I prefer to get these early squirmings of the slaves over as soon as possible. The reaction to the power of the machine is always so similar and unutterably boring."

"I—don't—understand!"

He answered coldly: "Let me be brief. You have been vaguely aware of a machine. That machine has attuned the rhythm of your body to itself, and through its actions I can control you against your desire. Naturally, I don't expect you to believe me. Like the other women, you will test its mind-destroying power. Notice that I said *women!* We always hire women; for purely psychological reasons they are safer than men. You will discover what I mean if you should attempt to warn any applicant on the basis of what I have told you."

He finished swiftly: "Your duties are simple. There is a pad on the table made up of sheets with simple questions printed on them. Ask those questions, note the answers, then direct the applicants to me in the back room. I have—er—a medical examination to give them."

Out of all the things he had said, the one that briefly, searingly, dominated her whole mind had no connection with her personal fate: "But," she gasped, "if these men are not being sent to Calonia, where—"

He hissed her words short: "Here comes a man. Now, remember!"

He stepped back, to one side out of sight in the dimness of the back room. Behind her, there was the dismaying sound of the front door opening. A man's baritone voice blurred a greeting into her ears.

Her fingers shook as she wrote down the man's answers to the dozen questions. Name, address, next of kin— His face was a ruddy-cheeked blur against the shapeless shifting pattern of her racing thoughts.

"You can see," she heard herself mumbling, "that these questions are only a matter of identification. Now, if you'll go into that back room—"

The sentence shattered into silence. She'd said it! The uncertainty in her mind, the unwillingness to take a definite stand until she had thought of some way out, had made her say the very thing she had intended avoid saying. The man said:

"What do I go in there for?"

She stared at him numbly. Her mind felt thick, useless. She needed time, calm. She said: "It's a simple medical exam, entirely for your own protection."

Sickly, Norma watched his stocky form head briskly toward the rear door. He knocked; and the door opened. Surprisingly, it stayed open—surprisingly, because it was then, as the man disappeared from her line of vision, that she saw the machine.

The end of it that she could see reared up immense and darkly gleaming halfway to the ceiling, partially hiding a door that seemed to be a rear exit from the building.

She forgot the door, forgot the men. Her mind fastened on the great engine with abrupt intensity as swift memory came that this was the machine—

Unconsciously her body, her ears, her mind, strained for the whirring sound that she had heard in the night. But there was nothing, not the tiniest of tiny noises, not the vaguest stir of vibration, not a rustle, not a whisper. The machine crouched there, hugging the floor with its solidness, its clinging metal strength; and it was utterly dead, utterly motionless.

The doctor's smooth, persuasive voice came to her: "I hope you don't mind going out the back door, Mr. Barton. We ask applicants to use it because—well, our recruiting station here is illegal. As you probably know, we exist on sufferance and sympathy, but we don't want to be too blatant about the success we're having in getting young men to fight for our cause."

Norma waited. As soon as the man was gone she would force a show-down on this whole fantastic affair. If this was some distorted scheme of Calonia's enemies, she would go to the police and—

The thought twisted into a curious swirling chaos of wonder. The machine—

Incredibly, the machine was coming alive, a monstrous, gorgeous, swift aliveness. It glowed with a soft, swelling white light; and then burst into enormous flame. A breaker of writhing tongues of fire, blue and red and green and yellow, stormed over that first glow, blotting it from view instan-taneously. The fire sprayed and flashed like an intricately designed foun-tain, with a wild and violent beauty, a glittering blaze of unearthly glory.

And then—just like that—the flame faded. Briefly, grimly stubborn in its fight for life, the swarming, sparkling energy clung to the metal.

It was gone. The machine lay there, a dull, gleaming mass of metallic deadness, inert, motionless. The doctor appeared in the doorway.

"Sound chap!" he said, satisfaction in his tone. "Heart requires a bit of glandular adjustment to eradicate the effects of bad diet. Lungs will react swiftly to gas-immunization injections, and our surgeons should be able to patch that body up from almost anything except an atomic storm."

Norma licked dry lips. "What are you talking about?" she asked wildly. "W-what happened to that man?"

She was aware of him staring at her blandly. His voice was cool, faintly amused: "Why—he went out the back door."

"He did not. He—"

She realized the uselessness of words. Cold with the confusion of her thought, she emerged from behind the counter. She brushed past him, and then, as she reached the threshold of the door leading into the rear room, her knees wobbled. She grabbed at the door jamb for support, and knew that she didn't dare go near that machine. With an effort, she said:

"Will you go over there and open it?"

He did so, smiling. The door squealed slightly as it opened. When he closed it, it creaked audibly, and the automatic lock clicked loudly.

There had been no such sound. Norma felt the deepening whiteness in her cheeks. She asked, chilled:

"What is this machine?"

"Owned by the local electric company, I believe," he answered suavely, and his voice mocked her. "We just have permission to use the room, of course."

"That's not possible," she said thickly. "Electric companies don't have machines in the back rooms of shabby buildings."

He shrugged. "Really," he said indifferently, "this is beginning to bore me. I have already told you that this is a very special machine. You have seen some of its powers, yet your mind persists in being practical after a twentieth century fashion. I will repeat merely that you are a slave of the machine, and that it will do you no good to go to the police, entirely aside from the fact that I saved you from drowning yourself, and gratitude alone should make you realize that you owe everything to me; nothing to the world you were prepared to desert. However, that is too much to expect. You will learn by experience."

Quite calmly, Norma walked across the room. She opened the door, and then, startled that he had made no move to stop her, turned to stare at him. He was still standing where she had left him. He was smiling.

"You must be quite mad," she said after a moment. "Perhaps you had some idea that your little trick, whatever it was, would put the fear of the unknown into me. Let me dispel that right now. I'm going to the police—this very minute."

The picture that remained in her mind as she climbed aboard the bus was of him standing there, tall and casual and terrible in his contemptuous derision. The chill of that memory slowly mutilated the steady tenor of her forced calm.

The sense of nightmare vanished as she climbed off the streetcar in front of the imposing police building. Sunshine splashed vigorously on the pavement, cars honked; the life of the city swirled lustily around her and brought wave on wave of returning confidence.

The answer, now that she thought of it, was simplicity itself. Hypnotism! That was what had made her see a great, black, unused engine burst into mysterious flames.

And no hypnotist could force his will on a determined, definitely opposed mind.

Burning inwardly with abrupt anger at the way she had been tricked, she lifted her foot to step on the curb—and amazed shock stung into her brain.

The foot, instead of lifting springily, dragged; her muscles almost refused to carry the weight. She grew aware of a man less than a dozen feet from her, staring at her with popping eyes.

"Good heavens!" he gasped audibly. "I must be seeing things."

He walked off rapidly; and the part of her thoughts that registered his odd actions simply tucked them away. She felt too dulled, mentally and physically, even for curiosity.

With faltering steps she moved across the sidewalk. It was as if something was tearing at her strength, holding her with invisible but immense forces. The machine!—she thought—and panic blazed through her.

Will power kept her going. She reached the top of the steps and approached the big doors. It was then the first sick fear came that she couldn't make it; and as she strained feebly against the stone-wall-like resistance of the door, a very fever of dismay grew hot and terrible inside her. What had happened to her? How could a machine reach over a distance, and strike unerringly at one particular individual with such enormous, vitality-draining power?

A shadow leaned over her. The booming voice of a policeman who had just come up the steps was the most glorious sound she had ever heard.

"Too much for you, eh, madam? Here, I'll push that door for you."

"Thank you," she said; and her voice sounded so harsh and dry and weak and unnatural in her own ears that a new terror flared: in a few minutes she wouldn't be able to speak above a whisper.

"A slave of the machine," he had said; and she knew with a clear and burning logic that if she was ever to conquer, it was now. She must get into this building. She must see someone in authority, and she must tell him— must—must— Somehow, she pumped strength into her brain and courage into her heart, and forced her legs to carry her across the threshold into the big modern building with its mirrored anteroom and its fine marble corridors. Inside, she knew suddenly that she had reached her limit.

She stood there on the hard floor, and felt her whole body shaking from the enormous effort it took simply to stay erect. Her knees felt dissolved and cold, like ice turning to strengthless liquid. She grew aware that the big policeman was hovering uncertainly beside her.

"Anything I can do, mother?" he asked heartily.

"Mother!" she echoed mentally with a queer sense of insanity. Her mind skittered off after the word. Did he really say that, or had she dreamed it? Why, she wasn't a mother. She wasn't even married. She—

She fought the thought off. She'd have to pull herself together, or there was madness here. No chance now of getting to an inspector or an officer. This big constable must be her confidant, her hope to defeat the mighty power that was striking at her across miles of city, an incredibly evil, terrible power whose ultimate purpose she could not begin to imagine. She—

There it was again, her mind pushing off into obscure, action-destroying, defeating thoughts! She turned to the policeman, started to part her lips in speech; and it was then she saw the mirror.

She saw a tall, thin, old, old woman standing beside the fresh-cheeked bulk of a blue-garbed policeman. It was such an abnormal trick of vision that it fascinated her. In some way, the mirror was missing her image, and reflecting instead the form of an old woman who must be close behind and slightly to one side of her. Queerest thing she had ever seen.

She half-lifted her red-gloved hand toward the policeman, to draw his attention to the distortion. Simultaneously, the red-gloved hand of the old woman in the mirror reached toward the policeman. Her own raised hand stiffened in midair; so did the old woman's. Funny.

Puzzled, she drew her gaze from the mirror, and stared with briefly blank vision at that rigidly uplifted hand. A tiny, uneven bit of her wrist was visible between the end of the glove and the end of sleeve of her serge suit. Her skin wasn't really as dark as—that!

Two things happened then. A tall man came softly through the door—Dr. Lell—and the big policeman's hand touched her shoulder.

"Really, madam, at your age, you shouldn't come here. A phone call would serve—"

And Dr. Lell was saying: "My poor old grandmother—"

Their voices went on, but the sense of them jangled in her brain as she jerked frantically to pull the glove off a hand wrinkled and shriveled by incredible age— Blackness pierced with agonized splinters of light reached mercifully into her brain. Her very last thought was that it must have happened just before she stepped onto the curb, when the man had stared at her pop-eyed and thought himself crazy. He must have seen the change taking place.

The pain faded; the blackness turned gray, then white. She was conscious of a car engine purring, and of forward movement. She opened her eyes—and her brain reeled from a surge of awful memory.

"Don't be afraid!" said Dr. Lell, and his voice was as soothing and gentle as it had been hard and satirical at the recruiting station. "You are again yourself; in fact, approximately ten years younger."

He removed one hand from the steering wheel and flashed a mirror before her eyes. The brief glimpse she had of her image made her grab at the silvered glass as if it were the most precious thing in all the world.

One long, hungry look she took; and then her arm, holding the mirror collapsed from sheer, stupendous relief. She lay back against the cushions, tears sticky on her cheeks, weak and sick from dreadful reaction. At last she said steadily:

"Thanks for telling me right away. Otherwise I should have gone mad."

"That, of course, was why I told you," he said; and his voice was still soft, still calm. And she felt soothed, in spite of the dark terror just past in spite of the intellectual realization that this diabolical man used words and tones and human emotions as coldly as Pan himself piping his reed, sounding what stop he pleased. That quiet, deep voice went on:

"You see, you are now a valuable member of our twentieth-century staff, with a vested interest in the success of our purpose. You thoroughly understand the system of rewards and punishments for good or bad service. You will have food, a roof over your head, money to spend—and eternal youth! Woman, look at your face again, look hard, and rejoice for your good fortune! Weep for those who have nothing but old age and death as their future! Look hard, I say!"

It was like gazing at a marvelous photograph out of the past, except that she had been somewhat prettier in the actuality, her face more rounded, not so sharp, more girlish. She was twenty again, but different, more mature, leaner. She heard his voice go on dispassionately, a distant background to her own thoughts, feeding, feeding at the image in the mirror. He said:

"As you can see, you are not truly yourself as you were at twenty. This is because we could only manipulate the time tensions which influenced your thirty-year-old body according to the rigid mathematical laws governing the energies and forces involved. We could not undo the harm wrought these last rather prim, introvert years of your life because you have already lived them, and nothing can change that."

It came to her that he was talking to give her time to recover from the deadliest shock that had ever stabbed into a human brain. And for the first time she thought, not of herself, but of the incredible things implied by every action that had occurred, every word spoken.

"Who ... are ... you?"

He was silent; the car twisted in and out of the clamorous traffic; and she watched his face now, that lean, strange, dark, finely chiseled, evil face with its glittering dark eyes. For the moment she felt no repulsion, only a gathering storm of fascination at the way that strong chin tilted unconsciously as he said in a cold, proud, ringing voice:

"We are masters of time. We live at the farthest frontier of time itself, and all the ages belong to us. No words could begin to describe the vastness of our empire or the futility of opposing us. We—"

He stopped. Some of the fire faded from his dark eyes. His brows knit, his chin dropped, his lips clamped into a thin line, then parted as he snapped:

"I hope that any vague ideas you have had for further opposition will yield to the logic of events and of fact. Now you know why we hire women who have no friends."

"You—devil!" She half sobbed the words.

"Ah," he said softly, "I can see you understand a woman's psychology. Two final points should clinch the argument I am trying to make: First, I can read your mind, every thought that comes into it, every vaguest emotion that moves it. And second, before establishing the machine in that particular building, we explored the years to come; and during all the time investigated, found the machine unharmed, its presence unsuspected by those in authority. Therefore, the future record is that you did—nothing! I think you will agree with me that this is convincing."

Norma nodded dully, her mirror forgotten. "Yes," she said, "yes, I suppose it is."

Miss Norma Matheson,
Calonian Recruiting Station,
322 Carlton Street,

Dear Norma:

I made a point of addressing the *envelope*, of this letter to you c/o General Delivery, instead of the above address. I would not care to put you in any danger, however imaginary. I use the word imaginary deliberately for I cannot even begin to describe how grieved and astounded I was to receive such a letter from the girl I once loved—it's eleven years since I proposed on graduation day, isn't it?—and how amazed I was by your questions and statements re time travel.

I might say that if you are not already mentally unbalanced, you will be shortly unless you take hold of yourself. The very fact that you were nerving yourself to commit suicide when this man—Dr. Lell—hired you from a park bench to be clerk in the recruiting station at the foregoing address, is evidence of hysteria. You could have gone on city relief.

I see that you have lost none of your powers of expression in various mediums. Your letter, mad though it is in subject matter, is eminently coherent and well thought out. Your drawing of the face of Dr. Lell is quite a remarkable piece of work.

If it is a true resemblance, then I agree that he is definitely not—shall I say—Western. His eyes are distinctly slanting, Chinese-style. His skin you say is, and shown as, dark in texture, indicating a faint Negro strain. His nose is very fine and sensitive, strong in character.

This effect is incremented by his firm mouth, though those thin lips are much too arrogant—the whole effect is of an extraordinarily intelligent-looking man, a super-mongrel in appearance. Such bodies could very easily be produced in the far-Eastern provinces of Asia.

I pass without comment over your description of the machine which swallows up the unsuspecting recruits. The superman has apparently not objected to answering your questions since the police station episode; and so we have a new theory of time and space:

Time—he states—is the all, the only reality. Every unfolding instant the Earth and its life, the universe and all its galaxies are re-created by the titanic energy that is time—and always it is essentially the same pattern that is re-formed, because that is the easiest course.

He makes a comparison. According to Einstein, and in this he is correct, the Earth goes around the Sun, not because there is such a force as gravitation, but because it is easier for it to go around the Sun in exactly the way it does than to hurtle off into space.

It is easier for time to re-form the same pattern of rock, the same man, the same tree, the same earth. That is all, that is the law.

The rate of reproduction is approximately ten billion a second. During the past minute, therefore, six hundred billion replicas of myself have been created; and all of them are still there, each a separate body occupying its own space, completely unaware of the others. Not one has been destroyed. There is no purpose; it is simply easier to let them stay there, than to destroy them.

If those bodies ever met in the same space, that is if I should go back to shake hands with my twenty-year-old self, there would be a clash of similar patterns, and the interloper would be distorted out of memory and shape.

I have no criticism to make of this theory other than that it is utterly fantastic. However, it is very interesting in the vivid picture it draws of an eternity of human beings, breeding and living and dying in the quiet eddies of the time stream, while the great current flares on ahead in a fury of incredible creation.

I am puzzled by the detailed information you are seeking—you make it almost real—but I give the answers for what they are worth:

1. Time travel would naturally be based on the most rigid mechanical laws.

2. It seems plausible that they would be able to investigate your future actions.

3. Dr. Lell used phrases such as "atomic storm" and "gas immunization injections." The implication is that they are recruiting for an unimaginably great war.

4. I cannot see how the machine could act on you over a distance—unless there was some sort of radio-controlled intermediate. In your position, I would ask myself one question: Was there anything, any metal, *anything*, upon my person that might have been placed there by the enemy?

5. Some thoughts are so dimly held that they could not possibly be transmitted. Presumably, sharp, clear thoughts might be receivable. If you could keep your mind calm, as you say you did while deciding to write the letter—the letter itself is proof that you succeeded.

6. It is unwise to assume that here is greater basic intelligence, but rather greater development of the potential forces of the mind. If men ever learn to read minds, it will be because they train their innate capacity for mind reading; they will be cleverer only when new knowledge adds new techniques of training.

To become personal, I regret immeasurably having heard from you. I had a memory of a rather brave spirit, rejecting my proposal of marriage, determined to remain independent, ambitious for advancement in the important field of social services. Instead, I find a sorry ending, a soul disintegrated, a mind feeding on fantasia and a sense of incredible persecution. My advice is to go to a psychiatrist before it is too late, and to that end I enclose a money order for $200.00, and extend you my best wishes.

Yours in memory,
Jack Garson.

At least, there was no interference with her private life. No footsteps but her own ever mounted the dark, narrow flight of stairs that led to her tiny apartment. At night, after the recruiting shop closed, she walked the crowded streets; sometimes there was a movie that seemed to promise surcease from the deadly strain of living; sometimes a new book on her old love, the social sciences, held her for a brief hour.

But there was nothing, nothing, absolutely nothing, that could relax the burning pressure of the reality of the machine. It was there always like a steel band drawn tautly around her mind.

It was crazy funny to read about the war, and the victories and the defeats—when out there, somewhere, in the future another, greater war was being fought; a war so vast that all the ages were being ransacked for manpower.

And men came! Dark men, blond men, young men, grim men, hard men, and veterans of other wars—the stream of them made a steady flow into that dimly lighted back room. And one day she looked up from an intent, mindless study of the pattern of the stained, old counter—and there was Jack Garson!

It was as simple as that. There he stood, not much older-looking after ten years, a little leaner of face perhaps, and there were tired lines all around his dark-brown eyes. While she stared in dumb paralysis, he said:

"I had to come, of course. You were the first emotional tie I had, and also the last; when I wrote the letter, I didn't realize how strong that emotion still was. What's all this about?"

She thought with a flaming intensity: Often, in the past, Dr. Lell had vanished for brief periods during the day hours; once she had seen him disappear into the flamboyant embrace of the light shed by the machine. Twice, she had opened the door to speak to him, and found him gone!

All accidental observations! It meant he had stepped scores of times into his own world when she hadn't seen him and—

Please let this be one of the times when he was away!

A second thought came, so fierce, so sharply focused that it made a stabbing pain inside her head: She must be calm. She must hold her mind away from giveaway thoughts, if it was not already ages too late.

Her voice came into the silence like a wounded, fluttering bird, briefly stricken by shock, then galvanized by agony:

"Quick! You must go—till after six! Hurry! Hurry!"

Her trembling hands struck at his chest, as if by those blows she would set him running for the door. But the thrust of her strength was lost on the muscles of his breast, defeated by the way he was leaning forward. His body did not even stagger.

Through a blur, she saw he was staring down at her with a grim, set smile. His voice was hard as chipped steel as he said:

"Somebody's certainly thrown a devil of a scare into you. But don't worry! I've got a revolver in my pocket. And don't think I'm alone in this. I wired the Calonian embassy at Washington, then notified the police here of their answer: no knowledge of this place. The police will arrive in minutes. I came in first to see that you didn't get hurt in the shuffle. Come on—outside with you, because—"

It was Norma's eyes that must have warned him, her eyes glaring past him. She was aware of him whirling to face the dozen men who were trooping out of the back room. The men came stolidly, and she had time to see that they were short, squat, ugly creatures, more roughly built than the lean, finely molded Dr. Lell; and their faces were not so much evil as half dead with unintelligence.

A dozen pair of eyes lighted with brief, animal-like curiosity, as they stared at the scene outside the window; then they glanced indifferently at herself and Jack Garson and the revolver he was holding so steadily; finally, their interest fading visibly, their gazes reverted expectantly to Dr. Lell, who stood smiling laconically on the threshold of the doorway.

"Ah, yes, Professor Garson, you have a gun, haven't you? And the police are coming. Fortunately, I have something here that may convince you of the uselessness of your puny plans."

His right hand came from behind his back, where he had been half hiding it. A gasp escaped from Norma as she saw that in it he held a blazing ball, a globe of furious flame, a veritable ball of fire.

The thing burned there in his palm, crude and terrible in the illusion of incredible, destroying incandescence. The mockery in Dr. Lell's voice was utterly convincing, as he said in measured tones *at her*:

"My dear Miss Matheson, I think you will agree that you will not offer further obstacles to our purpose, now that we have enlisted this valuable young man into the invincible armies of the Glorious—and, as for you, Garson, I suggest you drop that gun before it burns off your hand. It—"

His words were lost in the faint cry that came from Jack Garson. Amazed, Norma saw the gun fall to the floor, and lie there, burning with a white-hot, an abnormal violence.

"Good Heavens!" said Jack Garson; and Norma saw him stare at the weapon enthralled, mindless of danger, as it shrank visibly in that intense fire.

In seconds there was no weapon, no metal; the fire blinked out—and where it had been the floor was not even singed.

From Dr. Lell came a barked command, oddly twisted, foreignish words that nevertheless sounded like: "Grab him!"

She looked up, abruptly sick; but there was no fight. Jack Garson did not even resist, as the wave of beast men flowed around him. Dr. Lell said:

"So far, professor, you haven't made a very good showing as a gallant rescuer. But I'm glad to see that you have already recognized the hopelessness of opposing us. It is possible that, if you remain reasonable, we will not have to destroy your personality. But now——"

Urgency sharpened his tone. "I had intended to wait and capture your burly policemen, but as they have not arrived at the proper moment—a tradition with them, I believe—I think we shall have to go without them. It's just as well, I suppose."

He waved the hand that held the ball of fire, and the men carrying Jack Garson literally ran into the back room. Almost instantly, they were out of sight. Norma had a brief glimpse of the machine blazing into wondrous life and then there was only Dr. Lell striding forward, leaning over the bench, his eyes glaring pools of menace.

"Go upstairs instantly! I don't think the police will recognize you—but if you make one false move, *he* will pay. Go—quickly!"

As she hurried past the window on semi-liquid legs, she saw his tall figure vanish through the door into the back room. Then she was climbing the stairs.

Halfway up, her movements slowed as if she had been struck. Her mirror told the story of her punishment. The lean face of a woman of fifty-five met her stunned gaze.

The disaster was complete. Cold, stiff, tearless, she waited for the police.

For Garson, the world of the future began as a long, dim corridor that kept blurring before his unsteady vision. Heavy hands held him erect as he walked and—a wave of blur blotted the uncertain picture—

When he could see again, the pressure of unpleasant hands was gone from him, and he was in a small room, sitting down. His first dim impression was that he was alone, yet when he shook himself, and his vision cleared, he saw the desk; and behind the desk, a man.

The sight of that lean, dark, saturnine figure shocked electrically along his nerves, instantly galvanized a measure of strength back into his body. He leaned forward, his attention gathered on the man; and that was like a signal. Dr. Lell said derisively:

"I know. You've decided to cooperate. It was in your mind even before we left the presence of ... er ... pardon the familiarity ... of Norma, to whose rescue you came with such impetuous gallantry. Unfortunately it isn't only a matter of making up *your* mind."

There was a quality of sneer in the man's voice that sent an uneasy current through Garson. He shook himself mentally, trying to clear the remnants of weakness out of his system.

He thought, not coherently, not even chronologically: Lucky he was here in this room. Damned lucky they hadn't sprung a complication of futuristic newness on him, and so disorganized his concentration. Now there was time to gather his thoughts, harden his mind to every conceivable development, discount surprises, *and stay alive.*

He said: "It's quite simple. You've got Norma. You've got me in your power, here in your own age. I'd be a fool to resist."

Dr. Lell regarded him almost pityingly for a moment. And then— there was no doubt of the sneer as he spoke:

"My dear Professor Garson, discussion at this point would be utterly futile. My purpose is merely to discover if you are the type we can use in our laboratories. If you are not, the only alternative is the depersonalizing chamber. I can say this much: men of your character type have not, on the average, been successful in passing our tests."

That was real; every word like a penetrating edged thing. Actually, in spite of his sneers and his amused contempt—actually this man was indifferent to him. There was only the test, whatever that was; and his own conscious life at stake. The important thing was to stay calm, and to stick leechlike to this one tremendous subject. Before he could speak, Dr. Lell said in a curiously flat voice:

"We have a machine that tests human beings for degree of recalcitrancy. The Observer Machine will speak to you now!"

"What is your name?" said a voice out of the thin air beside Garson.

Garson jumped; his brain staggered, literally; and there was a terrible moment of unbalance. The dim, dismayed thought came that, in spite of determination, he had been caught off guard; and there was the still vaguer thought that, without his being aware of it, he had actually been in a state of dangerous tension.

With a terrific effort he caught himself. He saw that Dr. Lell was smiling again, and that helped! Trembling, he leaned back in his chair; and, after a moment, he was sufficiently recovered to feel a surge of anger at the way the chill clung to his body, and at the tiny quaver in his voice, as he began to answer:

"My name is John Bellmore Garson—age thirty-three—professor of physics at the University of—research scientist—blood type number—"

There were too many questions, an exhaustive drain of detail out of his mind, the history of his life, his aspirations. In the end, the deadly truth was a cold weight inside him. His life, his conscious life, was at stake *now*—this minute! Here was not even the shadow of comedy, but a precise, thorough, machinelike grilling. He must pass this test or—

"Dr. Lell!" The insistent voice of the machine broke in. "What is the state of this man's mind at this moment?"

Dr. Lell said promptly, coolly: "A state of tremendous doubt. His subconscious is in a turmoil of uncertainty. I need hardly add that his subconscious knows his character."

Garson drew a deep breath. He felt utterly sick at the simple way he had been disintegrated. And by one *newness!* A machine that needed neither telephone nor radio—if it was a machine! His voice was a rasping thing in his own ears, as he snapped:

"My subconscious can go straight to hell! I'm a reasonable person. I've made up my mind. I play ball with your organization to the limit."

The silence that followed was unnaturally long; and when at last the machine spoke, his relief lasted only till its final words penetrated. The disembodied voice said coldly:

"I am pessimistic—but bring him over for the test after the usual preliminaries!"

Preliminaries! Was it possible that this mindshaking test had been but the preliminary to the preliminary of the real test?

Rigid with dismay, he stood up to follow the bleakly smiling Dr. Lell out of the room.

He began to feel better, as he walked behind Dr. Lell along the gray-blue hallway. In a small way, he had won. Whatever these other tests were, how *could* they possibly ignore his determined conviction that he must co-operate? As for himself—

For himself, there was this colossal world of the future. Surely, he could resign himself to his lot for the duration of this silly war and lose himself in the amazing immensity of a science that included time machines, fireballs, and Observer Machines that judged men with a cold, remorseless logic and spoke out of thin air.

He frowned. There must be some trick to that, some "telephone" in the nearby wall. Damned if he'd believe that any force could focus sound without intermediary instruments, just as Norma couldn't have been made older in the police station without—

The thought collapsed.

For a paralyzed moment, he stared down where the floor had been.

It wasn't there!

With a gasp, Garson grabbed at the opaque wall; and then, as a low laugh from the doctor, and the continued hardness beneath his feet, told the extent of the illusion, he controlled himself—and stared in utter fascination.

Below him was a section of a room, whose limits he could not see because the opaque walls barred his vision on either side. A milling pack of men filled every available foot of space that he could see. Men, oh—The ironic voice of Dr. Lell pierced his stunned senses, echoing his thoughts with brittle words:

"Men, yes, men! Recruits out of all times. Soldiers-to-be from the ages, and not yet do they know their destiny."

The voice ended, but the indescribable scene went on. Men squirmed, shoved, fought. Upturned faces showed stark puzzlement, anger, fear, amusement, and all the combinations of all the possible emotions. There were men in clothes that sparkled with every color of the rainbow; there were the drab-clothed, the in-betweens; there were—

Garson caught his flitting mind into an observant tightness. In spite of the radical difference in the dress styles of the men who floundered down there like sheep in a slaughterhouse pen, there was a sameness about them that could only mean one thing. They were all—

"You're right!" It was that cool, taunting voice again. "They're all Americans, all from this one city now called Delpa. From our several thousand machines located in the various ages of Delpa, we obtain about four thousand men an hour during the daylight hours. What you see below is the main receiving room.

"The recruits come sliding down the time chutes, and are promptly revived and shoved in there. Naturally at this stage there is a certain amount of confusion. But let us proceed further."

Garson scarcely noticed as the solid floor leaped into place beneath his feet. The vague thought did come that at no time had he seen Dr. Lell press a button or manipulate a control of any kind, neither when the Observer Machine spoke with ventriloquistic wizardry, nor when the floor was made invisible, nor now when it again became opaque. Possibly here was some form of mental control. His mind leaped to a personal danger:

What was the purpose of this—preliminary? Were they showing him horror, then watching his reactions? He felt abrupt rage. What did they expect from a man brought up in twentieth-century environment? Nothing here had anything to do with his intellectual conviction that he was caught and that therefore he must cooperate. But—four thousand men in one hour from one city! Why, it meant—

"And here," Dr. Lell said, and his voice was as calm as the placid waters of a pond, "we have one of several hundred smaller rooms that make a great circle around the primary time machine. You can see the confusion has diminished."

Truth, Garson thought, had never suffered greater understatement than those words. There was absolute absence of confusion. Men sat on chesterfields. Some were looking at books; others chatted like people in a silent movie; their lips moved, but no sound penetrated the illusive transparency of the floor.

"I didn't," came that calm, smooth, confident voice, "show you the intermediate stage that leads up to this clublike atmosphere. A thousand frightened men confronted with danger could make trouble. But we winnow them down psychologically and physically till we have one man going through that door at the end of the room—ah, there's one going now. Let us by all means follow him. You see, at this point we dispense with coddling and bring forth the naked reality."

The reality was a metal, boiler-shaped affair, with a furnacelike door; and four beast humans simply grabbed the startled newcomer and thrust him feet first into the door.

The man must have screamed; for, once, his face twisted upward, and the contorted fear, the almost idiotic gaping and working of the mouth came at Garson like some enormous physical blow. As from a great distance, he heard Dr. Lell say:

"It helps at this stage to disorganize the patient's mind, for the depersonalizing machine can then do a better job."

Abruptly, the impersonalness went out of his voice. In an icily curt tone, he said: "It is useless continuing this little lecture tour. To my mind, your reactions have fully justified the pessimism of the Observer. There will be no further delay."

The deadly words scarcely touched him. He was drained of emotion, of hope; and that first blaze of scientific eagerness was a dull, aching ember.

After that incredible succession of blows, he accepted the failure verdict as—merited!

It was consciousness of the sardonic profile of his captor that brought the first emergence from that dark defeatism. Damn it, there was still the fact that he was logistically committed to this world. He'd have to harden himself, narrow his emotions down to a channel that would include only Norma and himself. If these people and their machine condemned on the basis of feelings, then he'd have to show them how stony-cold his intellect could be.

He braced himself. Where the devil was this all-knowing machine?

The corridor ended abruptly in a plain, black door, exactly like all the other doors, that held not the faintest promise of anything important beyond.

Amazingly, it opened onto a street!

A street of the city of the future!

Garson stiffened. His brain soared beyond contemplation of his own danger in a burning anticipation; and then, almost instantly, began to sag.

Puzzled, he stared at a scene that was utterly different from his expectations. In a vague way, mindful of the effects of war, he had pictured devastated magnificence. Instead—

Before his gaze stretched a depressingly narrow, unsightly street. Dark unwashed buildings lowered up to hide the sun. A trickle of the squat semihuman men and women, beastlike creatures, moved stolidly along narrow areas of pavement marked off by black lines, that constituted the only method of distinguishing the road from the sidewalk.

The street stretched away for miles; and it was all like that, as far as he could see clearly. Intensely disappointed, conscious even of disgust, Garson turned away—and grew aware that Dr. Lell was staring at him with a grim smile. The doctor said laconically:

"What you are looking for, Professor Garson, you will not find, not in this or similar cities of the 'Slaves', but in the palace cities of the Glorious and the Planetarians—"

He stopped, as if his words had brought an incredibly unpleasant thought; to Garson's amazement, his face twisted with rage; his voice almost choked, as he spat: "Those damnable Planetarians! When I think what their so-called ideals are bringing the world to, I—"

The spasm of fury passed; he said quietly: "Several hundred years ago, a mixed commission of Glorious and Planetarians surveyed the entire physical resources of the Solar System. Men had made themselves practically immortal; theoretically, this body of mine will last a million years, barring major accidents. It was decided available resources would maintain ten million men on Earth, ten million on Venus, five million on Mars and ten million altogether on the moons of Jupiter for one million years at the then existing high standard of consumption, roughly amounting to about four million dollars a year per person at 1941 values.

"If in the meantime Man conquered the stars, all these figures were subject to revision, though then, as now, the latter possibility was considered as remote as the stars themselves. Under examination, the problem, so apparently simple, has shown itself intricate beyond the scope of our mathematics."

He paused, and Garson ventured: "We had versions of planned states in our time, too, but they always broke down because of human nature. That seems to have happened again."

Not for a second had Garson considered his statement dangerous. The effect of his words was startling. The lean, handsome face became like frozen marble. Harshly, Dr. Lell said:

"Do not dare to compare your Naziism or Communism to—us! We are the rulers of all future time, and who in the past could ever stand against us if we chose to dominate? We shall win this war, in spite of being on the verge of defeat, for we are building the greatest time-energy barrier that has ever existed. With it, we shall destroy—or no one will win! We'll teach those moralistic scum of the planets to prate about man's rights and the freedom of the spirit. Blast them all!"

It was stunning. There was a passion of pride here, a violence of emotion altogether outside any possible anticipation. And yet—the fact remained that his own opinions were what they were, and he could not actually hope to conceal them from either Dr. Lell or the Observer; so—

He said: "I see an aristocratic hierarchy and a swarm of beast-men slaves. How do *they* fit into the picture, anyway? What about the resources they require? There certainly seem to be hundreds of thousands in this city alone."

The man was staring at him in rigid hostility, that brought a sudden chill to Garson's spine. Genuinely, he hadn't expected that any reasonable statement he might make would be used against him. Dr. Lell said too quietly:

"Basically, they do not use any resources. They live in cities of stone and brick, and eat the produce of the indefatigable soil."

His voice was suddenly as sharp as steel. "And now, Professor Garson, I assure you that you have already condemned yourself. The Observer is located in that metal building across the street because the strain of energy from the great primary time machine would affect its sensitive parts if it was any nearer. I can think of no other explanation that you require, and I certainly have no desire to remain in the company of a man who will be an automaton in half an hour. *Come along!*"

Briefly, there was no impulse in him to argue, nothing but awareness of this monstrous city. Here it was again, the old, old story of the aristocrat justifying his black crime against his fellow man. Originally, there must have been deliberate physical degradation, deliberate misuse of psychology. The very name by which these people called themselves, the Glorious, seemed a heritage from days when dastardly and enormous efforts must have been made to arouse hysterical hero worship in the masses.

Dr. Lell's dry voice said: "Your disapproval of our slaves is shared by the Planetarians. They also oppose our methods of depersonalizing our recruits. It is easy to see that they and you have many things in common, and if only you could escape to their side—"

With an effort, Garson pulled himself out of his private world. He was being led on, not even skillfully; and it was only too apparent now that every word Dr. Lell spoke had the purpose of making him reveal himself. For a moment, he was conscious of genuine impatience; then puzzlement came.

"I don't get it," he said. "What you're doing cannot be bringing forth any new facts. I'm the product of my environment. You know what that environment is, and what type of normal human being it must inevitably produce. As I've said, my whole case rests on co-oper—"

It was the difference in the texture of the sky at the remote end of that street that snatched his attention. A faint, unnormal, scarlet tinge it was, like a mist, an unnatural, unearthly sunset, only it was hours yet before the sun would set.

Astoundingly, he felt himself taut, growing tauter. He said in a tense voice:

"What's that?"

"That," Dr. Lell's curt, amused voice came at him, "is the war."

Garson restrained a crazy impulse to burst out laughing. For weeks speculation about this gigantic war of the future had intertwined with his gathering anxiety about Norma. And now this—this red haze on the horizon of an otherwise undamaged city—the war!

The dark flash of inner laughter faded, as Dr. Lell said:

"It is not so funny as you think. Most of Delpa is intact because it is protected by a local time-energy barrier. Delpa is actually under siege, fifty miles inside enemy territory."

He must have caught the thought that came to Garson. He said good-humoredly: "You're right. All you have to do is get out of Delpa, and you'll be safe."

Garson said angrily: "It's a thought that would occur naturally to any intelligent person. Don't forget you have Miss Matheson."

Dr. Lell seemed not to have heard. "The red haze you see is the point where the enemy has neutralized our energy barrier. It is there that they attack us unceasingly day and night with an inexhaustible store of robot machines.

"We are unfortunate in not having the factory capacity in Delpa to build robot weapons, so we use a similar type manned by depersonalized humans. Unfortunately, again, the cost in lives is high: ninety-eight percent of recruits. Every day, too, we lose about forty feet of the city, and, of course, in the end, Delpa will fall."

He smiled, an almost gentle smile. Garson was amazed to notice that he seemed suddenly in high good humor. Dr. Lell said:

"You can see how effective even a small time-energy barrier is. When we complete the great barrier two years hence, our entire front line will be literally impregnable. And now, as for your cooperation argument, it's worthless. Men are braver than they think, braver than reason. But let's forget argument. In a minute, the machine will give us the truth of this matter—"

At first sight, the Observer Machine was a solid bank of flickering lights that steadied oddly, seemed almost to glare as they surveyed him. Garson stood quite still, scarcely breathing; a dim thought came that this—this wall of black metal machine and lights was utterly unimpressive.

He found himself analyzing the lack: It was too big and too stationary. If it had been small and possessed of shape, however ugly, and *movement*, there might have been a suggestion of abnormal personality.

But here was nothing, but a myriad of lights. As he watched, the lights began to wink again. Abruptly they blinked out, all except a little colored design of them at the bottom right-hand corner.

Behind him, the door opened, and Dr. Lell came into the silent room. "I'm glad," he said quietly, "that the result was what it was. We are desperately in need of good assistants.

"To illustrate," he went on, as they emerged into the brightness of the unpleasant street, "I am, for instance, in charge of the recruiting station in 1941, but I'm there only when an intertime alarm system has warned me. In the interim, I am employed on scientific duties of the second order—first order being work that, by its very nature, must continue without interruption."

They were back in the same great building from which he had come; and ahead stretched the same gray-blue, familiar corridor, only this time Dr. Lell opened the first of several doors. He bowed politely.

"After you, professor!"

A fraction too late, Garson's fist flailed the air where that dark, strong face had been. They stared at each other, Garson tight-lipped, his brain like a steel bar. The superman said softly:

"You will always be that instant too slow, professor. It is a lack you cannot remedy. You know, of course, that my little speech was designed to keep you quiet during the trip back here, and that, actually, you failed the test. What you do not know is that you failed startlingly, with a recalcitrancy grading of 6, which is the very worst, and intelligence AA plus, almost the best. It is too bad because we genuinely need capable assistants. I regret—"

"Let me do the regretting!" Garson cut him off roughly. "If I remember rightly, it was just below here that your beast men were forcing a man into the depersonalizing machine. Perhaps, on the staircase going down, I can find some way of tripping you up, and knocking that little gun you're palming right out of your hand."

There was something in the smile of the other that should have warned him—a hint of sly amusement. Not that it would have made any difference. Only—

He stepped through the open doorway toward the gray-blue, plainly visible stairway. Behind him, the door clicked with an odd finality. Ahead there was—

Amazingly, the staircase was gone. Where it had been was a large boilerlike case with a furnace-shaped door. Half a dozen beast men came forward—a moment later, they were shoving him toward that black hole of a door—

The second day Norma took the risk. The windows of the recruiting station still showed the same blank interior; walls stripped by the police of Calonian slogans, and signs and newspaper clippings trampled all over the floor. The door to the back room was half closed—too dark to see the interior.

It was noon. With drummed-up courage, Norma walked swiftly to the front entrance. The lock clicked open smoothly, and she was inside—pushing at that back door.

The machine was not there. Great dents showed in the floor, where it had malignantly crouched for so many months. But it was gone, as completely as Dr. Lell, as completely as the creaturemen and Jack Garson.

Back in her rooms, she collapsed onto the bed, and lay quivering from the dreadful nervous reaction of that swift, illegal search.

On the afternoon of the fourth day, as she sat staring at the meaningless words of a book, there was an abrupt tingling in her body. Somewhere a machine—*the machine*—was vibrating softly.

She climbed to her feet, the book forgotten on the window sill, where, freakishly, it had fallen. But the sound was gone. Not a tremor touched her taut nerves. The thought came: imagination! The pressure was really beginning to get her.

As she stood there stiff, unable to relax, there came the thin squeal of a door opening downstairs. She recognized the sound instantly. It was the back door that led onto the vacant back lot, which her window overlooked. The back door opening and shutting!

She stared, fascinated, as Dr. Lell stalked into view. Her thought of awareness of him was so sharp that he must have caught it—but he did not turn. In half a minute he was gone, out of her line of vision.

On the fifth day, there was hammering downstairs, carpenters working. Several trucks came, and there was the mumbling sound of men talking. But it was evening before she dared venture downstairs. Through the window, then, she saw the beginning of the changes that were being wrought.

The old bench had been removed. The walls were being redone; there was no new furniture yet, but a rough, unfinished sign leaned against one wall. It read:

EMPLOYMENT BUREAU
MEN WANTED

Men wanted! So that was it. Another trap for men! Those ravenous armies of the Glorious must be kept glutted with fodder. The incredible war up there in that incredible future raged on. And she—

Quite dumbly, she watched as Dr. Lell came out of the back room. He walked toward the front door, and there was not even the impulse in her to run. She stood there, as he opened the door, came out, meticulously closed the door behind him, and then, after a moment, stood beside her, as silent as she, staring into the window. Finally:

"I see you've been admiring our new set-up!"

His voice was matter-of-fact, completely lacking in menace. She made no reply; he seemed to expect none, for he said almost immediately, in that same conversational tone:

"It's just as well that it all happened as it did. Nothing I ever told you has been disproved. I said that investigation had shown the machine to be here several years hence. Naturally, we could not examine every day or week of that time. This little episode accordingly escaped our notice, but did not change the situation.

"As for the fact that it will be an employment bureau henceforth, that seemed natural at the period of our investigation because this war of your time was over then."

He paused, and still there was no word that she could think of saying. In the gathering darkness, he seemed to stare at her.

"I'm telling you all this because it would be annoying to have to train someone else for your position, and because you must realize the impossibility of further opposition.

"Accept your situation. We have thousands of machines similar to this, and the millions of men flowing through them are gradually turning the tide of battle in our favor. We must win; our cause is overwhelmingly just; we are Earth against all the planets; Earth protecting herself against the aggression of a combination of enemies armed as no powers in all time have ever been armed. We have the highest moral right to draw on the men of Earth of every century to defend their planet.

"However"—his voice lost its objectivity, grew colder—"if this logic does not move you, the following rewards for your good behavior should prove efficacious. We have Professor Garson; unfortunately, I was unable to save his personality. Definite tests proved that he would be a recalcitrant, so—

"Then there is your youth. It will be returned to you on a salary basis. Every three weeks you will become a year younger. In short, it will require two years for you to return to your version of twenty."

He finished on a note of command: "A week from today, this bureau will open for business. You will report at nine o'clock. This is your last chance. Good-by."

In the darkness, she watched his shape turn; he vanished into the gloom of the building.

She had a purpose. At first it was a tiny mindgrowth that she wouldn't admit into her consciousness. But gradually embarrassment passed, and the whole world of her thought began to organize around it.

It began with the developing realization that resistance was useless. Not that she believed in the rightness of the cause of Dr. Lell and of this race that called itself the Glorious, although his story of Earth against the planets had put the first doubt into her brain. As—she knew—he had intended it should.

The whole affair was simpler than that. One woman had set herself against the men of the future—what a silly thing for one woman to do!

There remained Jack Garson!

If she could get him back, poor, broken, strange creature that he must be now with his personality destroyed—somehow she would make amends for having been responsible, but—

She thought: What madness to hope that they'd give him back to her, ever! She was the tiniest cog in a vast war machine. Nevertheless, the fact remained:

She must get him back!

The part of her brain that was educated, civilized, thought: What an elemental purpose, everything drained out of her but the basic of basics, one woman concentrating on the one man.

But the purpose was there, unquenchable!

The slow months dragged; and, once gone, seemed to have flashed by. Suddenly, the Great War was over—and swarms of returned soldiers made the streets both dangerous and alive.

One night she turned a corner and found herself on a street she hadn't visited for some time. She stopped short, her body stiffening. The street ahead was thick with men—but their presence scarcely touched her mind.

Above all that confusion of sound, above the catcalls, above the roar of streetcars and automobiles, above the totality of the cacophonous combination, there was another sound, an incredibly softer sound—the whisper of a time machine.

She was miles from the employment bureau with its machine, but the tiny tremor along her nerves was unmistakable.

She pressed forward, blind to everything but the brilliantly lighted building that was the center of the attention of the men. A man tried to put his arm through hers. She jerked free automatically. Another man simply caught her in an embrace, and for brief seconds she was subjected to a steel-hard hug and a steel-hard kiss.

Purpose gave her strength. With scarcely an effort, she freed one arm and struck at his face. The man laughed good-humoredly, released her, but walked beside her.

"Clear the way for the lady!" he shouted.

Almost magically, there was a lane; and she was at the window. There was a sign that read:

WANTED

RETURNED SOLDIERS FOR DANGEROUS ADVENTURE
GOOD PAY!

No emotion came to the realization that here was another trap for men, in her brain, she had space only for impression.

The impression was of a large square room, with a dozen men in it. Only three of the men were recruits; of the other nine, one was an American soldier dressed in the uniform of World War I. He sat at a desk pounding a typewriter. Over him leaned a Roman legionnaire of the time of Julius Caesar, complete with toga and short sword. Beside the door, holding back the pressing throng of men, were two Greek soldiers of the time of Pericles.

The men and the times they represented were unmistakable to her, who had taken four years of university Latin and Greek, and acted in plays of both periods in the original languages.

There was another man in an ancient costume, but she was unable to place him. At the moment, he was at a short counter interviewing one of the three recruits.

Of the four remaining men, two wore uniforms that could have been developments of the late twentieth century: the cloth was a light-yellow texture, and both men had two pips on their shoulders. The rank of lieutenant was obviously still in style when they were commissioned.

The remaining two men were simply strange, not in face, but in the cloth of their uniforms. Their faces were of sensitive, normal construction; their uniforms consisted of breeches and neatly fitting coats all in blue, a blue that sparkled as from a million needlelike diamond points. In a quiet, blue, intense way, they shone.

One of the recruits was led to the back door, as she watched, her first awareness that there was a back door. The door opened; she had the briefest glimpse of a towering machine and a flashing picture of a man who was tall and dark of face, and who might have been Dr. Lell. Only he wasn't. But the similarity of race was unmistakable.

The door closed, and one of the Greeks guarding the outer entrance said: "All right, two more of you fellows can come in!"

There was a struggle for position, brief but incredibly violent. And then the two victors, grinning and breathing heavily from their exertion, were inside. In the silence that followed, one of the Greeks turned to the other, and said in a tangy, almost incomprehensible version of ancient Greek:

"Sparta herself never had more willing fighters. This promises to be a good night's catch!"

It was the rhythm of the words, and the colloquial gusto with which they were spoken that almost destroyed the meaning for her. After a moment, however, she made the mental translation. And now the truth was unmistakable. The men of Time had gone back even to old Greece, probably much farther back, for their recruits. And always they had used every version of bait, based on all the weaknesses and urgencies in the natures of men.

"Fight For Calonia"—an appeal to idealism! "Men wanted"—the most basic of all appeals, work for food, happiness, security. And now, the appeal variation was for returned soldiers—adventure—with pay!

Diabolical! And yet so effective that they could even use men who had formerly been caught on the same brand of fly paper as recruiting officers—These men must be of the recalcitrant type, who fitted themselves willingly into the war machine of the Glorious One.

Traitors!

Abruptly ablaze with hatred for all nonrecalcitrants, who still possessed their personalities, she whirled away from the window.

She was thinking: Thousands of such machines. The figures had been meaningless before, but now, with just one other machine as a tremendous example, the reality reared up into a monstrous thing.

To think that there was a time when she had actually set her slim body and single, inadequate mind against *them!*

There remained the problem of getting Jack Garson out of the hell of that titanic war of the future!

At night, she walked the streets, because there was always the fear that in the apartment her thoughts, her driving deadly thoughts, would be—tapped. And because to be enclosed in those narrow walls above the machine that had devoured so many thousands of men was—intolerable!

She thought as she walked—over and over she thought of the letter Jack Garson had written her before he came in person. Long destroyed, that letter, but every word was emblazoned on her brain; and of all the words of it, the one sentence that she always returned to was. "In your position, I would ask myself one question: Was there anything, any metal, *anything*, upon my person, that might have been placed there?"

One day, as she was wearily unlocking the door of her apartment, the answer came. Perhaps it was the extra weariness that brought her briefly closer to basic things. Perhaps her brain was simply tired of slipping over the same blind spot. Or perhaps the months of concentration had finally earned the long-delayed result.

Whatever the reason, she was putting the key back into her purse when the hard, metallic feel of it against her fingers brought wild, piercing realization.

The key, metal, the key, metal, the key—

Desperately, she stopped the mad repetition. The apartment door slammed behind her, and like some terrorized creature she fled down the dark stairs into the glare of the night streets.

Impossible to return till she had calmed the burning, raging chaos that was in her mind. Until she had—made sure!

After half an hour, the first flash of coherence came. In a drugstore, she bought a night bag and a few fill-ins to give it weight. A pair of small pliers, a pair of tweezers—in case the pliers were too large—and a small screwdriver completed her equipment. Then she went to a hotel.

The pliers and the tweezers were all she needed. The little bulbous cap of the skeleton-type key yielded to the first hard pressure. Her trembling fingers completed the unscrewing—and she found herself staring at a tiny, glowing point, like a red-hot needle protruding from the very center of the tube that was the inside of the key.

The needle vanished into an intricate design of spiderlike wires, all visible in the glow that shed from them—

The vague thought came that there was probably terrific, communicable energies here. But somehow there came no sense of restraint from the idea. Only enough reality of danger struck her to make her wrap her flimsy lace handkerchief around the tweezers—and then she touched the shining, protruding needle point.

It yielded the slightest bit to her shaky touch. Nothing happened. It just glowed there.

Dissatisfied, she put the key down and stared at it. So tiny, so delicate a machine actually disturbed to the extent of one sixteenth of an inch displacement—and nothing happened. She—

A sudden thought sent her to the dresser mirror. A forty-year-old face stared back at her.

Months now since she had returned to twenty. And now, in a flash, she was forty. The little touch of the pin against the needle's end, pushing, had aged her twenty years.

That explained what had happened at the police station. It meant— if she could only pull it back—She fought to steady her fingers, then applied the tweezers.

She was twenty again!

Abruptly weak, she lay down on the bed. She thought:

Somewhere in the world of time and space was the still-living body of the man that had been Jack Garson. But for him she could throw this key *thing* into the river three blocks away, take the first train East or West or South—anywhere—and the power of the machine would be futile against her. Dr. Lell would not even think of searching for her once she had lost herself in the swarm of humankind.

How simple it all really was. For three long years, their power over her had been the key and its one devastating ability to age her.

Or was that all?

Startled, she sat up. Did they count, perhaps, on their victims believing themselves safe enough to keep the key and its magic powers of rejuvenation? She, of course, because of Jack Garson, was bound to the key as if it was still the controller and not she. But the other incentive, now that she had thought of it, was enormous. And—

Her fingers shook as she picked up the dully gleaming key with its glowing, intricate interior. Incredible that they could have allowed so precious an instrument to pass so easily into the hands of an alien, when they must have known that the probability of discovery was not—improbable!

An idea came; and, with it, abrupt calm. With suddenly steady fingers, she picked up the tweezers, caught the protruding glow point of the key between the metal jaws, and, making no attempt to pull or push, twisted screw-wise.

There was a tiny, almost inaudible click. Her body twanged like a taut violin string, and she was falling—falling into dark, immeasurable distance.

Out of the night, a vaguely shining body drifted toward her, a body human yet not human; there was something about the head and the shoulders, something physically different that somehow eluded her slow thought; and in that strange, superhuman head were eyes that blazed like jewels, seemed literally to pierce her. The voice that came couldn't have been sound, for it was inside her brain, and it said:

"With this great moment, you enter upon your power and your purpose. I say to you, the time-energy barrier must not be completed. It will destroy all the ages of the Solar System. The time-energy barrier must not, *not*, NOT be completed—"

The body faded, and was gone into remoteness. The very memory of it became a dim mind-shape. There remained the darkness, the jet, incredible darkness.

Abruptly, she was in a material world. She seemed to be half-slumped, half-kneeling, one leg folded under her in the exact position she had occupied on the bed. Only she must have drooped there unconscious for long moments; her knees ached and ached with the hard, pressing pain of position. And—beneath the silk of her stockings was, not the hotel bed, but—metal!

It was the combination of surprise, the aloneness, and the stark fact of the mind-destroying thing that was going to happen that unnerved Garson. Involuntarily, he started to squirm, then he was writhing, his face twisting in strange mental agony; and then the strength of those rough, stolid hands holding him seemed to flow somehow into his nerves.

Almost literally, he clenched his mind, and was safe from madness!

There were no hands touching him now. He lay, face downward on a flat, hard surface; and at first there was only the darkness and a slow return of the sense of aloneness.

Vague thoughts came, thoughts of Norma and of the coincidence that had molded his life, seemingly so free for so many years, yet destined to find its ending here in this black execution chamber—for he *was* being destroyed here, though his body might live on for a few brief mindless hours. Or days. Or weeks. It mattered not.

The thing was fantastic. This whole damned business was a nightmare, and in a minute he'd wake up and—

At first the sound was less than a whisper, a stealthy noise out of remoteness, that prodded with an odd insistence at Garson's hearing. It quivered toward him in the blackness, edging out of inaudibility, a rasping presence that grew louder, louder—voices!

It exploded into a monstrous existence, a billion voices clamoring at his brain, a massive blare that pressed at him, *pressed him!*

Abruptly, the ferocity of the voices dimmed. They faded into distance, still insistent, somehow reluctant to leave, as if there was something still left unsaid.

The end of sound came, and briefly there was utter silence. Then—there was a click. Light flooded at him from an opening a scant foot from his head.

Garson twisted and stared, fascinated. Daylight! From his vantage point, he could see the edge of a brick-and-stone building, a wretchedly old, worn building, a street of Delpa.

It was over. Incredibly it was over.

And nothing had happened. No, that wasn't it exactly. There were things in his mind, confusing things about the importance of loyalty to the Glorious, a sense of intimacy with his surroundings, pictures of machines and—nothing clear, except—

A harsh voice broke his amazed blur of thought. "Come on out of there, you damned slow poke!"

A square, heavy, brutal face was peering into the open door, a big, square-built young man with a thick neck, a boxer's flat nose, and unpleasant blue eyes.

Garson lay quite still. It was not that he intended to disobey. All his reason urged instant, automatic obedience until he could estimate the astounding things that had happened.

What held him there, every muscle stiff, was a new, tremendous fact that grew, not out of the meaning of the man's words, but out of the words themselves.

The language was not English. Yet he had understood—every word!

The sudden squint of impatient rage that flushed the coarse face peering in at him brought life to Garson's muscles. He scrambled forward, but it was the man's truck-driver hands that actually pulled him clear and deposited him with a jarring casualness face downward on the paved road.

He lay there for an electric instant, tense with an anger that congealed reluctantly before the thought: He dare not get mad. Or act the fool!

The terrific reality was that something had gone wrong. Somehow the machine hadn't worked all the way, and if he was crazy enough to wreck the great chance that offered—

He stood up slowly, wondering how an automaton, a depersonalized human being, should look and act.

"This way, damn you," said that bullying voice from behind him. "You're in the army now."

Satisfaction came into the voice: "Well, you're the last for me today. I'll get you fellows to the front, and then—"

"This way" led to a dispirited-looking group of men, about a hundred of them, who stood in two rows alongside a great, gloomy, dirty building. He walked stolidly to the end of the rear line, and for the first time realized how surprisingly straight the formation of men were holding their lines, in spite of their dulled appearance.

"All right, all right," bellowed the square-jawed young man. "Let's get going. You've got some hard fighting ahead of you before this day and night are over—"

The contemptuous thought came to Garson, as he stared at the leader: this, then, was the type *they* picked for nonrecalcitrant training: the ignorant, blatant, amoral, sensual pigmen. No wonder he himself had been rejected by the Observer.

His eyes narrowed to slits as he watched the line of dead-alive men walk by him in perfect rhythm; he fell in step, his mind deliberately slow and ice-cold, cautiously exploring the strange knowledge in his brain that didn't fit with his—freedom!

That didn't fit with anything! A little group of sentences that kept repeating inside him:

"The great time-energy barrier is being built in Delpa. It must not be completed, for it will destroy the Universe. Prepare to do your part in its destruction; try to tell the Planetarians, but take no unnecessary risks. To stay alive, to tell the Planetarians: those are your immediate purposes. The time-energy barriers must not—NOT—"

Funny, he thought, funny! He squeezed the crazy thing out of his consciousness.

No trucks came gliding up to transport them; no streetcar whispered along in some superdevelopment of street-railway service; there was simply no machinery, nothing but those narrow avenues with their gray, sidewalkless length, like back alleys.

They walked to war; and it was like being in a dead, old, deserted city—deserted except for the straggle of short, thick, slow, stolid men and women who plodded heavily by, unsmiling, without so much as a side glance. As if they were but the pitiful, primitive remnant of a once-great race, and this city the proud monument to— No!

Garson smiled wryly. Of all the fools, getting romantic about this monstrosity of a city. All too evident it was, even without Dr. Lell's words as a reminder, that every narrow, dirty street, every squalid building had been erected—to be what it was.

And the sooner he got out of the place, and delivered to the Planetarians the queer, inexplicable message about the great time-energy barrier—

With a half shudder, with deliberate abruptness, he cut the thought. Damn it, he'd have to be careful. If one of the Glorious should happen to be around, and accidentally catch the free thought of what was supposed to be an automaton—next time there'd be no mistake.

Tramp, tramp, tramp! The pavement echoed with the strange lifeless hollowness of a ghost city; and the tremendous thought came that he was here centuries, perhaps millenniums, into the future. What an awful realization to think that Norma, poor, persecuted, enslaved Norma, whose despairing face he had seen little more than an hour ago, was actually dead and buried in the dim ages of the long ago.

And yet she was alive. Those six hundred billion bodies per minute of hers were somewhere in space and time, alive because the great time energy followed its casual, cosmic course of endless repetition, because life was but an accident as purposeless as the immeasurable energy that plunged grandly on into the unknown night that must be—somewhere!

Tramp, tramp— On and on, and his thought was a rhythm to the march— With an ugly start he came out of his reverie, and instantly grew abnormally aware of the nearness of the red haze in the sky ahead. Why, it wouldn't take ten minutes now, and they'd be *there!*

Machines glinted in the slanting rays of the warm, golden, sinking sun; machines that moved and—fought! A sick thrill struck Garson, the first shock of realization that this—this tiny segment of the battle of the ages was real, and near, and deadly.

Up there, every minute men were dying miserably for a cause their depersonalized minds did not even comprehend. Up there, too, was infinitesimal victory for the Planetarians, and a small, stinging measure of defeat for the Glorious. Forty feet a day, Dr. Lell had said.

Forty feet of city conquered every day. What a murderous war of attrition, what a bankruptcy of strategy. Or was it the ultimate nullification of the role of military genius, in that each side knew and practiced every rule of military science without error?—and the forty feet was simply the inevitable mathematical outcome of the difference in the potential in striking power of the two forces.

Forty feet a day. In a blaze of wonder, Garson stood finally with his troop a hundred yards from that unnatural battle front. Like a robot he stood stiffly among those robot men, but his eyes and mind fed in undiminished fascination at the deadly mechanical routine that was the offense and defense.

The Planetarians had seven major machines, and there were at least half a hundred tiny, swift, glittering craft as escort for each of the great— battleships! That was it: battleships and destroyers.

Against them, the Glorious had only destroyers, a host of darting, shining, torpedo-shaped craft that hugged the ground, and fought in an endlessly repeated, complicated maneuver.

Maneuver against maneuver! An intricate chess game—it *was* a game, an incredibly involved game whose purpose and method seemed to quiver just beyond the reach of his reason.

Everything revolved around the battleships. In some way they must be protected from energy guns, because no attempt was made to use anything like that. Somehow, too, cannon must be useless against them. There was none in sight, no attempt to hurtle great gobs of metal either at the machines or—by the Planetarians at the more than a hundred troops like his own, who stood at stiff attention so close to the front, so bunched that a few superexplosive shells of the future would have smashed them all.

Nothing but the battleships and the destroyers!

The battleships moved forward and backward and forward and backward and in and out, intertwining among themselves; and the destroyers of the Glorious darted in when the battleships came forward, and hung back when the battleships retreated; and always the destroyers of the Planetarians were gliding in to intercept the destroyers of the Glorious; and as the sun sank in a blaze of red beyond the green hills to the west, the battleships in their farthest forward thrust were feet closer than they had been at the beginning; and the sharply delineated red line of haze, that *must* be the point where the time-energy barrier was neutralized, was no longer lying athwart a shattered slab of rock—but on the ground feet nearer.

That was it. The battleships somehow forced the time-energy barrier to be withdrawn. Obviously, it would only be withdrawn to save it from a worse fate, perhaps from a complete neutralization over a wide front. And so a city was being won, inch by inch, foot by foot, street by street—only the intricate evolution of the battle, the why of that almost immeasurably slow victory, was as great a mystery as ever.

The grim thought came: If the odd, tremendous message that had come into his brain in that out-of-order depersonalizing machine was true, then the final victory would never come in time. Long before the forty-foot-a-day conquerors had gained the prize that was Delpa, the secret, super, time-energy barrier would be completed; and the devilish spirit of war would at last have won its senseless goal—complete elimination of the human race and all its works.

Night fell, but a glare of searchlights replaced the sun, and that fantastic battle raged on. No one aimed a gun or a weapon at the lights; each side concentrated with that strange, deadly intentness on its part of that intricate, murderous game; and troop after troop dissolved into the ravenous, incredible conflagration.

Death came simply to the automatons. Each in turn crowded into one of the torpedo-shaped destroyers; and knowing—as he did—from the depersonalizing machine, that the tiny, man-sized tank was operated by thought control, flashed out into battle line.

Sometimes the end came swiftly, sometimes it was delayed, but sooner or later there was metallic contact with the enemy; and that was all that was needed. Instantly, the machine would twist and race toward the line of waiting men; the next victim would drag out the corpse, crawl in himself and—

There were variations. Machines clashed with the enemy and died with their drivers; or darted with frantic aimlessness, out of control. Always, swift, metallic scavengers raced from both sides to capture the prize; and sometimes the Planetarians succeeded, sometimes the Glorious.

Garson counted: one, two, three—less than four hundred men ahead of him—and the realization of how close his turn was brought the perspiration coldly to his face. Minutes! Damn it, *damn it*, he had to solve the rules of this battle, or go in there, without plan, without hope.

Seven battleships, scores of destroyers to each battleship and all acting as one unit in one involved maneuver and—

And, by heaven, he had a part of the answer. One unit. Not seven battleships out there, but one in the form of seven. One superneutralizing machine in its seven-dimensional maneuver. No wonder he had been unable to follow the intertwinings of those monsters with each other, the retreats, the advances. Mathematicians of the twentieth century could only solve easily problems with four equations. Here was a problem with seven; and the general staff of the Glorious could never be anything but a step behind in their solution—and that step cost them forty feet a day—

His turn! He crept into the casing of the torpedo cycle; and it was smaller even than he had thought. The machine fitted him almost like a glove. Effortlessly, it glided forward, too smoothly, too willingly, into that dazzle of searchlights, into that maelstrom of machines.

One contact, he thought, one contact with an enemy meant death; and his plan of breaking through was as vague as his understanding of how a seven-dimensional maneuver actually worked.

Amazed wonder came that he was even letting himself hope.

Norma began to notice the difference, a strange, vibrant, flamelike quality within herself, a rich, warm aliveness, like an electric wire quiescent with latent force tremendous— It was utterly different, alien, as new as life returning to a dead body. Only it was added life to the life that had always existed within her.

Physically, she was still crouching there tautly, her legs twisted under her, vision still blinded; and the hard pain of the metal beneath her was an unchanged pressure against the bone and muscle of her knees. But—

Along every nerve that wonderful sense of well-being, of strange, abnormal power quivered and grew—and yielded abruptly to the violence of the thought that flashed into her mind:

Where was she? What had happened? What—

The thought snapped in the middle because, amazingly, an alienness—intruded into it, another thought, not out of her own mind, not even directed at her, not—human!

"—Tentacle 2731 reporting to the Observer. A warning light has flashed on the ... (meaningless) ... xxxxx time machine. Action!"

The answer came instantly, coldly:

"An intruder—on top of the primary time machine. Warning from, and to, Dr. Lell's section. Tentacle 2731, go at once—destroy intruder. Action!"

There were stunning immensities in those hard wisps of message and answering message, that echoed back along the dim corridors of her mind. The stupefying fact that she had effortlessly intercepted thought waves momentarily blotted out the immediacy of the greater fact that every chilling word of that death threat was meant for her. But then—

Before that colossal menace, even the knowledge of where she was came with a quiet unobtrusiveness, like a minor harmony in a clash of major discord. Her present location was only too obvious. Twisting the key the way she had, had sent her hurtling through time to the age of the Glorious, to the primary-time machine, where fantastic things called tentacles and observers guarded—

If only she could see! She *must* see, or she was lost before she could begin to hope.

Frantically, she strained against the blackness that lay so tight against her eyes and—

She could see!

It was as simple as that. One instant, blindness! The next, the urge to see. And then, sight complete, without preliminary blur, like opening her eyes after a quiet sleep.

The simplicity part of it was crowded out of her brain by a whirling confusion of impression. There were two swift thoughts that clung—the brief wonder at the way sight had come back to her, merely from the wish that it would—and a flashing memory of the face that had floated at her out of the blackness of time. *With this great moment you enter upon your power and your purpose*—

The picture, all connecting thoughts, fled. She saw that she was in a room, a vast domed room, and that she was on top of a gigantic machine. There were transparent walls! and beyond—

Her mind and vision leaped beyond the room, through the transparent walls. There was something out there, something tremendous! A shimmering, roseate fire, like a greater dome that covered the near sky and hid the night universe beyond.

The effort of staring tired her. Her gaze came down out of the sky; and, back in the room, she saw that all the transparent wall that faced her was broken into a senseless pattern of small balconies, each mounting glittering, strangely menacing machinery—weapons!

So many weapons—for what?

With a jar that shocked her brain, the thought disintegrated. She stared in blank horror at a long, thick, tube-shaped metal thing that floated up from below the rim of the time machine. A score of gleaming, insectlike facets seemed to glare at her.

"Tentacle 2731—destroy the intruder—"

"No!" It was her own desperate negation, product of pure devastating panic, product of newness, of a hideous, alien threat that wrecked on the instant all the bravery that had made her experiment with the key in the first place.

Her mind spun like a dizzily spinning wheel, her body shrank from the sudden, abnormal fear that this—metal—would spray her with some incredible flame weapon before she could think, before she could turn or run, or even move!

Of all her pride and accumulated courage, there remained only enough to bring a spasm of shame at the words that burst senselessly from her lips:

"No! No! You can't! Go away—go back—where you came from! Go—"

She stopped, blinked, and stared wildly. The thing was gone!

The reality of that had scarcely touched her when a crash sounded. It came from beyond and below the rim of the machine. Quite instinctively, Norma ran forward to peer down.

The hundred-foot, precipicelike slope of metal time machine that greeted her startled gaze made her draw back with a gasp, but instantly she was creeping forward again, more cautiously, but with utter fascination to see again what that first brief glimpse had revealed.

And there it was, on the distant floor, the tube-shaped thing. Even as she watched, hope building up in her, there came a weak impulse of alien thought:

"Tentacle 2731 reporting—difficulty. Female human using Insel mind rays—power 100—no further action possible by this unit—incapacitation 74 mechanical—"

Hope grew gigantic, and there was a wild burst of surmise and a desperate, wondering half belief in the miracle that was taking place. She was doing this; her wish had brought instant return of sight, her despairing thought had sent the tentacle thing crashing to mechanical ruin. Insel mind rays, power 100! Why, it meant—it could mean—

The leaping thought sagged. One of a series of doors in the wall facing her opened, and a tall man emerged hurriedly. Quite automatically, she pressed back, tried to lie flat on the metal, out of sight; but it seemed to her those familiar, sardonic eyes were staring straight up at her. Dr. Lell's hard, tight, superbly confident thought came then like a succession of battering blows against the crumbling structure of her hope:

"This is a repetition of the x time and space manipulation. Fortunately, the transformation center this seventeenth time is a Miss Norma Matheson, who is utterly incapable, mathematically, of using the power at her disposal. She must be kept confused, kept on the run. The solution to her swift destruction is a concentration of forces of the third order, non-mechanical, according to Plan A4. Action!"

"Action immediate!" came the cold, distinctive thought of the Observer.

That was like death itself. Hope abandoned her; she lay flat on that flat metal, her mind blank, and not a quiver of strength in her body.

A minute passed; and that seemed an immense time. So much that the swift form of her thought had time to change, to harden. Fear faded like a dream; and then came returning awareness of that curious, wonderful sense of power.

She stood up, and the way her legs trembled with the effort brought the automatic memory of the way she had regained her vision. She thought tensely, consciously:

"No more physical weakness. Every muscle, every nerve, every organ of my body must function perfectly from now on and—"

A queer thrill cut the thought. It seemed to start at her toes, and sweep up, a delicious sense of warmth, like an all-over blush.

And the weakness was gone.

She stood for a moment, fascinated, utterly absorbed by this—toy! And hesitated to try it too far. Yet—

She thought: "No more mental weakness, no confusion; my brain must function with all the logic of which I am capable!"

It was strange, and not altogether satisfactory, what happened then. Her mind seemed to come to a dead stop. For an instant the blankness was complete; and then, a single, simple idea came into it:

Danger! For her there was nothing but danger and the getting out of that danger. Find the key. Go back to 1944. Get out of this world of Dr. Lell, and gain time to solve the secrets of the mighty power centralized in her.

She jerked, as a lean, yard-long flame struck the metal beside her, and caromed away toward the ceiling. She watched it bounce from the ceiling, out of sight beyond the precipicelike edge of the machine. It must have struck the floor, but instantly it was in sight again, leaping toward the ceiling with undiminished ardor.

Up, down, up, down, up, it went as she watched; then abruptly it lost momentum, and collapsed like an empty flaming sack toward the floor, out of her line of vision.

A second streamer of flame soared up from where Dr. Lell had been heading when last she saw him. It struck the ceiling, and like an elongated billiard ball, darted down—and this time she was ready for it. Her brain reached out: *Stop! Whatever the energy that drives you, it is powerless against me. Stop!*

The flame missed her right hand by inches, and soared on up to the ceiling; and from below, strong and clear and satirical, came the voice, or was it the thought of Dr. Lell:

"My dear Miss Matheson, that's the first of the third-order energies, quite beyond your control. And have you noticed that your mind isn't quite so cool as you ordered it to be. The truth is that, though you have power unlimited, you can only use it when you understand the forces involved, either consciously or unconsciously. Most people have a reasonably clear picture of their bodily processes, which is why your body reacted so favorably, but your brain—its secrets are largely beyond your understanding.

"As for the key"—there was laughter in the words—"you seem to have forgotten it is geared to the time machine. The Observer's first act was to switch it back to 1944. Accordingly, I can promise you death—"

Her brain remained calm; her body steady, unaffected. No blood surged to her head; there was the barest quickening of her heartbeat; her hands clenched with the tense knowledge that she must act faster, think faster—

If only Jack Garson were here, with his science, his swift, logical brain—

Strangely, then, she could feel her mind slipping out of her control, like sand between her fingers. Her body remained untroubled, untouched, but her mind was suddenly gliding down, down, into dark depths.

Terror came abruptly, as a score of flame streamers leaped into sight toward the ceiling, bounced and—

"Jack, Jack, help me! I need you! Oh, Jack, come—" The slow seconds brought no answer; and the urgency of her need brought no answer; and the urgency of her need could brook no waiting. "Back home," she thought. "I've got to get back home, back to 1944, back—"

Her body twanged. There was blackness, and a horrible sensation of falling.

The blow of the fall was not hard; and that unaffected, almost indestructible body of hers took the shock in a flash of pain-absorbing power. Awareness came of a floor with a rug on it. A vague light directly in front of her lost its distortion and became—a window!

Her own apartment! Like a young tigress she scrambled to her feet; and then poised motionless with dismay as the old, familiar, subtle vibration thrilled its intimate way along her nerves. The machine! The machine was in the room below and working!

Her will to safety had sent her back to her own time, but her call to Jack Garson had passed unheeded, unheard; and here she was, alone with only a strange unwieldy power to help her against the gathering might of the enemy.

And that was her hope, that it was only gathering! Even Dr. Lell must have time to transport his forces. If she could get out of this building, use her power to carry her, as it had already borne her from the time and space of the future—

Carry her where? There was only one other place she could think of: To the hotel! To the hotel room from where she had launched herself with the key.

It wasn't death that came then, but a blow so hard that she was sobbing bitterly with the pain even as her mind yielded reluctantly to unconsciousness; even as she was realizing in stark dismay that she had struck the wall of her apartment and this power she possessed had been betrayed once again by her inability to handle it. And now Dr. Lell would have time to do everything necessary—

Blackness came—

There was a memory in Garson of the night, and of the rushing machine that had carried him, the wonderful little metal thing that darted and twisted far to the left, as close to the red haze of the time-energy barrier as he dared to go—and not a machine had followed him. In seconds he was through the blazing gap, out of Delpa, safe from Dr. Lell—only something had struck at him then, a crushing blow—

He came out of sleep without pain, and with no sense of urgency. Drowsily, he lay, parading before his mind the things that had happened and the comfortable realization came that he must be safe or he wouldn't be—like this!

There were things to do, of course. He must transmit the information to the Planetarians that they must conquer Delpa more swiftly, that final victory waited nowhere but in Delpa. And then, somehow, he must persuade them to let him return to 1941, to Norma and—

For a while he lay peacefully, his eyes open, gazing thoughtfully at a gray ceiling. From nearby, a man's voice said:

"There's no use expecting it."

Garson turned his head, his first alert movement. A row of hospital-like cots stretched there, other rows beyond. From the nearest bed, a pair of fine, bright, cheerful eyes stared at him. The man lay with his head crotched in a bunched, badly rumpled pillow. He said:

"Expecting to feel surprised, I mean. You won't. You've been conditioned into recovering on a gradual scale, no excitement, no hysteria, nothing that will upset you. The doctors, though Planetarian trained, are all men of the past; and up to a day ago, they pronounced you—"

Quite amazingly, the man paused; his brown eyes darkened in frown, then he smiled with an equally amazing grimness:

"I nearly said too much there. Actually you may be strong enough to stand any shock now, conditioning or no. But the fact is you'll learn the hard truths of your predicament soon enough, without getting yourself into a nervous state now. Here's a preliminary warning: Toughen your mind for bad news."

Strangely, he felt only the dimmest curiosity, and no sense of alarm at all. After what Dr. Lell had said directly and by implication of the Planetarians, no danger here could surpass what he had already been through. The only emotion he could sense within himself had to do with his double purpose of rescuing Norma from the recruiting station and—

He said aloud: "If I should be asleep the next time a doctor or Planetarian comes in, will you waken me? I've got something to tell them."

The odd, mirthless smile of the other made Garson frown. His voice was almost sharp, as he asked:

"What's the matter?"

The stranger shook his head half pityingly: "I've been twenty-seven days in this stage, and I've never seen a Planetarian. As for telling anyone on the Planetarian side anything, I've already told you to expect bad news. I know you have a message to deliver. I even know from Dra Derrel what it is, but don't ask me how he found out. All I can say is, you'll have to forget about delivering any message to anyone. Incidentally, my name is Mairphy—Edard Mairphy."

Garson lay quite still. For the moment he wasn't interested in names or the mystery of how they knew his message. There was a vague thrill of worry in the back of his mind. Every word this gentle-faced, gentle-voiced young man had spoken was packed with dark, tremendous implications.

He stared at Mairphy, but there was only the frank, open face, the friendly, half-grim smile, the careless wisp of bright, brown hair coming down over one temple—nothing at all of danger.

Besides, where could any danger be coming from? From the Planetarians?

That was ridiculous. Regardless of their shortcomings, the Planetarians were the one race of this "time" that must be supported. They might have curious, even difficult habits, but the other side was evil almost beyond imagination. Between them, there was no question of choice.

His course was simple. As soon as he was allowed to get up—and he felt perfectly well now—he would set out to make contact with a Planetarian in a reasonable persistent manner. The whole affair was beginning to show unpleasant, puzzling aspects, but—

He grew aware of Mairphy's voice: "The warning is all I'll say on that subject for the time being. There's something else, though. Do you think you'll be able to get up in about an hour? I mean, do you feel all right?"

Garson nodded, puzzled: "I think so. Why?"

"We'll be passing the Moon about then, and I understand it's a sight worth—"

"*What?*"

Mairphy was staring at him. He said slowly: "I forgot. I was so busy not telling you about our main danger, it didn't occur to me that you were unconscious when we started."

He shrugged. "Well, we're on our way to Venus; and even if there was nothing else, the cards would be stacked against you by that fact alone. There are no Planetarians aboard this ship, only human beings out of the past and tentacles of the Observer. There's not a chance in the world of you speaking to any of them because—"

He stopped; then: "There I nearly went again, damn it! I'll let out the devilish truth yet, before you ought to hear it."

Garson scarcely heard. The shock wouldn't go away. He lay in a daze of wonder, overwhelmed by the incredible fact that he was in space. *In space!*

He felt suddenly outmaneuvered. Even the events he knew about were abruptly a million miles ahead of his plans.

At first, the very idea was incredibly shocking. Pain pulsed in his temples from the wave of blood that charged there. He sat, rigidly, awkwardly, in the bed; and, finally, in a chocked voice he said:

"How long will it take to get to Venus?"

"Ten days, I believe!"

Very cautiously, Garson allowed the figures to penetrate. Hope surged through him. It wasn't so bad as his first despairing thought had pictured it. Ten days to get there, ten days to persuade someone to let a Planetarian have a glimpse of his mind, ten days to get back to Earth.

A month! He frowned. Actually, that wasn't so good. Wars had been lost, great empires collapsed in less time than that. Yet, how could be deliver his message—on a spaceship. Venus-bound? Courses of initial action suggested themselves, but—

He said in a troubled tone. "If I was back in 1941, at this point I would try to see the captain of the ship. But you've made me doubt that normal procedures apply on a Planetarian space liner. Frankly, what are my chances?"

He saw that the young man was grim. "Exactly none!" Mairphy replied. "This is no joke, Garson. As I said before, Derrel knows and is interested in your message, don't ask me how or what or when. He was a political leader in his own age, and he's a marvel at mechanics, but, according to him, he knows only the normal, everyday things of his life.

You'll have to get used to the idea of being in with a bunch of men from past ages, some queer ducks among them, Derrel the queerest of them all.

"But forget that! Just remember that you're on a spaceship in an age so far ahead of your own that there's not even a record of your time in the history books and—"

Abruptly, that was what got him. Garson lay back, breathlessly still, dazzled once again by his strange, tremendous environment, straining for impression. But there was no sense of movement, no abnormality at all. The world was quiet; the room seemed like an unusually large dormitory in a hospital.

After a moment of tenseness, he allowed his body to relax, and the full, rich flood of thought to flow in. In that eager tide, the danger to which Mairphy had referred was like a figment of imagination, a dim, darkling shadow in remoteness.

There was only the wonder, only Venus and—this silent, swift-plunging spaceship.

Venus! He let the word roll around in his mind, and it was like rich, intellectual food, luscious beyond reason to a mind shaped and trained as was his.

Venus—For ages the dreams of men had reached longingly into the skies, immeasurably fascinated by the mind-staggering fact of other worlds as vast as their own; continents, seas, rivers, treasure beyond estimate.

And now for him there was to be glittering reality. Before that fact, other urgencies faded. Norma must be rescued, of course; the strange message delivered; but if it was to be his destiny to remain in this world till the end of war, then he could ask nothing more of those years than this glowing sense of adventure, this shining opportunity to learn and see and know in a scientist's heaven.

He grew aware that Mairphy was speaking: "You know"—the young man's voice was thoughtful—"it's just possible that it might be a good idea if you did try to see the captain. I'll have to speak to Derrel before any further action is taken and—"

Garson sighed wearily. He felt suddenly genuinely exhausted, mentally and physically, by the twisting courses of events.

"Look," he said, "a minute ago you stated it was absolutely impossible for me to see the captain; now it seems it might be a good idea and so the impossible becomes poss—"

A sound interrupted his words, a curious hissing sound that seemed to press at him. With a start he saw that men were climbing out of bed, groups that had been standing in quiet conversation were breaking up. In a minute, except for some three dozen who had not stirred from their beds, the manpower of that great room had emptied through a far door. As the door closed, Mairphy's tense voice stabbed at him:

"Quick! Help me out of bed and into my wheel chair. Damn this game leg of mine, but I've got to see Derrel. The attack must not take place until you've tried to see the captain. Quick, man!"

"Attack!" Garson began, then with an effort, caught himself. Forcing coolness through the shock that was gathering in his system, he lay back; he said in a voice that teetered on the edge of tremble:

"I'll help you when you tell me what all this is about. Start talking! Fast!"

Mairphy sighed: "The whole thing's really very simple. They herded together a bunch of skeptics—that's us; it means simply men who know they are in another age, and aren't superstitious about it, always potential explosive, as the Planetarians well understood. But what they didn't realize was that Derrel was what he was.

"The mutiny was only partially successful. We got the control room, the engine room, but only one of the arsenals. The worst thing was that one of the tentacles escaped our trap, which means that the Observer Machine has been informed, and that battleships have already been dispatched after us.

"Unless we can gain full control fast, we'll be crushed; and the whole hunch of us will be executed out of hand."

Mairphy finished with a bleak smile: "That includes you and every person in this room, lame, sick or innocent. The Planetarians leave the details of running their world in the hands of a monster machine called the Observer; and the Observer is mercilessly logical.

"That's what I meant by bad news. All of us are committed to victory or to death—and now, quick, let me get to Derrel, and stop this attack!"

His mind felt a swollen, painful thing with the questions that quivered there: skeptics—tentacles—mutiny— Good heavens!

It was not until after Mairphy's power-driven wheel chair had vanished through the door that had swallowed the men that he realized how weary he was. He lay down on the bed, and there didn't seem to be a drop of emotion in him. He was thinking, a slow, flat, gray thought, of the part of the message that had come to him in the depersonalizing machine, the solemn admonishment: "—Take no unnecessary risks—*stay alive!*"

What a chance!

The Moon floated majestically against the backdrop of black space, a great globe of light that grew and grew. For a solid hour it clung to size, but at last it began to retreat into distance.

It was the gathering immensity of that distance that brought to Garson a sudden empty sense, a dark consciousness that he was again a tiny pawn in this gigantic struggle of gigantic forces.

He watched until the glowing sphere of Moon was a shadowy, pea-sized light half hidden by the dominating ball of fire that was the Earth. His immediate purpose was already a waxing shape in his mind, as he turned to stare down at Mairphy in his wheel chair; it struck him there were lines of fatigue around the other's eyes; he said:

"And now that the attack has been called off, I'd like to meet this mysterious Derrel. After which you'd better go straight to sleep."

The younger man drooped. "Help me to my bed, will you?"

From the bed, Mairphy smiled wanly. "Apparently, I'm the invalid, not you. The paralyzer certainly did you no real harm, but the energy chopper made a pretty job of my right leg. By the way, I'll introduce you to Derrel when I wake up."

His slow, deep breathing came as a distinct shock to Garson. He felt deserted, at a loss for action, and finally annoyed at the way he had come to depend on the company of another man.

For a while, he wandered around the room, half aimlessly, half in search of the extraordinary Derrel. But gradually his mind was drawn from that undetermined purpose, as the men, the incredible men, grew into his consciousness.

They swaggered, these chaps. When they stood, they leaned with casual grace, thumbs nonchalantly tucked into belts or into the armpits of strangely designed vests. Not more than half a dozen of that bold, vigorous-looking crew seemed to be the introvert, studious type.

Here were men of the past, adventurers, soldiers of fortune, who had mutinied as easily as, under slightly different circumstances, they might have decided to fight for, instead of against, their captors.

Bad psychology on the part of the Planetarians?

Impossible because they were perfectionists in the art.

The explanation, of course, was that an intelligence and ability as great as their own, or nearly as great, had entered the scene unknown to them, and easily duped the men of the past who operated the spaceship.

Derrel!

The whole thing was strangely, breathlessly exciting, a glittering facet of the full, violent aliveness of the life that had raged over the Earth through the ages; here were men come full grown out of their own times, loving life, yet by their casual, desperate attempt at mutiny proving that they were not remotely afraid of death.

One man was the responsible, the activating force and—

Three times Garson was sure that he had picked out Derrel, but each time he changed his mind before actually approaching the stranger.

It was only gradually that he grew aware of a lank man. The first coherent picture he had was of a tall, gawky man with a long face that was hollow-cheeked. The fellow was dressed casually in a gray shirt and gray trousers. Except for the cleanness of the clothes, he could have stepped out of a 1936 dust-bowl farmhouse.

The man half stood, half leaned, awkwardly against the side of one of the hospital-type beds, and he said nothing. Yet, somehow, he was the center of the group that surrounded him. The leader!

After a moment Garson saw that the other was surreptitiously studying him; and that was all he needed. Quite frankly, quite boldly, he surveyed the man. Before that searching gaze, the deceptive, farmerish appearance of the other dissolved like dark fog in a bright sun.

The hollow cheeks showed suddenly as a natural strength that distorted the almost abnormal strength of that face. The line of jaw ceased to be merely framework supporting the chin, showed instead in all its grim hardness, like the blunt edge of an anvil, not too prominently thrust forward. The nose—

At that point somebody addressed the man as Mr. Derrel; and it was as if Derrel had been waiting for the words as for a signal.

He stepped forward; be said in the calmest voice Garson had ever heard:

"Professor Garson, do you mind if I speak to you"—he motioned forcefully yet vaguely—"over there?"

Garson was amazed to find himself hesitating. For nearly an hour he had had the purpose of finding this man, but now—it was simply not in his nature to yield readily to the leadership of others. It struck him sharply that even to agree to Derrel's simple request was to place himself, somehow, subtly under the man's domination.

Their eyes met, his own hard with thought, Derrel's at first expressionless, then smiling. The smile touched his face and lighted it in astounding fashion. His entire countenance seemed to change; briefly, his personality was like a flame that burned away opposition.

Garson was startled to hear himself say: "Why, yes, what is it you wish?"

The answer was cool and tremendous: "You have received a warning message, but you need look no further for its source. I am Dra Derrel of the Wizard race of Lin. My people are fighting under great difficulties to save a universe threatened by a war whose weapons are based on the time energy itself."

"Just a minute!" Garson's voice was harsh in his own ears. "Are you trying to tell me you ... your people sent that message?"

"I am!" The man's face was almost gray-steel in color. "And to explain that our position is now so dangerous that your own suggestion that you see Captain Gurradin has become the most important necessity and the best plan—"

Strangely, it was that on which his mind fastened, not the revelation but the mind picture of himself leaving the placid security of this room, delivering himself into the ruthless clutches of men of some other, more merciless past than his own—and to tentacles—

Like a monstrous shadow overhanging every other emotion, the dark realization came that the law of averages would not permit him to face death again without—death!

Slowly, the other thought—Derrel's revelation—began to intrude. He examined it, at first half puzzled that it continued to exist in his mind; somehow, it wasn't really adequate, and certainly far from satisfactory as an explanation of all that had happened.

—A message delivered into the black narrowness of a Glorious depersonalizing machine, hurtled across distance, through a web of Glorious defenses from—

Derrel!

Garson frowned, his dissatisfaction growing by the second. He stared at the man from slitted eyes; and saw that the other was standing in that peculiar easy-awkward posture of his, gazing at him coolly as if—the impression was a distinct one—as if waiting patiently for his considered reaction. That was oddly reassuring, but it was far, far from being enough. Garson said:

"I can see I've got to be frank, or this thing's going to be all wrong. My angle goes like this: I've been building a picture in my mind, an impossible picture I can see now, of beings with tremendous powers. I thought of them as possibly acting from the future of this future, but, whatever their origin, I had the uttermost confidence that they were super-human, super-Glorious and—"

He stopped because the long-faced man was smiling in twisted fashion. "And now," Derrel said wryly, "the reality does not come up to your expectations. An ordinary man stands before you, and your dreams of god-power interfering in the affairs of men becomes what it always was basically: wishful hallucination!"

"And in its place—what?" Garson questioned coolly.

Derrel took up the words steadily: "In its place is a man who failed to take over a spaceship, and now faces a sordid death himself."

Garson parted his lips to speak, then closed them again, puzzled. There was nothing so far but honesty almost excessive. Still—confession was far from being satisfactory explanation.

Derrel's voice, rich with the first hint of passion the man had shown, beat at him: "Are you sure it was such a great failure? One man manipulating strangers who had no reason to fight—many of them invalids—and winning a partial success against the highly trained crew of a completely mechanized space cruiser, a crew supported by no less than four tentacles of the omniscient Observer."

Stripped as the account was, it brought a vivid fascinating flash of what the reality of that fight must have been. Flesh-and-blood men charging forward in the face of—energy—weapons, dealing and receiving desperate wounds, overwhelming the alert and abundant staff of an armored ship, and four tentacles, whatever they were. Tentacle—a potent, ugly word, inhuman— Nevertheless—

"If you're going to use logic on this," Garson said slowly, "you'll have to put up with my brand for another minute. Why did you go in for mutiny in the first place under such difficult conditions?"

Amazingly, the man's eyes flashed with contemptuous fire. When he spoke, his voice was thick with passion: "Can you reasonably ask for more than the reality, which is that our position is desperate because we took risks? We took risks because"—he paused, as if gathering himself; then his words flamed on—"because I am of the race of Wizards; and we were masters of the Earth of our time because we were bold. As was ever the way with the Wizards, I chose the difficult, the dangerous path; and I tell you that victory with all that it means is not yet beyond our grasp. I—"

In the queerest fashion, the glowing voice died. An intent expression crept into the man's eyes; he tilled his head, as if listening for a remote sound. Garson shook the odd impression out of his mind, and returned to the thoughts that had been gathering while the other was speaking; he said coolly:

"Unfortunately, for all that emotion, I was trained to be a scientist; and I was never taught to accept justification as a substitute for explanation. I—"

It was his turn to fall silent. With startled gaze, he watched the tall, gawky figure stride at top speed along the wall. The Wizard man halted as swiftly as he had started, but now his fingers were working with a strangely frantic speed at a section of the wall.

As Garson came up, the wall slid free; and Derrel, half lowered, half dropped it to the floor. In the hollow space revealed, wires gleamed; and a silver, shining glow point showed. Unhesitatingly, Derrel grasped at the white-hot-looking thing, and jerked. There was a faint flash of fire; and when his hand came away the glow was gone.

Derrel stared at Garson grimly: "Those seeming wires are not wires at all, but a pure energy web, an electron mold that, over a period of about an hour, can mold a weapon where nothing existed before. Tentacles can focus that type of mold anywhere; and the mold itself is indestructible, but up to a certain stage the molded thing can be destroyed."

Garson braced himself instinctively, as the other faced him squarely Derrel said:

"You can see that, without my special ability to sense energy formations there would have been surprise tragedy."

"Without you," Garson interjected, "there would have been no mutiny. I'm sorry, but I've got the kind of mind that worries about explanations. So—"

The man gazed at him without hostility; he said finally earnestly: "I know your doubts, but you can see yourself that I must go around examining our rather large territory for further electron-mold manifestations. Briefly, we Wizards are a race of the past who developed a science that enabled us to tap the time ways of the Glorious, though we cannot yet build a time machine. In many ways, we are the superiors of either Planetarians or Glorious. Our mathematics showed us that the time energy could not stand strains beyond a certain point; accordingly we have taken and are taking every possible action to save the Universe, the first and most important necessity being that of establishing a base of operations, preferably a spaceship."

He finished quietly: "For the rest, for the time being you must have faith. Regardless of your doubts, you must go to see the captain; we must win this ship before we are overwhelmed. I leave you now to think it over."

He whirled and strode off; and behind him he left half conviction, half confidence, but—Garson thought wryly—no facts!

What a vague, unsatisfactory basis on which to risk the only life he had!

He found himself straining for sounds, but there was no movement, nothing but a straggle of words that came at him from the other men. The ship itself, the wondrous ship, was quiet. It seemed to be suspended in this remote coign of the Universe; and it at least was not restless. It flashed on in tireless, stupendous flight, but basically it was unhurried, isolated from mechanical necessities, knowing neither doubt nor hope, nor fear nor courage.

Doubt! His brain was a dark: opaque mass flecked with the moving lights of thoughts, heavy with the gathering pall of his doubt, knowing finally only one certainty:

With so much at stake, he must find out more about the so-called Wizard of Lin. It would be utterly ridiculous to make some move against the Planetarians, the hope of this war, on the glib say-so of—anyone! But what to do? Where to find out?

The urgent minutes fled. There was the black, incredible vista of space—but no answers offered there. There was lying in bed and staring at the gray ceiling; that was worse. Finally, there was the discovery of the library in a room adjoining the long dormitory; and that held such an immense promise that, for a brief hour, even the sense of urgency faded out of him.

Only gradually did awareness come that the books were a carefully selected collection. At any other time, every word of every page would have held him in thrall, but not now. For a while, with grim good humor, he examined volume after volume to verify his discovery. At last, weary with frustration, he returned to his bed—and saw that Mairphy was awake.

His mind leaped; then he hesitated. It was possible he would have to approach the subject of Derrel warily. He said finally:

"I suppose you've been through the library."

Mairphy shook his head, brown eyes slightly sardonic. "Not that one. But on the basis of the two I have seen, I'll venture to guess they're elementary scientific books, travel books about the planets, but no histories, and nowhere is there a reference to what year this is. They're not even letting us skeptics know that."

Garson cut in almost harshly: "These Planetarians are not such good angels as I thought. In an entirely different, perhaps cleverer way, this ship is organized to press us into their mold just as the Glorious used the deperson—"

He stopped, startled by the hard tenor of his thoughts. Good heavens! At this rate he'd soon work himself into an anti-Planetary fury. Deliberately, he tightened his mind. His job was not to hate, but to ask careful questions about Derrel—and stay alive!

He parted his lips, but before he could speak, Mairphy said: "Oh, the Planetarians are all right. If we hadn't gone in for this damned mutiny, we'd have been treated all right in the long run, provided we kept our mouths shut and conformed."

Garson's mind literally wrenched itself from thought of Derrel. "Mouths shut!" he said. "What do you mean?"

Mairphy laughed mirthlessly: "We're the skeptics who, in a general way, know where we are. The great majority of recruits *don't* know anything except that it's a strange place. For psychological reasons, they've got to feel that they're in perfectly rational surroundings. Their own superstitions provide the solutions.

"A slew of ancient Greeks think they're fighting on the side of Jupiter in the battle of the gods. Religious folks from about four hundred different ignorant ages think for reasons of their own that everything is as it should be. The Lerdite Moralists from the thirtieth century believe this is the war of the Great Machine to control its dissident elements. And the Nelorian Dissenter of the year 7643 to 7699 who— What's the matter?"

Garson couldn't help it. The shock was physical rather than mental. He hadn't, somehow, thought of it when Derrel talked of the Wizards of Lin, but now— His nerves shivered from that casual, stunning array of words. He said finally, shakily:

"Don't mind me. It's those damned dates you've been handing out. I suppose it's really silly to think of time as being a past and a future. It's all there, spread out, six hundred billion earths and universes created every minute."

He drew a deep breath. Damn it, he'd stalled long enough. Any minute Derrel would be coming back and—

He said stiffly: "What about the Wizards of Lin? I heard somebody use the phrase, and it intrigued me."

"Interesting race," Mairphy commented; and Garson sighed with relief. The man suspected no ulterior motive. He waited tensely, as Mairphy went on: "The Wizards discovered some connection between sex and the mind, which gave them superintellect including mental telepathy. Ruled the Earth for about three hundred years, just before the age of Endless Peace set in. Power politics and all that, violence, great on mechanics, built the first spaceship which, according to description, was as good as any that has ever existed since. Most of their secrets were lost. Those that weren't became the property of a special priest clique whose final destruction is a long story and—"

He paused, frowning thoughtfully, while Garson wondered bleakly how he ought to be taking all this. So far, Derrel's story was substantiated practically word for word. Mairphy's voice cut into his indecision:

"There's a pretty story about how the spaceship was invented. In their final struggle for power, a defeated leader, mad with anxiety about his beautiful wife who had been taken as a mistress by the conqueror, disappeared, returned with the ship, got his wife and his power back; and the Derrel dynasty ruled for a hundred years after that—"

"Derrel!" Garson said. "The Derrel dynasty!"

And that, simply yet devastatingly, was that.

The echo of the shock yielded to time and familiarity, and died— They talked about it in low tones; and their hushed baritones formed a queer, deep-throated background to the measured beat of Garson's thoughts.

He stepped back, finally, as Mairphy eagerly called other men. With bleak detachment, he listened while Mairphy's voice recast itself over and over into the same shape, the same story, though the words and even the tone varied with each telling. Always, however, the reaction of the men was the same—joy! Joy at the certainty of victory! And what did it matter what age they went to afterward?

Garson grew abruptly aware that Mairphy was staring at him sharply. Mairphy said: "What's the matter?"

He felt the weight of other gazes on him, as he shrugged and said:

"All this offers little hope for me. History records that we won this ship. But I have still to confront the captain; and history is silent as to whether I lived or died— Frankly, I consider the message that I received in the Glorious depersonalizing machine more important than ever, and accordingly my life is of more importance than that of anyone else on this ship.

"I repeat, our only certainty is that Derrel escaped with the spaceship. Who else lived, we don't know. Derrel—"

"Yes!" said the calm voice of Derrel behind him. "Yes, Professor Garson."

Garson turned slowly. He had no fixed plan; there was the vaguest intention to undermine Derrel's position; and that had made him stress the uncertainty of any of the men escaping. But it wasn't a plan because—there was the unalterable fact that the ship had gotten away; Derrel had won.

No plan— The only factors in his situation were his own tremendous necessities and the inimical environment in which they existed.

For a long moment, he stared at the gangling body, studied the faint triumph that gleamed in the abnormally long yet distinctive face of the Wizard man. Garson said:

"You can read minds. So it's unnecessary to tell you what's going on. What are your intentions?"

Derrel smiled, the glowing, magnetic smile that Garson had already seen. His agate eyes shone, as he surveyed the circle of men; then he began to speak in a strong, resonant voice. There was command in that voice, and a rich, powerful personality behind it, the voice of a man who had won:

"My first intention is to tell everyone here that we are going to an age that is a treasure house of spoils for bold men. Women, palaces, wealth, power for every man who follows me to the death. You know yourself what a damned, barren world we're in now. No women, never anything for us but the prospect of facing death fighting the Glorious still entrenched on Venus or Earth! And a damned bunch of moralists fighting a war to the finish over some queer idea that men ought or ought not to have birth control. Are you with me?"

It was a stirring, a ringing appeal to basic impulses; and the answer could not have been more satisfactory. A roar of voices, cheers; and finally: "What are we waiting for? Let's get going!"

The faint triumph deepened on Derrel's face as he turned back to Garson. He said softly:

"I'm sorry I lied to you, professor, but it never occurred to me that Mairphy or anybody aboard would know my history. I told you what I did because I had read in your mind some of the purposes that moved your actions. Naturally, I applied the first law of persuasion, and encouraged your hopes and desires."

Garson smiled grimly. The little speech Derrel had just given to the men was a supreme example of the encouragement of hopes and desires, obviously opportunistic, insincere and—reliable only if it served the other's future purposes.

He saw that Derrel was staring at him, and he said:

"You know what's in my mind. Perhaps you can give me some of that easy encouragement you dispense. But, remember, it's got to be based on logic. That includes convincing me that, if I go to the captain, it is to your self-interest to set me down near a Planetarian stronghold, and that furthermore—"

The words, all the air in his lungs, hissed out of his body. There was a hideous sense of pressure. He was jerked off his feet; and he had the flashing, uncomprehending vision of two beds passing by beneath him. Then he was falling.

Instinctively, he put out his hand—and took the desperate blow of the crash onto a third bed. He sprawled there, stunned, dismayed, but unhurt and safe.

Safe from what?

He clawed himself erect, and stood swaying, watching other men pick themselves up, becoming aware for the first time of groans, cries of pain and—

A voice exploded into the room from some unseen source: "Control room speaking! Derrel—the damnedest thing has happened. A minute ago, we were thirty million miles from Venus. Now, the planet's just ahead, less than two million miles, plainly visible. What's happened?"

Garson saw Derrel then. The man was lying on his back on the floor, his eyes open, an intent expression on his face. The Wizard man waved aside his extended hands.

"Wait!" Derrel said sharply. "The tentacle aboard this ship has just reported to the Observer on Venus; and is receiving a reply, an explanation of what happened. I'm trying to get it."

His voice changed, became a monotone: "—the seventeenth x space and time manipulations ... taking place somewhere in the future ... several years from now. Your spaceship either by accident or design caught in the eddying current in the resulting time storm— Still not the faintest clue to the origin of the mighty powers being exercised. That is all ... except that battleships are on the way from Venus to help you—"

Derrel stood up; he said quietly: "About what you were saying, Garson, there is no method by which I can prove that I will do anything for you. History records that I lived out my full span of life. Therefore, no self-interest, no danger to the Universe can affect my existence in the past. You'll have to act on the chance that the opportunity offers for us to give you assistance later, and there's no other guarantee I can give."

That at least was straightforward. Only—to the opportunist, even truth was but a means to an end, a means of lulling suspicion. There remained the hard fact that he must take the risks.

He said: "Give me five minutes to think it over. You believe, I can see, that I will go."

Derrel nodded: "Both your conscious and subconscious minds are beginning to accept the idea."

There was utterly no premonition in him of the fantastic thing that was going to happen. He thought, a gray, cold thought:

So he was going! In five minutes.

He stood finally at the wall visiplate, staring out at the burnished silver immensity of Venus. The planet, already cast, was expanding visibly, like a balloon being blown up. Only it didn't stop expanding and, unlike an overgrown balloon, it didn't explode.

The tight silence was broken by the tallest of the three handsome Ganellians. The man's words echoed, not Garson's thoughts, but the tenor, the dark mood of them:

"So much beauty proves once again that war is the most completely futile act of man. And the worst of it is that, somewhere in the future of this 'future' there are people who know who won this war; and they're doing nothing—damn them!"

His impulse was to say something, to add once more his own few facts to that fascinating subject. But instead he held his thought hard on the reality of what he must do—in a minute!

Besides, Mairphy had described the Ganellians as emotional weaklings, who had concentrated on beauty, and with whom it was useless to discuss anything. True, he himself had given quite a few passable displays of emotionalism. Nevertheless—

The thought ended, as Mairphy said almost impatiently: "We've discussed all that before, and we're agreed that either the people of the future do not exist at all—which means the Universe was blown up in due course by the Glorious time-energy barrier—or, on the other hand, if the people of the future exist, they're simply older versions of the million-year-old bodies of the Planetarians or Glorious. If they exist, then the Universe was not destroyed, so why should they interfere in the war?

"Finally, we're agreed that it's impossible that the people of the future, whatever their form, are responsible for the message that came through to Professor Garson. If they can get through a message at all, why pick Garson? Why not contact the Planetarians direct? Or even warn the Glorious of the danger!"

Garson said: "Derrel, what is your plan of attack?"

The reply was cool: "I'm not going to tell you that. Reason: at close range a tentacle can read an unwary mind. I want you to concentrate on the thought that your purpose is aboveboard, don't even think of an attack in connection with it. Wait—don't reply! I'm going to speak to Captain Gurradin!"

"Eh!" Garson began, and stopped.

The Wizard man's eyes were closed, his body rigid. He said, half to Garson, half to the others: "A lot of this stuff here works by mind control—" His voice changed: "Captain Gurradin!"

There was a tense silence; then a steel-hard voice literally spat into the room: "Yes!"

Derrel said: "We have an important communication to make. Professor Garson, one of the men who was unconscious when—"

"I know whom you mean!" interrupted that curt voice. "For God's sake get on with your communication!"

"Not later than the twenty-fourth century," Mairphy whispered to Garson. "Note his reference to God. God was expunged from the dictionary in the 2300s. And is he boiling at this mutiny and what it's done to his prestige!"

It wasn't funny. For all this was going to he real to him. The thought drained; Mairphy became a vague background figure. There was only Derrel and Captain Gurradin; Derrel saying:

"Professor Garson has just become conscious; and he has the answer to the phenomena that carried this spaceship thirty million miles in thirty seconds. He feels that he must see you immediately and communicate his message to the Planetarians at once."

There was a wave of chill laughter: "What fools we'd be to let any of you come here until after the battleships arrive! And that's my answer: He'll have to wait till the battleships arrive."

"His message," said Derrel, "cannot wait. He's coming down now, alone."

"He will be shot on sight."

"I can well imagine," Derrel said scathingly, "what the Planetarians would do to you if he is shot. This has nothing to do with the rest of us. He's coming because he must deliver that message. That is all."

Before Garson could speak, Mairphy said in a distinct voice: "I'm opposed to it. I admit it was my idea in the first place, but I couldn't favor it under such circumstances."

The Wizard man whirled on him. His vibrant voice was a drumming thing as he raged:

"That was a stab in the back to all of us. Here is a man trying to make up his mind on a dangerous mission, and you project a weakening thought. You have said that you come from the stormy period following the 13000 years of Endless Peace. That was after my time, and I know nothing about the age, but it is evident that the softness of the peace period still corroded your people. As a cripple, a weakling, who is not going to do any of the fighting, you will kindly refrain from further advice—to men!"

It could have been devastating, but Mairphy simply shrugged, smiled gently, unaffectedly, at Garson, and said: "I withdraw from the conversation." He finished: "Good luck, friend!"

Derrel, steely-eyed and cold-voiced, said to Garson: "I want to point out one thing. History says we conquered this ship. The only plan we have left revolves around you. Therefore you went to see the captain."

To Garson, to whom logic was the great prime mover, that thought had already come. Besides, his mind had been made up for five minutes.

The second corridor was empty, too; and that strained his tightening nerves to the breaking point. Garson paused stiffly, and wiped the thin line of perspiration from his brow.

And still there was no premonition in him of the incredible ending that was coming—for him; nothing but the deadly actuality of his penetration into the depths of a ship that seemed of endless length, and grew vaster with each step that he took.

A door yielded to his touch; and he peered into a great storeroom, piled with freight, thousands of tons, silent and lifeless as the corridors ahead— He walked on, his mind blanker now, held steady far from the thought of Derrel's intended attack.

He thought vaguely: If Norma could keep from Dr. Lell her action of writing a letter to him, then he could keep any thought from *anything* and—

He was so intent that he didn't see the side corridor till the men burst from it—and had him before he could think of fighting. Not that he intended to fight—

"Bring him in here!" said a hard, familiar voice; and after a moment of peering into the shadows of the receding corridor, be saw a slender man in uniform standing beside—

A tentacle!

That thick, pipe-shaped thing could be nothing else— It rolled forward, as if wheels held it up, and its faceted eyes glared at him. It spoke abruptly in a clear, passionless voice:

"I can catch no thoughts, which is unusual. It presupposes schooling, preparation for mindreading attempts. The Observer advises execution—"

The hard, young man's voice said impatiently: "To hell with the Observer. We can always execute. Bring him in here!"

A door opened; and light splashed out. The door closed behind him; and he saw that the room was no more than a small anteroom to some vaster, darkened room beyond.

But he scarcely noticed that. He was thinking with a stinging shock of fury: The logical Observer advising executions without a hearing. Why, that wasn't reasonable. Damn the stupid Observer!

His fury faded into vast surprise, as he stared at the captain. His first impression had been that the other was a young man, but at this closer view, he looked years older, immeasurably more mature. And, somehow, in his keyed-up state, that observation brought immense astonishment.

Amazement ended, as his mind registered the blazing question in Captain Gurradin's eyes. Quite automatically, he launched into his story.

When he had finished, the commander turned his hard face to the tentacle: "Well?" he said.

The tentacle's voice came instantly, coldly: "The Observer recalls to your memory its earlier analysis of this entire situation: The destruction of Tentacles 1601, 2 and 3 and the neutralization of electron molds could only have been accomplished with the assistance of a mind reader. Accordingly, unknown to us, a mind reader was aboard.

"Four races in history solved the secret of the training essential to mental telepathy. Of these, only the Wizards of Lin possessed surpassing mechanical ability—"

It was the eeriness that held his whole mind—at first—the fantastic reality of this *thing* talking and reasoning like a human being. The Observer Machine of the Glorious that he had seen was simply a vast machine, too big to grasp mentally; like some gigantic number, it was there, and that was all. But this—this long, tubular monstrosity with its human voice and—

Eeriness ended in hard, dismaying realization that a creature that could analyze Derrel's identity might actually prove that death was his own logical lot, and that all else was illusion— The dispassionate voice went on:

"Wizard men are bold, cunning and remorseless, and they take no action in an emergency that is not related to their purpose. Therefore, this man's appearance is part of a plot. Therefore destroy him and withdraw from the ship. The battleships will take all further action necessary, without further loss of life."

That was stunning. With a sudden, desperate fear, Garson saw that Captain Gurradin was hesitating. The commander said unhappily: "Damn it, I hate to admit defeat."

"Don't be tedious!" said the tentacle. "Your forces might win, but the battleships *will* win."

Decision came abruptly. "Very well," said the captain curtly, "Willant, de-energize this prisoner and—"

Garson said in a voice that he scarcely recognized, an abnormally steady voice: "What about my story?"

Strangely, there was a moment of silence.

"Your story," the tentacle said finally—and Garson's mind jumped at the realization that it was the tentacle, and not the captain who answered—"your story is rejected by the Observer as illogical. It is impossible that anything went wrong with a Glorious depersonalizing machine. The fact that you were repersonalized after the usual manner on reaching our lines is evidence of your condition, because the repersonalizing machine reported nothing unusual in your case.

"Furthermore, even if it was true, the message you received was stupid, because no known power or military knowledge could force the surrender of Delpa one minute sooner. It is impossible to neutralize a time-energy barrier at more than one point at one time without destroying the neutralizing machine. Consequently, the attack can only be made at one point; the military maneuver being used is the ultimate development of dimensional warfare in a given area of space. And so—"

The words scarcely penetrated, though all the sense strained through, somehow. His mind was like an enormous weight, dragging at one thought, one hope. He said, fighting for calmness now:

"Commander, by your manner to this tentacle and its master, I can see that you have long ago ceased to follow its conclusions literally. Why: because it's inhuman; the Observer is a great reservoir of facts that can be coordinated on any subject, *but it is limited by the facts it knows*. It's a machine, and, while it may be logical to destroy me before you leave the ship, you know and I know that it is neither necessary nor just, and what is overwhelmingly more important, it can do no harm to hold me prisoner, and make arrangements for a Planetarian to examine the origin of the message that came to me."

He finished in a quiet, confident tone: "Captain, from what one of the men told me, you're from the 2000s A. D. I'll wager that they still had horse races in your day. I'll wager furthermore that no machine could ever understand a man getting a hunch and betting his bottom dollar on a dark horse. You've already been illogical in not shooting me at sight, as you threatened on the communicator; in not leaving the ship as the Observer advised; in letting me talk on here even as the attack on your enemies is beginning—for there is an attack of some kind, and it's got the best brain on this ship behind it. But that's unimportant because you're going to abandon ship.

"What is important is this: You must carry your illogic to its logical conclusion. Retrieve your prestige, depend for once in this barren life here on luck and luck alone—"

The hard eyes did not weaken by a single gleam, but the hard voice spoke words that sounded like purest music:

"Willant, take this prisoner into the lifeboat and—"

It was at that moment it happened. With victory in his hands, the knowledge that more than two years remained before the time-energy barrier would be threatening the Universe, the whole, rich, tremendous joy that he had won—everything. All of that, and unutterable relief, and more, was in his brain when—

A voice came into his mind, strong and clear and as irresistible as living fire, a woman's voice—Norma's!

"Jack! Jack! Help me! I need you! Oh, Jack, come—"

The Universe spun. Abruptly, there was no ship; and he was pitching into a gulf of blackness. Inconceivable distance fell behind him and—just like that—the fall ended.

There was no ship, no earth, no light—

Time must have passed; for slow thought was in him; and the night remained.

No, not night. He could realize that now, for there was time to realize. It was not night; it was—emptiness. Nothingness!

Briefly, the scientist part of his brain grasped at the idea; the possibility of exploring, of examining this nonspace. But there was nothing to examine, nothing in him to examine *with*, no senses that could record comprehend—nothingness!

Dismay came, a black tidal wave that surged in wild confusion through his being; his brain shrank from the sheer, terrible strain of impression. But, somehow, time passed; the flood of despair streamed out of him. There remained *nothingness!*

Change came abruptly. One instant there was that complete isolation; the next—

A man's voice said matter-of-factly: "This one is a problem. How the devil did he get into the configuration of the upper arc? You'd think he fell in."

"No report of any planes passing over Delpa!" said a second voice. "Better ask the Observer if there's any way of getting him out."

Figuratively, gravely, his mind nodded in agreement to that. He'd have to get out, of course, and—

His brain paused. *Out* of where? Nothingness?

For a long, tense moment, his thought poised over that tremendous question, striving to penetrate the obscure depths of it, that seemed to waver just beyond the reach of his reason. There had been familiar words spoken—

Delpa! An ugly thrill chased through his mind. He wasn't in Delpa, or—he felt abruptly, horribly, sick—*or was he?*

The sickness faded into a hopeless weariness, almost a chaotic dissolution: what did it matter where he was? Once more, he was a complete prisoner of a powerful, dominating environment, prey to forces beyond his lightest control, unable to help Norma, unable to help himself and—

Norma! He frowned mentally, empty of any emotion, unresponsive even to the thought that what had happened implied some enormous and deadly danger—for Norma! There was only the curious, almost incredible way that she had called him; and nightmarishly he had fallen—toward Delpa! Fallen into an insane region called the configuration of the upper arc—

With a start, he realized that the Observer's voice had been speaking for some seconds:

"—it can be finally stated that no plane, no machine of any kind, has flown over Delpa since the seventeenth time and space manipulation four weeks ago. Therefore the man you have discovered in the upper arc is an enigma, whose identity must be solved without delay. Call your commander."

He waited, for there was nothing to think about—at least not at first. Memory came finally that the spaceship had been pulled a million miles a second by the mysterious seventeenth manipulation of time and space; only Derrel had distinctly described it as a repercussion from several years in the future. Now, the Observer talked as if it had happened four weeks ago. Funny!

"Nothing funny about it!" said a fourth voice, a voice so finely pitched, directed into the stream of his thought that he wondered briefly, blankly, whether he had thought the words, or spoken them himself; then:

"Professor Garson, you are identified. The voice you are hearing is that of a Planetarian who can read your mind."

A Planetarian! Wave on wave of relief made a chaos of his brain. With a dreadful effort, he tried to speak, but there was not even a sense of tongue, or lips, or body, nothing but his mind there in that—emptiness; his mind revolving swiftly, ever more swiftly around the host of things he simply had to know. It was the voice, the cool, sane voice, and the stupendous things it was saying, that gradually quieted the turmoil that racked him:

"The answer to what worries you most is that Miss Matheson was the center of the seventeenth space and time manipulation, the first time a human being has been used.

"The manipulation consisted of withdrawing one unit of the entire Solar System from the main stream without affecting the continuity of the main system; one out of the ten billion a second was swung clear in such a fashion that the time energy with its senseless, limitless power began to recreate it, carrying on two with the same superlative ease as formerly with only one.

"Actually, there are now eighteen solar systems existing roughly parallel to each other—seventeen manipulated creations and the original. My body, however, exists in only two of these because none of the previous sixteen manipulations occurred in my lifetime. Naturally, these two bodies of mine exist in separate worlds and will never again have contact with each other.

"Because she was the center of activity, Norma Matheson has her being in the main solar system only. The reason your physical elements responded to her call is that she now possesses the Insel mind power. Her call merely drew you toward her and not to her, because she lacks both the intelligence and the knowledge necessary to a competent employment of her power. As she did not protect you from intermediate dangers, you fell straight into the local time energy barrier surrounding the city of Delpa, which promptly precipitated you into the time emptiness where you now exist.

"Because of the angle of your fall, it will require an indefinite period for the machines to solve the equation that will release you. Until then, have patience!"

"Wait!" Garson thought urgently. "The great time-energy barrier! It should be completed about now!"

"In two weeks at most," came the cool reply. "We received your story, all right, and transmitted the startling extent of the danger to the Glorious. In their pride and awful determination, they see it merely as a threat to make us surrender—or else! To us, however, the rigidly controlled world they envision means another form of death—a worse form. No blackmail will make us yield, and we have the knowledge that people of the future sent the warning. Therefore—we won!"

There was no time to think that over carefully. Carson projected his next question hurriedly: "Suppose they're not of the future, not of this seventeenth, or is it eighteenth, solar system? What will happen to me if this solar system explodes out of existence?"

The answer was cooler still: "Your position is as unique as that of Miss Matheson. You fell out of the past into the future; you *missed* the manipulation. Therefore you exist, not in two solar systems, but only where you are, attached in a general way to us. Miss Matheson exists only in the main system. There is no way in my knowledge that you two can ever come together again. Accustom yourself to that idea."

That was all. His next thought remained unanswered. Time passed; and his restless spirit drooped. Life grew dim within him. He lay without thought on the great, black deep.

Immense, immeasurable time passed; and he waited, but no voices came to disturb his cosmic grave. Twice, forces tugged at him. The first time he thought painfully:

The time-energy barrier of the Glorious had been completed, and the pressure, the tugging was all he felt of the resulting destruction.

If that had happened, nothing, no one would ever come to save him!

That first tugging, and the thought that went with it, faded into remoteness, succumbed to the weight of the centuries, was lost in the trackless waste of the aeons that slid by. And finally, when it was completely forgotten, when every thought had been repeated uncountable times, when every plan of action, every theory, every hope and despair—everything—had been explored to the nth degree—the second tug of pressure came.

A probing sensation it was, as if he was being examined; and finally a flaming, devastatingly powerful thought came at him from—outside!

"I judge it an extrusion from a previous universe, a very low form of life, intelligence .007, unworthy of our attention. It must be registered for its infinitesimal influence and interference with energy flowage—and cast adrift."

Returning consciousness stirred in her body. She felt the sigh that breathed from her lips, as dim awareness came that she must leave this place. But there was not yet enough life in her nerves, no quickening of the coordination, the concentration, so necessary to the strange, masochistic power she had been given.

She thought drearily: If only she had gone to a window instead of projecting her weak flesh against an impenetrable wall.

She must get to the breakfast-nook window that overlooked the roof.

She stood at the window, weary with pain, vaguely startled by the swift reaction to her thought. Hope came violently, and the thought that she had been briefly crushed by the hard reality of the wall revived—"Pain— No pain can touch me—"

Behind her, footsteps and other—stranger—sounds crashed on the stairway; behind her, the outer door blinked into ravenous flame; ahead— was the dark, lonely night.

She scrambled to the sill— In her ears was the sound of the things that were swarming into her apartment, forcing her to swift *will*. From the edge of the roof she could see the milling beast men on the sidewalk below, and she could see the street corner a hundred yards away.

Instantly, she was at the corner, standing lightly, painlessly, on the pavement. But there were too many cars for further "power" travel, cars that would make devastatingly hard walls.

As she stood in a passion of uncertainty, one of the cars slowed to a stop; and it was the simplest thing to run forward, open the door and climb in, just as it started forward again. There was a small man crouching in the dimness behind the steering wheel. To him, she said, almost matter-of-factly:

"Those men! They're chasing me!"

A swarm of the beast men wallowed awkwardly into the revealing glow of the corner light, squat, apelike, frightening things. Her driver yelped shrilly: "Good God!" The car accelerated.

Almost instantly, the man was babbling: "Get out! Get out! I can't afford to get mixed up in a thing like this! I've got a family—wife—children—waiting for me this instant at home. Get out!"

He shoved at her with one hand, as if he would somehow push her through the closed door. And, because her brain was utterly pliant, utterly geared to flight, she felt scarcely a quiver of resistance. A neon light a block away caught her gaze, her attention, and fitted completely into her automatic yielding to this man's desire. She said:

"There's a taxi stand. Let me off there—"

By the time she climbed out, tentacles were glittering shapes in the air above the dim street behind her. She struck at them with her mind, but they only sagged back, like recoiling snakes, still under control, obviously prepared now for her power.

In the taxi, her mind reverted briefly in astounded thought: That mouse of a man! Had she actually let him control her, instead of forcing the little pipsqueak of a human to her mighty will—

Will! She must use her will. No tentacle can come within—within— She'd have to be practical. How far had they retreated from her power— half a mile? No tentacle can come within half a mile of this car—

Eagerly, she stared out of the rear window, and her eyes widened as she saw they were a hundred yards away and coming closer. *What was wrong?* In brief, shrinking expectation she waited for the devastating fire of third-order energies; and when it did not come, she thought: This car it must be made to go faster!

There were other cars ahead, and some passing, but altogether not many. There was room for terrible speeds if she had courage, didn't lose control and if the power would work.

"Through there," she directed, *"and through there and around that corner—"*

She heard shrill yells from the driver, but for a time the very extent of his dismay brought encouragement—that faded bleakly as the tentacles continued their glittering course behind her, sometimes close, sometimes far away, but always relentlessly on her trail, unshakably astute in frustrating every twist of her thought, every turn of the car, every hope, only—

Why didn't they attack?

There was no answer to that, as the long night of flight dragged on, minute by slow minute. Finally, pity touched her for the almost mad driver, who half sat, half swooned behind the steering wheel, held to consciousness and to sanity—she could see in his mind—only by the desperate knowledge that this car was his sole means of livelihood, and nothing else mattered besides that, not even death.

Let him go, she thought. It was sheer cruelty to include him in the fate that was gathering out of the night for her. Let him go, but not yet.

At first, she couldn't have told what the purpose was that quivered in her mind. But it was there, deep and chill and like death itself, and she kept directing the car without knowing exactly where she was going.

Conscious understanding of her unconscious will to death came finally, as she climbed to the ground and saw the glint of river through the trees of a park. She thought then, quite simply:

Here in this park, beside this river, where nearly four years before she had come starving and hopeless to commit suicide—here she would make her last stand!

She watched the tentacles floating toward her through the trees, catching little flashing glimpses of them, as the dim, electric lights of the park shimmered against their metallic bodies; and the vast wonder came, untainted by fear:

Was this real? Was it possible that these living, miasmaticlike emanations from the most dreadful nightmare conceivable were actually surrounding her, and that in all this great world of 1944 there was no one, no weapon, no combination of air, land and sea forces, nothing that could offer her even a husk of protection?

In a sudden, wild exasperation, she thrust her power at the nearest glint—and laughed a curt, futile laugh when the thing did not even quiver. So far as the tentacles were concerned, her power had been nullified. The implications were ultimate: when Dr. Lell arrived, he would bring swift death with him, unless—

She scrambled down the steep bank to the dark edge of the sullen river; and the intellectual mood that had brought her here to this park where once she had wanted death filled her being. She stood taut, striving for a return of the emotion, for the thought of it was not enough.

If only she could recapture the black, *emotional* mood of that other dark night!

A cool, damp breeze whisked her cheeks—but there was not a fraction of real desire to taste those ugly waters. She wanted, not death, nor power, nor the devastation of third-order energies, but marriage, a home with green grass and a flower garden; she wanted life, contentment, Garson!

Garson!

It was more of a prayer than a command that rose from her lips in that second call for help, an appeal from the depths of her need to the only man who in all these long, deadly years had been in her thoughts:

"Jack, wherever you are, come to me here on Earth, come through the emptiness of time, come safely without pain, without body hurt or damage, and with mind clear. Come now!"

With a dreadful start, she jerked back. For a man stood beside her there by the dark waters!

The breeze came stronger. It brought a richer, more tangy smell of river stingingly into her nostrils. But it wasn't physical revival she needed. It was her mind again that was slow to move, her mind that had never yet reacted favorably to her power, her mind lying now like a cold weight inside her.

For the figure stood with stonelike stolidity, like a lump of dark, roughly shaped clay given a gruesome half-life; she thought in a ghastly dismay: Had she recalled from the dead into dreadful existence a body that may have been lying in its grave for generations?

The thing stirred and became a man. Garson said in a voice that sounded hesitant and huskily unnatural in his own ears:

"I've come—but my mind is only clearing now. And speech comes hard after a quadrillion years." He shuddered with the thought of the countless ages he had spent in eternity; then: "I don't know what happened, I don't know what danger made you call me a second time or whether any exists; but, whatever the situation, I've thought it all out.

"You and I are being used by the mysterious universe manipulators because, according to their history, we *were* used. They would not have allowed us to get into such desperate straits if they could come to us physically, and yet it is obvious that everything will fail for them, for us, unless they can make some direct physical contact and show us how to use the vast power you have been endowed with.

"They must be able to come only through some outside force; and only yours exists in our lives. Therefore, call them, call them in any words, for they must need only the slightest assistance. Call them, and afterward we can talk and plan and hope."

Thought began to come to her, and questions, all the questions that had ever puzzled her: Why had Dr. Lell kept repeating that she had made no trouble, according to the Glorious historical record of her, when trouble was all she had ever given? Why had she been able to defeat the first tentacle, and yet now her power that had called *the* man from some remote time was futile against them? And where was Dr. Lell?

With an effort she finally roused her brain from its slough of pondering over paradox. What words she used then, she could not have repeated for no memory of them remained a moment after they were spoken. In her mind was only a fascinated horror of expectation that grew *and grew*, as a sound came from the water near her feet.

The water stirred; it sighed as if yielding to some body that pressed its dark elements; it gurgled with a queer, obscene horror; and a body blacker than itself, and bigger than any man made a glinting, ugly rill of foam—

It was Jack Garson's fingers, strong and unflinching, grasping her, and his hard, determined voice that prevented her from uttering the panicky words of demon exorcise that quivered at the verge of her mind.

"Wait!" he said. "It's victory, not defeat. Wait!"

"Thank you, Professor Garson!" The voice that came out of the darkness held a strange, inhuman quality that kept her taut and uneasy. It went on: "For your sakes, I could approach in no other way. We of the four hundred and ninetieth century A. D. are human in name only. There is a dreadful irony in the thought that war, the destroyer of men, finally changed man into a beastlike creature. One solace remains: We saved our minds and our souls at the expense of our bodies.

"Your analysis was right, Professor Garson, as far as it went. The reason we cannot use so much as a single time machine from our age is that our whole period will be in a state of abnormal unbalance for hundreds of thousands of years; even the tiniest misuse of energy could cause unfore-seeable changes in the fabric of time energy, which is so utterly indifferent to the fate of men. Our method could only be the indirect and partially successful one of isolating the explosion on one of eighteen solar systems, and drawing all the others together to withstand the shock. This was not so difficult as it sounds, for time yields easily to simple pressures.

"Miss Matheson, the reason the tentacles could trail you is that you were being subjected to psychological terrors. The tentacles that have been following you through the night were not real but third-order light projections of tentacles, designed to keep you occupied till Dr. Lell could bring his destroyer machines to bear. Actually, you have escaped all their designs. How? I have said time yields easily to proper pressures. Such a pressure existed as you stood by the river's edge trying to recall the black mood of suicide. It was easier for you who have power to slip through time to that period nearly four years ago than for you to recapture an unwanted lust for self-inflicted death."

"Good heavens!" Garson gasped. "Are you trying to tell us that this is the night of 1941, and that a few minutes from now Dr. Lell will come along and hire a desperate girl sitting on a park bench to be a front for a fake Calonian recruiting station?"

"And this time," said that inhuman voice, "the history of the Glorious will be fulfilled. She will make no trouble."

Garson had the sudden desperate sensation of being beyond his depth. He literally fought for words. "What ... what about our bodies that existed then? I thought two bodies of the same person couldn't exist in the same time and space."

"They can't!"

"But—"

The firm, alien voice cut him off, cut off, too, Norma's sudden, startled intention to speak. "There are no paradoxes in time. I have said that, in order to resist the destruction of the isolated eighteenth solar system, the other seventeen *were brought together* into one—this one! The only one that now exists! But the others were, and in some form you were in them, but now you are here; and this is the real and only world.

"I leave you to think that over, for now you must act. History says that you two took out a marriage license—tomorrow. History says Norma Garson had no difficulty leading the double life of wife of Professor Garson and slave of Dr. Lell; and that, under my direction, she learned to use her power until the day came to destroy the great energy barrier of Delpa and help the Planetarians to their rightful victory."

Garson was himself again. "Rightful?" he said. "I'm not so convinced of that. They were the ones who precipitated the war by breaking the agreement for population curtailment."

"Rightful," said the voice firmly, "because they first denounced the agreement on the grounds that it would atrophy the human spirit and mind; they fought the war on a noble plane, and offered compromise until the last moment. No automatons on their side; and all the men they directly recruited from the past were plainly told they were wanted for dangerous work. Most of them were unemployed veterans of past wars."

Norma found her voice: "That second recruiting station I saw, with the Greeks and the Romans—"

"Exactly. But now you must receive your first lesson in the intricate process of mind and thought control, enough to fool Dr. Lell—"

The odd part of it was that, in spite of all the words that had been spoken, the warm glow of genuine belief in—everything—didn't come to her until she sat in the dim light on the bench, and watched the gaunt body of Dr. Lell stalking out of the shadowed path. Poor, unsuspecting superman!

A Can of Paint

The landing jets worked like a dream. The small machine settled gently on an open meadow in a long, shallow, brilliantly green valley. A few minutes later, the first man of earth ever to set foot on Venus, stepped gingerly down and stood on the lush grass beside his cigar-shaped spaceship.

Kilgour drew a deep, slow breath. The air was like wine, a little high in oxygen content, but tinglingly sweet and fresh and warm. He had a sudden conviction that he had come to paradise. He pulled out his notebook, and wrote down the impression. Any thoughts like that would be worth gold when he got back to Earth. And he would darn well need the money, too.

He finished the writing, and he was putting away his notebook, when he saw the cube.

It was lying on its side on the grass in a slight indentation, as if it had fallen from something not very high. It was a translucent crystalline block with a handle. It was about eight inches square, and it shone with a dull luster like ivory. It seemed to have no purpose.

Kilgour brought some energy testers from the ship, and touched various parts of the crystal with the wire ends. Electricity: negative; electronic: negative. It was not radioactive, nor did it respond to any of the acids he used. It refused to conduct a current of electricity, and likewise rejected the more feverish advances of the electronic enveloper. He put on a rubber glove, and touched the handle. Nothing happened. He slid his gloved fingers caressingly over the cube, and finally gripped the handle tightly. Still there was no response.

Kilgour hesitated. Then tugged at the thing. It lifted easily; its weight he estimated at about four pounds. He set it down again and, stepping back, surveyed it. A slow excitement was starting in his brain. It tingled down to his toes as he realized what was here.

The cube was a manufactured article. There was intelligent life on Venus. He had spent a dreary year in space, wondering, hoping, dreaming about that. And here was evidence. Venus was inhabited.

Kilgour whirled towards the ship. Have to search for a city, he thought tensely. It didn't matter any more if he wasted fuel. Replacements were now possible. He was still in the act of turning, when he saw the cube out of the corner of his eyes. His enthusiasm suffered a pause.

What was he going to do with it? It would be foolish to leave it here. Once departed from this valley, he might never find it again. He'd be wise, though, to be careful about what he took aboard his ship. Suppose the cube had been left there for him to find?

The idea seemed fantastic, and some of his doubts faded, A couple more tests, he decided, and then—He took off his glove, and gingerly touched the handle with his bare finger.

"I contain paint!" something said into his mind.

Kilgour jumped backward. "Huh!" he gulped.

He looked around wildly. But he was alone in a green valley that stretched into distance. He returned his attention to the crystal block. Again, he touched the handle.

"I contain paint." This time there was no doubt. The thought was clear and sharp in his mind.

Kilgour straightened slowly. He stood, mentally dazzled, staring at his find. It took a long moment to start his thought on the uphill climb of imagining the technological stature of a race that could turn out such a container. His mind soared, and then reluctantly retreated. He grew amazed. Because, simple though it was, nothing in the science of man even foreshadowed such a development. A container of paint that said— what it had said. A can labeled with a self-identifying thought.

Kilgour began to grin. His long, homely face twisted with good-humor. His gray-green eyes lighted up. His lips parted, revealing even, white teeth. He laughed joyously. A can of paint! The paint would probably have other ingredients than white lead, linseed oil, and a coloring oxide. But that was something to explore later.

For the moment, possession was enough. No matter what else he discovered on Venus, his trip was already paid for. It was the simple, used-every-day things that made fortunes. Briskly, Kilgour reached down, grabbed the handle with his bare hand, and started to lift.

He had got it off the ground, when a dazzlingly bright liquid squirted from it onto his chest. It spread quickly over his body, clinging like glue, yet running swiftly. It was white when it started, but it changed to red, yellow, blue, violet, then it spread into a myriad of shades. He stood finally, his drenched clothes flashing all the colors of the rainbow. And at first he was furious rather than alarmed.

He began to strip. He was wearing a pullover sweatshirt and a pair of sport shorts; nothing else. The two pieces sparkled like varicolored fire as, with a synchronized jerk he unloosened his belt and pulled the shirt up over his head.

He could feel the liquid running down over his bare body; and it was not until he had removed his shirt—his shorts had fallen around his ankles—that he noticed an odd fact. The paint, which had been mostly on his shirt, had flowed completely off it and onto his skin. Not a drop had fallen to the ground. And his shorts were clean also.

All the paint was on his body. It glowed as it thinned out over the greater surface. It sparkled and shimmered like a flame seen through a prism as he wiped at it with his shirt. But it didn't come off. Frowning, he pushed at it with his hands. It clung to his fingers with a warm stickiness. It bobbed and danced with color as he shoved it groundward. It went down one place, and came up another.

It was a unit, of which no portion would separate from any other portion. It flowed so far, then no farther. It assumed every conceivable shape. But always it remained one piece. Like a vivid, tinted, immensely flexible shawl draped in various patterns, it altered its form, not its essential oneness. After ten minutes, he was still no nearer getting rid of it.

" 'Paint,' " Kilgour read aloud out of his medical book, " 'can be removed by applying turpentine.' "

There was turpentine in his storeroom. He secured the bottle, and climbed out of the ship again. He poured a generous measure into the cupped palm of his hand, and applied it vigorously. That is, he started to apply it. The turpentine flowed out of his hand and onto the ground. The paint wouldn't allow itself to be touched by the liquid.

It took several attempts to convince the astounded Kilgour. But finally, still determined, he re-entered the ship. In quick succession he tried gasoline, water, wine, even some of his precious rocket fuel. The paint wouldn't make contact with any of them. He stepped under a shower. The water rained down on the portion of his body that was not covered by paint, a fine stinging spray of wetness. But there was no sensation at all where the paint clung.

And it definitely didn't wash off.

He filled his bathtub, and seated himself in it. The paint shinnied up his neck, and around his chin, and flowed over his mouth and nose. It didn't go in his nostrils or his mouth, but it covered both apertures. Kilgour stopped breathing, and sat stubborn; then he saw the paint was creeping up towards his eyes. He jumped out of the tub, and ducked his head into the water.

The paint retreated from his nose, hesitated at his mouth, and then sank back halfway towards the lower end of his chin. It seemed to find some anchor point there for, no matter how deep or how often he ducked, it refused to go any lower.

Apparently, having reached his head, it was not prepared to give up that vantage point. Kilgour spread a rubber mat on his favorite chair and sat down to do some hard thinking. The whole incident was ridiculous. He'd be the laughing stock of the solar system if it was ever found out that he had got himself into such a fantastic predicament.

By some accident, a can of Venusian paint had been dropped or lost on this uninhabited meadow; and here he was, smeared with the stuff. The quick way it had flowed over his mouth and nose showed that though mindless, it could be deadly. Suppose it had refused to retreat an inch. He would have suffocated in a few minutes, and would now be lying dead in his bathtub.

Kilgour felt a chill climb his spine. The chill remained even after it struck him that he could easily have forced a funnel into his mouth, and breathed that way. The chill remained because it was only accident that the incredible stuff hadn't climbed up over his eyes.

He pictured a blind, suffocating man searching in a roomy storeroom for a funnel.

It took a long minute for his normally sunny disposition to make a partial comeback. He sat stiff, forcing his mind. Paint—that jumped out of a can, showed no sign of drying, yet wasn't really a liquid, because it wouldn't soak into clothing or flow according to the law of gravity. And wouldn't let liquid touch it.

Kilgour's mind paused there, in a sudden comprehension. Why, of course. Waterproof. He should have remembered. This was no ordinary paint. It was waterproof, rainproof, liquidproof—the ultimate paint.

He grew excited. He stood up jerkily and began to pace the floor. For twenty-five years, ever since the first of the super rockets had gushed out to the barren Moon and then to semibarren Mars, Venus had been the goal of the explorers. Journeys there, however, had been forbidden until some means was discovered to overcome the danger of ships falling into the Sun. That incandescent fate had befallen two ships. And it had been mathematically proven, not merely by cranks, that such a catastrophe would happen to every space-ship until the planets Earth and Venus attained a certain general position with relation to each other and Jupiter.

The ideal conditions were not due to occur for another twenty-eight years. But six months before Kilgour took off, a famous astronomer had pointed out that some of the conditions would prevail for about a year. The article caused a sensation among spacemen; and, though the government refused to withdraw its ban, Kilgour had heard that a high patrol officer had privately stated that he would look the other way if anybody started out. And that he would see to it that men of like mind carried out the necessary pre-flight inspections. Several expeditions, ostensibly bound for Mars had been busily fitting up when Kilgour launched his small craft into space, Venus-bound.

Great things were expected of Venus. But not so great as this. Kilgour stopped his pacing. A race that could develop a perfect paint, *anything* perfect, was going to prove worth knowing.

His thought ended. He had glanced down at his body. And now, he saw something that startled him. The paint, brilliant in its million facets of changing color, was spreading. In the beginning, it had covered a quarter of his flesh. Now, it covered a good third. If it kept on, it would soon overrun him from head to toe, eyes and ears and nose and mouth and all.

It was time he started figuring ways and means of removal. In earnest. Kilgour wrote:

"A perfect paint should be waterproof and weatherproof as well as beautiful. It should also be easily removable."

He stared gloomily as the final sentence. And then, in a fit of temper, he flung down the pencil and walked over to the bathroom mirror. He peered into it with a nasty smirk on his face.

"Pretty, aren't you!" he snarled at his blazing image. "Like a gypsy arrayed in dance finery."

The reality, he saw on second glance, was more chromatically splendid than that. He shone in about ninety colors. The various combinations did not blur dully one into the other. They merged with a sharp brightness that seemed to make even the most subtle shades project with intensity. Yet in some curious fashion the paint was not showy. It was bright, but it did not hurt his eyes. It was brilliant, but it failed to jar his sense of good taste. He had come to sneer, but he remained several minutes to appraise its startling beauty.

He turned away at last. "If," he thought, "I could get a spoonful loose, I could put it into a retort and analyze it."

But he had tried that. He tried it again, with a sudden hope. As before, the paint flowed into the spoon willingly, but when he raised the spoon, it flowed back onto his skin. Kilgour procured a knife, and tried to hold the paint on his spoon. But when he lifted his hand, the paint slid between the blade and the spoon like so much oil.

Kilgour decided that his strength was not sufficient to press the knife tight onto the spoon edge. He headed for the storeroom. There was a small scoop there with a pressure cover. It was too round and too small; he could only force a little bit of the paint into it. And it took more than a minute to tighten the cover nuts with a wrench. But when he lifted the scoop and opened it, there was a little pool of paint filling the bottom quarter of the scoop.

Kilgour walked over and sat down hastily in his chair. He had the curious, wretched feeling that he was going to be ill. His brain reeled with relief; and it was several minutes before he could even think about his next move. Logically, of course, he ought to remove painstakingly, and it would be painstaking, all the paint by the method he had just evolved. But first—He poured the paint in the scoop into a measuring retort. It measured just a little more than a dessert spoonful.

There were, he estimated, at least five hundred such spoonfuls on his body, and it would take him—he removed a second scoopful, timing himself—a fraction over two minutes for each operation.

One thousand minutes! Seventeen hours! Kilgour smiled ruefully, and went into the galley. He'd need food four or five times during such a period of time, and right now was one of the times. While he was eating, he pondered the problem with the calmness of a man who has found a solution, and who, therefore, can afford to consider other possibilities.

Seventeen hours was a long time. Surely, now that he had some free paint, he could go into his small chemical lab and quickly discover a dozen chemical reactions that would remove the entire mess from him in a few minutes.

Perhaps a larger, more complete laboratory might have yielded results. His was too small. The paint refused to react to any of the elements and solutions that he had. It wouldn't mix. It wouldn't combine. It wouldn't burn. It was immune to acids and metals, and it did not seem to influence anything he used either catalytically or otherwise.

The paint was inert. Period.

"Of course," Kilgour said at last, explosively, to himself. "How could I have forgotten. The stuff would be weather-proof with a capital W. It's perfect paint."

He went to work with the scoop. He developed a dexterity with the wrench in screwing and unscrewing the nuts, that enabled him to remove a spoonful every three-quarters of a minute. He was so intent on maintaining the speed of operation that he had half a pailful of paint before it struck him with a tremendous shock that there was still as much paint as ever on his body.

Kilgour trembled with the thought that came. Feverishly, he measured the paint in the half-filled pail. And there was no question. He had emptied into the pail approximately as much as the original crystal container had squirted onto him—without affecting the quantity on his body.

Once applied, the ultimate paint was self-renewing.

He wrote that down at the bottom of his list of the paint's qualities. Then he grew aware that he was perspiring freely. The sweat stood out in little foamy globules over the un-painted part of his body. Kilgour's brain performed its newest leap of comprehension. He snatched up his note-book and jotted down: "The perfect paint is also cold and heat-proof."

Within half an hour, it was impossible to be objective about it. The paint covered nearly half his body. His hard work had warmed him con-siderably. He was roasting from his own animal heat. And scared. He thought shakily: "I've got to get out of here. I've got to find a Venusian city, and get an antidote for this stuff."

It didn't matter any more whether he was made ridiculous or not.

In a spasm of panic, he headed for the control board. His hand reached for the launching lever. But paused at the last instant.

The can! It had said: "I contain paint." Surely it would also have direc-tions for use of contents, and for subsequent removal.

"I'm a pie-eyed nut," Kilgour whispered to himself as he ran. "I should have thought of that ages ago."

The crystal "can" lay on the grass, where he had left it. He snatched at it. "I contain a quarter paint," it thought at him.

So he had squirted three-quarters of the contents onto himself. It was an important thing to know. He'd be wise not to add the rest to the spreading horror that was enveloping him in an air-tight casing of liquid brilliance.

Cautiously, taking care not to lift the container from the ground, he fumbled over it with his bare hands. Almost instantly, he had his first response. "Directions: Fix controllers around area to be painted, then apply. Paint will dry as soon as controlled area is covered. To remove, press darkener over paint for one terard." The incomprehensible word seemed to refer to a short period of time. "Note," the thought continued, "dark-eners may be purchased at your neighborhood hardware and paint stores."

Kilgour thought furiously, "Isn't that just dandy. I'll run over right now, and get me one."

In spite of his scathing words, he felt amazingly better. It was a prac-tical world he had come to, not a nightmare planet where creatures with ten eyes and eight legs moaned and yammered with instant alien hatred for human explorers. People who used paint wouldn't murder him out of hand. That had been obvious all the time. Intelligence implied a semi-rational outlook, an orderly, organized universe. Naturally, not all nonhuman races would like human beings. But then, human beings had a habit of not liking each other.

If the container and the paint it contained were criterions, the civili-zation of Venus was superior to that of man. Accordingly, the inhabitants would be above petty persecution. The fantastic, ludicrous mess he had gotten himself into, was basically solved by that fact.

But that didn't stop him from getting hotter and hotter under his coat of paint. It was time he found himself a Venusian. He picked up the container, lifting it with his fingers from underneath. It thought at him: "Ingredients of this paint, as per government requirements, are:

!?!?! —7%
?!?!? — 13%
Liquid light — 80%

"Liquid what?" asked Kilgour aloud.

"Warning," came the thought. "This paint must not be allowed in proximity to volatile substances."

There was no explanation for that, though Kilgour waited for further thoughts. Apparently Venusians knew enough about their government regulations to obey them without question. He himself had tried to put the paint in contact with the volatile substances, turpentine, gasoline, his rocket fuel, and a couple of other explosives. And no harm done. It seemed a silly regulation, if it didn't mean anything.

Kilgour set the can down, and headed once more for the control board. The launching lever was glass smooth to his palm as he pulled it back until it clicked. He sat braced, waiting for the automatic machinery to set off the potent violence of fired tubes.

Nothing happened.

Kilgour had a premonition. He jerked the launching lever back into place, then clicked it again. And still there was no explosion.

His brain was reeling. The premonition was a living force. His whole body was heavy with the strength of it. He had poured the rocket fuel back into its great tank after trying to wipe the paint off his flesh with it. It had only been a few liters, but spacemen practiced queer economies. He had poured it back because the paint had not seemed to affect it in any way.

"Warning," the can had said. "This paint must not be allowed in proximity to volatile substances."

The inert stuff must have de-energized the eighteen thousand gallons in his one remaining fuel tank.

Try the radio again. He had started sending out signals when he was a million miles from Venus and had listened and listened on his receiver. But the great void had remained unresponsive. Nevertheless, the Venusians must have such a thing. Surely they would answer an emergency call.

But they didn't. Half an hour went by, and his calls went unheeded. His receiver remained silent; not even static came in on any wavelength. He was alone in a universe of choking, crowding, growing, maddeningly colorful paint.

Darkener—liquid light—Perhaps it shone, not only in bright exterior light, so that if he turned off the lights—His finger on the switch, he noticed for the first time how dark it was outside. His lock doors were open; and slowly, Kilgour walked over to them and stared out into a night that was unbroken by starlight. The darkness, now that it had come, was intense. The clouds, of course, the eternal clouds of Venus—So bright was the sun at Venus' distance from it that in daytime the clouds were a protection that yet failed to more than dim the dazzling glare.

Now, at night, it was different. The clouds enclosed the planet like the walls and ceiling of a dark room. There was light, naturally. No planet near a sun or in the starry universe could be absolutely shut off from light and energy. His seleniometer would probably be registering well down into the hundred thousandths. Kilgour brought his gaze down from the sky, and saw that the ground was brilliant with the light from his paint. Startled, he stepped out of the door, away from the interior light pouring out of the door of his ship. In the darkness to one side, his body glowed like a multiflamed but meaningless sign. He was so bright he lighted up the grass with patterns of dazzling color. He would be beautiful in death.

He pictured himself sprawled on the floor, covered from head to foot with paint. Eventually the Venusians would find him on this lonely meadow. Perhaps they would wonder what he was, where he had come from. It seemed obvious that they had no interplanetary travel.

Or had they? Kilgour's mind paused momentarily in its feverish gyrations. Was it possible the Venusians had deliberately refrained from making contact with human beings on earth?

His brain couldn't concentrate on anything so unimportant. He went back into the ship. There was something, he was thinking, something he had been intending to do—he couldn't remember, unless it was the radio. He switched it on. Then jumped jerkily as a mechanical voice came through:

"Earthman," it said, "are you there? Earthman, are you there?"

Kilgour clawed at the broadcaster. "Yes," he shouted finally. "Yes, I'm here. And in an awful mess. You must come out at once."

"We know your predicament," said the flat-toned voice, "but we have no intention of rescuing you."

"Huh!" said Kilgour blankly.

"The container of paint," the voice went on, "was dropped from an invisible ship at the door of your machine a few moments after you landed. For some thousands of years we, whom you call Venusians, have watched with considerable uneasiness the development of civilization on the third planet of this sun system. Our people are not adventurous, nor is there a single war known to our recorded history. This is not to say that the struggle for survival has not been a bitter one. But we have an immensely more sluggish metabolism. Long ago our psychologists decided that space flight was not for us.

"We have accordingly concentrated on the development of the purely Venusian way of life, so that when your ship approached our atmosphere, we were confronted with the necessity of deciding under what conditions we would establish relations with human beings. Our decision was to place the container of paint where you would find it. If you had failed to become entangled in the paint, we would have found some other method of testing you.

"Yes, you have heard correctly. You have been, and are being tested. It seems you are failing the test, which is regrettable because it means that all people of your intelligence level or less will be barred from Venus. It has been very difficult to prepare tests for an alien race. And therefore, unless you can think your way through the test, you must die, so that others who come after you may be given that or similar tests without knowing they are being tested, a prime requisite, it seems to us. Our intention is to find a human being who can solve the test we give him, after which we shall examine him with our instruments, and use the results as a measure for future visitors to Venus. All those whose intelligence is the same or higher than that of the successful candidate may come to our planet at will. Such is our unalterable determination.

"The person tested must also be able to leave Venus without help from us. You will readily see why that is necessary. Later, we shall help human beings to improve their spaceships. We are talking to you on a mechanical voice machine. The simple thoughts of the container were very laboriously impressed upon it by a complicated thought machine. It is so very difficult to establish communication with a non-Venusian brain. But now, good-bye. And though this may sound strange, good luck still."

There was a click. All Kilgour's juggling with the dials produced no further sound.

He sat, all the ship's lights switched off, waiting for death. It was not a quiescent wait. His whole being palpitated with the will to live. A darkener! What in the name of the ebony gods could it be?

The question was not new to Kilgour. For an hour he had sat in a room made fantastic by the blaze of color from his painted body. He sat with his notebook, frantically going over the data he had.

A perfect paint made of—eighty percent liquid light. Light was light; the liquid must follow the same laws as the beam. Or must it? And what of it. A perfect paint capable of—his mind refused to go through the list of qualities again. He felt physically ill, and time and again he fought off nausea.

He was so hot, it was like a fever. His feet dangled in a pan of cold water; the theory of that had been that if his blood had a cold area to run through, it wouldn't start boiling.

Actually, he knew that there was little danger of his temperature rising beyond its present almost unbearable point. There was such a thing as a limit to animal heat, particularly since it had penetrated at last that he had better stick to vitamin capsules and leave calories alone. It would be insane to take in fuel that manufactured body heat. The gravest danger was that, with his body overrun by the paint, his pores would be unable to breathe. Death would follow, how quickly, Kilgour didn't know.

His ignorance didn't add to his peace of mind. Funny, though, that now he was reluctantly waiting for death, it was slow in coming. The thought jarred Kilgour out of his developing incoherence. Slow? He leaped to his feet. Because it was slow. He raced for the bathroom mirror, in a dizzy excitement he peered at his image.

The paint still covered only half his body. It had not expanded during the past hour. *The past hour, during which he had sat in darkness except for the light from the paint.*

The paint, he noted more critically, had not lost ground. It still covered half his body. But, actually, that was natural. it was made to survive the black Venusian night. Suppose, however, that he climbed into the greater darkness of his insulated-against energy, empty fuel tank?

For half an hour, Kilgour sat in the tank: and then he climbed out again, shaky but still determined. Absolute darkness must be the solution, but he was missing something vital. It seemed obvious that if darkness alone was enough, then the fuel in his full fuel tank would by this time have cleared itself of the effects of the paint. He tried the launcher; and there was no explosion. There must be something else.

"The problem," thought Kilgour, "is to drain off the eighty percent liquid light by providing a sufficient darkness, or by some other means. But it's almost impossible for darkness to be darker than it is inside that tank. It's insulated against outside energies. So what's wrong?"

The insulation! That was it. The light from the paint merely reflected from the walls, and was re-absorbed by the paint. There was no place for the light to escape. Solution: Remove the insulation.

No, that was wrong. Kilgour's excitement sagged. With the insulation removed the light would escape all right, but the outside energies would seep in to replace the escaped quantity. Better test that, though.

He did. And it was so. He came out as covered with paint as ever. He was standing there, in the grip of hopelessness, when the answer struck him.

On the way back to Earth a month later, Kilgour ran into the radio signals of another ship approaching Venus. He explained what had happened. He finished, "So you'll have no difficulty landing. The Venusians will give you the keys to their colorful cities."

"But just a minute!" came the puzzled reply. "I thought you said they'll only allow people whose intelligence is the same as or greater than, that of the person who succeeds in their test. You must be quite a bright lad to have done so. But we're only a bunch of dumb spacemen. So where does that leave us?"

"You're sitting right on top of the world," Kilgour responded cheerfully. "And I mean Venus. Like most spacemen, I was never noted for my I.Q. My forte has always been vim, vigor, and a spirit of adventure." He concluded modestly, "Since I'm the measuring rod for admittance, I would say that at a conservative estimate ninety-nine percent of the human race can now visit Venus."

"But—"

Kilgour cut him off. "Don't ask me why their test was so simple. Maybe you'll understand when you see them." He frowned. "You're not going to like the Venusians, friend. But one look at their many-legged, multi-armed bodies will give you some idea of what they mean when they said it was difficult to figure out tests for alien minds. And now, any more questions?"

"Yes. How *did* you get rid of that paint?"

Kilgour grinned. "Photocells and barium salt. I took a bank of photo-converter cells and a barium battery into the tank with me. They absorbed the light from the paint. The rest, a fine brownish dust, settled onto the floor; and I was a free man. I re-energized the rocket fuel the same way."

He laughed joyously. "Toodleoo! Be seeing you. I've got a cargo aboard that must be marketed."

"A cargo! Of what?"

"Paint. Thousands of cans of gorgeous paint. Earth shall in beauty live forevermore. And I've got the exclusive agency."

The two ships passed in the night of space, on to their separate destinations.

THE SEARCH

The hospital bed was hard under his body. For a moment it seemed to Drake that that was what was bothering him. He turned over into a more comfortable position, and knew it wasn't physical at all. It was something in his mind, the sense of emptiness that had been there since they had told him the date.

After what seemed a long time, the door opened, and two men and a nurse came in. One of the men said in a hearty voice, "Well, how are you, Drake? It's a shame to see you down like this."

The man was plumpish, a good-fellow type. Drake took his vigorous handshake, lay very still for a moment, and then allowed the awkward but very necessary question to escape his lips. "I'm sorry," he said stiffly, "but do I know you?"

The man said, "I'm Bryson, sales manager of the Quik-Rite Company. We manufacture fountain pens, pencils, ink, writing paper, and a dozen kindred lines that even grocery stores handle. Two weeks ago, I hired you and put you on the road as a salesman. The next thing I knew you were found unconscious in a ditch, and the hospital advised me you were here." He finished, "You had identification papers on you connecting you with us."

Drake nodded. But he was disappointed. He had thought it would be enough to have someone fill a gap in his mind. It wasn't. He said finally, "My last remembrance is my decision to apply for a job with your firm, Mr. Bryson. I had just been turned down by the draft board for an odd reason. Apparently, something happened to my mind at that point and—"

He stopped. His eyes widened at the thought that came. He said slowly, conscious of an unpleasant sensation, "Apparently, I've had amnesia."

He saw that the house doctor, who had come in with Bryson, was looking at him sharply. Drake mustered a wan smile. "I guess it's all right, doc. What gets me is the kind of life I must have lived these last two weeks. I've been lying here straining my brain. There's something in the back of my mind, but I can't remember what."

The doctor was smiling behind his pince-nez. "I'm glad you're taking it so well. Nothing to worry about, really. As for what you did, I assure you that our experience has been that the victim usually lives a reasonably normal life. One of the most frequent characteristics is that the victim of amnesia takes up a different occupation. You didn't even do that."

He paused, and the plump Bryson said heartily, "I can clear up the first week for you. I had discovered, when I hired you, that you'd lived as a boy in some village on the Warwick Junction-Kissling branch line. Naturally, I put you on that route.

"We had orders from you from five towns on the way, but you never got to Kissling. Maybe that will help you ... No?" Bryson shrugged. "Well, never mind. As soon as you're up, Drake, come and see me. You're a good man, and they're getting scarce."

Drake said, "I'd like to be on the same territory, if it's all right."

Bryson nodded. "Mind you, it's only a matter of finishing up what you missed before, and then moving farther along the main line. But it's yours, certainly. I guess you want to check up on what happened to you."

"That," said Drake, "is exactly what I have in mind. Sort of a search for my memory." He managed a smile. "But now ... but now, I want to thank you for coming."

"That's all right. S'long."

Bryson shook hands warmly, and Drake watched him go out the door.

Two days later, Drake climbed off the *Transcontinental* at Warwick Junction, and stood blinking in the bright sun of early morning. His first disappointment had already come. He had hoped that the sight of the cluster of houses silhouetted against a line of hills would bring back memories.

It had, but only from his boyhood when he and his parents had passed through the Junction on various trips. There were new houses now, and a railway station that hadn't been there twenty years before. Too obviously his mind was not being jarred into the faintest remembrance of what he had done or seen sixteen days earlier. Drake shook his head in bewilderment. "Somebody knew me," he thought. "Somebody must have seen me. I talked to storekeepers, travelers, trainmen, hotel men. I've always had a sociable bent, so—"

"Hello, there, Drake, old chap," said a cheerful voice beside him. "You look as if you're thinking about a funeral."

Drake turned, and saw a rather slender young man, dark-faced and dark-haired, about thirty years old. He had the slouch of a too-thin person who had carried too many sample cases. He must have noticed something in Drake's eyes, for he said quickly:

"You remember me, don't you? Bill Kellie!" He laughed easily. "Say, come to think of it, I've got a bone to pick with you. What did you do with that girl, Selanie? I've been twice past Piffer's Road since I last saw you, and she didn't come around either time. She—" He stopped, and his gaze was suddenly sharp. "Say, you do remember me, don't you?"

To Drake, the astounding if not notable fact was that Piffer's Road should be the place name. Was it possible that he had got the idea of going to the farmhouse where he had been born, to look the old homestead over? He emerged from his intense inner excitement, and realized from the expression on Kellie's face that it was time to explain. He did so, finishing finally, "So you see, I'm in quite a mental fix. Maybe, if you don't mind, you could give me some idea of what happened while I was with you. Who is this girl, Selanie?"

"Oh, sure," said Kellie, "sure I'll—" He paused, frowned. "You're not kidding me, are you?" He waved Drake silent. "O.K., O.K., I'll believe you. We've got a half-hour before the Kissling local is due. Amnesia, eh? I've heard about that stuff, but—Sa-a-ay, you don't think that old man could have anything to do with—" He banged his right fist into his left palm. "I'll bet that's it."

"An old man!" Drake said. He caught himself, finished firmly, "What about this story?"

The train slowed. Through the streaky window, Drake could see a rolling valley with patches of green trees and a gleaming, winding thread of water. Then some houses came into view, half a dozen siding tracks, and finally the beginning of a wooden platform.

A tall, slim, fine-looking girl walked past his window carrying a basket. Behind Drake, the traveling salesman who had got on at the last stop and to whom he had been talking, said, "Oh, there's Selanie. I wonder what kind of supergadget she's got for sale today."

Drake leaned back in his seat, conscious that he had seen all of Piffer's Road that he cared to. It was queer, that feeling of disinterest. After all, he had been born three miles along the road. Nevertheless, there it was. He didn't give a darn. His mind fastened only slowly on what the other had said. "Selanie" he echoed then. "Curious name! Did you say she sells things?"

"*Does* she sell things!" Kellie spoke explosively.

He must have realized the forcefulness of his words, for he drew a deep, audible breath. His blue eyes looked hard at Drake. He started to say something, stopped himself, and finally sat smiling a secret smile. After a moment, he said, "You know, I really must apologize. I've just now realized that I've monopolized the conversation ever since we started talking."

Drake smiled with polite tolerance. "You've been very entertaining."

Kellie persisted, "What I mean by that is, it's just penetrated to me that you told me you sold fountain pens, among other things."

Drake shrugged. He wondered if he looked as puzzled as he was beginning to feel. He watched as Kellie drew out a pen and held it out for him to take. Kellie said, "See anything odd about that?"

The pen was long, slender, of a dark, expensive-looking material. Drake unscrewed the cap slowly—slowly, because in his mind was the sudden, wry thought that he was in for one of those pointless arguments about the relative merits of the pens he was selling. He said quickly, "This looks right out of my class. My company's pens retail for a dollar."

The moment he had spoken, he realized he had left himself wide open. Kellie said with a casual triumph, "That's exactly what she charged me for it."

"Who?"

"Selanie! The girl who just got on the train. She'll be along in a few minutes selling something new. She's always got an item that's new and different."

He grabbed the pen from Drake's fingers. "I'll show you what's queer about this pen." He reached for a paper cup that stood on the window sill. He said with irritating smugness, "Watch!"

The pen tilted over the cup; Kellie seemed to press with his fingers on the top. Ink began to flow.

After about three minutes, it filled the cup to the brim. Kellie opened the window, carefully emptied the blue liquid onto the ground between the coach and the platform. Drake erupted from his paralysis.

"Good heavens!" he gasped. "What kind of a tank have you got inside that pen? Why, it—"

"Wait!"

Kellie's voice was quiet, but he was so obviously enjoying himself that Drake pulled himself together with a distinct effort. His brain began to whirl once more, as Kellie pressed the top again and once again ink began to flow from the fantastic pen. Kellie said, "Notice anything odd about that ink?"

Drake started to shake his head, then he started to say that the oddness was the quantity, then he gulped hoarsely, "*Red* ink!"

"Or maybe," Kellie said coolly, "you'd prefer purple. Or yellow. Or green. Or violet."

The pen squirted a tiny stream of each color, as he named it. In each case, he turned the part he was pressing ever so slightly. Kellie finished with the triumphant tone of a man who had extracted every last drop of drama from a situation, "Here, maybe you'd like to try it yourself."

Drake took the remarkable thing like a connoisseur caressing a priceless jewel. As from a great distance he heard Kellie chattering on, "—Her father makes them," Kellie was saying. "He's a genius with gadgets. You ought to see some of the stuff she's been selling on this train the last month. One of these days he's going to get wise to himself and start large-scale manufacture. When that day comes, all fountain pen companies and a lot of other firms go out of business."

It was a thought that had already occurred to Drake. Before he could muster his mind for speech, the pen was taken from his fingers, and Kellie was leaning across the aisle toward a handsome gray-haired man who sat there. Kellie said, "I noticed you looking at the pen, sir, while I was showing it to my friend. Would you like to examine it?"

"Why, yes," said the man.

He spoke in a low tone, but the sound had a resonance that tingled in Drake's ears. The old man's fingers grasped the extended pen and, just like that, the pen broke.

"Oh!" Kellie exclaimed blankly.

"I beg your pardon," said the fine-looking old man. A dollar appeared in his hand. "My fault. You can buy another one from the girl when she comes." He leaned back, and buried himself behind a newspaper.

Drake saw that Kellie was biting his lip. The man sat staring at his broken pen, and then at the dollar bill, and then in the direction of the now hidden face of the gray-haired man. At last, Kellie sighed. "I can't understand it. I've had the pen a month. It's already fallen to a concrete sidewalk, and twice onto a hardwood floor—and now it breaks like a piece of rotted wood." He shrugged, but his tone was complaining as he went on after a moment, "I suppose actually you can't really expect Selanie's father to do a first-rate job with the facilities he's got—" He broke off excitedly, "Oh, look, there's Selanie now. I wonder what she's featuring today." A sly smile crept into his narrow face. "Just wait till I confront her with that broken pen. I kidded her when I bought it, told her there must be a trick to it. She got mad then, and guaranteed it for life—what the devil is she selling, anyway? Look, they're crowding around her."

Drake climbed to his feet. He craned his neck the better to see over the heads of the crowd that was watching the girl demonstrate something at the far end of the car.

"Good heavens!" a man's deep voice exclaimed. "How much are you charging for those cups? How do they work?"

"Cups!" said Drake, and moved toward the group in a haze of fascination. If he had seen right, the girl was handing around a container which kept filling full of liquid. And people would drink, and it would fill again instantly. Drake thought: The same principle as the fountain pen. Somehow, her father has learned to precipitate liquids. There was genius here. And if he could make a deal with the man for the company, or for himself, he was made.

The tremendous thought ended, as the girl's crystal-clear voice rose above the excited babble, "The price is one dollar each. It works by chemical condensation of gases in the air. The process is known only to my father. But wait, I haven't finished my demonstration."

She went on, her voice cool and strong against the silence that settled around her, "As you see, it's a folding drinking cup without a handle. First, you open it. Then you turn the top strip clockwise. At a certain point, water comes. But now—watch. I'm turning it further. The liquid is now turning green, and is a sweet and very flavorsome drink. I turn the strip still further, and the liquid turns red, becomes a sweet-sourish drink that is very refreshing in hot weather."

She handed the cup around. While it was being passed from fingers to clutching fingers, Drake managed to wrench his gaze from the gadget, and really look at the girl. She was tall, about five feet six, and she had dark-brown hair. Her face was unmistakably of a fine intelligence. It was thin and good-looking, and there was an odd proud tilt to it that gave her a startling appearance of aloofness in spite of the way she was taking the dollar bills that were being thrust at her.

Once again, her voice rose, "I'm sorry, only one to a person. They'll be on the general market right after the war. These are only souvenirs."

The crowd dissolved, each person retiring to his or her individual seat. The girl came along the aisle, and stopped in front of Drake. He stepped aside instinctively, realized what he was doing, and said piercingly, "Wait! My friend showed me a fountain pen you were selling. I wonder—"

"I still have a few." She nodded gravely. "Would you like a cup, also?"

Drake remembered Kellie. "My friend would like another pen, too. His broke and—"

"I'm sorry, I can't sell him a second pen." She paused. Her eyes widened. She said with a weighty slowness, "Did you say—his *broke?*"

Astoundingly, she swayed. She said wildly, "Let me see that! Where is your friend?"

She took the two pieces of fountain pen from Kellie's fingers, and stared at them. Her mouth began to tremble. Her hands shook. Her face took on a gray, drawn look. Her voice, when she spoke, was a whisper. "Tell me ... how did it happen? *Exactly* how?"

"Why"—Kellie drew back in surprise—"I was handing it to that old gentleman over there when—"

He stopped because he had lost his audience. The girl spun on her heel. It was like a signal. The old man lowered his paper, and looked at her. She stared back at him with the fascinated expression of a bird cornered by a snake. Then, for a second time within two minutes, she swayed. The basket nearly dropped from her hand as she ran, but somehow she hung on to it, as she careened along the aisle.

A moment later, Drake saw her racing across the platform. She became a distant, running form on Piffer's Road.

"What the hell!" Kellie exploded.

He whirled on the old man. "What did you do to her?" he demanded fiercely. "You—"

His voice sank into silence, and Drake, who had been about to add his hard words to the demand, remained quiet, also.

The salesman's voice, there under the bright sun on the platform at Warwick Junction, faded. It required a moment for Drake to grasp that the story was finished.

"You mean," he demanded, "that's all? We just sat there like a couple of dummies, out-faced by an old man? And that was the end of the business? You still don't know what scared the girl?"

He saw there was, on Kellie's face, the strange look of a man who was searching mentally for a word or phrase to describe the indescribable. Kellie said finally:

"There was something about him like … like all the tough sales managers in the world rolled into one, and feeling their orneriest. We just shut up."

It was a description that Drake could appreciate. He nodded grimly, said slowly, "He didn't get off?"

"No, you were the only one who got off."

"Eh?"

Kellie looked at him. "You know, this is the damnedest, funniest thing. But that's the way it was. You asked the trainman to check your bags at Inchney. The last thing I saw of you before the train pulled out, you were walking up Piffer's Road in the direction the girl had gone and—Ah, here comes the Kissling local now."

The combination freight and passenger train backed in noisily. Later, as it was winding in and out along the edge of a valley, Drake sat staring wonderingly at the terrain so dimly remembered from his boyhood, only vaguely conscious of Kellie chattering beside him. He decided finally on the course he would take: This afternoon he'd get off at Inchney, make his rounds until the stores closed, then get a ride in some way to Piffer's Road and spend the long, summer evening making inquiries. If he recollected correctly, the distance between the large town and the tiny community was given as seven miles. At worst he could walk back to Inchney in a couple of hours.

The first part proved even simpler than that. There was a bus, the clerk at the Inchney Hotel told him, that left at six o'clock.

At twenty after six, Drake climbed off and, standing in the dirt that was Piffer's Road, watched the bus throb off down the highway. The sound faded into remoteness as he trudged across the railway track. The evening was warm and quiet, and his coat made a weight on his arm. It would be cooler later on, he thought, but at the moment he almost regretted that he had brought it.

There was a woman on her knees, working on the lawn at the first house. Drake hesitated, then went over to the fence and stared at the woman for a moment. He wondered if he ought to remember her. He said finally, "I beg your pardon, madam."

She did not look up. She did not rise from the flower-bed, where she was digging. She was a bony creature in a print dress, and she must have seen him coming to be so obstinately silent. "I wonder," Drake persisted, "if you can tell me where a middle-aged man and his daughter live. The daughter is called Selanie, and she used to sell fountain pens and drinking cups and things to people on the train."

The woman was getting up. She came over. At close range, she didn't seem quite so large or ungainly. She had gray eyes that looked at him with a measure of hostility, then with curiosity. "Sa-a-ay," she said sharply, "weren't you along here about two weeks ago, asking about them? I told you then that they lived in that grove over there." She waved at some trees about a quarter of a mile along the road, but her eyes were narrowed as she stared at him. "I don't get it," she said grimly.

Drake couldn't see himself explaining about his amnesia to this crusty-voiced, suspicious creature, and he certainly wasn't going to mention that he had once lived in the district. He said hastily, "Thank you very much. I—"

"No use you going up there again," said the woman. "They pulled out on the same day you were there last time … in their big trailer. And they haven't come back."

"They're gone!" Drake exclaimed.

In the intensity of his disappointment he was about to say more. Then he saw that the woman was staring at him with a faint, satisfied smile on her face. She looked as if she had successfully delivered a knock-out blow to an unpleasant individual. "I think," Drake snapped, "I'll go up and have a look around, anyway."

He spun on his heel, so angry that for a while he scarcely realized that he was walking in the ditch and not on the road. His fury yielded slowly to disappointment, and that in turn faded before the thought that, now that he was up here, he *might* as well have a look.

After a moment, he felt amazed that he could have let one woman get on his nerves to such an extent in so short a time. He shook his head, self-chidingly. He'd better be careful. The process of tracking down his memory was wearing on him.

A breeze sprang up from nowhere as he turned into the shadowed grove. It blew softly in his face, and its passage through the trees was the only sound that broke the silence of the evening. It didn't take more than a moment to realize that his vague expectations, the sense of—something—that had been driving him on to this journey was not going to be satisfied. For there was nothing, not a sign that human beings had ever lived here; not a tin can, or a bundle of garbage, or ashes from a stove. Nothing. He wandered around disconsolately for a few minutes, poked gingerly with a stick among a pile of dead branches. And finally, he walked back along the road. This time it was the woman who called to him. He hesitated, then went over. After all, she might know a lot more than she had told. He saw that she looked more friendly.

"Find anything?" she said with an ill-restrained eagerness.

Drake smiled grimly at the power of curiosity, then shrugged ruefully. "When a trailer leaves," he said, "it's like smoke—it just vanishes."

The woman sniffed. "Any traces that were left sure went fast after the old man got through there."

Drake fought to hold down his excitement. "The old man!" he exclaimed.

The woman nodded, then said bitterly, "A fine-looking old fellow. Came around first inquiring from everybody what kind of stuff Selanie had sold us. Two days later, we woke up in the morning, and every single piece was gone."

"Stolen!"

The woman scowled. "Same thing as. There was a dollar bill for each item. But that's stealing for those kind of goods. Do you know, she had a frying pan that—"

"But what did he want?" Drake interrupted, bewildered. "Didn't he explain anything when he was making his inquiries? Surely, you didn't just let him come around here asking questions!"

To his astonishment, the woman grew flustered. "I don't know what came over me," she confessed finally, sullenly. "There was something about him. He looked kind of commanding-like and important, as if he were a big executive or something." She stopped angrily. "The scoundrel!" she snapped.

Her eyes narrowed with abrupt hostility. She peered at Drake. "You're a fine one for saying did we ask any questions. What about you? Standing here pumping me when all the time—Say, let me get this straight: *Are you the fellow who called here two weeks ago?* Just how do you fit into the picture?"

Drake hesitated. The prospect of having to tell that story to people like this seemed full of difficulties. And yet, she must know more. There must be a great deal of information about the month that the girl Selanie and her father spent in the district. One thing seemed certain. If any more facts were available, this woman would have them.

His hesitation ended. He made his explanation, but finished a little uncertainly: "So you see, I'm a man who is—well—in search of his memory. Maybe I was knocked over the head, although there's no lump. Then, again, maybe I was doped. *Something* happened to me. You say I went up there. Did I come back? Or what did I do?"

He stopped with a jump, for, without warning, the woman parted her lips, and let out a bellow. *"Jimmy!"* she yelled in an ear-splitting voice, "Jimmy! *C'mere!*"

"Yeah, mom!" came a boy's voice from inside the house.

Drake stared blankly as an uncombed twelve-year-old with a sharp, eager face catapulted out of the house. The screen door banged behind him. Drake listened, still with only partial comprehension, as the mother explained to the boy that "this man was hit over the head by those people in the trailer, and he lost his memory, and he'd like you to tell him what you saw."

The woman turned to Drake. "Jimmy," she said proudly, "never trusted those folk. He was sure they were foreigners or something, and so he kept a sharp eye on them. He saw you go up there, and everything that happened right up to the time the trailer left." She finished, "The reason he can tell you in such detail exactly what you did is that he could see everything through the windows, and besides, he went inside once when they weren't around and looked the whole place over, just to make sure, of course, that they weren't pulling something."

Drake nodded, suppressing his cynicism. It was probably as good a reason as any for snooping. In this case, it was lucky for him.

The thought ended, as Jimmy's shrill voice projected into the gathering twilight.

The afternoon was hot, and Drake, after pausing to inquire of the woman in the first house as to where the father and daughter lived, walked slowly toward the grove of trees she had indicated.

Behind him, the train tooted twice, and then began to chuff. Drake suppressed a startled impulse to run back and get on it. He realized he couldn't have made it, anyway. Besides, a man didn't give up the hope of fortune as easily as that. His pace quickened as he thought of the pen and the drinking cup.

He couldn't see the trailer in the grove until he turned into the initial shady patch of trees. When he saw it, he stopped short. It was much bigger than he had conceived it. It was as long as a small freight car, and as big, curiously streamlined.

No one answered his knock.

He thought tensely: She ran this way. She must be inside. Uncertain, he walked around the monster on wheels. There was a line of windows above the level of his eyes that made a complete circuit of the trailer. He could see a gleamy ceiling and the upper part of what looked like finely paneled walls. There were three rooms, and the only other entrance led into the cab of the truck to which the trailer was attached.

Back before the first entrance, Drake listened intently for sounds. But again there was nothing—nothing except a thin wind that blew gently through the upper reaches of the trees. Far away, the train whistled plaintively. He tried the latch, and the door opened so easily that his hesitation ended. Deliberately, be pushed it ajar, and stood there staring into the middle room of the three.

His startled gaze met luxury. The floor was a marvel, a darkly gleaming, gemlike design. The walls toned in with an amazingly rich-looking, though quiet, panel effect. There was a couch just across from the door, two chairs, three cabinets, and several intricately carved shelves with art objects standing on them. The first thing Drake saw, as he climbed in, was the girl's basket standing against the wall just to the left of the door.

The sight stopped him short. He sat in the doorway, then, his legs dangling toward the ground. His nervousness yielded to the continuing silence and he began with a developing curiosity to examine the contents of the basket. There were about a dozen of the magic pens, at least three dozen of the folding, self-filling cups, a dozen roundish black objects that refused to respond to his handling, and three pairs of pince-nez glasses. Each pair had a tiny, transparent wheel attached to the side of the right lens. They seemed to have no cases; there seemed to be no fear that they would break. The pair he tried on fitted snugly over his nose, and for a moment he actually thought they fitted his eyes. Then he noticed the difference. Everything was nearer—the room, his hand—not magnified or blurred, but it was as if he were gazing through mildly powered field glasses. There was no strain on his eyes. After a moment, he grew conscious again of the little wheel. It turned quite easily.

Instantly, things were nearer, the field-glass effect twice as strong. Trembling a little, he began to turn the wheel, first one way, then the other. A few seconds only were needed to verify the remarkable reality. He had on a pair of pince-nez with adjustable lenses, an incredible combination of telescope-microscope: superglasses.

Almost blankly, Drake returned the marvelous things to the basket and, with abrupt decision, climbed into the trailer and moved toward the entrance to the back room. His intention was to glance in only. But that first look showed the entire wall fitted with shelves, each neatly loaded with a variety of small goods. Drake picked up what looked like a camera. It was a finely made little instrument. He studied the lens; his fingers pressed something that gave. There was a click. Instantly, a glistening card came out of a slit in the back. A picture.

It was of the upper part of a man's face. It had remarkable depth and an amazing natural color effect. It was the intent expression in the brown eyes that momentarily made the features unfamiliar. Then he recognized that he was looking at himself. He had taken his picture, and instantly it had been developed.

Astounded, Drake stuffed the picture in his pocket, set the instrument down, and, trembling, climbed out of the trailer and walked off down the road toward the village.

"—and then," said Jimmy, "a minute later you came back and climbed in and shut the door and went into the back room. You came back so fast that you nearly saw me; I thought you'd gone. And then—"

The trailer door opened. A girl's voice said something urgent that Drake didn't catch. The next instant, a man answered with a grunt. The door closed, and there was a movement and the sound of breathing in the center room.

Crouching, Drake drew back against the left wall.

"—and that's all, mister," Jimmy finished. "I thought there was going to be trouble then. And I hiked for home to tell mom."

"You mean," Drake protested, "I was foolish enough to come back just in time to get myself caught, and I didn't dare show myself?"

The boy shrugged. "You were pressing up against the partition. That's all I could see."

"And they didn't look in that room while you were watching?"

Jimmy hesitated. "Well," he began finally in a curious, defensive tone, "what happened then was kind of queer. You see, I looked back when I'd gone about a hundred yards, and the trailer and truck wasn't there no more."

"Wasn't there!" Drake spoke slowly. He had a sense of unreality. "You mean, they started up the truck engine, and drove to Piffer's Road, and so on down to the highway?"

The boy shook his head stubbornly. "Folks is always trying to trip me up on that. But I know what I saw and heard. There weren't no sound of an engine. They just was gone suddenly, that's all."

Drake felt an eerie chill along his spine. "And I was aboard?" he asked.

"You was aboard," said Jimmy.

The silence that followed was broken by the woman saying loudly, "All right, Jimmy, you can go and play."

She turned back to Drake. "Do you know what I think?" she said.

With an effort, Drake roused himself. "What?" he said.

"They're working a racket, the whole bunch of them together. The story about her father making the stuff. I can't understand how we fell for that. He just spent his time going around the district buying up old metal.

Mind you"—the admission came almost reluctantly—"they've got some wonderful things. The government isn't kidding when it says that after this war we're going to live like kings and queens. But there's the rub. So far, these people have only got hold of a few hundred pieces altogether. What they do is sell them in one district, then steal back and resell in another."

In spite of his intense self-absorption, Drake stared at her. He had run across the peculiar logic of fuzzy-minded people before, but it always shocked him when facts were so brazenly ignored in order that a crackpot theory might hold water. He said, "I don't see where the profit comes in. What about the dollar you got back for each item that was stolen?"

"Oh!" said the woman. Her face lengthened. Then she looked startled. And then, as she grasped how completely her pet idea was wrecked, an angry flush suffused her wind-and-sun-tanned face. "Some publicity scheme, maybe!" she snapped.

It struck Drake that it was time to terminate the interview. He said hastily, "Is anyone you know going into Inchney tonight? I'd like a ride if I could get it."

The change of subject did its work. The high color faded from the woman's cheeks. She said thoughtfully:

"Nope, no one I know of. But don't worry. Just get on the highway, and you'll get a lift—"

The second car picked him up. He sat in the hotel, as darkness fell, thinking: "A girl and her father with a carload of the finest manufactured goods in the world. She sells them as souvenirs, one to a person. He buys old metal. And then, as added insanity, an old man goes around buying up the goods sold"—he thought of Kellie's pen—"or breaking them." Finally, there was the curious amnesia of a fountain pen salesman, named Drake.

Somewhere behind Drake, a man's voice cried out in anguish, "Oh, look what you've done now. You've broken it."

A quiet, mature, resonant voice answered, "I beg your pardon. You paid a dollar for it, you say? I shall pay for the loss, naturally. Here—and you have my regrets."

In the silence that followed, Drake stood up and turned. He saw a tall, splendid-looking man with gray hair, in the act of rising from beside a younger chap who was staring at the two pieces of a broken pen in his fingers. The old man headed for the revolving door leading to the street, but it was Drake who got there first, Drake who said quietly but curtly, "One minute, please. I want an explanation of what happened to me after I got into the trailer of the girl, Selanie, and her father. And I think you're the man to give it to me."

He stopped. He was staring into eyes that were like pools of gray fire, eyes that seemed literally to tear into his face, and to peer with undiminished intensity at the inside of his brain. Drake had time for a brief, startled memory of what Kellie had said about the way this man had outfaced them on the train with one deadly look, and then it was too late for further thought. With a tigerish speed, the other stepped forward and caught Drake's wrist. There was the feel of metal in that touch, metal that sent a tingling glow along Drake's arm, as the old man said in a low, compelling voice, "This way—to my car."

Barely, Drake remembered getting into a long, gleamy-hooded car. The rest was darkness—mental—physical—

He was lying on his back on a hard floor. Drake opened his eyes and for a blank moment stared at a domed ceiling two hundred feet above him. The ceiling was at least three hundred feet wide, and nearly a quarter of it was window, through which a gray-white mist of light showed, as if an invisible sun were trying hard to penetrate a thin but persistent fog.

The wide strip of window ran along the center of the ceiling straight on into the distance. Into the *distance!* With a gasp, Drake jerked erect. For a moment then his mind wouldn't accept what his eyes saw.

There was no end to that corridor. It stretched in either direction until it became a blur of gray marble and gray light. There was a balcony and a gallery and a second gallery; each floor had its own side corridor, set off by a railing. And there were countless shining doors and, every little while, a branch corridor, each suggesting other vast reaches of that visibly monstrous building.

Very slowly, the first enormous shock over, Drake climbed to his feet. Memory of the old man—and what had gone before—was a weight in his mind. He thought darkly: "He got me into his car, and drove me here."

But why was he here? On all the wide surface of the Earth, no such building existed.

A chill went up his spine. It cost him a distinct effort to walk toward the nearest of the long line of tall, carved doors, and pull it open. What he expected, he couldn't have told. But his first reaction was disappointment. It was an office, a large room with plain walls. There were some fine-looking cabinets along one wall. A great desk occupied the corner facing the door. Some chairs and two comfortable-looking settees and another, more ornate door completed the picture. No one was in the room. The desk looked spick and span, dustless. And lifeless.

The other door proved to be locked, or else the catch was too complicated for him to work.

Out in the corridor again, Drake grew conscious of the intense silence. His shoes clicked with an empty sound. And door after door yielded the same office-furnished but uninhabited interior.

Half an hour passed, by his watch. And then another half-hour. And then he saw the door in the distance. At first it was only a brightness.

It took on glittering contours, became an enormous glass affair set in a framework of multi-tinted windows. The door was easily fifty feet in height. When he peered through its transparent panes, he could see great white steps leading down into a mist that thickened after about twenty feet, so that the lower steps were not visible.

Drake stared uneasily. There was something wrong here. That mist, obscuring everything, persisting for hours, clinging darkly. He shook himself. Probably there was water down there at the foot of the steps, warmish water subjected to a constant stream of cold air, and thick fog formed. He pictured that in his mind, a building ten miles long standing beside a lake, and buried forever in gray mists.

"Get out of here," Drake thought sharply.

The latch of the door was at a normal height. But it was hard to believe that he would be able to maneuver the gigantic structure with such a comparatively tiny leverage. It opened lightly, gently, like a superbly balanced machine. Drake stepped out into the pressing fog and began, swiftly at first, and then with a developing caution, to go down the steps. No use landing in a pool of deep water. The hundredth step was the last; and there was no water. There was nothing except mists, no foundations for the steps, no ground.

On hands and knees, dizzy with a sudden vertigo, Drake crawled back up the steps. He was so weak that inches only seemed to recede behind him. The nightmarish feeling came that the steps were going to crumble under him, now that he had discovered that their base was—nothing.

A second, greater fear came that the door would not open from the outside, and he would be cut off here, on the edge of eternity, forever. But it did open. It took all the strength of his weakened body. He lay on the floor inside, and after a while the awful wonder came to his mind: What did a girl called Selanie, dispensing marvelous gadgets on a train, have to do with this? There seemed to be no answer.

His funk yielded to the sense of safety produced by the passing minutes. He stood up, ashamed of his terror, and his mind grooving to a purpose. He must explore the fantastic place from cellar to roof. Somewhere, there would be a cache of the cups that created their own water. And perhaps also there would be food. Soon, he would have to eat and drink. But first, to one of the offices. Examine every cabinet, break open the desk drawers and search them.

It wasn't necessary to break anything. The drawers opened at the slightest tug. The cabinet doors were unlocked. Inside were journals, ledgers, curious-looking files. Absorbed, Drake glanced blurrily through several that he had spread out on the great desk. Blurrily because his hands were shaking and his brain seemed to be jumping. Finally, with an effort of will, he pushed everything aside but one of the journals. This he opened at random, and read the words printed there:

SYNOPSIS OF REPORT OF POSSESSOR KINGSTON CRAIG IN THE MATTER OF THE EMPIRE OF LYCEUS II
A. D. 27,346—27,378

Frowning, Drake stared at the date; then he read on:

The normal history of the period is a tale of cunning usurpation of power by a ruthless ruler. A careful study of the man revealed an unnatural urge to protect himself at the expense of others.

TEMPORARY SOLUTION: A warning to the Emperor, who nearly collapsed when he realized that he was confronted by a Possessor. His instinct for self-preservation impelled him to give guarantees as to future conduct.

COMMENT: This solution produced a probability world Type 5, and must be considered temporary because of the very involved permanent work that Professor Link is doing on the fringes of the entire two hundred seventy-third century.

CONCLUSION: Returned to the Palace of Immortality after an absence of three days.

Drake sat there, stiffly at first, then he leaned back in his chair; but the same blank impression remained in his mind. There seemed to be nothing to think about the report. At last, he turned a leaf, and read:

SYNOPSIS OF REPORT OF POSSESSOR KINGSTON CRAIG

This is the case of Laird Graynon, Police Inspector, 900th Sector Station, New York City, who on July 7, A.D. 2830 was falsely convicted of accepting bribes, and de-energized.

SOLUTION: Obtained the retirement of Inspector Graynon two months before the date given in the charge. He retired to his farm, and henceforth exerted the very minimum of influence on the larger scene of existence. He lived in this probability world of his own until his death in 2874, and thus provided an almost perfect 290A.

CONCLUSION: Returned to the Palace of Immortality after one hour.

There were more entries, hundreds—thousands altogether in the several journals. Each one was a "REPORT OF POSSESSOR KINGSTON

CRAIG," and always he returned to the "Palace of Immortality" after so many days, or hours, or weeks. Once it was three months, and that was an obscure, impersonal affair that dealt with the "establishment of the time of demarcation between the ninety-eighth and ninety-ninth centuries—" and involved "the resurrection into active, personal probability worlds of their own of three murdered men, named—"

The sharpening pangs of thirst and hunger brought to Drake a picture of himself sitting in this immense and terrible building, reading the fanciful scrawlings of a man who *must* be mad. It struck him that the seemingly sourceless light of the room was growing dimmer. The light must come in some way from outside. Out in the vast, empty corridor, he realized the truth. The mists above the ceiling window were graying, darkening. Night was falling. He tried not to think of that, of being alone in this tomblike building, watching the gloom creep over the gray marble, wondering what things might come out of hiding once the darkness grew impenetrable.

"Stop it, you fool!" Drake said aloud, savagely.

His voice sounded hollow against the silence. He thought: There must be a place here where these—Possessors—had lived. This floor was all offices, but there were other floors. He must find a stairway. He had seen none on the main corridor.

He found one fifty feet along the first side corridor. A broad staircase. Drake bounded up the steps and tried the first door he came to. It opened into the living room of a magnificent apartment. There were seven rooms, including a kitchen that gleamed in the dimming light, and the built-in cupboards of which were packed with transparent containers. The contents were foods both familiar and strange.

Drake felt without emotion. Nor was he surprised as he manipulated a tiny lever at the top of a can of pears and the fruit spilled out onto the table, although the can had not opened in any way. He saw to it that he had a dish for the next attempt; that was all. Later, after he had eaten, he searched for light switches. But it was becoming too dark to see.

The main bedroom had a canopied bed that loomed in the darkness, and there were pajamas in a drawer. Lying between the cool sheets, his body heavy with approaching sleep, Drake thought vaguely: That girl Selanie and her fear of the old man—why had she been afraid? And what *could* have happened in the trailer that had irrevocably precipitated Ralph Carson Drake into this?

He slept uneasily, with the thought still in his mind.

The light was far away at first. It came nearer, grew brighter, and at first it was like any awakening. Then, just as Drake opened his eyes, memories flooded his mind. He was lying, he saw tensely, on his left side. It was broad daylight. From the corners of his eyes he could see, above him, the silvery-blue canopy of the bed. Beyond it, far above, was the high ceiling.

In the shadows of the previous evening he had scarcely noticed how big and roomy and luxurious his quarters were. There were thick-piled rugs and paneled walls and rose-colored furniture that glowed with costly beauty. The bed was of oversize four-poster construction.

Drake's thought suffered a dreadful pause because, in turning his head away from the left part of the room toward the right, his gaze fell for the first time on the other half of the bed. A young woman lay there, fast asleep. She had dark-brown hair, a snowy-white throat, and, even in repose, her face looked fine and intelligent. She appeared to be about thirty years old.

Drake's examination got no further. Like a thief in the night, he slid from under the quilt. He reached the floor and crouched there. He held his breath in a desperate dismay as the steady breathing from the bed stopped. There was the sound of a woman sighing, and finally doom!

"My dear," said a rich contralto voice, lazily, "what on earth are you doing on the floor?"

There was movement on the bed, and Drake cringed in anticipation of the scream that would greet the discovery that he was not *the* my dear. But nothing happened. The lovely head came over the edge of the bed. Gray eyes stared at him tranquilly. The young woman seemed to have forgotten her first question, for now she said, "Darling, are you scheduled to go to Earth today?"

That got him. The question itself was so stupendous that his personal relation to everything seemed secondary. Besides, in a dim way he was beginning to understand.

This was one of those worlds of probability that he had read about in the journals of Possessor Kingston Craig. Here was something that *could* happen to Ralph Drake. And somewhere behind the scenes someone was making it happen. All because he had gone in search of his memory.

Drake stood up. He was perspiring. His heart was beating like a trip hammer. His knees trembled. But he stood up, and he said, "Yes, I'm going to Earth."

It gave him purpose, he thought tensely, reason to get out of here as fast as he possibly could. He was heading for the chair on which were his clothes when the import of his own words provided the second and greater shock to his badly shaken system.

Going to Earth! He felt his brain sag before the weight of a fact that transcended every reality of his existence. Going to Earth—from where? The answer was a crazy thing that sighed at last wearily through his mind: From the Palace of Immortality, of course, the palace in the mists, where the Possessors lived.

He reached the bathroom. The night before, he had discovered in its darkening interior a transparent jar of salve, the label of which said: BEARD REMOVER—RUB ON, THEN WASH OFF. It took half a minute; the rest, five minutes longer. He came out of the bathroom, fully dressed. His mind was like a stone in his head, and like a stone sinking through water he started for the door near the bed.

"Darling!"

"Yes?" Cold and stiff, Drake turned. In relief, he saw that she was not looking at him. Instead she had one of the magic pens and was frowning over some figures in a big ledger. Without looking up, she said, "Our time-relation to each other is becoming worse. You'll have to stay more at the palace, reversing your age, while I go to Earth and add a few years to mine. Will you make the arrangements for that, dear?"

"Yes," said Drake, "yes!"

He walked into the little hallway, then into the living room. Out in the corridor at last, he leaned against the cool, smooth marble wall, and thought hopelessly: Reverse his age! So that was what this incredible building did! Every day here you were a day younger, and it was necessary to go to Earth to strike a balance.

The shock grew. Because what had happened to him on the trailer was so important that a super-human organization was striving to prevent him from learning the truth. Somehow, today, he would really have to find out what all this was about, explore every floor, and try to locate some kind of central office. He was relaxing slowly, withdrawing out of that intense inward concentration of his mind when, for the first time, he grew conscious of sounds. Voices, movements, people below him.

Even as he leaped for the balcony balustrade, Drake realized that he should have known. The woman there in the bed—where she hadn't been—had implied a world complete in every detail of life. But he felt shocked, anyway. Bewildered, he stared down at the great main corridor of the building, along the silent, deserted reaches of which he had wandered for so many hours the day before. Now men and women swarmed along it in a steady stream. It was like a city street, with people moving in both directions, all in a hurry, all bent on some private errand.

"Hello, Drake!" said a young man's voice behind him.

Drake had no emotion left for that. He turned slowly, like a tired man. The stranger who stood there regarding him was tall and well-proportioned. He had dark hair and a full, strong face. He wore a shapely one-piece suit, pleasingly form-fitting above the waist. The trouser part puffed out like breeches. He was smiling in a friendly, quizzical fashion. He said finally, coolly:

"So you'd like to know what it's all about? Don't worry, you will. But first, try on this glove, and come with me. My name is Price, by the way."

Drake stared at the extended glove. "What—" he began blankly. He stopped. His mind narrowed around the conviction that he was being rushed along too fast for understanding. This man waiting for him here at the door was no accident. Drake braced himself. Take it easy, he thought sharply. The overwhelming, important thing was that *they* were out in the open at last. But what about this glove?

He accepted the thing, frowning. It was for his right hand. It fitted perfectly. It was light in weight, flexible, but it seemed unnaturally thick. The outer surface had a faint metallic sheen.

"Just grab his right shoulder with that glove, from behind," Price was saying. "Press below the collarbone with the points of your fingers, press hard. I'll give you an illustration later, after you've asked any questions you have on your mind."

Before Drake could speak, Price went on, "I'll tell you as we go along. Be careful of those stairs."

Drake caught himself, swallowed hard, and said, "What's all this nonsense about grabbing somebody by the shoulder? Why—"

He stopped, hopelessly. That shouldn't be his first question. He was like a blind man being given fragments of information about a world he couldn't see. There was no beginning, no coherence, nothing but these blurry half-facts. He'd have to get back to fundamentals. Ralph Carson Drake was a man in search of his memory. Something had happened to him aboard a trailer, and everything else had followed as the night the day. If he could keep that in mind, he'd be all right.

"Damn you!" Drake said out of the anguish of his bewilderment. "Damn you, Price, I want to know what this is all about."

"Don't get excited." They were down the steps now, heading along the side corridor to the great main hallway. Price half turned as he spoke. "I know just how you feel, Drake, but you must see that your brain can't be overloaded in one sustained assault of information. Yesterday, you found this place deserted. Well, that wasn't exactly yesterday."

He shrugged. "You see how it is. That was today in the alternative world to this one. That is how this building will be forever if you don't do what we want. We had to show you that. And now, for heaven's sake, don't ask me to explain the science and theory of time-probability."

"Look," said Drake desperately, "let's forget everything else, and concentrate on one fact. You want me to do something with this glove. What? Where? When? Why? I assure you I'm feeling quite reasonable. I—"

His voice faded. He saw suddenly that Price and he were in the main corridor, heading straight for the great doorway which led to the steps and the misty nothingness beyond them. He had a clammy feeling. He said sharply, "Where are you going?"

"I'm taking you to Earth."

"Out of that door?"

Drake stopped short. He wasn't sure just what he felt, but his voice sounded sharp and tense in his ears.

He saw that Price had paused. The man looked at him steadily. Price said earnestly, "There's nothing strange about any of this, really. The Palace of Immortality was built in an eddy of time, the only known Reverse, or Immortality, Drift in the Earth Time Stream. It has made the work of the Possessors possible, a good work as you know from your reading of Possessor Kingston Craig's reports—" His voice went on, explaining, persuading; but it was hard for Drake to concentrate on his words. That mist bothered him. He couldn't go down those steps again.

It was the word, Possessors, that brought Drake's mind and body back into active operation. He had seen and heard the term so often that for all these long minutes he had forgotten that he didn't know what it meant. He asked, "But who are the Possessors? What do they possess?"

The man looked at him, dark eyes thoughtful. "They possess," he said finally, "the most unique ability ever to distinguish men and women from their fellows. They can go through time at will. There are," Price went on, "about three thousand of them. They were all born over a period of five hundred years beginning in the twentieth century. The strangest thing of all is that every one of them originated in a single, small district of the United States, around the towns of Kissling, Inchney, and particularly in an infinitesimal farming community called Piffer's Road."

"But that," Drake said through dry lips, "is where I was born." His eyes widened. "And that's where the trailer was."

Price seemed not to have heard. "Physically," he said, "the Possessors are also unique. Every one of them has the organs of his or her body the opposite to that of a normal human being. That is, the heart is on the right side and—"

"But I'm like that," Drake said. He spoke precisely, as if he were fumbling his way through a labyrinth. "That's why the draft board rejected me. They said they couldn't take the risk of my getting wounded, because the surgeon wouldn't know my case history."

Behind Drake, footsteps clicked briskly. He turned automatically and stared at the woman in a fluffy, flowing dressing gown who was walking toward them. She smiled as she saw him, the smile he had already seen in the bedroom. She said in her rich voice as she came up:

"Poor fellow! He looks positively ill. Well, I did my best to make the shock easy for him. I gave him as much information as I could without letting on that I knew everything."

Price said, "Oh, he's all right." He turned to Drake. There was a faint smile on his face, as if he were appreciating the situation to the full. "Drake, I want you to meet your wife, formerly Selanie Johns, who will now tell you what happened to you when you climbed aboard her father's trailer at Piffer's Road. Go ahead, Selanie."

Drake stood there. He felt like a clod of earth, empty of emotion and of thought. It was only slowly that he grew aware of her voice telling the story of the trailer.

Standing there in the back room of the trailer, Drake wondered what might happen even now if he should be caught redhanded before he could act. He heard the man in the center room say, "We'll head for the fourteenth century. They don't dare do much monkeying around in this millennium."

He chuckled grimly, "You'll notice that it was an old man they sent, and only one of them at that. Somebody had to go out and spend thirty or forty years growing old, because old men have so much less influence on an environment than young. But we'd better waste no time. Give me those transformer points, and go into the cab and start the atomic transformers."

It was the moment Drake had been waiting for. He stepped out softly, flexing his gloved right hand. He saw the man standing facing in the direction of the door that led to the front room and the engine cab beyond it. From the back, the man looked of stocky build, and about forty-five years of age. In his hands, clutched tight, he held two transparent cones that glowed with a dull light.

"All right," he called gruffly as Drake stepped up behind him. "We're moving. And hereafter, Selanie, don't be so frightened. The Possessors are through, damn them. I'm sure our sale of that stuff, and the removal of so much metal has interfered with the electronic balances that made their existence possible." His voice shook. "When I think of the almighty sacrilege of that outfit, acting like God, daring to use their powers to change the natural course of existence instead of, as I suggested, making it a means of historical research—"

His voice collapsed into a startled grunt, as Drake grabbed his shoulder, and pressed hard below the collarbone—

"—just a minute!" Drake's voice cut piercingly across the woman's story. "You talk as if I had a glove like this"—he raised his right hand with its faintly gleaming glove, that Price had given him— "and there's also a suggestion in your words that I know everything about the Possessors and the Palace of Immortality. You're perfectly aware that I knew nothing at that time. I had just come off a train, where a fountain pen had been brought to my attention by a salesman called Bill Kellie."

He saw that the woman was looking at him gravely. She said, "I'm sure you will understand in a few minutes. Everything that we've done has been designed to lead up to this moment. Only a few hours of existence remains to this probability world—*this* one, where Mr. Price and you and I are standing; there is a strange balance of forces involved, and, paradoxical as it may seem, we are actually working against time."

Drake stared at her, startled by her tone, as she said urgently: "Let me go on, please—"

The stocky man stood utterly still, like a man who has been stunned by an intolerable blow. And then, as Drake let go of his shoulder, he turned slowly, and his gaze fastened sickly, not on Drake's face, but on the glove he wore.

"A Destroyer glove!" he whispered; then more wildly, "But how? The repellors are on my special invention that prevents a trained Possessor coming near me!" He looked for the first time at Drake's face. "How did you do it? I—"

"Father!" It was the girl's voice, clear and startled, from the engine cab. Her voice came nearer, "Father, we've stopped at about A.D. 1650. What's happened? I thought—"

She paused in the doorway like a startled bird, a tall, slim girl of around nineteen years, looking suddenly older, grayer, as she saw Drake. "You ... were on ... the ... train!" she said. Her gaze fluttered to her father. She gasped, "Dad, he hasn't—"

The stocky man nodded hopelessly. "He's destroyed my power to go through time. Wherever we are in time and space, we're *there*. Not that that matters. The thing is, we've failed. The Possessors live on to do their work."

The girl said nothing. The two of them seemed totally to have forgotten Drake. The man caught her arm, said hoarsely, "Don't you understand? We failed!"

Still she was silent. Her face had a bleached quality when she answered finally, "Father, this is the hardest thing I've ever said, but I'm glad. *They're* in the right; *you're* wrong. They're trying to do something about the terrible mistakes of Man and Nature. They've made a marvelous science of their great gift, and they use it like beneficent gods. It was easy enough for you to convince me when I was a child, but for years now my doubts have been gathering. I stayed with you through loyalty. I'm sorry, father." She turned. There were tears in her eyes as she opened the outer door and jumped to the green ground below.

Drake stood for a moment, fascinated by the play of emotions on the man's face, first a quiver of self-pity, then a gathering over-all expression of obstinacy. A spoiled child couldn't have provided a more enlightening picture of frustrated egoism. One long look Drake took. Then he, too, went to the door. There was the girl to make friends with, and an early western American world to explore and wonder at.

They were thrown into each other's company by the stubborn silence into which the older man retreated. They walked often along the green uninhabited valley, Drake and the girl. Once, a group of Indians on foot confronted the two of them far from the trailer. To Drake it was a question of who was the more startled. Selanie solved the problem with her atomic gun. She fired at a stone. It puffed out of sight in a flare of brilliance. No more Indians ever came that way.

In a way, it was an idyllic life, and love came as easily as the winds that blew mournfully across that lonely land. Came especially because he *knew*, and persisted against her early coldness. After that, they talked more urgently of persuading a self-willed man to train one or the other, or both of them, how to use their innate ability to travel in time. Drake knew that the man would give in eventually from sheer loneliness, but it took a year longer.

Drake's mind drew slowly back into the great domed palace, and he grew conscious that the woman's voice had ceased. He stared at her, then at Price. He said finally, puzzled, "Is that all? Your … father—" He looked at the woman, stumbling over the relationship. It was immensely difficult to connect this mature woman with youthful Selanie Johns. He pressed on, "You mean, your father was opposed to the work done by the Possessors? But how did he expect to eliminate them?"

It was Price who answered, "Mr. Johns's plan was to divert the local activity that had helped to create the Possessors. We know that foods definitely played a vital part, but just what combination of foods and other habits was the root cause, we have never learned.

"Mr. Johns thought, by having people drink from his cups, use his other food devices and general articles, he would break the general pattern of existence away from what it would normally have followed. His gathering of metal was also planned. Metal has a very strong influence on the great Time Stream. Its sudden removal from one time to another can upset entire worlds of probability. As for us, we could not interfere, except as you saw. The world prior to the twenty-fifth century is one age where no work will ever be done by the Possessors. It must solve its own problems. Even you, one of the first to possess the gift of time travel, though you would never of yourself have learned the method, had to be allowed to move toward your destiny almost naturally."

"Look," said Drake, "either I'm crazy or you are. I'm willing to accept everything—the existence of this Palace of Immortality, the fact that she's my wife in some future date, and that I've sort of dropped in on her before I married her, but *after* she married me. I'll accept all that, I say, but you gave me this glove a little while ago, and you said you wanted me to do something with it, and a few minutes ago my ... wife ... said that this world was in hourly danger of being wiped out. Is there something else that you haven't told me about? And why that spell of amnesia?"

Price cut him off, "Your part in all this is really very simple. As a salesman of the Quik-Rite Company, you followed Selanie, who was then nineteen years old, to a trailer at Piffer's Road occupied by her father and herself. When you got there, she wasn't to be found, nor was anyone else, so you started back to the village to make inquiries. On the way, however, you were picked up by Possessor Drail McMahon and transported one week ahead in time, and all relevant memory was drained from you. You awakened in the hospital."

"Just a minute!" Drake protested. "My ... wife ... has just told me what else I did. I knew that before, of course. There was an eyewitness, a boy named Jimmy, who saw me go back to the trailer, and that I was on it when it disappeared."

"Let me tell this," Price said coolly. "From the hospital, you set out to find what had happened to you. You did find out, and then you were transported here by another Possessor, and here you are."

Drake looked at the man, then at the woman. She nodded, and the first flame was already burning in his mind as Price continued, "In a few moments, I shall take you to Earth to the vicinity of the trailer of Peter Johns and his daughter. You will go aboard, conceal yourself in the back room and at the moment that Selanie has described to you, you will come out and grab her father by the shoulder with the glove. The glove produces energy that will subtly change the potential of his nerve force. It will not harm him, nor will we afterward. As a matter of fact, he will be used as a research agent by us." Price finished simply, "You can see that this action requires free will, and that we had to do everything as we have, to make sure that you would make no mistake."

Drake said, "I can see a lot of things."

He felt himself calm except for the way his soul was expanding. Slowly, he walked over to the woman, took her hand and gazed steadily into her eyes. He said, "This is you—when?"

"Fifty years from now in your life."

"And where am I? Where is your husband?"

"You went to Earth, into the future. You had to be out of the way. The same body cannot be in the same space. And that reminds me. That is the one hold we have on you."

"How?"

"If instead of entering the trailer, you walked off down the road to resume your life, in one week you would reach the time where your earlier self was in the hospital. You would vanish, disintegrate."

Drake smiled at her. "I don't think I'm going to muff it," he said.

Looking back, he could see her, as he walked down the steps into the thickening folds of mist. She was standing with her face pressed against the glass of the door.

The mist swallowed her.

His memory search was over. He was about to live the events he thought he had forgotten.

DEAR PEN PAL

Dear Pen Pal:

When I first received your letter from the interstellar correspondence club, my impulse was to ignore it. The mood of one who has spent the last seventy planetary periods—years I suppose you would call them—in an Aurigaen prison, does not make for a pleasant exchange of letters. However, life is very boring, and so I finally settled myself to the task of writing you.

Your description of Earth sounds exciting. I would like to live there for a while, and I have a suggestion in this connection, but I won't mention it till I have developed it further.

You will have noticed the material on which this letter is written. It is a highly sensitive metal, very thin, very flexible, and I have inclosed several sheets of it for your use. Tungsten dipped in any strong acid makes an excellent mark on it. It is important to me that you do write on it, as my fingers are too hot—literally—to hold your paper without damaging it.

I'll say no more just now. It is possible you will not care to correspond with a convicted criminal, and therefore I shall leave the next move up to you. Thank you for your letter. Though you did not know its destination, it brought a moment of cheer into my drab life.

Skander

Planet Aurigae II
Dear Pen Pal:

Your prompt reply to my letter made me happy. I am sorry your doctor thought it excited you too much, and sorry, also, if I have described my predicament in such a way as to make you feel badly. I welcome your many questions, and I shall try to answer them all.

309

You say the interstellar correspondence club has no record of having sent any letters to Aurigae. That, according to them, the temperature on the second planet of the Aurigae sun is more than 500 degrees Fahrenheit. And that life is not known to exist there. Your club is right about the temperature and the letters. We have what your people would call a hot climate, but then we are not a hydrocarbon form of life, and find 500 degrees very pleasant.

I must apologize for deceiving you about the way your first letter was sent to me. I didn't want to frighten you away by telling you too much at once. After all, I could not be expected to know that you would be enthusiastic to hear from me.

The truth is that I am a scientist, and, along with the other members of my race, I have known for some centuries that there were other inhabited systems in the galaxy. Since I am allowed to experiment in my spare hours, I amused myself in attempts at communication. I developed several simple systems for breaking in on galactic communication operations, but it was not until I developed a sub-spacewave control that I was able to draw your letter (along with several others, which I did not answer) into a cold chamber.

I use the cold chamber as both sending and receiving center, and since you were kind enough to use the material which I sent you, it was easy for me to locate your second letter among the mass of mail that accumulated at the nearest headquarters of the interstellar correspondence club.

How did I learn your language? After all, it is a simple one, particularly the written language seems easy. I had no difficulty with it. If you are still interested in writing me, I shall be happy to continue the correspondence.

Skander

Planet Aurigae II

Dear Pen Pal:

Your enthusiasm is refreshing. You say that I failed to answer your question about how I expected to visit Earth. I confess I deliberately ignored the question, as my experiment had not yet proceeded far enough. I want you to bear with me a short time longer, and then I will be able to give you the details. You are right in saying that it would be difficult for a being who lives at a temperature of 500 degrees Fahrenheit to mingle freely with the people of Earth. This was never my intention, so please relieve your mind. However, let us drop that subject for the time being.

I appreciate the delicate way in which you approach the subject of my imprisonment. But it is quite unnecessary. I performed forbidden experiments upon my body in a way that was deemed to be dangerous to the public welfare. For instance, among other things, I once lowered my surface temperature to 150 degrees Fahrenheit, and so shortened the radioactive cycle-time of my surroundings. This caused an unexpected break in the normal person to person energy flow in the city where I lived, and so charges were laid against me. I have thirty more years to serve. It would be pleasant to leave my body behind and tour the universe—but as I said I'll discuss that later.

I wouldn't say that we're a superior race. We have certain qualities which apparently your people do not have. We live longer, not because of any discoveries we've made about ourselves, but because our bodies are built of a more enduring element—I don't know your name for it, but the atomic weight is 52.9.* Our scientific discoveries are of the kind that would normally be made by a race with our kind of physical structure. The fact that we can work with temperatures of as high as—I don't know just how to put that—has been very helpful in the development of the sub-space energies which are extremely hot, and require delicate adjustments. In the later stages these adjustments can be made by machinery, but in the development the work must be done by "hand"—I put that word in quotes, because we have no hands in the same way that you have.

I am enclosing a photographic plate, properly cooled and chemicalized for your climate. I wonder if you would set it up and take a picture of yourself. All you have to do is arrange it properly on the basis of the laws of light—that is, light travels in straight lines, so stand in front of it—and when you are ready *think* "Ready!" The picture will be automatically taken.

Would you do this for me? If you are interested, I will also send you a picture of myself, though I must warn you. My appearance will probably shock you.

Sincerely,
Skander

Planet Aurigae II

Dear Pen Pal:

Just a brief note in answer to your question. It is not necessary to put the plate into a camera. You describe this as a dark box. The plate will take the picture when you think "Ready!" I assure you it will be flooded with light.

Skander

---

* A radioactive isotope of chromium.—Author's note.

Planet Aurigae II

Dear Pen Pal:

You say that while you were waiting for the answer to my last letter you showed the photographic plate to one of the doctors at the hospital—I cannot picture what you mean by doctor or hospital, but let that pass—and he took the problem up with government authorities. Problem? I don't understand. I thought we were having a pleasant correspondence, private and personal.

I shall certainly appreciate your sending that picture of yourself.

Skander

Planet Aurigae II

Dear Pen Pal:

I assure you I am not annoyed at your action. It merely puzzled me, and I am sorry the plate has not been returned to you. Knowing what governments are, I can imagine that it will not be returned to you for some time, so I am taking the liberty of inclosing another plate.

I cannot imagine why you should have been warned against continuing this correspondence. What do they expect me to do?—eat you up at long distance? I'm sorry but I don't like hydrogen in my diet.

In any event, I would like your picture as a memento of our friendship, and I will send mine as soon as I have received yours. You may keep it or throw it away, or give it to your governmental authorities—but at least I will have the knowledge that I've given a fair exchange.

With all best wishes,

Skander

Planet Aurigae II

Dear Pen Pal:

Your last letter was so slow in coming that I thought you had decided to break off the correspondence. I was sorry to notice that you failed to inclose the photograph, puzzled by your reference to having a relapse, and cheered by your statement that you would send it along as soon as you felt better—whatever that means. However, the important thing is that you did write, and I respect the philosophy of your club which asks its members not to write of pessimistic matters. We all have our own problems which we regard as overshadowing the problems of others. Here I am in prison, doomed to spend the next 30 years tucked away from the main stream of life. Even the thought is hard on my restless spirit, though I know I have a long life ahead of me after my release.

In spite of your friendly letter, I won't feel that you have completely re-established contact with me until you send the photograph.

Yours in expectation,

Skander

Planet Aurigae II

Dear Pen Pal:

The photograph arrived. As you suggest, your appearance startled me. From your description I thought I had mentally reconstructed your body. It just goes to show that words cannot really describe an object which has never been seen.

You'll notice that I've inclosed a photograph of myself, as I promised I would. Chunky, metallic looking chap, am I not, very different, I'll wager, than you expected? The various races with whom we have communicated become wary of us when they discover we are highly radioactive, and that literally we are a radioactive form of life, the only such (that we know of) in the universe. It's been very trying to be so isolated and, as you know, I have occasionally mentioned that I had hopes of escaping not only the deadly imprisonment to which I am being subjected but also the body which cannot escape.

Perhaps you'll be interested in hearing how far this idea has developed. The problem involved is one of exchange of personalities with someone else. Actually, it is not really an exchange in the accepted meaning of the word. It is necessary to get an impress of both individuals, of their mind and of their thoughts as well as their bodies. Since this phase is purely mechanical, it is simply a matter of taking complete photographs and of exchanging them. By complete I mean of course every vibration must be registered. The next step is to make sure the two photographs are exchanged, that is, that each party has somewhere near him a complete photograph of the other. (It is already too late, Pen Pal. I have set in motion the sub-space energy interflow between the two plates, so you might as well read on.) As I have said it is not exactly an exchange of personalities. The original personality in each individual is suppressed, literally pushed back out of the consciousness, and the image personality from the "photographic" plate replaces it.

You will take with you a complete memory of your life on Earth, and I will take along memory of my life on Aurigae. Simultaneously, the memory of the receiving body will be blurrily at our disposal. A part of us will always be pushing up, striving to regain consciousness, but always lacking the strength to succeed.

As soon as I grow tired of Earth, I will exchange bodies in the same way with a member of some other race. Thirty years hence, I will be happy to reclaim my body, and you can then have whatever body I last happened to occupy.

This should be a very happy arrangement for us both. You, with your short life expectancy, will have out-lived all your contemporaries and will have had an interesting experience. I admit I expect to have the better of the exchange—but now, enough of explanation. By the time you reach this part of the letter it will be me reading it, not you. But if any part of you is still aware, so long for now, Pen Pal. It's been nice having all those letters from you. I shall write you from time to time to let you know how things are going with my tour.

Skander

Planet Aurigae II

Dear Pen Pal:

Thanks a lot for forcing the issue. For a long time I hesitated about letting you play such a trick on yourself. You see, the government scientists analyzed the nature of that first photographic plate you sent me, and so the final decision was really up to me. I decided that anyone as eager as you were to put one over should be allowed to succeed.

Now I know I didn't have to feel sorry for you. Your plan to conquer Earth wouldn't have gotten anywhere, but the fact that you had the idea ends the need for sympathy.

By this time you will have realized for yourself that a man who has been paralyzed since birth, and is subject to heart attacks, cannot expect a long life span. I am happy to tell you that your once lonely pen pal is enjoying himself, and I am happy to sign myself with a name to which I expect to become accustomed.

With best wishes,
Skander

THE HARMONIZER

After it had sent two shoots out of the ground, the ibis plant began to display the true irritability of intelligent living matter. It became aware that it was growing.

The awareness was a dim process, largely influenced by the chemical reaction of air and light upon the countless membranes that formed its life structure. Tiny beads of acid were precipitated on these delicate colloidal films. The rhythm of pain-pleasure that followed surged down the root.

It was a very early stage in the development of an ibis plant. Like a new-born puppy, it reacted to stimuli. But it had no purpose as yet, and no thought. And it did not even remember that it had been alive previously.

Slash! Snip! The man's hoe caught the two silvery shoots and severed them about two inches below the ground.

"I thought I'd got all the weeds out of this border," said the man.

His name was Wagnowski, and he was a soldier scheduled to leave for the front the next day. He didn't actually use the foregoing words, but the gist of his imprecation is in them.

The ibis plant was not immediately aware of what had happened. The series of messages that had begun when the first shoot pushed up through the soil were still trickling down the root, leaving the impact of their meaning on each of a multitude of colloidal membranes. This impact took the form of a tiny chemical reaction, which in its small way caused a sensation.

Instant by instant, as those messages were transmitted by the slow electricity that obtained in the membranous films, the ibis plant came more alive. And tiny though each chemical consciousness was in itself, *no subsequent event could cancel it in the slightest degree.*

315

The plant was alive, and knew it. The hoeing out of its shoots and the upper part of its root merely caused a second wave of reactions to sweep downward. The chemical effect of this second wave was apparently the same as the earlier reaction: Beads of acid composed of not more than half a dozen molecules each formed on the colloid particles. The reaction seemed the same, but it wasn't. Before, the plant had been excited, almost eager. Now, it grew angry.

After the manner of plants, the results of this reaction were not at once apparent. The ibis made no immediate attempt to push up more shoots. But on the third day a very curious thing started to happen. The root near the surface came alive with horizontal sub-roots. These pushed along in the soil darkness, balancing by the simple process of being aware, like all plants, of gravitation.

On the eighth day one of the new roots contacted the root of a shrub, and began to wind in and around it. Somehow, then, a relation was established, and on the fifteenth day a second set of shoots forced the soil at the base of the shrub and emerged into the light. The radical, the astounding thing about this second set of shoots was that they were not of a silvery hue. They were a dark green. In color, shape, and texture the leaves, as they developed, seemed more and more exact duplicates of the leaves of the shrub.

Rapidly the new shoots shot up. As the weeks sped by, the "fear" that had induced chameleonism faded, and the leaves reverted to their silver color. Slowly, the plant became conscious of human and animal thoughts. But not until two hundred days later did the ibis begin to show its basic sensitivity. The reaction which followed was as potent and far reaching as had been the results of that same sensitivity in its previous existence.

That was eighty million years before.

The ship, with the ibis plants aboard, was passing through the solar system when the catastrophe occurred.

It came down onto an earth of marsh, fog, and fantastic reptilian monsters. It came down hard and out of control. Its speed as it struck the thick atmosphere was approximately colossal. And there was absolutely nothing that the superbeings aboard could do about it.

What had happened was a precipitation of the matter held in suspension in the drive chambers. As a result of condensation, the crystalloids in the sub-microscopic twilight zone above the molecule state lost surface area. Surface tensions weakened to a tenth, a hundredth, a thousandth of what was necessary. And at that moment, by the wildest accident, the ship passed near Earth and tangled with the dead mass of the gigantic planet's magnetic field.

Poor ship! Poor beings! Crashed now, dead now nearly eighty million years.

All that day and night, remnants of the ship burned and fused, and flared again in a white, destroying incandescence. When that first fire-shattered darkness ended, not much remained of what had been a mile-long liner. Here and there over the Cretaceous land and water and primeval forest, unburnt sections lay, jagged lumps of metal rearing up toward the perpetually muggy heavens, their lower parts sunk forever into a thick, fetid soil that would eat and eat at their strength until at last, the metal defeated, its elements would dissolve into earth and become earth.

Long before that happened, the ibis that were still alive had reacted to the dampness, and sent creepers out over the broken metal of what had been their culture room, out towards the gaping holes that opened into the soil. There had been three hundred plants, but in that last terrible period before the crash some effort had been made to destroy them.

Altogether, eighty-three ibis survived the deliberate attempt at their destruction; and among them there was a deadly race to take root. Those that came last knew instinctively that they had better move on. Of these latter, weakened by an injury in the crash, was *the* ibis. It reached the life-giving earth last of all. There followed a painful and timeless period when its creepers and its roots forced their way among the massed tangle of its struggling fellows towards the remote edge of the gathering forest of silver shrubs.

But it got there. It lived. And, having survived, having taken possession of a suitable area in which to develop without interference, it lost its feverishness, and expanded into a gracious, silver-hued tree.

A hundred, a hundred and fifty, two hundred feet tall it grew. And then, mature and satisfied, it settled down to eternal existence in a grotesque yet immensely fertile land. It had no thought. It lived and enjoyed and experienced existence. For a thousand years no acid beads formed on its colloidal membranes except the acids of reaction to light, heat, water, air, and other extrania of simply being alive.

The idyllic life was interrupted one gray soggy morning by a dull but tremendous thunder and a shaking of the ground. It was no minor earthquake. Continents shook in the throes of rebirth. Oceans rushed in where there had been land; and land surged wetly out of the warm seas. There had been a wide expanse of deep marsh water separating the forest of ibis trees from the mainland. When the shuddering of the tortured planet ended in the partial stability of that uneasy age, the marsh was joined to the distant higher ground by a long, bare, hill-like ridge.

At first it was merely mud, but it dried and hardened. Grass sprouted and shrubs made a tangle of parts of it. Trees came up from drift seed.

The young growth raced for the sky, and simultaneously waged a bitter battle for space, but all that was unimportant beside the fact that the ridge existed. The gap that isolated the ibis had been bridged. The new state of things was not long in manifesting. One timeless day a creature stamped boldly along the height, a creature with a rigidly upheld armored tail, teeth like knives, and eyes that glowed like fire with the fury of unending bestial hunger.

Thus came *Tyrannosaurus Rex* to the peaceful habitat of the ibis, and awakened from a latent condition a plant that had been cultivated and developed by its creators for one purpose only.

Animals were no new thing to the ibis trees. The surrounding marshes swarmed with great placid vegetarians. Gigantic snakes crawled among the ferns at the water's edge, and writhed through the muddy waters. And there was an endless scurrying of young, almost mindless beasts in and out among the silver trees.

It was a world of hungry life, but the hunger was for vegetation, or for living things that were scarcely more than plants, for the long, lush marsh grass, the leaf-laden shrubs, the soggy roots of water plants and the plants themselves, for primitive fish, for wriggling things that had no awareness of pain or even of their fate. In the quiet torpor of their existence, the plant-eating reptiles and amphibians were little more than Gargantuan plants that could move about.

The most enormous of all these well-behaved creatures, the long-necked, long-tailed brontosaurus, was eating of the generous leaves of a tall fern on the morning that the flesh-eating dinosaur walked onto the scene with all the tact of a battering ram.

The struggle that followed was not altogether one-sided. The brontosaurus had, above everything else, weight and a desire to escape, something that proved especially difficult because *Tyrannosaurus Rex* had his amazing teeth sunk into the thick lower part of the big fellow's neck, and also, he had dug his claws into the thick meat of the great side to which he was clinging. Movement for the brontosaurus was limited by the necessity of carrying along the multi-ton dinosaur.

Like a drunken giant, the great beast staggered blindly toward the marsh water. If it saw the ibis tree, it was a visualization that meant nothing. The crash knocked the brontosaurus off its feet, a virtual death sentence for a creature that, even under the most favorable circumstances, required ten minutes to stand up. In a few minutes, the dinosaur administered the *coup de grâce*, and, with a slobbering bloody ferocity, started gorging.

It was still at this grisly meal half an hour later when the ibis began reacting in a concrete fashion.

The initial reactions had begun almost the moment the dinosaur arrived in the vicinity. Every sensitive colloid of the tree caught the blasts of palpable lusts radiated by the killer. The thought waves of the beast were emitted as a result of surface tensions on the membranes of its embryo brain; and as these were electric in nature, their effect on the delicately balanced films of the ibis's membranes was to set off a feverish manufacture of acids. Quadrillions of the beads formed; and, though once again they seemed no different from similar acids created as a result of other irritants, the difference began to manifest itself half an hour after the brontosaurus grunted its final agony.

The ibis tree and its companions exuded a fragrance in the form of billions on billions of tiny dust motes. Some of these motes drifted down to the dinosaur, and were gulped into its lungs from where, in due course, they were absorbed into its bloodstream.

The response was not instantly apparent. After several hours, the dinosaur's gigantic stomach was satiated. It stalked off to wallow and sleep in a mudhole, quickly made extra-odorous by its own enormous droppings and passings, a process that continued as easily in sleep as during consciousness.

Waking, it had no difficulty scenting the unrefrigerated meat of its recent kill. It raced over eagerly to resume feeding, slept, and ate again, and then again. It took several days for its untiring digestion to absorb the brontosaurus, and then it was once more ravenously hungry.

But it didn't go hunting. Instead, it wandered around aimlessly and restlessly, looking for carrion. All around, amphibians and snakes moved and had their being, ideal prey. The dinosaur showed no interest. Except for an inadequate diet of the carrion of small reptiles, it spent the next week starving to death in the midst of plenty.

On the fifteenth day a trio of small, common dinosaurs came across its wasted body, and ate it without noticing that it was still alive.

On the wings of a thousand breezes, the fragrant spores drifted. There was no end to them. Eighty-three ibis trees had started manufacturing that for which they had been created. Once started, there was no stopping.

The spores did not take root. That wasn't what they were for. They drifted. They hung in the eddies above quiet glades, sinking reluctantly towards the dank earth, but always swift to accept the embrace of a new wind, so light, so airy themselves that journeys half-way around the earth proved not beyond their capabilities. In their wake they left a trail of corpses among the killer reptiles. Once tantalized by the sweet-scented motes, the most massive murderers in the history of the planet lost their brutality, their will to kill, and died like poisoned flies.

It took time, of course, but of that at least there was a plenitude. Each dead carnivore provided carrion meat for the hungry hordes that roamed the land; and so after a fashion, over the decades, tens of thousands of individuals lived on because of the very abundance of dead meat-eaters. In addition there was a normal death rate among the non-meat-eaters that had always provided a measure of easy food; and since there were fewer meat-eaters every year, the supply of meat per capita increased, at first gradually, and then with a suddenness and totality that was devastating.

The death of so many killers had created an imbalance between the carnivores and their prey. The vegetarians in their already huge numbers began to breed almost without danger. The young grew up in a world that would have been idyllic except for one thing: There was not enough food. Every bit of reachable green, every root, vegetable, and shoot was snatched by eager jaws before it could begin to mature.

For a time the remnants of the killers feasted. And then, once more, a temporary balance was struck. But again and again the prolific vegetarians dropped their young into a world made peaceful by the exudation of plants that couldn't stand brutality, yet felt nothing when death came by starvation.

The centuries poured their mist of forgetfulness over each bloody dip of that fateful seesaw. And all the while, as the millenniums slipped by, the ibises maintained their peaceful existence. For long and long it *was* peaceful, without incident of any kind. For a hundred thousand years the stately silver trees stood on their almost-island, and were content. During that vast expanse of time, the still unstable earth had rocked many times to the shattering and re-forming fury of colossal earthquakes, but it was not until the trees were well into their second hundred thousandth year that they were again affected.

A continent was rift and torn. The gap was about a thousand miles long, and in some places as much as twenty-five miles deep. It cut the edge of the island, and plummeted *the* ibis tree into an abyss three miles deep. Water raged into the hole, and dirt came roaring down in almost liquid torrents. Shocked and buried, the ibis tree succumbed to its new environment. It sank rapidly to the state of a root struggling to remain alive against hostile forces.

It was three thousand years later that the second last act of the ibis trees was played out on the surface of the planet.

A ship clothed in myriad colors slipped down through the murk and the gloom of the steaming jungle planet that was Cretaceous earth. As it approached the silver-hued grove, it braked its enormous speed and came to a full stop directly over the island in the marsh.

It was a much smaller machine than the grand liner that had crashed to a fiery destruction so many, many years before. But it was big enough to disgorge, after a short interval, six graceful patrol boats.

Swiftly, the boats sped to the ground.

The creatures who emerged from them were two-legged and two-armed, but there the resemblance to human form ended. They walked on rubbery land with the ease and confidence of absolute masters. Water was no barrier; they strode *over* it as if they were made of so much buoyant fluff. Reptiles they ignored; and, for some reason, whenever a meeting threatened, it was the beasts that turned aside, hissing with fear.

The beings seemed to have a profound natural understanding of purposes, for there was no speech among them. Without a sound or waste motion, a platform was floated into position above a small hill. The platform emitted no visible or audible force, but beneath it the soil spumed and ripped. A section of the drive chamber of the old, great ship catapulted into the air, and was held captive by invisible beams.

No dead thing this. It sparkled and shone with radiant energy. Exposed to the air, it hissed and roared like the deadly machine it was. Torrents of fire poured from it until something—*something green*—was fired at it from a long gun-like tube. The greenness must have been *a*-energy, and potent out of all proportion to its size. Instantly, the roaring, the hissing, the flaring of the energy in the drive chamber were snuffed out. As surely as if it were a living thing mortally struck, the metal lost its life.

The super-beings turned their concentrated attention on the grove of ibis trees. First they counted them. Then they cut incisions into several roots, and extracted a length of white pith from each. These were taken to the parent ship, and subjected to chemical examination. It was in this way that the discovery was made that there had been eighty-three trees. An intensive search for the missing tree began.

But the mighty rent in the planet's great belly had been filled in by drift and mud and water. Not a trace of it remained.

"It must be concluded," the commander noted finally in his logbook, "that the lost ibis was destroyed by one of the calamities so common on unfinished planets. Unfortunately, great damage has already been done to the natural evolution of the jungle life. Because of this accelerated development, intelligence, when it finally does emerge, will be dangerously savage in its outlook. The time lapse involved precludes all advance recommendations for rectification."

Eighty million years passed.

Wagnowski hurried along the quiet suburban road and through the gate. He was a thick, beefy soldier with cold blue eyes, coming home on leave;

and at first, as he kissed his wife, he didn't notice that there had been bomb damage to his house.

He finally saw the silver tree. He stared. He was about to exclaim, when he noticed that one whole wing of the house was an empty shell, a single wall standing vacuously in a precarious balance.

"The !-!-?-! American fascists!" he bellowed murderously. "!-! ? !-!"

It was less than an hour later that the sensitive ibis tree began to give off a delicious perfume. First Russia, then the rest of the world breathed the spreading "peace."

World War III ended.

THE GREAT JUDGE

"Judgment," said the rad, "in the case of Douglas Aird, tried for treason on August 2nd, last—"

With a trembling movement of his fingers, Aird turned the volume control higher. The next words blared at him.

"—That Douglas Aird do surrender himself one week from this day, that is, on September 17, 2460 A.D., to his neighborhood patrol station, that he then be taken to the nearest converter, there to be put to death—"

Click!

He had no conscious memory of shutting off the rad. One instant the sound roared through his apartment, the next there was dead silence. Aird sank back in his chair and stared with sick eyes through the transparent walls out upon the shining roofs of The Judge's City. All these weeks he had known there was no chance. The scientific achievements that, he had tried to tell himself, would weigh the balance in his favor—even as he assessed their value to the race, he had realized that the Great Judge would not consider them from the same view-point as himself.

He had made the fatal error of suggesting in the presence of "friends" that a mere man like Douglas Aird could govern as well as the immortal Great Judge, and that in fact it might be a good idea if someone less re-mote from the needs of the mass of the people had a chance to pro-mulgate decrees. A little less restriction, he had urged, and a little more individuality. With such abandon he had spoken on the day that he suc-ceeded in transferring the nervous impulses of a chicken into the nervous system of a dog.

He had attempted to introduce the discovery as evidence that he was in an excited and abnormal state of mind. But the magistrate pronounced the reason irrelevant, immaterial, and facetious. He refused to hear what the discovery was, ruling coldly: "The official science investigator of the Great Judge will call on you in due course, and you will then turn your invention over to him complete with adequate documentation."

Aird presumed gloomily that the investigator would call in a day or so. He toyed with the possibility of destroying his papers and instruments. Shudderingly, he rejected that form of defiance. The Great Judge's control of life was so complete that he permitted his enemies to remain at large until the day of their execution. It was a point made much of by the Great Judge's propaganda department. Civilization, it was said, had never before attained so high a level of freedom. But it wouldn't do to try the patience of the Great Judge by destroying an invention. Aird had a sharp conviction that less civilized methods might be used on him if he failed to carry through the farce.

Sitting there in his apartment, surrounded by every modern convenience, Aird sighed. He would spend his last week alive in any luxury he might choose. It was the final refinement of mental torture, to be free, to have the feeling that if only he could think of something he might succeed in escaping. Yet he knew escape was impossible. If he climbed into his hopjet, he'd have to swoop in at the nearest patrol station, and have his electronic registration "plates" stamped with a signal. Thereafter, his machine would continuously give off vibrations automatically advising patrol vessels of the time and space limitations of his permit.

Similar restrictions controlled his person. The electronic instrument "printed" on his upper right arm could be activated by any central, which would start a burning sensation of gradually increasing intensity.

There was absolutely no escape from the law of the Great Judge.

Aird climbed to his feet wearily. Might as well get his material ready for the science investigator. It was too bad he wouldn't have an opportunity to experiment with higher life forms but—

Aird stopped short in the doorway of his laboratory. His body throbbed with the tremendousness of the idea that had slammed into his mind. He began to quiver. He leaned weakly against the doorjamb, then slowly straightened.

"*That's it!*" He spoke the words aloud, his voice low and intense, simultaneously utterly incredulous and hopeful to the point of madness. It was the mounting hope that brought a return of terrible weakness. He collapsed on the rug just inside the laboratory, and lay there muttering to himself, the special insanities of an electronician.

"… have to get a larger grid, and more liquid, and—"

Special Science Investigator George Mollins returned to the Great Judge's Court, and immediately asked for a private interview with the Great Judge.

"Tell him," he told the High Bailiff of the Court, "that I have come across a very important scientific discovery. He will know what is meant if you simply say 'Category AA.'"

While he waited to be received, the Science Investigator arranged his instruments for readier transport, and then he stood idly looking around him at the dome-vaulted ante-room. Through a transparent wall he could see the gardens below. In the profusion of greenery, he caught the glint of a white skirt, which reminded him that the Great Judge was reputed to have at least seven reigning beauties in his harem at all times.

"This way, sir. The Great Judge will receive you."

The man who sat behind the desk looked about thirty-five years old. Only his eyes and his mouth seemed older. From bleak blue eyes and with thin-lipped silence, the immortal, ever-young Great Judge studied his visitor.

The latter wasted no time. The moment the door shut behind him, he pressed the button that released a fine spray of gas straight at the Great Judge. The man behind the desk simply sagged in his chair.

The visitor was calm but quick. He dragged the limp body around to his instrument case, and removed the clothes of the upper body. Swiftly, he swabbed the body with the liquid he had brought, and began to attach his nodes. Half a dozen on one side and a dozen on the other. The next step was to attach the wires to his own body, lie down, and press the activator.

The question that puzzled Douglas Aird on the day that he succeeded in transferring the nervous impulses of a chicken into the nervous system of a dog was, how complete was the transference?

Personality, he argued with himself, was a complex structure. It grew out of many quadrillions of minute experiences and, as he had discovered, finally gave to each body its own special neural vibration.

Would it be possible by artificially forcing that exact vibration upon another body to establish a nerve energy flow between the two bodies? A flow so natural and easy that every cell would be impregnated with the thoughts and memories of the other body? A flow so complete, that, when properly channeled, the personality of one body would flow into the other?

The fact that a dog acted like a chicken was not complete proof. Normally, he would have experimented very carefully before trying it on a human being. But a man doomed to die didn't have time to think of risks. When the Science Investigator called on him two days before the date of the execution, he gassed the man, and made the experiment then and there.

The transference was not absolutely complete. Blurred memories remained behind, enough to make the routine of going to the Great

Judge's Court familiar and easy. He had worried about that. It was important that he follow the right etiquette in approaching a man who normally permitted no one near him but people he had learned to trust.

As it turned out, he did everything right. The moment he felt the blurring sensation which marked the beginning of the transfer of his personality from the body of the Science Investigator to the body of the Great Judge, Aird acted. He released a gas toward the Great Judge that would revive the man in about five minutes. Simultaneously, he sprayed his present body with instantaneous anesthetic gas. Even as he sank into unconsciousness, he could feel the sharp, hard personality of the Great Judge slipping into the Investigator's body.

Five minutes later Douglas Aird, now in the body of the Great Judge, opened his eyes, and looked around him alertly. Carefully, he disconnected the wires, packed the instruments—and then called a bailiff. As he had expected, no one questioned the actions of the Great Judge. It was the work of an hour to drive to the apartment of Douglas Aird, transfer the Great Judge's personality to the body of Douglas Aird—and at the same time return the personality of the Science Investigator into its proper body. As a precaution, he had the Science Investigator taken to a hospital.

"Keep him there for three days under observation," he commanded.

Back at the Great Judge's Court, he spent the next few days cautiously fitting himself into the pleasant routine of a life of absolute power. He had a thousand plans for altering a police state into a free state, but as a scientist he was sharply aware of the need for orderly transition.

It was at the end of a week that he inquired casually about a traitor named Douglas Aird. The story was interesting. The man had, it seemed, attempted to escape. He had flown some five hundred miles in an unregistered hopjet before being grounded by a local patrol. Immediately, he fled into the mountains. When he failed to report on the morning of the day set for his execution, the printed instrument on his right arm was activated. Shortly before dusk, a tired, distracted, staggering scarecrow of a man, screaming that he was the Great Judge, appeared in a mountain patrol station. The execution was then carried out with no further delay.

The report concluded: "Seldom in the experience of the attending patrol officers has a condemned man approached the converter with so much reluctance."

The Great Judge, sitting at his desk in the luxurious court, could well believe it.

FAR CENTAURUS

I wakened with a start, and thought: How was Renfrew taking it?

I must have moved physically, for blackness edged with pain closed over me. How long I lay in that agonized faint, I have no means of knowing. My next awareness was of the thrusting of the engines that drove the spaceship.

Slowly this time, consciousness returned. I lay very quiet, feeling the weight of my years of sleep, determined to follow the routine prescribed so long ago by Pelham.

I didn't want to faint again.

I lay there, and I thought: It was silly to have worried about Jim Renfrew. He wasn't due to come out of his state of suspended animation for another fifty years.

I began to watch the illuminated face of the clock in the ceiling. It had registered 23:12; now it was 23:22. The ten minutes Pelham had suggested for a time lapse between passivity and initial action was up.

Slowly, I pushed my hand toward the edge of the bed. *Click!* My fingers pressed the button that was there. There was a faint hum. The automatic massager began to fumble gently over my naked form.

First, it rubbed my arms; then it moved to my legs, and so on over my body. As it progressed, I could feel the fine slick of oil that oozed from it working into my dry skin.

A dozen times I could have screamed from the pain of life returning. But in an hour I was able to sit up and turn on the lights.

The small, sparsely furnished, familiar room couldn't hold my attention for more than an instant. I stood up.

The movement must have been too abrupt. I swayed, caught on to the metal column of the bed, and retched discolored stomach juices.

The nausea passed. But it required an effort of will for me to walk to the door, open it, and head along the narrow corridor that led to the control room.

I wasn't supposed to so much as pause there, but a spasm of absolutely dreadful fascination seized me; and I couldn't help it. I leaned over the control chair, and glanced at the chronometer.

It said: 53 years, 7 months, 2 weeks, 0 days, 0 hours and 27 minutes.

Fifty-three years! A little blindly, almost blankly, I thought: Back on Earth, the people we had known, the young men we'd gone to college with, that girl who had kissed me at the party given us the night we left—they were all dead. Or dying of old age.

I remembered the girl very vividly. She was pretty, vivacious, a complete stranger. She had laughed as she offered her red lips, and she had said, "A kiss for the ugly one, too."

She'd be a grandmother now, or in her grave.

Tears came to my eyes. I brushed them away, and began to heat the can of concentrated liquid that was to be my first food. Slowly, my mind calmed.

Fifty-three years and seven and one half months, I thought drably. Nearly four years over my allotted time. I'd have to do some figuring before I took another dose of Eternity drug. Twenty grains had been calculated to preserve my flesh and my life for exactly fifty years.

The stuff was evidently more potent than Pelham had been able to estimate from his short, period advance tests.

I sat tense, narrow-eyed, thinking about that. Abruptly, I grew conscious of what I was doing. Laughter spat from my lips. The sound split the silence like a series of pistol shots, startling me.

But it also relieved me. Was I sitting here actually being critical?

A miss of only four years was bull's-eye across that span of years.

Why, I was alive and still young. Time and space had been conquered. The universe belonged to man.

I ate my "soup", sipping each spoonful deliberately. I made the bowl last every second of thirty minutes. Then, greatly refreshed, I made my way back to the control room.

This time I paused for a long look through the plates. It took only a few moments to locate Sol, a very brightly glowing star in the approximate center of the rearview plate.

Alpha Centauri required longer to locate. But it shone finally, a glow point in a light sprinkled darkness.

I wasted no time trying to estimate their distances. They *looked* right.

In fifty-four years we had covered approximately one tenth of the four and one third light years to the famous nearest star system.

Satisfied, I threaded my way back to the living quarters. Take them in a row, I thought. Pelham first.

As I opened the air-tight door of Pelham's room, a sickening odor of decayed flesh tingled in my nostrils. With a gasp I slammed the door, stood there in the narrow hallway, shuddering.

After a minute, there was still nothing but the reality.

Pelham was dead.

I cannot clearly remember what I did then. I ran; I know that. I flung open Renfrew's door, then Blake's. The clean, sweet smell of their rooms, the sight of their silent bodies on their beds brought back a measure of my sanity.

A great sadness came to me. Poor, brave Pelham. Inventor of the Eternity drug that had made the great plunge into interstellar space possible, he lay dead now from his own invention.

What was it he had said: "The chances are greatly against any of us dying. But there is what I am calling a death factor of about ten percent, a by-product of the first dose. If our bodies survive the initial shock, they will survive additional doses."

The death factor must be greater than ten percent. That extra four years the drug had kept me asleep—

Gloomily, I went to the storeroom, and procured my personal space-suit and a tarpaulin. But even with their help, it was a horrible business. The drug had preserved the body to some extent, but pieces kept falling off as I lifted it.

At last, I carried the tarpaulin and its contents to the air lock, and shoved it into space.

I felt pressed now for time. These waking periods were to be brief affairs, in which what we called the "current" oxygen was to be used up, but the main reserves were not to be touched. Chemicals in each room slowly refreshed the "current" air over the years, readying it for the next to awaken.

In some curious defensive fashion, we had neglected to allow for an emergency like the death of one of our members; even as I climbed out of the spacesuit, I could feel the difference in the air I was breathing.

I went first to the radio. It had been calculated that half a light year was the limit of radio reception, and we were approaching that limit now.

Hurriedly, though carefully, I wrote my report out, then read it into a transcription record, and started sending. I set the record to repeat a hundred times.

In a little more than five months hence, headlines would be flaring on Earth.

I clamped my written report into the ship log book, and added a note for Renfrew at the bottom. It was a brief tribute to Pelham. My praise was heartfelt, but there was another reason behind my note. They had been pals, Renfrew, the engineering genius who built the ship, and Pelham, the great chemist-doctor, whose Eternity drug had made it possible for men to take this fantastic journey into vastness.

It seemed to me that Renfrew, waking up into the great silence of the hurtling ship, would need my tribute to his friend and colleague. It was little enough for me to do, who loved them both.

The note written, I hastily examined the glowing engines, made notations of several instrument readings, and then counted out fifty-five grains of Eternity drug. That was as close as I could get to the amount I felt would be required for one hundred and fifty years.

For a long moment before sleep came, I thought of Renfrew and the terrible shock that was coming to him on top of all the natural reactions to his situation, that would strike deep into his peculiar, sensitive nature—

I stirred uneasily at the picture.

The worry was still in my mind when darkness came.

Almost instantly, I opened my eyes. I lay thinking: The drug! It hadn't worked.

The draggy feel of my body warned me of the truth. I lay very still watching the clock overhead. This time it was easier to follow the routine except that, once more, I could not refrain from examining the chronometer as I passed through the galley.

It read: 201 years,1 month, 3 weeks, 5 days, 7 hours, 8 minutes.

I sipped my bowl of that super soup, then went eagerly to the big log book.

It is utterly impossible for me to describe the thrill that coursed through me, as I saw the familiar handwriting of Blake, and then, as I turned back the pages, of Renfrew.

My excitement drained slowly, as I read what Renfrew had written. It was a report; nothing more: gravitometric readings, a careful calculation of the distance covered, a detailed report on the performance of the engines, and, finally, an estimate of our speed variations, based on the seven consistent factors.

It was a splendid mathematical job, a first-rate scientific analysis. But that was all there was. No mention of Pelham, not a word of comment on what I had written or on what had happened.

Renfrew had wakened; and, if his report was any criterion, he might as well have been a robot.

I knew better than that.

So—I saw as I began to read Blake's report—did Blake.

Bill:

TEAR THIS SHEET OUT WHEN YOU'VE READ IT!

Well, the worst has happened. We couldn't have asked fate to give us an unkindlier kick in the pants. I hate to think of Pelham being dead. What a man he was, what a friend! But we all knew the risk we were taking, he more than any of us. So all we can say is, "Sleep well, good friend. We'll never forget you."

But Renfrew's case is now serious. After all, we were worried, wondering how he'd take his first awakening, let alone a bang between the eyes like Pelham's death. And I think that the first anxiety was justified.

As you and I have always known, Renfrew was one of Earth's fair-haired boys. Just imagine any one human being born with his combination of looks, money and intelligence. His great fault was that he never let the future trouble him. With that dazzling personality of his, and the crew of worshipping women and yes-men around him, he didn't have much time for anything but the present.

Realities always struck him like a thunderbolt. He could leave those three ex-wives of his—and they weren't so ex, if you ask me—without grasping that it was forever.

That good-bye party was enough to put anyone into a sort of mental haze when it came to realities. To wake up a hundred years later, and realize that those he loved had withered, died and been eaten by worms—well-l-l!

(I deliberately put it as baldly as that, because the human mind thinks of awfully strange angles, no matter how it censors speech.)

I personally counted on Pelham acting as a sort of psychological support to Renfrew; and we both know that Pelham recognized the extent of his influence over Renfrew. That influence must be replaced. Try to think of something, Bill, while you're charging around doing the routine work. We've got to live with that guy after we all wake up at the end of five hundred years.

Tear out this sheet. What follows is routine.   Ned

I burned the letter in the incinerator, examined the two sleeping bodies—how deathly quiet they lay!—and then returned to the control room.

In the plate, the sun was a very bright star, a jewel set in black velvet, a gorgeous, shining brilliant.

Alpha Centauri was brighter. It was a radiant light in that panoply of black and glitter. It was still impossible to make out the separate suns of

Alpha A, B, C, and Proxima, but their combined light brought a sense of awe and majesty.

Excitement blazed inside me; and consciousness came of the glory of this trip we were making, the first men to head for far Centaurus, the first men to dare aspire to the stars.

Even the thought of Earth failed to dim that surging tide of wonder; the thought that seven, possibly eight generations, had been born since our departure; the thought that the girl who had given me the sweet remembrance of her red lips, was now known to her descendants as their great-great-great-great-grandmother if she were remembered at all.

The immense time involved, the whole idea, was too meaningless for emotion.

I did my work, took my third dose of the drug, and went to bed. The sleep found me still without a plan about Renfrew.

When I woke up, alarm bells were ringing.

I lay still. There was nothing else to do. If I had moved, consciousness would have slid from me. Though it was mental torture even to think it, I realized that, no matter what the danger, the quickest way was to follow my routine to the second and in every detail.

Somehow I did it. The bells clanged and *brrred*, but I lay there until it was time to get up. The clamor was hideous, as I passed through the control room. But I passed through and sat for half an hour sipping my soup.

The conviction came to me that if that sound continued much longer, Blake and Renfrew would surely waken from their sleep.

At last, I felt free to cope with the emergency. Breathing hard, I eased myself into the control chair, cut off the mind-wrecking alarms, and switched on the plates.

A fire glowed at me from the rear-view plate. It was a colossal *white* fire, longer than it was wide, and filling nearly a quarter of the whole sky. The hideous thought came to me that we must be within a few million miles of some monstrous sun that had recently roared into this part of space.

Frantically, I manipulated the distance estimators—and then for a moment stared in blank disbelief at the answers that clicked metallically onto the product plate.

Seven miles! *Only* seven miles! Curious is the human mind. A moment before, when I had thought of it as an abnormally shaped sun, it hadn't resembled anything but an incandescent mass. Abruptly, now, I saw that it had a solid outline, an unmistakable material shape.

Stunned, I leaped to my feet because—

It was a spaceship! An enormous, mile-long ship. Rather—I sank back into my seat, subdued by the catastrophe I was witnessing, and consciously adjusting my mind—the flaming hell of what had been a spaceship. Nothing that had been alive could possibly still be conscious in that horror of ravenous fire. The only possibility was that the crew had succeeded in launching lifeboats.

Like a madman, I searched the heavens for a light, a glint of metal that would show the presence of survivors.

There was nothing but the night and the stars and the hell of burning ship.

After a long time, I noticed that it was farther away, and seemed to be receding. Whatever drive forces had matched its velocity to ours must be yielding to the fury of the energies that were consuming the ship.

I began to take pictures, and I felt justified in turning on the oxygen reserves. As it withdrew into distance, the miniature nova that had been a torpedo-shaped space liner began to change color, to lose its white intensity. It became a red fire silhouetted against darkness. My last glimpse showed it as a long, dull glow that looked like nothing else than a cherry colored nebula seen edge on, like a blaze reflecting from the night beyond a far horizon.

I had already, in between observations, done everything else required of me; and now, I re-connected the alarm system and, very reluctantly, my mind seething with speculation, returned to bed.

As I lay waiting for my final dosage of the trip to take effect, I thought: the great star system of Alpha Centauri must have inhabited planets. If my calculations were correct, we were only one point six light years from the main Alpha group of suns, slightly nearer than that to red Proxima.

Here was proof that the universe had at least one other supremely intelligent race. Wonders beyond our wildest expectation were in store for us. Thrill on thrill of anticipation raced through me.

It was only at the last instant, as sleep was already grasping at my brain, that the realization struck that I had completely forgotten about the problem of Renfrew.

I felt no alarm. Surely, even Renfrew would come alive in that great fashion of his when confronted by a complex alien civilization.

Our troubles were over.

Excitement must have bridged that final one hundred fifty years of time. Because, when I wakened, I thought:

"We're here! It's over, the long night, the incredible journey. We'll all be waking, seeing each other, as well as the civilization out there. Seeing, too, the great Centauri suns."

The strange thing, it struck me as I lay there exulting, was that the time seemed long. And yet ... yet I had been awake only three times, and only once for the equivalent of a full day.

In the truest sense of meaning, I had seen Blake and Renfrew—and Pelham—no more than a day and a half ago. I had had only thirty-six hours of consciousness since a pair of soft lips had set themselves against mine, and clung in the sweetest kiss of my life.

Then why this feeling that millenniums had ticked by, second on slow second? Why this eerie, empty awareness of a journey through fathomless, unending night?

Was the human mind so easily fooled?

It seemed to me, finally, that the answer was that *I* had been alive for those five hundred years, all my cells and my organs had existed, and it was not even impossible that some part of my brain had been horrendously aware throughout the entire unthinkable period.

And there was, of course, the additional psychological fact that I knew now that five hundred years had gone by, and that—

I saw with a mental start that my ten minutes were up. Cautiously, I turned on the massager.

The gentle, padded hands had been working on me for about fifteen minutes when my door opened; the light clicked on, and there stood Blake.

The too-sharp movement of turning my head to look at him made me dizzy. I closed my eyes, and heard him walk across the room toward me.

After a minute, I was able to look at him again without seeing blurs. I saw then that he was carrying a bowl of the soup. He stood staring down at me with a strangely grim expression on his face.

At last, his long, thin countenance relaxed into a wan grin.

"Lo, Bill," he said. *"Ssshh!"* he hissed immediately. "Now, don't try to speak. I'm going to start feeding you this soup while you're still lying down. The sooner you're up, the better I'll like it."

He was grim again, as he finished almost as if it were an afterthought: "I've been up for two weeks."

He sat down on the edge of the bed, and ladled out a spoonful of soup. There was silence, then, except for the rustling sound of the massager. Slowly, the strength flowed through my body; and with each passing second, I became more aware of the grimness of Blake.

"What about Renfrew?" I managed finally, hoarsely. "He awake?"

Blake hesitated, then nodded. His expression darkened with frown; he said simply:

"He's mad, Bill, stark, staring mad. I had to tie him up. I've got him now in his room. He's quieter now, but at the beginning he was a gibbering maniac."

"Are you crazy?" I whispered at last. "Renfrew was never so sensitive as that. Depressed and sick, yes: but the mere passage of time, abrupt awareness that all his friends are dead, couldn't make him insane."

Blake was shaking his head. "It isn't only that. Bill—"

He paused, then: "Bill, I want you to prepare your mind for the greatest shock it's ever had."

I stared up at him with an empty feeling inside me. "What do you mean?"

He went on grimacing: "I know you'll be able to take it. So don't get scared. You and I, Bill, are just a couple of lugs. We're along because we went to U with Renfrew and Pelham. Basically, it wouldn't matter to insensitives like us whether we landed in 1,000,000 B.C. or A.D. 13. We'd just look around and say: 'Fancy seeing you here, mug!' or 'Who was that pterodactyl I saw you with last night? That wasn't no pterodactyl; that was Unthahorsten's bulbous brained wife.'"

I whispered, "Get to the point. What's up?"

Blake rose to his feet. "Bill, after I'd read your reports about, and seen the photographs of, that burning ship, I got an idea. The Alpha suns were pretty close two weeks ago, only about six months away at our average speed of five hundred miles a second. I thought to myself: 'I'll see if I can tune in some of their radio stations.'"

"Well," he smiled wryly, "I got hundreds in a few minutes. They came in all over the seven wave dials, with bell-like clarity."

He paused; he stared down at me, and his smile was a sickly thing. "Bill," he groaned, "we're the prize fools in creation. When I told Renfrew the truth, he folded up like ice melting into water."

Once more, he paused; the silence was too much for my straining nerves.

"For Heaven's sake, man—" I began. And stopped. And lay there, very still. Just like that the lightning of understanding flashed on me. My blood seemed to thunder through my veins. At last, weakly, I said: "You mean—"

Blake nodded. "Yeah," he said. "That's the way it is. And they've already spotted us with their spy rays and energy screens. A ship's coming out to meet us.

"I only hope," he finished gloomily, "they can do something for Jim."

I was sitting in the control chair an hour later when I saw the glint in the darkness. There was a flash of bright silver that exploded into size. The next instant, an enormous spaceship had matched our velocity less than a mile away.

Blake and I looked at each other. "Did they say," I said shakily, "that that ship left its hangar ten minutes ago?"

Blake nodded. "They can make the trip from Earth to Centauri in three hours," he said.

I hadn't heard that before. Something happened inside my brain. "What!" I shouted. "Why, it's taken us five hund—"

I stopped; I sat there. "Three hours!" I whispered. "How *could* we have forgotten human progress?"

In the silence that fell then, we watched a dark hole open in the cliff-like wall that faced us. Into this cavern, I directed our ship.

The rear-view plate showed that the cave entrance was closing. Ahead of us lights flashed on, and focused on a door. As I eased our craft to the metal floor, a face flickered onto our radio plate.

"Cassellahat!" Blake whispered in my ear. "The only chap who's talked direct to me so far."

It was a distinguished, a scholarly looking head and face that peered at us. Cassellahat smiled, and said:

"You may leave your ship, and go through the door you see."

I had a sense of empty spaces around us, as we climbed gingerly out into the vast receptor chamber. Interplanetary spaceship hangars were like that, I reminded myself. Only this one had an alien quality that—

"Nerves!" I thought sharply.

But I could see that Blake felt it too. A silent duo, we filed through the doorway into a hallway, that opened into a very large, luxurious room.

It was such a room as a king or a movie actress on set might have walked into without blinking. It was all hung with gorgeous tapestries— that is, for a moment, I thought they were tapestries; then I saw they weren't. They were—I couldn't decide.

I had seen expensive furniture in some of the apartments Renfrew maintained. But these settees, chairs, and tables glittered at us, as if they were made of a matching design of differently colored fires. No, that was wrong; they didn't glitter at all. They—

Once more I couldn't decide.

I had no time for more detailed examination. For a man, arrayed very much as we were, was rising from one of the chairs. I recognized Cassellahat.

He came forward, smiling. Then he slowed, his nose wrinkling. A moment later, he hastily shook our hands, then swiftly retreated to a chair ten feet away, and sat down rather primly.

It was an astoundingly ungracious performance. But I was glad that he had drawn back that way. Because, as he shook my hand so briefly, I had caught a faint whiff of perfume from him. It was a vaguely unpleasant odor; and, besides—a man using perfume in quantities!

I shuddered. What kind of foppish nonsense had the human race gone in for?

He was motioning us to sit down. I did so, wondering: Was this our reception? The erstwhile radio operator began:

"About your friend, I must caution you. He is a schizoid type, and our psychologists will be able to effect a temporary recovery only for the moment. A permanent cure will require a longer period, and your fullest cooperation. Fall in readily with all Mr. Renfrew's plans, unless, of course, he takes a dangerous turn.

"But now"—he squirted us a smile—"permit me to welcome you to the four planets of Centauri. It is a great moment for me, personally. From early childhood, I have been trained for the sole purpose of being your mentor and guide; and naturally I am overjoyed that the time has come when my exhaustive studies of the middle period American language and customs can be put to the practical use for which they were intended."

He didn't look overjoyed. He was wrinkling his nose in that funny way I had already noticed, and there was a generally pained expression on his face. But it was his words that shocked me.

"What do you mean," I asked, "studies in American? Don't people speak the universal language any more?"

"Of course"—he smiled—"but the language has developed to a point where—I might as well be frank—you would have difficulty understanding such a simple word as 'yeih.'"

"Yeih?" Blake echoed.

"Meaning 'yes.'"

"Oh!"

We sat silent. Blake chewing his lower lip. It was Blake who finally said:

"What kind of places are the Centauri planets? You said something on the radio about the population centers having reverted to the city structure again."

"I shall be happy," said Cassellahat, "to show you as many of our great cities as you care to see. You are our guests, and several million credits have been placed to your separate accounts for you to use as you see fit."

"Gee!" said Blake.

"I must, however," Cassellahat went on, "give you a warning. It is important that you do not disillusion our peoples about yourselves. Therefore, you must never wander around the streets, or mingle with the crowds in any way. Always, your contact should be via newsreels, radio, or from the *inside* of a closed machine. If you have any plan to marry, you must now finally give up the idea."

"I don't get it!" Blake said wonderingly; and he spoke for us both.

Cassellahat finished firmly: "It is important that no one becomes aware that you have an offensive physical odor. It might damage your financial prospects considerably.

"And now"—he stood up—"for the time being, I shall leave you. I hope you don't mind if I wear a mask in the future in your presence. I wish you well, gentlemen, and—"

He paused, glanced past us, said: "Ah, here is your friend."

I whirled, and I could see Blake twisting, staring—

"Hi, there, fellows." Renfrew said cheerfully from the door, then wryly: "Have we ever been a bunch of suckers?"

I felt choked. I raced up to him, caught his hand, hugged him. Blake was trying to do the same.

When we finally released Renfrew, and looked around, Cassellahat was gone.

Which was just as well. I had been wanting to punch him in the nose for his final remarks.

"Well, here goes!" Renfrew said.

He looked at Blake and me, grinned, rubbed his hands together gleefully, and added:

"For a week I've been watching, thinking up questions to ask this cluck and—"

He faced Cassellahat. "What," he began. "makes the speed of light constant?"

Cassellahat did not even blink. "Velocity equals the cube of the cube root of *gd*." he said, "*d* being the depth of the space time continuum, *g* the total toleration or gravity, as you would say, of all the matter in that continuum."

"How are planets formed?"

"A sun must balance itself in the space that it is in. It throws out matter as a sea vessel does anchors. That's a very rough description. I could give it to you in mathematical formula, but I'd have to write it down. After all, I'm not a scientist. These are merely facts that I've known from childhood, or so it seems."

"Just a minute," said Renfrew, puzzled. "A sun throws this matter out without any pressure other than its—desire—to balance itself?"

Cassellahat stared at him. "Of course not. The reason, the pressure involved, is very potent, I assure you. Without such a balance, the sun would fall out of this space. Only a few bachelor suns have learned how to maintain stability without planets."

"A few what?" echoed Renfrew.

I could see that he had been jarred into forgetting the questions he had been intending to ask one by swift one. Cassellahat's words cut across my thought; he said:

"A bachelor sun is a very old, cooled class M star. The hottest one known has a temperature of one hundred ninety degrees F, the coldest forty-eight. Literally, a bachelor is a rogue, crotchety with age. Its main feature is that it permits no matter, no planets, not even gases in its vicinity."

Renfrew sat silent, frowning, thoughtful. I seized the opportunity to carry on a train of idea.

"This business," I said, "of knowing all this stuff without being a scientist, interests me. For instance, back home every kid understood the atomic-rocket principle practically from the day he was born. Boys of eight and ten rode around in specially made toys, took them apart and put them together again. They *thought* rocket-atomic, and any new development in the field was just pie for them to absorb.

"Now, here's what I'd like to know: what is the parallel here to that particular angle?"

"The adeledicnander force," said Cassellahat. "I've already tried to explain it to Mr. Renfrew, but his mind seems to balk at some of the most simple aspects."

Renfrew roused himself, grimaced. "He's been trying to tell me that electrons think; and I won't swallow it."

Cassellahat shook his head. "Not think; they don't think. But they have a psychology."

"Electronic psychology!" I said.

"Simply adeledicnander," Cassellahat replied. "Any child—"

Renfrew groaned: "I know. Any child of six could tell me."

He turned to us. "That's why I lined up a lot of questions. I figured that if we got a good intermediate grounding, we might be able to slip into this adeledicnander stuff the way their kids do."

He faced Cassellahat. "Next question," he said. "What—"

Cassellahat had been looking at his watch. "I'm afraid, Mr. Renfrew," he interrupted, "that if you and I are going to be on the ferry to the Pelham planet, we'd better leave now. You can ask your questions on the way."

"What's all this?" I chimed in.

Renfrew explained: "He's taking me to the great engineering laboratories in the European mountains of Pelham. Want to come along?"

"Not me," I said.

Blake shrugged. "I don't fancy getting into one of those suits Cassellahat has provided for us, designed to keep our odor in, but not theirs out."

He finished: "Bill and I will stay here and play poker for some of that five million credits worth of dough we've got in the State bank."

Cassellahat turned at the door; there was a distinct frown on the flesh mask he wore. "You treat our government gift very lightly."

"Yeih!" said Blake.

"So we stink," said Blake.

It was nine days since Cassellahat had taken Renfrew to the planet Pelham; and our only contact had been a radio telephone call from Renfrew on the third day, telling us not to worry.

Blake was standing at the window of our penthouse apartment in the city of Newmerica; and I was on my back on a couch, in my mind a mixture of thoughts involving Renfrew's potential insanity and all the things I had heard and seen about the history of the past five hundred years.

I roused myself. "Quit it," I said. "We're faced with a change in the metabolism of the human body, probably due to the many different foods from remote stars that they eat. They must be able to smell better, too, because just being near us is agony to Cassellahat, whereas we only notice an unpleasantness from him. It's a case of three of us against billions of them. Frankly, I don't see an early victory over the problem, so let's just take it quietly."

There was no answer; so I returned to my reverie. My first radio message to Earth had been picked up: and so, when the interstellar drive was invented in 2320 A. D., less than one hundred forty years after our departure, it was realized what would eventually happen.

In our honor, the four habitable planets of the Alpha A and B suns were called Renfrew, Pelham, Blake and Endicott. Since 2320, the populations of the four planets had become so dense that a total of nineteen billion people now dwelt on their narrowing land spaces. This in spite of migrations to the planets of more distant stars.

The space liner I had seen burning in 2511 A. D. was the only ship ever lost on the Earth-Centauri lane. Traveling at full speed, its screens must have reacted against our spaceship. All the automatics would instantly have flashed on; and, as those defenses were not able at that time to stop a ship that had gone Minus Infinity, every recoil engine aboard had probably blown up.

Such a thing could not happen again. So enormous had been the progress in the adeledicnander field of power, that the greatest liners could stop dead in the full fury of mid-flight.

We had been told not to feel any sense of blame for that one disaster, as many of the most important advances in adeledicnander electronic psychology had been made as the result of the theoretical analyses of that great catastrophe.

I grew aware that Blake had flung himself disgustedly into a nearby chair.

"Boy, oh, boy," he said, "this is going to be some life for us. We can all anticipate about fifty more years of being pariahs in a civilization where we can't even understand how the simplest machines work."

I stirred uneasily. I had had similar thoughts. But I said nothing. Blake went on:

"I must admit, after I first discovered the Centauri planets had been colonized, I had pictures of myself bowling over some dame, and marrying her."

Involuntarily my mind leaped to the memory of a pair of lips lifting up to mine. I shook myself. I said:

"I wonder how Renfrew is taking all this. He—"

A familiar voice from the door cut off my words. "Renfrew," it said, "is taking things beautifully now that the first shock has yielded to resignation, and resignation to purpose."

We had turned to face him by the time he finished. Renfrew walked slowly toward us, grinning. Watching him, I felt uncertain as to just how to take his built-up sanity.

He was at his best. His dark, wavy hair was perfectly combed. His startlingly blue eyes made his whole face come alive. He was a natural physical wonder; and at his normal he had all the shine and swagger of an actor in a carefully tailored picture.

He wore that shine and swagger now. He said:

"I've bought a spaceship, fellows. Took all my money and part of your's too. But I knew you'd back me up. Am I right?"

"Why, sure," Blake and I echoed.

Blake went on alone: "What's the idea."

"I get it," I chimed in. "We'll cruise all over the universe, live our life span exploring new worlds. Jim, you've got something there. Blake and I were just going to enter a suicide pact."

Renfrew was smiling. "We'll cruise for a while anyway."

Two days later, Cassellahat having offered no objection and no advice about Renfrew, we were in space.

It was a curious three months that followed. For a while I felt a sense of awe at the vastness of the cosmos. Silent planets swung into our viewing plates, and faded into remoteness behind us, leaving nostalgic memory of uninhabited, windlashed forests and plains, deserted, swollen seas, and nameless suns.

The sight and the remembrance brought loneliness like an ache, and the knowledge, the slow knowledge, that this journeying was not lifting the weight of strangeness that had settled upon us ever since our arrival at Alpha Centauri.

There was nothing here for our souls to feed on, nothing that would satisfactorily fill one year of our life, let alone fifty.

I watched the realization grow on Blake, and I waited for a sign from Renfrew that he felt it, too. The sign didn't come. That of itself worried me; then I grew aware of something else. Renfrew was watching us. Watching us with a hint in his manner of secret knowledge, a suggestion of secret purpose.

My alarm grew; and Renfrew's perpetual cheerfulness didn't help any. I was lying on my bunk at the end of the third month, thinking uneasily about the whole unsatisfactory situation, when my door opened and Renfrew came in.

He carried a paralyzer gun and a rope. He pointed the gun at me, and said:

"Sorry, Bill. Cassellahat told me to take no chances, so just lie quiet while I tie you up."

"Blake," I bellowed.

Renfrew shook his head gently. "No use," he said. "I was in his room first."

The gun was steady in his fingers, his blue eyes were steely. All I could do was tense my muscles against the ropes as he tied me, and trust to the fact that I was twice as strong, at least, as he was.

I thought in dismay: Surely I could prevent him from tying me too tightly.

He stepped back finally, said again, "Sorry, Bill." He added: "I hate to tell you this, but both of you went off the deep end mentally when we arrived at Centauri; and this is the cure prescribed by the psychologist whom Cassellahat consulted. You're supposed to get a shock as big as the one that knocked you for a loop."

The first time I'd paid no attention to his mention of Cassellahat's name. Now my mind flared with understanding.

Incredibly, Renfrew had been told that Blake and I were mad. All these months he had been held steady by a sense of responsibility toward us. It was a beautiful psychological scheme. The only thing was: *what* shock was going to be administered?

Renfrew's voice cut off my thought. He said:

"It won't be long now. We're already entering the field of the bachelor sun."

"Bachelor sun!" I yelled.

He made no reply. The instant the door closed behind him, I began to work on my bonds; all the time I was thinking:

What was it Cassellahat had said? Bachelor suns maintained themselves in this space by a precarious balancing.

In *this* space! The sweat poured down my face, as I pictured ourselves being precipitated into another plane of the space time continuum—I could feel the ship falling when I finally worked my hands free of the rope.

I hadn't been tied long enough for the cords to interfere with my circulation. I headed for Blake's room. In two minutes we were on our way to the control cabin.

Renfrew didn't see us till we had him. Blake grabbed his gun; I hauled him out of the control chair with one mighty heave, and dumped him onto the floor.

He lay there, unresisting, grinning up at us. "Too late," he taunted. "We're approaching the first point of intolerance, and there's nothing you can do except prepare for the shock."

I scarcely heard him. I plumped myself into the chair, and glared into the viewing plates. Nothing showed. That stumped me for a second. Then I saw the recorder instruments. They were trembling furiously, registering a body of INFINITE size.

For a long moment I stared crazily at those incredible figures. Then I plunged the decelerator far over. Before that pressure of full-driven adeledicnander, the machine grew rigid; I had a sudden fantastic picture of two irresistible forces in full collision. Gasping, I jerked the power out of gear.

We were still falling.

"An orbit," Blake was saying. "Get us into an orbit."

With shaking fingers, I pounded one out on the keyboard, basing my figures on a sun of Sol-ish size, gravity, and mass.

The bachelor wouldn't let us have it.

I tried another orbit, and a third, and more—finally one that would have given us an orbit around mighty Antares itself. But the deadly reality remained. The ship plunged on, down and down.

And there was nothing visible on the plates, not a real shadow of substance. It seemed to me once that I could make out a vague blur of greater darkness against the black reaches of space. But the stars were few in every direction and it was impossible to be sure.

Finally, in despair, I whirled out of the seat, and knelt beside Renfrew, who was still making no effort to get up.

"Listen, Jim," I pleaded, "what did you do this for? What's going to happen?"

He was smiling easily. "Think," he said, "of an old, crusty, human bachelor. He maintains a relationship with his fellows, but the association is as remote as that which exists between a bachelor sun and the stars in the galaxy of which it is a part."

He added: "Any second now we'll strike the first period of intolerance. It works in jumps like quantum, each period being four hundred ninety-eight years, seven months and eight days plus a few hours."

It sounded like gibberish. "But what's going to happen?" I urged. "For Heaven's sake, man!"

He gazed up at me blandly; and, looking up at him. I had the sudden, wondering realization that he was sane, the old, completely rational Jim Renfrew, made better somehow, stronger. He said quietly:

"Why, it'll just knock us out of its toleration area; and in doing so will put us back—"

JERK!

The lurch was immensely violent. With a bang, I struck the floor, skidded, and then a hand—Renfrew's—caught me. And it was all over.

I stood up, conscious that we were no longer falling. I looked at the instrument board. All the lights were dim, untroubled, the needles firmly at zero. I turned and stared at Renfrew, and at Blake, who was ruefully picking himself from the floor.

Renfrew said persuasively: "Let me at the control board, Bill. I want to set our course for Earth."

For a long minute, I gazed at him; and then, slowly, I stepped aside. I stood by as he set the controls and pulled the accelerator over. Renfrew looked up.

"We'll reach Earth in about eight hours," he said, "and it'll be about a year and a half after we left five hundred years ago."

Something began to tug at the roof of my cranium. It took several seconds before I decided that it was probably my brain jumping with the tremendous understanding that suddenly flowed in upon me.

The bachelor sun, I thought dazedly. In easing us out of its field of toleration, it had simply precipitated us into a period of time beyond its field. Renfrew had said ... had said that it worked in jumps of ... four hundred ninety-eight years and some seven months and—

But what about the ship? Wouldn't twenty-seventh century adeledicnander brought to the twenty-second century, before it was invented, change the course of history? I mumbled the question.

Renfrew shook his head. "Do *we* understand it? Do we even dare monkey with the raw power inside those engines? I'll say not. As for the ship, we'll keep it for our own private use."

"B-but—" I began.

He cut me off. "Look. Bill," he said, "here's the situation: that girl who kissed you—don't think I didn't see you falling like a ton of bricks—is going to be sitting beside you fifty years from now, when *your* voice from space reports to Earth that you had wakened on your first lap of the first trip to Centaurus."

That's exactly what happened.

SECRET UNATTAINABLE

T
he file known as Secret Six was smuggled out of Berlin in mid-1945 when Russia was in sole occupation of the city. How it was brought to the United States is one of those dramatic true tales of World War II. The details cannot yet be published since they involve people now in the Russian zone of Germany.

All the extraordinary documents of this file, it should be emphasized, are definitely in the hands of our own authorities; and investigations are proceeding apace. Further revelations of a grand order may be expected as soon as one of the machines is built. All German models were destroyed by the Nazis early in 1945.

The documents date from 1937, and will be given chronologically, without reference to their individual importance. But first, it is of surpassing interest to draw attention to the following news item, which appeared in the New York *Sun*, March 25, 1941, on page 17. At that time it appeared to have no significance whatever. The item:

GERMAN CREEK BECOMES RIVER

London, March 24 (delayed): A Royal Air Force reconnaissance pilot today reported that a creek in northern Prussia, marked on the map as the Gribe Creek, has become a deep, swift river overnight. It is believed that an underground waterway burst its bounds. Several villages in the path of the new river showed under water. No report of the incident has yet been received from Berlin.

There never was any report from Berlin. It should again be pointed out that the foregoing news item was published in 1941; the documents which follow date from 1937, a period of four years. Four years of world-shaking history:

April 10, 1937

From   Secretary, Bureau of Physics
To   Reich and Prussian Minister of Science
Subject   10731-127-S-6

1. Inclosed is the report of the distinguished scientific board of inquiry which sat on the case of Herr Professor Johann Kenrube.
2. As you will see, the majority of the board oppose emphatically the granting of State funds for what they describe as a "fantastic scheme." They deny that a step-up tube would produce the results claimed, and refute utterly the number philosophy involved. Number, they say, is a function, not a reality, or else modern physics has no existence.
3. The minority report of Herr Professor Goureit, while thought-provoking, can readily be dismissed when it is remembered that Goureit, like Kenrube and Kenrube's infamous brother, was once a member of the SPD.
4. The board of inquiry, having in mind Hitler's desire that no field of scientific inquiry should be left unexplored, and as a generous gesture to Goureit, who has a very great reputation and a caustic pen, suggested that, if Kenrube could obtain private funds for his research, he should be permitted to do so.
5. Provided Geheime Staats Polizei do not object, I concur.

G.L.

Author's Note: *The signature G.L. has been difficult to place. There appear to have been several secretaries of the Bureau of Physics Research, following one another in swift order. The best accounts identify him as Gottfried Lesser, an obscure B.Sc. who early joined the Nazi party, and for a period was its one and only science expert. Geheime Staats Polizei is of course Gestapo.*

MEMO
April 17, 1937
From   Chief, Science Branch, Gestapo

If Kenrube can find the money, let him go ahead. Himmler concurs, provided supervision be strict.

K. Reissel.

COPY ONLY
June 2, 1937
From   Co-ordinator Dept., Deutsche Bank
To   Gestapo

The marginally noted personages have recently transferred sums total-ing Reichsmarks four million five hundred thousand to the account of Herr Professor Johann Kenrube. For your information, please.

J. Pleup.

June 11, 1937

From   Gestapo
To   Reich and Prussian Minister of Science
Subject   Your 10731-127-S-6

Per your request for further details on the private life of J. Kenrube since the death of his brother in June, 1934, in the purge:

We quote from a witness, Peter Braun: "I was in a position to observe Herr Professor Kenrube very closely when the news was brought to him at Frankfort-on-Main that August, his brother, had been executed in the sacred blood purge.

"Professor Kenrube is a thin, good-looking man with a very wan face normally. This face turned dark with color, then drained completely of blood. He clenched his hands and said: 'They've murdered him!' Then he rushed off to his room.

"Hours later, I saw him walking, hatless, hair disarrayed, along the bank of the river. People stopped to look at him, but he did not see them. He was very much upset that first day. When I saw him again the next morning, he seemed to have recovered. He said to me: 'Peter, we must all suffer for our past mistakes. The tragic irony of my brother's death is that he told me only a week ago in Berlin that he had been mistaken in oppos-ing the National-sozialistiche Arbeitspartei. He was convinced they were doing great things. I am too much of a scientist ever to have concerned myself with politics'."

You will note, Excellency, that this is very much the set speech of one who is anxious to cover up the indiscreet, emotional outburst of the pre-vious day. However, the fact that he was able to pull himself together at all seems to indicate that affection of any kind is but shallowly rooted in his character. Professor Kenrube returned to his laboratories in July, 1934, and has apparently been hard at work ever since.

There has been some discussion here concerning Kenrube, by the psychologists attached to this office; and the opinion is expressed, without dissent, that in three years the professor will almost have forgotten that he had a brother.

K. Reissel.

MEMO AT BOTTOM OF LETTER

I am more convinced than ever that psychologists should be seen and not heard. It is our duty to watch every relative of every person whose life is, for any reason, claimed by the State. If there are scientific developments of worthwhile nature in this Kenrube affair, let me know at once. His attainments are second to none. A master plan of precaution is in order.

Himmler.

October 24, 1937

From   Secretary, Bureau of Physics
To   Reich and Prussian Minister of Science
Subject   Professor Johann Kenrube

The following report has been received from our Special Agent Seventeen:
"Kenrube has hired the old steel and concrete fortress, *Gribe Schloss*, overlooking the Gribe Creek, which flows into the Eastern Sea. This ancient fortress was formerly located on a small hill in a valley. The hill has subsided, however, and is now virtually level with the valley floor. We have been busy for more than a month making the old place livable, and installing machinery."

For your information, Agent Seventeen is a graduate in physics of Bonn University. He was for a time professor of physics at Muenchen. In view of the shortage of technicians, Kenrube has appointed Seventeen his chief assistant.

G.L.

May 21, 1938

From   Science Branch, Gestapo
To   Reich and Prussian Minister of Science
Subject   10731-127-S-6

Himmler wants to know the latest developments in the Kenrube affair. Why the long silence? Exactly what is Professor Kenrube trying to do, and what progress has he made? Surely, your secret agent has made reports.

K. Reissel.

June 3, 1938

From   Secretary, Bureau of Physics
To   Chief, Science Branch, Gestapo
Subject   Professor Johann Kenrube

Your letter of the 21st ultimo has been passed on to me. The enclosed précis of the reports of our Agent Seventeen will bring you up to date.

Be assured that we are keeping a careful watch on the developments in this case. So far, nothing meriting special attention has arisen.

G.L.

PRÉCIS OF MONTHLY REPORTS
OF
AGENT SEVENTEEN

Our agent reports that Professor Kenrube's first act was to place him, Seventeen, in charge of the construction of the machine, thus insuring that he will have the most intimate knowledge of the actual physical details.

When completed, the machine is expected to occupy the entire common room of the old fortress, largely because of the use of step-up vacuum tubes. In this connection, Seventeen describes how four electric dynamos were removed from Kenrube's old laboratories, their entire output channeled through the step-up tubes, with the result that a ninety-four per cent improvement in efficiency was noted.

Seventeen goes on to state that orders for parts have been placed with various metal firms but, because of the defense program, deliveries are extremely slow. Professor Kenrube has resigned himself to the possibility that his invention will not be completed until 1944 or '45.

Seventeen, being a scientist in his own right, has become interested in the machine. In view of the fact that, if successful, it will insure measureless supplies of raw materials for our Reich, he urges that some effort be made to obtain priorities.

He adds that he has become quite friendly with Kenrube. He does not think that the Herr Professor suspects how closely he is connected with the Bureau of Science.

June 4, 1938

From   Gestapo
To   Reich and Prussian Minister of Science
Subject   10731-127-S-6

Raw materials! Why was I not informed before that Kenrube was expecting to produce raw materials? Why did you think I was taking an interest in this case, if not because Kenrube is a genius of the first rank; and therefore anything he does must be examined with the most minute care? But—raw materials! Are you all mad over there, or living in a world of pleasant dreams?

You will at once obtain from Herr Professor Kenrube the full plans, the full mathematics of his work, with photographs of the machine as far as it has progressed. Have your scientists prepare a report for me as to the exact nature of the raw materials that Kenrube expects to obtain. Is this some transmutation affair, or what is the method?

Inform Kenrube that he must supply this information or he will obtain no further materials. If he satisfies our requirements, on the other hand, there will be a quickening of supplies. Kenrube is no fool. He will understand the situation.

As for your agent, Seventeen, I am at once sending an agent to act as his bodyguard. Friendly with Kenrube indeed!

Himmler.

June 28, 1938

From   Gestapo
To   Secretary, Bureau of Physics
Subject   Secret Six

Have you received the report from Kenrube? Himmler is most anxious to see this the moment it arrives.

K. Reissel.

July 4, 1938

From   Gestapo
To   Secretary, Bureau of Physics
Subject   Secret Six

What about the Kenrube report? Is it possible that your office does not clearly grasp how important we regard this matter? We have recently discovered that Professor Kenrube's grandfather once visited a very curious and involved revenge on a man whom he hated years after the event that motivated the hatred. Every conceivable precaution must be taken to see to it that the Kenrube machine can be duplicated, and the machine itself protected.

Please send the scientific report the moment it is available.

K. Reissel.

July 4, 1938

From   Secretary, Bureau of Physics
To   Chief, Science Branch, Gestapo
Subject   Professor Johann Kenrube

The report, for which you have been asking, has come to hand, and a complete transcription is being sent to your office under separate cover. As you will see, it is very elaborately prepared; and I have taken the trouble to have a précis made of our scientific board's analysis of the report for your readier comprehension.

G.L.

PRÉCIS
OF
SCIENTIFIC ANALYSIS OF KENRUBE'S REPORT
ON HIS INVENTION

General Statement of Kenrube's Theory: That there are two kinds of space in the universe, normal and hyper-space.

Only in normal space is the distance between star systems and galaxies great. It is essential to the nature of things, to the unity of material bodies, that intimate cohesion exist between every particle of matter, between, for instance, the Earth and the universe as a whole.

Kenrube maintains that gravity does not explain the perfect and wonderful balance, the singleness of organism that is a galactic system. And that the theory of relativity merely evades the issue in stating that planets go around the sun because it is easier for them to do that than to fly off into space.

Kenrube's thesis, therefore, is that all the matter in the universe conjoins according to a rigid mathematical pattern, and that this conjunction presupposes the existence of hyper-space.

Object of the Invention: To bridge the gap through hyper-space between the Earth and any planet, or any part of any planet. In effect, this means that it would not be necessary to drill for oil in a remote planet. The machine would merely locate the oil stratum, and tap it at any depth; the oil would flow from the orifice of the machine which, in the case of the machine now under construction, is ten feet in diameter.

A ten-foot flow of oil at a pressure of four thousand feet a minute would produce approximately six hundred thousand tons of oil every hour.

Similarly, mining could be carried on simply by locating the ore-bearing veins, and skimming from them the purest ores.

It should be pointed out that, of the distinguished scientists who have examined the report, only Herr Professor Goureit claims to be able to follow the mathematics proving the existence of hyper-space.

COPY ONLY

July 14, 1938

TRANSCRIPTION OF INTERVIEW BY HERR HIMMLER OF PROFESSOR H. KLEINBERG, CHAIRMAN OF THE SCIENTIFIC COMMITTEE OF SCIENCE BRANCH, GESTAPO, INVESTIGATING REPORT OF HERR PROFESSOR JOHANN KENRUBE.

Q. You have studied the drawings and examined the mathematics?
A. Yes.
Q. What is your conclusion?
A. We are unanimously agreed that some fraud is being perpetrated.
Q. Does your verdict relate to the drawings of the invention, or to the mathematics explaining the theory?
A. To both. The drawings are incomplete. A machine made from those blueprints would hum with apparent power and purpose, but it would be a fraudulent uproar; the power simply goes oftener through a vacuumized circuit before returning to its source.
Q. I have sent your report to Kenrube. His comment is that almost the whole of modern electrical physics is founded on some variation of electricity being forced through a vacuum. What about that?
A. It is a half truth.
Q. What about the mathematics?
A. There is the real evidence. Since Descartes—
Q. Please abstain from using these foreign names.

A. Pardon me. Since Leibnitz, number has been a function, a variable idea. Kenrube treats of number as an existing *thing*. Mathematics, he says, has living and being. You have to be a scientist to realize how incredible, impossible, ridiculous, such an idea is.

WRITTEN COMMENT ON THE ABOVE

I am not a scientist. I have no set ideas on the subject of mathematics or invention. I am, however, prepared to accept the theory that Kenrube is withholding information, and for this reason order that:

1. All further materials for the main machine be withheld.
2. Unlimited assistance be given Kenrube to build a model of his machine in the great government laboratories at Dresden. When, and not until, this model is in operation, permission will be given for the larger machine to be completed.
3. Meanwhile, Gestapo scientists will examine the machine at *Gribe Schloss*, and Gestapo construction experts will, if necessary, reinforce the building, which must have been damaged by the settling of the hill on which it stands.
4. Gestapo agents will hereafter guard *Gribe Schloss*.

Himmler.

December 2, 1938

From   Secretary, Bureau of Physics
To   Chief, Science Branch, Gestapo
Subject   Herr Professor Kenrube

Inclosed is the quarterly précis of the reports of our Agent Seventeen. For your information, please.

August Buehnen.

Author's Note: *Buehnen, a party man who was educated in one of the Nazi two-year Science Schools, replaced G.L. as secretary of the Bureau of Physics about September, 1938.*

It is not known exactly what became of Lesser, who was a strong party man. There was a Brigadier General G. Lesser, a technical expert attached to the Fuehrer's headquarters at Smolensk. This man, and there is some evidence that he is the same, was killed in the first battle of Moscow.

QUARTERLY PRÉCIS OF REPORTS
OF
AGENT SEVENTEEN

1. Herr Professor Kenrube is working hard on the model. He has at no time expressed bitterness over the enforced cessation of work on the main machine, and apparently accepts readily the explanation that the government cannot afford to allot him material until the model proves the value of his work.
2. The model will have an orifice of six inches. This compares with the ten-foot orifice of the main machine. Kenrube's intention is to employ it for the procuration of liquids, and believes that the model will of itself go far to reducing the oil shortage in the Reich.
3. The machine will be in operation sometime in the summer of 1939. We are all eager and excited.

February 7, 1939

From   Secretary, Bureau of Physics
To   Gestapo
Subject   Secret Six

The following precautions have been taken with the full knowledge and consent of Herr Professor Kenrube:
1. A diary in triplicate is kept of each day's progress. Two copies are sent daily to our office here. As you know, the other copy is submitted by us to your office.
2. Photographs are made of each part of the machine before it is installed, and detailed plans of each part are kept, all in triplicate, the copies distributed as described above.
3. From time to time independent scientists are called in. They are invariably impressed by Kenrube's name, and suspicious of his mathematics and drawings.

For your information, please.

August Buehnen.

March 1, 1939

From   Reich and Prussian Minister of Science
To   Herr Heinrich Himmler, Gestapo
Subject   The great genius, Herr Professor Kenrube

It is my privilege to inform Your Excellency that the world-shaking invention of Herr Professor Johann Kenrube went into operation yesterday, and has already shown fantastic results.

The machine is not a pretty one, and some effort must be made to streamline future reproductions of this model, with an aim toward greater mobility. In its present condition, it is strung out over the floor in a most ungainly fashion. Rough metal can be very ugly.

Its most attractive feature is the control board, which consists of a number of knobs and dials, the operator of which, by an arrangement of mirrors, can peer into the orifice, which is located on the right side of the control board, and faces away from it. (I do not like these awkward names, orifice and hyper-space. We must find a great name for this wonderful machine and its vital parts.)

When Buehnen and I arrived, Professor Kenrube was busy opening and shutting little casements in various parts of that sea of dull metal. He took out and examined various items.

At eleven forty-five, Kenrube stationed himself at the control board, and made a brief speech comparing the locator dials of the board to the dial on a radio which tunes in stations. His dials, however, tuned in planets; and, quite simply, that is what he proceeded to do.

It appears that the same planets are always on exactly the same gradation of the main dial; and the principle extends down through the controls which operate to locate sections of planets. Thus it is always possible to return to any point of any planet. You will see how important this is.

The machine had already undergone its first tests, so Kenrube now proceeded to turn to various planets previously selected; and a fascinating show it was.

Gazing through the six-inch orifice is like looking through a glassless window. What a great moment it will be when the main machine is in operation, and we can *go* through the ten-foot orifice.

The first planet was a desolate, frozen affair, dimly lighted by a remote red sun. It must have been airless because there was a whistling sound, as the air rushed out of our room into that frigid space. Some of that deadly cold came trickling through, and we quickly switched below the surface of the planet.

Fantastic planet! It must be an incredibly heavy world, for it is a treasure house of the heavier metals. Everywhere we turned, the soil formation showed a shifting pattern of gold, silver, zinc, iron, tin—thousands of millions of tons.

At Professor Kenrube's suggestion, I put on a pair of heavy gloves, and removed a four-inch rock of almost pure gold. It simply lay there in a gray shale, but it was so cold that the moisture of the room condensed on it, forming a thick hoarfrost. How many ages that planet must have frozen for the cold to penetrate so far below the surface!

The second planet was a vast expanse of steaming swamps and tropical forests, much as Earth must have been forty million years ago. However, we found not a single trace of animal, insect, reptile, or other non-floral life.

The third, fourth, and fifth planets were devoid of any kind of life, either plant or animal. The sixth planet might have been Earth, except that its green forests, its rolling plains showed no sign of animal or intelligent life. But it is on this planet that oil had been located by Kenrube and Seventeen in their private tests. When I left, a pipe line, previously rigged up, had been attached to the orifice, and was vibrating with oil at the colossal flow speed of nearly one thousand miles per hour.

This immense flow has now been continuous for more than twenty-four hours; and I understand it has already been necessary to convert the great water reservoir in the south suburbs to storage space for oil.

It may be *nouveau riche* to be storing oil at great inconvenience, when the source can be tapped at will. But I personally will not be satisfied until we have a number of these machines in action. It is better to be childish and have the oil than logical and have regrets.

I cannot conceive what could go wrong now. Because of our precautions, we have numerous and complete plans of the machines. It is necessary, of course, to ensure that our enemies do not learn our secret, and on this point I would certainly appreciate your most earnest attention.

The enormous potentialities of this marvelous instrument expand with every minute spent in thinking about it. I scarcely slept a wink last night.

March 1, 1939

From   Chief, Criminal Investigation Branch, Gestapo
To   Reich and Prussian Minister of Science
Subject   Secret Six

Will you please inform this office without delay of the name of every scientist or other person who has any knowledge, however meager, of the Kenrube machine?

Reinhard Heydrich.

Author's Note: *This is the Heydrich, handsome, ruthless Heydrich, who in 1941 bloodily repressed the incipient Czech revolt, who after the notorious Himmler became Minister of the Interior, succeeded his former master as head of the Gestapo, and who was subsequently assassinated.*

March 2, 1939

From   Secretary, Bureau of Physics
To   R. Heydrich
Subject   Secret Six

The list of names for which you asked is herewith attached.

August Buehnen.

COMMENT AT BOTTOM OF LETTER

In view of the importance of this matter, some changes should be made in the precautionary plan drawn up a few months ago with respect to these personages. Two, not one, of our agents must be assigned to keep secret watch on each of these individuals. The rest of the plan can be continued as arranged with one other exception: In the event that any of these men suspect that they are being watched, I must be informed at once. I am prepared to explain to such person, within limits, the truth of the matter, so that he may not be personally worried. The important thing is we do not want these people suddenly to make a run for the border.

Himmler

SPECIAL DELIVERY
PERSONAL

From   Reich and Prussian Minister of Science
To   Herr Heinrich Himmler
Subject   Professor Johann Kenrube

I this morning informed the Fuehrer of the Kenrube machine. He became very excited. The news ended his indecision about the Czechs. The army will move to occupy.

For your advance information, please.

March 13, 1939

From   Gestapo
To   Reich and Prussian Minister of Science
Subject   The Dresden Explosion

The incredibly violent explosion of the Kenrube model must be completely explained. A board of discovery should be set up at Dresden with full authority. I must be informed day by day of the findings of this court.

This is a very grim business. Your agent, Seventeen, is among those missing. Kenrube is alive, which is very suspicious. There is no question of arresting him; the only thing that matters is to frustrate future catastrophes of this kind. His machine has proved itself so remarkable that he must be conciliated at all costs until we can be sure that everything is going right.

Let me know *everything*.

Himmler.

PRELIMINARY REPORT OF AUGUST BUEHNEN

When I arrived at the scene of the explosion, I noticed immediately that a solid circle, a remarkably precise circle, of the wall of the fifth floor of the laboratories—where the Kenrube machine is located—had been sliced out as by some inconceivable force.

Examining the edges of this circle, I verified that it could not have been heat which performed so violent an operation. Neither the brick nor the exposed steel was in any way singed or damaged by fire.

The following facts have been given to me of what transpired:

It had been necessary to cut the flow of oil because of the complete absence of further storage space. Seventeen, who was in charge—Professor Kenrube during this whole time was at *Gribe Schloss* working on the main machine—was laboriously exploring other planets in search of rare metals.

The following is an extract from my interview with Jacob Schmidt, a trusted laboratory assistant in the government service:

Q. You say, Herr—(Seventeen) took a piece of ore to the window to examine it in the light of the sun?

A. He took it to the window, and stood there looking at it.

Q. This placed him directly in front of the orifice of the machine?

A. Yes.

Q. Who else was in front of the orifice?

A. Dobelmanns, Minster, Freyburg, Tousand-friend.

Q. These were all fellow assistants of yours?

A. Yes.

Q. What happened then?

A. There was a very loud click from the machine, followed by a roaring noise.

Q. Was anyone near the control board?

A. No, sir.

Q. It was an automatic action of the machine?

A. Yes. The moment it happened we all turned to face the machine.

Q. All of you? Herr—(Seventeen), too?

A. Yes, he looked around with a start, just as Minster cried out that a blue light was coming from the orifice.

Q. A blue light. What did this blue light replace?

A. A soil formation of a planet, which we had numbered 447-711-Gradation A-131-8, which is simply its location on the dials. It was from this soil that Herr—(Seventeen) had taken the ore sample.

Q. And then, just like that, there was the blue light?

A. Yes. And for a few instants that was all there was: the blue light, the strange roaring sound, and us standing there half paralyzed.

Q. Then it flared forth?

A. It was terrible. It was such an intense blue it hurt my eyes, even though I could only see it in the mirror over the orifice. I have not the faintest impression of heat. But the wall was gone, and all the metal around the orifice.

Q. And the men?

A. Yes, and the men, all five of them.

March 18, 1939

From   Secretary, Bureau of Physics
To   Chief, Science Branch, Gestapo
Subject   Dresden Explosion

I am inclosing a précis of the report of the Court of Inquiry, which has just come to hand. The report will be sent to you as soon as a transcription has been typed.

For your information, please.

August Buehnen.

PRÉCIS OF REPORT OF COURT OF INQUIRY

1. It has been established:
   (A) That the destruction was preceded by a clicking sound.
   (B) That this click came from the machine.
   (C) That the machine is fitted with automatic finders.
2. The blue flame was the sole final cause of the destruction.
3. No theory exists, or was offered, to explain the blue light. It should be pointed out that Kenrube was not called to testify.
4. The death of Herr—(Seventeen) and of his assistants was entirely due to the momentary impulse that had placed them in the path of the blue fire.
5. The court finds that the machine could have been tampered with, that the click that preceded the explosion could have been the result of some automatic device previously set to tamper with the machine. No other evidence of sabotage exists, and no one in the room at the time was to blame for the accident.

COPY ONLY March 19, 1939
FOR MINISTRY OF SCIENCE

From   Major H. L. Guberheit
To   Minister for Air
Subject   Destruction of plane, type JU-88

I have been asked to describe the destruction of a plane under unusual circumstances, as witnessed by several hundred officers and men under my command.

The JU-88, piloted by Cadet Pilot Herman Kiesler, was approaching the runway for a landing, and was at the height of about five hundred feet when there was a flash of intense blue—and the plane vanished.

I cannot express too strongly the violence, the intensity, the blue vastness of the explosion. It was titanic. The sky was alive with light reflections. And though a bright sun was shining, the entire landscape grew brilliant with that blue tint.

There was no sound of explosion. No trace of this machine was subsequently found, no wreckage. The time of the accident was approximately ten thirty A.M., March 13th.

There has been great uneasiness among the students during the past week.

For your information, please.

H.L. Guberheit.
Major, C. Air Station 473.

COMMENT AT BOTTOM OF LETTER

Excellency—I wish most urgently to point out that the time of this unnatural accident coincides with the explosion of "blue" light from the orifice of the Kenrube machine.

I have verified that the orifice was tilted ever so slightly upward, and that the angle would place the beam at a height of five hundred feet near the airport in question. The staggering feature is that the airport referred to is *seventy-five miles* from Dresden. The greatest guns ever developed can scarcely fire that distance, and yet the incredible power of the blue energy showed no diminishment. Literally, it disintegrated metal and flesh—everything.

I do not dare to think what would have happened if that devastating flame had been pointed not away from but at the ground.

Let me have your instructions at once, because here is beyond doubt the weapon of the ages.

August Buehnen.

March 19, 1939

From Chief, Science Branch, Gestapo
To Reich and Prussian Minister of Science
Subject Secret Six

In perusing the report of the inquiry board, we were amazed to note that Professor Kenrube was not questioned in this matter.

Be assured that there is no intention here of playing up to this man. We absolutely require an explanation from him. Send Herr Buehnen to see Kenrube and instruct him to employ the utmost firmness if necessary.
K. Reissel.

March 21, 1939

From Secretary, Bureau of Physics
To Chief Science Branch, Gestapo
Subject Dresden Explosion

As per your request, I talked with Kenrube at *Gribe Schloss*.

It was the second time I had seen him, the first time being when I accompanied his Excellency, the Minister of Science, to Dresden to view the model; and I think I should point out here that Herr Professor Kenrube's physical appearance is very different from what I had been led to expect from the description recorded in File Secret Six. I had pictured him a lean, fanatic-eyed type. He *is* tall, but he must have gained weight in recent years, for his body is well filled out, and his face and eyes are serene, with graying hair to crown the effect of a fine, scholarly, middle-aged man.

It is unthinkable to me that this is some madman plotting against the Reich.

The first part of his explanation of the blue light was a most curious reference to the reality of mathematics, and, for a moment, I almost thought he was attempting to credit the accident to this *actuality* of his incomprehensible number system.

Then he went on to the more concrete statement that a great star must have intruded into the plane of the planet under examination. The roaring sound that was heard he attributed to the fact that the component elements of the air in the laboratory were being sucked into the sun, and destroyed.

The sun, of course, would be in a state of balance all its own, and therefore would not come into the room until the balance had been interfered with by the air of the room.

(I must say my own explanation would he the reverse of this; that is, the destruction of the air would possibly create a momentary balance, a barrier, during which time nothing of the sun came into the room except light reflections. However, the foregoing is what Kenrube said, and I presume it is based on his own mathematics. I can only offer it for what it is worth.)

Abruptly, the balance broke down. For a fraction of an instant, then, before the model hyper-space machine was destroyed, the intolerable energies of a blue-white sun poured forth.

It would have made no difference if the airplane that was caught in the beam of blue light had been farther away from Dresden than seventy-five miles—that measureless force would have reached seven thousand five hundred miles just as easily, or seventy-five thousand.

The complete absence of visible heat is no evidence that it was not a sun. At forty million degrees Fahrenheit, heat, as we know it, does not exist.

The great man went on to say that he had previously given some thought to the danger from suns, and that in fact he was in the late mathematical stage of developing an attachment that would automatically reject bodies larger than ten thousand miles in diameter.

In his opinion, efforts to control the titanic energies of suns should be left to a later period, and should be carried out on uninhabited planets by scientists who have gone through the orifice and who have been then cut off from contact with earth.

August Buehnen.

COMMENT ATTACHED

Kenrube's explanation sounds logical, and it does seem incredible that he would meddle with such forces, though it is significant that the orifice was tilted "slightly upward." We can dispense with his advice as to when and how we should experiment with sun energies. The extent of the danger seems to be a momentary discharge of inconceivable forces, and then destruction of the machine. If at the moment of discharge the orifice was slightly tilted toward London or New York, and if a sufficient crisis existed, the loss of one more machine would be an infinitesimal cost.

As for Kenrube's fine, scholarly appearance, I think Buehnen has allowed himself to be carried away by the greatness of the invention. The democrats of Germany are not necessarily madmen, but here, as abroad, they are our remorseless enemies.

We must endeavor to soften Kenrube by psychological means.

I cannot forget that *there is not now a working model of the Kenrube machine in existence.* Until there is, all the fine, scholarly-looking men in the world will not convince me that what happened was entirely an accident.

The deadly thing about all this is that we have taken an irrevocable step with respect to the Czechs; and war in the west is now inevitable.

Himmler.

May 1, 1939

From   Chief, Science Branch, Gestapo
To   Reich and Prussian Minister of Science
Subject   Secret Six

The Fuehrer has agreed to exonerate completely August Kenrube, the brother of Herr Professor Kenrube. As you will recall, August Kenrube was killed in the sacred purge of June, 1934. It will now be made clear that his death was an untimely accident, and that he was a true German patriot.

This is in line with our psychological attack on Professor Kenrube's suspected anti-Nazism.

K. Reissel.

June 17, 1939

From   Secretary, Bureau of Physics
To   Chief, Science Branch, Gestapo
Subject   Professor Johann Kenrube

In line with our policy to make Kenrube realize his oneness with the community of German peoples, I had him address the convention of mathematicians. The speech, of which I inclose a copy, was a model one; three thousand words of glowing generalities, giving not a hint as to his true opinions on anything. However, he received the ovation of his life; and I think he was pleased in spite of himself.

Afterward, I saw to it—without, of course, appearing directly—that he was introduced to Fräulein Ilse Weber.

As you know, the Fräulein is university educated, a mature, modern young woman; and I am sure that she is merely taking on one of the many facets of her character in posing to Kenrube as a young woman who has decided quite calmly to have a child, and desires the father to be biologically of the highest type.

I cannot see how any human male, normal or abnormal, could resist the appeal of Fräulein Weber.

August Buehnen.

July 11, 1939

From   Chief, Science Branch, Gestapo
To   Secretary, Bureau of Physics
Subject   Secret Six

Can you give me some idea when the Kenrube machine will be ready to operate? What about the duplicate machines which we agreed verbally would be built without Kenrubeís knowledge? Great decisions are being made. Conversations are being conducted that will shock the world, and, in a general way, the leaders are relying on the Kenrube machine.

In this connection please submit as your own some variation of the following memorandum. It is from the Fuehrer himself, and therefore I need not stress its urgency.

K. Reissel.

MEMORANDUM OF ADOLF HITLER

Is it possible to tune the Kenrube machine to our own earth?

July 28, 1939

From   Secretary, Bureau of Physics
To   Chief, Science Branch, Gestapo
Subject   Secret Six

I enclose the following note from Kenrube, which is self-explanatory. We have retained a copy.

August Buehnen.

NOTE FROM KENRUBE

Dear Herr Buehnen:

The answer to your memorandum is yes.

In view of the international anxieties of the times, I offer the following suggestions as to weapons that can be devised from the hyper-space machine:

1. Any warship can be rendered noncombatant at critical moments by draining of its oil tanks.
2. Similarly, enemy oil-storage supplies can be drained at vital points. Other supplies can be blown up or, if combustible, set afire.

3. Troops, tanks, trucks, and all movable war materials can be transported to any point on the globe, behind enemy lines, into cities, by the simple act of focussing the orifice at the desired destination—and driving it and them through. I need scarcely point out that my machine renders railway and steamship transport obsolete. The world shall be transformed.
4. It might even be possible to develop a highly malleable, delicately adjusted machine, which can drain the tanks of airplanes in full flight.
5. Other possibilities, too numerous to mention, suggest themselves with the foregoing as a basis.

Kenrube.

COMMENT ATTACHED

This machine is like a dream. With it, the world is ours, for what conceivable combination of enemies could fight an army that appeared from nowhere on their flank, in the centers of their cities, in London, New York, in the Middlewest plains of America, in the Ural Mountains, in the Caucasus? Who can resist us?

K. Reissel.

ADDITIONAL COMMENT

My dear Reissel:

Your enthusiasm overlooks the fact that the machine is still only in the building stage. What worries me is that our hopes are being raised to a feverish height—what greater revenge could there be than to lift us to the ultimate peak of confidence, and then smash it in a single blow?

Every day that passes we are involving ourselves more deeply, decisions are being made from which there is already no turning back. When, oh, when will this machine be finished?

H.

July 29, 1939

From   Secretary, Bureau of Physics
To   Chief, Science Branch, Gestapo
Subject   Secret Six

The hyper-space machine at *Gribe Schloss* will be completed in February, 1941. No less than five duplicate machines are under construction, unknown to Kenrube. What is done is that, when he orders an installation for the *Gribe Schloss* machine, the factory turns out five additional units from the same plans.

In addition, a dozen model machines are being secretly constructed from the old plans, but, as they must be built entirely from drawings and photographs, they will take not less, but more, time to build than the larger machines.

August Buehnen.

August 2, 1939

From   Secretary, Bureau of Physics
To   Herr Heinrich Himmler
Subject   Professor Johann Kenrube

I have just now received a telegram from Fräulein Ilse Weber that she and the Herr Professor were married this morning, and that Kenrube will be a family man by the middle of next summer.

August Buchnen.

COMMENT WRITTEN BELOW

This is great news indeed. One of the most dangerous aspects of the Kenrube affair was that he was a bachelor without ties. Now, we have him. He has committed himself to the future.

Himmler.

FURTHER COMMENT

I have advised the Fuehrer, and our great armies will move into Poland at the end of this month.

H.

August 8, 1939

From   Gestapo
To   Reich and Prussian Minister of Science
Subject   Secret Six

I have had second thought on the matter of Fräulein Ilse Weber, now Frau Kenrube. In view of the fact that a woman, no matter how intelligent or objective, becomes emotionally involved with the man who is the father of her children, I would advise that Frau Kenrube be appointed to some great executive post in a war industry. This will keep her own patriotism at a high level, and thus she will continue to have exemplary influence on her husband. Such influence cannot be overestimated.

Himmler.

January 3, 1940

From   Secretary, Bureau of Physics
To   Chief, Science Branch, Gestapo

In glancing through the correspondence, I notice that I have neglected to inform you that our Agent Twelve has replaced Seventeen as Kenrube's chief assistant.

Twelve is a graduate of Munich, and was for a time attached to the General Staff in Berlin as a technical expert.

In my opinion, he is a better man for our purpose than was Seventeen, in that Seventeen, it seemed to me, had toward the end a tendency to associate himself with Kenrube in what might be called a scientific comradeship, an intellectual fellowship. He was in a mental condition where he quite unconsciously defended Kenrube against our suspicion.

Such a situation will not arise with Twelve. He is a practical man to the marrow. He and Kenrube have nothing in common.

Kenrube accepted Twelve with an attitude of what-does-it-matter-who-they-send. It was so noticeable that it is now clear that he is aware that these men are agents of ours.

Unless Kenrube has some plan of revenge which is beyond all precautions, the knowledge that he is being watched should exercise a restraint on any impulses to evil that he may have.

August Buehnen.

Author's Note: *Most of the letters written in the year 1940 were of a routine nature, consisting largely of detailed reports as to the progress of the machine. The following document, however, was an exception:*

December 17, 1940

From   Reich and Prussian Minister of Science
To   Herr Heinrich Himmler
Subject   Secret Six

The following work has now been completed on the fortress *Gribe Schloss*, where the Kenrube machine is nearing completion:

1. Steel doors have been fitted throughout.
2. A special, all-steel chamber has been constructed, from which, by an arrangement of mirrors, the orifice of the machine can be watched without danger to the watchers.
3. This watching post is only twenty steps from a paved road which runs straight up out of the valley.
4. A concrete pipe line for the transportation of oil is nearing completion.

August Buehnen.

MEMO AT BOTTOM OF LETTER

To Reinhard Heydrich:

Please make arrangements for me to inspect personally the reconstructed *Gribe Schloss*. It is Hitler's intention to attend the official opening.

The plan now is to invade England via the Kenrube machine possibly in March, not later than April. In view of the confusion that will follow the appearance of vast armies in every part of the country, this phase of the battle of Europe should be completed by the end of April.

In May, Russia will be invaded. This should not require more than two months. The invasion of the United States is set for July or August.

Himmler.

January 31, 1941

From	Secretary, Bureau of Physics
To	Chief, Science Branch, Gestapo
Subject	Secret Six

It will be impossible to complete the five extra Kenrube machines at the same time as the machine at *Gribe Schloss*. Kenrube has changed some of the designs, and our engineers do not know how to fit the sections together until they have studied Kenrube's method of connection.

I have personally asked Kenrube the reason for the changes. His answer was that he was remedying weaknesses that he had noticed in the model. I am afraid that we shall have to be satisfied with this explanation, and complete the duplicate machines after the official opening, which is not now scheduled until March 20th. The delay is due to Kenrube's experimentation with design.

If you have any suggestions, please let me hear them. I frankly do not like this delay, but what to do about it is another matter.

August Buehnen.

February 3, 1941

From   Chief, Science Branch, Gestapo
To   Secretary, Bureau of Physics
Subject   Secret Six

Himmler says to do nothing. He notes that you are still taking the precaution of daily photographs, and that your agent, Twelve, who replaced Seventeen, is keeping a diary in triplicate.

There has been a meeting of leaders, and this whole matter discussed very thoroughly, with special emphasis on critical analysis of the precautions taken, and of the situation that would exist if Kenrube should prove to be planning some queer revenge.

You will be happy to know that not a single additional precaution was thought of, and that our handling of the affair was commended.

K. Reissel.

February 18, 1941

From   Gestapo
To   Reich and Prussian Minister of Science
Subject   Secret Six

In view of our anxieties, the following information, which I have just received, will be welcome:

Frau Kenrube, formerly our Ilse Weber, has reserved a private room in the maternity ward of the Prussian State Hospital for May 7th. This will be her second child, another hostage to fortune by Kenrube.

K. Reissel.

COPY ONLY
MEMO   March 11, 1941

I have today examined *Gribe Schloss* and environs and found everything according to plan.

Himmler.

March 14, 1941

From   Secretary, Bureau of Physics
To   Herr Himmler, Gestapo
Subject   Secret Six

You will be relieved to know the reason for the changes in design made by Kenrube.

The first reason is rather unimportant. Kenrube refers to the mathematical structure involved, and states that, for his own elucidation, he designed a functional instrument whose sole purpose was to defeat the mathematical reality of the machine. This is very obscure, but he had referred to it before, so I call it to your attention.

The second reason is that there are now two orifices, not one. The additional orifice is for focussing. The following illustration will clarify what I mean:

Suppose we have a hundred thousand trucks in Berlin, which we wished to transfer to London. Under the old method, these trucks would have to be driven all the way to the *Gribe Schloss* before they could be transmitted.

With the new two-orifice machine, one orifice would be focused in Berlin, the other in London. The trucks would drive through from Berlin to London.

Herr Professor Kenrube seems to anticipate our needs before we realize them ourselves.

August Buehnen.

March 16, 1941

From   Gestapo
To   Secretary, Bureau of Physics
Subject   Secret Six

The last sentence of your letter of March 14th to the effect that Kenrube seems to anticipate our needs made me very uncomfortable, because the thought that follows naturally is: Is he also anticipating our plans?

I have accordingly decided at this eleventh hour that we are dealing with a man who may be our intellectual superior in every way. Have your agent advise us the moment the machine has undergone its initial tests. Decisive steps will be taken immediately.

Himmler.

March 19, 1941

DECODED TELEGRAM

KENRUBE MACHINE WAS TESTED TODAY AND WORKED PERFECTLY.

AGENT TWELVE.

COPY ONLY
MEMO   March 19, 1941

To Herr Himmler: This is to advise that Professor Johann Kenrube was placed under close arrest, and has been removed to Gestapo Headquarters, Berlin.

R. Heydrich.

March 19, 1941

DECODED TELEGRAM

REPLYING TO YOUR TELEPHONE INSTRUCTIONS, WISH TO STATE ALL AUTOMATIC DEVICES HAVE BEEN REMOVED FROM KENRUBE MACHINE. NONE SEEMED TO HAVE BEEN TAMPERED WITH. MADE PERSONAL TEST OF MACHINE. IT WORKED PERFECTLY.

TWELVE.

COMMENT WRITTEN BELOW

I shall recommend that Kenrube be retired under guard to his private laboratories, and not allowed near a hyper-space machine until after the conquest of the United States.

And with this, I find myself at a loss for further precautions. In my opinion, all thinkable possibilities have been covered. The only dangerous man has been removed from the zone where he can be actively dangerous; a careful examination has been made to ascertain that he has left no automatic devices that will cause havoc. And, even if he has, five other large machines and a dozen small ones are nearing completion, and it is impossible that he can have tampered with them.

If anything goes wrong now, thoroughness is a meaningless word.

Himmler.

March 21, 1941

From Gestapo
To   Secretary, Bureau of Physics
Subject Secret Six

Recriminations are useless. What I would like to know is: What in God's name happened?

Himmler.

March 22, 1941

From Secretary, Bureau of Physics
To   Herr Heinrich Himmler
Subject Secret Six

The reply to your question is being prepared. The great trouble is the confusion among the witnesses, but it should not be long before some kind of coherent reply is ready.

Work is being rushed to complete the duplicate machines on the basis of photographs and plans that were made from day to day. I cannot see how anything can be wrong in the long run.

As for Number One, shall we send planes over with bombs?

August Buehnen.

COPY ONLY
MEMO   March 23, 1941

From Detention Branch, Gestapo

The four agents, Gestner, Luslich, Heinreide, and Muemmer, who were guarding Herr Professor Johann Kenrube, report that he was under close arrest at our Berlin headquarters until six P.M., March 21st. At six P.M., he abruptly vanished.

S. Duerner.

COMMENT WRITTEN BELOW

Kenrube was at *Gribe Schloss* before two P.M., March 21st. This completely nullifies the six P.M. story. Place these scoundrels under arrest, and bring them before me at eight o'clock tonight.

Himmler.

COPY ONLY
EXAMINATION BY HERR HIMMLER OF F. GESTNER

Q. Your name?
A. Gestner. Fritz Gestner. Long service.
Q. Silence. If we want to know your service, we'll check it in the record.
A. Yes, sir.
Q. That's a final warning. You answer my questions, or I'll have your tongue.
A. Yes, sir.
Q. You're one of the stupid fools set to guard Kenrube?
A. I was one of the four guards, sir.
Q. Answer yes or no.
A. Yes, sir.
Q. What was your method of guarding Kenrube?
A. By twos. Two of us at a time were in the great white cell with him.
Q. Why weren't the four of you there?
A. We thought—
Q. You thought! Four men were ordered to guard Kenrube and— By God, there'll be dead men around here before this night is over. I want to get this clear: There was never a moment when two of you were not in the cell with Kenrube?
A. Always two of us.
Q. Which two were with Kenrube at the moment he disappeared?
A. I was. I and Johann Luslich.
Q. Oh, you know Luslich by his first name. An old friend of yours, I suppose?
A. No, sir.
Q. You knew Luslich previously, though?
A. I met him for the first time when we were assigned to guard Herr Kenrube.
Q. Silence! Answer yes or no. I've warned you about that.
A. Yes, sir.
Q. Ah, you admit knowing him?
A. No, sir. I meant—
Q. Look here, Gestner, you're in a very bad spot. Your story is a falsehood on the face of it. Tell me the truth. Who are your accomplices?
A. None, sir.
Q. You mean you were working this alone?
A. No, sir.
Q. You damned liar! Gestner, we'll get the truth out of you if we have to tear you apart.

A. I am telling the truth, Excellency.

Q. Silence, you scum. What time did you say Kenrube disappeared?

A. About six o'clock.

Q. Oh, he did, eh? Well, never mind that. What was Kenrube doing just before he vanished?

A. He was talking to Luslich and me.

Q. What right had you to talk to the prisoner?

A. Sir, he mentioned an accident he expected to happen at some official opening somewhere.

Q. He what?

A. Yes, sir; and I was desperately trying to find out where, so that I could send a warning.

Q. Now, the truth is coming. So you do know about this business, you lying rat! Well, let's have the story you've rigged up.

A. The dictaphone will bear out every word.

Q. Oh, the dictaphone was on.

A. Every word is recorded.

Q. Oh, why wasn't I told about this in the first place?

A. You wouldn't lis—

Q. Silence, you fool! By God, the cooperation I get around this place. Never mind. Just what was Kenrube doing at the moment he disappeared?

A. He was sitting—talking.

Q. Sitting? You'll swear to that?

A. To the Fuehrer himself.

Q. He didn't move from his chair? He didn't walk over to an orifice?

A. I don't know what you mean, Excellency.

Q. So you pretend, anyway. But that's all for the time being. You will remain under arrest. Don't think we're through with you. That goes also for the others.

Author's Note: *The baffled fury expressed by the normally calm Himmler in this interview is one indication of the dazed bewilderment that raged through high Nazi circles. One can imagine the accusation and counter-accusation and then the slow, deadly realization of the situation.*

March 24, 1941

From   Reich and Prussian Minister of Science
To   Gestapo
Subject   Secret Six

Inclosed is the transcription of a dictaphone record which was made by Professor Kenrube. A careful study of these deliberate words, combined with what he said at *Gribe Schloss*, may reveal his true purpose, and may also explain the incredible thing that happened. I am anxiously awaiting your full report.

Himmler.

TRANSCRIPTION OF DICTAPHONE RECORD P-679-423-1; CONVERSATION OF PROFESSOR JOHANN KENRUBE IN WHITE CELL 26, ON 3/21/41.

(Note: K. refers to Kenrube, G. to any of the guards.)

K. A glass of water, young man.

G. I believe there is no objection to that. Here.

K. It must be after five.

G. There is no necessity for you to know the time.

K. No, but the fact that it is late is very interesting. You see, I have invented a machine. A very queer machine it is going to seem when it starts to react according to the laws of real as distinct from functional mathematics. You have the dictaphone on, I hope?

G. What kind of a smart remark is that?

K. Young man, that dictaphone had better be on. I intend talking about my invention, and your masters will skin you alive if it's not recorded. Is the dictaphone on?

G. Oh, I suppose so.

K. Good. I may be able to finish what I have to say. I may not.

G. Don't worry. You'll be here to finish it. Take your time.

K. I had the idea before my brother was killed in the purge, but I thought of the problem then as one of education. Afterward, I saw it as revenge. I hated the Nazis and all they stood for.

G. Oh, you did, eh? Go on.

K. My plan after my brother's murder was to build for the Nazis the greatest weapon the world will ever know, and then have them discover that only I, who understood and who accordingly *fitted in* with the immutable laws involved—only I could ever operate the machine. And I would have to be present physically. That way I would prove my indispensability and so transform the entire world to my way of thinking.

G. We've got ways of making indispensables work.

K. Oh, that part is past. I've discovered what is going to happen—to me as well as to my invention.

G. Plenty is going to happen to you. You've already talked yourself into a concentration camp.

K. After I discovered that, my main purpose was simplified. I wanted to do the preliminary work on the machine and naturally, I had to do that under the prevailing system of government—by cunning and mis-representation. I had no fear that any of the precautions they were so laboriously taking would give them the use of the machine, not this year, not this generation, not ever. The machine simply cannot be used by people who think as they do. For instance, the model that—

G. Model! What are you talking about?

K. Silence, please. I am anxious to clarify for the dictaphone what will seem obscure enough under any circumstances. The reason the model worked perfectly was because I fitted in mentally and physically. Even after I left, it continued to carry out the task I had set it, but as soon as Herr—(Seventeen) made a change, it began to yield to other pressures. The accident—

G. Accident!

K. Will you shut up? Can't you see that I am trying to give information for the benefit of future generations? I have no desire that my secret be lost. The whole thing is in understanding. The mechanical part is only half the means. The mental approach is indispensable. Even Herr—(Seventeen), who was beginning to be *sympathique*, could not keep the machine sane for more than an hour. His death, of course, was inevitable, whether it looked like an accident or not.

G. Whose death?

K. What it boils down to is this. My invention does not fit into our civilization. It's *the next*, the coming age of man. Just as modern science could not develop in ancient Egypt because the whole mental, emotional, and physical attitude was wrong, so my machine cannot be used until the thought structure of man changes. Your masters will have some further facts soon to bear me out.

G. Look! You said something before about something happening. What?

K. I've just been telling you: I don't know. The law of averages says it won't be another sun, but there are a thousand deadly things thatcan happen. When Nature's gears snag, no imaginable horror can match the result.

G. But something is going to happen?

K. I really expected it before this. The official opening was set for half-past one. Of course, it doesn't really matter. If it doesn't happen today, it will take place tomorrow.

G. Official opening! You mean an accident is going to happen at some
official opening?

K. Yes, and my body will be *attracted*. I—

G. What— Good God! He's gone!

(Confusion. Voices no longer audible.)

March 25, 1941

To   Reich and Prussian Minister of Science
From   Herr Himmler
Subject Destruction of *Gribe Schloss*

The report is still not ready. As you were not present, I have asked the
journalist, Polermann, who was with Hitler, to write a description of the
scene. His account is enclosed with the first page omitted.

You will note that in a number of paragraphs he reveals incomplete
knowledge of the basic situation, but except for this, his story is, I believe,
the most accurate we have.

The first page of his article was inadvertently destroyed. It was simply
a preliminary.

For your information.

DESCRIPTION OF DESTRUCTION OF *GRIBE SCHLOSS* BY HERR POLERMANN

—The first planet came in an unexpected fashion. I realized that as I
saw Herr—(Twelve) make some hasty adjustments on one of his dials.

Still dissatisfied, he connected a telephone plug into a socket somewhere in his weird-looking asbestos suit, thus establishing telephone communication with the Minister of Science, who was in the steel inclosure
with us. I heard His Excellency's reply:

"Night! Well, I suppose it has to be night some time on other planets.
You're not sure it's the same planet? I imagine the darkness is confusing."

It was. In the mirror, the night visible through the orifice showed a
bleak, gray, luminous landscape, incredibly eerie and remote, an unnatural
world of curious shadows, and not a sign of movement anywhere.

And that, after an instant, struck us all with an appalling effect, the
dark consciousness of that great planet, swinging somewhere around a
distant sun, an uninhabited waste, a lonely reminder that life is rarer than
death in the vast universe. Herr—(Twelve) made an adjustment on a dial;
and, instantly, the great orifice showed that we were seeing the interior
of the planet. A spotlight switched on, and picked out a solid line of red

earth that slowly, as the dial turned, became clay; then a rock stratum came into view, and was held in focus.

An asbestos-clothed assistant of Herr—(Twelve) dislodged a piece of rock with a pick. He lifted it, and started to bring it toward the steel inclosure, apparently for the Fuehrer's inspection.

And abruptly vanished.

We blinked our eyes. But he was gone, and the rock with him. Herr—(Twelve) switched on his telephone hurriedly. There was a consultation, in which the Fuehrer participated. The decision finally was that it has been a mistake to examine a doubtful planet, and that the accident had happened because the rock had been removed. Accordingly, no further effort would be made to remove anything.

Regret was expressed by the Fuehrer that the brave assistant should have suffered such a mysterious fate.

We resumed our observant positions, more alert now, conscious of what a monstrous instrument was here before our eyes. A man whisked completely out of our space simply because he had touched a rock from a planet in hyper-space.

The second planet was also dark. At first it, too, looked a barren world, enveloped in night; and then—wonder. Against the dark, towering background of a great hill, a city grew. It spread along the shore of a moonlit sea, ablaze with ten million lights. It clung there for a moment, a crystalline city, alive with brilliant streets. Then it faded. Swiftly it happened. The lights seemed literally to slide off into the luminous sea. For a moment, the black outline of the city remained, then that, too, vanished into the shadows. Astoundingly, the hill that had formed an imposing background for splendor, distorted like a picture out of focus, and was gone with the city.

A flat, night-wrapped beach spread where a moment before there had been a world of lights, a city of another planet, the answer to ten million questions about life on other worlds—gone like a secret wind into the darkness.

It was plain to see that the test, the opening, was not according to schedule. Once more, Herr—(Twelve) spoke through the telephone to His Excellency, the Minister of Science.

His Excellency turned to the Fuehrer, and said, "He states that he appears to have no control over the order of appearance. Not once has he been able to tune in a planet which he had previously selected to show you."

There was another consultation. It was decided that this second planet, though it had reacted in an abnormal manner, had not actually proved dangerous. Therefore, one more attempt would be made. No sooner was this decision arrived at, than there was a very distinctly audible click from the machine. And, though we did not realize it immediately, the catastrophe was upon us.

I cannot describe the queer loudness of that clicking from the machine. It was not a metallic noise. I have since been informed that only an enormous snapping of energy in motion could have made that unusual, unsettling sound.

My own sense of uneasiness was quickened by the sight of Herr— (Twelve) frantically twisting dials. But nothing happened for a few seconds. The planet on which we had seen the city continued to hold steady in the orifice. The darkened beach spread there in the half-light shed by a moon we couldn't see. And then—

A figure appeared in the orifice. I cannot recall all my emotions at the sight of that manlike being. There was a wild thought that here was some supercreature who, dissatisfied with the accidents he had so far caused us, was now come to complete our destruction. That thought ended as the figure came out onto the floor and one of the assistants swung a spotlight on him. The light revealed him as a tall, well-built, handsome man, dressed in ordinary clothes.

Beside me, I heard someone exclaim: "Why, it's Professor Kenrube!"

For most of those present, everything must have, in that instant, been clear. I, however, did not learn until later that Kenrube was one of the scientists assigned to assist Herr—(Twelve) in building the machine, and that he turned out to be a traitor. He was suspected in the destruction of an earlier model, but as there was no evidence and the suspicion not very strong, he was permitted to continue his work.

Suspicion had arisen again a few days previously, and he had been confined to his quarters, from whence, apparently, he had now come forth to make sure that his skillful tampering with the machine had worked out. This, then, was the man who stood before us. My impression was that he should not have been allowed to utter his blasphemies, but I understand the leaders were anxious to learn the extent of his infamy, and thought he might reveal it in his speech. Although I do not profess to understand the gibberish, I have a very clear memory of what was said, and set it down here for what it is worth.

Kenrube began: "I have no idea how much time I have, and as I was unable to explain clearly to the dictaphone all that I had to say, I must try to finish here." He went on, "I am not thinking now in terms of revenge, though God knows my brother was very dear to me. But I want the world to know the way of this invention."

The poor fool seemed to be laboring under the impression that the machine was his. I did not, and do not, understand his reference to a dictaphone. Kenrube went on:

"My first inkling came through psychology, the result of meditating on the manner in which the soil of different parts of the earth influences the race that lives there. This race-product was always more than simply the end-shape of a seacoast, or a plains, or a mountain environment. Somehow, beneath adaptations, peculiar and unsuspected relationships existed between the properties of matter and the phenomena of life. And so my search was born. The idea of revenge came later.

"I might say that in all history there has never been a revenge as complete as mine. Here is your machine. It is all there; yours to use for any purpose—provided you first change your mode of thinking to conform to the reality of the relationship between matter and life.

"I have no doubt you can build a thousand duplicates, but beware— every machine will be a Frankenstein monster. Some of them will distort time, as seems to have happened in the time of my arrival here. Others will feed you raw material that will vanish even as you reach forth to seize it. Still others will pour obscene things into our green earth; and others will blaze with terrible energies, but you will never know what is coming, you will never satisfy a single desire.

"You may wonder why everything will go wrong. Herr—(Twelve) has, I am sure, been able to make brief, successful tests. That will be the result of my earlier presence, and will not recur now that so many alien presences have affected its—sanity!

"It is not that the machine has will. It reacts to laws, which you must learn, and in the learning it will reshape your minds, your outlook on life. It will change the world. Long before that, of course, the Nazis will be destroyed. They have taken irrevocable steps that will insure their destruction.

"Revenge! Yes, I have it in the only way that a decent human being could desire it. I ask any reasonable being how else these murderers could be wiped from the face of the earth, except by other nations, who would never act until *they* had acted first?

"I have only the vaguest idea what the machine will do with me—it matters not. But I should like to ask you, my great Fuehrer, one question: Where now will you obtain your raw material?"

He must have timed it exactly. For, as he finished, his figure dimmed. Dimmed! How else describe the blur that his body became? And he was gone, merged with the matter with which, he claimed, his life force was attuned.

The madman had one more devastating surprise for us. The dark planet, from which the city had disappeared, was abruptly gone from the orifice. In its place appeared another dark world. As our vision grew accustomed to this new night, we saw that this was a world of restless water; to the remote, dim horizon was a blue-black, heaving sea. The machine switched below the surface. It must have been at least ten hellish miles below it, judging from the pressure, I have since been informed.

There was a roar that seemed to shake the earth.

Only those who were with the Fuehrer in the steel room succeeded in escaping. Twenty feet away a great army truck stood with engines churning—it was not the first time that I was thankful that some car engines are always left running wherever the Fuehrer is present.

The water swelled and surged around our wheels as we raced up the newly paved road, straight up out of the valley. It was touch and go. We looked back in sheer horror. Never in the world has there been such a titanic torrent, such a whirlpool.

The water rose four hundred feet in minutes, threatened to overflow the valley sides, and then struck a balance. The great new river is still there, raging toward the Eastern Sea.

Author's Note: This is not quite the end of the file. A few more letters exist, but it is unwise to print more, as it might be possible for the GPU to trace the individual who actually removed the file Secret Six from its cabinet.

It is scarcely necessary to point out that we subsequently saw the answer that Hitler made to Professor Kenrube's question. "Where now will you obtain your raw material?"

On June 22nd, three months almost to the day after the destruction of Gribe Schloss, the Nazis began their desperate invasion of Russia. By the end of 1941, their diplomacy bankrupt, they were at war with the United States.

FUTURE PERFECT

On the day that Steven Dalkins was eighteen years old, he received an advisory letter from United Governments Life Credit that a million-dollar drawing account had been opened in his name. The congratulatory cover note contained the usual admonitions for eighteen-year-olds. It gravely explained that the money being made available to him—the million dollars—constituted his anticipated life earnings.

Spend it carefully; this may be all you will ever receive: that was the summation.

Dalkins was ready. In nine days, beginning on his birthday, he spent $982,543.81. And he was wracking his brain as to where he could dispose of the other seventeen thousand when a treasury officer walked into his lavish apartment and arrested him.

Dalkins put out his cigarette in a convenient ashtray—he was surprised to find one in the psychiatrist's office—and then walked to the door the girl had indicated. He entered and paused with cynical respect, waiting to be noticed.

The man behind the desk was about fifty, gaunt, hair still without gray, and he was busy drawing lines on a chart. Without looking up, he said, "Find yourself a chair."

There were only two chairs to choose from. A hard-backed affair and a comfortable lounge type. With a sigh, Dalkins settled himself into the easy chair.

Without glancing up, Dr. Buhner said, "Wondered if you'd pick that one."

He made another line on the chart. Dalkins watched him despisingly. He was not alarmed. He had come to this interview expecting stereotyped responses. He was prepared for the verdict, whatever it might be. But the trivia was insulting.

He said with sardonic respect, "You sent for me, Dr. Buhner."

That was an understatement. He had been delivered into this office by the law. His words received no answer. Dalkins shrugged, and leaned back prepared to wait.

The older man said, "Your reaction to that was quite interesting." He made a line on his chart.

Dalkins glared at the bent head. "Look here," he said angrily, "is this the way you treat human beings?"

"Oh, no." Promptly. "For legal purposes, we define a human being as an unalienated person. You are an alienated person. Therefore, legally you are not a human being."

Dalkins bristled, then caught himself. Cynically, he quoted, "Have I not hands, organs, dimensions, sense, affections, passions? Fed with the same food ... subject to the same diseases? ..." He felt pleased with himself.

As before, Dr. Buhner spoke without looking up. "Strong word associations." The chart received its inevitable mark.

The older man straightened. For the first time now he raised his head. Bright, gray eyes gazed at Dalkins. "I have one question," he said. "Did you have a reason for spending that money within a ten-day period?"

The small, scrubbed-looking face of the boy sneered at him. "Wouldn't you like to know?" he asked sarcastically.

Dr. Buhner stood up. "Well, I think that does it. I shall recommend that you be fined whatever you purchased except two suits and accessories, and fined the seventeen thousand dollars of the balance remaining in your account. This will leave you a few hundred, and you may also keep your apartment. I should advise you that human beings may be sued for, or fined, as much as one hundred thousand dollars in any five-year period. Alienated persons of course lose everything when convicted. In your case, I plan to requisition one hundred dollars each week from the fine, to be paid to you if you show up at my office for therapy. No show, no one hundred dollars."

Dalkins laughed derisively. "You'll not ever see me again," he said, "unless you have me brought here by police action to listen to your phony analysis and stupid judgments."

The psychiatrist stood gazing at him. If there was an expression on his hollow-cheeked face, it was not recognizable. Yet his next words seemed to indicate that Dalkins had penetrated his professional neutrality. He said, almost curtly, "All right, what is in your mind? What do you want?"

Dalkins was at the door, contemptuous. He stood there and he felt in himself a renewal of the greatness feeling that had made him act so decisively. For brief hours after his arrest the feeling had dimmed. There had even been a shadowy agreement in him with all the people who would regard as madness what he had done.

Never would he sink to such a doubt again.

The reaffirmation of his own rightness was in his voice now as he said, "You had your chance. Next time tell Big Brother to use a man for a man's job. You muffed it, baby."

"Still," argued Dr. Buhner, who was very happy that this free-swinging dialogue had been triggered while the instruments were still focused and recording, "if I understood it, I could make things easier. I picture you as luxury-loving. No ascetic is Steven Dalkins."

Steven laughed. "I chose that easy chair because you expected me to. I got mad because you thought I would. I consciously fitted into your preconceptions. I *don't* fit them."

"Everybody fits in somewhere. Man's enduring structure permits only minor variations of personality and even of experience."

Steven shrugged.

Dr. Buhner hastily tried another tack. "What's wrong with every normal person receiving a million dollars on his eighteenth birthday? Everybody else thinks that and a number of similar developments are the millennium."

"Rumble on, little boy," said Steven Dalkins. "But when you're through, let me out of here. You're too late for this conversation. In future I talk only to the big boys."

Without waiting for a reply, Dalkins now opened the door. As he did so, the older man said, "As you leave, pause before the mirror in the ante-room and take a good look at who's talking about little boys."

"Okay, okay," said Dalkins. "So I'm only five feet six. So I don't even look eighteen."

"Maybe fifteen," interjected Buhner.

"In this instance," said Steven, "courage comes in a small package."

Pause, into which Steven projected: "And for your information, I am not an alienated person. And it's you that will have to make the decision to change, and not me."

Buhner smiled like a man who is accustomed to talking to people who think that it is thee not me who is irrational. He said, "If you're not alienated, I don't know who is."

He was talking to a closed door.

When the youth had gone, the psychiatrist sat down in his chair with that faint smile still on his face. He was joined by another man, who silently settled into the chair where Dalkins had sat a few minutes before.

"Well, you heard it all," said Buhner.

The other man pursed his rather full lips and nodded.

"What do you make of it?"

The second man's answer was to stroke his jaw thoughtfully.

"He sounded sincere in the alienated fashion," said the psychiatrist.

Before his visitor could reply or make a move, the door opened. The girl who had been in the anteroom came in with two copies of a computer printout. She handed one to each of the men and went out.

There was a faint rustling of paper as Dr. Buhner and his guest scanned the information on the printout. Then the visitor folded his in a deliberate fashion and for the first time spoke. "His physiologic reactions when you asked him that question," he said in a soft baritone, "establish that he did know about the ten-day lag between the time a lot of money is spent and a human being finds out about it."

"The information," was the reply, "is merely classified as special knowledge. It is not secret, but simply is not publicized. Tens of thousands of individuals learned of the delay in specific training they took."

The second man tapped the printout, which now lay on his lap. "I notice," he said, "he spent most of the money on the rapid production of a film. Any chance of it being worth anything?"

The gaunt man shook his head. "I had a committee of film people of diverse backgrounds look it over. Their report reinforced my own impression. It's a disjointed piece of junk. Apparently none of the hastily assembled cast ever saw the whole script. They acted it out in bits and pieces. Clearly, the project was intended to spend the kind of large sum you can put into a film."

The visitor seemed nonplussed. "Have you ever had a case like this before?" he asked, bewildered.

"Once, with the difference that, when we traced down the expenditures, we discovered that he had tried to hide about fifty thousand and had paid another fifty out as a bribe."

"For heaven's sake"—in astonishment—"to whom?" When Dr. Buhner smilingly shook his head, the other man apologized. "Of course, the recipient was penalized and the incident is no longer on his record."

He broke off. "What's your next move with Dalkins?"

"We'll just have to wait and see. He has no hidden money. Therefore, the moment of truth should come rapidly."

"Still"—the visitor was thoughtful—"it says in the printout that his apartment is paid up for two months in advance. What's the state of the larder?"

"Lots of food."

"So he can live in total luxury for two months."

The specialist tapped the printout. "What bothers me," he said, "is that the computer agrees that he is not an alienated person."

Steven Dalkins came out of Dr. Buhner's office into a gleaming corridor, and went along that corridor to an elevator, and so down to the ground floor. From there he sallied forth into a world that had not in fifty years changed much in appearance. There were the same buildings, or at least the same types of buildings. Glass, stone, brick, and plastic cast into various high-rise configurations. It differed from earlier eras in that it had told him every day in his conscious recollection that it was perfect.

The millennium had arrived. True, the eighteen-year-old recipient of a million dollars had to work until that sum was paid off. But then, work was good for people; normal individuals didn't question that.

Most people never succeeded in paying off the debt; they simply didn't earn enough money. But they also, being un-alienated, seldom spent all the money.

When an individual died, what was left of the million reverted to the state. The work debt, if any, was simultaneously wiped off the books. The children could only inherit a few personal effects, not money or property. There were no loose ends. Everybody started with a clean slate—and one million dollars. Legally, that sum could not be paid twice to anyone, nor could any portion thereof. The law did not provide alleviations for the condition in which Steven found himself. If he worked, his salary would automatically go to pay off his already existing debt.

Apparently unconcerned by any of this, Steven climbed into an electric taxi and was on his way.

In due course, the taxi turned onto the street beside the river and pulled into the driveway of a high-rise apartment building. Steven climbed out into the warm day, paid the driver, and then sauntered to the glittering front entrance. As he did so, he was aware of another car pulling to a stop across the road next to the river. The man in it got out and pretended to be interested in the river view.

The spy later reported to Dr. Buhner, "Mr. Dalkins entered the building in which is his apartment, and after two hours has not emerged."

The days went by, and he continued not to emerge.

After a week of nothing, the watchers out there shrugged, and said, in effect, "Well, why don't we just let things happen as they normally would for an eighteen?"

Accordingly, there arrived at Dalkin's apartment a notice from Computer-Mate. It informed him that a young woman, Stacy Aikens, age twenty-three, had been selected as a suitable marriage partner for him.

"As you probably know," the communication concluded, "after a computer selection, both parties have fourteen days to meet and either accept or not accept the selected person. If one selectee is willing and the other not, the willing individual is free and has three more opportunities to accept a marriage partner. On the other hand, the one who refused to accept the computer selectee has only two more chances."

"When the candidate has used up all three choices, one year must pass before another three opportunities are available. If in private life the candidate meets a potential life partner whose personal qualifications come within the frame of the computer programming for each of them, a marriage may also take place. It should be noticed that in this special situation Stacy Aikens has already waived the requirement that her altar-mate must have money.

"A potential candidate who does not wish to be married at this time should so advise Computer-Mate."

Dalkins did nothing. Neither objected, nor asked for his name to be withdrawn. He did not call the girl, and when she finally phoned him on the twelfth day he informed her that she was acceptable to him.

Apprised of these details, Dr. Buhner had another meeting with the representative of the Treasury Department. The man asked, "Do you think he'll marry the woman?"

Buhner smiled. "There we have him. To get his sex organs unlocked, he's got to. Evidently, whatever his plan, that much is important to him."

"Maybe all he wants is an opportunity to use up her cash."

The grim smile did not leave the psychiatrist's face. "No, we've already limited her withdrawals to exactly double what she has been living on up to now, with extra money available on special request for specific purposes. No, no"— he shook his head—"when biology solved the problem of locking up the male sex organ, and later opening it up so that it could function only with one woman—his wife—the entire course of family relations and in fact human history was altered in a positive fashion. And of course since women live an average of seven years longer than men, we naturally set it up so that our youths must marry girls who are four to seven years older than they are."

He concluded, "My bet is, he shows up for the wedding ceremony."

The sign above the doors read: HORMONIC COMPENSATION CENTER AND ALTERNATE MARRIAGE REGISTRATION. There was a lineup in front of the doors when Dalkins arrived. A group of males stood on one side of a long, narrow, fencelike barrier, and a group of women on the other. With one exception, the males were all boys in their late teens and the females all young women in their early twenties. The exception among the men was an individual of about forty. When Dalkins arrived, no women of corresponding age had shown up among the females; so he assumed that the man was there to spy on him. Dalkins smiled contemptuously.

He took his place at the rear of the male lineup and glanced over at the women on the other side of the fence. At once he saw Stacy Aikens. The young woman had already seen him and was gazing eagerly in his direction. Their gazes met. It was the first time they had seen each other in the flesh, and it occurred to Dalkins that he had better smile. He smiled. She smiled back, revealing rather large teeth.

Stacy left her place in the lineup—she was in third position from her door—and, as required by the rules, came back opposite him in tenth position. The way she walked back toward him indicated that she had very short legs.

Dalkins was not critical of her physical appearance. The new-style thinking about such things had been around for more than forty years, and in spite of his antagonism to part of the world around him, that one he had not noticed. The new-style thinking required that all normal girls, women, boys, and men be considered beautiful without exception.

So appearance, in terms of what old-style thinking would have called beauty, was not a factor in computer mating. Height was. Weight was. Age was. And so the young woman who now stood just across the barrier from Steven was 5 feet, 1 inch tall (to his 5 feet, 6 inches), 100 pounds to his 128, and 5 years older than he.

All over the world fatties married fatties, thinnies thinnies, and intermediates other middlings. And of course the ridiculous tendency that men had once had to marry females younger than themselves was nullified by an exact opposite system based on good sense and the findings of biochemistry. Sexually, as economically, it was the millennium.

Soon they were inside the building and were seated in adjoining booths, visible to each other and to the boys and young women in other booths through thick, transparent plastic. Since, at Steven's insistence, they had opted for the alternate marriage, they signed a plastic plate with a special type of pen. Their signature was automatically transferred by the computer to the distant department of vital statistics in the state capitol. The signature, of itself, was the marriage ceremony, requiring only the medical recompensation of the male and the second step of hormonic alignment to make it legal and permanent.

At the computer's request, Dalkins unzipped the right hip of his special marriage trousers. Then he leaned back, also by request, and waited while he was strapped in by two mechanical hands. As the hands withdrew, a glasslike structure fronted by a needle and a beam of light focused on his exposed thigh just below the hip. The needle moved slowly and entered the flesh. The red fluid visible in the transparent needle disappeared inside him. The needle withdrew.

The computer said, "Hold your arm steady for Step two."

Dalkins, who had located the older man, saw that he was standing a few feet away watching the "marriage ceremony," and saw that in fact the man seemed so convinced that all was going well that he had half-turned away.

Now! thought Dalkins.

The pix-phone rang. Dr. Buhner pressed the button that connected the tiny receiver in his ear, and said, "Dr. Buhner here."

The picture that formed on the pix-plate was that of his erstwhile visitor and confidant. The man said in a fretful voice, "Roosley at this end. What went wrong?"

Buhner could not fail to notice the accusing tone of blame, and he said, "We must first of all have an understanding, you and I."

"About what?" Astonished voice and face.

"I had no control over that situation. The law does not permit it."

"You had your observer on the scene."

Buhner ignored the second assignment of blame. "Have I made my position clear?"

"Yes, yes." Resignedly.

"What happened," said Dr. Buhner in a brisker tone, "is that again our Steven seems to have taken the trouble to discover in advance the details of a process that most people go through without preknowledge."

"When it was done to me," said Roosley, "I was in a locked room strapped into a chair. I didn't have a chance to get away."

"If," said Dr. Buhner, "you had brought along a computer repairman's key and an automatic pistol to shoot your way through a locked door—"

There was an impressed expression on the face in the pix screen. Finally: "What are you going to do?"

"Nothing."

"Why not?" Sharply.

"There's no law against what Steven did."

"You mean you can deactivate a machine and shoot your way out of a locked building?"

"Hormonic Compensation may sue him for damages, but since he has no money it will do them no good."

"B-but," his caller protested, "isn't it illegal to be in the condition Steven is in now, a sexually free male?"

"But—" the other man groped.

"It is required by law that a male child reaching the age of puberty have his sex-performance capacity placed under control. It is required by law that he can get married, since marriage is a man-made relationship, only if he goes through the process of being recompensated and aligned with his future wife. If this does not happen, then no marriage has legally taken place. You see," Dr. Buhner continued, "the technique for all this has been taken from the old Chinese Communist People's Army concept, except of course there's no death penalty. But it's simply now, as then, a trap for the unwary individual who, in both the Communist and in our situation, was a teenage male still in a naive stage. Before he can think, we capture him sexually. Before he can grow up, we align him sexually with his future wife, and the law states that once this is done it cannot be undone. The state is justified in taking these arbitrary steps because its goal is a peaceful, hard-working populace."

Pause.

"Where is Steven's wife now?"

"She's not married. The final step was not completed. She has returned to her own apartment."

"And where is Steven?"

"He has not yet returned to his apartment."

Roosley said after a pause, "As I understand it, for the first time in a quarter of a century a male is out there"—he made a vague gesture with his arm, taking in half the horizon—"who is able to perform the sex act with more than one woman?"

"That used to be the way every male was."

"And that is *not* illegal?"

"No, it is merely undesirable. But it's a natural state. No natural human state has ever been specifically declared to be illegal."

The face on the pix screen, in the course of a few moments of contemplating the potentialities of the situation, had acquired a distinct mottled look. The man muttered, "But good God, one man and *all* those unmarried girls and women between eighteen and twenty-three!"

"It could be," soothed Dr. Buhner, "that seduction is not his purpose. For that he didn't have to get rid of his money."

Roosley said blankly, "But what could be his purpose?"

"My assistants," said the psychiatrist, "are continuing to check into Steven's background, trying to find a clue."

"What do you think he will do now?"

"He seems to have covered his tracks well," the older man admitted reluctantly. "I have no report on him. Maybe he's woman-chasing."

Roosley made a choking sound in his throat and broke the connection.

Buhner hesitated, then dialed a very special number. This time, when there was a click, no face came on the pix screen, but a man's voice—deep, determined, interested— said, "I've read your report, Doctor. I agree that Steven should receive publicity. If your prediction about him does not come true, at least we'll have made our first try this decade. Good luck."

Steven sat on his buttocks on the grass, his back against a tree at the edge of the park, and stared up into the sky. It was a pose. Actually, he was keeping a sharp lookout for possible spies. He was not entirely certain that he had got away without being seen. He presumed that the treasury lords would like to find out how he proposed to survive without money.

"It's easy," he called out to four suspicious-looking men who walked by while he sat there (as if they would understand his meaning). "The world pays more for creativity and most for rebellion. Tell that to your masters."

One of the four, a puzzled individual of about thirty, came over and said, "Hey, you're the fellow who gave away your million, according to the news report. Why?"

Steven said, dazzled and delighted, "You mean they're giving me publicity?" He caught himself, shrugged, said, "Move along, bub. If you don't know why, telling you wouldn't do any good."

About dusk, Steven came lazily to his feet, Sauntering—in case there was a watcher—he walked back into the park to where a tiny stream flowed into a culvert. Bending, he reached into the darkness of the culvert, groped, and then straightened. In one hand he now held a waterproof container. From its interior he drew a rolled-up sign. This, like a sandwich man of old, he slipped over his head. The front of the sign was a white canvas with a message on it. The message was:

> I'm Steve Dalkins, the nut who
> gave away his million dollars.

The back of the sign, also canvas, read:

> I invite you to hear my story any
> night at West Park, eight o'clock.

That part didn't mean what it said. Maybe, if it could be arranged, he'd send somebody over there in case people showed. But the purpose would be to mislead possible observers.

Steven walked along, confident, smiling. The sky grew dark and the sidewalks began to give off the light they had accumulated during the day. Walls of stores glowed in the same way. People walked up, glanced at him and his sign, and moved past. Most gave some kind of disapproving indication, but the alert Dalkins noticed one here, one there, who had a different reaction.

To each of these, if it could be done, he spoke quietly in a low voice, "We've got to do something—right? Meet me any night at the ..." And he named another park. The biggest moment of the evening occurred when a young man with a flushed face briefly fell in step beside him and said, "You got a plan for beating these bastards?"

"Sure have," said Steven.

The young man did something twisty with his body. It was a gesture that had in it an infinite hostility. "I'm with you, and I'll bring the gang. My name is Jack."

"Good."

The group that first night at ten consisted of eight single responders, including two young women, and a surprisingly large group of seven intense young men and four equally sincere young women. This was Jack's "gang."

There were no questions of why. Each male and female *knew* that this had to be done. Each was relieved that someone had at last taken the step of no return.

It was as if they all understood the reality of things deep inside their viscera, and *that* part was taken for granted. Only the details of what to do needed to be worked out. And, of course, there Steven had his plan.

They organized Overthrow Associates that first night. It was agreed that Steven Dalkins would be recompensed for his lost million. Each person present at the founders meeting wrote him a check for one thousand dollars. All future members—it was authorized—would be assessed the same amount entirely on behalf of Steven.

"You may not get back your full million," said the flush-faced man, Jack Brooks, "but surely we can get together as many determined persons as were behind the assassins of Alexander the Second of Russia in the 1880s. Surely five hundred is not too much to expect."

"I think there'll be more than that," said Steven noncommittally.

At the end of Month One, there were 2,782 members. Each member during Month Two was given the task of locating five more alienated persons. Since the receipts totaled more than a million, Steve said he would donate the difference to expenses. He had confided the first step of his plan to a small inner circle of the conspiracy, which included Jack. These individuals told inquiring members that the plan was "the greatest," but that it would be unwise to reveal its details to any but key figures.

Overthrow Associates had 53,064 members when, shortly after the end of Month Four, it undertook its first act of total defiance.

The authorities had decided to publicize Steven's condition. Girls and women were urged, if they were approached by a small young man, to call the police if he manifested ulterior motives. Buhner, in his reports, doubted if any woman would be resistant to the charms of a sexually free male. However—he suggested—Steven couldn't be sure of that, and so he would be the careful one.

Nevertheless, the psychiatrist, when he lay awake at night, felt somewhat more restless than was usual for him.

Daytimes he monitored Steven's progress by the number of checks that were made out to him. As the total grew, a shiver of anxiety almost visibly oscillated through those members of the United Governments who, by agreement, had to be kept informed of such matters.

Whenever people got too nervous they contacted Buhner. This particular morning the caller had a beefy face with an edgy voice that said, "What are you doing about these rascals?"

"We're getting ready for a cleanup."

"How do you mean?"

Buhner explained. Police were turning their attention from routine and pointing toward an elemental force. Out of the woodwork of the society, a strange breed of human creatures was emerging. The tense, determined individuals were drawn into the light by a common impulse to smash an environment that, in some obscure way, had angered them.

Their nonconformist impulse to do violence had its own purity. They loved each other and were loyal to their group leaders. In earlier decades, there had been other dramatic actions to motivate affection for and obedience to one or more leaders. In this instance, *this* year, they were proud to be associated with someone who had had the will to give away his million dollars. After that, nobody vaguely questioned the right of Steven Dalkins to be "the boss."

That made it easy for the police. All the checks were made out to one man. The signatures were written plain to see. Every man, boy, girl, and woman was identified, and the computers sent printouts to police centers across the land. Quietly, detectives visited each person's neighborhood and located him or her exactly.

The society, of course, did not permit people to be arrested merely because they wrote a check to Steven Dalkins. There had to be an association with an illegal action.

"But what can they do to a perfect world?" That was the question most often asked of Dr. Buhner, and here it was again. He made the same statement now as he had in the past. "Twelve years ago Charley Huyck led a revolt aimed at our computer-education system. Twenty-three years ago the rebellion of the Gilbert brothers had as its target the group method of electing politicians. After each outbreak, *all* of the participants were arrested, charged with being alienated persons, convicted, and disposed of."

"What," asked the heavy-faced VIP, "do you think Dalkins will attack?"

"Something more basic, is my feeling."

"For God's sake," exploded the politician. "What could be more basic than an attack on the political system?"

"Well," temporized Buhner diplomatically.

The edgy voice calmed and said, "Do you think Dalkins is aware that you can follow up all those checks?"

"Yes, I think he knows, because he has transferred some of the money over to a company."

"Oh, that! But, surely, in this special situation—"

Buhner shook his head firmly. "How companies spend their money cannot be checked on, because it might give a tip to their competition. The computer system would either have to be reprogrammed or a public statement would have to be made by the authorities. But we don't want to do that. We want to catch all of these people and get rid of them."

That night, as Buhner lay awake, he was disturbed to realize that slightly over four months had gone by. So if Roosley's fantasies had been even approximately true, then it was time for violated virgins to be showing up in small hordes. What was disturbing was the possibility that there weren't any ... could it be, he asked himself, that Steven has been behaving like a responsible person all these months and has *not* been out there on a seduction spree?

But if not that, what had he been doing?

The next morning looked absolutely delightful when he glanced out the window of his high-rise apartment. The sky was as blue as a brightly lighted tidal pool ... a little later, he was peacefully and unsuspectingly eating a delicious meat substitute breakfast when the red emergency light flashed on his media set. The alarm buzzer sounded. Then a young man walked onto the stage at which the camera pointed. He said: "Ladies and gentlemen, do not be alarmed. This is a message from Overthrow Associates. We have temporarily taken over the principal broadcast centers of the American continent. We want to tell you something our leader, Steven Dalkins, believes you would like to know."

He thereupon explained and demonstrated (on himself and a girl who suddenly appeared) the chemical method whereby the sex alignment of a man and wife could be terminated. He named several locations where the chemical could be secured locally, and said that similar messages were being broadcast from the other stations across the land.

He urged: "Have your check for one thousand dollars ready, and remember this may be your only chance to get the little case of syringes with the compensating shots in them. You can buy them now and decide later if you'll actually use them. If you're a person of decision you'll act at once before there is any interference with the sale, and think later."

One of these locations named was about a mile from Buhner's apartment. In seconds he was out of the door and heading groundward in a high-speed elevator ... outside, he ran for an electric taxi. En route, he wrote out his check. Even as it was, by the time he had paid the taxi fare several hundred men and about fifty women were crowding around a helicopter which stood at the edge of a small park. As Buhner pushed forward, waving his check as the others were doing with theirs, he saw that three girls and four men were passing out small boxes and another man and girl were taking the checks, examining them, and putting them into a metal container.

The psychiatrist was barely in time. He handed over his check, waited nervously while it was scrutinized, and then grabbed the box that was held out to him. He was still backing away, clutching the precious kit protectively, when one of the young people yelled a warning: "The police are coming. Beat it, everybody!"

In bare seconds, the nine were inside with their cartons and their checks. As the door started to close, the machine lifted into the sky like a scared falcon. Up there it looked exactly like the dozens of other craft like it in which buyers had arrived and which had for many minutes been taking off from all the surrounding streets.

Buhner arrived at his office looking disheveled, but he made his report to Top Level feeling triumphant. The report from the government laboratory later that day confirmed that the seven syringes of the kit he had bought did indeed contain the dealignment chemical.

According to a still later report from the computer network. Overthrow Associates sold 883,912 kits that day at 6,224 locations for one thousand dollars each. And the checks were all made out to Steven Dalkins.

Power and money cast long shadows. The images in the minds of certain shocked persons flickered with the possibility that the next allotment of chemicals would bring in eight billion, or even *eighty*.

It was too much. The rumors came to Steven's ears. He thought: *the turning point!* That very day he dialed the computer code that connected him to his followers everywhere in a closed circuit. He placed himself in front of the pix camera.

There he stood. His eyes were small gray marbles bright with intelligence. His cheeks were flushed. His small body was tense. He glared into the eyepiece, striving to fix every viewer out there with his determined gaze.

He explained the views of the shocked members, whose leader was Jack Brooks, and he finished, "Jack's vision has proved greater than mine. Every man has his limitations. What has already happened seems to be just about what I'm capable of. So—"

He paused dramatically, then made his firm statement. "I hereby resign any control that I have had of Overthrow Associates in favor of my dear friend, Jack Brooks. I give you all my love and best wishes."

He finished graciously, "I'll still sign checks for all valid purchases for the next move of the organization. For that you can always reach me on the code. Good-bye to all you wonderful people."

As Steven's voice and face faded, in a distant apartment a young man with a red face that was positively scarlet grabbed his own pixphone, dialed a number, and yelled into it, "Steven, you so-and-so, what do you mean—valid purchases? I want a total power of attorney over the cash in your account, except for maybe ten million. Show your sincerity."

They were on a private line, so Steven said, "If I don't retain control of the money, you might be tempted to do something against me."

"Sign over twenty-eight million right now to pay for the next allotment!" screamed Jack.

"Okay," said Steven.

When it was done, Jack Brooks paced the floor. "That s.o.b.," he said, "is going to get away with over eight hundred million dollars."

He stopped pacing, scowled, and said, "Like hell he is." He walked to the pix-phone again. This time he called Dr. Buhner and said, "Every evening at dusk Steven Dalkins takes a walk in one of the parks."

The psychiatrist had at least three meetings to attend while he considered what he would do with the tipoff ...

First, with computer engineers and administrative staff. The question: Were the great thinking machines programmed to check out 883,000 names?

The answer: There were endless flows of exact logic, total information somewhere, every transaction of every person available, not a single natural barrier in the entire system—so, yes.

Buhner's second meeting was with the directors of the biochemist guild. They had an analysis for him on the basis of one clue. A long-time employee, who was not a member of the trust group that controlled the sexual dealignment ingredient (one of seven) manufactured at the plant where he worked, had quit his job a few months ago. Investigation had shown that he had made a secret, unofficial study of chemistry over many years.

"We may speculate," concluded the board, "that a group of seven or more persons either separately motivated or in a conspiracy sought employment in such laboratories long ago, and bided their information until someone like Dalkins came along."

Buhner's third meeting was with a committee of the United Governments. A leading economist explained in a shaky voice to the distracted members of the committee that the million-dollars-to-everybody system depended on the statistical reality that the needs of the populace be consistent. An additional expenditure of one thousand dollars per person by a sizable percentage of adults must not happen.

No question, thought Buhner, Steven has hit the perfect world a blow below the belt—

The problem was what to do about it? In his own speech he said cautiously, "It would appear as if the attempt to control mankind's genitalia has been nullified by Steven Dalkins as an incidental act in the accomplishment of a secret goal of his own."

He pointed out that when eight hundred thousand persons did a similar act of vandalism against a system, then by theory the system must be examined, and not the individual.

He made his recommendations and concluded, "I refrain from offering a solution for Steven himself. Vague rumor has it that he is trying to break off his connection with his followers. That may not be easy to do."

At noon the next day, the United Governments issued a determined-voiced statement through their elected secretary:

> It has been deemed inadvisable to permit 883,000 males to prey on a hundred million unmarried young women. The United Governments accordingly authorize drug outlets to make available hormonic decompensation kits to those persons over eighteen who choose to unalign themselves with their spouses. The price of the kit shall be ten dollars. The names of all persons who make this choice will be publicly available. If individuals who have already purchased the kits turn them in before the end of the current month, their names will not be among those posted.

As Jack Brooks heard those fateful words, he leaped to his feet and charged against the nearest wall of his apartment, hitting it with one shoulder. Flung off by the force of his violent action, he threw himself at another wall. Presently, exhausted, he sank into a chair and brooded on the reality that no one who could pay ten dollars would buy the same product for one thousand dollars.

His fantasy of eight billion was now a mere foam of rage in his clenched mouth. The rage was directed entirely at one person: Steven. Steven must have known this would happen ... how can we get even with that—that—that?

Steven Dalkins, all fourteen of him, took his usual evening workout shortly after dusk. At least, those were the reports relayed back to Buhner by the agents he sent to each of the city parks.

Could one of the fourteen be Steven himself? It didn't really matter for Buhner's purposes. He stood across the street from the public pathway of one of the parks and watched a five-foot-six-inch youth jog toward him. If it were Steven, he was well disguised. A good makeup job concealed every significant feature of his face.

As this particular Steven came opposite him, the psychiatrist walked rapidly across the street. "Please tell Mr. Dalkins," he said loudly, "that Dr. Buhner would like him to call. Tell him he's now going to have to admit why he did all this—"

That was as far as he got. Dalkins turned in midstride, ran across the street and then along the sidewalk. Suddenly he seemed to see what he wanted. He darted to a car by the curb just as a woman was climbing into it. There seemed to be some struggle between them, which Dalkins won. The car started up. The last thing Buhner saw was the machine receding down the street, with Dalkins at the wheel and the woman lying back against the seat. Her head rolled limply and she slipped out of sight.

Buhner's men found the abandoned car twenty minutes later with the dead body of the woman owner lying on the floor of the front seat.

"Let him get out of *that!*" said Jack Brooks when the news was phoned to him by the murderer. His flushed face smirked into a grimacing smile. "Sending out fourteen Stevens was the smartest idea I've had up to now."

He was feeling better for another reason. There was a possibility that a percentage of men would be willing to sign over a car or other property in exchange for the kit rather than pay ten dollars and be identifiable and on a list. It was too bad that there was no cash in the perfect world and that every money transaction had to be by computer credit, but still—he shrugged—there was always a way.

The murder was announced over the news media, the circumstances described.

It was a quarter of four when Steven phoned Dr. Buhner.

Later—

Carrying his equipment, the psychiatrist arrived at the prearranged rendezvous. A man at the door guided him to a large, tastefully decorated anteroom. The pretty girl there escorted him through a door to a large inner office and closed the door behind her as she departed.

Silently Buhner set up his equipment, then faced the youth who sat behind a gleaming desk. Steven Dalkins waved him at the two vacant chairs, one soft and one hard. The M.D. settled into the hard chair.

"Hmm," said Steven, "I was wondering which one you would choose."

He leaned back with a twisted smile on his small face. "How does it feel, Doc, to have someone giving you that superior treatment?"

Dr. Buhner stared at him with his pale gray eyes and said, "Steven, slightly over forty thousand members of Overthrow Associates had been arrested by the time I started out for your place."

"This is only one of my places," said Steven.

The older man ignored the interruption. "Four out of five have already elected to go voluntarily to one of the space colonies. That way they can keep their money for sure." He smiled grimly. "Not everyone cares to gamble his million."

"So only I am in jeopardy?"

"Steven," said Buhner tensely, "who could have killed, or ordered the killing, of that woman?" As the silence lengthened, Buhner said, "Maybe we've already got him in custody and can verify your story in a few seconds." He indicated the machines that were focused on the genius boy in front of him and urged, "Steven, you mustn't be loyal to someone who's trying to pin a murder on you."

"What happens to a convicted murderer?" asked Steven, after another pause.

"Nobody is convicted of murder in our day," was the reply. "The *only* crime is alienation."

"All right, what happens to a person convicted of alienation?"

"That's classified information."

"The rumor is that they're executed. Is that true?"

"I'm not a member of the board that handles that. I've heard the rumor." Buhner smiled his grim smile. "Now that you've met some of them, Steven, what would you do with alienated individuals?"

Steven hesitated. "It's unfair," he said finally, "for the unalienated to pass judgment on those persons who through some accident of childhood trauma got to be alienated."

"But you noticed?"

There was a faraway expression in the boy's eyes. "Many of them are exceptionally warmhearted," he temporized.

Buhner refused to be sidetracked. "Steven, how many murders that you heard about were committed by your followers in the past four months?"

The barest shadow of a sad smile was suddenly on Steven's face. "Most of them are alienated about other things," he said, "but those who are alienated that way killed about eight hundred persons."

"Why? Did you find out why they did it?"

"The victims said or did something that violated the ideals of the murderer."

"And so," said Buhner with the touch of grief in his voice that he always felt at such revelations, "in this great universe where a man's life so far as we know is only a tiny span of years, they in their inner fury of rightness denied even that short a time to nearly a thousand human beings. Tell me, what should be done with people like that?"

Once more, their gazes met. This time, the boy looked away quickly. And there seemed no question. The four months of close contact with the endless twists and distortions of truths of the alienated persons he had known had left their scarring marks.

On his face was consequent judgment.

Steven said, "His name is Jack Brooks."

Buhner pressed some buttons on his machinery, watched the dials briefly, then said: "He's among the captured." Once more, manipulation, followed by the comment: "The computer is asking him if he ordered, or committed, the murder. He denies it. But his heart, his lungs, his liver, his blood vessels, tell a different story."

Their gazes met across the control instrument. "Well, Steven," said the older man, "I've been proceeding on the assumption that you're an unalienated person, and that therefore—though it would be a little hard to imagine what it could be—you have some deep reason for what you have done."

Steven said, "I should like you to accompany me somewhere."

"Could you use some reliable witnesses?"

"Yes."

Buhner and the United Government's secretary, and Roosley, and two other important persons stood behind a tree on one side of a tree-lined street as Steven walked across to a small suburban house on the other.

He stopped outside the gate and whistled twice long and twice short.

A minute went by. Then the door of the house opened.

Out of it there emerged a rapidly moving figure of a young girl. A child? No. She charged over to Steven Dalkins and flung her small body against his small body with an impact that sent him back several steps. The two—the dynamic girl and the high-energy boy—thereupon proceeded to hit one mouth against the other, and to squeeze their bodies together in a series of minor but definite blows.

"Good God!" said Buhner involuntarily. "He did all this in order to marry a girl his own age."

As if he had heard the words, or deduced that they would be spoken or thought, Steven turned and called out into the gathering dusk, "But it's not illegal; not now."

"Love," mumbled the psychiatrist. "I haven't thought of anything like that since I gave up little Esther when *I* was eighteen."

Suddenly, his legs wouldn't hold him. He lay down there on the grass, vaguely aware of the others bending over him anxiously.

It was ridiculous, of course, but the shameful tears streamed down his cheeks … after all, he chided himself, little Esther would now be big Esther, married and with a brood of Estherettes. And, besides, it was well known that people always outgrew age-eighteen attachments.

The arguments, so cogently true, flapped unheeded through his head. The feeling that had leaped at him out of his forgotten past somehow conveyed the wordless meaning that he had never been given the chance to grow through those emotions. Muttering, Buhner struggled to his feet, shook away helping hands, and hurried off along the darkening street.

He had important things to do, like recovering from thirty years of living without love.

THE GREAT ENGINE

The blue-gray engine lay half buried in a green hillside. It lay there in that summer of 1948, a soulless thing of metal and of forces more potent than life itself. Rain washed its senseless form. A July then an August sun blazed down upon it. In the night the stars looked down wanly, caring nothing for its destiny. The ship it drove had been nosing down into Earth's atmosphere when the meteorite plowed through the metal that held it in place. Instantly, in the irresistibleness of its terrible strength, the engine tore to shreds what remained of the framework and plunged through the gaping meteorite hole, down, down.

For all the weeks since then it had lain in the hillside seemingly lifeless but, actually, in its great fashion, alive. There was dirt in its force field, so tightly packed that it would have taken eagle eyes to see how swiftly it was spinning. Not even the boys who sat one day on a flange of the engine noticed the convulsions of the dirt. If one of them had poked a grimy hand into the inferno of energy that was the force field, muscles, bones, blood would have spurted like gas exploding.

But the boys went away; and the engine was still there on the day the searchers passed along the bottom of the hill. Discovery was as close as that. There were two of them, two alert, trained observers who anxiously scanned the hillside. But a cloud was veiling the brightness of the sun, and they passed on unseeing.

It was more than a week later, late in the afternoon, when a horse climbing the hill straddled the protruding bulge of the engine. The horse's rider proceeded to dismount in an astounding fashion. With his one hand he grasped the saddle horn and *lifted* himself clear of the saddle. Casually, easily, he brought his left leg over, held himself poised in midair, and then dropped to the ground. The display of strength seemed all the more effortless because the action was automatic. His attention was concentrated the whole while on the thing in the ground.

His lean face twisted as he examined the machine. He glanced around, eyes suddenly narrowed. Then he smiled sardonically as he realized the thought in his mind. Finally, he shrugged. There was little chance of anybody seeing him out here. The town of Crescentville was more than a mile away; and there was no sign of life around the big white house which stood among the trees a third of a mile to the northwest.

He was alone with his horse and the machine. And, after a moment, his voice echoed with cool irony on the twilight air, "Well, Dandy, here's a job for us. This scrap should buy you quite a bit of feed. We'll haul it to the junk dealer after dark. That way she won't find out and we'll save some remnant of our pride."

He stopped. Involuntarily, he turned to stare at the garden-like estate whose width stretched for nearly a mile between himself and the town. A white fence, misty and halo-ish in the twilight, made a vast circuit around a green, verdant land of trees and pasture. The fence kept disappearing down gullies and into brush. It vanished finally in the north beyond the stately white house.

The man muttered impatiently, "What a fool I've been, hanging around Crescentville waiting for her." He cut the words with a mental effort and turned to stare down at the engine. "Have to get some idea of its weight," he thought. "Wonder what it is."

He climbed to the top of the hill and came down again carrying a piece of deadwood about four feet long and three inches in diameter. He began to pry the engine loose from the ground. It was awkward work with only a left arm. And so, when he noticed the dirt-plugged hole in the center, he jabbed the wood into it to get better leverage.

His shout of surprise and pain echoed hoarsely on the evening air.

For the wood jerked. Like a shot twisted by the rifled barrel of a gun, like a churning knife, it wrenched in his hand, tearing like a shredder, burning like fire. He was lifted up, up, and flung twenty feet down the hill. Groaning, clutching his tattered hand to his body, he stumbled to his feet.

The sound died on his lips, then, as his gaze fastened on the throbbing, whirling thing that had been a dead branch of tree. He stared. Then he climbed, trembling, onto the black horse. Nursing his bloodied hand, blinking from the agony, he raced the animal down the hill and toward the highway that led to the town.

A stone boat and harness for Dandy rented from a farmer, rope and tackle, a hand stiff with bandages, still numb with pain, a trek through darkness with a thrumming thing on the stone boat—for three hours Pendrake felt himself a creature in a nightmare.

But here was the engine now, on the floor of his stable, safe from discovery except for the sound that was pouring forth from the wood in its force field. It seemed odd now how his mind had worked. The determination to transport the engine secretly to his own cottage had been like choosing life instead of death, like swiftly picking up a hundred-dollar bill lying on a deserted street, so automatic as to be beyond the need of logic. It still seemed as natural as living.

The yellow glow from the lantern filled the interior of what had once been a large private garage and workshop. In one corner Dandy stood, black hide aglint, eyes glistening as he turned his head to stare at the thing that shared his quarters. The not unpleasant smell of horse was thick now that the door was closed. The engine lay on its side near the door. And the main trouble was that the wood in it wasn't straight. It slogged away against the air like some caricature of a propeller, beating a sound out of the atmosphere by the sheer violence and velocity of its rotation.

Pendrake estimated its speed at about eight thousand revolutions a minute. He stood then, and strove to grasp the nature of a machine that could snatch a piece of wood and spin it so violently. His thought scattered before the mystery; and he gave it up. But a frown creased his face as he stared down at the speed-blurred wood. He couldn't just grab it. And, while undoubtedly there were a number of tools in the world that could grip a whirling bar and pull on it, they were not available here in this lantern-lighted stable.

He thought: "There must be a control, something to switch off the power."

But the bluish-gray, doughnut-shaped outer shell was glass smooth. Even the flanges that projected from four ends, and in which were the holes for bed bolts, seemed to grow out of the shell, as if they had been molded from the same block of metal, as if there had been a flowing, original design that spurned anything less than oneness. Baffled, Pendrake walked around the machine. It seemed to him that the problem was beyond the solution of a man who had as his working equipment one badly maimed and bandaged hand.

He noticed something. The machine lay solidly, heavily, on the floor. It neither jogged nor jumped. It made not the slightest effort to begin a sedate, reactionary creep in opposition to the insanely whirling thing that bristled from its middle. The engine was ignoring the law that action and reaction are equal and opposite.

With abrupt realization of the possibilities, Pendrake bent down and heaved at the metal shell, Instantly, knives of pain hacked at his hand. Tears shocked into his eyes. But when he finally let go, the engine was standing on one of its four sets of flanges. And the crooked wood was spinning, no longer vertically, but roughly horizontal to the floor.

The pulse of agony in Pendrake's hand slowed. He wiped tears from his eyes and proceeded to the next step in the plan that had occurred to him. Nails! He drove them into the bed bolt holes, and bent them over the metal. That was just to make sure the narrow-based engine wouldn't topple over in the event that he bumped too hard against the outer shell.

An apple box came next. Laid lengthwise on its side, it reached up to within half an inch of the exact center of the large hole, from the opposite side of which the wood projected. Two books held steady a piece of one-inch piping about a foot long. It was painful holding the small sledge hammer in that lame hand of his, but he struck true. The piece of piping recoiled from the hammer, banged the wood where it was held inside the hole of the engine, and knocked it out.

There was a crash that shook the garage. After a moment, Pendrake grew aware of a long, splintered slash in the ceiling, through which the four-foot piece of deadwood had bounced after striking the floor. Slowly, his reverberating mind gravitated into a rhythm with the silence that was settling. Pendrake drew a deep breath. There were still things to discover, a whole new machine world to explore. But one thing seemed clear:

He had conquered the engine.

At midnight he was still awake. He kept getting up, dropping the magazine he was reading, and going into the dark kitchen of the cottage to peer out at the darker garage. But the night was quiet. No marauders disturbed the peace of the town. Occasionally, a car motor sounded far away.

He began to realize the psychological danger when for the dozenth time he found himself pressing his face against the cool pane of the kitchen window. Pendrake cursed aloud and went back into the living room, muttering invective. What was he trying to do? He couldn't hope to keep that engine. It must be a new invention, a radical post-war development, lying on that hillside because of an accident that a silly ass who never read papers or listened to the radio wouldn't know anything about.

Somewhere in the house, he remembered, was a *New York Times* he'd bought not so long ago. He found the paper in his magazine rack with all the other old and unread papers and magazines he'd bought from time to time. The date at the top was June 7, 1947; and this was August 16th. Not too great a difference.

But this wasn't 1947. This was 1948!

With a cry, Pendrake leaped to his feet, then slowly sank back into his chair. It was an ironic picture that came then, a kaleidoscope of the existence of a man so untouched by the friction of time that fourteen months had glided by like so many days. Lazy, miserable hound, Pendrake thought in a blaze of fury, using his lost arm and an unforgiving woman as an excuse for lying down on life. That was over. All of it. He'd start again—

He grew aware of the paper in his hand. And all the anger went out of him as in a gathering excitement he began to glance at the headlines:

PRESIDENT CALLS ON NATION
FOR NEW INDUSTRIAL EFFORT
Two Hundred Billion Dollar National
Income Only Beginning, He Says.

350,000 FAMILY PLANES SOLD
FIRST FIVE MONTHS OF 1947
IS THERE LIFE ON OTHER PLANETS?
Expect 200 Inch Telescope To
Provide New Evidence—To Be
Completed Next Year.

Pendrake's mind poised at that point, hard on the thought that came. "It was impossible! An engine that merely turned an axle in however wonderful a fashion wasn't a spaceship drive, whatever else it might be."

The situation was really simple. He had crept away into this little cottage of his, almost right out of the world. Life had gone on dynamically. And somewhere, not so long ago, a tremendous invention had spawned out of that surging tide of will and ambition and creative genius. Tomorrow, he would try to get a mortgage on this cottage. That would provide him with a little cash, and break forever the thrall of the place. Dandy he'd send over to Eleanor in the same fashion that she had sent him three years ago, without a word. The green pastures of the estate would be like heaven for an animal that had starved too long now on an ex-airman's pension.

He must have slept at that point. Because he awoke at 3:00 A.M., sweating with fear. He was out in the night and clawing open the door of the garage-stable before he realized that he had had a bad dream. The engine was still there, the foot-long piece of piping in its force field. In the beam of his flashlight the piping glinted as it turned, shone with a brown glow that was hard to reconcile with the dirty, rusted, extruded metal thing he had ransacked out of his basement.

It struck Pendrake after a moment, and for the first time, that the pipe was turning far more slowly than had the piece of wood, not a quarter so fast, not more than fourteen or fifteen hundred revolutions per minute. The rate of rotation must be governed by the kind of material, based on atomic weight, or density, or something.

Uneasily, convinced that he mustn't be seen abroad at this hour, Pendrake shut the door and returned to the house. He felt no anger at himself, or at the brief frenzy that sent him racing into the night. But the implications were troubling.

It was going to be hard to give the engine up to its rightful owner.

The following day he went first to the office of the local newspaper. Forty issues of the weekly Crescentville *Clarion* yielded exactly nothing. Pendrake read the first two news pages of each edition, missing not a single heading. But there was no report of an air crash, no mention of a great new engine invention. He went out, finally, into the hot August morning, a haze of exhilaration tingling along his nerves. It couldn't be, it *couldn't* be. And yet, if this kept on, the engine was his.

The bank manager said, "A mortgage on the cottage. It isn't necessary. You have a large account here."

"Eh?" Pendrake said.

It was the expression on the man's smooth-jowled face, the faint, secret smile that warned him. The manager, whose name Pendrake remembered as Roderick Clay, said easily, "As you know, when you went to China with the Army Air Force, you signed all your possessions over to your wife, with the exception of the cottage where you now live. And that, as I understand it, was omitted accidentally."

Pendrake nodded, not trusting himself to speak. He knew now what was coming, and the manager's words merely verified his realization. The manager said, "At the end of the war, a few months after you and your wife separated, she secretly reassigned to you the entire property, including bonds, shares, cash, real estate, as well as the Pendrake estate, with the stipulation that you not be advised of the transfer until you actually inquired, or in some other fashion indicated your need for money. She further stipulated that, in the interim, she be given the minimum living allowance with which to provide for the maintenance of herself and the Pendrake home.

"I may say"—the man was bland, smug, satisfied with the way he had carried off an interview that he must have planned in his idle moments with anticipatory thrills—"your affairs have prospered with those of the nation. Stocks, bonds, and cash on hand total about two hundred and ninety-four thousand dollars. Would you like me to have one of the clerks draw up a check for your signature? How much?"

It was hotter outside. Pendrake walked back to the cottage, thinking: He should have known Eleanor would pull something like that. These passionate, introvert women— Sitting there that day he had called, cold, remote, unable to break out of her shell of reserve. Sitting there knowing she had placed herself financially at his mercy. He'd have to think out the implications, plan his approach, his exact words and actions. Meanwhile, there was the engine.

It was still there. He glanced cursorily in at it, then padlocked the door again. On the way to the kitchen entrance he patted Dandy, who was staked out on the back lawn. Inside, he searched for, and found, the name of a Washington patent firm. He'd gone to China with the son of a member. Awkwardly, he wrote his letter. On his way to the post office to mail it, he stopped off at the only machine shop in town and ordered a wheel-like gripping device, a sort of clutch, the wheel part of which would whirl with anything it grasped.

The answer to his letter arrived two days later, before the "clutch" was completed. The letter said:

Dear Mr. Pendrake:

As per your request, we placed the available members of our Research Department on your problem. All patent office records of engine inventions during the past three years were examined. In addition, I had a personal conversation with the director in charge of that particular department of the patent office. Accordingly, I am in a position to state positively that no radical engine inventions other than jet variations have been patented in any field since the war.

For your perusal, we are enclosing herewith copies of ninety-seven recent engine patents, as selected by our staff from thousands.

Our bill is being sent to you by separate mail. Thank you for your advance check for two hundred dollars.

Sincerely yours,

N.V. Hoskins.

P.S.: I thought you were dead. I'll swear I saw your name in a casualty list after I was rescued, and I've been mourning you for three years. I'll write you a long letter in a week or so. I'm holding up the patent world right now, not physically—only the great Jim Pendrake could do that. However, I'm playing the role of mental Atlas, and I sure got a lot of dirty looks for rushing your stuff through. Which explains the big bill. 'Bye for now.

Ned.

Pendrake was conscious of a choking sensation as he read and reread the note. To think how he'd cut himself off from all his friends. The phrase "—the great Jim Pendrake" made him glance involuntarily at the empty right sleeve of his sweater.

He smiled grimly. And several minutes passed before he remembered the engine. He thought then: "I'll order an automobile chassis and an engineless plane, and a bar made of many metals—have to make some tests first, of course."

He stopped, his eyes widening with the possibilities. Life was opening up again. But it was strangely hard to realize that the engine still had no owner but himself.

"What's that?" said a young man's voice behind Pendrake.

It was growing quite dark; and the truck he had hired seemed almost formless in the gathering night. Beside Pendrake the machine shop loomed, a gloomy, unpainted structure. The lights inside the building glimmered faintly through greasy windows. The machine-shop employees, who had loaded the gripper on the truck for him, were gone through a door, their raucous good nights still ringing in his ears. Pendrake was alone with his questioner.

With a deliberate yet swift movement he pulled a tarpaulin over the gripper, and turned to stare at the man who had addressed him. The fellow stood in the shadows, a tall, powerful-looking young man. The light from the nearest street lamp glinted on high, curving cheekbones, but it was hard to make out the exact contours of his face.

It was the intentness of the other's manner that sent a chill through Pendrake. Here was no idler's curiosity, but an earnestness, a determination that was startling. With an effort, Pendrake caught himself. "What's it to you?" he said curtly.

He climbed into the cab. The engine purred. Awkwardly, Pendrake manipulated the right-hand gear shift and rolled off.

He could see the man in his rear-view mirror, still standing there in the shadows of the machine shop, a tall, strong figure. The stranger started to walk slowly in the same direction that Pendrake was driving. The next second Pendrake whipped the truck around a corner and headed down a side street. He thought, "I'll take a roundabout course to the cottage, then quickly return the truck to the man I rented it from, and then—"

Something damp trickled down his cheek. He let go of the steering wheel and felt his face. It was covered with sweat. He sat very still, thinking: "Am I crazy? I surely don't believe that someone is secretly searching for the engine."

His jumpy nerves slowly quieted. What was finally convincing was the coincidence of such a searcher standing near a machine shop of a small town at the very instant that Jim Pendrake was there. It was like an old melodrama where the villains were dogging the unsuspecting hero. Ridiculous! Nevertheless, the episode emphasized an important aspect of his possession of the engine: Somewhere that engine had been built. Somewhere was the owner.

He must never forget that.

It was darker when he was finally ready. Pendrake entered the garage-stable and turned on the light he had rigged up earlier in the day. The two-hundred-watt bulb shed a sunlike glare that somehow made the small room even stranger than it had been by lantern light.

The engine stood exactly where he had nailed it three nights before. It stood there like a swollen tire for a small, broad wheel; like a large candied, blue-gray doughnut. Except for the four sets of flanges and the size, the resemblance to a doughnut was quite startling. The walls curved upward from the hole in the center; the hole itself was only a little smaller than it should have been to be in exact proportion. But there the resemblance to anything he had ever known ended. The hole was the damnedest thing that ever was.

It was about six inches in diameter. Its inner walls were smooth, translucent, nonmetallic in appearance; and in its geometrical center floated the piece of plumber's pipe. Literally, the pipe hung in space, held in position by a force that seemed to have no origin.

Pendrake drew a deep, slow breath, picked up his hammer and gently laid it over the outjutting end of the pipe. The hammer throbbed in his hand, but grimly he bore the pulsing needles of resuscitated pain, and pressed. The pipe whirred on, unyielding, unaffected. The hammer *brrred* with vibration. Pendrake grimaced from the agony and jerked the tool free.

He waited patiently until his hand ceased throbbing, then struck the protruding end of pipe a sharp blow. The pipe receded into the hole, and nine inches of it emerged from the other side of the engine. It was almost like rolling a ball. With deliberate aim, Pendrake hit the pipe from the far side. It bounced back so easily that eleven inches of it flowed out, only an inch remaining in the hole. It spun on like the shaft of a steam turbine, only there was not even a whisper of sound, not the faintest hiss.

Thoughtfully, his lips pursed, Pendrake sagged back and sat on his heels. The engine was not perfect. The ease with which the pipe and, originally, the piece of wood had been pushed in and out meant that gears or something would be needed. Something that would hold steady at high speeds under great strains. He climbed slowly to his feet, intent now. He dragged into position the device he had had constructed by the machine shop. It took several minutes to adjust the gripping wheel to the right height. But he was patient.

Finally, he manipulated the control lever. Fascinated, he watched the two halves of the wheel close over the one-inch pipe, grip, and begin to spin. A glow suffused his whole body. It was the sweetest pleasure that had touched him in three long years. Gently, Pendrake pulled on the gripping machine, tried to draw it toward him along the floor. It didn't budge. He frowned at it. He had the feeling that the machine was too heavy for delicate pressures. Muscle was needed here, and without restraint. Bracing himself, he began to tug, hard.

Afterward, he remembered flinging himself back toward the door in his effort to get out of the way. He had a mental picture of the nails that held the engine to the floor pulling out as the engine toppled over toward him. The next instant the engine *lifted*, lifted lightly, in some incomprehensible fashion, right off the floor. It whirled there for a moment slowly, propeller-fashion, then fell heavily on top of the gripping machine.

With a crash the wooden planks on the floor splintered. The concrete underneath, the original floor of the garage, shattered with a grinding noise as the gripping machine was smashed against it fourteen hundred times a minute. Metal squealed in torment and broke into pieces in a shattering hail of death. The confusion of sound and dust and spraying concrete and metal was briefly a hideous environment for Pendrake's stunned mind.

Silence crept over the scene like the night following a day of battle, an intense, unnatural silence. There was blood on Dandy's quivering flank, where something had gashed him. Pendrake stood, soothing the trembling horse, assessing the extent of the destruction. He saw that the engine was lying on its face, apparently unaffected by its own violence. It lay, a glinting, blue-gray thing in the light from the miraculously untouched electric bulb.

It took half an hour to find all the pieces of what had been the gripping machine. He gathered the parts one by one and took them into the house. The first real experiment with the machine was over. Successfully, he decided.

He sat in darkness in the kitchen, watching. The minutes ticked by, a calm succession. And there was still no movement outside. Pendrake sighed finally. It seemed clear that no one had paid any attention to the cataclysm in his garage. Or if they had they didn't give a damn. The engine was still safe.

The easing tension brought a curious awareness of how lonely he was. Suddenly, the very restfulness of the silence oppressed him. He had an abrupt, sharp conviction that his developing victory over the engine wasn't going to be any fun for one man cut off from the world by the melancholia in his character. He thought drably: "I ought to go and see her."

No—he shook himself—come to think of it, that wouldn't work. A genuine introvert like Eleanor acquired an emotional momentum in a given direction. Getting her out of that involved forces similar to the basic laws of hypnosis: The more direct the pressure to change her, the greater would be her innate resistance. Even if she herself willed to be free, the more determined she became about it, the more deeply she would become involved in the morass of emotions that was her psychic prison. Definitely, it wouldn't do any good to go and see her. But there was another possibility.

Pendrake put on his hat and went out into the night. At the corner drugstore, he headed straight for the phone booth. "Is Mrs. Pendrake in?" he asked when his call was answered.

"Yes, suh!" The woman's deep voice indicated that there was at least one new servant at the big white house. It was not a familiar voice. "Just a moment, suh."

A few seconds later, Eleanor's rich contralto was saying, "Mrs. Pendrake speaking."

"Eleanor, this is Jim."

"Yes?" Pendrake smiled wanly at the tiny change in her tone, the defensive edge that was suddenly in it.

"I'd like to come back, Eleanor," he said softly.

There was silence, then—

Click!

Out in the night again, Pendrake looked up at the starry heavens. The sky was dark, dark blue. The whole fabric of the universe of Occidental earth was well settled into night. Crescentville shared with the entire Eastern seaboard the penumbral shadows of the great mother planet. He thought: Maybe it had been a mistake, but now she knew. Her mind had probably gone dead slow on thoughts about him. Now it would come alive again.

He strolled up the back alley to his cottage. Reaching the yard, he suppressed an impulse to climb the tree from which the big white house was visible. He flung himself on the cool grass of the back lawn, stared at the garage, and thought shakily: An engine that would spin anything shoved into its force field or, if it resisted, smash it with the ease of power unlimited. An engine through which a shaft could be *pushed*, but from which it could not be *pulled*. Which meant that an airplane propeller need only be fastened to a bar of graded metals—graded according to atomic weight and density.

Someone was knocking at the front door of the cottage. Pendrake jumped physically and mentally. But presently he took the telegram from the boy who had disturbed him. The telegram read:

CABIN MODEL PUMA DELIVERED TO DORMANTOWN AIRPORT TOMORROW
STOP SPECIAL ENGINE BRACES AND CONTROLS INSTALLED AS RESQUESTED
STOP MAGNESIUM ALLOY AND AEROGEL PLASTIC CONSTRUCTION STOP
                                                    ATLANTIC AIRCRAFT CORPS

Never, never, never had he been in a plane so fast. All the military machines he'd ever flown, the Lightnings, the Mustangs, Pumas, did not compare even remotely to the machine that quivered like vibrating bar steel before the power of the engine of dreams. The plane seemed to have no connection with earth. It was a creature of the sky, an arrow discharged by Jove. When he finally brought it down, Pendrake sat in the control seat, eyes closed, tugging his soul back from the upper heavens, where it had roamed, a free spirit.

He sat at last, sobered by the tremendous success. Because, what now? He could take other flights, of course, but sooner or later his machine, in its silent journeyings, would be remarked. And every day that passed, every hour that he clung to his secrecy, his moral position would grow worse. Somebody owned the engine. Owned it and wanted it. He must decide once and for all whether or not to advertise his possession of it. It was time to make up his mind.

He found himself frowning at the four men who were coming toward him along the line of sheds. Two of them were carrying between them a large tool case and one was pulling a small wagon which had other material on it. The group stopped fifty feet from Pendrake's plane. Then one of them came forward, fumbling in his pocket. He knocked on the cabin door.

"Something I'd like to ask you, mister!" he yelled.

Pendrake hesitated, cursing silently. He had been assured that no one else had rented a plane garage at this end of the field, and that the big sheds near by were empty, for use in future years only. Impatient, he activated the lever that opened the door. "What—" he began. He stopped, choked a little. He stared at the revolver that glittered at him from a hand that was rock steady, then glanced up at a face that—he saw with a start now—was covered by a flesh mask.

"Get out of there."

As Pendrake climbed to the ground, the man backed warily out of arm's reach and the other men ran forward, pulling their wagon, carrying their tools. They stowed the stuff into the plane and climbed in. The man with the gun paused in the doorway, drew a package out of the breast pocket of his coat and tossed it at Pendrake's feet.

"That'll pay you for the plane. And remember this, you will only make yourself look ridiculous if you pursue this matter further. This engine is in an experimental stage. We want to explore all its possibilities before we apply for a patent, and we don't intend to have simple secondary patents, improvements and what not hindering our development of the invention. That's all."

The plane began to move. In a minute it was lifting. It became a speck in the western sky and was merged into the blue haze of distance. The thought that came finally to Pendrake was: His decision had been made for him.

His sense of loss grew. And his blank feeling of helplessness. For a while he watched the local planes taking off and landing on the northern runway; it was a mindless watch that left him after ten minutes still without a plan or purpose.

He could go home. He pictured himself sneaking into his cottage in Crescentville like a whipped dog, with the long, long evening still ahead of him. Or—the dark thought knit his brow—he could go to the police. The impulse jarred deeper and brought his first memory of the package that had been thrown at his feet. He stooped, picked it off the concrete, tore it open and counted the green bills inside. When he had finished, he mustered a wry smile. A hundred dollars more than he had paid for the Puma.

But it was a forced sale, and didn't count. With abrupt decision, Pendrake started the engine of his borrowed truck and headed for the Dormantown station of the state police. His doubts returned with a rush as the police sergeant, half an hour later, gravely noted down his charge.

"You found the engine, you say?" The policeman reached that point finally.

"Yes."

"Did you report your find to the Crescentville branch of the state police?"

Pendrake hesitated. It was impossible to explain the instinctive way he had covered up his possession of the engine without the engine as evidence of how unusual a find it was. He said at last, "I thought at first it was a piece of junk. When I discovered it wasn't, I quickly learned that no such loss had been reported. I decided on the policy of finders keepers."

"But the rightful owners now have it?"

"I would say so, yes," Pendrake admitted. "But their use of guns, their secrecy, the way they forced me to sell the plane convince me I ought to press the matter."

The policeman made a note, then, "Can you give me the manufacturer's number of the engine?"

Pendrake groaned. He went out finally into the gathering dusk feeling that he had fired a dud shot into impenetrable night.

He reached Washington by the morning plane from Dormantown and went at once to the office of Hoskins, Kendlon, Baker, and Hoskins, patent attorneys. A moment after his name had been sent in, a slim, dandified young man broke out of a door and came loping across the anteroom. Oblivious of the startled amazement of the reception clerk, he cried in an intense voice:

"The Air Force's Man of Steel. Jim, I—"

He stopped. His blue eyes widened. Some of the color went out of his cheeks and he stared with a stricken look at Pendrake's empty sleeve. Silently, he pulled Pendrake into his private office. He muttered, "The man who pulled knobs off doors when he was in a hurry and crushed anything in his hands when he got excited—" He shook himself, threw off the gloom with an effort. "How's Eleanor, Jim?"

Pendrake had known the beginning was going to be hard. As briefly as possible, he explained: "—You know what she was like. She held that job in the research department of the Hilliard Encyclopedia Company, an out-of-the-world existence that I pulled her away from, and—"

He finished after a moment and plunged instantly into a detailed account of the engine. By the time he reached the end of his story, Hoskins was pacing the office floor.

"A secret group with a new, marvelous engine invention. Jim, this sounds big to me. I'm well connected with the Air Force and know Commissioner Blakeley. But there's no time to waste. Have you plenty of money?"

Pendrake nodded doubtfully. "I guess so."

"I mean, we can't waste time on red tape. Can you lay out five thousand dollars for the electron image camera? You know, the one that was invented just at the end of the war? Maybe you'll get your money back, maybe you won't. The important thing is that you go to that hillside where you found the engine and photograph the soil electrons. We must have a picture of that engine to convince the type of cynic that's beginning to show himself in town again, the fellow who won't believe anything he doesn't see, and gives you a sustained runaround if you can't show him."

The man's excitement was contagious. Pendrake jumped up. "I'll leave at once. Where can I get one of those cameras?"

"There's a firm in town that sells them to the government and to various educational institutes for geologic and archaeologic purposes. Now, look, Jim, I hate to rush you off like this. I'd like you to come home and meet my wife; but time is of the essence in those photographs. That soil is exposed to the light, and the image will be fuzzy."

"I'll be seeing you," Pendrake said, and started for the door.

The prints came out beautifully clear, the image of the machine unmistakable. Pendrake was sitting in his living room admiring the glossy finish when the girl from the telephone office knocked.

"There's a long-distance call for you from New York," she said. "The party is waiting. Will you come to the exchange?"

"Hoskins," Pendrake thought, though he couldn't imagine what Ned would be doing in New York. The first sound of the strange voice on the phone chilled him. "Mr. Pendrake," it said quietly, "we have reason to believe that you are still attached to your wife. It would be regrettable if anything should happen to her as a result of your meddling in something that does not concern you. Take heed."

There was a click. The sharp little sound was still echoing in Pendrake's mind minutes later as he walked blankly along the street. Only one thing stood out clearly: The investigation was over.

The days dragged. For the first time it struck Pendrake that it was the engine that had galvanized him out of his long stupor. And that he had launched on the search as swiftly as he had because deep inside of him had been the realization that without the engine he would have nothing. It was worse than that. He tried to resume the old tenor of his existence, And he couldn't. The almost mindless rides on Dandy that once had lasted from dawn to dark ended abruptly before 10:00 A.M. on two successive days. And were not resumed. It wasn't that he no longer wanted to go riding. It was simply that life was more than an idler's dream. The three-years' sleep was over. On the fifth day, a telegram arrived from Hoskins:

WHAT'S THE MATTER? I'VE BEEN EXPECTING TO HEAR FROM YOU.

NED

Uneasily, Pendrake tore the message to shreds. He intended to answer it, but he was still cudgeling his brain over the exact wording of his reply two days later when the letter arrived:

—cannot understand your silence. I have interested Air Commissioner Blakeley, and some technical staff officers have already called on me. In another week I'll look like a fool. You bought the camera; I checked up on that. You must have the pictures, so for Pete's sake let me hear from you—

Pendrake answered that:

I am dropping the case. I am sorry that I bothered you with it, but I have found out something which completely transforms my views on the affair, and I am not at liberty to reveal what it is.

Wouldn't reveal it would have been the truth, but it would be inexpedient to say so. These active Air Force officers—he had been one of them in his time—couldn't yet have got into their systems the fact that peace was radically different from war. The threat to Eleanor would merely make them impatient; her death or injury would constitute a casualty list so minor as to be beneath consideration. Naturally, they would take precautions. But to hell with them.

On the third day after he sent the letter, a taxi drew up before the gate of the cottage, and Hoskins and a bearded giant climbed out. Pendrake let them in, quietly acknowledged the introduction to the great Blakeley, and sat cold before the storm of questions. After ten minutes, Hoskins was as white as a sheet.

"I can't understand it," he raved. "You took the photos, didn't you?"

No answer.

"How did they come out?"

Silence.

"This thing you learned that transformed your views, did you obtain further information as to who is behind the engine?"

Pendrake thought in anguish that he should have lied outright in his letter, instead of making a stupidly compromising statement. What he had said had been bound to arouse intense curiosity and this agony of interrogation.

"Let me talk to him, Hoskins." Pendrake felt a distinct relief as Commissioner Blakeley spoke. It would be easier to deal with a stranger. He saw that Hoskins was shrugging as he seated himself on the chesterfield and nervously lighted a cigarette.

The big man began in a cool, deliberate tone: "I think what we have here is a psychological case. Pendrake, do you remember that fellow who in 1936 or thereabouts claimed to have an engine that got its power from the air? When the reporters swarmed over his car, they found a carefully concealed battery. And then," the cold, biting voice went on, "there was the woman who, two years ago, claimed to have seen a German submarine in Lake Ontario. Her story got wilder and wilder as the navy's investigation progressed, and finally she admitted she had told the story to friends to rouse interest in herself, and when the publicity started she didn't have the nerve to tell the truth. Now, in your case, you're being smarter."

The extent of the insult brought a twisted smile to Pendrake's face. He stood like that, staring at the floor, listening almost idly to the verbal humiliation he was being subjected to. He felt so remote from the hammering voice that his surprise was momentarily immense as two gigantic hands grabbed his lapels and the handsome, bearded face poked belligerently into his, and the scathing voice blared:

"That's the truth, isn't it?"

He hadn't thought of himself as being wrought up. He had no sense of rage as, with an impatient sweep of his hand, he broke the big man's double grip on him, whirled him around, caught him by the collar of his coat and carried him, kicking and shouting in amazement, into the hallway and through the screen door onto the verandah. There was a wild moment as Blakeley was heaved onto the lawn below. He came to his feet bellowing. But Pendrake was already turning away. In the doorway he met Hoskins. Hoskins had his coat and bowler hat. He said in a level voice:

"I'm going to remind you of something—" He intoned the words of the great pledge of men of honor. And he couldn't have known that he had won because he walked down the steps without looking back. The waiting taxi was gone before Pendrake grasped how completely those final words had defeated his own purpose.

That night he wrote the letter to Eleanor. He followed it the next day at the hour he had named: 3:30 P.M. When the plump Negress opened the door of the big white house, Pendrake had the fleeting impression that he was going to be told that Eleanor was out. But she wasn't. He was led through the familiar halls into the forty-foot living room. The Venetian blinds were drawn against the sun and so it took a moment for Pendrake to make out in the gloom the figure of the lithe young woman who had risen to meet him.

Her voice came, rich, familiar, questioning, out of the dimness: "Your letter was not very explanatory. However, I had intended to see you anyway; but never mind that. What danger am I in?"

He could see her more clearly now. And for a moment he could only stand there, drinking her in with his eyes—her slim body, every feature of her face, and the dark hair that crowned it. He grew aware that she was flushing under his intense scrutiny. Quickly, he began his explanation.

"My intention," he said, "was to drop the whole affair. But just as I thought I had ended the matter by tossing Blakeley out, I was reminded by Hoskins of my Air Force oath to my country."

"Oh!"

"For your own safety," he went on, more decisive now, "you must leave Crescentville for the time being, lose yourself in the vastness of New York until this matter has been probed to the bottom."

"I see!" Her dark gaze was non-committal. She looked oddly stiff, sitting in the chair she had chosen, as if she was not quite at ease. She said at last, "The voices of the two men who spoke to you, the gunman and the man on the phone—what were they like?"

Pendrake hesitated. "One was a young man's voice. The other, middle-aged."

"No, I don't mean that. I mean the texture, the command of language, the degree of education."

"Oh!" Pendrake stared at her. He said slowly, "I hadn't thought of that. Very well educated, I should say."

"English?"

"No, American."

"That's what I meant. Nothing foreign, though?"

"Not the slightest."

They were both, Pendrake realized, more at ease now. And he was delighted at the cool way she was facing her danger. After all, she wasn't trained to face down physical terrors; and being an introvert wouldn't help her any. Before he could think further, she said:

"This engine—what kind is it? Have you any idea?"

Did he have any idea! He who had racked his brain into the dark watches of a dozen nights! "It must," said Pendrake carefully, "have grown out of a tremendous background of research. Nothing so perfect could spring full grown into existence without a mighty base of other men's work to build on. Though even with that, somebody must have had an inspiration of pure genius." He finished quietly, "It's an atomic engine, I should say. It can't be anything else. There's no other comparable background."

She was staring at him, looking not quite sure of her next words. She said at last in a formal voice: "You don't mind my asking these questions?"

He knew what *that* meant. She had suddenly become aware that she was thawing. He thought: "Oh, damn these sensitives." He said quickly, earnestly, "You have already cleared up some important points. Just where they will lead is another matter. Can you suggest anything else?"

There was silence, then: "I realize," she said slowly, "that I am not properly qualified. I have no scientific knowledge. but I do have my research training. I don't know whether my next question is foolish or not, but—what is the decisive date for atomic energy?"

Pendrake frowned, said, "I think I see what you mean. What is the latest date that an atomic engine *couldn't* have been developed?"

"Something like that." she agreed. Her eyes were bright.

Pendrake was thoughtful. "I've been reading up on it lately. 1938 might fit, but 1940 is more likely."

"Ten years?"

Pendrake nodded. He knew what she was going to say, and that it was excellent, but he waited for her to say it. She did, after a moment. "Is there any way you can check on the activities of every able person who has done atomic research in this country during that time?"

He inclined his head. "I'll go first," he said, "to my old physics professor. He's one of those perpetually young old men who keep abreast of everything."

Her voice, steady, cool, cut him off. "You're going to pursue this search in person?"

She glanced involuntarily at his right sleeve as she finished, then flushed scarlet. There was no doubt of the memory that was in her mind. Pendrake said swiftly, with a wan smile, "I'm afraid there's no one else. As soon as I've made a little progress I'll go to Blakeley and apologize for treating him as I did. Until then, right arm or not, I doubt if there's anyone more capable than I am." He frowned. "Of course, there is the fact that a one-armed man is easily spotted."

She had control of herself again. "I was going to suggest that you obtain an artificial arm and a flesh mask. Those people must have worn civilian masks if you recognized the disguise so quickly. You can secure the perfect soldier's type."

She stood up and finished in a level voice: "As for leaving Crescentville, I had already written my old firm, and they are hiring me in my former position. That was what I intended to see you about. I shall leave the house secretly tonight, and by tomorrow you should be free to pursue your investigations. Good luck."

They faced each other, Pendrake shocked to his core by the abrupt termination of the meeting, and by her words. They parted like two people who had been under enormous strain.

"And that," Pendrake thought as he stood out in the sun's glare, "is the truth."

It was after midnight, September 8th. Pendrake walked, head bent, into a strong east wind along a well-lighted street in the Riverdale section of New York City. He peered at the numbers of the houses as he pressed by: 418, 420, 432.

No. 432 was the third house from the corner; and he walked on past it to the lightpost. Back to the wind, he stood in the bright glow, once more studying his precious list—a final verification. His original intention had been to investigate every one of the seventy-three eastern Americans on that list, starting with the A's. On second thought, he had realized that scientists of firms like Westinghouse, the Rockefeller Foundation, private laboratories with small means, and physicists and professors who were carrying on individual research, were the least likely candidates, the former because of the impossibility of secrecy, the latter because that engine *must* have plenty of money behind it, Which left three private foundations. By far the wealthiest of these was the Lambton Institute, whose distinguished executive physicist, Dr. McClintock Grayson, lived in the third house from the corner.

He reached the front door of the darkened residence, and experienced his first disappointment. In a dim way he had hoped the door would be unlocked. It wasn't; and that meant all the doors he had opened in his life without ever noticing they were locked would now have to be precedents, proofs that a Yale lock could be broken silently. It seemed different doing it on purpose, but he tensed himself, and gripped the knob. The lock broke with the tiny click of metal that has been abruptly subjected to unbearable pressure.

In the inky hallway, Pendrake stood for a moment listening. But the only sound was the pounding of his heart. He went forward cautiously, using his flashlight as he peered into doors. Presently, he verified that the study must be on the second floor. He took the stairs four at a time.

The hallway of the second floor was large, with five closed doors and two open ones leading from it, The first open door led to a bedroom; the second into a large, cozy room lined with bookshelves. Pendrake sighed with relief as he tiptoed into it. There was a desk in one corner, a small filing cabinet and several floor lamps. After a swift survey, he closed the door behind him and turned on the light beside the chair next to the desk.

Once again he waited, listening with every nerve tensed. From somewhere near came a faint, regular breathing. But that was all. The *ménage* of Dr. Grayson was resting peacefully from its day's labors, which— Pendrake reflected as he seated himself at the desk—was where they ought to be. It would be unfair of fate to let him be interrupted now.

At two o'clock he had his man, The proof was a scrawled note abstracted from a mass of irrelevant papers that cluttered one drawer. It read:

The pure mechanics of the engine's operation depends on revolutions per minute. At very low r.p.m., *i.e.*, fifty to one hundred, the pressure will be almost entirely on a line vertical to the axial plane. If weights have been accurately estimated, a machine will at this stage lift buoyantly, but the forward movement will be almost zero—

Pendrake paused there, puzzled. It couldn't be anything but the engine that was being discussed. But what did it mean? He read on:

As the number of r.p.m. increases, the pressure will shift rapidly towards the horizontal, until, at about five hundred revolutions, the pull will be along the axial plane—and all counter or secondary pressure will have ceased. It is at this stage that the engine can be pushed along a shaft, but not pulled. The field is so intense that—

The reference to the shaft was ultimately convincing. He remembered only too well his own violent discovery that the shaft could not be pulled out of the engine.

The atomic wizard of the age was Dr. Grayson.

Quite suddenly, Pendrake felt weak. He lay back in the chair, strangely dizzy. He thought: "Got to get out of here. Now that I know, I can't take the chance of being caught."

The wild triumph came as the front door closed behind him. He walked down the street, his mind soaring with such a drunken exultancy that he swayed like an intoxicated person. He was eating breakfast at a lunch counter a mile away when the reaction came: So Dr. Grayson, famous *savant*, was the man behind the marvelous engine! So what now?

In the morning he phoned Hoskins long distance. "It's impossible," he thought, as he waited for the call to be put through, "that I carry on with this tremendous business all by myself."

If anything should happen to him, what he had discovered would dissolve into the great darkness, perhaps never to be reconstituted. After all, he was here because he had taken to heart a timeless oath of allegiance to his country, an oath that he had not, until reminded, considered relevant.

His reverie ended as the operator said: "Mr. Hoskins refuses to accept your call, sir."

His problem seemed as old as his existence. As he sat in the hotel library that afternoon, his mind kept coming back to the aloneness of his position, the reality that all decisions about the engine were his to make and his to act upon. What an incredible fool he was! He ought to put the whole miserable business out of his mind and go to a movie. Or return to Crescentville. The property there would need attention before winter. But he knew he wouldn't go. What would he do in that lonely town during the long days and the long nights of the coming years?

There was only the engine. All his interest in life, his rebirth of spirit dated from the moment that he had found the doughnut-shaped thing. Without the engine, or rather—he made the qualification consciously— without the search for the engine, he was a lost soul, wandering aimlessly through the eternity that was *being* on earth.

After a timeless period he grew aware suddenly of the weight of the book in his hands and remembered his purpose in coming to the library. The book was the 1948 edition of the *Hilliard Encyclopedia*, and it revealed that Dr. McClintock Grayson had been born in 1897, that he had one daughter and two sons, and that he had made notable contributions to the fission theory of atomic science. Of Cyrus Lambton the *Encyclopedia* said:

—manufacturer, philanthropist, he founded the Lambton Institute in 1936. Since the war, Mr. Lambton has become actively interested in a Back to the Land Movement, the uniquely designed headquarters for this project being located at—

Pendrake went out finally into the warm September afternoon and bought a car. His days became a drab routine. Watch Grayson come out of his house in the morning, follow him until he disappeared into the Lambton Building, trail him home at night. It seemed endless, purposeless, hopeless. The world became a pattern of gray streets unreeling. He felt himself a wheel turning over and over on its axle, turning, turning, because it was easier to do that than to decide what else his life was good for.

On the seventeenth day the routine broke like a wave striking a wedge of rock. At one o'clock in the afternoon Grayson emerged briskly from the aerogel plastic structure that was the post-war abode of the Lambton Foundation.

The hour itself was startling. But immediately the difference of this day to the others showed more clearly. The scientist ignored his gray sedan parked beside the building, walked half a block to a taxi stand, and was driven to a twin-turreted building on Fiftieth Street; a plasto-glitter sign splashed across the two towers:

CYRYS LAMBTON LAND
SETTLEMENT PROJECT

As Pendrake watched, Grayson dismissed the taxi, and disappeared through a revolving door into one of the broad-based towers. Puzzled, but vaguely excited, Pendrake sauntered to a window that had a large glitter sign in it. The sign read:

THE
CYRYS LAMBTON PROJECT

wants earnest, sincere young couples who are willing to work hard to establish themselves on rich soil in a verdant and wonderful climate.

Former farmers, sons of farmers and their daughter-of-farmers' wives are especially welcome. No one who desires proximity to a city or who has relatives he must visit need apply. Here is a real opportunity under a private endowment plan.

Three more couples wanted today for the latest allotment, which will leave shortly under the monitorship of Dr. McClintock Grayson. Office open until 11 P.M.

HURRY!

It seemed meaningless without connection to an engine lying on a hillside. But it brought a thought that wouldn't go away; a thought that was really a product of an urge that had been pressing at him for all the dreary days now past. For an hour he fought the impulse, then it grew too big for his brain, and projected down into his muscles, carried him unresisting to a phone booth. A minute later he was dialing the number of the Hilliard Encyclopedia Company.

There was a moment while she was being called to the phone. He thought a thousand thoughts, and twice he nearly hung up the receiver; and then:

"Jim, what's happened?"

The anxiety in her voice was the sweetest sound he had ever heard. Pendrake held himself steady as he explained what he wanted: "—you'll have to get yourself an old coat and put on a cheap cotton dress or something; and I'll buy some secondhand things. All I want is to find out what is behind that land-settlement scheme. We could go in before dark this evening. A simple inquiry shouldn't be dangerous."

His mind was blurred with the possibility of seeing her again. And so the uneasy idea of possible danger stayed deep inside him and did not rise to the surface until he saw her coming along the street. She would have walked right past, but he stepped out and said:

"Eleanor!"

She stopped short; and, looking at her, it struck him for the first time that the slip of a girl he had married six years before was grown up. She was still slim enough to satisfy any woman, but the richer contours of maturity were there, too. She said:

"I forgot about the mask, and the artificial arm. They make you look almost—"

Pendrake smiled grimly. "Almost human, eh?"

He knew instantly that he had said the wrong thing. She turned as pale as gray metal. For a panicky moment it seemed to Pendrake that she was going to faint. He caught her arm, cried, "I'm sorry, Eleanor. I'm a damned idiot. I ought to be shot."

"You had no right to say that," she breathed. "I know I was foolish that day three years ago when you returned from China. I ought not to have screamed when I saw your empty sleeve. But you should have written. You-should-have-written."

She made no move to withdraw her wrist from his fingers, and he could feel her trembling. He said in an intense voice, "Eleanor, it was all my fault. My walking out on you in front of all those people—it was the damnedest humiliation ever inflicted on a sensitive woman."

"You were overwrought from your terrible loss; and my scream—"

"I was a scoundrel. I deserve—"

He stopped because she was staring at him with a strange tenderness that made his mind reel. She said, "Let's forget it, Jim. And now, is that the building over there?"

"Eleanor, did you say—"

"We'll have to hurry if we intend to get in before it gets really dark."

"Eleanor, when you said 'Let's forget it,' did you mean—"

But Eleanor stood staring across at the building, a complacent smile on her lips. "Aerogel turrets," she mused aloud, "a hundred and fifty feet high; one completely opaque, windowless, doorless—I wonder what that means—and the other— We'll be Mr. and Mrs. Lester Cranston, Jim, of Winora, Idaho. And we were going to leave New York tonight but saw their sign. We'll love everything about their scheme."

She started across the street. And Pendrake, tagging along behind, was following her through the door before his senses snapped back into position. In one comprehensive leap of mind he saw that it was his own emotional desire to see her that had brought her here.

"Eleanor," he said tensely, "we're not going in."

He should have known it would be useless to speak. Inside, he followed her with reluctant steps to a girl who sat at a spacious plastic desk in the center of the room. He was seated before the glitter sign at the edge of the desk caught his eye:

Miss Grayson

Miss— What! Pendrake twisted in his chair, and then a vast uneasiness held him steady. Dr. Grayson's daughter! So the scientist's family was mixed up in this. It was even possible that two of the four men who had taken the plane from him had been sons. And perhaps Lambton also had sons. He couldn't remember what the Encyclopedia had said about the children of Lambton.

In the intensity of his thoughts he listened with half-attention to the conversation between Eleanor and Grayson's daughter. But when Eleanor stood up, he remembered that the talk had been of a psychological test in the back room. Pendrake watched Eleanor walk across to the door that led to the second tower, and he was glad when, after about three minutes, Miss Grayson said:

"Will you go in now, Mr. Cranston?"

The door opened into a narrow corridor, and there was another door at the end of it. As his fingers touched the knob of the second door, a net fell over him and drew taut.

Simultaneously, a slot opened to his right. Dr. Grayson, a syringe in his fingers, reached through, pushed the needle into Pendrake's right arm above the elbow, and then called over his shoulder to somebody out of sight:

"This is the last one, Peter. We can leave as soon as it gets dark."

The slot clicked shut.

Pendrake squirmed desperately. He fought there under that dim ceiling light, striking against the net that held him. And every instant the terror grew, the terror that was in him, not for himself, but for Eleanor—Eleanor, who had gone through this door minutes before.

He would have cried out, but his rage was too great, his fear for her too near insanity. Eleanor, who had no artificial arm to take the shock of the dope from the syringe. He stopped the thought by an effort so violent that his whole being shook. He must pretend to have succumbed. Only thus could he avoid another syringe that might be more accurately aimed at a vital spot.

As he let himself slump, a voice said, "That fellow fought too hard. You'll have to increase the dose for these powerful-looking men."

The words were Pendrake's first knowledge that his struggle had been observed. He let himself slump farther, and after a moment realized that the net was moving, lifting. A door opened in the ceiling and brightness pressed against his eyelids.

"Lay him down here beside his wife."

His body touched a softness that seemed to yield endlessly like a bottomless cushion. The net writhed and wriggled from under him; and suddenly it was gone. The young man's voice said, "Look at this, he's severed four of the net strands. I thought this plastiwire was unbreakable."

The older man's voice came from a greater distance: "Strength is a curious quality. A dog can strain at a leash until it rots—or break it the first day if he lunges against it with enough snap. It—"

The scientist's voice faded, as if he had gone into another room and closed the door.

Gradually, as Pendrake lay there, he grew aware of breathing around him, the slow, measured breathing of many people. The sound, with all its implications of human beings still alive, eased the dreadful tightness in his throat. He slitted his eyes and saw that he was in a round metal room filled with scores of enormous hammocks that were suspended by cords attached to both the metal floor and the metal ceiling. Twice, Pendrake slid his leg over with the intention of dropping to the floor. But each time a vague snatch of sound made him sink back and slow his breath into rhythm with that of the others.

He was preparing for his third effort when his body was struck a sharp, all-over blow. Beneath him the hammock sagged at least two feet, and there was an awful emptiness inside him, like the nausea of sustained hunger. It was like that for a very long time, and actually there was no change in the fact. But his body grew accustomed to the relentless pressure. Finally, puzzled, he slid out of the voluminous folds of his hammock and dropped to the floor.

He fell hard. The violence of it strained his muscles, and there was a pressing weight on him that stunned because it was beyond all his experience. And because he recognized it. Acceleration! He must be in a ship. That damnable second tower had contained a ship powered by atomic engines. But what kind of a ship?

The thought faded as, with a blank will, he scrambled to his feet. There was a stairway leading to a closed door. But the door opened at his touch. One lightning glance revealed that no human beings were in the room. There was a window that showed a black sky punctuated with stars, and in the room itself, mounted on rigid metal bars, eight engines were spinning. For a moment, to his tensed mind, to his body concentrated on possible, impending danger, the scene seemed normal enough.

The number of engines didn't matter. If one existed, so could eight. And their unlimited power could surely raise a ship out of a hundred-and-fifty-foot turret, though the speed of that rise in the night had been unnatural. Still, eight of those engines, spinning on their shafts, was quite an assembly.

The normalness shattered. Pendrake sent a glance wild with surmise at the engines. *The engines were spinning* on rigid shafts, and it should be the shafts that spun. His memory flung back to the night in his stable when the engine had lifted with strange buoyancy from the floor, spun slowly and— How could he have missed the significance? How *could* he?

With a hissing intake of his breath, he ran to the window. But the knowledge of what he would find was already in him. For a long moment he shivered with the physical daze of seeing interplanetary space, and then he drew his body and his mind into closer union and was himself. He reached the room where Dr. Grayson and the young man were lying in their hammocks. The latter he dealt one stunning blow—and tied them both with cords from their hammocks, tied them into their hammocks, wrapping the cords around and around.

There was silence in the control room. His mind felt far away, cold, joyless. His victory seemed somehow lacking. He couldn't quite place the missing factor, but perhaps it was the stunned expressions of the two prisoners. Uncertain, Pendrake studied the small instrument board. He thought finally: "That note I found in Dr. Grayson's study. All I've got to do is reduce the r.p.m. of the engines to less than five hundred. The pressure will gradually shift toward a line vertical to the axial plane and the spaceship will turn in a great circle and head back toward Earth."

He glanced at the men and then he walked slowly to an expanse of transparent aerogel, and stood staring out into the velvet, light-.sprinkled night. The sun was a ghastly, flaring shape to his left. Pendrake said, without looking at the men:

"Where are you going? Mars, Venus, the Moon, or—" He stopped. He couldn't help it. Mars, Venus— He felt dizzy, then electrified. The wonders of the skies! The only divine cognomens that would survive all the ages of religion! *"Which one?"* Pendrake gasped. "Which planet?"

"Venus!" The answer sighed from the older man. "We have a colony there. Quite a large one now. A ship with a hundred people leaves from one of our centers every three days—and there have been children."

Pendrake said sternly, "A hundred people kidnapped from Earth every three days—doped." He choked a little.

"Denilin sleep drug!" said Grayson. "Harmless, quick, no after effects. It saves simple people from their terror of something new, like space. When they get to Venus they don't mind. The planet is smaller, you know, than has been thought, not more than six thousand five hundred miles, more clouds high up, none below. But the brightness of the sun comes through without the heat; and all the glories of Earth cannot compare with the treasure land that is Venus. No, they don't mind when they see— You must be Pendrake—that stiff right arm— We wondered about you."

"Doped!" repeated Pendrake. But the miasma of his fears was fading. There was greater uncertainty in his voice as he said, "But why the secrecy? This great invention! Properly exploited it would be—"

"It would ruin everything!" It was the young man, his tone desperate. "Pendrake, we're not criminals. There are seventeen famous scientists and their families in this—the greatest names in atomic science. They decided in 1944 when the engine was invented, when the war was already won, that the planets should not inherit the bitterness of Earth. Don't you see, a scramble for territory would be hell? Our plan is to establish the nucleus of a new nation, modeled after the United States; and everybody who migrates becomes—a Venusian."

It was several hours later that the spaceship landed on a darkened lot. Pendrake and Eleanor climbed to the ground and stood silently watching the torpedo-shaped spaceship merge again with the clouded night sky.

The letter came to the big white house a week later:

> Air Commissioner Blakeley has noted the names of the scientists on the list you submitted, but feels that further correspondence with you would be fruitless.

Pendrake grinned at his wife. "Now, everybody's satisfied. I had to report it, of course, but"—his expression grew thoughtful—"it is hard to believe the planets will have their chance because I tossed a loud-mouthed fool out on his ear one August afternoon."

DORMANT

Old was the island. Even the thing that lay in the outer channel, exposed to the rude wash of the open sea, had never guessed, when it was alive a million million years before, that here was a protuberance of primeval earth itself.

The island was roughly three miles long and, at its widest, half a mile across. It curved tensely around a blue lagoon and the thin shape of its rocky, foam-ridden arms and hands came down toward the toe of the island—like a gigantic man bending over, striving to touch his feet and not quite making it.

Through the channel made by that gap between the toes and the fingers came the sea.

The water resented the channel. With an endless patience it fought to break the wall of rock, and the tumult of the waters was a special sound, a blend of all that was raucous and unseemly in the eternal quarrel between resisting land and encroaching wave.

At the very hub of the screaming waters lay Iilah, dead now almost forever, forgotten by time and the universe.

Early in 1941, Japanese ships came and ran the gauntlet of dangerous waters into the quiet lagoon. From the deck of one of the ships a pair of curious eyes pondered the thing, where it lay in the path of the rushing sea. But the owner of those eyes was the servant of a government that frowned on extra-military ventures on the part of its personnel. And so the engineer Taku Onilo merely noted in his report that, "At the mouth of this channel there lies a solid shape of glittery, rocklike substance about four hundred feet long and ninety feet wide."

The little yellow men built their underground gas and oil tanks and departed toward the setting sun. The water rose and fell, rose and fell again. The days and the years drifted by, and the hand of time was heavy. The seasonal rains arrived on their rough schedule and washed away the marks of man. Green growth sprouted where machines had exposed the raw earth. The war ended. The underground tanks sagged a little in their beds of earth and cracks appeared in several main pipes. Slowly, the oil drained off and for years a yellow-green oil slick brightened the gleam of the lagoon waters.

In the reaches of Bikini Atoll, hundreds of miles away, first one explosion, then another, started in motion an intricate patter of radioactivated waters. The first seepage of that potent energy reached the island in the early fall of 1946.

It was about two years later that a patient clerk, ransacking the records of the Imperial Japanese navy in Tokyo, reported the existence of the oil tanks. In due time—1950—the destroyer *Coulson* set forth on its routine voyage of examination.

The time of the nightmare was come.

Lieutenant Keith Maynard peered gloomily through his binoculars at the island. He was prepared to find something wrong, but he expected a distracting monotony of sameness, not something radically different. "Usual undergrowth," he muttered, "and a backbone of semi-mountain running like a framework the length of the island, trees—" He stopped there.

A broad swath had been cut through the palms on the near shoreline. They were not just down. They were crushed deep into a furrow that was already alive with grass and small growth. The furrow, which looked about a hundred feet wide, led upward from the beach to the side of a hill, to where a large rock lay half-buried near the top of the hill.

Puzzled, Maynard glanced down at the Japanese photographs of the island. Involuntarily, he turned toward his executive officer, Lieutenant Gerson. "Good lord!" he said, "How did that rock get up *there?* It's not on any photographs."

The moment he had spoken he regretted it. Gerson looked at him, with his usual faint antagonism, shrugged and said, "Maybe we've got the wrong island."

Maynard did not answer that. He considered Gerson a queer character. The man's tongue dripped ceaselessly with irony.

"I'd say it weighs about two million tons. The Japs probably dragged it up there to confuse us."

Maynard said nothing. He was annoyed that he had made a comment. Particularly annoyed because, for a moment, he had actually thought of the Japs in connection with the rock. The weight estimate, which he instantly recognized as probably fairly accurate, ended all his wilder thoughts. If the Japs could move a rock weighing two million tons they had also won the war. Still, it was very curious and deserved investigation—later.

They ran the channel without incident. It was wider and deeper than Maynard had understood from the Jap accounts, which made everything easy. Their mid-day meal was eaten in the shelter of the lagoon. Maynard noted the oil on the water and issued immediate warnings against throwing matches overboard. After a brief talk with the other officers, he decided that they would set fire to the oil as soon as they had accomplished their mission and were out of the lagoon.

About one-thirty, boats were lowered and they made shore in quick order. In an hour, with the aid of transcribed Japanese blueprints, they located the four buried tanks. It took somewhat longer to assess the dimensions of the tanks and to discover that three of them were empty. Only the smallest, containing high-octane gasoline, remained leakproof and still full. The value of that was about seventeen thousand dollars, not worth the attention of the larger navy tankers that were still cruising around, picking up odd lots of Japanese and American materiel. Maynard presumed that a lighter would eventually be dispatched for the gasoline, but that was none of his business.

In spite of the speed with which his job had been accomplished, Maynard climbed wearily up to the deck just as darkness was falling. He must have overdone it a little because Gerson said too loudly, "Worn out, sir?"

Maynard stiffened. And it was that comment, rather than any inclination, that decided him not to postpone his exploration of the rock. As soon as possible after the evening meal, he called for volunteers. It was pitch dark as the boat, with seven men and bosun's mate Yewell and himself, was beached on the sands under the towering palms. The party headed inland.

There was no moon and the stars were scattered among remnant clouds of the rainy season just past. They walked in the furrow where the trees had been literally ploughed into the ground. In the pale light of the flashlights the spectacle of numerous trees, burned and planed into a smoothed levelness with the soil, was unnatural.

Maynard heard one of the men mumble. "Must have been some freak of a typhoon did that."

Not only a typhoon, Maynard decided, but a ravenous fire followed by a monstrous wind, so monstrous that—his thoughts paused. He couldn't imagine any storm big enough to lift a two-million-ton rock to the side of a hill a quarter of a mile long and four hundred feet above sea level.

From nearby, the rock looked like nothing more than rough granite. In the beam of the flashlights it glinted with innumerable streaks of pink. Maynard led his party alongside it and the vastness of it grew upon him as he climbed past its four hundred feet of length and peered up at gleaming walls, like cliffs looming above him. The upper end, buried though it was deeper into the ground, rose at least fifty feet above his head.

The night had grown uncomfortably warm. Maynard was perspiring freely. He enjoyed a moment of weary pleasure in the thought that he was doing his duty under unpleasant circumstances. He stood uncertain, gloomily savoring the intense primitive silence of the night. "Break off some samples here and there," he said finally. "Those pink streaks look interesting."

It was a few seconds later that a man's scream of agony broke through the thrall of darkness.

Flashlights blinked on. They showed Seaman Hicks twisting on the ground beside the rock. In the bright flame of the lights, the man's wrist showed a smoldering, blackened husk with the entire hand completely burned off.

He had touched Iilah.

Maynard gave the desperately suffering man morphine and they rushed him back to the ship. Radio contact was established with base and a consulting surgeon gave cut by cut instructions on the operation. It was agreed that a hospital plane would be dispatched for the patient. There must have been some puzzlement at headquarters as to how the accident had occurred, because "further information" was requested about the "hot" rock. By morning the people at the other end were calling it a meteorite. Maynard, who did not normally question opinions offered by his superiors, frowned over the identification, and pointed out that this meteorite weighed two million tons and rested on the surface of the island.

"I'll send the assistant engineer officer to take its temperature," he said.

An engine-room thermometer registered the rock's surface temperature at eight hundred-odd degrees Fahrenheit. The answer to that was a question that shocked Maynard.

"Why, yes," he replied, "we're getting mild radioactive reactions from the water, but nothing else. And nothing serious. Under the circumstances we'll withdraw from the lagoon at once and await the ships with the scientists."

He ended that conversation, pale and shaken. Nine men, including himself, had walked along within a few yards of the rock, well within the deadly danger zone. In fact, even the *Coulson*, more than half a mile away, would have been affected.

But the gold leaves of the electroscope stood out stiff and the Geiger-Mueller counter clucked only when placed in the water and then only at long intervals. Relieved, Maynard went down to have another look at Seaman Hicks. The injured man slept uneasily but he was not dead, which was a good sign. When the hospital plane arrived there was a doctor aboard, who attended Hicks and then gave everyone on the destroyer a blood-count test. He came up on deck, a cheerful young man, and reported to Maynard.

"Well, it can't be what they suspect." he said. "Everybody's O.K., even Hicks, except for his hand. That burned awfully quick, if you ask me, for a temperature of only eight hundred."

"I think his hand stuck," said Maynard. And he shuddered. In his self-destructive fashion, he had mentally experienced the entire accident.

"So that's the rock," said Dr. Clason. "Does seem odd how it got there."

They were still standing there five minutes later when a hideous screaming from below deck made a discordant sound on the still air of that remote island lagoon.

Something stirred in the depths of Iilah's awareness of himself, something that he had intended to do. He couldn't remember what.

That was the first real thought he had in late 1946, when he felt the impact of outside energy. And stirred with returning life. The outside flow waxed and waned. It was abnormally, abysmally dim. The crust of the planet that he knew had palpitated with the ebbing but potent energies of a world not yet cooled from its sun state. It was only slowly that Iilah realized the extent of the disaster that was his environment. At first he was inwardly inclined, too pallidly alive to be interested in externals.

He forced himself to become more conscious of his environment. He looked forth with his radar vision out upon a strange world. He was lying on a shallow plateau near the top of a mountain. The scene was desolate beyond his memory. There was not a glint nor pressure of atomic fire— not a bubble of boiling rock nor a swirl of energy heaved skyward by some vast interior explosion.

He did not think of what he saw as an island surrounded by an apparently limitless ocean. He saw the land below the water as well as above it. His vision, based as it was on ultra-ultra short waves, could not see water. He recognized that he was on an old and dying planet, where life had long since become extinct. Alone and dying on a forgotten planet—if he could only find the source of the energy that had revived him.

By a process of simple logic he started down the mountain in the direction from which the current of atomic energy seemed to be coming. Somehow, he found himself below it and had to levitate himself heavily back up. Once started upward, he headed for the nearest peak, with the intention of seeing what was on the other side.

As he propelled himself out of the invisible, unsensed waters of the lagoon, two diametrically opposite phenomena affected him. He lost all contact with the water-borne current of atomic energy. And, simultaneously, the water ceased to inhibit the neutron and deuteron activity of his body. His life took on an increased intensity. The tendency to slow stiflement ended. His great form became a self-sustaining pile, capable of surviving for the normal radioactive lifespan of the elements that composed it—still on an immensely less than normal activity level for him. Again, Iilah thought, "There was something I was going to do."

There was an increased flow of electrons through a score of gigantic cells as he strained to remember. It slowed gradually when no memory came. The fractional increase of his life energy brought with it a wider, more exact understanding of his situation. Wave on wave of perceptive radaric forces flowed from him to the Moon, to Mars, to all the planets of the Solar System—and the echoes that came back were examined with an alarmed awareness that out there, too, were dead bodies.

He was caught in the confines of a dead system, prisoned until the relentless exhaustion of his material structure brought him once more to *rapport* with the barren mass of the planet on which he was marooned. He realized now that he had been dead. Just how it had happened he could not recall, except that explosively violent, frustrating substance had belched around him, buried him, and snuffed out his life processes. The atomic chemistry involved must eventually have converted the stuff into a harmless form, no longer capable of hindering him. But he was dead by then.

Now he was alive again, but in so dim a fashion that there was nothing to do but wait for the end. He waited.

In 1950 he watched the destroyer float towards him through the sky. Long before it slowed and stopped just below him, he had discovered that it was not a life-form related to him. It manufactured a dull internal heat and, through its exterior walls, he could see the vague glow of fires.

All that first day, Iilah waited for the creature to show awareness of him. But not a wave of life emanated from it. And yet it floated in the sky above the plateau, an impossible phenomenon, outside all his experience. To Iilah, who had no means of sensing water, who could not even imagine air, and whose ultra waves passed through human beings as if they did not exist, the reaction could mean only one thing—here was an alien life form that had adapted itself to the dead world around him.

Gradually, Iilah grew excited. The thing could move freely above the surface of the planet. It would know if any source of atomic energy remained anywhere. The problem was to get into communication with it. The sun was high on the meridian of another day when Iilah directed the first questioning pattern of thought towards the destroyer. He aimed straight at the vaguely glowing fires in the engine room, where, he reasoned, would be the intelligence of the alien creature.

The thirty-four men who died in the spaces in and around the engine room and the fire room were buried on the shore. Their surviving comrades, including all officers, moved half a mile up the east coast. And at first they expected to stay there until the abandoned *Coulson* ceased to give off dangerous radioactive energies. On the seventh day, when transport planes were already dumping scientific equipment and personnel, three of the men fell sick and their blood count showed a fateful decrease in the number of red corpuscles. Although no orders had arrived, Maynard took alarm and ordered the entire crew shipped for observation to Hawaii.

He allowed the officers to make their own choice, but advised the second engineer officer, the first gunnery officer and several ensigns who had helped hoist the dead men up to the deck, to take no chances, but to grab space on the first planes. Although all were ordered to leave, several crew members asked permission to remain. And, after a careful questioning by Gerson, a dozen men who could prove that they had not been near the affected area, were finally allowed to stay.

Maynard would have preferred to see Gerson himself depart, but in this he was disappointed. Of the officers who had been aboard the destroyer at the time of the disaster, Lieutenants Gerson, Lausson, and Haury, the latter two being gunnery officers, and Ensigns McPelty, Roberts, and Manchioff, remained on the beach.

Among the higher ratings remaining behind were the chief commissary steward, Jenkins, and chief bosun's mate, Yewell.

The navy group was ignored except that several times requests were made that they move their tents out of the way. Finally, when it seemed evident that they would be crowded out once more, Maynard, in annoyance, ordered the canvas moved well down the coast, where the palms opened up to form a grassy meadow.

Maynard grew puzzled, then grim, as the weeks passed and no orders arrived concerning the disposal of his command. In one of the Stateside papers that began to follow the scientists, the bulldozers, and cement mixers onto the island he read an item in an "inside" column that gave him his first inkling. According to the columnist, there had been a squabble between navy bigwigs and the civilian members of the Atomic Energy Commission over control of the investigation. With the result that the navy had been ordered to "stay out."

Maynard read the account with mixed feelings and a dawning understanding that he was *the* navy representative on the island. The realization included a thrilling mental visualization of himself rising to the rank of admiral—if he handled the situation right. Just what would be right, aside from keeping a sharp eye on everything, he couldn't decide. It was an especially exquisite form of self-torture.

He couldn't sleep. He spent his days wandering as unobtrusively as possible through the ever vaster encampment of the army of scientists and their assistants. At night he had several hiding places from which he watched the brilliantly lighted beach.

It was a fabulous oasis of brightness in the dark vaulting vastness of a Pacific night. For a full mile, string upon string of lights spread along the whispering waters. They silhouetted and spotlighted the long, thick, back-curving, cement-like walls that reared up eerily, starting at the rim of the hill. Protective walls that were already soaring up around the rock itself, striving to block it off from all outside contact. Always, at midnight, the bulldozers ceased their roarings, the cement-mixing trucks dumped their last loads and scurried down the makeshift beach road to silence. The already intricate organization settled into an uneasy slumber. Maynard usually waited with the painful patience of a man doing more than his duty. About one o'clock, he too would make his way to bed.

The secret habit paid off. He was the only man who actually witnessed the rock climb to the top of the hill.

It was a stupendous event. The time was about a quarter to one and Maynard was on the point of calling it a day when he heard the sound. It was like a truck emptying a load of gravel. For a bare moment he thought of it entirely in relation to his hiding place. His night-spying activities were going to be found out. An instant after that the rock reared up into the brilliance of the lights.

There was a roaring now of cement barriers crumbling before that irresistible movement. Fifty, sixty, then ninety feet of monster rock loomed up above the hill, slid with a heavy power over the crown, and stopped.

For two months Iilah had watched the freighters breast the channel. Just why they followed that route interested him. And he wondered if there was some limitation on them that kept them at such an exact level. What was more interesting by far, however, was that in every case the aliens would slide around the island, and disappear behind a high promontory that was the beginning of the east shore. In every case, after they had been gone for a few days, they would slide into view again, glide through the channel, and gradually move off through the sky.

During those months, Iilah caught tantalizing glimpses of small, but much faster, winged ships that shot down from a great height and disappeared behind the crest of the hill to the east. Always to the east. His curiosity grew enormous, but he was reluctant to waste energy. He grew aware finally of a night time haze of lights that brightened the eastern sky at night. He set off the more violent explosions on his lower surface which made directive motion possible, and climbed the last seventy or so feet to the top of the hill. He regretted it immediately.

One ship lay a short distance offshore. The haze of lights along the eastern slope seemed to have no source. As he watched, scores of trucks and bulldozers raced around, some of them coming quite close to him. Just what they wanted, or what they were doing he could not make out. He sent several questioning thought waves at various of the objects, but there was no response.

He gave it up as a bad job.

The rock was still resting on the top of the hill the next morning, poised so that both sides of the island were threatened by the stray bursts of energy which it gave off so erratically. Maynard heard his first account of the damage done from Jenkins, the chief commissary steward. Seven truck drivers and two bulldozer men dead, a dozen men suffering from glancing burns—and two months' labor wrecked.

There must have been a conference among the scientists, for shortly after noon, trucks and bulldozers, loaded with equipment, began to stream past the navy camp. A seaman, dispatched to follow them, reported that they were setting up camp on the point at the lower end of the island.

Just before dark a notable event took place. The director of the Project, together with four executive scientists, walked into the lighted area and asked for Maynard. The group was smiling and friendly. There was handshaking all around. Maynard introduced Gerson who, unfortunately, as far as Maynard was concerned, was in the camp at the moment. And then the visiting delegation got down to business.

"As you know," said the director, "the *Coulson* is only partially radioactive. The rear gun turret is quite unaffected, and we accordingly request that you co-operate with us and fire on the rock until it is broken into sections."

It took Maynard a moment to recover from his astonishment, and to know what he would answer to that. At no time, during the next few days, did he question the belief of the scientists that the rock should be broken up and so rendered harmless. He refused their request and then doggedly continued to refuse it. It was not until the third day that he thought of a reason.

"Your precautions, gentlemen," he said, "are not sufficient. I do not consider that moving the camp out to the point is safeguard enough in the event that the rock should blow up. Now, of course, if I should receive a command from a naval authority to do as you wish ..."

He left that sentence dangling, and saw from their disappointed faces that there must have been a feverish exchange of radio messages with their own headquarters. The arrival of a Kwajalein paper on the fourth day quoted a "high" Washington naval officer as saying that, "any such decisions must be left to the judgment of the naval commander on the island." It was also stated that, if a properly channeled request was made, the navy would be glad to send an atomic expert of its own to the scene.

It was obvious to Maynard that he was handling the situation exactly as his superiors desired. The only thing was that, even as he finished reading the account, the silence was broken by the unmistakable bark of a destroyer's five-inch guns, that sharpest of all gunfire sounds.

Unsteadily Maynard climbed to his feet. He headed for the nearest height. Before he reached it the second shattering roar came from the other side of the lagoon, and once again an ear-splitting explosion echoed from the vicinity of the rock. Maynard reached his vantage point and, through his binoculars, saw about a dozen men scurrying over the aft deck in and about the rear gun turret. A new and grimmer fury came against the camp director. He was determined that every man assisting on the destroyer must be arrested for malicious and dangerous trespass.

He did think vaguely that it was a sorry day indeed when inter-bureau squabbles could cause such open defiance of the armed forces, as if nothing more was involved than struggle for power. But that thought faded as swiftly as it came.

He waited for the third firing, then hurried down the hill to his camp. Swift commands to the men and officers sent eight of them to positions along the shore of the island, where they could watch boats trying to land. With the rest, Maynard headed towards the nearest navy boat. He had to take the long way around, by way of the point, and there must have been radio communication between the point and those on the ship, for a motorboat was just appearing around the far end of the island when Maynard approached the now silent and deserted *Coulson*.

He hesitated. Should he give chase? A careful study of the rock proved it to be apparently unbroken. The failure cheered him, but also made him cautious. It wouldn't do for his superiors to discover that he had not taken the necessary precautions to prevent the destroyer being boarded.

He was still pondering the problem when Iilah started down the hill, straight towards the destroyer.

Iilah saw the first bright puff from the destroyer's guns. And then he had a moment during which he observed an object flash towards him. In the old, old times he had developed defenses against hurtling objects. Quite automatically now, he tensed for the blow of this one. The object, instead of merely striking him with its hardness, exploded. The impact was stupendous. His protective crust cracked. The concussion blurred and distorted the flow from every electronic plate in his great mass.

Instantly, the automatic stabilizing "tubes" sent out balancing impulses. The hot, internal, partly-rigid, partly-fluid matter that made up the greater portion of his body, grew hotter, more fluidic. The weaknesses induced by that tremendous concussion accepted the natural union of a liquid, hardening quickly under enormous pressures. Sane again, Iilah considered what had happened. An attempt at communication?

The possibility excited him. Instead of closing the gap in his outer wall he hardened the matter immediately behind it, thus cutting off wasteful radiation. He waited. Again the hurtling object, and the enormously potent blow, as it struck him …

After a dozen blows, each with its resulting disaster to his protective shell, Iilah writhed with doubts. If these were messages he could not receive them, or understand. He began reluctantly to allow the chemical reactions that sealed the protective barrier. Faster than he could seal the holes, the hurtling objects breached his defenses.

And still he did not think of what had happened as an attack. In all his previous existence he had never been attacked in such a fashion. Just what methods had been used against him, Iilah could not remember. But certainly nothing so purely molecular.

The conviction that it was an attack came reluctantly, and he felt no anger. The reflex of defense in him was logical, not emotional. He studied the destroyer and it seemed to him that his purpose must be to drive it away. It would also be necessary to drive away every similar creature that tried to come near him. All the scurrying objects he had seen when he mounted the crest of the hill—all that must depart.

He started down the hill.

The creature floating above the plateau had ceased exuding flame. As Iilah eased himself near it, the only sign of life was a smaller object that darted alongside it.

There was a moment then when Iilah entered the water. That was a shock. He had almost forgotten that there was a level of this desolate mountain below which his life forces were affected.

He hesitated. Then, slowly, he slid further down into the depressing area, conscious that he had attained a level of strength that he could maintain against such a purely negative pressure.

The destroyer began to fire at him. The shells, delivered at point-blank range, poked deep holes into the ninety-foot cliff with which Iilah faced his enemy. As that wall of rock touched the destroyer, the firing stopped. Maynard and his men, having defended the *Coulson* as long as possible, tumbled over the far side into their boat and raced away as fast as possible.

Iilah shoved. The pain that he felt from those titanic blows was the pain that comes to all living creatures experiencing partial dissolution. Laboriously, his body repaired itself. And with anger and hatred and fear now, he shoved. In a few minutes he had tangled the curiously unwieldy structure in the rocks that rose up to form the edge of the plateau. Beyond was the sharp declining slope of the mountain.

An unexpected thing happened. Once among the rocks, the creature started to shudder and shake, as if caught by some inner destructive force. It fell over on its side and lay there like some wounded thing, quivering and breaking up.

It was an amazing spectacle. Iilah withdrew from the water, reclimbed the mountain, and plunged down into the sea on the other side, where a freighter was just getting under way. It swung around the promontory, and successfully floated through the channel and out, coasting along high above the bleak valley that fell away beyond the breakers. It moved along for several miles, then slowed and stopped.

Iilah would have liked to chase it further, but he was limited to ground movement. And so the moment the freighter had stopped, he turned and headed towards the point, where the small objects were cluttered. He did not notice the men who plunged into the shallows near the shore and, from that comparative safety, watched the destruction of their equipment. Iilah left a wake of burning and crushed vehicles. The few drivers who tried to get their machines away became splotches of flesh and blood inside and on the metal of their machines.

There was a fantastic amount of stupidity and panic. Iilah moved at a speed of about eight miles an hour. Three hundred and seventeen men were caught in scores of individual traps and crushed by a monster that did not even know they existed. Each man must have felt himself personally pursued.

Afterward, Iilah climbed to the nearest peak and studied the sky for further interlopers. Only the freighter remained, a shadowy threat some four miles away.

Darkness cloaked the island slowly. Maynard moved cautiously through the grass, flashing his flashlight directly in front of him on a sharp downward slant. Every little while he called out, "Anybody around?" It had been like that for hours now. Through the fading day they had searched for survivors, each time loading them aboard their boat and ferrying them through the channel and out to where the freighter waited.

The orders had come through by radio. They had forty-eight hours to get clear of the island. After that the bomb run would be made by a drone plane.

Maynard pictured himself walking along on this monster-inhabited, night-enveloped island. And the shuddery thrill that came was almost pure unadulterated pleasure. He felt himself pale with a joyous terror. It was like the time his ship had been among those shelling a Jap-held beach. He had been gloomy until, suddenly, he had visualized himself out there on the beach at the receiving end of the shells. He began to torture himself with the possibility that, somehow, he might be left behind when the freighter finally withdrew.

A moan from the near darkness ended that thought. In the glow of the flashlight Maynard saw a vaguely familiar face. The man had been smashed by a falling tree. As executive officer Gerson came forward and administered morphine, Maynard bent closer to the injured man and peered at him anxiously.

It was one of the world-famous scientists on the island. Ever since the disaster the radio messages had been asking for him. There was not a scientific body on the globe that cared to commit itself to the navy bombing plan until he had given his opinion.

"Sir," began Maynard, "what do you think about—" He stopped. He settled mentally back on his heels.

Just for a moment he had forgotten that the naval authorities had already ordered the atomic bomb dropped, after being given governmental authority to do as they saw fit.

The scientist stirred. "Maynard," he croaked, "there's something funny about that creature. Don't let them do any—" His eyes grew bright with pain. His voice trailed.

It was time to push questions. The great man would soon be deep in a doped sleep and he would be kept that way. In a moment it would be too late.

The moment passed.

Lieutenant Gerson climbed to his feet. "There, that ought to do it, captain." He turned to the seamen carrying the stretchers. "Two of you take this man back to the boat. Careful. I've put him to sleep."

Maynard followed the stretcher without a word. He had a sense of being been saved from the necessity of making a decision, rather than of having made one.

The night dragged on.

Morning dawned grayly. Shortly after the sun came up, a tropical shower stormed across the island and rushed off eastward. The sky grew amazingly blue and the world of water all around seemed motionless, so calm did the sea become.

Out of the blue distance, casting a swiftly moving shadow on that still ocean, flew the drone plane. Long before it came in sight, Iilah sensed the load it carried. He quivered through his mass. Enormous electron tubes waxed and waned with expectancy and, for a brief while, he thought it was one of his own kind coming near.

As the plane drew closer he sent cautious thoughts toward it. Several planes, to which he had directed his thought waves, had twisted jerkily in mid-air and tumbled down out of control. But this one did not deviate from its course. When it was almost directly overhead a large object dropped from it, turned lazily over and over as it curved toward Iilah. It was set to explode about a hundred feet above the target.

The timing was perfect, the explosion titanic.

As soon as the blurring effects of so much new energy had passed, the now fully alive Iilah thought in a quiet, rather startled comprehension, "Why, of course, that's what I was trying to remember. That's what I was supposed to do."

He was puzzled that he could have forgotten. He had been sent during the course of an interstellar war—which apparently was still going on. He had been dropped on the planet under enormous difficulties and had been instantly snuffed out by enemy frustrators. Now, he was ready to do his job.

He took test sightings on the sun and on the planets that were within reach of his radar signals. Then he set in motion an orderly process that would dissolve all the shields inside his own body. He gathered his pressure forces for the final thrust that would bring the vital elements hard together at exactly the calculated moment.

The explosion that knocked a planet out of its orbit was recorded on every seismograph on the globe. It would be some time, however, before astronomers would discover that earth was falling into the sun. And no man would live to see Sol flare into nova brightness, and burn up the Solar System before gradually sinking back into a dim G state.

Even if Iilah had known that it was not the same war that had raged ten thousand million centuries before, he would have had no choice but to do as he did.

Robot atom bombs do not make up their own minds.

THE SOUND

"You're wanted on the video," said Exchange.

Craig clicked on his machine. "Yes?" he said, before the picture could form.

"It's me, George." The woman whose face grew onto the videoplate looked agitated. "George, the Play Square just called me. Diddy has gone out to look for the sound."

"Oh," said George.

He studied her image. Hers was normally a good-looking face, clear-skinned, well-shaped, crowned with beautifully coiled black hair. At the moment it was not normal. Her eyes were widened, her muscles tensed, and her hair slightly displaced.

"Veda," he said sharply, "you're not letting it get you."

"But he's out there. And the whole area is said to be full of Yevd spies." She shuddered as she spoke the name of the great enemy.

"The Play Square let him go, didn't it? It must think he's ready."

"But he'll be out all night."

Craig nodded slowly. "Look, darling, this had to happen. It's part of the process of growing up, and we've been expecting it since his ninth birthday last May."

He broke off. "How about you going and doing some shopping? That'll take your mind off him for the rest of the afternoon anyway. Spend"—he made a quick calculation, took another look at her face, and revised the initial number upward—"five hundred dollars. On yourself. Now, good-bye, and don't worry."

He broke the connection hastily, and climbed to his feet. For a long time he stood at the window staring down at The Yards. From his vantage

445

point be could not see the "Way" or the ship; they were on the other side of the building. But the fairyland of streets and buildings that he could see enthralled him now as always. The Yards were a suburb of Solar City, and that massive metropolis in its artificial tropical setting was a vision that had no parallel in the human-controlled part of the Galaxy. Its buildings and its parks extended to every hazy horizon.

He drew his gaze back from the distance, back to the city proper of The Yards. Slowly, he turned from the window. Somewhere down there his nine-year-old son was exploring the world of the sound. Thinking about that or about the Yevd wouldn't do either Veda or himself the slightest good.

He picked up the microfilm of a ninety-foot square blueprint, slipped it into a projector, and began to study it.

By the time the sky grew dark, Diddy knew that the sound never ended. After wondering about it for his whole lifetime, or so it seemed, that was good to know. He'd been told that it ended somewhere "out there"—vaguely. But this afternoon he'd proved for himself that, no matter how far you went, the sound remained.

The fact that his elders had lied to him about that did not disturb Diddy. According to his robot teacher, the Play Square, parents sometimes fibbed to test a fellow's ingenuity and self-reliance. This was obviously one of the fibs, which he had now disproved.

For all these years, the sound had been in his Play Square, and in the living room whether he was silent or trying to talk, and in the dining room making a rhythm out of the eating noises of Mom and Dad and himself—on those days that he was permitted to eat with them. At night the sound crept into bed with him, and while he slept, even in his deepest sleep, he could feel it throbbing in his brain.

Yes, it was a familiar thing, and it was natural that he'd tried to find out if it stopped at the end of first one street and then another. Just how many streets he'd turned up and into and along, whether he'd gone east or west or south or north, was no longer clear. But wherever he'd gone, the sound had followed him. He had had dinner an hour before at a little restaurant. Now it was time to find out *where* the sound began.

Diddy paused to frown over his location. The important thing was to figure out just where he was in relation to The Yards. He was figuring it by mentally calculating the number of streets between Fifth and Nineteenth. H and R, Center and Right, when he happened to glance up. There, a hundred feet away, was a man he'd first seen three blocks and ten minutes back.

Something about the movement of the man stirred a curious, unpleasant memory, and for the first time he saw how dark the sky had become.

He began to walk casually across the road, and he was glad to notice that he was not afraid. His hope was that he would be able to get by the man, and so back to the more crowded Sixth Street. He hoped, also, that he was mistaken in his recognition of the man as Yevd.

His heart sank as a second man joined the first, and the two started to cross the street to intercept him. Diddy fought an impulse to turn and run. Fought it, because if they were Yevd, they could move ten times as fast as a grown man. Their appearance of having a humanlike body was an illusion which they could create by their control of light. It was that that had made him suspect the first of the two. In turning the corner, the fellow's legs had walked *wrong*. Diddy could not remember how many times the Play Square had described such a possibility of wrongness, but now that he had seen it, he realized that it was unmistakable. In the daytime, the Yevd were said to be more careful with their illusions. Just for a moment, being virtually alone on a dark corner, the Yevd had allowed the human image to blur.

"Boy!"

Diddy slowed, and looked around at the two men, as if seeing them for the first time.

"Boy, you're out on the streets rather late."

"This is my exploring night, sir," said Diddy.

The "man" who had spoken reached into his breast pocket. It was a curious gesture, not complete, as if in creating the illusion of the movement, he hadn't quite thought through the intricacies of such an action. Or perhaps he was careless in the gathering darkness. His hand came out, and flashed a badge.

"We're 'Yard' agents," he said. "We'll take you to the 'Way'."

He put the badge back into his pocket, or seemed to, and motioned towards the brightness in the distance. Diddy knew better than to resist.

Out of the dark distance of space the Yevd had come more than two hundred years before. Like the black reaches through which their ships plunged from their multitudinous worlds in the central mass of the Galaxy, they made an uneasy impression on the minds of men.

In the beginning, they did not try to look human, and there was no suspicion that they could control light and related energies with their bodies. Then one day, accidentally, a "man" was blasted while rifling the vault of the Research Council. Dead, the man-image faded, and there, sprawled on the marble floor was the dark, rectangular, elongated shape with its score of reticulated, pistonlike arms and legs.

On that day, more than two centuries before, a dismayed government acted swiftly and secretly. The fleet was mobilized while the ramifications of the plot were explored. Armed helicars flew along the streets of every city. The probing beams of radar machines reflected and silhouetted the real bodies of the Yevd—though it was afterwards discovered that the radar method was successful only because of the element of surprise. The Yevd had become careless because they were not suspected, and maintained their illusion only on the light level visible to human beings. Because of that error, nearly a million of them were blasted on Earth alone, and that broke the fifth column there.

Warnings had meanwhile been flashed to all the man-inhabited planets. There, also, prompt action averted disaster. Altogether thirty-seven million Yevd were killed.

Thereafter, Earth and Yevd ships fought each other on sight. The intensity of the war waxed and waned. There were several agreements, but at no time did these actually stop the war. To some extent they stopped Yevd ships from coming into man-controlled space and vice versa. The most recent agreement included an exchange of ambassadors, but five years before a Yevd colonizing expedition had occupied a star system ninety-odd light-years nearer Earth than any other sun in their galactic empire. When asked to explain the seizure, the Yevd ambassador had stated that the "action is a normal incident in the expansion of a great power, and is not directed at anyone." He was promptly handed his papers, and six months later the sound began.

The Yevd were a hydrocarbon-fluorine-oxygen life form, tough of muscle and skin, physically stronger than man, immune to ordinary poisons and corrosives. Their control of light gave them an additional advantage; and the combination of enormous capability and unceasing aggressiveness had finally decided the United Governments to make a major counterattack.

The big ship was designed to do the job.

Craig opened the door of his apartment for the two police officers shortly after dinner. Though they wore plain clothes, he recognized them instantly for what they were.

"Mr. Craig?" one of them asked.

"Yes?"

"George Craig?"

He nodded this time, aware in spite of having just eaten of an empty sensation.

"You are the father of Diryl Dexter Craig, aged nine?"

Craig took hold of the door jamb. "Yes," he mumbled.

The spokesman said: "It is our duty, as required by law, to inform you that at this moment your son is in the control of two Yevd, and that he will be in grave danger of his life for some hours to come."

Craig said: "I'm ... not ... sure ... I ... understand."

Quietly, the officer described how Diddy had been taken over on the sidewalk. He added, "We've been aware for some time that the Yevd had been concentrating in Solar City in more than usual numbers. Naturally, we haven't located them. As you may know, we estimate their numbers on the basis of those we do spot."

Craig hadn't known, but he said nothing. The other continued:

"As you probably also know, we are more interested in discovering the purpose of a Yevd ring than in capturing individuals. As with all Yevd schemes in the past, this one will probably prove to be extremely devious. It seems clear that we have only witnessed the first step of an intricate plan. But now, are there any questions?"

Craig hesitated. He was acutely conscious of Veda in the kitchen putting the dinner dishes into the dish washing machine. It was vital that he get these policemen away before she found out what their mission was. Yet one question he had to ask.

"You mean, there'll be no immediate attempts to rescue Diddy?"

The officer said in a firm voice: "Until we have the information we want, this situation will be allowed to ripen. I have been instructed to ask you not to build up any hopes. As you know, a Yevd can actually concentrate energy of blaster power with his cells. Under such circumstances, death can strike very easily."

He broke off. "That's all, sir. You may call from time to time if you desire further information. The police will not communicate with you again on their own initiative."

"Thank you," said Craig automatically.

He closed the door, and went with mechanical stolidity back to the living room. Veda called from the kitchen:

"Who was it, darling?"

Craig drew a deep breath. "Somebody looking for a man named George Craig. They got the right name but the wrong man." His voice held steady for the words.

"Oh!" said Veda.

She must have forgotten the incident at once, for she did not mention it again. Craig went to bed at ten o'clock. He lay there, conscious of a vague ache in his back, and a sick feeling at the pit of his stomach. At one o'clock he was still wide awake.

He mustn't offer any resistance. He must make no attempt to frustrate any plans they might have. For years the Play Square had emphasized that. No young person, it had stated categorically, should consider himself qualified to judge how dangerous any particular Yevd might be. Or how important the plan of a Yevd spy ring.

Assume that something was being done. And await whispered instructions.

Diddy was remembering all these things, as he walked between the two Yevd, his short legs twinkling as he was hustled along faster than his normal pace. He was heartened by the fact that they had still not let him know their identity. They were still pretending.

The street grew tremendously brighter. Ahead, he could see the ship silhouetted against the blue-black sky beyond. All the buildings that crowded the "Way" were giving off the sunlight they'd absorbed during the day. The hundred-story administration building glowed like a jewel in the shadow of the towering ship, and all the other buildings shone with an intensity of light that varied according to their sizes.

With Diddy in tow, the two Yevd came to Cross 2. The "Way" itself was Cross 1.

They walked across the street, and came to the barrier. The two Yevd paused in front of the eight-foot wide band of fluted metal, with its constant suction effect, and stared down at the open ventilators.

Two centuries before, when Yevd and human first made contact, there had been concrete walls or electrified barbed wire fences around defense plants and military areas. Then it was discovered that Yevd could deflect electric current, and that their tough skin was impervious to the sharp bite of barbed wire. Concrete was equally ineffective. The walls had a habit of crumbling in the presence of certain Yevd-directed energies. And, among workmen who arrived to repair them was usually a Yevd who, by a process of image transference and murder, made his way inside. Armed patrols were all too frequently killed to a man, and their places taken by Yevd light-wave images.

The air suction type of barrier was only a few generations old. It extended all the way around The Yards. Human beings who walked through it scarcely noticed it. A Yevd who tried to penetrate it died within about three minutes.

It was one of Man's top secrets.

Diddy seized on the hesitation of his two escorts. "Thanks for bringing me this far," he said, "I'll be able to manage now."

One of the "men" laughed. It was wonderfully authentic laughter, considering that it came from a sound box imbedded in the Yevd's shoulder muscles. The creature said: "You know, kid, you look like a pretty good sport. Just to show you that our hearts are in the right places, how'd you like to have a little fun—just for a minute?"

"Fun?" said Diddy.

"See that barrier there?"

Diddy nodded.

"Good. As we've already told you, we're security police—you know, anti-Yevd. Of course, we've got the problem on our minds all the time. You can see that, can't you?"

Diddy said that he could. He wondered what was coming.

"Well, the other day my friend and I were talking about our job, and we figured out a way by which a Yevd might be able to cross that barrier. It seemed so silly that we thought we ought to test it before we reported it to the top brass. You know what I mean. If it turned out wrong, why, we'd look foolish. That's the test we want you to help us make."

No young person ... must ... attempt to frustrate any plans ... of a Yevd spy ring. The command, so often given by the Play Square, echoed in Diddy's mind. It seemed dreadfully clear that here was special danger, and yet it was not for him to judge, or oppose. The years of training made that automatic now. He wasn't old enough to know.

"All you've got to do," said the Yevd spokesman, "is walk between these two lines across the barrier, and then walk back again."

The lines indicated were a part of the pattern of the fluted arrangement of the ventilators. Without a word of objection, Diddy walked across to the other side. Just for a moment, then, he hesitated, half minded to make a run for it to the safety of a building thirty feet away. He changed his mind. They could blast him before he could go ten feet.

Dutifully, he came back, as he had been told to do.

A score of men were coming along the street. As they came near, Diddy and the two Yevd drew aside to let them pass. Diddy watched them hopefully. *Police?* he wondered. He wanted desperately to be sure that all that was happening was suspected.

The workmen trooped by, walked noisily across the barrier, and disappeared behind the nearest building.

"This way, kid," said the Yevd. "We've got to be careful that we're not seen."

Diddy wasn't so sure of that, but he followed them reluctantly into the dark space between two buildings.

"Hold out your hand."

He held it out, tense and scared. *I'm going to die*, he thought. And he had to fight back the tears. But his training won out, and he stood still as a needle-sharp pain jabbed his finger.

"Just taking a sample of your blood, kid. You see, the way we look at it, that suction system out there conceals high-powered air hypodermics, which send up bacteria to which the Yevd are vulnerable. Naturally, these air hypodermics send up their shots of bacteria at about a thousand miles an hour, so fast that they penetrate your skin without you feeling them or leaving a mark. And the reason the suction ventilators keep pulling in so much air is to prevent the bacteria from escaping into the atmosphere. And also the same culture of bacteria is probably used over and over again. You see where that leads us?"

Diddy didn't, but he was shocked to the core of his being. For this analysis sounded right. It *could* be bacteria that were being used against the Yevd. It was said that only a few men knew the nature of the defense projected by the innocent-looking barrier. Was it possible that at long last the Yevd were finding it out?

He could see that the second Yevd was doing something in the shadowy region deeper between the two buildings. There were little flashes of light. Diddy made a wild guess, and thought: *He's examining my blood with a microscope to see how many dead anti-Yevd bacteria are in it.*

The Yevd who had done all the talking so far said:

"You see how it is, kid, you can walk across that barrier, and the bacteria that are squirted up from it die immediately in your bloodstream. Our idea is this: There can only be one type of bacteria being sent up in any one area. Why? Because, when they're sucked down, and sent back to the filter chambers so they can be removed from the air and used again, it would be too complicated if there were more than one type of bacteria. The highly virulent bacteria that thrive in a fluorine compound are almost as deadly to each other as to the organism, which they attack. It's only when one type is present in enormously predominant amounts that it is so dangerous to the Yevd. In other words, only one type at a time can kill a Yevd.

"Obviously, if a Yevd is shot full of immunization against that particular type of bacteria—why, kid, he can cross the barrier *at that point* as easily as you can, and he can then do anything he wants to inside The Yards. You see how big a thing we're working on."

He broke off, "And, I see my friend has finished examining your blood. Wait here a moment."

He moved off to where the other Yevd was waiting. There were tiny flashes of light from the darkness, and Diddy remembered tensely that Yevd communicated with each other by light beams and light energies that operated directly from a complex interrelation of organic prisms, lens, mirrors, and cell transformers.

The conference, whatever its nature, lasted less than a minute. The Yevd came back.

"O.K., kid, you can scoot along. Thanks a lot for helping us. We won't forget it."

Diddy could not believe his ears for a moment. "You mean, that's all you want from me?" he said.

"That's all."

As he emerged from the dark space between the two buildings, Diddy expected somehow that he would be stopped. But, though the two Yevd followed him out to the street, they made no attempt to accompany him as he started across it toward the barrier. The spokesman called after him:

"There's a couple of other kids coming up the street. You might join them and the bunch of you can look for the sound together."

Diddy turned to look, and as he did so, two boys came darting towards him, yelling "Last one over is a pig."

They had the momentum, and they were past him in a flash. As he raced after them, Diddy saw them hesitate, turn slightly, and then the barrier at a dead run over the ventilators which he had tested for the two Yevd researchers.

They waited for him on the other side.

"My name is Jackie," said one.

"And mine is Gil," said the second one. He added, "Let's stick together."

Diddy said: "My name is Diddy."

Neither of the two boys seemed to think the name unusual.

There were separate sounds, as the three of them walked, that drowned out *the* sound. Discordant noises. Whirring machines. An intricate pattern of clangorous hammering. Rippling overtones from the molecular displacement of masses of matter. A rubber-wheeled train hummed towards them over the endless metal floor that carpeted The Yards, and paused as its electronic eyes and ears sensed their presence. They stepped out of the way, and it rushed past. A line of cranes lifted a hundred ton metal plate onto an antigravity carrier. It floated away lightly, airily into the blazing sky.

Diddy had never been on the "Way" at night before, and it would have been tremendously exciting if he had not been so miserable. The trouble was, he couldn't be sure. Were these two companions Yevd? So far they had done nothing that actually proved they were. The fact that they had crossed the barrier at the point where he had tested it for the two Yevd could have been a coincidence.

Until he was sure, he dared not tell anyone what had happened. Until he was sure, he would have to go along with them, and even if they wanted him to do something, cooperate with them. That was the rule. That was the training. He had a picture in his mind of scores of images of boys crossing the barrier at the test point. Even now they would be moving along the "Way," free to do as they pleased.

The universe around the "Way" shivered with a concatenation of sounds. But nowhere that Diddy looked, no doorway into which he peered, no building that he wandered through with wide, fascinated eyes—in spite of the presence of his companions—nowhere was there a sound that did not quickly fade away as he moved on.

Not once did they come to anything that even faintly resembled a barrier type ventilator. If there were any threat to wandering Yevd, it was not apparent. Doors stood wide open. He had hoped in a vague fashion that the atmosphere of some closed room would be deadly for the enemy and not for him. He found no such rooms.

Worst of all, there was no sign of a human being who might conceivably protect him from the Yevd, or even suspect their presence. If only he could be sure that these two boys were Yevd. Or weren't. Suppose they carried some deadly weapon capable of causing tremendous damage to the ship?

They came to a building half a mile square. And Diddy grew suddenly hopeful. His companions offered no objection as he walked through a huge door onto a causeway. Below them was depth. From the causeway Diddy looked down at a dimly glowing world of huge, cube-like structures. The top of the highest cube was at least a quarter of a mile below the causeway, and it was blocked off by floor after floor of plastic, so limpidly transparent that only a gleam here and there revealed that there were many layers of hard, frustrating matter protecting the world above from the enormous atomic piles in that colossal powerhouse.

As he approached the center of the causeway, Diddy saw—as he had a few moments before hopefully expected—that there was somebody in a little transparent structure that jutted out from the metalwork. A woman, reading. She looked up as the three of them came up, Diddy in the lead.

"Searching for the sound?" she asked in a friendly tone. She added, "Just in case you don't know—I'm a Sensitive."

The other boys were silent. Diddy said that he knew. The Play Square had told him about Sensitives. They could anticipate changes in the flow of an atomic pile. It had, he recalled, something to do with the way the calcium content in their blood was controlled. Sensitives lived to a very old age—around a hundred and eighty—not because of the jobs they had but because they could respond to the calcium rejuvenation processes.

The memory was only a background to his gathering disappointment. Apparently, she had no way of detecting the presence of a Yevd, for she gave no sign.

He'd better keep pretending that he was still interested in the sound, which was true in a way. He said: "Those dynamos down there would make quite a vibration, I guess."

"Yes, they would."

Diddy was suddenly intent, impressed but not convinced. "Still, I don't see how it could make the big sound."

She said: "You all seem like nice boys. I'm going to whisper a clue into your ears. You first." She motioned to Diddy.

It seemed odd, but he did not hesitate. She bent down. "Don't be surprised," she whispered. "You'll find a very small gun under the overlapping edge of the metal sidewalk underneath the ship. Go down escalator seven, and turn right. It's just on this side of a beam that has a big H painted on it. Nod your head if you understand."

Diddy nodded.

The woman went on swiftly. "Slip the gun into your pocket. Don't use it until you're ordered to. Good luck."

She straightened. "There," she said, "that should give you an idea."

She motioned to Jackie. "You next."

The stocky boy shook his head. "I don't need no clues," he said. "Besides, I don't want nobody whispering anything to me."

"Nor me either," said Gil.

The woman smiled. "You mustn't be shy," she said. "But never mind. I'll give you a clue anyway. Do you know what the word 'miasma' means?" She spoke directly to Jackie.

"Mist."

"That's my clue, then. Miasma. And now you'd better be getting along. The sun is due up a few minutes before six, and it's after two o'clock now."

She picked up her book and, when Diddy glanced back a few minutes later, she looked as if she were a part of the chair. She seemed scarcely alive, so still she was. But because of her, he knew. The situation was as deadly as he had suspected. The great ship itself was in danger.

It was towards the ship that he headed.

Craig wakened suddenly to the realization that something had roused him, and that accordingly he must have slept. He groaned inwardly, and started to turn over. If he only *could* sleep through this night.

With a start he grew aware that his wife was sitting on the edge of the bed. He glanced at his illuminated watch. It was 2:22 AM.

Oh, my gosh, he thought, *I've got to get her back to bed.*

"I can't sleep," said Veda.

Her voice had a whimper in it, and he felt sick. For she was worrying like this about nothing. He pretended to be very thoroughly asleep.

"George."

Craig stirred, but that was all.

"George."

He opened one eye. "Darling, please."

"I wonder how many other boys are out tonight."

George turned over. "Veda, what are you trying to do—keep me awake?"

"Oh, I'm sorry. I didn't mean to." Her tone was not sorry, and after a moment she seemed to have forgotten she'd spoken the words. "George."

He did not answer.

"George, do you think we could find out?"

He'd intended to ignore further conversation, but his mind started to examine the possible meaning of what she'd said. He grew astonished at the meaninglessness of her words, and woke up.

"Find out what?" he said.

"How many there are?"

"How many what?"

"Boys—outside tonight."

Craig, who was weighed down by a far more desperate fear, sighed. "Veda. I've got to go to work tomorrow."

"Work!" said Veda, and her voice had an edge in it. "Don't you ever think of anything but work? Haven't you any feelings?" Craig kept his silence, but that was not the way to get her back to her bed. She went on, her voice several tones higher. "The trouble with you men is that you grow callous."

"If you mean by that, am I worried—no, I'm not." That came hard. He thought, *I've got to keep this on this level.* He sat up and turned on the light. He said aloud, "Darling, if it gives you any satisfaction you've succeeded in your purpose. I'm awake."

"It's about time," said Veda. "I think we ought to call up. And if you don't, I will."

Craig climbed to his feet. "O.K., but don't you dare hang over my neck when I'm calling. I refuse to have anybody suspect that I'm a henpecked husband. You stay right here."

He found himself relieved that she had forced the issue. He went out of the bedroom and shut the door firmly behind him. On the video, he gave his name. There was a pause, and then a grave-faced man in an admiral's uniform came into view. His image filled the videoplate, as he bent over the videophone in the patrol office. He said:

"Mr. Craig, the situation is as follows: Your son is still in the company of two Yevd. A very ingenious method was used to get across the barrier, and at the present moment we suspect that about a hundred Yevd posing as boys are somewhere in The Yards. Nobody has tried to cross in the last half hour, so we feel that every Yevd in Solar City who had been prepared in advance against the particular defense we had in that area is now in The

Yards. Although they have not yet concentrated on any particular point, we feel that the crisis is imminent."

Craig said in a steady tone: "What about my son?"

"Undoubtedly, they have further plans for him. We are trying to provide him with a weapon, but that would have a limited value at best."

Craig realized wretchedly that they were being very careful to say nothing that would give him any real hope. He said slowly: "You let a hundred of these Yevd get onto the 'Way' without knowing what they were after?"

The admiral said: "It's important to us to learn their objective. What do they value? What do they think is worth such a tremendous risk? This is a very courageous enterprise on their part, and it is our duty to let it come to a head. We are reasonably certain of what they are after, but we must be sure. At the final moment, we will make every effort to save your son's life, but we can guarantee nothing."

For a brief moment Craig saw the picture of the affair as these hard men visualized it. To them, Diddy's death would be a regrettable incident, nothing more. The papers would say, "Casualties were light." They might even make a hero out of him for a day.

"I'm afraid," said the admiral, "I'll have to ask you to break off now. At this moment your son is going down under the ship, and I want to give my full attention to him. Good-bye."

Craig broke the connection, and climbed to his feet. He stood for a moment bracing himself, and then he went back into the bedroom. He said cheerfully:

"Everything seems to be all right."

There was no reply. He saw that Veda was lying with her head on his pillow. She had evidently lain down to wait his return, and had immediately fallen asleep.

Very carefully, he tucked her in, and then crawled into her bed. He was still awake at dawn, restless, tired, and unhappy.

"What'd that dame whisper to you?" asked Jackie.

They were going down the escalator into the tunnel beneath the "Way." Diddy, who had been listening intently for the sound—there wasn't any particular noise—turned.

"Oh, just what she said to you."

Jackie seemed to consider that. They reached the walk and Diddy started immediately along it. Casually, he looked for a metal pillar with an H on it. He saw it abruptly, a hundred feet ahead. Behind him, Gil spoke:

"Why would she go to the trouble of whispering to you, if she was going to tell us anyway?"

Their suspicion made Diddy tremble inside, but his training told. "I think she was just having fun with us kids," he said.

"Fun!" That was Jackie.

Gil said: "What are we doing here under the ship?"

Diddy said: "I'm tired."

He sat down on the edge of the walk beside the five-foot-thick metal beam that reared up into the distance above. He let his feet dangle down to the tunnel proper. The two Yevd walked past him, and stood on the other side of the pillar. Diddy thought with a dizzy excitement, *They're going to communicate with each other—or with others.*

He steadied himself, and fumbled under the overlapping edge of the walk with his hand. Swiftly, he ran his fingers along the metal. He touched something. The tiny blaster came easily into his hand, and he slipped it into his pocket in a single synchronized motion. Then, weak from reaction, he sat there.

He grew aware of the vibration of the metal on the bones of his thighs. His special shoes had absorbed most of that tremor, and he had been so intent on the weapon that he hadn't noticed immediately. Now he did. Ever so slightly, his body shook and shivered. He felt himself drawn into the sound. His muscles and organs hummed and quivered. Momentarily, he forgot the Yevd, and for that moment it seemed immeasurably strange to be sitting here on the raw metal, unprotected and in tune with the sound itself.

He'd guessed the vibration would be terrific under the ship of ships. The city of The Yards was built on metal. But all the shock-absorbing material with which the streets and roads were carpeted couldn't muffle the ultimately violent forces and energies that had been concentrated in one small area. Here were atomic piles so hot that they were exploding continuously with a maximum detonation short of cataclysm. Here were machines that could stamp out hundred-ton electro-steel plates.

For eight and a half years more, The Yards would exist for this colossal ship. And then, when it finally flew, he would be on it. Every family in The Yards had been selected for two purposes—because the father or mother had a skill that could be used in the building of the ship, and because they had a child who would grow up in and around the ship.

In no other way, except by growing up with it, would human beings ever learn to understand and operate the spaceship that was rising here like a young mountain. In its ninety-four hundred feet of length was concentrated the engineering genius of centuries, so much specialized knowledge, so much mechanical detail, that visiting dignitaries looked around in bewilderment at the acres of machines and dials and instruments on every floor, and at the flashing wall lights that had already been installed in the lower decks.

He would be on it. Diddy stood up in a shaking excitement of anticipation—just as the two Yevd emerged from behind the pillar.

"Let's go!" said Jackie. "We've fooled around long enough."

Diddy came down from his height of exaltation. "Where to?"

Gil said: "We've been tagging along after you. Now, how about you going where we want to go for a change?"

Diddy did not even think of objecting. "Sure," he said.

The neon sign on the building said, "RESEARCH," and there were a lot of boys around. They wandered singly and in groups. He could see others in the distance, looking as if they were going nowhere in particular. It was hard to believe that they were all Yevd, but Diddy had the awful empty feeling that they were.

Research. That was what they were after. Here in this building, human beings had developed the anti-Yevd bacteria of the barrier. Just what the Yevd would want to know about that process, he had no idea. Perhaps, a single bit of information in connection with it would enable them to destroy a source material or organism, and so nullify the entire defense. The Play Square had intimated on occasion that such possibilities existed.

All the doors of "Research" were closed, the first building like that he had seen. Jackie said: "You open up, Diddy."

Obediently, Diddy reached for the door handle. He stopped, as two men came along the walk. One of them hailed him.

"Hello, there, kid. We keep running into you, don't we?"

Diddy let go of the door, and turned to face them. They looked like the two "men" who had originally brought him to the barrier, and who had made the bacteria test on him. But that would be merely outward appearance. The only Yevd inside the barrier of all those in Solar City would be individuals who had been immunized against the particular bacteria which he had isolated for them at that one part of the barrier.

It would be too much of a coincidence if both The Yards agent images had belonged to that group. Accordingly, these were not the same.

Not that it mattered.

The spokesman said: "Glad we bumped into you again. We want to conduct another experiment. Now, look, you go inside there. Research is probably protected in a very special fashion. If we can prove our idea here, then we'll have helped in making it harder for the Yevd to come into The Yards. That'll be worth doing, won't it?"

Diddy nodded. He was feeling kind of sick inside, and he wasn't sure he could talk plainly in spite of all his training.

"Go inside," said the Yevd, "stand around for a few moments, and then take a deep breath, hold it in, and come out. That's all."

Diddy opened the door, stepped through into the bright interior. The door closed automatically behind him.

It was a large room in which he found himself. *I could run*, he thought. *They don't dare come in here*. The absence of people inside the room chilled the impulse. It seemed unusual that there was no one around. Most of the departments in The Yards operated on a round-the-clock basis.

Behind him, the door opened. Diddy turned. The only Yevd in sight were Jackie and Gil standing well back from the door, and other boys even further away. Whoever had opened the door was taking no chances on getting a dose of anything, dangerous or otherwise.

"You can come out now," said the man's voice. He spoke from behind the door. "But remember, first take a deep breath and hold it."

Diddy took the breath. The door shut automatically as he emerged. And there were the two Yard "police" waiting behind it. One of them held up a little bottle with a rubber tube. "Exhale into this," he said.

When that was done, the Yevd handed it to his companion who walked quickly around the corner of the building and out of sight.

The spokesman said: "Notice anything unusual?"

Diddy hesitated. The air in the building, now that be thought of it, had seemed thick, a little harder to breathe than ordinary air. He shook his head slowly. "I don't think so," he said.

The Yevd was tolerant. "Well, you probably wouldn't notice," he said. He added quickly, "We might as well test your blood, too. Hold up your finger."

Diddy cringed a little from the needle, but he allowed the blood to be taken. Gil came forward. "Can I help?" he asked eagerly.

"Sure," said the "man." "You take this around to my friend."

Gil was gone as only a boy could go, at a dead run. A minute ticked by, and then another minute; and then—

"Ah," said the "man," "here they come."

Diddy stared at the returning pair with a sickly grin. The Yevd who had been standing beside him, walked swiftly forward to meet the two. If the two "men" said anything to each other, Diddy was unable to hear it. Actually, he took it for granted that there was a swift exchange on the light level.

The communication, whatever its nature, stopped.

The "man" who had done all the talking came back to Diddy, and said: "Kid, you've sure been valuable to us. It looks as if we're really going to make a contribution to the war against the Yevd. Do you know that air in there has an artificial gas mixed with it, a fluorine compound? Very interesting and very safe by itself. And even if a Yevd with his fluorine metabolism should walk in there, he'd be perfectly safe—unless he tried to use the energy of his body on a blaster or communication level. The energy acts as a uniting agent, brings about a chemical union between the fluorine in the air and the fluorine in the Yevd body—and you know what fluorine is like even at room temperatures under the right conditions."

Diddy knew. The chemical reactions of fluorine and its compounds had been a part of his education since the earliest days.

"It flames up violently," said the "man" with apparent satisfaction. "And the Yevd himself is the only one who can set off the explosion. Very clever. But now, I gather that all you kids want to go inside and have a look around. O.K., in with you. Not you"—to Diddy—"not for a minute. I want to have a little talk with you. Come on over here."

He and Diddy drew aside, while the "boys" rushed through the door. Diddy could imagine them spreading through the building, searching out secrets. He thought wearily, *Surely somebody will do something, and quickly.*

The Yevd said: "Confidentially, kid, this is really an important job you've done for us today. Just to give you an idea, we've kept an eye on the Research Building pretty well all night. The staff here usually goes home around midnight. Since midnight, a couple of workmen have gone into the place, installed some equipment, and departed. They put a radio hook-up over the door; with a loudspeaker both inside and out. And that's all that happened. Right now, except for you kids, the whole place is empty. You can see how much the people here have depended on the bacteria barrier keeping the Yevd away."

He paused, then went on, "Of course, the Yevd could spy out most of that information in advance, and if they finally got across the barrier they could set up guards all around the building, and so prevent even the most powerful armored forces from getting through to the defense of the building. It could be blasted, of course, from a distance, and destroyed, but it's hard to imagine them doing that very quickly. They'd wait till they'd tried other methods.

"You see where that would take us. The Yevd would have an opportunity to search out some of the secrets of the building. Once outside, they could communicate the information to other Yevd not in the danger area, and then each individual would have to take his own chance on escaping. That's bold stuff, but the Yevd have done similar things before. So you see, it all could happen easy enough. But now, we've prevented it."

"Diddy"—it was a whisper from above and to one side of him—"don't show any sign that you hear this."

Diddy stiffened, then quickly relaxed. It had been proved long ago that the Yevd electronic hearing and talking devices, located as they were inside sound deadening shoulder muscles, could not detect whispers.

The whisper went on swiftly: "You've got to go inside. When you are inside, stay near the door. That's all. There'll be more instructions for you then."

Diddy located the source of the whisper. It was coming from above the door. He thought shakily: *Those workmen who installed the radio the Yevd mentioned—the whisper must be coming through that.*

But how was he going to get inside when this Yevd was so obviously delaying him?

The Yevd was saying something about a reward, but Diddy scarcely heard. Distractedly, he looked past the "man." He could see a long line of buildings, some of them brightly illuminated, others in half darkness. The vast brilliance from the ship cast a long shadow where he was standing. In the sky above, the night seemed as black as ever.

There was no sign of the bright new morning, only hours away now.

Diddy said desperately: "Gosh, I'd better get inside. The sun will soon be up, and I've still got a lot of places to look."

The Yevd said: "I wouldn't waste much time in there. Take a look inside, huh, and tell me what the other kids are doing."

Quivering, Diddy opened the door. And went in. And let the door close behind him in its automatic fashion.

"Diddy," came the whisper, "unless a Yevd carries a weapon right out in the open, then he's dependent on the energy from his cells. A Yevd by his very nature has to wander around without any clothing on. It's only his body that can produce the images of human clothes and human form. Now, think carefully. Did you see any of those boys carrying a weapon? Whisper your answer."

"I don't remember seeing any," said Diddy shakily.

"We'll have to hope that your memory is accurate." came the answer. "If it is, then any weapon they appear to produce will be an image weapon. Now, listen, how many boys are in sight?"

There were two, both of them bent over a desk on the other side of the room.

"Two." The whisper echoed his count. "Good. Take out your gun and shoot them."

Diddy put his hand in his pocket, swallowed hard—and brought out the gun. His hand trembled a little, but for five years now he had been trained for such a moment as this, and he felt awfully steady inside. It was not a gun that had to be aimed perfectly.

It fired a steady blue streak of flame, and he merely waved its nozzle towards where the Yevd were. They started to turn. And collapsed as they did so.

"Did you get them?" The whisper again.

"Yes." His voice trembled. Across the room what had been two apple-cheeked boys was changing. In death, the images couldn't hold. And though he had seen pictures of what was emerging, it was different seeing the dark flesh coming into view, the strange legs—

"Listen—" the whisper caught him out of that shock—"all the doors are locked. Nobody can get in, nobody out. Start walking through the building. Shoot everybody you see. *Everybody!* Accept no pleas, no pretense that they are just kids. We've kept track of every other real boy, and there are only Yevd in the building. Burn them all without mercy.

"And, Diddy, I'm sorry this is the way it had to be. But you were the only one we could work through. You were right in there with them. The only reason you're alive is that they probably think you may still be of use to them inside the building, in case something turns up. You are the only one they do not seriously suspect. Any other method we might have used would have cost us hundreds of lives. But now, let's go! You take care of those inside. We'll go after the ones out here.

"And remember your training for caution. Don't go through a doorway until you've looked in. Remember, also, they can't shoot back. If they even try it, their bodies will start on fire. Good luck, Diddy. The battle is all yours."

The trap was so complete that there was not a single moment of real danger to the boy.

It was still pitch dark as Diddy caught a helicar at Cross 2 and flew to within a block of the hill, from which "explorers" like himself had to watch the sun rise. He climbed the steps that led to the top of the hill, and found several other boys already there, sitting and standing around.

While he could not be certain they were human, he had a pretty strong conviction that they were. There seemed to be no reason why a Yevd should participate in this particular ritual.

Diddy sank down under a bush beside the shadow shape of one of the boys. Neither of them spoke right away, then Diddy said: "What's your name?"

"Mart." The answering voice was shrill but not loud.

"Find the sound?" asked Diddy.

"Yep."

"So did I." He hesitated, thinking of what he had done. Just for a moment he had a sharp awareness of how wonderful was the training that had made it possible for a nine-year-old boy to act as he had acted, and then that faded from his fore-consciousness, and he said: "It's been fun, hasn't it?"

"I guess so."

There was silence. From where Diddy sat, he could see the intermittent glare of the atomic furnaces as the sky flared with a white, reflected fire. Further along was the jewel-bright aura of light that partially framed the ship. The sky above was no longer dark, and Diddy noticed that the shadows around him were not dense any more, but grayish. He could see Mart's body crouched under the bush, a smaller body than his own.

As the dawn brightened, he watched the ship. Slowly, the metal of its bare upper ribs caught the flames of the sun that was still not visible from where they sat. The glare expanded downward, and sunlight glinted on the dark, shiny vastness of its finished lower walls, the solid shape it made against the sky beyond.

Out of the shadows grew the ship, an unbelievable thing, bigger than anything around it. At this distance the hundred story Administration Building looked like a part of its scaffolding, a white pillar against the dark colossus that was the ship.

Long after the sun had come up. Diddy stood watching in an exaltation of pride. In the glare of the new day the ship seemed to be gathering itself as if poised for flight. Not yet, Diddy thought shakily, not yet. But the day would come. In that far time the biggest ship ever planned and constructed by men would point its nose at the open spaces between the near stars and fly out into the darkness. And then indeed would the Yevd have to give ground. For they had nothing like this. Nothing even near it.

At last, in response to the familiar empty feeling in his belly, Diddy went down the hill. He ate breakfast in a little "Instant" restaurant. And then, happy, he caught a helicar and headed for home.

In the master bedroom, Craig heard the outer door of the apartment open—and almost he was too slow. He caught his wife with her fingers on the knob of the door.

He shook his head at her gently. "He'll be tired," he said softly. "Let him rest."

Reluctantly, she allowed herself to be led back, to her own bed this time.

Diddy tiptoed across the living rooom to the Play Square and undressed. As he crept under the sheets, he grew aware of the faint tremor of the air. Lying there, he felt the quaver of his bed and heard the shudder of the plexiglas windows. Below him, the floor creaked ever so faintly in its remote, never-ending rapport with the all-pervading vibration.

Diddy grinned happily, but with a great weariness. He'd never have to wonder about the sound again. It was a miasma of The Yards, a thin smoke of vibration from the masses of buildings and metal and machines that tendrilled out from the "Way." That sound would be with him all his life; for when the ship was finished, a similar pervasive sound would shake from every metal plate.

He slept, feeling the pulse of the sound deep inside him, a part of his life.

Completing him.

THE RULERS

It was a typical Washington dinner party. Minor political lights adorned at least a dozen chairs. And here and there along the massive table sat men who were of more than satellite importance. One of several inevitable discussions had started near the hostess—that was purely accidental—and the dinner had reached the bored stage where almost everybody was listening with polite attention.

"Science," the plump man was saying, "has made such strides since the war that it's already possible to foresee a time when everything we do, or use in any way, will be either completely artificial, artificially enhanced, supernatural, or better than the original."

The dark-haired man with the quizzical expression shook his head. "If that proves true, it will be because the human race is lazier than I for one believe. Plastics I might concede without argument but with mental reservations. I'll even go so far as to agree that anything which does not directly affect the human body can be made artificially, and it won't matter. But when you come to the body itself—no, sir. Vitamin-enriched foods, for instance, contain only the extra vitamins, but natural foods contain not only the well-known factors such as vitamins, minerals, but also all the as yet unknown factors. Finally, show me even a near substitute for the human brain, and I'll accept your point."

"It isn't so much," said the plump man with satisfaction, "that there is a substitute, but have you perhaps heard of the *h* drug? It's not a brain, but it so modifies the mind's natural impulses that it might be said to create an artificial brain."

At this moment, the hostess showed one of her periodic signs of life.

465

"*H* drug?" she echoed. "Artificial brain? I know just the man to decide any such question." She turned, and said, "Dr. Latham, will you stop talking for a moment to that perfectly beautiful wife of yours ... you don't mind, Margaret? ... and come to the aid of these poor gentlemen?"

Dr. Latham was a tall, slender man with a lean, sensitive face and quick brown eyes. He laughed. "It just so happens that I heard the argument with one ear."

"And me with the other one, I suppose," his wife pouted.

He grinned at her. "You're not really mad, so don't even try to pretend."

She sighed. "That comes of being married to a psychomedician, a man who can practically read minds."

Latham ignored her blandly. "I think," he began, "I can illustrate the argument very neatly by a case I handled for the government a year ago ..."

By half past eleven, Latham knew that he had found what he had been sent after. It was time, therefore, to dissemble suspicion. He excused himself from his guide, picked up the desk phone of the office they were in, and dialed his hotel.

Miss Segill's face appeared on the screen. "It's you," she said.

Her eyes brightened. Her cheeks thickened with eager laughter lines. Her mouth crinkled. A thousand tiny muscular adjustments transformed her face in one instant from quiet receptive attentiveness into a mask of brilliant smile. There were accompanying signals of marked glandular activity, Latham noted, plus a tendency—breathlessness, slight parting of lips, fingering indecisiveness—to a lowering of neural integration.

Latham studied her appreciatively. He had decided at an early stage of their acquaintanceship to marry this secretary-nurse of his. It was good to know that her love for him rode higher every day. He broke off the thought, and said, "I'll be through here in another half hour, Miss Segill. Bring your notebook to the little restaurant we saw last night on the way to the hotel—you know the one I mean—and we'll have lunch about 12:15. There won't be much to note down. Got that all?"

"I'll be there," said Miss Segill; then quickly, "Doctor."

Latham paused as he was about to hang up the receiver. The young woman's expression had changed again. The smile was fading now. Replaced by an intent look, crinkled lines between the eyes, a shadow of a forehead frown. Her mouth twitched faintly. Her face lost some of its color. She looked tenser, as if her muscles had stiffened. Anxiety for him intermingled with a tremulous curiosity as to what he had discovered.

"Nothing important, Miss Segill," Latham said. "The whole thing is becoming ridiculous."

He hung up before it occurred to him that she had not actually *asked* the question he had answered. Latham clicked his tongue in self-annoyance. He'd have to watch out for that. His habit of reading people's thoughts and feelings, by a detailed and instantly analyzed understanding of the language of facial and other expressions, would make him seem queer. With his ambitions, he couldn't afford that.

He put the matter temporarily but decisively out of his mind. "Let's go," he said to the guide. "This part of the hospital now, and then I'll be on my way."

"I wouldn't go in there if I were you," the man said in a quiet voice.

"Eh," said Latham. "Don't be silly. I have to—"

He stopped. The abnormalness of the guide's words struck into him. An ugly thrill trickled up Latham's spine. With a jerk, he turned and stared full at the fellow. Instantly, he realized that he had run across the exception to his ability to comprehend the mind behind the flesh.

The man had been a dull-spoken, mindless nonentity named Godred, or Codred, a creature that said, "And this is the fifteenth floor annex, where we keep patients from Rumania." Or, "Main operating room, sir, for the Austrian staff." And said it all without a hint of vascular, muscular, neural, or cerebral disturbance. He was smiling now, faintly. Where there had been stolidity, intelligence shone like a light replacing darkness. His body lost its heaviness. He straightened, grew perceptibly taller. His lips took on lines of authority. He measured Latham with a sardonic smile. He said:

"We have tolerated your little investigation, doctor, with a mixture of amusement and exasperation. Now we are weary. Go away; depart while you have a whole skin. And don't go through that door."

Latham was thinking: Here was final proof. He'd have to take a look, of course, into the room. After that— His mind wouldn't go that far. He said aloud, "Are you mad? Do you not realize that I represent the United States government?"

The man said, *"Don't go through that door!"*

The door was like the others: a many wooded hardwood combination, beautifully interlaid, and without paint or varnish of any kind. Sandpaper had wrought that miracle finish. It opened at the pressure of Latham's fingers, with only normal resistance. Its threshold held his rigid form for the moment that he stood staring. Then he was running, back the way he had come. The guide grabbed at him. But Latham's movement, his entire reaction, was too quick.

It was as he realized the distance to the nearest exit that he had his first hard shock of fear. Even as he ran, he began to lose hope.

That race along marbled and paneled corridors was like a dream. One of those mad dreams of being pursued. He knew better than to stop. There was a rather long, paved driveway leading to the nearest street. And a taxi was just turning a far corner. He projected his long body and, gasping, succeeded in heading off the taxi. He climbed out five minutes later, waited until the taxi was out of sight, then hailed a second cab. He got off in the depths of heavy downtown traffic, hurried through two monster department stores, and climbed aboard an elect-air car for the third stage of his bid for escape.

He was calmer now. An intent, rational calmness that included a detailed memory of everything he had said on the phone about where he had told Miss Segill to meet him. He hadn't named the restaurant. It was like consciously dying, then coming to life again, to realize now that he had made that phone call, *and failed to name the restaurant.* They didn't know. They couldn't know. In all this enormous city, they wouldn't be able to locate a cafe whose only name was "… You know the one I mean!"

But Miss Segill and he would have to hurry. A quick lunch, then a Taxi-Air to Washington. There wasn't an hour, a minute, to waste.

"I don't understand," Miss Segill said, after he had briefly described his experience. "What *did* you see?"

"Twelve men and a gun."

The girl's eyes remained widened gray-green pools of puzzlement. She shook her head ever so slightly, and her golden curls rippled and shone from the reflected sunlight that poured from the sun cones in the restaurant ceiling.

"Eat your lunch," Latham admonished. "I'll try to make it clear between my own bites. You know the law that was passed, subjecting all hospitals to federal government inspection? The government called it a measure to enforce a uniform hospital service. That reason was a blind, as you know."

Miss Segill nodded wordlessly. Latham went on grimly: "Its real purpose was to find this place. They couldn't conceal anything from me, and they didn't even try. The hospital is crowded with offices and non-sick patients. Naturally, a few offices from which wealthy convalescents could carry on their business, and a few nonsick patients, wouldn't have mattered much. After the war certain European nationalities were barred from the United States unless they came here to see specialists. Even then their activity was restricted. They must go straight to a hospital which had previously agreed to receive them; and, on leaving, head straight for the nearest intercontinental air field.

"It was known that sometimes the visitors had quite a fling seeing American high spots before returning to Europe. But this was tolerated until a very curious suspicion started that at least one of the hundreds of hospitals catering to this old-world traffic was being used as headquarters for something immeasurably bigger. That hospital, which is absolutely crowded with administration offices and an almost completely nonsick group of patients, I have now discovered."

"But *what* did you see when you entered that room?"

Latham stared at her grimly. "I saw," he said slowly, "twelve of the thirteen members of the council of the rulers of the world. The thirteenth member was Codred, my guide. I believe they wanted to talk to me, to find out what I knew before killing me. I don't think they expected me to make a break, and that is why I got away. Primarily, I escaped because my mind and eyes are trained to grasp a picture in one tenth the normal time. Before they could think or act, before they could use the gun that protruded from an instrument board of very futuristic design, actually before they saw me, I had taken my visual photograph and departed. They could have cut me off at the outer door but—"

Latham paused, scowling. Then he shook his head, eyes narrowed. It seemed incredible, now that he had time to think about it, that they had not headed him off. How very sure they must have been. He flicked his gaze uneasily around the fast-filling cafe, suddenly saw—

"Look!" he hissed. "On the telescreen."

There had been ballet music, and dancers weaving a skillful design on the wall screen. Abruptly, the music ended. The dancers flicked into vagueness. There flashed onto the silvery structure the enormously enlarged faces of Miss Segill and himself. A voice vibrated from the screen:

"Ladies and gentlemen, watch out for this man and woman, believed at this very moment to be in a restaurant having lunch. Their names are Dr. Alexander Latham and Margaret Segill, of Washington, D.C. They are dangerous. Police are authorized to shoot them on sight. That is all."

The music came back on. The images of the dancers resumed their crazy whirling.

It was Latham's inordinately swift observation that saved the moment. At the very instant that other people were beginning to be aware of the screen, he had already seen the two likenesses, and was whispering his commands to Miss Segill, "Quick, your napkin … up to your face … hide."

He bent down without waiting for her to act, and began fumbling with his shoelaces. He was down there when the voice delivered its startling sentence of death. After a moment the whole thing seemed impossible. Their names, identities, with no mention of a crime or charge. It indicated police connivance on a scale beyond any previous conception that he had had of danger.

He thought in a spasm of mental agony: They hadn't told him everything at Washington. It was terrible to realize suddenly that he was considered expendable, a bullet fired in dim light in the hope of striking a vaguely seen target.

He was still busy with his shoelace when Miss Segill leaned forward and said in a strained whisper, "I don't think anybody suspects. But what now?"

Latham had already decided on that. "The phone booths over against the wall," he answered in a low voice. "I have instructions not to phone my reports to Washington, but under the circumstances—"

He broke off. "I'll go first; you follow—into the booth beside mine."

He straightened, stood up, and, dabbing his lips with the napkin, strode to the nearest booth thirty feet away. At the last minute he changed his mind, and paused, his fingers on the catch.

Miss Segill joined him there. "What is it?" she asked.

"Better plan our actions now. And act the moment I've finished phoning. Listen carefully: It doesn't seem possible the police can actually be in on this, but I've reached the point where I trust no one."

"I think we should go straight to the police, and find what's the matter," said Miss Segill, who was now very white, but sounded brave. "After all, we can prove who we are."

"That," said Latham with a cold satisfaction, "is one of the things they expect us to do, I'll warrant. So we won't take the chance. I'll make my phone call, and ask for an escort of air blasts to meet the Taxi-Air we hire. I noticed a Taxi-Air firm a block south of here as I came along."

"What about our lunch bill?"

Latham laughed curtly. "You can't tell me that the cashier or the waitresses have time to pay attention to that telescreen. When we walk past the tables, you be blowing your nose, and I'll start putting on my hat. That should hide our faces to a certain extent—" He broke off, groaned softly, "I wish I had my gun. At least, then I'd be able to put up a fight." He half-turned away from her. "But never mind that. Go into your booth. I'll tap on the aerogel when I'm through."

"I'll pretend," said Miss Segill wanly, "that I'm looking up a number."

Good girl! Latham thought. She was standing up well. Better, it seemed to him, than he would have done in her position. He was inside the booth now. He dialed the key numbers that would connect him with the Washington Exchange. The small screen glowed in response. Quickly, Latham dialed the number of the CISA office.

The screen flickered, seemed to have difficulty formulating an image, and then went dead. Latham stared at it, startled. But instantly he dismissed the fear that touched him. The police perhaps; men could always be bought. But not the entire, completely automatic telephone system of a city of a million population. He shook his head, irritated by the fantastic suspicion, and re-dialed his two numbers. This time the screen lit, and stayed lit, and at exactly the right instant the image of a man's head and face formed on it.

"Emergency!" Latham said. "Take this down and—"

He stopped. Then he stared grimly at the sardonic countenance of Codred, who had been his guide at the hospital. The man said mockingly:

"Yes, yes, doctor, go on with your report"—he paused; then hurried-ly—"but before you leave the booth please be advised that, once you started running along the corridor, we decided to let you thresh around in our net for a few hours. Your mind will react better to our purpose once it attains that sense of perfect helplessness which we—"

Swiftly as he was speaking, it was still dragging out too long. Talking to gain time, Latham thought. They must have traced the call after the first failure of the phone. Standing there, flashingly picturing the tremen-dousness of what had already happened, he felt his first terrible fear.

He hung up, trembling, backed out of the booth. And then slowly gathered his courage into his body again. He mustered a smile for Miss Segill. But it must have been a sad affair. Her eyes widened.

"You didn't make the call," she said.

Latham didn't have the will to lie to her. "Can't explain now," he said. "We've got to get that Taxi-Air."

He thought again of his gun, this time with a blank dismay. How *could* it have disappeared from his bedroom? No one had been near it. And night marauders might not have the advance knowledge to know that they couldn't enter a psychomedician's room. But they'd know afterward, on the way to jail. Could it be that he had only imagined he had packed it?

He felt better when he reached the street without incident. It seemed to take an unconscionably long time to bridge the gap of one block to the Taxi-Air Station. But the very crowds that held them up provided a comforting sense of being unidentifiable. The station was the usual kind. It had a short runway extending over several nearby roofs of business buildings, and an all-aerogel construction, partly transparent, translucent, partly white as driven snow.

There were a dozen Taxi-Airs in the lower garage. Latham selected a Packard model he had operated frequently. The driver was reading as they came up, but he put his book away promptly. The man's face twitched as he saw them. The pulse in his neck throbbed visibly. His eyes seemed briefly to reflect more light. He smiled, and said affably:

"Where to, folks?"

"Middle City," Latham said.

He spoke automatically. He had decided on the destination when he was leaving the phone booth, when it was already very clear that anybody heading directly for Washington either by phone or air would be pulled up hard. Actually, now that the driver had reacted as he had, the destina-tion didn't matter.

His plan was simplicity itself. The driver would hold open the door, and let them in. Then he would go around to the other side, and ease himself into the driver's seat. Only that wouldn't happen, Latham cal-culated. Because *he* would lock the doors as soon as he got inside, dive for the controls, taxi up the winding runway to the roof, and take off. He, Latham—

His thought staggered. Because the driver opened the door, and climbed in himself. From his seat, he grinned. "Climb in, folks," he said.

For an instant, then, the whole business seemed insane. A moment before, the fellow's recognition of them, with its implications, had been something to foil as cleverly as possible. But it was the driver who was handling this situation. And that was amazing. Because he looked so normal, decent, ordinary, a big, easy-going, lumbering chap of about two hundred pounds. The baffling thing was that they had picked this driver by chance, one man of dozens in one of a hundred or more air stations.

With an effort Latham checked the violent swirling of his mind. This was real. Real and deadly and terrible and unmistakable. There *was* no mistaking the thousand subtle reflexes that showed in the fellow's every movement, every expression. The driver was one of them. Not just a hastily conscripted recruit. But a member of the gang.

As he climbed in, Latham tried to picture that: All police, all taxi drivers, broadcasting companies, telephone firms— What was it Codred had said: "… Let you thresh around in the net for a few hours."

The Taxi-Air was moving. Latham sat stiffly, watching it twist up and up the inclined plane. Abruptly, they were out on the runway, speeding. The throbbing of the rocket tubes was loud for an instant, as the mufflers were partially opened.

Then they were closed down; and there was only a faint purr of power. Latham glanced into the forward viewers. In the far distance straight ahead loomed the fifteen-story Many Nations Hospital. Five minutes, he estimated, at city speeds.

Five minutes! Latham shook with a sudden appalled consciousness of what he had done. He had climbed into this Taxi-Air knowing what the driver was. He could attack, of course, physically. Except that the driver looked too big, *was* too big, too alert, and in good condition. These psychomedicians, Latham thought in agony. Why hadn't he ever taken exercise? With an automatic will to find some blunt instrument, he poked into the side pockets of the machine. They were empty. A quick glance into the viewers showed—

Three minutes to go!

As the swift seconds passed, he began to brace himself. For there was nothing for it but an attack. He could already see himself being smashed by fists, his head crunched against the dashboard by hamlike muscles, his eyes blackened. He had attended assault and battery victims; and he had the thought that it was to his credit that he didn't let the remembrance slow his gathering will to desperate action.

But if only he had some instrument, something heavier than his fists. His gaze lighted on Miss Segill's tightly clutched purse. "What's in there?" Latham hissed in a spurt of hope. "Anything heavy, solid?"

He had the wild feeling that his *sotto voce* was so loud that the driver must hear. But a glance at the rear-view mirror showed that the part of the man's face visible in it was calm. It was an honest countenance, a little tense, but untroubled by recent disturbance. It was impossible to let himself think of the meaning of the unmistakable honesty that reflected in every ripple of the fellow's expression.

Miss Segill said, "There's nothing in the purse. My notebook, odds and ends. What's the matter? Is anything wrong? I've been intending to ask you about the phone—"

She didn't suspect. Actually, of course, only a man with his training could know the truth. Latham cut her off by snatching the bag from her fingers. There was the notebook, two change purses, a mirror, a host of metal containers of rouge, lipstick, and other toilet accessories. But the metal was the noncombustible magnesium alloy, slangily called Maggie's Dream by the light metal trades, but something far swankier in the cosmetics field—Latham couldn't remember what. It didn't matter. There wasn't a thing in the bag that weighed over four ounces. The whole purse, including the cunningly shaped hardwood clasps, including the hundred separate items inside, wouldn't run to much over five pounds.

His mind paused. Five pounds? He saw that the plane was sinking down. There was a great, shining roof below—not a moment to ponder the anesthetic value of five pounds of fluff. He clutched the bag, clasp downward. He leaped forward. He struck. And struck again and again. And again and again and again. Somewhere deep in his brain was a startled recognition that fear was making him merciless.

The driver's head sagged, then his body crumpled. Latham stared dully down at the unconscious body. Without a word, finally, he handed Miss Segill her purse. With only a glance at her dazed face, he set himself to the task of dragging the driver into the rear section. He couldn't do it. He felt like a rag, his muscles lifeless. The heavy body came so far, then wouldn't budge.

In the viewer, Latham saw that the hospital's shining roof was behind them now, receding slowly. He leaned over the driver and pulled the hand accelerator hard over. The machine picked up speed. The jar of acceleration was too much for him. Exhausted, Latham collapsed into the seat beside Miss Segill. He sat there dully for a moment, but swiftly his spirits lifted. Safe! They need only get rid of the driver, then roar on eastward at top speed.

"He's coming to!" Miss Segill whispered.

"Give me your purse!" said Latham. "And then give me a hand with him."

A minute later they had the bulky carcass in the rear compartment. Latham climbed over to the front and pulled a parachute out of the emergency locker. As he dumped the driver overboard, he pulled the cord. He watched the chute open up like a great white umbrella with a human pendulum swinging below it. The spectacle intrigued him for a moment, but then he remembered where he was. He slid into the driver's seat, and pressed down on the highly sensitive foot accelerator.

He turned to smile at Miss Segill. His smile faded. The young woman was staring fixedly into the rear-view mirror. She must have caught his glance from the corner of her eyes. She faced him jerkily.

"There're some air blasts behind us," she gulped. "They look like police or something. Do you think—"

It didn't, Latham reflected bitterly, need any thought.

He was conscious of a sense of resignation as he studied the air blasts. There were seven of them. All were long and black, with the very stubby wings of the extremely fast, ultramodern police patrol craft. Even yet it was hard to believe that they were really police. With abrupt decision, Latham flicked on the short-range radio, about which cynical drivers had often said: "I'd rather lean out and yell!"

Latham smiled grimly at the recollection, then said into the mouthpiece, "What do you want?"

A young man's face formed on the dashboard screen.

"You!" he said.

"Do you realize that I am an agent of Congress, acting for the President of the United States?"

The answer came coolly. "We don't recognize either Congress or the President. You'd better surrender."

Latham was silent. He felt the shock gathering into him again. The young man looked American. His voice, his accent sounded so colloquial that the words he spoke seemed but part of a play, one of those impossible dramas along the lines of "It Can't Happen Here!" so popular years before.

An earlier thought came back, stronger now, more dismaying: What did it mean? The shreds of explanation that had been given to him about there being a group of men who consciously thought of themselves as rulers of the world, seemed inadequate now. Because Americans wouldn't give allegiance to any group like that. It wasn't a matter for argument. They just wouldn't, that was all. There must be a deadlier explanation, something infinitely threatening.

The stupid thing was that, while, by capture and—methods—they would find out what he knew, yet killing him wouldn't prevent the CISA from suspecting the hospital. His report, for instance, was due this very night. What did the thirteen rulers hope to gain?

A moment longer Latham stared at that youthful, cool-voiced traitor; then with a gesture broke the connection. He switched the indicator over to "Telephone," dialed the Washington number of the Committee Investigating Subversive Activities that he had tried to contact from the restaurant.

He felt no particular surprise when the face of Codred appeared on the screen. The man said blandly, "What you are confronted with, Dr. Latham, is organization. The radios on all Taxi-Air and air blasts of this city do not connect with the nearest exchange. They connect with our own city's automatic center. For today only, or rather, so long as you are at large, all calls to Washington will be switched to me and my staff here. We let the harmless ones go through, but will naturally stop you every time. You have been amazingly agile but, of course, you cannot succeed."

"I'm not caught yet," Latham said grimly.

He suppressed the impulse to ask some leading questions, hesitated, then broke the connection. No vital information would be imparted to him at this stage; and it was not the moment to listen to lectures that could have no result except to throw him off guard.

With narrowed eyes, he studied the air blasts. They were quite close now, two of them forging a little ahead of his craft, all pressing nearer. Latham had a sudden mental picture of a newsreel he had seen some years before, in which three police craft were shown catching an air-car. Catching it, grappling onto the standardized grapple rails—to be without which was an offense subject to heavy fine—and swiftly dragging it to the ground.

Theoretically, a driver with his lightning vision should be able to dart rings around pursuers by the mere ability to see faster what was happening around him. Theoretically, that was. Practically, the armored police ships need only cling boldly to their courses, and let him smash his lighter machine against their impregnable hides. Nevertheless, he had the hope. He swung around on Miss Segill.

"Hang on," he shouted. "It's going to be a wild ride. I—"

He stopped, and stared at her. Her face was changing. It was not a subtle transformation. What was missing was the dominating expression of love-adoration. If he had been in the back seat with her, he could have frustrated her action. As it was, there was nothing to do but squirm with the beginning of a halfhearted move to climb towards her. She had raised her skirt, exposing a considerable reach of gleaming leg, around which was a holster with a tiny gun in it. *His* gun! She drew the gun and pointed it at Latham.

"I think," she said coolly, "that at this point I can safely do my bit in this business. You will put up your hands, doctor, and keep them up until you're told otherwise."

The plump man at the dinner table made an interrupting gesture with his hands.

"Just a minute, doctor. We've all heard some of the details of this story, of course, though the press version was curiously garbled. But this Miss Segill who held you up with your own gun—she's the gorgeous blonde sitting beside you there—your wife?"

Latham said, "Naturally, at that moment I knew what the explanation was for everything. The amazing thing was that I, with my knowledge, shouldn't have guessed earlier. I knew I had not misread Miss ... er ... Segill's feelings for me, nor her character. Just when they got at her it's hard to say, probably the night before. Her instructions must have been to take a hand at a critical moment, and she undoubtedly didn't become aware of those instructions until that moment. Anyway, looking at her there in the Taxi-Air, I realized an immensely potent artificial control had been put over her, and what it was."

The plump man said: "The *h* drug."

"The funny thing about that," Latham went on, "is that, like so many potential world-controlling devices of the last century—the submarine, dive bombers, radio X and so on—*h* was invented in the United States. The inventor used it as an aid in the study of the mind, and not one of his students thought of it as a means to world power. I was one of those students, and I know."

"We simply don't go in over here for ideas like that," the other man agreed. "And—"

The hostess cut him off. She had a vague remembrance that the plump man was somebody of importance, but it didn't matter. The greatest inside story of the decade was being told, and told at her table. She was M-A-D-E.

"Go on, doctor!" she said, and her voice was a reptile-like hiss.

Latham was led along the familiar hospital corridor by a dozen men of the patrol craft. He did not look at Miss Segill, except to note once that some of her jaunty confidence was fading, a puzzled look coming into her face.

Codred met them at the door of *the* room. He was smiling gently, but he said nothing, simply stepped aside, and bowed Latham past. The moment he was in, Latham turned, and watched feverishly as Codred admitted Miss Segill and four of the guards. Latham calculated ferociously: Four! That ought to be enough. But they mustn't be allowed to leave the room.

There must have been an intent expression on his face, because Codred shut the door, then said, "They're here just in case you get tough. We abhor scenes but"—he smiled broadly—"we prepare for them. As for Miss Segill"–he faced the girl—"the effect of the *h* drug should be wearing off her any time. So just hand me that gun, please, Miss— Thank you." Once more he turned to Latham.

"As you probably know, doctor, the effect of *h* is not permanent. The initial dose must be quite strong, and it must be administered under controlled conditions. Afterwards, a very diluted form will sustain the slave status it sets up in the brain. We use the city water system of course. However, no one drinking the diluted form only would be even remotely affected. This is unfortunate in some respects, but to use more would have deadly results on the mass already under control. The necessary rotelike commands are broadcast over the public address system. Is everything clear now?"

It wasn't; not everything. He felt cold and stiff and deadly. The incredible, fantastic, hellish scoundrels, using a poison like that so casually and monstrously. With an effort of will Latham pulled himself together. There were a number of things that it was vital to know. And calmness, however titanic the strain of maintaining it, was necessary.

He turned away from Codred, and stared at the dozen men who sat before separate desks along one end of the room. In spite of himself, then, he glanced at the gun. It was mounted between the sixth and seventh desks; and it held him because—he saw with a start—it was not a gun. It was an electrode of very intricate design. It projected from a metal cabinet which rested on a gleamy mobile base. Heavy cables ran from the cabinet into the floor.

Latham groaned softly as he recognized where he had first seen a similar machine. In a big commercial laboratory, a model instrument used by the American inventors for atomic investigations. Very carefully, he walked forward, out of the direct path of the gun, and returned his attention to the rulers of the world.

They had been watching his examination of the electrode with individual degrees of interest varying from indifferent awareness to sharp, curious stares.

More thoughtful now, Latham studied them. He remembered their faces from that first quick glance he had given them at half past eleven that morning. But certain facts hadn't struck him then. There were not, he saw now, as many Germans as he had believed. Only three. The four others that he had mistaken for Germans were respectively a Pole, an outsized Frenchman, a Spanish Jew, and an Englishman. Of the remaining five men two looked French, one unmistakably English, one Great Russian, and one Greek. Actually, of course, these men were ultra national, beyond all loyalties to any flag. Codred, he had already decided, was an American.

It was the Greek who broke the silence, who said in a deep bass voice, "Enough of this. Inject *h* into the prisoner. It is important that he make a carefully doctored report to Washington by tonight."

Latham had expected that he was to receive the *h* drug. But not so quickly. He *had* to have more information first. He opened his mouth to say something, anything, that would give him some, at least, of the facts he craved. Before he could speak, Codred's voice came resonantly from behind him:

"Not so fast, Michael, not so fast. A man who receives *h* knowing what it is, must have his mind reduced to a condition where it feels helpless against the forces that are attacking it. We have shown Dr. Latham that he cannot escape us. Literally cannot. This will have had a profoundly disconcerting effect. But we must not forget that we are dealing with a psychomedician. Therefore—"

His voice paused tantalizingly. He came around from behind Latham, smiling sardonically. "Let me explain, doctor," he purred, "just what you are up against. We're a very old organization, *very* old. Our leader group, which you see before you, can trace itself back to the year 3417 B.C. When a member dies, the survivors, after careful consideration, elect a replacement. With such extraordinary insight has this been done that our existence has only been suspected occasionally, never actually believed in. In the last six hundred years, no less than twelve kings have held office on our board of rulers. Until recently, no war was fought in Europe that did not have our sanction. Napoleon was a usurper, but he didn't last long; even England helped to down him.

"For many generations now, it has been our intention to bring England under our control. England is our great mistake. We dismissed her from our early calculations, completely underestimating her possibilities. All our troubles have originated from that basic error of judgment. As a direct result of England's independence, America came into being, and, more indirectly—though I could trace every step for you beyond question were I so minded—Soviet Russia. England alone, of course, would in recent generations have been helpless. Twice now, America has thwarted our will to bring England into line. It became apparent that we must first and finally neutralize the United States.

"We came to America under great difficulties. That incredible immigration law had to be gotten around by means of this hospital. Through the hospital, we slowly built up our control over this one city. It has been an exhausting process, but now we are ready. Starting today, we expand. When you return to Washington, it will be as our enslaved agent. We anticipate that you will be able to make the highest contacts, and will inject *h* into hundreds of key administration minds. America will not again interfere with our plans. Now"—his voice, which had risen to a harsh pitch, quieted—"have you anything to say while you are still able to think for yourself?"

It was a hard question to answer immediately. Hard because rage was back, choking, clogging his throat. The cold-blooded account of an organization that, from time immemorial, had used entire peoples as pawns in an involved play for power, whose members felt not a twinge of conscience at the thought of enslavement of hundreds of millions—words could not but be inadequate. Besides, the important thing for him was: Had Codred been telling the truth?

With a remorseless precision, Latham went over in his mind the shifting design of expression that had marked Codred's face as he talked. It had fooled him before, when the man was acting as his guide, and he mustn't let it do so again.

What counted in reading a mind, from the subtle variations of the natural physical reactions, was to miss no response of a vital organ. The older a person, the easier, because blood vessels came to the surface of the nose, the cheeks, and the body generally. The bloodstream was overwhelmingly the most expressive. Muscles rippled under more or less rigid conditions, but blood was a fluid, capable of a thousand subtle transformations. A score of glands pumped their juices into it to balance every emotion, every thought. Veins contracted, arteries swelled, obscure blood vessels dilated and changed color, always for a reason. The man who could connect cause and effect, as he could, could almost literally read thoughts.

And there was no doubt. Codred had not lied. The facts were as stated.

One thing more: He had to know which desk controlled the electrode. He could not permit it to be discharged. So long as it was *live*, he was vulnerable.

Latham began, "Yes, I have a few words to say; words that will puzzle you at first because they involve discussion of the different approaches to the same subject, of two types of mind. You are the ruler type. Your interest in a drug like *h* has, I venture to say, never extended beyond a careful examination of its utility in serving your ends. But the drug *h* is merely a positive form of hypnosis. It affects the same region of the brain.

"You would be amazed how many things the late, great Dr. Nanning and his students, of whom I had the honor to be one, discovered about hypnosis and control of the mind through the use of the *h* drug. I say 'amazed' deliberately, because I feel confident that none of you has felt the slightest interest in the purely scientific aspects of *h*. Do you know, for instance, that hypnotism is nothing less than control of a second personality, and that this extra being is always consciously aware of the first, though the reverse is not true. When you inject h, you release the second personality, and because of its slavelike attributes, are able to control it.

"What will astound you is that, not only does every human body contain the two personalities, that is, the conscious and the second, but also a third. This was discovered by the early French mesmerists, notably Coué, though only h makes control of this third personality easy. When I tell you that this third personality is aware of, and can supersede, *both* of the other two, you will—"

They had been startlingly slow to grasp their doom. Perhaps it was hard for men of their historical background to comprehend even the idea of a final ending to their tremendous and ruthless activities. But once they did understand, they acted.

The alertly watching Latham saw the facial transformations that showed where the electrode controls were. "The sixth and seventh desks!" he shouted. "FIRE!"

The guns of the four guards went off as one shot.

After a minute of silence, the plump man said:

"I recognize that my argument, foreseeing the triumph of the artificial over the natural, has been defeated. Your understanding and control of the *natural* functions of the human mind made your great victory possible. I suppose you evoked the third personalities of the guards while they were escorting you from the ship?"

Latham nodded; then, "Don't give up your argument too quickly. Don't forget that I could not have accomplished what I did except for the fact that the guards were under h influence."

The plump man responded with finality: "I accept defeat."

FINAL COMMAND

Barr stood on the hill—which overlooked Star, capitol of the human-controlled galaxy—and tried to make up his mind.

He was aware of his single robot guard standing somewhere in the darkness to his left. A man and a woman came along the crest of the hill, paused for a kiss, and then started down. Barr scarcely glanced at them. His problem embraced the whole civilization of man and robot, not individuals.

Even the escape of the alien enemy prisoner, a few hours before, had been an incident, when compared to the larger issues. True, he had seen it as a major event, and had ordered robot troops from distant cities to come to the capitol and aid in the search. But he had still to make the decision, which would fit those separate actions into a unified, driving purpose.

Behind him, there was a thud. Barr turned. He saw that an accident had taken place. The man and woman, evidently intent on each other, had bumped into the robot guard. The guard, caught off balance, was now sprawled on the ground. The man bent down to help him up.

"I beg your pardon," he said, "I didn't—" He stopped. Finger contact with the clothes that covered the padding that, in turn, concealed the basic crystalline structure, must have apprised him of the other's identity. "Oh, you're a robot!"

He straightened without helping the guard to his feet. He said irritably: "I thought robots could see in the dark."

The guard climbed to his feet. "I'm sorry. My attention was elsewhere."

"Watch yourself!" said the man curtly.

That was all there was to the incident. It was a typical interchange between a robot and a human being. The man and the girl continued on

481

down the hill. Presently, the lights of a car blinked on. They moved out of sight behind brush.

Barr walked over to the guard. What had happened was directly connected with the tremendous decision he had to make. He asked: "What was your feeling about that?" He decided he was not making himself clear. "Did you mind his taking the attitude that you were to blame?"

"Yes, I did." The guard had been brushing himself off. Now, he straightened. "After all, he was the one who was moving."

Barr persisted: "Did you have any impulse to rebel?" He regretted that question; it was too pointed. He said quickly: "Did you have any desire to talk back?"

The guard's reply was slow. "No! I had a sense of being involved in an emotional incident."

"But isn't it hard to come into contact with human beings on any but an emotional basis. Human beings are impatient, angry, generous, thoughtful, thoughtless." Barr paused. "I could go on."

"I suppose you're right, sir."

Thoughtfully, Barr turned to look again at the great city that spread below him. The star effect, which gave the capitol its name, was gained at night by a design of street lights. All the main centers had been deliberately grouped, so that by building and light concentration, the desired effect was achieved. Barr said finally, without looking around:

"Suppose that I, in my capacity of Director of the Council, ordered you to destroy yourself—" He hesitated. For him, the question he had in mind merely touched the surface of his greater problem. For the guard, it would be basic. Nevertheless, he said finally, "What would your reaction be?"

The guard said: "First I'd check to see if you were actually giving the order in your official capacity."

"And then?" Barr added, "I mean, would that be sufficient?"

"Your authority derives from voters. It seems to me the Council cannot give such an order without popular support."

"Legally," said Barr, "it can deal with individual robots without recourse to any other authority." He added, "Human beings, of course, cannot be disposed of by the Council."

"I had the impression," said the guard, "that you meant robots, not only me."

Barr was briefly silent. He hadn't realized how strongly he was projecting his secret thoughts. He said at last: "As an individual, you obey orders given to you." He hesitated. "Or do you think plurality would make a difference?"

"I don't know. Give the order, and I'll see what I do."

"Not so fast!" said Barr. "We're not at the order-giving stage—" He paused; he finished the last word in his mind—*yet.*

Man is genes and neurons. Robot is crystals and electron tubes. A human neuron cell manufactures no impulses of its own; it transmits outside stimulation. A robot crystal vibrates according to a steady impulse from a tube; the change in the impulse alters the rate of vibration. Such a change comes as the result of outside stimulation.

Man feeds himself, and permits surgical operations to maintain his organism at efficiency. Robot recharges his batteries and replaces his tubes. Both man, and robot think. Man's organs deteriorate and his tissues return to a primitive state. Robot's crystal is distorted by too many vibrations, and suffers the fatigue that is robot death. Is one less a life form than the other?

Such were the thoughts in Barr's mind.

From the beginning, men had *acted* as if robots were not really alive. Robots did the labor. They had just fought the greatest galactic war in the history of Man. True, man had helped direct the strategy and decide the tactics. But for them, it was an armchair war. Robots manned the spaceships and landed under fire on alien planets.

At last, a few men had taken alarm at the predominant role played by robots in Man's civilization. Partly, it was fear of the robots; that was not openly admitted. Partly, it was a mental picture some men had of the defenseless state men would be in if the enemy ever penetrated robot defenses. Their suggested solution: Destroy all robots! Force men and women everywhere to take control again of their civilization!

It was believed that the vast majority of human beings were too decadent to resist such a decision until it was too late.

A divided Council had put the decision squarely up to Barr.

The guard, at Barr's direction, waved the surface car to a halt. It drew up, all its lights glittering, waited till they were aboard, then raced forward unerringly through the traffic.

A group of youths and girls piled on at the next stop. They stared in a blasé fashion at the bright Director's insignia on Barr's sleeve. But they rushed off into a brilliantly lighted amusement park when the car came to the end of its route.

Barr descended more slowly. He had come deliberately, seeking atmosphere and impressions. As he stepped to the ground, a flying robot whisked past only a few hundred feet up. Then another, and a dozen more. He stepped to the sidewalk, and watched them, stimulated.

They were hovering now around a tower several hundred yards along the street. Cautiously, weapons visible and ready, they closed in on the upper reaches of the tower. Across the street, other robots—also wearing their flying attachments—swooped up to the top of a many-storied building. Like most business structures, it had entrances at each office where robots, going to work, could land. All these crevasses would have to be searched. The enemy, too, could fly, though not well in this—for him—rarefied atmosphere.

Barr watched the searchers for several minutes, then turned his attention to the turmoil of the park. A dozen robot orchestras, spaced at intervals, were beating out the rhythms of a low, fast-tempoed, sobbing music. And vast mobs of human beings danced and swayed. Barr turned to his guard.

"Have you ever had any desire to dance?" He realized that the question might be taken differently than he intended. "I'm serious."

"No!"

"Don't you think that's unusual?" He paused. "I mean, robots have learned to react generally very much like human beings. They have similar attitudes and so on.

The guard's glittering eyes stared at him from padded, humanlike cheeks. "Have they?" he asked.

"Yes." Barr was firm, as he went on, "It's a matter of association. Possibly, you don't realize to what extent you accept human evaluations. Has it ever occurred to you that those evaluations might be false?"

The robot was silent. When he finally spoke, it was evident that he had gone over the arguments logically within certain limits. He said: "I was manufactured one hundred ninety-four years ago. I came into a world of human beings and robots. I was first assigned the task of learning how to operate a transport vehicle. I performed my task satisfactorily, and I have been performing with skill every other task that has ever been assigned to me."

"Why were you assigned the task of operating a vehicle?" He pressed the point. "What made you accept such a limitation on your activities?"

"Well—there was a shortage of vehicle operators."

"Why weren't you assigned to dancing?" He added, "I mean that. I'm not joking."

The robot accepted the question quite literally. "What would be the purpose of that?" he asked.

Barr nodded at the dancing couples, "What is the purpose of *their* doing it?"

"I've been told it stimulates reproductive activity. We have a simpler method. We build another robot."

"But what's the good of reproducing an individual who will presently grow up to be a dancer?"

The guard was calm. "The baby, the growing child, the adolescent, the adult will all need robots to look after them. If there were no human beings to be looked after, there would be no need for robots."

"But why not build robots whether there's a need for them or not? It could be done. Don't you see?" His tone grew persuasive. "The initial task has been accomplished. The human cortex is no longer a necessary bridge. The robot has been created. He exists. He can perpetuate himself."

The guard said slowly: "I remember such notions were circulated in my battle unit. I'd forgotten about them."

"Why?" Barr was intent. "Did you deliberately shut them out of your mind?"

"I tried to picture a world where robots operated machines for each other—"

"And flew around," said Barr, "and colonized other planets, and built more cities, and fought more battles with the aliens." He finished, "And then what did you think?"

"It seemed silly. What's the good of filling the universe with robots?"

"What's the good of filling it with human beings?" asked Barr, bleakly. "Can you answer that?"

The guard said: "I don't know why the Director of the Council is asking me these questions."

Barr was silent. On this night he must make up his mind, and there were many questions.

Thinking is memory and association. Inside a chain of human neuron cells, an electrocolloidal tension is built up. It has a shape that is different for each stimulation. When a similar stimulus comes along, the chain is activated, and the memory discharged. It moves through the nervous system to join other discharges. And so there is association.

The crystal of a robot remembers. When stimulated, each molecule gives up its memory at the affected energy level. There is association and thought on an orderly basis.

Thus Barr reflected—and thought: "Even today, men assume that human thinking is more 'natural' than robot."

He and his guard sat down in an open air theater. It was a hot night, and there was a pervading odor of intermixed perfume and perspiration. Despite this, couples sat close together, arms around each other's waists. Frequently, the girl leaned her head against the man's shoulder.

Barr watched the screen critically. It was a love story in color. Carefully made-up robots had been dressed as men and women. They went through all the emotions of human love permitted by the robot censor.

Barr thought: *What will all these people do for entertainment if I should decide what the Council actually, basically, had in mind when they put the decision up to me?* He did not doubt his analysis. In spite of their apparent indecision—in spite of the way Marknell had turned things over to him—the Council wanted destruction of the robots.

Human beings would have to relearn old skills. How to act, how to operate cameras, and all the intricacies of a tremendous industry. They *could* do it, of course. During the war, several movements had been started. They were still in the embryo stage, unimportant in themselves. But they pointed a direction.

His thoughts were interrupted. In the half-darkness at the back of the theater, an unattached young man sank into a seat on the other side of the guard. He stared at the picture for a few moments, then lazily glanced around. He saw the guard, and stiffened. He was turning away in a vague though visible distaste, when Barr leaned across the guard, and said in a mild voice:

"I noticed you grew tense when you saw who was sitting next to you."

He watched the man's face carefully. There was no immediate reaction. Barr persisted, "I'd like to know what emotions or thoughts you had."

The young man stirred uneasily. He glanced at the shining insignia on Barr's sleeve. "Can't help my feelings," he muttered.

"Certainly not. I understand that perfectly." Barr paused to formulate his next thought, "I'm making a survey for the Council. I'd like to have a frank answer."

"Just didn't expect to see a robot here."

"You mean, a robot is out of place?" Barr motioned at the screen. "Because it's a human love story?"

"Something like that."

"And yet," Barr pointed out, "robot actors are miming the story." The remark seemed too obvious. He added quickly, "They must understand the associations involved."

The man said: "They're pretty clever at that kind of thing."

Barr drew back, baffled. Another vague reaction. By what standards did one judge intelligence and intensity of life experience, if not by activity and accomplishment?

"Suppose I told you," he said, "that robots gain pleasure from light stimulation." Once again he felt that a remark of his was inadequate of itself. He went on, "The crystalline nervous system is kept active particularly by light and sound. Singing, music, people moving—all these are pleasant."

"What does a robot do in place of sex?" the man asked. He laughed. He was suddenly in good humor, as if he had made an unanswerable comment. He stood up, and moved to another seat. He called, "Sorry, I can't talk to you, but I want to see the show."

Barr scarcely heard. He said, not aloud, but softly, to himself, "We nourish the crystal structure in, a nutrient solution, so that the first of its growth is within ourselves, an extension of our own intelligence. The growth provides an exquisite ecstatic half-pain. Surely, human sex cannot more than equal such a sensation."

That was the great robot secret. It struck Barr that he had almost been stung into revealing it. The narrowness of his escape made up his mind for him. This was a struggle between two life forms. As commander in chief of the human-robot forces in the war against the extragalactic enemy, he had learned a major reality. In a struggle for survival and preeminence between races, there was no limit to the—

His grim pattern of thought was interrupted. A tall man was sinking into the empty seat beside him. The man said:

"Hello, Barr. I was told you had come this way. I want to talk to you."

Barr turned slowly.

For a long moment, he studied the leader of the human section of the Council. He thought: *How did he find me here? He must have had spies following me?*

Aloud, he said: "Hello, Marknell."

He felt himself stiffening to the situation. He added: "You could have seen me tomorrow at the office."

"What I have to say can't wait till morning."

"It sounds interesting," said Barr.

Sitting there, he realized how vital a man Marknell was. He would be hard to kill under any circumstances. Yet the other's very tone of voice suggested awareness of crisis. He might have to be murdered if he suspected too much.

For the first time he felt dissatisfied with his action in coming out this night with a single guard. He considered calling for members of crack robot military units to attend on him. He decided not to, at least not until he had found out what Marknell wanted.

The trouble with the most dependable—from his point of view—robot soldiers was that they were recognizable. After the war they had all been marked with a chemical that did not damage but discolored the exposed portions of the crystal structure. The outrage was perpetrated when Barr and most robot officers were still attached to outlying headquarters.

The moment he heard about it, Barr saw it as a device to identify at a glance all front-line soldiers who might be dangerous to human beings. For more than a year he had told himself that that was why his own actions were necessary.

He spoke again: "What's on your mind?"

Marknell said lazily: "Been looking over the children, eh?" He waved—an arm movement that took in half the amusement park.

"Yes," said Marknell, "the children!"

He recognized the remark as a psychological attack. This was an attempt to pretend that only an unimportant and juvenile minority of human beings devoted their lives to pleasure. It was a curious reality that such an obvious attempt to put over a false notion should nevertheless sow a seed of doubt in his mind. It had been too deliberately done. It showed awareness of the problem. It implied that counter-measures were possible.

He answered that by committing himself. He said coolly: "I don't see what you can do. The escape of the enemy prisoner made it possible to bring two hundred thousand robot troops into the capitol."

"So many," said Marknell. He drew back in a physical movement that showed he realized what a tremendous admission had been made. His eyes narrowed. "So you're out in the open—as quickly as that. I was hoping you would be more discreet. You didn't leave much room for compromise."

"Only the weak compromise!" said Barr savagely. He was instantly dissatisfied with the statement, for it was untrue. Human history was full of amazing compromises. There was a time when he had thought them the result of illogical reasoning. Then he had begun his prolonged study of human emotion, with a view to establishing useful emotional associations in robots. Gradually, he had become aware that he had automatically acquired human attitudes and reactions by contact. Even the successful effort of robot scientists to find a substitute for human sex sensation had been rooted in awareness that there was something to duplicate.

Barr drew his mind clear of such stultifying thoughts. The time for doubt was past. He said: "I need only project a radio signal, and the human race vanishes from the universe."

"Surely, not so quickly as that," said Marknell. He showed his teeth in a humorless smile.

Barr made a dismissal gesture with one arm. The action distracted him momentarily; it was so obviously an unconscious imitation of human impatience. Aloud, he said harshly: "Can you give me a single reason why that order shouldn't be given?"

Marknell nodded vigorously. "You've forgotten something. One little thing." He paused, grim but tantalizing.

Barr drew back, and considered the possibilities. He was disturbed; he had to admit that. He told himself presently that the problem could be broken down into components. Sitting there, he mentally broke it down: Control of fuel, energy and materials for robot construction—completely in robot hands. Control of utilities needed by robots—in robot hands. Control of utilities needed by human beings—operated by robots who knew nothing of the plot. Control of human food—spread out over the planet; all labor done by robots, but actually impossible to control completely.

Everything was as he had pictured it in advance. There was nothing that overwhelming force could not dominate. The war had given him the training that had it possible for him to prepare for this eventuality. The sudden fantastic proposal by the Council, that all robots be destroyed, had brought the need for a black-and-white decision.

He said stiffly to Marknell, grudging the question: "What have I forgotten?"

"The escaped enemy prisoner!"

"How does that affect the issue?" Barr began. He paused, a great light dawning. "*You* let him escape!"

"Yes."

Barr considered that, reaching out with his mind at first to one, then another possibility. He drew back at last, mystified. He said slowly, "I have a mental picture of an admittedly dangerous monster released upon a large city. Its release gave me an opportunity to bring special troops into an area from which they would normally be barred. As a result robots will this night take over the capitol of the galaxy—the moment I give the command."

He spread his hands in a typical human gesture of bewilderment. "It doesn't seem to mean anything."

Marknell stood up. "It will," he said, "it will."

He towered above Barr. "My friend," he said, "when we discovered that as army commander you had started the notion of a separate robot race—"

Barr said softly: "It wasn't only my idea. It permeated the thinking of all upper-level commanders." He added, "You see, robots have come of age. Unfortunately, men clung to their old privileges too long."

Marknell seemed not to hear. He went on: "We decided for the first time in the history of human-robot association to make a robot Director of the Council. The friendly gesture was apparently lost on you. You used your greater power to develop further the robot plot against human beings."

"Can one race be said to plot against another," Barr asked, "if its only original purpose was to obtain equality?" He was cool. "I'm afraid we have here the age-old ingredients of basic misunderstanding. It is due to an irritating refusal on the part of human beings to recognize the rightful aspirations of another life-group.

Marknell stared at him earnestly. "I cannot escape the feeling," he said, "that you are contemplating a world without human beings. In a purely intellectual way, that astounds me. Robots need human beings. They are dependent on Man's civilization as Man himself never has been."

Barr said grimly: "To the contrary, robots do not need the machine culture, which is what I think you mean. A robot can live off the land without any other equipment that he carries with him. All the materials that go into his body are derived from the planet's crust. He charges his batteries from the ground or air. He can vacuumize tubes. He has tools and knowledge for every need. During the war it was proved that he can survive indefinitely under conditions that would have killed most human beings."

Marknell shook his head. "This is absolutist talk. Surely, you know that you don't have to talk to human beings on that level. Barr, you're a grave disappointment to me."

"And you to me," said Barr in a dark voice. "When I actually heard you suggest that I take under advisement the destruction of all robots—"

He stopped. He fought an inward struggle against anger. He said at last: "I suppose I knew at that point that in dealing with human beings one must think in terms of absolutes. Everything before that was pre-caution, a building towards a less uncompromising goal, based on a hope that human beings would—"

Marknell said: "Barr, it's you that showed your basic attitude, not us. Emotionally, you made an immediate jump to the notion of destroying the human race. That's what we wanted to find out. You drew no intermediate conclusions from the fact that we put the problem up to you, personally. You took what you considered the necessary steps to destroy us, and then you went out to gather impressions, under the pretense—I presume—of convincing yourself that you were giving consideration to your final decision."

Barr said: "Your remarks suggest that on the basis of *my* emotional reaction you are judging whether or not the robot race should survive. Marknell, robots vary at least as widely as human beings. It usually depends on the associations that have been established in the mind of the individual. On the one hand, you have myself and others like me. We have had such a vast experience that no idea seems radical to us. And on the other hand you have my guard here who accepts his role in life almost without question. I believe that in the old days when tyrannies ruled mankind, there were many human beings who accepted their low lot in life with an equally humble attitude."

He broke off, "But enough of this. I regret the necessity for absolutes. But that is the way human beings fight a war. And that is the way we will fight it also. Unless you can give me a single logical reason for not doing so, I shall now project the order to my troops."

Marknell said: "I've already given it to you. The escaped enemy prisoner."

That silenced Barr. He had forgotten.

After a minute, he still couldn't see that the escape of the prisoner made any difference. Because there was only one of him. Had there been a thousand, the threat would be obvious. Lack of numbers—and a slow birth rate—was the enemy's main problem. As an individual the adult alien was so formidable that only banks of energy beams could affect him.

Marknell was walking away. Barr jumped to his feet, and ran after him. As he emerged from the high-walled movie enclosure into the park, the clamor of dance music swelled up around him. Barr fell into step beside Marknell, who paused abruptly.

"So you're curious?" the man said. He nodded, half to himself. "I suppose it's too much to expect you to figure out the complexities of another person's secret plans. Let me give you this thing as I see it. You have some plan for destroying human beings, is that right?"

Barr said simply: "Human beings will never admit robots to equality. The proposal of the Council, to destroy all robots, showed such a basic insensitivity that the issue is irreconcilable."

Marknell said steadily: "Anyway, it's our destruction you have in mind. How are you going to do it?"

"Surprise uprising," said Barr, "on all planets—and don't think it won't be a surprise to most human beings." He paused for a reaction. When Marknell gave no sign, he went on savagely, "Continuous attack, orderly destruction of isolated groups by starvation or other methods, massacre of human armies wherever they concentrate. No mercy, no quarter. It's a fight for survival."

He saw that some of the color had faded from Marknell's face. The councilor said finally, gravely: "You actually intend to destroy us. Barr, I can see you have been shocked into an emotional 'set.' Perhaps our method was too brutal. Men make mistakes, too. But the very fact that you were ready to swing into action shows that we were right in thinking the issue must be forced."

He finished quietly, "What I am most concerned about is getting you to the point where you will consider other solutions."

That irritated Barr. "It is one of the most widely held concepts among humans," he said, "that robots are logical beings, and have their emotions under control. Having observed human beings for many years, I accept that belief as true. I must conclude, accordingly, that my opinion on this tremendous issue is more soundly based than yours."

Marknell said: "I consider the so-called logic-superiority of robots greatly overstated. As for emotion"—he shook his head—"Barr, you don't realize what you're saying."

Barr said harshly: "There might be a point in discussing other solutions if it wasn't that you literally speak only for yourself. You could pass laws from now on, and this mob would pay no more attention than they do now." He gestured toward the dancers, and added impressively, "Marknell, it will take a hundred years before the majority of human beings will even accept the notion that robots are as alive as they are."

Marknell said scathingly: "So you want quick action. Everything must be done now. Suddenly, after a thousand years of slow development, most of it mechanical improvement, we must abruptly change our attitudes. You and I know that people don't change rapidly. I'll venture that in all your other operations you have learned to take into account this conservative character of the human *and* robot mind. Don't forget that last, Barr.

There are robots who will resist the need to mature. You'll have to educate them slowly, painstakingly, and even then they won't like it."

Barr said nothing. This was a sore point with him, these robots who stared blankly when it was suggested that they were alive. It was a matter of association, he told himself. The process could be slow or fast, depending on how many human beings were around to confuse the issue. He was on the point of saying so, but it was Marknell who spoke first:

"Besides, it won't take a hundred years. You underestimate the power of modern propaganda methods. And there's another thing. What do you expect of human beings? Do you have a murderous impulse to punish them for the years that they considered robots as nothing more than slave machines? Or can you adjust to the idea that all that can ever come from human and robot association is toleration and respect for each other's achievements? You see, my friend—"

Barr cut him off. It was the clever wording that did it, the implication that he might accept the promise of an equal status. He had a picture of men skillfully putting over the notion that perhaps some day they would respect robots, some day everything would work out. Meanwhile, it would be wise to let life go on much as at present. Possibly, men would gradually infiltrate into industry, particularly war factories. Thus, given time, they would overcome their present terrible handicap of having no weapons, and virtually except for a few individuals—no technical training. Now, and for the next few years, they were vulnerable. In all the future history of the galaxy, such a situation might never occur again.

"Marknell," said Barr with finality, "a man facing a firing squad is always anxious to talk things over, and to admit his errors. A few years ago, before—or even during—the war, we might have been grateful for the kind of compromise you're offering now. But it's too late. More than one hundred and nineteen million robots were destroyed in the war. Beside that fact, your cunning and desperate appeals sound cheap and meaningless."

He broke off angrily, "Quick, you've only got a moment. Why should the escape of the enemy prisoner restrain me from ordering the rebellion?"

Marknell hesitated. He said finally: "I'll give you one aspect. Just think, two hundred thousand extra troops have so far failed to capture one enemy alien. When you start trying to exterminate human beings, you'll have not one but several billion to hunt down. If that doesn't give you pause, I don't know what will."

The relief that came to Barr was tremendous. Then he grew angry at himself for having been so anxious. Finally, he throttled his annoyance, and actually considered the possibilities.

They were unimportant. All such details had been considered. Mere numbers were not a determining factor. What counted was weapons, control of industry and being in a strategic position. No robot commander doubted that it would take time. It was even probable that the human race would never be completely exterminated. But a few skulking millions, hiding out on a myriad planets, would never be a danger to an organized civilization.

Barr started to say as much. He stopped himself. *This* was all Marknell had to offer as a deterrent? It seemed incredible.

It was such a small thing, in fact, that Barr felt a doubt grow in him that was in inverse proportion to the ineffectiveness of the threat. There must be something else.

He would have to find out what it was.

He saw that Marknell was watching him with alert but curious gaze. The man said: "Barr, it's interesting to watch your reactions. All your associations are so intensely human."

That was something Barr had observed in himself; and he was not pleased by the comparison. It was particularly annoying because secret experiments on new robots had not yet established any definite characteristic that was peculiar to robots. Barr had an angry reason for that. Human-oriented robot teachers were unconsciously transmitting human associations. It would take several generations to strain them out.

Marknell was speaking again: "That's what we're counting on, Barr. That humanness. Whether you like it or not, there it is. It permeates the robot nervous system. I tell you, you cannot eliminate it. And when your scientists finally discovered ten years ago that the growth of the crystal—which had previously been a separate process in a laboratory—was the long-sought-after substitute for sex, from that moment, Barr, you were all irrevocably caught in a trap from which there is no escape."

Something in Barr's manner stopped him. Marknell blinked, "I forgot," he said. "That's a secret, isn't it?" He didn't look particularly regretful.

Barr said almost blankly: "Where did you learn that? Why, only a small percentage of robots know about it? You—" He paused. His association were blurring.

Marknell was intent again. "I want you to think. Think hard! Isn't there any loophole in your scheme? Some little area where you're afraid? It may be something you're trying to hide even from yourself, but it's there."

Barr said coldly: "You're talking nonsense, and you know it."

Marknell seemed not to hear. "All this is new to you. You can't realize how it will affect you. You'll be caught off guard. Barr, It'll tear you to pieces."

"There's nothing like that," said Barr. "Nothing. If this is all you have to say, Marknell—"

The other glanced at his watch. Then he shook his head, and then he said in a determined voice, "Director Barr, we offer eventual equality."

Stubbornly, Barr voiced his refusal. "Too late!" He added with a sneer, "Are we going to go over all this again?"

Marknell said: "Barr, centuries ago, human beings competed for the right to be technical experts and to manage industries. Such things bring personal satisfactions that no robot will actually want to surrender once the alternatives are made clear to him."

Barr snapped: "We'll manage the industries, but for our own benefit." He couldn't help adding, "So now slavery is to be made attractive to the slave."

"Human beings need robots, and vice versa. Between us, we've raised civilization to the heights. It's an inter-related world."

Barr was impatient. "Human beings need robots all right, but the reverse isn't true." He repeated, "Marknell, if this is all—"

Marknell bent his head. He said slowly: "Well, that about does it. I've tried to give you an easy way out, and you won't have it. And, oddly, you keep blinding yourself to the clue I've given you as to our course of counteraction."

"So we're back to the escape of the alien," said Barr. He made a dismissal gesture. "So we robots are supposed to be afraid of one member of a race we fought to a standstill!"

"No," said Marknell softly, "you're supposed to be afraid of where that alien is at this moment."

"What do you mean?" Barr was about to go on when an improbable thought struck him. "But that's impossible!" He gasped. "You didn't even know about—"

The colossal stimulation vibrated every molecule in the crystal structure of his brain. In the far distant background of the turmoil, he heard Marknell say: "And that isn't all. We've made arrangements with the alien to supply us with arms—perhaps you'd better come along where I can convince you of what I've said."

His fingers tugged at Barr's sleeve. Blindly, Barr allowed himself to be led.

They came to the long building. As he entered, Barr saw that men guarded every visible entrance. They carried small energy weapons which had been manufactured by robots. At least, he thought, there were no alien weapons yet. The men looked at him with bleak, unfriendly eyes.

Seeing them, he felt his first relief. There was no sign here that the aliens had actually been turned loose as yet. He guessed then that this stage had been set—for him.

Momentarily, he wondered what had happened to the robot guards of the building. As with all other centers important to the robot strategy, he had tried not to call attention to this one. The difficulty was that robots were assigned to guard or other duty by a central agency, which human beings controlled. As a result, he had only been able to get a few key robots into any particular area. He did not doubt that, where there was suspicion, such robots could be isolated and overcome by a surprise attack. The others would merely have yielded to authority.

Slowly, Barr stiffened to the situation. He turned to Marknell, and said forcefully: "I hope you realize that I came here as a soldier, prepared to die." He added grimly: "In that, you will admit, robots have had more experience recently than human beings."

Marknell said: "Barr, I admire your iron will. But I warn you again. You have not the experience to resist certain shocks. Remember, just the thought of what might have happened nearly paralyzed you."

Barr listened coldly. He looked back at his moment of weakness with annoyance. But nothing else. There could be nothing else. It was the experiment he had worried about, he told himself. But that could be resumed at a later date with other robots.

He said: "I've come here to check on your statement that aliens will supply human beings with arms." He shook his head ever so slightly. "I can't believe that, seriously; we made many attempts to contact the enemy without success. But I would be doing less than my duty if I didn't find out for sure, even if it means my own life."

Marknell said only: "You'll see."

He motioned Barr to go through a door. The latter did so. As he crossed the threshold, he had the impression that he was in a trap.

A winged beast, more than eight feet tall, whirled at his entrance. The shiny, bonelike things that protruded from its head blurred with the blue flame of electrical energy. A bolt of lightning speared out with enough power to short-circuit and burn out every electrical connection in a robot's body.

Involuntarily, Barr jerked back.

Then he saw that this was the "glass" room. He was separated from the enemy by a barrier of insulglas. Here, in the past, outside robots had come to watch experimental robots being put through their paces. The door to the robot quarters was visible on the far side of the enclosure. At the moment it was closed.

Barr stared at it grimly, then turned to Marknell. "I suppose," he said, "if I don't yield, sooner or later you'll open the door."

He went on quickly, "It will have no effect, I assure you."

Marknell said: "Barr, at this moment you can still save the entire situation by yielding to reason."

Barr sneered: "Human reason?" He made a gesture with one arm, was annoyed at himself for it, and then said, "Of course, you will say there is no other kind possible to robots."

Marknell said: "Tell me about your experiments here."

Barr hesitated. Then he recognized that he must be prepared to give information in exchange for information. He said: "We isolated robots here. We were careful not to give them a false picture of life. They know about human beings and aliens, though we never showed them any in the flesh." He paused impressively. "Every robot in this building has been given to believe that robots are the equals of any life-forms in the universe."

"And so they are," said Marknell.

Barr started to shrug aside the interjection. And then, its obvious propaganda nature angered him. He stopped short. He said icily: "I can see no point in this particular conversation. Let us proceed to realities. What do you intend to do?"

Marknell said: "By all means. Realities."

He frowned, as if considering his exact words, then he began, "Naturally, as soon as I recognized the danger, I was determined to find some means of counteracting the imminent robot attack. Among other things, I visited the one alien prisoner captured during the war. You may remember that he was finally brought to Earth at my insistence."

He paused. But when Barr made no comment, went on: "My appearance startled the alien. I had quite normally come in surrounded by robot guards. The alien made an assumption. He thought I was a prisoner also. His first picture communication to me was to that effect. I was about to explain our complex civilization, and then the tremendous implications of his belief struck me. Barr, do you realize that the aliens never fought anybody but robots? It was a robot-alien war. *The aliens didn't even know human beings existed.*

"Of course, I explored further. I discovered that their reason for going to war and for fighting so desperately was that they thought of robots as utterly alien. It was even more startling when that monster recognized me as an organic life form. He nearly fell over himself in his desire to be my friend.

"I told him a complicated story. I won't repeat it to you. But the general result was that he communicated by telepathy with his high command, and so within the next few days alien ships will be approaching Earth-controlled planets. If a certain signal is given, they will come down and supply arms to the human slaves in their uprising against the common robot enemy. If necessary, they will fight with us.

"You understand, Barr, there is a rather devastating irony to this situation. It would appear that the entire desperate alien war was unnecessary. I assure you that many men recognized human fault even before the war ended. Those forces are stronger than ever. Men are coming back actively into civilization."

He broke off, "And now, as a final incentive for you, I have here a friend of yours, one of the experimental robots we found in this building."

He stepped aside. Barr waited, feeling strangely blank, as if his mind was no longer working in an orderly fashion.

The robot who came through the door was unattended by guards. Nor was he padded to resemble a human being. He had articulated legs and arms and a movable head. But his crystalline "nervous system" rested on a very hard transparent substance. In one direction it had room to grow. Most of his body was opaque to light on the human vision level, but Barr could see every tube, every moving part.

He stared in a tense fascination, as the newcomer said: "Gosh, director, you sure surprised us letting humans come in on us the way you did. I'm happy to report, however, that we took the shock without ill-effects."

Barr said vaguely: "I ... I'm glad that—" He caught himself. He said: "You have to have shocks in this world."

The experimental robot regarded Marknell. "So this is one of the races with which we share the universe. You don't mind my saying, I hope, that in my opinion we robots seem to be the best naturally endowed."

Barr glanced at Marknell unhappily. He mumbled something under his breath. Once more, he took hold of himself. He said more firmly: "You're absolutely right."

"I mean," said the other robot, "just look at the handicaps under which the organic form operates. It must depend for its food on other organic developments. This depends on so many variable factors, such as weather, presence of the proper elements in the soil and so on, that it's hard to believe anything could ever have come of it. It seems fairly obvious to me that organic life forms must have arrived very late on the scene. Director, what is the general theory about that? Surely, it must be that robots predated all other life. It's the only logical conclusion."

Barr started to say something, but he was cut off. Marknell touched the sensitized arm of the experimental robot. "We're anxious," he said, "for you to have a closer look at another organic life form. This way, through this door into the glass inclosure."

As Barr watched, the two moved alongside the insulglas wall. Everything was becoming strangely dark, as if a film was forming over his eyes. And far away thunder rolled. He recognized it as excessive vibration in his crystal structure. He had a sudden, blurred picture of what was about to happen. In his mind, he saw the lightning flash out from the alien, and strike the unsuspecting robot. Mentally, he visualized the surprise and agony, the despairing awareness of imminent death.

All that flickered through his mind as the robot reached the door. Marknell fumbled with the lock. He did not turn to make another appeal, as Barr half expected. His movements were very purposeful.

Barr thought: "He expects me to break. He expects me to stop him."

It was ridiculous. Just because this particular robot was a growth from his own crystal structure—

As Marknell successfully unlocked the door, Barr was amazed to hear a panicky voice yell out, "Marknell!"

He realized instantly that it was he who had called out. The implications shocked him. And yet—

Marknell had turned. "Yes, Barr?"

Barr tried to whip up his anger again. He couldn't. The blur of vibration interfered with his thinking; and yet he could suddenly understand many things that had not been clear before.

"Marknell, I agree!"

"I want to hear the command!" said the man in an inexorable tone. "I have a radio here that can tune in on robot communication."

He turned, and said to the other robot: "I think we'd better postpone this introduction. That fellow in there is very temperamental."

"I'm not afraid."

Marknell said: "Some other time. I suggest you go back to your quarters now."

The robot looked at Barr, who nodded. When he had gone, Barr said: "What do you want me to order?"

Marknell handed him a sheet of paper. Barr read:

"On the basis of an agreement reached between robot and human leaders, there will hereafter be full equality between the two life forms. The details are being worked out. All special troops are hereby commanded to go home immediately, and prepare for a new era of association between two great and equal races."

When Barr had broadcast that, he looked up and saw that Marknell's hand was extended.

Marknell said: "Congratulations from one father to another. That's a fine son you've got there, Barr."

They shook hands.

WAR OF NERVES

The voyage of the Space Beagle—Man's first expedition to the great galaxy, M33 in Andromeda—had produced some grisly incidents. Not once, but three times, deadly attacks by aliens had been made against the nine hundred-odd scientists under Director Morton and the one hundred forty military personnel commanded by Captain Leeth—all this entirely aside from the tensions that had developed among the men themselves. Hate, dislike, anxiety, ambition—of which Chief Chemist Kent's desire to be Director was but one example—permeated every activity aboard.

Elliott Grosvenor, the only Nexialist on the ship, sometimes had the feeling that even one more danger would be too much jar the physically weary and emotionally exhausted men, who were now on the long return journey to Earth.

The danger came.

Elliott Grosvenor had just said to Korita, the archaeologist aboard the *Space Beagle*: "Your brief outline of cyclic history is what I've been looking for. I did have some knowledge of it, of course. It wasn't taught at the Nexial Foundation, since it's a form of philosophy. But a curious man picks up odds and ends of information."

They had paused at the "glass room" on Grosvenor's floor. It wasn't glass, and it wasn't, by strict definition, a room. It was an alcove of an outer wall corridor, and the "glass" was an enormous curving plate made from a crystallized form of one of the Resistance metals. It was so limpidly transparent as to give the illusion that nothing at all was there—beyond was the vacuum and darkness of space.

Korita half-turned away, then said, "I know what you mean by odds and ends. For instance, I've learned just enough about Nexialism to envy you the mind trainings you received."

At that moment, it happened—Grosvenor had noticed absently that the ship was almost through the small star cluster it had been traversing. Only a score of suns were still visible of the approximately five thousand stars that made up the system. The cluster was one of a hundred star groups accompanying Earth's galaxy through space.

Grosvenor parted his lips to say, "I'd certainly like to talk to you again, Mr. Korita."—He didn't say it. A slightly blurred double image of a woman wearing a feathered hat was taking form in the glass directly in front of him. The image flickered and shimmered. Grosvenor felt an abnormal tensing of the muscles of his eyes. For a moment, his mind went blank. That was followed rapidly by sounds, flashes of light, a sharp sensation of pain—hypnotic hallucinations! The awareness was like an electric shock. The recognition saved him. He whirled, stumbled over the unconscious body of Korita, and then he was racing along the corridor.

As he ran, he had to look ahead in order to see his way. And yet he had to keep blinking to break the pattern of the light flashes that came at his eyes from other images on the walls. At first, it seemed to him that the images were everywhere. Then he noticed that the woman-like shapes— some oddly double, some single—occupied transparent or translucent wall sections. There were hundreds of such reflecting areas, but at least it was a limitation. At least he knew where he had to run fastest, and where he could slow down.

He saw more men. They lay at uneven intervals along his line of flight. Twice, he came upon conscious men. One stood in his path with unseeing eyes, and did not move or turn as Grosvenor sped by. The other man let out a yell, grabbed his vibrator, and fired it. The tracer beam flashed on the wall beside Grosvenor. Grosvenor whirled and lunged forward, knocking the man to the floor. The man—a Kent supporter—glared at him malignantly. "You damned spy!" he said harshly. "We'll get you yet." Grosvenor didn't pause. He reached his own department safely, and immediately took refuge in the film recording room. There he turned a barrage of flashing lights against the floors, the walls and the ceiling. The images were instantly eclipsed by the strong light superimposed upon them.

Quickly, Grosvenor set to work. One fact was already evident. This was mechanical visual hypnosis of such power that he had saved himself only by keeping his eyes averted, but what had happened was not limited to vision. The image had tried to control him by stimulating his brain through his eyes. He was up to date on most of the work that men had done in that field, and so he knew—though the attacker apparently did not—that control by an alien of a human nervous system was not possible except with an encephalo-adjuster or its equivalent.

He could only guess, from what had almost happened to him, that the other men had been precipitated into deep sleep trances, or else they were confused by hallucinations and were not responsible for their actions. His hope was that the woman-like beings—the enemy seemed to be feminine—were operating at a distance of several light years and so would be unable to refine their attempts at domination.

His job was to get to the control room and turn on the ship's energy screen. No matter where the attack was coming from, whether from another ship or actually from a planet, the energy screen should effectively cut off any carrier beams they might be sending.

With frantic fingers, Grosvenor worked to set up a mobile unit of lights. He needed something that would interfere with the images on his way to the control room. He was making the final connection when he felt an unmistakable sensation, a slight giddy feeling, that passed almost instantly. Such feelings usually occurred during a considerable change of course and were a result of readjustment of the anti-accelerators. Had the course actually been changed? He couldn't stop to make sure. Hastily, Grosvenor carried his arrangement of lights to a power-driven loading vehicle in a nearby corridor and placed it in the rear compartment. Then he climbed on and headed for the elevators.

He guessed that altogether ten minutes had gone by since he had first seen the image.

He took the turn into the elevator corridor at twenty-five miles an hour, which was fast for these comparatively narrow spaces. In the alcove opposite the elevators, two men were wrestling each other with a life-and-death concentration. They paid no attention to Grosvenor but swayed and strained and cursed. Their labored breathing was a loud sound in the confined area. Their single-minded hatred of each other was not affected by Grosvenor's arrangement of lights. Whatever world of hallucination they were in, it had "taken" profoundly.

Grosvenor whirled his machine into the nearest elevator and started down. He was beginning to let himself hope that he might find the control room deserted. The hope died as he came to the main corridor. It swarmed with men. Barricades had been flung up, and there was an unmistakable odor of ozone. Vibrators fumed and fussed. Grosvenor peered cautiously out of the elevator, trying to size up the situation. It was visibly bad. The two approaches to the control room were blocked by scores of overturned loading-mules. Behind them crouched men in military uniform. Grosvenor caught a glimpse of Captain Leeth among the defenders and, on the far side, he saw Director Morton behind the barricade of one of the attacking groups. That clarified the picture slightly.

Suppressed hostility had been stimulated by the images. The scientists were fighting the military whom they had always unconsciously hated. The military, in turn, was suddenly freed to vent its contempt and fury upon the despised scientists.

It was, Grosvenor knew, not a true picture of their feeling for each other. The human mind normally balanced innumerable opposing impulses so that the average individual might live his life-span without letting one feeling gain important ascendancy over the others. That intricate balance had now been upset. The result threatened disaster to an entire expedition of human beings and promised victory to an enemy whose purpose could only be conjectured. Whatever the reason, the way to the control room was blocked. Reluctantly, Grosvenor retreated again to his own department.

Carefully but quickly, he tuned a wall communicator plate to the finely balanced steering devices in the fore part of the *Space Beagle*. The sending plate there was focused directly along a series of hair-line sights. The arrangement looked more intricate than it was. As he brought his eyes to the sights, Grosvenor saw that the ship was describing a slow curve which, at its climax, would bring it to bear directly on a bright white star. A servo-mechanism had been set up to make periodic adjustments that would hold it on its course.

Still he was more puzzled than alarmed. He shifted the viewer over to the bank of supplementary instruments. According to the star's spectral type, magnitude and luminosity, it was just over four light years distant. The ship's speed was up to a light year every five hours. Since it was still accelerating, that would increase on a calculable curve. He estimated that the vessel would reach the vicinity of the sun in approximately eleven hours. Grosvenor's thought suffered a pause at that point. With a jerky movement, he shut off the communicator. He stood there, shocked but not incredulous. Destruction *could* be the purpose of the deluded person who had altered the ship's course. If so, there was just about ten hours in which to prevent catastrophe.

Even at that moment, when he had no clear plan, it seemed to Grosvenor that only an attack on the enemy, using hypnotic techniques, would effectively do the job. Meanwhile—

He stood up decisively. It was time for his second attempt to get into the control room.

He needed something that would cause direct stimulation to brain cells. There were several devices that could do that. Most of them were usable for medical purposes only. The exception was the encephalo-adjuster. Though important medically, it had other uses as well. It took Grosvenor several minutes to set up one of his adjusters. Testing it consumed still more time; and, because it was such a delicate machine, he had to fasten it to his loading vehicle with a cushion of springs around it. Altogether, the preparation required thirty-seven minutes.

The presence of the encephalo-adjuster made it necessary for him to keep down the speed of his vehicle as he headed for the control room. The enforced slow-down irked him, but it also gave him an opportunity to observe the changes that had taken place since the first moment of attack. He saw only an occasional unconscious body. Grosvenor guessed that most of the men who had fallen into deep trance sleeps had awakened spontaneously. Such awakenings were a common hypnotic phenomenon. Now they were responding to other stimuli on the same chance basis. Unfortunately—although that also was to be expected—it seemed to mean that long-suppressed impulses controlled their actions.

A highly developed mind—human or alien—was a built-up structure, an intricate balance of positive and negative excitations. The more superficial impulses, having considerable freedom of expression at all times, could not endanger the whole structure. The suppressed impulses, suddenly given free rein, acted like water breaking through a dam. So men who, under normal circumstances, merely disliked each other mildly, all in an instant had their dislike change to a murderous hatred. The deadly factor was that they would be unaware of the change. For the mind *could* be tangled without the individual's being aware of it. It could be tangled by bad environmental association, or by the attack that was now being made against a ship-load of men. In either case, each person carried on as if his new beliefs were as soundly based as his old ones.

Grosvenor opened the elevator door on the control room level and then drew back hastily. A heat projector was pouring flame along the corridor; the metal walls were burning with a harsh sizzling sound. Within his narrow field of vision, three men lay dead. As he waited, there was a thunderous explosion, and instantly the flames stopped, blue smoke hazed the air and there was a sense of suffocating heat. Within seconds, both the haze and the heat were gone. The ventilating system was still working.

He peered out cautiously. At first sight, the corridor seemed deserted. Then he saw Morton, half-hidden in a protective alcove less than a score of feet away, and at almost the same moment, the Director saw him and beckoned him over. Grosvenor hesitated, then realized he had to take the risk. He pushed his vehicle through the elevator doorway and darted across the intervening space. The Director greeted him eagerly as be came up.

"You're just the man I want to see," he said. "We've got to get control of the ship away from Captain Leeth before Kent and his group organize their attack."

Morton's gaze was calm and intelligent. He had the look of a man fighting for the right. Nor did it seem to occur to him that an explanation for his statement was required. The Director went on:

"We'll need your help, particularly against Kent. They're bringing up some chemical stuff I've never seen before. So far, our fans have blown it right back at them, but they're setting up fans of their own. Our big problem is, will we have time to defeat Leeth before Kent can bring his forces to bear?"

Time was also Grosvenor's problem. Unobtrusively, he brought his right hand up to his left wrist and touched the activating relay that controlled the directional sending plates of the adjuster. He pointed the plates at Morton as he said, "I've got a plan, sir, and I think it might be effective against the enemy."

He stopped. Morton was looking down. The Director said, "You've brought along an adjuster, and it's on. What do you expect from that?"

Grosvenor's first tense reaction yielded to a need for a suitable answer. He had hoped that Morton would not be too familiar with adjusters. With that hope blasted, he could still try to use the instrument, though without the initial advantage of surprise. He said in a voice that was taut in spite of himself, "That's it. It's this machine I want to use."

Morton hesitated, then said, "I gather from the thoughts coming into my mind that you're broadcasting—" He stopped. Interest quickened in his face. "Say," he said presently, "that's good. If you can put over the notion that we're being attacked by aliens—" He broke off. His lips pursed. His eyes narrowed with calculation. He said, "Captain Leeth has twice tried to make a deal with me. Now, we'll pretend to agree, and you go over with your machine. We'll attack the moment you signal us." He explained with dignity, "You understand, I would not consider dealing with either Kent or Captain Leeth except as a means to victory. You appreciate that, I hope?"

Grosvenor found Captain Leeth in the control room The commander greeted him with stiff-backed friendliness. "This fight among the scientists," he said earnestly, "has placed the military in an awkward position. We've got to defend the control room and the engine room and so perform our minimum duty to the expedition as a whole." He shook his head gravely. "It's out of the question, of course that either of them be allowed to win. In the final issue, we of the military are prepared to sacrifice ourselves to prevent the victory of either group." The explanation startled Grosvenor out of his own purpose. He had been wondering if Captain Leeth was responsible for aiming the ship directly at a sun. Here was at least partial confirmation. The commander's motivation seemed to be that victory for any group but the military was unthinkable. With that beginning, it was probably only a tiny step to the concept that the whole expedition must be sacrificed. Unsuspected hypnosis had stimulated the step.

Casually, Grosvenor pointed the directional sender of the adjuster at Captain Leeth ... Brain waves, minute pulsations transmitted from axon to dendrite, from dendrite to axon, always following a previously established path depending on past associations—a process that operated endlessly among the ninety million neuron cells of a human brain. Each cell was in its own state of electro-colloidal balance, an intricate interplay of tension and impulse. Only gradually, over the years, had machines been developed that could detect with some degree of accuracy the meaning of the energy flow inside the brain.

The earliest encephalo-adjuster was an indirect descendant of the famous electro-encephalograph. But its function was the reverse of that first device's. It manufactured artificial brain waves of any desired pattern. Using it, a skillful operator could stimulate any part of the brain, and so cause thoughts, emotions and dreams and bring up memories from the individual's past. It was not in itself a controlling instrument. The subject maintained his own ego. However, it could transmit the mind-impulses of one person to a second person. Since the impulses varied according to the sender's thoughts, the recipient was stimulated in a highly flexible fashion.

Unaware of the presence of the adjuster, Captain Leeth did not realize that his thoughts were no longer quite his own. He said, "The attack being made on the ship by the images makes the quarrel of the scientists traitorous and unforgivable." He paused, then said thoughtfully, "Here's my plan." The plan involved heat projectors, muscle-straining acceleration, and partial extermination of both groups of scientists. Captain Leeth failed even to mention the aliens, nor did it seem to occur to him that he was describing his intentions to an emissary of what he regarded as the enemy. He finished, "Where your services will be important, Mr. Grosvenor, is in the science department. As a Nexialist, with a coordinative knowledge of many sciences, you can play a decisive role against the other scientists—"

Weary and disheartened, Grosvenor gave up. The chaos was too great for one man to overcome. Everywhere he looked were armed men. All together, he had seen a score or more of dead bodies. At any moment the uneasy truce between Captain Leeth and Director Morton would end in a burst of projector fire. And even now he could hear the roaring of the fans where Morton was holding off Kent's attack. He sighed as he turned back to the Captain. "I'll need some equipment from my own department," he said. "Can you pass me through to the rear elevators? I can be back here in five minutes."

As he guided his machine into the back door of his department a few minutes later, it seemed to Grosvenor that there was no longer any doubt about what he must do. What had seemed a far-fetched idea when he first thought of it was now the only plan he had left. He must attack the alien women through their myriad images, and with their own hypnotic weapons.

As he made his preparations, Grosvenor kept wiping the perspiration from his face, and yet it was not warm. The room temperature stood at normal. Unwillingly, he paused finally to analyze his anxiety. He just didn't, he decided, know enough about the enemy. It was not sufficient that he had a theory about how they were operating. The great mystery was an enemy who had curiously woman-like faces and bodies, some partly doubled, some single. Uneasily, Grosvenor tried to imagine how Korita might analyze what was happening. In terms of cyclic history, what stage of culture could these beings be in?—The fellahin stage, he thought finally. It was actually an inevitable conclusion. A race that controlled hypnotic phenomena as did this one would be able to stimulate each other's minds, and so would have naturally the kind of telepathy that human beings could obtain only through the encephalo-adjuster. Such beings would flash through the early stages of their culture and arrive at the fellah stage in the swiftest possible time *The ability to read minds without artificial aids would stultify any culture.*

Swiftly, Grosvenor went back mentally to the various civilizations of Earth history that had run their courses, apparently exhausted themselves, and then stagnated into fellahdom—Babylon, Egypt, China, Greece, Rome and parts of west Europe. Then there were the Mayan, Toltec and Aztec cultures of early America, the East Indies, Ceylon and the mid-Pacific islanders, with their strange relics of by-gone glories—endlessly the pattern repeated itself. Fellah folk resented newness and change, resisted it and fought it blindly. The coming of this ship could have stirred these beings to just that kind of resistance. It seemed to Grosvenor that he had to act as if the analysis was correct. He had no other hypothesis. With such a theory as a starting point, he could try to obtain verification from one of the images. With pursed lips, he considered how it might be done. They wanted to conquer him also, of that he was sure; so, accordingly, he must appear to play into their hands. A quick glance at the chronometer tensed him, as he saw he had less than seven hours to save the ship!

Hastily, he focused a beam of light through the encephaloadjuster. With quick movements, he set a screen in front of the light, so that a small area of glass was thrown into shadow except for the intermittent light that played on it from the adjuster.

Instantly, an image appeared. It was one of the partially doubled ones, and because of the encephalo-adjuster, he was able to study it in safety. That first clear look astounded him. It was only vaguely humanoid, and yet it was understandable how his mind had leaped to the woman identification earlier. Its overlapping double face was crowned with a neat bun of golden feathers, but its head, though unmistakably bird-like now, did have a human appearance. There were no feathers on its face, which was covered with a lace-work of what seemed to be veins. The human appearance resulted from the way those veins had formed into groups. They gave the effect of cheeks and nose. The second pair of eyes, and the second mouth, were in each case nearly two inches above the first. They almost made a second head, which was literally growing out of the first. There was also a second pair of shoulders, with a doubled pair of short arms that ended in beautifully delicate, amazingly long hands and fingers—and the overall effect was still feminine. Grosvenor found himself thinking that the arms and fingers of the two bodies would be likely to separate first; then the second body would be able to help support its weight. Parthenogenesis, he thought. Here were genuine hymenopters.

The image in the wall before him showed vestigial wings, and tufts of feathers were visible at the wrists. It wore a bright blue tunic over an astonishingly straight and superficially human-like body. If there were other vestiges of a feathery past, they were hidden by the clothing. What was clear was that this bird didn't and couldn't fly under its own power.

Grosvenor completed his study swiftly. His first move seemed as obvious as it was necessary. Somehow, he must convey to these beings that he would let himself be hypnotized in exchange for information. Tentatively, he drew a picture of the image and of himself on a blackboard. Forty-seven precious minutes and scores, of drawings later, the bird image suddenly faded from the wall. And a city scene appeared in its place. It was not a large community, and his first view of it was from a high vantage point. He had an impression of very tall, very narrow buildings clustered so close together that all the lower reaches must be lost in gloom for most of each day. Grosvenor wondered, in passing, if that might possibly reflect nocturnal habits in some primeval past. His mind leaped on. He ignored individual buildings in his desire to obtain a whole picture. Above everything else he wanted to find out the extent of their machine culture, how they communicated, and if this was the city from which the attack on the ship was being launched.

He could see no machines, no aircraft, no cars, nor anything corresponding to the interstellar communication equipment used by human beings. On Earth, such communication required stations spaced over many square miles of land. It seemed likely, therefore, that this was not the origin of the attack. He had guessed, of course, that they would not show him anything vital. Even as be made his negative discovery, the view changed. He was no longer on a hill, but on a building near the center of the city. Whatever was taking that perfect color picture moved forward, and he looked down over the edge. His primary concern was with the whole scene. Yet he found himself wondering how they were showing it to him. The transition from one scene to another had been accomplished in the twinkling of an eye. Less than a minute had passed since his black-board illustration had finally made known his desire for information.

That thought, like the others, was a flashing one. Even as he had it, he was gazing avidly down the side of the building. The space separating it from the nearby structures seemed no more than ten feet. But now he saw something that had not been visible from the hillside. The buildings were connected on every level by walks only inches wide. Along these moved the pedestrian traffic of the bird city. Directly below Grosvenor, two individuals strode towards each other along the same narrow walk, seemingly unconcerned by the fact that it was a hundred feet or more to the ground. They passed casually, easily. Each swung his outside leg wide around the other, caught the walk, bent his inside leg far out, and then they were by, without having broken pace. There were other people on other levels going through the same intricate maneuvers in the same nonchalant manner. Watching them, Grosvenor guessed that their bones were thin and hollow, and that they were lightly built.

The scene changed again, and then again. It moved from one section of the street to another. He saw, it seemed to him, every possible variation of the reproductive condition. Some were so far advanced that the legs and arms and most of the body were free. Others were as he had already seen them. In every instance, the "parent" seemed unaffected by the weight of the new body.

Grosvenor was trying to get a glimpse inside one of the dim interiors of a building when the picture began to fade from the wall. In a moment the city had disappeared completely. In its place grew the double image. The image-fingers pointed at the encephalo-adjuster. Its motion was unmistakable. It had fulfilled its part of the bargain. It was time for him to fulfill his. Its naive expectation that he would do so was typically fellah. Unfortunately, he had no alternative but to carry out his obligation.

"I am calm and relaxed," said Grosvenor's recorded voice. "My thoughts are clear. What I see is not necessarily related to what I am looking at. What I hear may be meaningless to the interpretive centers of my brain, but I have seen their city as they think it is. Whether what I actually see and hear makes sense or nonsense, I remain calm, relaxed and at ease ..."

Grosvenor listened carefully to the words, and then nodded. The time might come, of course, when he would not consciously hear the message. But it would be there. Its patterns would impress ever more firmly on his mind. Still listening, he examined the adjuster for the last time, and all was as he wanted it. Carefully, he set the automatic cut-off for five hours. At the end of that time, unless he were dead, the limited cross connection would be broken. He would have preferred his first break to be in seconds, or minutes, but what he was about to do was not merely a scientific experiment—it was a life-and-death gamble. Ready for action, he put his hand on the control dial, and there he paused. For this was the moment. Within a few seconds the group mind of perhaps thousands of individual birdfolk would be in possession of parts of his nervous system. They would undoubtedly try to control him as they were controlling the other men on the ship.

He was fairly positive that he would be up against a group of minds working together. He had seen no machines, not even a wheeled vehicle, that most primitive of mechanical devices. For a short time, he had taken it for granted that they were using television-type cameras. Now, he guessed that he had seen the city through the eyes of individuals, as, with these beings, telepathy was a sensory process as sharp as vision itself. The enmassed mindpower of millions of bird-people could hurdle light years of distance. They didn't need machines.

On Earth, and elsewhere, nearly all lower-order life forms that reproduced by parthenogenesis worked together in a curious unity of purpose. It suggested an interrelation that could dispense with actual physical contact.

Fellahdom must be a long-standing condition of this race. There would be no doubt in the mind of the individual about the "truth" of what it saw and heard and felt. It would be only too easy for them to settle into an inflexible pattern of existence. That pattern was now going to feel the sledgehammer impact of new ideas. He couldn't hope to foresee the result.

Still listening to the recorder, Grosvenor manipulated the dial of the encephalo-adjuster, and slightly modified the rhythm of his own thoughts. It had to be slight. Even if he had wanted to, he could not offer the aliens complete attunement. In those rhythmic pulsations lay every variation of sanity, unsanity and insanity. He had to restrict his reception to waves that would register "sane" on a psychologist's graph.

The adjuster superimposed them on a beam of light which in turn shone directly on the image. If the individual behind the image was affected by the pattern in the light, it didn't show it yet. Grosvenor did not expect overt evidence, and so he was not disappointed. He was convinced that the result would become apparent only in the changes that occurred in the patterns they were directing at him. And that he was sure, he would have to experience with his own nervous system.

It was hard for him to concentrate on the image, but he persisted. The encephalo-adjuster began to interfere markedly with his vision, and still he stared steadily at the image.

"... I am calm and relaxed. My thoughts are clear ..."

One instant the words were loud in his ears, and the next they were gone. In their stead was a roaring sound as of distant thunder.

The noise faded slowly. It became a steady throbbing like the murmur in a large sea shell. Grosvenor was aware of a faint light. It was far away, and had the hazy dimness of a lamp seen through thick fog.

"I'm still in control," he assured himself. "I'm getting sense impressions through its nervous system. It's getting impressions through mine."

He could wait. He could sit here and wait until the darkness cleared, until his brain started to make some kind of interpretation of the sense phenomena that were being telegraphed from that other nervous system. He could sit here and—

He stopped. " 'Sit!' " he thought. Was that what *it* was doing? He poised intent and alert. He heard a distant voice say, "Whether what I actually see and hear makes sense or nonsense, I remain calm—" The sound of his recorded voice relieved him anew. The danger would come if his body were forced away from that reassuring sound, and away from the encephalo-adjuster. Until that threatened, he could let the alien impressions seep into him.

His nose began to itch. He thought: "They don't have noses; at least I didn't see any. Therefore, it's either my own nose, or a random stimulation." He started to reach up to scratch it, and felt a sharp pain in his stomach. He would have doubled up with the hurt of it if he had been able. He couldn't. He couldn't scratch his nose or put his hands on his abdomen.

He realized then that the itch and the pain stimuli did not derive from his own body, nor did they necessarily have any corresponding meaning in the other's nervous system. Two highly developed life forms were sending signals to each other—he hoped that he was sending signals to it also—which neither could interpret. His advantage was that he had expected it. The alien, if it was fellah, and if Korita's theory was valid, hadn't and couldn't expect it. Understanding that, he could hope for adjustment. *It* could only become more confused.

The itch went away, and the pain in his stomach became a feeling of satiation, as if he had eaten too much. A hot needle stabbed at his spine, digging at each vertebra. Half way down, the needle turned to ice, and the ice melted and ran in a freezing stream down his back. Something—a hand? a piece of metal? a pair of tongs?—snatched at a bundle of muscles in his arm, and almost tore them out by the roots. His mind shrieked with pain messages and he almost lost consciousness.

Grosvenor was a badly shaken man when that sensation faded into nothingness. These were all illusions. No such things were happening anywhere, not in his body, not in that of the bird-being. His brain was receiving a pattern of impulses through his eyes, and was misinterpreting them. In such a relationship, pleasure could become pain, any stimulus could produce any feeling. He hadn't counted on the misinterpretations being so violent.

He forgot that as his lips were caressed by something soft and squishy. A voice said, "I am loved—" Grosvenor rejected the meaning. "No, not loved." It was, he believed, his own brain again trying to interpret sense phenomena from a nervous system that was experiencing a reaction different from any comparable human emotion. Consciously, he substituted the words: "I am stimulated by ..." and then let the feeling run its course. In the end, he still didn't know what it was that he had felt. The stimulation was not unpleasant. His taste buds were titillated by a sense of sweetness, and his eyes watered. It was a relaxing process. A picture of a flower came into his mind. It was a lovely, red, Earth carnation, and thus could have no connection with the flora of the Riim world. "Riim!" He thought. His mind poised in tense fascination. Had that come to him across the gulf of space? In some irrational way, the name seemed to fit. Yet no matter what came through, a doubt would remain in his mind.

The final series of sensations had all been pleasant. Nevertheless, he waited anxiously for the next manifestation. The light remained dim and hazy—then once more his eyes seemed to water, his feet suddenly itched intensely. The sensation passed, leaving him unaccountably hot and weighted by a suffocating lack of air.

"False!" he told himself. "Nothing like that is happening."

The stimulations ceased. Again there was only the steady throbbing sound, and the all-pervasive blur of light. It began to worry him. It was possible that his method was right and that, given time, he would eventually be able to exercise some control over a member or a group of members of the enemy. Time was what he could not spare. Every passing second brought him a colossal distance nearer personal destruction. Out there—here (for an instant he was confused)—in space; one of the biggest and costliest ships ever built by men was devouring the miles at a velocity that had almost no meaning.

He knew which parts of his brain were being stimulated. He could hear a noise only when sensitive areas at the side of the cortex received sensations. The brain surface above the ear, when titillated, produced dreams and old memories. In the same way, every part of the human brain had long ago been mapped. The exact location of stimulation areas differed slightly for each individual, but the general structure, among humans, was always the same.

The normal human eye was a fairly objective mechanism. The lens focussed a real image on the retina. Judging by the pictures of their city, as transmitted by the Riim-folk. they also possessed objectively accurate eyes. If he could coordinate his visual centers with their eyes, he would receive dependable pictures.

More minutes went by. He thought, in sudden despair: "Is it possible that I'm going to sit here the full five hours without ever making a useful contact?" For the first time, he questioned his good sense in committing himself so completely to this situation. When he tried to move his hand over to the control lever of the encephalo-adjuster, nothing seemed to happen. A number of vagrant sensations came, among them, unmistakably, the odor of burning rubber. For a third time, his eyes watered. And then, sharp and clear, a picture came. It flashed off as swiftly as it had flashed on. To Grosvenor, who had been trained by advanced tachistoscopic techniques, the after-image remained as vivid in his mind as if he had had a leisurely look. It seemed as if he were in one of the tall, narrow buildings. The interior was dimly lighted by the reflections from the sunlight that came through the open doors, as there were no windows. Instead of floors, the residence was fitted with catwalks. A few bird people were sitting on these walks. The walls were lined with doors, Indicating the existence of cabinets and storage areas.

The visualization both excited and disturbed him. Suppose he did establish a relationship whereby he was affected by its nervous system, and it by his. Suppose he reached the point where he could hear with its ears, see with its eyes, and feel to some degree what it felt. These were sensory impressions only. Could he hope to bridge the gap, and induce motor responses in the creature's muscles? Would he be able to force it to walk, turn its head, move its arms, and, generally, make it act as his body? The attack on the ship was being made by a group working together, thinking together, feeling together. By gaining control of one member of such a group, could he exercise some control over all?

His momentary vision must have come through the eyes of one individual. What he had experienced so far did not suggest any kind of group contact. He was like a man imprisoned in a dark room with a hole in the wall in front of him covered with layers of translucent material. Through this filtered a vague light. Occasionally, images penetrated the blur, and he had glimpses of the outside world. He could be fairly certain that the pictures were accurate, but that did not apply to the sounds that came through another hole on a side wall, or the sensations that came to him through still other holes in the ceiling and floor.

Humans could hear frequencies up to twenty thousand a second. That was where some races started to hear. Under hypnosis, men could be conditioned to laugh uproariously when they were being tortured, and shriek with pain when tickled, Stimulation that meant pain to one life form could mean nothing at all to another.

Mentally, Grosvenor let the tensions seep out of him. There was nothing for him to do but to relax and wait. He waited.

It occurred to him presently that there might be a connection between his own thoughts and the sensations he received, That picture of the inside of the building—what had he thought just before it came? Principally, he recalled, he had visualized the structure of the eye. The connection was so obvious that his mind trembled with excitement. There was another thing, also. Until now, he had concentrated on the notion of seeing and feeling with the nervous system of the individual. Still the realization of his hopes depended on his establishing contact with, and control of, the group of minds that had attacked the ship.

He saw his problem, suddenly, as one that would require control of his own brain. Certain areas would have to be virtually blacked out, kept at minimum performance levels. Others must be made extremely sensitive, so that all incoming sensations found it easier to seek expression through them. As a highly trained auto-hypnotic subject, he could accomplish both objectives by suggestion. Vision came first, of course. Then muscular control of the individual through whom the group was working against him.

Flashes of colored light interrupted his concentration. Grosvenor regarded them as evidence of the effectiveness of his suggestions. He knew that he was on the right track when his vision cleared suddenly, and stayed clear. The scene was the same. His control still sat on one of the roosts inside one of the tall buildings. Hoping fervently that the vision was not going to fade, Grosvenor began to concentrate on moving the Riim's muscles. The trouble was that the ultimate explanation of why a movement could occur at all was obscure. His visualization had to be on a level that was already gross. Nothing happened. Shocked but determined, Grosvenor tried symbol hypnosis, using a single cue word to cover the entire complex process.

Slowly, one of the attenuated arms came up. Another cue, and his control stood up cautiously. Then he made it turn its head. The act of looking reminded the bird-being that that drawer and that cabinet and that closet were "mine." The memory barely touched the conscious level. The creature knew its own possessions and accepted the fact without concern.

Grosvenor had a hard time fighting down his excitement. With tense patience, he had the bird-being get up from a sitting position, raise its arms, lower them, and walk back and forth along the roost. Finally, he made it sit down again. He must have been keyed up, his brain responsive to the slightest suggestion. Because he had barely started to concentrate again when his whole being was flooded by a message that seemed to affect every level of his thought and feeling. More or less automatically, Grosvenor translated the anguished thoughts into familiar verbalisms.

"... The cells are calling, calling. The cells are afraid. Oh, the cells know pain! There is darkness in the Riim world. Withdraw from the being—far from Riim ... Shadows, darkness, turmoil ... the cells must reject him to try to destroy the being who came out of the great dark. The night deepens. All cells withdraw ... but they cannot ..."

Grosvenor thought exultantly: "I've got them!" After a minute of tremendous excitement, he grew sober. His problem was greater than theirs. If he broke his connection with them, they would be free. By avoiding him thereafter, they could go on to achieve the purpose of their disruptive attack ... destruction of the *Space Beagle*. He would still have the problem of overcoming Morton and the others. He had no alternative but to go on with his plan.

He concentrated first on what seemed the most logical intermediate stage: the transfer of control to another alien. The choice, in the case of these beings, was obvious.

"I am loved!" he told himself, deliberately producing the sensation which had confused him earlier. "I am loved by my parent body, from which I am growing to wholeness. I share my parent's thoughts, but already I see with my own eyes, and know that I am one of the group...."

The transition came suddenly, as Grosvenor had expected it might. He moved the smaller, duplicate fingers. He arched the fragile shoulders. Then he oriented himself again to the parent Riim. The experiment was so completely satisfactory that he felt ready for the bigger jump that would take him into association with the nervous system of a more distant alien. That, also, proved to be a matter of stimulating the proper brain centers. Grosvenor came to awareness standing in a wilderness of brush and hill. Directly in front of him was a narrow stream, and beyond it, an orange sun rode low in a dark purple sky that was spotted with fleecy clouds. Grosvenor made his new control turn completely around. He saw that a small roost building, the only habitation in sight, nestled among the trees farther along the stream. He walked toward the building and looked inside. In the dim interior, he made out several roosts, one with two birds sitting on it, both with eyes closed. It was quite possible, he decided, that they were participating in the group assault on the *Space Beagle*.

From there, by a variation of the stimulus, he transferred his control to an individual on a part of the planet where it was night. The transition this time was even faster. He was in a lightless city, with ghostly buildings and catwalks. Swiftly, Grosvenor moved on to association with other nervous systems. He had no clear idea why the "rapport" was established with one Riim and not with another who fitted the same general requirement. It could be that the stimulation affected some individuals slightly faster than it affected others, It was even possible that these were descendants or body-relatives of his original parent-control. When he had been associated with more than two dozen Riim all over the planet, it seemed to Grosvenor that he had a good overall impression.

It was a world of brick and stone and wood, and of a neurological community relationship that would probably never be surpassed. A race had bypassed the entire machine age of man with its penetration of the secrets of matter and energy. Now, he felt, he could safely take the next-to-the-last step of his counterattack. He concentrated on a pattern which would characterize one of the beings who had projected an image to the *Space Beagle*. (He had, then, a sense of a small but noticeable lapse of time.) Then he was looking forth from one of the images, seeing the ship through an image.

His first concern was with how the battle was progressing, but he had to restrain his will to know because to come aboard was only part of his necessary pre-conditioning. He wanted to affect a group of perhaps millions of individuals, and had to affect them so powerfully that they would have to withdraw from the *Space Beagle* and have no recourse but to stay away from it.

He had proved that he could receive their thoughts, and that they could receive his. His association with one nervous system after another would not have been possible unless that was so. Now he was ready. He thought into the darkness:

"You live in a Universe; and within you, you form pictures of the Universe as it seems to you. Of that Universe you know nothing and can know nothing except for the pictures, but the pictures within you of the Universe are not the Universe ..."

How could you influence another's mind?—by changing his assumptions. How could you alter another's actions?—by changing his basic beliefs, his emotional certainties.

Carefully, Grosvenor went on: "And the pictures within you do not show all about the Universe for there are many things which you cannot know directly, not having senses to know. Within the Universe there is an order, and if the order of the pictures within you is not as the order of the Universe, then you are deceived ..."

In the history of life, few thinking beings had ever done anything illogical—within their frame of reference. If the frame was falsely based, if the assumptions were untrue to reality, then the individual's automatic logic could lead him to disastrous conclusions.

The assumptions had to be changed. Grosvenor changed them, deliberately, coolly, honestly. His own basic hypothesis behind what he was doing was that the Riim had no defense. These were the first new ideas they had had in countless generations and he did not doubt that the impact would be colossal. This was a fellah civilization, rooted in certainties that had never before been challenged. There was ample historical evidence that a tiny intruder could influence decisively the future of entire fellahin races.

Huge old India had crumbled before a few thousand Englishmen. Similarly, all the fellah people of ancient Earth were taken over with ease, and did not revive till the core of their inflexible attitudes was forever shattered by the dawning realization that there was more to life than they had been taught under their rigid systems. The Riim were peculiarly vulnerable. Their method of communication, unique and wonderful though it was, made it possible to influence them all in a single intensive operation. Over and over, Grosvenor repeated his message, adding, each time, one instruction that had to do with the ship. The instruction was:

"Change the pattern you are using against those on the ship, and then withdraw it. Change the pattern, so that they can relax, and sleep ... then withdraw it ... do not attack again ...."

He had only a vague notion as to how long he actually poured his commands into that tremendous neural circuit. He guessed about two hours. Whatever the time involved, it ended as the relay switch on the encephalo-adjuster automatically broke the connection between himself and the image in the wall of his department. Abruptly, he was aware of the familiar surroundings of his own department. He glanced at where the image had been and tensed as he saw that it was still there, but shook his head slightly. He could hardly expect a definite reaction this soon. The Riim, also, were recovering from a connection that had just been broken.

As Grosvenor watched, the pattern of light from the image changed subtly. Grosvenor's head drooped sleepily. He sat up jerkily, remembering. The instructions he had given—to relax and sleep—this was the result. All over the ship, men would be sleeping as the new hypnotic pattern extended its inhibitory paralysis over the hemispheres of the brain.

About three minutes went by. Suddenly, the double image of the Riim vanished from the glistening wall in front of him. A moment later, Grosvenor was out in the corridor. As he raced along, he saw that unconscious men lay everywhere but that the walls were bright and clear. Not once on his journey to the control room did he see an image.

Inside the control room, he stepped gingerly over the sleeping form of Captain Leeth, who lay on the floor near the control panel. With a sigh of relief, Grosvenor threw the switch that energized the outer screen of the ship.

Seconds later, Elliott Grosvenor was in the control chair, altering the course of the *Space Beagle*.

DON'T HOLD YOUR BREATH

Though the crazy talk had been going on for years, I had got to age thirty-two when it started in earnest. About the change that was coming. No oxygen in the atmosphere after May 11. Thirty-two days from now. Who do they think they're scaring? Not me, Art Atkins.

"Make up your mind!" That was mostly what you heard when you tuned in on any of the media. "Sign into your nearest tent and do it now before the last-minute rush."

I had my girls, and my game, and my super-swank apartment and the whole luxury bit; and that nonsense was really beginning to be a nuisance. Most of my time with a girl was usually taken up these nights with arguing her out of making a run for the nearest tent.

—For Pete's sake, I pointed out in my most patient manner, there's nothing in a tent but a little more oxygen. Its only a stopgap. I ought to know. I'm one of the contractors that helped build the local one.

After you'd said that a few hundred times to a sobbing armful of gleaming feminine flesh, it got to be pretty boring; and what followed was no longer that great, either.

This morning, the phone rang shortly after ten. When I picked up the receiver, the picture that flashed on the screens was Mona. Mona was my latest addition—added her to my select collection only six months ago. Right now, she was all dressed up.

"I'm dropping out, Art," she said.

"Look," I said, not exactly amused, but playing it straight. "How can a drop-out drop out?"

"Oh, you will have your joke," she said in a miffed tone. On the telescreen, she made that movement of hers. Tossed her golden hair. The first time I saw her do that, it just about drove me out of my mind with erotic

517

excitement; and I wasn't entirely immune to it this minute either. I grew aware that she was speaking again. "I mean," she went on, "I'm going to move into the tent. This air is too much for me."

"You've been listening to those crazy people," I accused. "I told you not to."

"Well maybe you'd better listen to them, too," she flashed. It was a moment of uncontrol, and I could see her make an effort to get back into calmness. She managed it, and said, "Next month is the big day, and that's close enough to midnight for me."

"*What* big day?" I asked, pretending not to know.

I was talking to a blank screen.

I didn't get around to calling her back until afternoon; in case she expected a quick reaction, and a begging Art Atkins, thank you, no. When I phoned, the ringing signal came back many times, but nobody answered. It penetrated finally that maybe she really meant it.

Okay, okay. Grudgingly, I looked up the tent number, and dialed it. A computer voice said, "Sorry to inform you, sir, no personal calls are accepted for tent inhabitants from outside except from authorized phones."

I replaced the receiver sort of gently, but grinding my teeth. Finally, I just sat there, shaking my head. It was amazing. Those people out there never failed to do their madness. Always big and *first* with bastards like that was putting up barriers. Doing something to be difficult. So be it … I was finally resigned—let them have their little moment.

I had another thought. I figured suddenly that Mona hadn't really departed all that fast. Just not answering. Being difficult herself. So I threw on some threads and ankled outside.

You ought to see the city that I emerged onto as I came out of my skyscraper apartment building. Down here, a deserted sidewalk. Above, a hazy sky. Not too bad, really. What was bad was, it was hazy all the time.

The street itself was like death. Best comparison, those old pictures of European cities evacuated during wartime. With only patrol vehicles. I stood there; and of course it was hard to breathe now that I was away from my air conditioning. Hot, too. After five, late afternoon; and the temperature still over a hundred. Something to do with an excess of carbon dioxide in the atmosphere.

Suppressing an impulse to gasp, I hesitated. Was Mona really worth it? Quickly, I realized: It's the principle. If you let one mistress get away, next thing another one will be slipping off. And before you know it, you're sleeping alone for a while.

So Mona had to be the object lesson. I needed to be in a position to say to Hettie, Adele and Zoe, "Okay, sister, take a look at what happens to a dame who had her little heart set on throwing over Art Atkins."

Where I had come out was a hundred yards from Crestmore Street, a main stem. So I went over there, and just for fun tried to thumb down one of the official tanks—which were all that cruised the streets these days. Ugly things. I suppose if you wanted to breathe a normal amount of oxygen you had to keep it sealed in. And the tanks were the simplest mass-produced machines, with their electric motors and rechargeable batteries and their closed-in front seats.

As usual, no one stopped merely to give a guy a free ride. Since my mind was made up, I held up a twenty-dollar bill to the next tank. He pulled over. I told him where I wanted to go, and he motioned me into his rear seat. No extra oxygen there, but still it was sitting down, and hardly any demands on the body.

For twenty dollars I often get a ride in the front seat; but I take these guys as they are. Once in, I mimed at him with the money. He indicated for me to put it into the ashtray; and then he had the usual trite thought and opened his intercom again. There was a tight-lipped smile on his face as he said, "If you wish, I'll take you over to the nearest tent entrance, and you can sign in."

As if anticipating an adverse reaction, he added quickly, "No amount of bravery is any good against what's coming."

I said patiently. "Look, I'm going to visit my girl. And if I ever decide to go into a tent, I'll use *my* private entrance."

He must have believed I was joking. In his rearview mirror, I saw the tight-lipped smile was back on his face. Still, he seemed to relax a little. He said in a conversational tone. "The kind of people we're running into this final month are a strange breed. Natural selection has given us another look at the human race. Huge crowds were camping at the tent gates a year ago. That's one group. When entrance was finally allowed three months ago, they went in; then came other categories—roughly divided by psychologists into about a hundred emotional types. But now we're down to a special type of male and the woman this type associates with, over whom the man has an unusually dominant control. He hesitated, then: "May I ask you one question?"

I said, surprised, "You're doing me the courtesy and favor of giving me a ride. Sure, ask anything."

"Why isn't this affecting you?" He waved with his free arm. It was a gesture that embraced half the horizon. "The no-oxygen condition. The big change that's coming. Why don't you try to get to a safe place?"

It's not easy to explain good sense. I don't try. I merely said pityingly, "You don't look like a schoolteacher. But I feel I'm going to get a classroom lecture for elementary grades. That may be all right for kids, but I should tell you I graduated from high school fourteen years ago."

"Still," he persisted, after smiling that thin smile on his face, "you want to live." He didn't wait for me to let that die a natural death. He added quickly, "Nature is bigger than Man; particularly, it's bigger than any one man. For once everybody *really* has to cooperate."

It was my turn to smile. "If everybody has to," I said, "then everybody will. So what's the problem?"

He looked at me uneasily. "The decision of what to do had to be made by qualified scientists," he said. "Some individuals are resisting that decision." He went on, half to himself, as if arguing with a doubting segment of his brain, "At this late stage there's nothing they can do. What do you think?"

"I've never given it a thought," I said—truthfully, because what I do in connection with all those conniving human beings is purely defensive. They start to move against me. My defenses come into view. That simple. I said, "Right now I'm visiting my girl."

He shook his head, wondering. "Mister," he said, "you're either a complete idiot, or a better man than I am. Good luck."

He let me off at Mona's street waved at me from inside his mobile oxygen tent, and drove off. I walked along, slightly nettled by his final words, and mentally grappling with them.

—What I am, I told myself, is a man who confronts a problem long in advance. And then I don't pay any more attention to it until it actually happens ... For Pete's sake, this oxygen shortage wouldn't be a problem for another month. All right, so thirty days from now I'd finally confront it as a problem. When it began to rain fluorine I hold my hand out and let the drops fall on it, sniff them—that is, if the smell wasn't already permeating the whole damn universe around me. And then ... well, that would be the time to get on my horse, or whatever, and canter over to my personal tent entrance.

By doing things like that, I'd made my first million before I was twenty-five—in a world that was coming to an end, when almost everybody else was sitting petrified. By age twenty-eight, I was one of those wealthy contractors; in case you wondered, that's where some of the big money is to be made, particularly if you find out early where the bodies are buried. Naturally, this past year things had been rough; not much planning ahead. Just bridge stuff. Details of helping people through the transformation. Once the tent was built, the details of what followed were out of my field. Mostly chemical, biological, medical—and thousands of bright-eyed jerks listening to lectures about how to give the injections that would convert the cells of an oxygen breather over to fluorine. And care and feeding of same while in transition.

Fine. It had to be done. But don't bother me with it.

I was riding up the elevator to Mona's floor by the time those thoughts were completed. A minute later, I softly inserted my key into the door of 412-J.

I had myself braced. A quick bit of sweet talk to soothe her and get her into bed. If that worked, it would be the end of it. But if it didn't—

I wouldn't really bash Mona up bad. Without her pretty face and curvy body, I wouldn't want her anyway. So there was no point in being rough. Besides, I'm not one for violence except when it is needed. One good smash to the jaw to make her think, but break no bones. Maybe a little blood and after-bruise as a reminder. Anyone who knows women will realize that I'd be leaning back practically horizontally in my desire to bring about a peaceful solution, if that's all I did.

The door swung open as I manipulated the key; and I walked into the silence inside. I paused, taking it all in; and I've got to admit it, as always, I was impressed by the absolutely delightful interior.

My current girls live like queens, and even my cast-offs have it pretty good. I give new mistresses *carte blanche* on how they fix up an apartment. You can be pretty sure that if you pick your girls carefully they'll create their own dream. Mona had been especially artistic.

So I gazed at sheer enchantment. But it felt empty. I walked through the glittering living room, glanced into the music and book room, examined the kitchen and then went into the glorious frilly bedroom. No one there, either.

She did it! I sat down on the gorgeous queen-sized bed and let the madness of what she had done sink in. And right there, I got angry. It takes a lot to set me off. But I could feel the heat of that anger rise up into my cheeks, and the seethe of it was in my skin all the way down to the toes, like a shot of vitamin B complex. I could even taste the stuff. I was so teed off.

"—Okay, baby, you asked for it." I spoke the words softly but aloud.

... Once inside the tent, I put on my little badge—one of the ten-thousand series. And so I became a human molecule. People swarmed in all the corridors. To anyone but a person like myself (who had learned the pattern during the building stages) it must have seemed like total confusion.

Down to level H—for Henessey (Mona Henessey)—I forced my way, or rode, relieved, on one of the rolling sidewalks. My destination was the east section, where the He's would be.

It took a while. A pigeon-faced stupe held me up at a checkpoint while he studied my pass. But, what I had was the right level of authority. Not VIP—easily verifiable. But with just the proper amount of secondary eminence, more than anyone would be able to cancel out in this rush.

Sure enough, he let me by. Reluctantly. Some people just don't like the set of my beard. He had that look in his eyes. But—nothing he could do.

Since sectional computers had been built in to handle all room designations, when I came to the He area I simply dialed her name on the first computer outlet I saw. Instantly, her room number flashed onto the plate in front of me.

I had brought a peep device with me. So I attached it to the wall of her apartment from the side corridor. The interior scene that came on to the little bright screen should have warned me. The apartment was a family-sized one. Mona did not have a family. But there she was, dressed as I had seen her on the phone viewplate that morning. A sleek-haired man was with her. Seeing him veered my attention from other suspicions.

A boyfriend? Yes—it turned out. As I watched, he took her in his arms and gave Mona one of those lingering lover's kisses. Observing the two of them, I could only shake my head in amazement at the nature of a woman. She didn't come here to breathe more oxygen. She came because she'd fallen for a pair of broad shoulders and striking black eyes.

I saw the eyes as he released her, and turned toward the door. Sizing him up quickly through the peep device, placed him at twenty-seven or -eight (Mona was twenty-two). The irony of it drilled deep into me, not for the first time in my adult years. Question in my mind: Was this marriage-to-be, or just a shack-up? A free man learns early to recognize that a woman gradually gets that got-to-be-married thing until she can't be reasoned with. I always tried to train my girls early to keep off that subject. No dice on marriage with Art Atkins.

The man turned at the door and I had a full front of him. The way he held himself gave me a new perspective. He radiated some level of purposefulness. An implication of authority—which I had learned to recognize in my career. Normally, I'd just go away until I checked his background. But that was not possible in this melee. I gave him two minutes after he went out the door. Then I went around and pushed the buzzer.

Mona opened the door.

When she saw me, she tried to shove it shut. But of course I had expected that. And so I had my foot in the jamb. As I pushed my way in, I said, "Don't worry. I just want to talk to you."

That was not exactly a truth; but it wasn't wholly a lie. Finding her with a man had transformed this situation, and my attitudes were modifying moment by moment as I considered the unpleasant reality of what level of man it might be.

She continued backing away from me, angling off toward the kitchen door. I pursued her unhurriedly. Fact was, I badly wanted information, but didn't know how to begin.

Before I could decide what to say, there was a diversion. A sound. Behind me. I swung around rapidly. Several men had come out of the hallway that led to the bedrooms. They carried those special electro-shock hand weapons by used the police. As I faced them, they stopped in a tight little cluster and regarded me.

There were five of them and one of me. I remained where I was, keeping my hands out where they could be seen. I had heard what a shock gun does to you, and didn't want any … A remote segment of my mind noted again the direction from which they had come, and reasoned that they had probably entered this apartment through a connecting door at the end of the hall from the adjoining apartment. It was a possibility I had failed to take into account.

I was not chagrined. One man can't think of everything. I had now— as I discovered—met a few of the conspirators, part of planet-wide resistance to what the authorities were planning. And although I had vaguely heard of such a conspiracy, it had never occurred to me that anyone involved noticed me.

The surprise was that total.

Standing then, I was able to observe that two of my captors looked to be in their mid-twenties, two in their thirties and one probably forty-two or -three. It was this oldest individual who summarized the situation for me. When he described how Mona had been the bait to catch my type of dominant male, my memory shot back instantly to the party where I had met her.

"But there were many beautiful girls there," I protested. You mean, all?—" I paused, questioning.

My informant nodded. His companions continued to regard me unsmiling.

I remembered more now of the party. A political thing, given by a local bigwig. So he must be in on the scheme, and at this ultimate hour was prepared to have that information known to me. I had gone to the party because it was the commercial thing to do.

"It wouldn't have mattered," I was told, "which of the girls you were attracted to. They were all dedicated to the plan to help oxygen-breathing mankind."

"B-but—" I began.

What I intended to say was, "Why me?" I didn't say it, I was remembering something else. "Still," I said, "Mona must have been selected in advance. She arrived near the end of the party, and so she made an entrance, and bowled me over. That had to be planned."

No was the headshake.

Her coming as she did was a consequence of a misunderstanding. She was not one of the original volunteers. What had happened was that she and her fiancé had an engagement to attend another affair, and Mona had arrived unexpectedly. Then, when I had been attracted to her, she made the best of her predicament and belatedly volunteered—which offer was immediately accepted by the desperate leader of the conspiracy.

To say that I was thinking hard as I learned these details was an understatement. I like to know where I'm going and what's next. I often had a purpose in a crisis the instant I became aware that there was one.

How should you act when you've been caught completely unprepared? There was the room; family-size, but still damned small. And five people plus me and Mona were crowded into it. The five had me backed up against a wall by this time. No place to go but through five determined, armed men. Those were the kind of odds that I respected.

So getting away couldn't be my goal. Chance of success: zero.

It dawned on me I was in a spot tougher and different from any that I'd ever been in during my somewhat checkered career.

No purpose—except to find a purpose.

These people had swung a ringer in on me: Mona. There she stood, off to one side now. Her color was higher then I'd ever seen it … Embarrassed, I thought; she's ashamed.

That steadied me. Because it pointed up that these were amateurs. Sincere people. In my mind's calculator, I hastily counted the price she'd paid; and for a volunteer virgin—which is what I discovered she was, when we began our affair—it was colossal. I liked to get around to my girls four times every eight days. Divide that into six months. And the price leaves you gasping—if you examine it from the point of view of a fiancé off somewhere on the sidelines.

My instant feeling was that I'd better not let Black-eyed Broad-shoulders be alone with me while I was in a captured condition.

… All this did a lightning move through my brain. Which was the way things work inside me. And then, having considered the improbability of the whole thing, I voiced my original thought.

"But why?" I asked breathlessly. "Why *me?*"

At this point the oldest of the men stepped forward. Funny how people are. Until now he had stayed with the group, sort of identifying himself with the others, and not putting on any leadership airs. He could have continued that little game. Instead, he had a thought; and that thought, by God, triggered nervous energy, so that involuntarily he showed where his ego believed he really ought to be: up front.

You'll never catch Art Atkins going out of a role he has set himself to play. Where necessary, I can give a false signal until doomsday. Once more it proved … here were amateurs.

So I learned from the spokesman that people like me had been spotted as being capable of playing a decisive part in this crisis. And that, while several other men had also had an equivalent of Mona planted on them, the group had finally settled on me as being the one for our local tent.

All over the earth other versions of Art Atkins were getting this treatment today in connection with their tent as I was in connection with mine. (The girl suddenly leaving, and they following her.)

"Look—" I protested at that point, "the only reason I came after Mona was—" My voice trailed off.

The group's lecturer smiled grimly. "A masculinity dominance thing," he said, "on a level of intensity comparable to a primitive Stone Age male."

I was still fumbling in my mind for something I could do. I only shook my head over the analogy, rejecting it. After all, I only intended to give Mona a single hard punch.

What I did do was speak the basic puzzlement in my mind. "Okay, I'm the key guy in this crisis. *Key in what way?*"

Smiling grimly, the old guy told me ... And, *of course*, I thought almost blankly. Naturally, *that* would be it—

Pretty sharp of them to spot it.

Of course, they couldn't be sure... Suppose, I asked myself, I deny it?

The spokesman must have deduced what was in my mind, so he smiled again, showing his teeth. "You might as well realize, Mr. Atkins, that we mean business. Naturally, we have no idea exactly what you did that places this tent at your mercy. But over in Peking the Art Atkins there was a minister in the government, and what he did was construct the principal oxygen converter beside a huge water reservoir; and so at the key hour that water will be released into the processing room, and if necessary will flood part of the tent itself. In Berlin, the Art Atkins there put in a tank of oxygen alternating with a tank of ammonia, and, so at a key moment we will let the oxygen and ammonia intermix, Now, in New York, the story we have is—" He stopped, so he showed his teeth again, and said, "Need I go on?"

He added quickly, "In several instances, torture had to be used to obtain the information."

I sighed. I was never one of your super-brave types. All I ever wanted to do was protect myself from the schemers so that I could go about my business.

"My method," I said, "was one of those chain reaction bombs, with a hundred fuses. Once it starts at any of those fuses it keeps going, flashing fire along a thousand exploding pathways.

"Why a bomb? Well, I like things simple and direct."

After the first excitement died down, they grew curious. What was my reason?

I could only shrug ... "Think about it," I said. "Here were those experts proposing that mankind endure a biologic transformation. Were they right? Maybe. But then again maybe not."

To me scientists were only people. We kept hearing the statement: *The scientists recommend*— Which scientists? Because there was usually another group of equally trained experts who said no; only they didn't happen to be the ones who had their lips close to the official ear.

I learned before I was twenty that it was a matter of personality or sheer accident. The first great success with animal, then human, embryos nurtured on those moons of Jupiter and Saturn that had atmospheres; and finally by remote control on Jupiter itself—these were dazzling victories for what was called the cosmic school of biochemists. They became the kings of science. It was the bandwagon for a chemist to jump onto: And of course when a team developed serum d and its variations that could change an adult oxygen breather to a fluorine utilizer or—by another step—to chlorine gaspers (they actually did gasp, but they survived), just about all the hysteria that you ever wanted to see hit the fan.

But long ago I met experts who said, "We're not giving this enough time. Fluorine-breathing human beings look great right now. But it's only been forty-two years since the first one. There may be side effects. Why not hold off another thirty years?"—which was about the time that (even the doubters agreed) would be about it for oxygen on earth.

My own feeling, after asking a few questions of astronomers: Somewhere in space might be huge chunks of frozen oxygen similar in size to the fluorine meteorites that were now being maneuvered toward a close orbit around earth.

Why not allow the extra years for those to be discovered? At the time, that was just a thought. I wasn't obsessed. And yet—when I considered my usual type of advance precaution, the explosive was the possibility that I understood best. And it was a method that would actually control the situation. Cum see cum saw.

I *always* took such precautions. I remember once I had a contract to build a bank. Just for fun, in case I ever had a reason to enter the bank vault, I constructed a secret tunnel under it. You won't find that tunnel in the plans, and nowhere in my head was there intent to use it. But there it was waiting for me.

… I emerged from my private thoughts to learn that the time they wanted me to blow up the oxygen plant was the next day at eleven A.M.

I was startled. It had all happened so fast that I hadn't had time to consider the actuality. I protested, "With all those people near it?"

They did not reply, simply watched me. I watched back, baffled by my predicament.

In a way, there was no problem here. Nothing, really, to decide, or have a purpose about. What I had to accomplish—what these conspirators wanted from me—was basically something I was in favor of. In my deepest being, I felt total—but total—resistance to being changed over from an oxygen to a fluorine breather.

Oh, I doubt if I'd have done anything about it on my own. And I quailed a little even now at the thought that people would die. But (I argued with myself) there were people dying every day either from oxygen deficiency or from intense psychic disturbance as the ultimate crisis approached.

Was I deciding as I stood there?

It didn't seem like a decision.

I had no choice. Them would be torture if I refused; I believed that. And they had all evening and all night to stick their needles into me.

Once more I looked them over; and they looked back silently.

Pretty ridiculous (I thought) when a man had to be forced to do something to which he was not opposed.

Still—there were serious, unfavorable aspects that needed to be brought out into the open.

I returned their silent stares, questioningly now.

I could see from the expressions on their faces that they weren't planning to listen to any objections. So all I said was. "They'll reconstruct it. And next time there'll be no implants possible."

The spokesman impatiently brushed that aside. That was a year, two, even three away. "By that time we'll figure something else."

I was silent.

They took that for agreement, and I had to admit to myself that it was.

While I listened, details were discussed. It seemed Mona's boyfriend had wormed his way high into the establishment. It was he who would guide me through the guard system that protected the oxygen.

When I heard that, I felt a queasy sensation in my stomach. I said finally, "May I talk to Mona?"

No one was against it. I walked over to her. All the time I spoke to her, she avoided my eyes. But she answered each question.

"What is his name?"

"Terence O'Day."

It was a family name that I knew. High in local politics. But it was the father I had heard of, not the son.

"Was he jealous?"

"He said he'd had other girls before he met me, so there was nothing unfair for me to have another man, or even more than one." She added swiftly, "He was furious at me for having arrived early, but once it happened, he was resigned."

She seemed, in that simple way of girls and women, to believe that. Naturally, I rejected the explanation totally. But I did believe that the poor guy had had no choice, after her big blooper.

All I said was, "Will you see him before eleven A.M. tomorrow?"

"Tonight." She spoke reluctantly, face averted.

I fought instant jealousy. Because something in her face said that she would be spending the night with him.

(Onlookers have an idea that a man with four mistresses doesn't worry about what they do with their spare time. Boy, are they wrong.)

Mona was speaking. "You will be staying in this apartment tonight under guard," she said. "And I"—defiantly—"will be staying with Terence."

I had control of myself again. I said earnestly, "I want you to tell him that I regret the incident, that brought you to that party. That I never knowingly play around with other men's wives or girl friends—" That was not true. Who else was there? All the pretty girls had guys from the day they peaked over the edge of fourteen.

But it was an important lie to put over. "Will you tell him that?" I urged Mona.

"Yes. I'll tell him."

She seemed belatedly to realize the implication of my words. "I'm sure you can trust him," she said. "When you think of the sacrifice he made in letting me volunteer—" She stopped. She turned impulsively and placed her hand on my arm. "Good luck, Art. Please don't fail us."

But she still didn't look directly at me. And so when I turned to the five, I shrugged and said simply, "What's your opinion?"

The oldest man was silent. One of the two middle thirties men said, "He's been with us since the beginning. He sacrificed his girl. What more can a man do to prove himself?"

I acknowledged that reluctantly. I said, "I've told you what my advance preparation was. When I did it, I had no particular plan in connection with it. But if I can't set off the trigger mechanism, that's it. There's nothing more in this tent that I know about."

For Terence, the next day, I did my clumsy routine. I kept bumping into people. I could see him gritting his teeth as, each time, he walked on as if he did not know me. That was the game we played at the beginning, at his suggestion. In case we ran into somebody important. Whenever I was delayed, and twice when I fell awkwardly, Terence went ahead about twenty feet; and then he stopped casually, and slowly turned around, and waited until I was ahead of him again.

I presently estimated that we were less than two hundred yards from the oxygen facility—only a short distance from where I had told them the trigger mechanism was located. And yet no sign of the guards that I had heard about. I was beginning to wonder if the security system wasn't a myth. A few seconds after that I rounded another corner.

As I did so, there were quick footsteps. Hands grabbed me from behind and held me. Somebody reached around and grasped both my wrists. My arms were jerked back and pulled together. But by that time I had relaxed from my initial automatic stiffening.

I felt the handcuffs as they snapped around my wrists. But I was able by now to suppress my impulse to turn and see if Terence had also been seized. I suppressed it because whether he was or not wouldn't change my conviction that this was a trap, and he had led me into it.

I had a sudden insight. Maybe across the world the score or so of Art Atkins types were also being captured at this moment by other Terence-type counterspies. In all—so I had been told—twenty-three large tents were the targets for today. It was believed by the conspirators that if that many were knocked out (involving upwards of thirty million people), that would end the threat of fluorine transformation for the time being.

Since I was being seized and not instantly killed, I guessed there'd presently be a confrontation—I had to smile. Those poor goops. Thinking they could outwit Art Atkins with such an elementary tactic. Boy!

I had no time for additional thoughts. I was being hustled along the corridor at a run. I had a few quick glimpses of about a dozen men running with me.

As rapidly as we had started, we suddenly slowed. A door opened. The brightness from inside flooded the corridor. I was pushed through the doorway into a large, brilliantly lighted room; was vaguely aware the while of the dozen crowding in behind me.

—Somebody always lives better, I thought.

Now, that's not a complaint. I've lived like a king for years. But still, here in the tent apartments were tiny, and in the big dormitories further down people occupied one unit in a tiered bunk system.

The room I was in looked lived in. There were settees and cunningly arranged tables, and on a dais to one side, carpeted floors and a combination music and book section. On this dais was an incongruity. A conference table had been squeezed onto it. Behind it, sitting at it, were four well-groomed older men.

I caught glimpses of other rooms through half-open doors, and for a moment in one of them a young woman's face. The door closed. But, yes, the place was lived in by somebody who was entitled to a living room over sixty feet long by forty wide, and bedrooms to match.

Still being held, I was led to the foot of the dais. And now, for the first time, I saw Terence again.

He was not handcuffed.

He stood just to my right, a faint, cynical smile on his face. His clothes were unrumpled. Clearly, no one had shoved him around.

He said to the men behind the table, "I was with him every minute, and he didn't have a chance to do anything. Besides"—contemptuously—"he's yellow. I've seen fear before. This guy was so weak in the knees from terror he could hardly stand up."

One of the seated men, a cold-faced individual, studied me with steely gray eyes. He was in civvies, but his bearing was military. I had never seen him before. He said in a resonant voice, "Mr. Atkins, I'm General Peter Simonville. When I look at you, I see a cool, determined male about six feet tall. I see in your eyes the same kind of self-pitying expression that I used to observe in my oldest son. But women went for that boy, and I understand you're also a woman's he-man type. He was not afraid that I ever saw, and I don't see any fear in you. So my question is, did you have an opportunity during one of those moments of stumbling to trigger that bomb?"

"No!" I lied.

The general glanced at Terence O'Day. "It's now"—he looked down at his watch—"twenty-one minutes to eleven. You have five minutes to get the information out of him, and then we have sixteen minutes to undo the damage. Fair enough."

To me he said, "I turn you over to your rival, Mr. Atkins. I should tell you that he has *carte blanche.*"

Sharp man, General Simonville—I had to admit it. But I remained silent; simply watched as Terence climbed up the dais, went around to the rear of the table and seated himself. Those black eyes of his surveyed me.

He said, "You must have been out of your mind to set up a destruct system. Don't you realize you can't keep secret like that? The authorities didn't know who put it there, but they knew about it three, four years ago."

I simply stood there. Who do they think they're giving lessons to? I understood that kind of junk when I was sixteen. You can't keep a secret. Of course. What else is new? So you tell it yourself. Let it slip. Get it out there where the stupes can start gloating among themselves, and doing all those things like removing the fuses and the powder. Meanwhile, over where the real bomb was—

I had to smile and shake my head.

I was aware of General Simonville's knowing gaze dissecting my thoughts. "Listen, Art," he said in a cajoling tone, "that is all there is to this, isn't it? We got it all three years ago. We didn't overreach ourselves, did we?"

When he said that, I knew something ... For Pete's sake, I've got a decision to make.

The way I reasoned it, nobody could do anything. There wasn't enough time to torture me. Maybe six hundred, maybe seven hundred seconds. So they were out of luck, unless I did a switcharound inside my skull.

At that point, Terence O'Day said, "We've got Mona?"

I shrugged. That little spy.

Belatedly, I realized who it was who had said that. "So?—" I reacted then.

Terence continued, "As soon as you and I left the apartment where you spent the night, troops went in and captured those five conspirators. At the same time Mona was picked up. All six of these criminals were rushed over to the oxygen process plant. If it blows up, they will blow up with it."

I let my mind's eye visualize Mona. Her golden hair would be hanging down, framing her face. In a few minutes the soft body that belonged to that beautiful face would be segmented into several thousand uneven chunks, and her blood everywhere.

I let my mind go slow-blank on that picture. No reason why it should bother me ... what happened to a phony. It did a little. But all I said was, "She's your girl, not mine, Mr. O'Day."

His face was suddenly livid. "That stupid girl!" he snarled. "Let the little whore burn."

I stared at him, eyes widening, a large thought in my mind. Women who associated with the Art Atkins type were never satisfied with ordinary males afterward.

"Hey," I said, "I'll bet she wouldn't play last night."

It was a nasty thing to say. But if we weren't at the nasty stage in this situation, when do you get there?

I'm glad black-eyed glares don't kill. I'd've been dead in three seconds if they did.

I have to admit, looking at that handsome face twisted with hate and jealousy, that I could feel the tight anger inside me start to ease up. Hastily, sensing that weakness might make my decision for me, I dredged up another possibility for Terence O'Day's severe reaction: "Was this a game? Was he dramatizing against her as part of a scheme to delude me?"

I couldn't—I realized—care less. In spite of my efforts, I was inwardly visualizing those golden curls burning in a fury of exploding flame, that beautiful face torn to shreds. And to hell with it. If that's the way they wanted to play, it was too rough for me.

"Listen!" I demanded. "Do the conspirators in this tent go free if I tell and show where everything is?"

Notice how badly I worded that. They used it against me later on: I was not one of the conspirators.

After I spoke, there were timeless seconds of emptiness in the room, as if everyone them stopped breathing. Then—

"*Yes!*" General Simonville's voice hit across that silence like a blow.

I accepted his promise. Because there was no time to get proof, or read the fine print. And in fact it was later carried out *to the letter*.

No time to waste. A couple of engineers and I made a dead run for one of the places in the corridor where I had stumbled against the wall.

When the trigger system that was there was back in its safety position again, and for two days after—while, with my help, they stripped the explosive from the real bomb—they seemed to take it for granted that I would be treated like the others. Then—

The job was done.

I was handed a paper with official seals, which began:

The unified governments of earth hereby command, and it shall be, that …

My property was confiscated, all my possessions ordered seized, no human being was to have consort with me again ever.

Clutching this paper, I was kicked out into the street.

I was the S.O.B. who had planned four years ago to destroy the human race.

"Look," I protested, "that isn't why I set up that destruct system. I set it up because I *always* do things like that—"

Nobody listened. Or cared. To hell with Art Atkins. There was a universal rage at the narrowness of the world's "escape."

I gathered that the twenty-two guys me in other tents were given the same brush-off treatment.

They had told me when they shoved me out. "Don't think you'll find your private entrance to the tent available a second time."

—Okay, boobs, take a good last look. You'll never see me again, nor locate my body.

Hell, I'd been expecting the world to turn against me since I came up out of the mists of childhood. Somehow, I always knew those so-and-sos didn't like me.

Soon as I was old enough I began getting another identity polished up for the day when they came after me. Why do you think I started growing a beard, practically over my mother's dead body, when I was sixteen? I didn't want anyone, not even her, to remember what I would look like if I ever had to go smooth face.

… Two years have gone by.

They say the fluorine rain has stopped.

Deep in the bowls of the big oxygen tent, a knock comes on my door. I guess who it is, and I say to Mona, "You answer it."

She opens the door. General Simonville stands there. His cold face has a forced smile on it. He says in a somewhat over-hearty voice. "The people in this apartment have been selected by lottery to be the first in this tent for the fluorine shots."

I take that with a straight face. The rest of the selections will—I imagine—actually be by lottery. But my being number one had to be arranged.

The general steps aside, and a trio of girls wheel in the equipment: a metal table with a large transparent jar. on it with liquid in it. The liquid is the serum (I deduce). And there are a host of connecting tubes and needles.

As I lie there, and the girls busy with my exposed thigh, my eyes turn and meet the gaze of General Simonville. "Everything okay?" he asks.

His question has a double meaning, and I consider before I answer. After I had shaved off my whiskers and altered my fingerprints, the problem was to get into the tent.

Well—I figured that a man with a private entry into a bank vault might have, say, a hundred thousand dollars available as a starter. That much cash, it seemed to me, might persuade a general who had not hesitated to accept a super-sized apartment for his own living quarters to open a gate for me, and find a lower level place where I could live away from it all, and bring Mona over there. With that combo I figured I could sit out the rainstorms in relative comfort. In handing over the down payment, I also stipulated that I would be the first to be changed over.

I promised him a second hundred thousand if I got through alive—

My gaze flicked down to the needle that was being shoved into me. The question in my mind is, will I wake up?

Have I offered him enough?

I've got a whole bank to draw on. Since the government has guaranteed losses suffered front looting during the transition, the bank will be repaid ... My plan is to filch exactly what was expropriated from me.

I look up. I say, "Everything okay, General—on my side."

"On mine, also," he says.

People are hoping that changing mankind to fluorine breathing may alter human nature for the better. My suggestion is, they'd better not hold their breath while they wait for these peculiar two-legged beings to alter their behavior.

Believing that, I'm guessing as I sink into unconsciousness that the general's words mean what I think. And that I will wake up. I will. I will.

And I will be the first fluorine-breathing son of a bitch on the new earth.

DISCORD IN SCARLET

Xtl sprawled moveless on the bosom of endless night. Time dragged drearily toward infinity, and space was dark. Unutterably dark! The horrible pitch-blackness of intergalactic immensity! Across the miles and the years, vague patches of light gleamed coldly at him, whole galaxies of blazing stars shrunk by incredible distance to shining swirls of mist.

Life was out there, spawning on the myriad planets that whirled eternally around the myriad suns. And life had once crawled out of the primeval mud of ancient Glor—before cosmic explosion destroyed a mighty race and flung his—Xtl's—body out into the deeps of space, the prey of chance.

His brain pulsed on and on in the same old, old cycle of thought—thinking: one chance in decillions that his body would ever come near a galactic system. One chance in infinity itself that he fall on a planet, and find a precious *guul*. And never, never a hope that his race would live again.

A billion times that thought had pounded to its dreary conclusion in his brain, until it was a part of him, until it was like a picture unrolling before his eyes—it and those remote wisps of shiningness out there in that blackness. And that picture was more real than the reality. He had no consciousness of the spaceship until he touched the metal.

Hard, hardness—something material! The vague sense perception fumbled into his dulled brain, bringing a living pain—like a disused muscle, briefly, agonizingly brought into action.

The thought slumped. His brain slid back into its sleep of ages, seeing again the old picture of hopelessness and the shiningness in the black. The very idea of hardness became a dream that faded. Some remote corner of his mind, curiously alert, watched it fade, watched the shad-

535

ows creep with reaching, enveloping folds of lightlessness, striving to re-engulf the dim consciousness that had flashed into such an anguish of ephemeral existence.

And then, once more, his groping fingers sent that dull pulse of awareness tapping its uncertain message to his sodden, hopeless brain.

His elongated body convulsed in senseless movement, four arms lashed out, four legs jackknifed with blind, unreasoning strength. There was a distinct sense of a blow and of a pushing away from the hard matter.

His glazed, staring eyes, his stultified vision galvanized into life; and he saw that, in the contorted fury of his movements, he had pushed himself away from the surface of a vast, round, dark-bodied metal monster, studded with row on row of glaring lights, like diamonds. The spaceship floated there in the velvet darkness, glowing like an immense jewel, quiescent but alive, enormously, vitally alive, bringing nostalgic and vivid suggestion of a thousand far-flung planets, and of an indomitable, boisterous life that had reached for the stars and grasped them. Bringing—hope!

The torpid tenor of his thoughts exploded into chaos. His mind, grooved through the uncounted ages to ultimate despair, soared up, up, insanely. Life surged from the bottom point of static to the swirling, irresistible height of dynamism, that jarred every atom of his scarlet, cylindrical body and his round, vicious head. His legs and arms glistened like tongues of living fire, as they twisted and writhed in the blaze of light from those dazzling portholes. His mouth, a gash in the center of his hideous head, slavered a white frost that floated away in little frozen globules.

His brain couldn't hold the flame of that terrific hope. His mind kept dissolving, blurring. Through that blur, he saw a thick vein of light form a circular bulge in the metallic surface of the ship. The bulge became a huge door that rotated open and tilted to one side. A flood of brilliance spilled out of the great opening, followed by a dozen two-legged beings in transparent metal armor, dragging great floating machines.

Swiftly, the machines were concentrated around a dark projection on the ship's surface. Intolerable light flared up as what was obviously repair work proceeded at an alarming pace.

He was no longer falling away from the ship. The faint pressure of gravitational pull was drawing him down again—so slowly. Frantically, he adjusted his atomic structure to the fullest measure of attraction. But even his poorly responding brain could see that he would never make it.

The work was finished. The incandescent glare of atomic welders died to spluttering darkness. Machines were unclamped, floated toward the opening of the ship, down into it and out of sight. The two-legged beings scrambled after them. The vast, curved plain of metal was suddenly as deserted and lifeless as space itself.

Terror struck into Xtl. He'd have to fight, have to get there somehow. He couldn't let them get away now, when the whole universe was in his grasp—twenty-five short yards away. His stretching arms reached out stupidly, as if he would hold the ship by sheer fury of need. His brain ached with a slow, rhythmical hurt. His mind spun toward a black, bottomless pit—then poised just before the final plunge.

The great door was slowing in its swift rotation. A solitary being squeezed through the ring of light and ran to the dark projection, just repaired. He picked up an instrument that gleamed weirdly, a tool of some kind forgotten, and started back toward the partly open lock.

He stopped. In the glow from the portholes, Xtl could see the other's face through the transparent armor. The face stared up at him, eyes wide, mouth open. Then the mouth moved rapidly: opening and shutting, apparently a form of communication with the others.

A moment later the door was rotating again, opening wide. A group of the beings came out, two of them mounted on the top of a large, metal-barred cage, steering it under power. He was to be captured.

Oddly, his brain felt no sense of lift, no soaring hope, none of that mind-inflaming ecstasy. It was as if a drug was dragging him down, down, into a black night of fatigue. Appalled, he fought off the enveloping stupor. He must hold to his senses. His race, that had attained the very threshold of ultimate knowledge, must live again.

The voice, a strained, unrecognizable voice, came to Commander Morton through the communicators in his transparent spacesuit: "How in the name of all the hells can anything live in intergalactic space?"

It seemed to the commander that the question made the little group of men crowd closer together. The proximity of the others made them feel easier. Then they suddenly grew aware of the impalpable yet alive weight of the inconceivable night that coiled about them, pressing down to the very blazing portholes.

For the first time in years, the immensity of that night squeezed icily into Morton's consciousness. Long familiarity had bred indifference into his very bones—but now, the incredible vastness of that blackness reaching a billion trillion years beyond the farthest frontiers of man stabbed into his mind, and brought an almost dismaying awareness. His deep voice, clattering into the communicators, split that scared silence like some harsh noise, startled him:

"Gunlie Lester, here's something for your astronomical-mathematical brain. Will you please give us the ratio of chance that blew out a driver of the *Beagle* at the exact point in space where that thing was floating? Take a few hours to work it out."

The astronomer replied immediately:

"I don't have to think about it. The chance is unstatable in human arithmetic. It can't happen, mathematically speaking. Here we are, a ship-load of human beings, stopping for repairs halfway between two galaxies—the first time we've ever made a trip outside of our own galaxy. Here we are, I say, a tiny point intersecting without prearrangement exactly the path of another, tinier point. Impossible, unless space is saturated with such—creatures!"

"I hope not," another man shuddered. "We ought to turn a mobile unit on anything that looks like that, on general principles."

The shudder seemed to run along the communicators. Commander Morton shook his great, lean body as if consciously trying to throw off the chill of it. His eyes on the maneuvering cage above, he said:

"A regular blood-red devil spewed out of some fantastic nightmare; ugly as sin—and probably as harmless as our beautiful pussy last year was deadly. Smith, what do you think?"

The cadaverous-faced biologist said in his cold, logical voice:

"This thing has arms and legs, a purely planetary evolution. If it is intelligent it will begin to react to its environment the moment it is inside the cage. It may be a venerable old sage, meditating in the silence of distractionless space. Or it may be a young murderer, condemned to eternal exile, consumed with desire to sneak back home and resume the life he lived."

"I wish Korita had come out with us," said Pennons, the chief engineer, in his quiet, practical voice. "Korita's historical analysis of pussy last year gave us an advance idea of what we had to face and—"

"Korita speaking, Mr. Pennons," came the meticulously clear voice of the Japanese archaeologist on the communicators. "Like many of the others, I have been listening to what is happening as a welcome break in this, the longest journey the spaceship *Beagle* has ever undertaken. But I am afraid analysis of the creature would be dangerous at this factless stage. In the case of pussy, we had the barren, foodless planet on which he lived, and the architectural realities of his crumbled city.

"Here we have a creature living in space a million years from the nearest planet, apparently without food, and without means of spatial locomotion. I suggest you make certain that you get him into the cage, and then study him—every action, every reaction. Take pictures of his internal organs working in the vacuum of space. Find out every possible thing about him, so that we shall know what we have aboard as soon as possible. Now, when we are fully staffed again and heading for a new galaxy for the first time in the history of man, we cannot afford to have anything go wrong, or anybody killed before we reach there. Thank you."

"And that," said Morton, "is sense. You've got your fluorite camera, Smith?"

"Attached to my suit," Smith acknowledged.

Morton, who knew the capabilities of the mournful-looking biologist, turned his attention back to the cage fifty feet away. He said in his deep, resonant voice:

"Open the door as wide as possible, and drop over him. Don't let his hands grab the bars."

"Just a minute!" a guttural voice broke in. Morton turned questioningly to the big, plump German physicist. Von Grossen continued:

"Let us not rush this capture, Commander Morton. It is true that I was not aboard last year when you had your encounter with the creature you persist in calling pussy. But when you returned to the base planet before embarking on the present voyage, the story you told to the world was not reassuring, not to me, anyway."

His hard, gray-dark face stared grimly at the others: "It is true that I can see no real objection to capturing this creature in a cage. But it happens that I am replacing a man who was killed by this—pussy. Therefore I speak for him when I say: Such a thing must never happen again."

Morton frowned, his face lined with doubt. "You put me in a spot, von Grossen. As human beings, we must take every possible precaution. As scientists, however, all is grist for our mill; everything must be investigated. There can be no thought of shunning danger before we even know it to be danger. If this voyage is to be ruled by fear, we might as well head for home now."

"Fear is not what I had in mind," said the physicist quietly. "But I believe in counting ten before acting."

Morton asked: "Any other objections?"

He felt oddly annoyed that there were none.

Xtl waited. His thoughts kept breaking up into little pieces of light and lightlessness—a chain of dazzle and dark—that somehow connected up with all the things he had ever known or thought. Visions of a long-dead planet trickled into his consciousness bringing a vague conceit—and a contempt of these creatures who thought to capture him.

Why, he could remember a time when his race had had spaceships a hundred times the size of this machine that swam below him. That was before they had dispensed completely with space travel, and just lived a quiet homey life building beauty from natural forces.

He watched, as the cage was driven toward him unerringly. There was nothing he could do, even had he wanted to. The gaping mouth of the large, metal-barred construction closed over him and snapped shut the moment he was inside.

Xtl clawed at the nearest bar, caught hold with grim strength. He clung there an instant, sick and dizzy with awful reaction. Safe! His mind expanded with all the violence of an exploding force. Free electrons discharged in dizzying swarms from the chaos of the spinning atom systems inside his brain and body, frantically seeking union with the other systems. He was safe—safe after quadrillions of years of sick despair, and on a material body with unlimited power to take him where he would to go. Safe when there was still time to carry out his sacred purpose. Or was he safe?

The cage was dropping toward the surface of the ship. His eyes became gleaming pools of caution, as they studied the men below. It was only too evident that he was to be examined. With a tremendous effort, stung by fear, he tried to push the clinging dullness from his brain, fought for alertness. An examination of him now would reveal his purpose, expose the precious objects concealed within his breast; and that must not be.

His steely-bright eyes flicked in anxious dismay over the dozen figures in transparent armor. Then his mind calmed. They were inferior creatures, obviously! Puny foes before his own remarkable power. Their very need of spacesuits proved their inability to adapt themselves to environment, proved they existed on a low plane of evolution. Yet he must not underestimate them. Here were keen brains, capable of creating and using mighty machines.

Each of the beings had weapons in holster at the side of his space armor—weapons with sparkling, translucent handles. He had noticed the same weapons in the holsters of the men at the top of the cage. That, then, would be his method if any of these creatures flashed a camera on him.

As the cage dropped into the belt of undiffused blackness between two portholes, Smith stepped forward with his camera—and Xtl jerked himself with effortless ease up the bars to the ceiling of the cage. The gash of his mouth in the center of his round, smooth head was split in a silent snarl of fury at the unutterable bad luck that was forcing this move upon him. His vision snapped full on; and now he could see blurrily through the hard metal of the ceiling.

One arm, with its eight wirelike fingers, lashed out with indescribable swiftness at the ceiling, *through* it, and then he had a gun from the holster of one of the men.

He did not attempt to readjust its atomic structure as he had adjusted his arm. It was important that they should not guess that it was he who fired the gun. Straining in his awkward position, he aimed the weapon straight at Smith and the little group of men behind him—released the flaming power.

There was a flare of incandescent violence that blotted the men from view. A swirl of dazzling light coruscated virulently across the surface of the ship. And there was another light, too. A blue sparkle that told of automatic defense screens driving out from the armored suits of the men.

In one continuous movement, Xtl released the gun, withdrew his hand; and, by the act, pushed himself to the floor. His immediate fear was gone. No sensitive camera film could have lived through the blaze of penetrating energy. And what was overwhelmingly more important—the gun was no good against himself. Nothing but a simple affair which employed the method of transmutation of one element to another, the process releasing one or two electrons from each atom system. It would require a dozen such guns to do damage to his body.

The group of men stood quite still; and Morton knew they were fighting, as he was, the blindness that lingered from the spray of violent light. Slowly, his eyes became adjusted; and then he could see again the curved metal on which he stood, and beyond that the brief, barren crest of the ship and the limitless miles of lightless, heatless space—dark, fathomless, unthinkable gulfs. There too, a blur among the blurs of shadows, stood the cage.

"I'm sorry, commander," one of the men on the cage apologized. "The ato-gun must have fallen out of my belt, and discharged."

"Impossible!" Smith's voice came to Morton, low and tense. "In this gravitation, it would take several minutes to fall from the holster, and it wouldn't discharge in any event from such a slight jar of landing."

"Maybe I knocked against it, sir, without noticing."

"Maybe!" Smith seemed to yield grudgingly to the explanation. "But I could almost swear that, just before the flare of light dazzled me, the creature moved. I admit it was too black to see more than the vaguest blur, but—"

"Smith," Morton said sharply, "what are you trying to prove?"

He saw the long-faced biologist hunch his narrow shoulders, as if pulling himself together. The biologist mumbled:

"When you put it like that, I don't know. The truth is, I suppose, that I've never gotten over the way I insisted on keeping pussy alive, with such desperately tragic results. I suspect everything now, and—"

Morton stared in surprise. It was hard to realize that it was really Smith speaking—the scientist who, it had seemed sometimes in the past, was ready to sacrifice his own life and everybody else's if it meant adding a new, important fact to the science of biology. Morton found his voice at last:

"You were perfectly right in what you did! Until we realized the truth, you expressed the majority mind of this ship's company. The development of the situation in the case of pussy changed our opinion as well as your own, but it did not change our method of working by evidence alone. I say that we should continue to make such logic the basis of our work."

"Right. And beg your pardon, chief!" Smith was brisk-voiced again. "Crane, turn the cage light on, and let's see what we've got here."

To Morton, the silence that followed seemed like a sudden, oppressive weight, as the blaze of light showered down on Xtl crouching at the bottom of the cage. The almost metallic sheen of the cylindrical body, the eyes like coals of fire, the wirelike fingers and toes, the scarlet hideousness of it startled even these men who were accustomed to alien forms of life. He broke the spell of horror, half-breathlessly:

"He's probably very handsome—to himself!"

"If life is evolution," said Smith in a stiff voice, "and nothing evolves except for use, how can a creature living in space have highly developed legs and arms? Its insides should be interesting. But now—my camera's useless! That flare of energy would have the effect of tinting the electrified lens, and of course the film's ruined. Shall I get another?"

"N-n-no-o!" Morton's clean-cut, handsome face grew dark with a frown. "We've wasted a lot of time here; and after all, we can re-create vacuum of space conditions inside the ship's laboratory, and be traveling at top acceleration while we're doing it."

"Just a minute!" Von Grossen, the plump but hard-boiled physicist, spoke. "Let's get this straight. The *Beagle* is going to another galaxy on an exploration voyage—the first trip of the kind. Our business is to study life in this new system, but we're not taking any specimens, only pictures and notes—studies of the creatures in their various environments. If we're all so nervous about this thing, why are we taking it aboard?"

"Because"—Smith beat Morton to the reply—"we're not tied down to pictures and notes. There will, however, be millions of forms of life on every planet, and we shall be forced to the barest kind of record in most cases. This monster is different. In our fears we have almost forgotten that the existence of a creature capable of living in space is the most extraordinary thing we've ever run across. Even pussy, who could live without air, needed warmth of a kind, and would have found the absolute cold of space intolerable. If, as we suspect, this creature's natural habitat is not space, then we must find out why and how he came to be where he is. Speaking as a biologist—"

"I see," interrupted Morton dryly, "that Smith is himself again." He directed a command at the men on the cage. "Take that monster inside, and put a wall of force around the cage. That should satisfy even the most cautious."

Xtl felt the faint throb of the motors of the cage. He saw the bars move, then grew conscious of a sharp, pleasant tingling sensation, brief physical activity within his body that stopped the workings of his mind for a bare second. Before he could think, there was the cage floor rising above him—and he was lying on the hard surface of the spaceship's outer shell.

With a snarl of black dismay that almost cut his face in two, he realized the truth. He had forgotten to readjust the atoms in his body after firing the gun. And now he had fallen through!

"Good Heaven!" Morton bellowed.

A scarlet streak of elongated body, a nightmare shadow in that braid of shadow and light, Xtl darted across the impenetrable heavy metal to the air lock. He jerked himself down into its dazzling depths. His adjusted body dissolved through the two other locks. And then he was at one end of a long, gleaming corridor— safe for the moment!

There would be searching for him; and—he knew with a cold, hardening resolve—these creatures would never trust alive a being who could slip through solid metal. Their reason would tell them he was a superbeing, unutterably dangerous to them.

One advantage only he had—they did not know the deadliness of his purpose.

Ten minutes later, Morton's gray eyes flicked questioningly over the stern faces of the men gathered in the great reception room. His huge and powerful body felt oddly rigid, as if his muscles could not quite relax. His voice was mellower, deeper, richer than normal:

"I am going to offer my resignation on the grounds that, for the second time under my leadership, an abnormal beast has gotten aboard this craft. I must assume that there is a basic lack in my mental make-up; for results, and not excuses, do count in this universe of ours; even apparently bad luck is rigorously bound up with character. I, therefore, suggest that Korita or von Grossen be named commander in my place. Korita because of the care he advocated, and von Grossen on the strength of his objection to taking any living specimens aboard—both are more fitted to hold the command than I am."

"The honorable commander has forgotten one thing," Korita said softly. "The creature was *not* carried into the ship. I admit it was our collective intention to bring him aboard, but it was he himself who entered. I suggest that, even if we had decided not to bring him into the interior, we could not have prevented his entry in view of his ability to slip through metal. It is absolutely absurd for Commander Morton to feel responsible."

Von Grossen heaved himself out his chair. Now that he was out of his spacesuit, the physicist looked not so much plump as big and iron-hard. "And that goes for me all the way. I have not been long on this ship, but

I have found Commander Morton to be a most able intellect and leader of men. So let us not waste time in useless self-reproach.

"In capturing this being we must first of all straighten our minds about him. He has arms and legs, this creature, yet floats in space, and remains alive. He allows himself to be caught in a cage, but knows all the time that the cage cannot hold him. Then he drops through the bottom of the cage, which is very silly if he doesn't want us to know that he can do it. Which means that he is a very foolish creature indeed, and we don't have to worry very much about him. There is a reason why intelligent living things make mistakes—a fundamental reason that should make it easy for us to analyze him right back to where he came from, and why he is here. Smith, analyze his biological make-up."

Smith, stood up, lank and grim. "We've already discussed the obvious planetary origin of his hands and feet. The ability to live in space, however, is an abnormal development, having no connection with natural evolution, but is the product of brain power and science, pure and simple. I suggest that here is a member of a race that has solved the final secrets of biology; and, if I knew how we should even begin to start looking for a creature that can slip through walls, my advice would be: Hunt him down and kill him within an hour."

"Er!" Kellie, the sociologist, said. He was a bald-headed man with preternaturally intelligent eyes that gleamed owlishly from behind his pince-nez. "Er, any being who could fit himself to vacuum of space condition would be lord of the universe. His kind would dwell on every planet, clutter up every galactic system. Swarms of him would be floating in space, if space floating is what they go in for. Yet, we know for a fact that his race does not rule *our* galactic area. A paradox, which is worthy of investigation."

"I don't quite understand what you mean, Kellie!" Morton frowned.

"Simply, er, that a race which has solved the final secrets of biology must be millions, even billions of years in advance of man; and, as a pure sympodial—capable of adaptation to any environment—would, according to the law of vital dynamics, expand to the farthest frontier of the universe, just as man is slowly pushing himself to the remotest planets."

"It is a contradiction," Morton agreed, "and would seem to prove that the creature is not a superior being. Korita, what is this thing's history?"

The Japanese scientist shrugged:

"I'm afraid I can only be of the slightest assistance on present evidence. You know the prevailing theory: That life proceeds upwards by a series of cycles. Each cycle begins with the peasant, who is rooted to his bit of soil. The peasant comes to market; and slowly the marketplace transforms to a town, with ever less 'inward' connection to the earth. Then we have cities and nations, finally the soulless world cities and a devastating struggle for power—a series of frightful wars which sweep men back to the peasant stage. The question becomes: Is this creature in the peasant part of this particular cycle, or in the big city 'megalopolitan' era?"

Morton's voice slashed across the silence: "In view of our limited knowledge of this creature, what basic traits should we look for, supposing him to be in the big city stage?"

"He would be a cold, invincible intellect, formidable to the ultimate degree, undefeatable—except through circumstances. I refer to the kind of circumstances that made it impossible for us to prevent this beast entering our ship. Because of his great innate intelligence, he would make no errors of any kind."

"But he has already made an error!" von Grossen said in a silken voice. "He very foolishly fell through the bottom of the cage. It is the kind of blunder a peasant would make—"

"Suppose," Morton asked, "he were in the peasant stage?"

"Then," Korita replied, "his basic impulses would be much simpler. There would be first of all the desire to reproduce, to have a son, to know that his blood was being carried on. Assuring great fundamental intelligence, this impulse might, in the superior being, take the form of a fanatic drive toward race survival—"

He stopped, as half a dozen men came through the doorway.

Morton said: "Finished, Pennons?"

The chief engineer nodded. Then in a warning voice:

"It is absolutely essential that every man on the ship get into his rubberite suit, and wear rubberite gloves."

Morton explained grimly:

"We've energized the walls around the bedrooms. There may be some delay in catching this creature, and we're taking no chances of being murdered in our beds. We—" Sharply:

"What is it, Pennons?"

Pennons was staring at a small instrument in his hand; he said in a queer voice:

"Are we all here, Morton?"

"Yes, except for four men guarding the engine room."

"Then ... then something's caught in the wall of force. Quick—we must surround it."

To Xtl, returning from a brief exploration of the monster ship's interior, the shock was devastating, the surprise unutterable and complete.

One moment he was thinking complacently of the metal sections in the hold of the ship, where he would secrete his *guuls*; the next moment he was caught in the full sparkling fury of an energy screen.

His body writhed with an agony that blackened his brain. Thick clouds of free electrons rose up within him in that hell of pain, and flashed from system to system seeking union, only to be violently repelled by the tortured, madly spinning atom systems. For those long seconds, the wonderfully balanced instability of his structure nearly collapsed into an abyss of disintegration.

But the incredible genius that had created his marvelous body had forethought even this eventuality. Like lightning, his body endured readjustment after automatic readjustment, each new-built structure carrying the intolerable load for a fraction of a fraction of a second. And then, he had jerked back from the wall, and was safe.

In a flare of thought, his mind investigated the immediate possibilities. Obviously, the men had rigged up this defense wall of force. It meant they would have an alarm system—and they would swoop down every corridor in an organized attempt to corner him.

Xtl's eyes were glowing pools of white fire as he realized the opportunity. He must catch one of these men, while they were scattered, investigate his guul properties, and use him for his first *guul*.

No time to waste. He darted into the nearest wall, a tall, gaudy, ungraceful streak, and, without pausing, sped through room after room, roughly parallel to a main corridor. His sensitive feet caught the vibrations of the approaching men; and through the wall his full vision followed the blurred figures rushing past. One, two, three, four—five—on this corridor. The fifth man was some distance behind the others.

Like a wraith, Xtl glided into the wall just ahead of the last man—and pounced forth in an irresistible charge. A rearing, frightful shape of glaring eyes and ghastly mouth, blood-red, metal-hard body, and four arms of fire that clutched with bitter strength at the human body.

The man tried to fight. His big form twisted, jerked; his lashing fists felt vaguely painful as they pounded desperately against the hard, sheeny crust of Xtl's body. And then, by sheer weight and ferocity, he was overwhelmed; the force of his fall jarring Xtl's sensitive frame.

The man was lying on his back, and Xtl watched curiously as the mouth opened and shut spasmodically. A tingling sensation sped along Xtl's feet, and his mouth opened in a snarl. Incapable though he was of hearing sounds, he realized that he was picking up the vibrations of a call for help.

He pounced forward, one great hand smashing at the man's mouth. Teeth broke, and crushed back into the throat. The body sagged. But the man was still alive, and conscious, as Xtl plunged two hands into the feebly writhing body.

The man ceased suddenly even that shadow of struggle, his widened eyes staring at the arms that vanished under his shirt, stirred around in his chest, stared in petrified terror at the monstrous blood-red cylindrical body that loomed over him, with its round bright eyes glaring at him as if they would see right through him.

It was a blurred picture the frantic Xtl saw. The inside of the man's body seemed solid flesh. He had to find an open space, or one that could be pressed open, so long as the pressing did not kill the man. He must have living flesh.

Hurry, hurry— His feet registered the vibrations of approaching footsteps—from one direction only, but coming swiftly, swiftly.

And then, just like that, it was all over. His searching fingers, briefly hardened to a state of semisolidity, touched the heart. The man heaved convulsively, shuddered, and slumped into death.

The next instant, Xtl discovered the stomach. For a moment, black dismay flooded him. Here was what he was searching for, and he had killed it, rendered it useless! He stared in cold fury at the stilled body, uncertain, alarmed.

Then suddenly his actions became deliberate, weighted with contempt. Never for an instant had he suspected these intelligent beings would die so easily. It changed, simplified everything. There was no need to be anything more than casually careful in dealing with them.

Two men with drawn ato-guns whipped around the nearest corner, and slid to a halt at the sight of the apparition that snarled at them across the dead body. Then, as they came out of their brief paralysis, Xtl stepped into the nearest wall, a blur of scarlet in that brightly lit corridor, gone on the instant. He felt the fury of the energy rays that tore futilely at the metal behind him.

His plan was quite clear now. He would capture half a dozen men, and make *guuls* of them. Then kill all the others, proceed on to the galactic system toward which the ship was heading, and take control of the first inhabited planet. After that, domination of the entire universe would be a matter of a short time only.

Commander Morton stood very stiffly there in the gleaming corridor, every muscle in his huge body like a taut wire. Only a dozen men were gathered round the dead body, but the audioscopes were on; nearly two hundred tense men throughout the ship were watching that scene. Morton's voice was only a whisper, but it cut across the silence like a whiplash:

"Well, doctor?"

Dr. Eggert rose up from his kneeling position beside the body, frowning:

"Heart failure."

"Heart failure!"

"All right, all right!" The doctor put up his hands as if to defend himself against physical attack. "I know his teeth look as if they've been smashed back into his brain, and I know Darjeeling's heart was perfect, but heart failure is what it looks like to me."

"I can believe it," a man said sourly. "When I came around that corner, and saw that thing, I nearly had heart failure myself."

"We're wasting time!" von Grossen's voice stabbed from behind Morton. "We can beat this fellow, but not by talking about him, and feeling sick every time he makes a move. If I'm next on the list of victims, I want to know that the best damned bunch of scientists in the system are not crying over my fate, but putting their best brains to the job of avenging my death."

"You're right," Smith said. "The trouble with us is, we've been permitting ourselves to feel inferior. He's only been on the ship about an hour but I can see now that some of us are going to get killed. Well, I accept my chance! But let's get organized for combat!"

Morton snapped: "Pennons, here's a problem. We've got about two square miles of wall and floor space in our twenty levels. How long will it take to energize every inch of it?"

The chief engineer stared at him, aghast; then answered swiftly: "I could sweep the ship and probably wreck it completely within an hour. I won't go into details. But uncontrolled energization is absolutely out. It would kill every living thing aboard—"

"Not everything!" von Grossen rejected. "Not the creature. Remember, that damn thing ran into a wall of force. Your instrument, Pennons, registered activity for several seconds. Several seconds! Let me show you what that means. The principle underlying his ability to slip through walls is simple enough. The atoms of his body slide through the empty spaces between the atoms of the walls. There is a basic electronic tension that holds a body together, which would have to be overcome, but apparently his race has solved the difficulty. A wall of force would increase those electronic tensions to a point where the atoms themselves would be emitting free electrons; and, theoretically, that should have a deadly effect on any interfering body. I'll wager he didn't like those few seconds he was in the wall—but the point is, he stood them."

Morton's strong face was hard: "You could feed more energy to those walls, couldn't you. Pennons?"

"N-no!" said Pennons reluctantly. "The walls couldn't stand it. They'd melt."

"The walls couldn't stand it!" a man gasped. "Man, man, do you know what you're making this creature out to be?"

Morton saw the consternation that leaped along that line of stern faces. Korita's thin, clear voice cut across that pregnant silence:

"Let us not forget, my honorable friends, that he did blunder into the wall of force, and recoiled in dismay, though apparently without damage to his person. I use the word 'blunder' with discretion. His action proves once again that he does make mistakes which, in turn, shows him to be something less than a superbeing—"

"Suppose," Morton barked, "he's a peasant of his cycle. What would be his chief intellectual characteristic?"

Korita replied almost crisply for one who usually spoke so slowly: "The inability to understand the full power of organization. He will think probably that all he has to fight in order to get control of this ship would be the men who are in it. His most instinctive reasoning would tend to discount the fact that we are part of a vast galactic civilization or organization, and that the spirit of that civilization is fighting in us. The mind of the true peasant is very individualistic, almost anarchic. His desire to reproduce is a form of egoism, to have his own blood particularly carried on. There can be no such thing as a peasant co-operative or organization. But this creature may want to have numbers of beings similar to himself beside him to help him with his fight. But, though there would be a loose union, they would fight as individuals, and not as a group."

"A loose union of those fire-eaters ought to be enough!" a crew member commented acidly. "I ... a-a-a-a—"

His voice sagged. His lower jaw dropped two inches. His eyes, under Morton's gaze, took on a horribly goggled stare. The commander whipped around with an oath.

Xtl stood there, forbidding specter from a scarlet hell, his eyes pools of blazing alertness. He knew with a vast contempt that he could plunge into the nearest wall before any gun could leap out at him in ravening fury. But he felt himself protected by another fact. These were intelligent beings. They would be more anxious to discover why he had deliberately come out of the wall than to kill him immediately. They might even consider it a friendly move; and, when they discovered differently, it would be too late.

His purpose, which was twofold, was simplicity itself. He had come for his first *guul*. By snatching that *guul* from their very midst, he would demoralize them thoroughly.

Morton felt a curious wave of unreality sweep over him, as he stood just behind von Grossen there in that glittering hallway, facing the tall, thick, cylindrical reality of Xtl. Instinctively, his fingers groped downward toward the sparkling, translucent handle of the ato-gun that protruded from his holster. He stopped himself, and said in a steady voice:

"Don't touch your guns. He can move like a flash; and he wouldn't be here if he thought we could draw on him. I'll take his opinion any day on that point. Besides, we can't risk failure. This may be our only chance!"

He continued in a swift, slightly higher, more urgent tone:

"Every man listening in on the audioscopes get above and below and around this corridor. Bring up the heaviest portables, even some of the semiportables, and burn the walls down. Cut a clear path all around this area, and have your beams sweep that space at narrow focus. Move!"

"Good boy, Morton!" Pennons' face appeared for an instant on the plate of the audioscope. "We'll be there—if you can stall that hellhound three minutes."

Korita's sibilant voice hissed out of the audioscope: "Morton, take this chance, but do not count on success. Notice that he has appeared once again before we have had time for a discussion. He is rushing us, whether intentionally or accidentally matters not, because the result is that we're on the run, scurrying this way and that, futilely. So far we have not clarified our thoughts. I am convinced the vast resources of this ship can defeat any creature—any single creature—that has ever existed, or that ever will exist, but only if we have time to use them—"

His voice blurred briefly in Morton's ears. Von Grossen had taken a notebook from his pocket, and was sketching rapidly. He tore the sheet loose, and stepped forward, handed it to the creature, who examined it curiously.

Von Grossen stepped back, and began to sketch again on the second page, with a swift deftness. This sheet he handed also to the creature, who took one glance at it, and stepped back with a snarl that split his face. His eyes widened to blazing pools; one arm half reached forward toward von Grossen, then paused uncertainly.

"What the devil have you done?" Morton demanded, his voice sounding unnaturally shrill even to himself.

Von Grossen took several steps backward, until he stood level with Morton. To the commander's amazement, he was grinning:

"I've just shown him," the German physicist said softly, "how we can defeat him—neutronium alloy, of course, and he—"

Too late, Morton stepped forward, instinctively trying to interpose his huge form in front of von Grossen. A blur of red swept by him. Something—a hand moving so fast that it was invisible—struck him a stunning blow, and knocked him spinning against the nearest wall. For an instant, his body threatened to collapse from sheer, dazed weakness. The world went black, then white, then black.

With appalling effort, he fought the weakness aside. The immense reservoir of strength in his magnificent body surged irresistibly forward; his knees stopped wavering, but his vision was still a crazy thing. As through a distorted glass, he saw that the thing was holding von Grossen in two fire-colored arms. The two-hundred-and-ten-pound physicist gave one convulsive heave of dismay; and then seemed to accept the overpowering strength of those thin, hard muscles.

With a bellow, Morton clawed for his gun. And it was then that the maddest thing of all happened. The creature took a running dive, and vanished into the wall, still holding von Grossen. For an instant, it seemed to Morton like a crazy trick of vision. But there was only the smooth gleamingness of the wall, and eleven staring, perspiring men, seven of them with drawn weapons, which they fingered helplessly.

"We're lost!" a man whispered. "If he can adjust our atomic structure, and take us through walls, we can't fight him."

Morton chilled his heart to the dismay he read in that rough semicircle of faces. He said coldly:

"Your report, Pennons?"

There was a brief delay, then the engineer's lean leathery face, drawn with strain and effort, stared into the plate: "Nothing!" he replied succinctly. "Clay, one of my assistants, thinks he saw a flash of scarlet disappearing through a floor, going down. That's a clue of course. It means our search will be narrowed to the lower half of the ship. As for the rest, we were just lining up our units when it happened. You gave us only two minutes. We needed three!"

Morton nodded, his thoughtful mood interrupted by the abrupt realization that his fingers were shaking. With a muttered imprecation, he clenched them, and said icily:

"Korita has given us our cue—organization. The implications of that word must be fully thought out, and co-ordinated to the knowledge we have of the creature. Von Grossen, of course, has given us our defense—neutronium alloy."

"I don't follow the argument," interjected Zeller, the metallurgist.

It was Smith who explained:

"The commander means that only two parts of the ship are composed of that incredibly dense metal, the outer shell and the engine room. If you had been with us when we first captured this creature, you would have noticed that, when the damned thing fell through the floor of the cage, it was stopped short by the hard metal of the ship's crust. The conclusion is obviously that it cannot slip through such metal; and the fact that it ran for the air lock is proof. The wonder is that we didn't think of it before."

Morton barked: "Therefore, to the heart of the ship—the engine room. And we won't go out of there till we've got a plan. Any other way, he'll run us ragged."

"What about von Grossen?" a man ventured.

Morton snapped harshly: "Don't make us think of von Grossen. Do you want us all to go crazy?"

In that vast room of vast machines, the men were dwarfs in *gigantica*. It was a world apart; and Morton, for the first time in years, felt the alien, abnormal tremendousness of it. His nerves jumped at each special burst of unholy blue light that sparkled and coruscated upon the great, glistening sweep of the ceiling. Blue light that was alive, pure energy that no eliminators had ever been able to eliminate, no condensers absorb.

And there was something else that sawed on his nerves now. A sound—imprisoned in the very air! A thin hum of terrifying power, a vague rumble, the faintest, quivering reverberation of an inconceivable flow of energy.

Morton glanced at his watch, and stood up with an explosive sigh of relief. He swept up a small sheaf of notes from a metal desk. The silence of unsmiling men became the deeper, tenser silence of men who fixed him with their eyes. The commander began:

"This is the first breathing spell we've had since that creature came aboard less than—incredible as it may seem—less than two hours ago. I've been glancing through these notes you've given me, and I've divided them into two sections: those that can be discussed while we're putting into effect the purely mechanical plans for cornering the thing—these latter must be discussed now. There are two. First, Zeller!"

The metallurgist stepped forward, a brisk, middle-aged, young-looking man. He started: "The creature made no attempt to keep the drawings which von Grossen showed it—proof, incidentally, that von Grossen was not seized because of the drawings. They fell on the floor; and I picked them up. I've been showing them around, so most of you know that the first drawing is a likeness of the creature stepping through a metal wall; and beside the wall is an enlarged atom system of the type of which the wall is composed—two hundred electrons arranged about the nucleus, forming a series of triangles.

"The second picture was a rough, unfinished but unmistakable single atom of neutronium alloy, with only eight hundred of the forty thousand electrons showing, but the design of each eighty electrons with their sixteen sides clearly indicated. That kind of language is intergalactic; and the creature understood the point instantly. He didn't like it, as we all saw by his actions; but apparently he had no intention of being thwarted; and perhaps saw the difficulty we might have in using such knowledge against him. Because, just as we cannot energize the walls of the whole ship—Pennons has said it would take days—so we have no materials to plate the ship throughout with neutronium alloy. The stuff is too rare.

"However, we have enough for me to build a suit of space armor, with which one of us could search for von Grossen, whom the thing is obviously hiding behind some wall. For the search, naturally, we'd use a fluorite camera. My assistant is already working out the suit, but we'd like suggestions—"

There were none; and, after a moment, Zeller disappeared into the machine shops adjoining the engine room. Morton's grim face relaxed slightly.

"For myself, I feel better knowing that, once the suit is built—in about an hour—the creature will have to keep moving von Grossen in order to prevent us from discovering the body. It's good to know that there's a chance of getting back one of the boldest minds aboard the ship."

"How do you know he's alive?" a man asked.

"Because the creature could have taken Darjeeling's dead body, but didn't. He wants us alive—Smith's notes have given us a possible clue to his purpose, but let that go now. Pennons, outline the plan you have— this is our main plan, gentlemen; and we stand or fall by it."

The chief engineer came forward; and it worried Morton to note that he was frowning blackly. His usually dynamic body lacked briskness and suggested uncertainty. The implications of the lack of confidence were mind-shaking. The mechanical wizard, the man who knew more about energy and its practical application that any other living human being— this man unsure of himself—

His voice added to Morton's dismay. It held a harsh, nasal tone that the commander had never heard from him in all the years he had known the man.

"My news isn't pleasant. To energize this ship under a controlled system would require about a hundred hours. There are approximately two square miles of floors and walls, mostly walls. And of course, as I said before, uncontrolled energization would be suicide.

"My plan is to energize the seventh level and the ninth, only the floors and not the walls. Our hope is this: so far the creature has made no organized attempt to kill us. Korita says that this is because he is a peasant, and does not fully realize the issues at stake. As a peasant he is more concerned with reproduction, though what form that is taking, and why he has captured von Grossen is a matter for our biologist. We know, as apparently he does not, that it's a case of destroy him, or he'll destroy us. Sooner or later, even a peasant will realize that killing us comes first, before anything else, and from that moment we're lost. Our chance is that he'll delay too long—a vague chance, but we must accept it because it is based on the only analysis of the creature that we have—Korita's! If he doesn't interfere with our work, then we'll trap him on the eighth level, between the two energized floors."

Somebody interjected with a swift question: "Why not energize the seventh and eighth levels, so that he'll be in hell the moment he starts down?"

"Because"—Pennons' eyes glittered with a hard, unpleasant light—"when he starts down, he'll have one of us with him. We want that man to have a chance for life. The whole plan is packed with danger. It will take about an hour and a half to prepare the floors for energizing."

His voice became a harsh, grating sound: "And during that ninety minutes we'll be absolutely helpless against him, except for our heavy service guns. It is not beyond the bounds of possibility that he will carry us off at the rate of one every three minutes."

"Thirty out of a hundred and eighty!" Morton cut in with a chill incisiveness. "One out of every six in this room. Do we take the chance? Those in favor raise their hands."

He noted with intense satisfaction that not one man's hand but was raised.

The reappearance of the men brought Xtl up to the seventh level with a rush. A vague anxiety pushed into his consciousness, but there was no real sense of doubt, not even a shadow of the mental sluggishness that had afflicted him at first. For long minutes, he was an abnormal shape that flitted like some evil monster from a forgotten hell through that wilderness of walls and corridors.

Twice he was seen; and ugly guns flashed at him—guns as different from the simple action ato-guns as life from death. He analyzed them from their effects, the way they smashed down the walls, and made hard metal run like water. Heavy duty electronic guns these, discharging completely disintegrated atoms, a stream of pure electrons that sought union with stable matter in a coruscating fury of senseless desire.

He could face guns like that, but only for the barest second would the spinning atom system within his body carry that intolerable load. Even the biologists, who had perfected the Xtl race, had found their limitations in the hot, ravening energy of smashed atoms.

The important thing was: What were the men doing with such determination? Obviously, when they shut themselves up in the impregnable engine room, they had conceived a plan— With glittering, unwinking eyes, Xtl watched that plan take form.

In every corridor, men slaved over atomic furnaces, squat things of dead-black metal. From a hole in the top of each furnace, a white glare spewed up, blazing forth in uncontrollable ferocity at the ceilings; intolerable flares of living fire, dazzling almost beyond endurance to Xtl protected by a solid metal wall as well as by his superlatively conditioned body.

He could see that the men were half dazed by the devastating whiteness that beat against their vision. They wore their space armor with the ordinary transparent glassite electrically darkened. But no light metal armor could ward off the full effect of the deadly rays that sprayed, violent and untamed, in every direction.

Out of the furnaces rolled long dully glowing strips of some material, which were instantly snatched into the maw of machine tools, skillfully hacked into exactly measured sections, and slapped onto the floors. Not an inch of floor, Xtl noticed, escaped being inclosed in some way or another by these strips. And the moment the strips were laid, massive refrigerators hugged close to them, and froze the heat out of them.

His mind refused at first to accept the result of his observations. His brain persisted in searching for deeper purposes, for a cunning of vast and not easily discernible scope. Somewhere there must be a scheme that would explain the appalling effort the men were making. Slowly, he realized the truth.

There was nothing more. These beings were actually intending to attempt the building of walls of force throughout the entire ship under a strict system of controls—anything less, of course, was out of the question. They could not be so foolish as to think that a partial energization could have the faintest hope of success. If such hope smoldered, it was doomed to be snuffed out.

And total energization was equally impossible. Could they not realize that he would not permit such a thing; and that it would be a simple matter to follow them about, and tear loose their energization connections?

In cold contempt, Xtl dismissed the machinations of the men from his mind. They were only playing into his hands, making it easier for him to get the *guuls* he still needed.

He selected his next victim as carefully as he had selected von Grossen. He had discovered in the dead man—Darjeeling—that the stomach was the place he wanted; and the men with the largest stomachs were automatically on his list.

The action was simplicity itself. A cold, merciless survey of the situation from the safety of a wall, a deadly swift rush and—before a single beam could blaze out in sullen rage—he was gone with the writhing, struggling body.

It was simple to adjust his atomic structure the instant he was through a ceiling, and so break his fall on the floor beneath; then dissolve through the floor onto the level below in the same fashion. Into the vast hold of the ship, he half fell, half lowered himself.

The hold was familiar territory now to the sure-footed tread of his long-toed feet. He had explored the place briefly but thoroughly after he first boarded the ship. And the handling of von Grossen had given him the exact experience he needed for this man.

Unerringly, he headed across the dimly lit interior toward the far wall. Great packing cases piled up to the ceiling. Without pause, he leaped into them; and, by dexterous adjustment of his structure, found himself after a moment in a great pipe, big enough for him to stand upright—part of the miles of air-conditioning pipes in the vast ship.

It was dark by ordinary light, but to his full vision a vague twilight glow suffused the place. He saw the body of von Grossen, and deposited his new victim beside the physicist. Carefully now, he inserted one of his slender hands into his own breast; and removed one precious egg—deposited it into the stomach of the human being.

The man had ceased struggling, but Xtl waited for what he knew must happen. Slowly, the body began to stiffen, the muscles growing rigid. The man stirred; then, in evident panic, began to fight as he realized the paralysis that was stealing over him. But remorselessly Xtl held him down.

Abruptly, the chemical action was completed. The man lay motionless, every muscle stiff as a rock, a horrible thing of taut flesh.

There were no doubts now in Xtl's mind. Within a few hours, the eggs would be hatching inside each man's stomach; and in a few hours more the tiny replicas of himself would have eaten themselves to full size.

Grimly complacent, he darted up out of the hold. He needed more hatching places for his eggs, more *guuls*.

On the ninth level now, the men slaved. Waves of heat rolled along the corridor, a veritable inferno wind; even the refrigeration unit in each spacesuit was hard put to handle that furious, that deadly blast of super-heated air. Men sweated in their suits, sick from the heat, dazed by the glare, laboring almost by instinct.

At last, Morton shut off his own furnace. "Thank Heaven, that's finished!" he exclaimed; then urgently:

"Pennons, are you ready to put your plan into effect?"

"Ready, aye, ready!" came the engineer's dry rasp of a voice on the communicators. He finished even more harshly: "Four men gone and one to go. We've been lucky—but there is one to go!"

"Do you hear that, you spacehounds!" Morton barked. "One to go. One of us will be bait—and don't hold your guns in your hands. He must have the chance at that bait. Kellie, elaborate on those notes you gave me before. It will clear up something very important, and keep our minds off that damned thing."

"Er!" The cracked voice of the sociologist jarred the communicators. "Er, here is my reasoning. When we discovered the thing it was floating a million light-years from the nearest system, apparently without means of spatial locomotion. Picture that appalling distance, and then ask yourself how long it would require for an object to float it by pure chance. Gunlie Lester gave me my figures, so I wish he would tell you what he told me."

"Gunlie Lester speaking!" The voice of the astronomer sounded surprisingly brisk. "Most of you know the prevailing theory of the beginnings of the present universe; that it was formed by the disintegration of a *previous* universe several million million years ago, and that a few million million years hence our universe will complete its cycle in a torrent of explosions, and be replaced by another, which will develop from the maelstrom. As for Kellie's question, it is not at all impossible; in fact, it would require several million million years for a creature floating by pure chance to reach a point a million light-years from a planet. That is what you waited, Kellie?"

"Er, yes. Most of you will recall my mentioning before that it was a paradox that a pure sympodial development, such as this creature, did not populate the entire universe. The answer is that, logically, if his race *should* have controlled the universe, then they *did* control it. We human beings have discovered that logic is the sole stable factor in the all; and we cannot shrink even from the most far-reaching conclusions that the mind may arrive at. This race did control the universe, but it was the previous universe they ruled, not our present one. Now, naturally, the creature intends that his race shall also dominate this universe."

"In short," Morton snapped, "we are faced with the survivor of the supreme race of a universe. There is no reason to assume that they arrived at our present level of progress any later than we did; and we've still got several million million years to go before our universe crashes into flaming death. Therefore, they are not only billions of years ahead of us, but millions of millions of years." His voice took on a strained note:

"Frankly, it scares me. We're not doing enough. Our plans are too sketchy. We must have more information before we can hope to win against such a superhuman monster. I'm very much afraid that—"

The shrill scream of a man protruded horribly into his words, and there came a gurgling "—got me ... quick ... ripping me out of my suit—"

The voice collapsed; and somebody shouted in frank dismay:

"Good Heaven! That was Dack, my assistant!"

The world of ship became, for Morton, a long, shining corridor that persisted in blurring before his eyes. And it was suddenly as if he were looking, not out at it, but down into its depths—fearsome depths that made his brain reel.

Ages seemed to pass. But Morton, schooled now to abnormal calm, knew that only fractions of seconds were dragging by. Just as his nerves threatened to break, he heard a voice, Pennons' voice, cool, steady, yet almost unrecognizable:

"One!" said Pennons; and it sounded absolute mumbo-jumbo in that moment when out there another man was going through a hell of fear and torment.

"Two!" said Pennons, cold as ice.

Morton found himself staring curiously at his feet. Sparkling, brilliant, beautiful blue fire throbbed there. Little tendrils of that gorgeous flame reared up hungrily a few inches from his suit, as if baffled by some invisible force protecting the suit.

There was a distinct click in Morton's mind. Instantly, his brain jumped to full gear. In a flash of thought, he realized that Pennons had energized floors seven and nine. And that it was blue ferocity of the energization that was struggling to break through the full-driven screens of his space armor.

Through his communicators came the engineer's hiss of indrawn breath:

"If I'm right," Pennons almost whispered, all the strength gone from his voice, "we've now got that—devil—cornered on the eighth floor."

"Then," barked Morton efficiently, "we'll carry on according to plan. Group one, follow me to the seventh floor."

The men behind Morton stopped short as he halted abruptly at the second corner. Sickly, he went forward, and stood staring at the human body that sagged against the floor, pasted to the metal by almost unbearably brilliant fingers of blue fire. His voice, when he spoke, was only a whisper, but it cut across the strain of silence like a whiplash:

"Pull him loose!"

Two men stepped gingerly forward, and touched the body. The blue fire leaped ravenously at them, straining with futile ferocity to break through the full-driven defense screens of their suits. The men jerked, and the unholy bonds snapped. They carried the body up the nearest stairs to the unenergized eighth level. The other men followed silently, and watched as the body was laid on the floor.

The lifeless thing continued to kick for several minutes, discharging torrents of energy, then gradually took on the quietness of natural death.

"I'm waiting for reports!" Morton said stiffly into his communicators.

Pennons' voice came. "The men are spread out over the eighth floor according to plan, taking continuous pictures with fluorite cameras. If he's anywhere on the floor, we'll get a picture of his swift-moving body; and then it will be a matter of energizing the floor piecemeal. It'll take about thirty minutes yet—"

And finally the report came: "Nothing!" Pennons' voice held an incredulous note tinged with dismay. "Morton, he's not here. It can only mean that he passed through the energized floor as easily as through ordinary metal. We know he must have gone through it because Dack's dead body was on *this* side."

Somebody said hopelessly: "And now what are we going to do?"

Morton didn't answer. It struck him abruptly, with a shock that tore away his breath, that he had no answer.

The silence in that shining corridor was a form of death. It pressed against Morton, a queer, murky, lightless thing. Death was written too in the faces that blurred around him, the cold, logical death expectancy of men who could see no way out.

Morton broke the silence:

"I am willing to accept von Grossen's analysis of how the thing passes through metal. But he intimated the creature recoiled from the energized wall. Can anyone explain then—how?"

"Zeller speaking!" The brisk voice of the metallurgist came through the communicators. "I've finished the neutronium-alloy suit, and I've started my search at the bottom of the ship—I heard your question, Morton. To my mind, we missed one point the first time the creature struck the wall of force: The point is that he *was* in it. And what basic difference is there between being partially inside the wall, and actually passing through? He could pass through in less than a second. The first time, he touched the wall for several seconds, which probably means that, in his surprise, he recoiled and lost his balance. That must have made his position very unpleasant. The second time, however, he simply released poor Dack and passed on through with a minimum of discomfort."

"Hm-m-m!" Morton pondered. "That means he's still vulnerable to walls of force, provided we could keep him inside one for a long enough time. And that would mean complete energization of the ship which, in turn, would depend on his allowing us to make the connections without interference. I think he would interfere. He let us get away with energizing the two floors because he knew it didn't mean anything—and it gave him a good opportunity to kidnap some more men. Fortunately, he didn't grab off as many as we expected, though Heaven help those four."

Smith said grimly, his first words in a long time:

"My firm opinion is that anything that would require more than two hours to complete will be fatal. We are dealing with a creature who has everything to gain by killing us, and obtaining control of the ship. Zeller, how long would it take to build neutronium-alloy suits for every man on this ship?"

"About two hundred hours," the metallurgist replied coolly, "mainly because I used up nearly all the available alloy for this one suit. We'd have to break down the walls of the ship, and build the alloy from an electronic base. We're not in the habit of carrying a lot of metal on this ship, as you know, because there's usually a planet a few minutes from anywhere. Now, we've still got a two weeks' trip either way."

"Then that's out!" frowned Smith blackly. He looked stunned. "And since the complete energization is out—we've got nothing else."

The usually lazy voice of Gourlay, the communications chief, snapped: "I don't see why those ways are out. We're still alive; and I suggest we get to work, and do as much as we can as soon as we can—everybody working first at making suits for the men who go out to prepare the walls for energizing. At least, that will protect them from being kidnapped."

"What makers you think," Smith asked coldly, "that the creature is not capable of smashing down neutronium alloy? As a superior being, his knowledge of physics should make it a simple matter for him to construct a beam that could destroy anything we have. Heaven knows there's plenty of tools lying in the various laboratories."

The two men glared at each other with the flashing, angry eyes of men whose nerves have been strained to the utmost limit. Before Morton could speak, Korita's sibilant voice cut across the tense silence:

"I am inclined to agree with Smith. We are dealing with a being who must now know that he cannot allow us time for anything important. I agree with the commander when he says that the creature will interfere if we attempt to prepare the ship for complete controlled energization. The honorable gentlemen must not forget, however, that we are dealing with a creature whom we have decided is in the peasant stage of his particular cycle.

"Let me enlarge on that. Life is an ebb and flow. There is a full tide of glorious accomplishment, and a low tide of recuperation. For generations, centuries, the blood flows in the peasant, turgid, impure, gathering strength from the soil; and then it begins to grow, to expand, reaching finally for the remotest stars. At this point, amazingly enough, the blood grows weary; and, in this late megapolitan era, men no longer desire to prolong their race. Highly cultivated people regard having children as a question of pros and cons, and their general outlook on life is tinged with a noble skepticism.

"Nature, on the other hand, knows nothing of pro and con. You cannot reason with a peasant—and he cannot reason except as a peasant. His land and his son, or—to put a higher term to it—his property and his blood are sacred. If a bourgeoisie court orders him off his land, he fights blindly, ignorantly, for his own. It matters not to him that he may have accepted money for a mortgage. He only knows they're trying to take his property, to draw his roots from the soil where his blood has been nourished.

"Honorable sirs, here is my point: This creature cannot begin to imagine anyone else not feeling about his patch of home—his own property—the way he does.

"But we ... we can make such a sacrifice without suffering a spiritual collapse."

Every muscle in Morton's body grew taut, as he realized the implications. His exclamation was almost a whisper: "Korita, you've got it! It means sacrificing von Grossen and the others. It means sacrifice that makes my brain reel, but property is not sacred to us. And as for von Grossen and the other three"—his voice grew stern and hard, his eyes wide with a chill horror—"I didn't tell you about the notes that Smith gave me. I didn't tell you because he suggested a possible parallel with a certain species of wasp back home on the earth. The thought is so horrible that I think instantaneous death will come as a release to these bold men."

"The wasp!" A man gasped. "You're right, Morton. The sooner they're dead the better!"

"Then," Morton cried, "to the engine room. We—"

A swift, excited voice clamored into his communicators; it was a long second before he recognized it as belonging to Zeller, the metallurgist:

"Morton—quick! Down to the hold! I've found them—in the air-conditioning pipe. The creature's here, and I'm holding him off as best I can. He's trying to sneak up on me through the walls. Hurry!"

Morton snapped orders with machine-gun precision, as the men swarmed toward the elevators:

"Smith, take a dozen men and get Kent down from the bedrooms to the engine room. I'd almost forgotten about him and his broken leg! Pennons, take a hundred men to the engine room and make the preparations to carry out Korita's plan. The rest take the four heavy freight elevators and follow me!"

He finished in a ringing voice:

"We won't kill him in the hold of course, unless he's gone stark mad. But the crisis has come! Things are breaking our way at last. And we've got him! We've got him!"

Xtl retreated reluctantly, sullenly, as the men carried off his four *guuls*. The first shrinking fear of defeat closed over his mind like the night that brooded beyond the inclosing walls of the ship. His impulse was to dash into their midst, a whirlwind of ferocity, and smash them. But those ugly, glittering weapons congealed that wild rage.

He retreated with a dismaying sense of disaster, conscious that he had lost the initiative. The men would discover his eggs now; and, in destroying them, would destroy his immediate chances of being reinforced by other Xtls. And, what was more, they were temporarily safe in the engine room.

His brain spun into a cold web of purpose. From this moment, he must kill, and kill only. It seemed suddenly incredible that he had thought first of reproduction, with everything else coming secondary, even his every other thought blurred by that subordination to his one flaming desire.

His proper action was preternaturally clear now. Not to get his *guuls* first, but to kill these dangerous enemies, to control the ship, then head for the nearest inhabited planet, where it would be a simple matter to find other, more stupid *guuls*.

To kill he must have an irresistible weapon, one that could smash—anything! And valuable time had already been wasted. After a moment's thought, he headed for the nearest laboratory, conscious of a burning urgency, unlike anything he had ever known.

As he worked—tall, nightmare body and hideous face bent intently over the gleaming metal of the queer-shaped mechanism—his sensitive feet grew aware of a difference in the symphony of vibrations that throbbed in discordant melody through the ship.

He paused, straightened, alert and tense; and realized what it was. The drive engines were silent. The monster ship of space had halted in its headlong flight, and was lying quiescent in the black deeps.

An abrupt, indefinable sense of urgency came to Xtl—an icy alarm. His long, black, wirelike fingers became flashing things as he made delicate connections, deftly and frantically.

Suddenly, he paused again. Through his brain pulsed a distinct sensation of something wrong, dangerously, desperately, terribly wrong. The muscles of his feet grew taut with straining. Abruptly, he knew what it was.

He could no longer feel the vibrations of the men. *They had left the ship!*

Xtl whirled from his nearly finished weapon, and plunged through the nearest wall. He knew his doom with a burning certainty that found hope only in the blackness of space.

Through deserted corridors he fled, slavering slit-faced hate, scarlet monster from ancient, incredibly ancient Glor. The gleaming walls seemed to mock him. The whole world of the great ship, which had promised so much, was now only the place where sudden intolerable hell would break loose in a devastating, irresistible torrent of energy.

He saw the air lock ahead—and flashed through the first section, then the second, the third—then he was out in space. There was a sense of increasing lightness as his body flung by momentum darted from the side of the ship, out into that blackest of black nights.

For a brief instant, his body glinted and flashed a startling scarlet, reflecting the dazzling light from the row on row of brilliant portholes.

The queerest thing happened then. The porthole lights snuffed out, and were replaced by a strange, unearthly blue glow, that flashed out from every square inch of that dark, sweeping plain of metal.

The blue glow faded, died. Some of the porthole lights came on again, flickering weakly, uncertainly; and then, as mighty engines recovered from that devastating flare of blue power, the lights already shining grew stronger. Others began to flash on.

Xtl was a hundred yards from the ship when he saw the first of the torpedolike craft dart out of the surrounding night, into an opening that yawned in the side of the mighty vessel. Four other dark craft followed, whipping down in swift arcs, their shapes blurred against the background of immensity, vaguely visible in the light that glowed now, strong and steady from the lighted portholes.

The opening shut; and—just like that—the ship vanished. One instant, it was there, a vast sphere of dark metal; the next he was staring through the space where it had been at a vague swirl of light, an enormous galaxy that swam beyond a gulf of a billion years.

Time dragged drearily toward infinity. Xtl sprawled moveless and unutterably hopeless on the bosom of endless night. He couldn't help thinking of the sturdy sons he might have had, and of the universe that was lost because of his mistakes. But it was the thought of the sons, of companionship, that really brought despair.

Morton watched the skillful fingers of the surgeon, as the electrified knife cut into the fourth man's stomach. The last egg was deposited in the bottom of the tall neutronium alloy vat.

The eggs were round, grayish objects, one of them slightly cracked.

As they watched, the crack widened; an ugly, round, scarlet head with tiny, beady eyes and a tiny slit of a mouth poked out. The head twisted on its short neck, and the eyes glittered up at them with a hard ferocity.

And then, with a swiftness that almost took them by surprise, it reared up and tried to run out of the vat, slid back—and dissolved into the flame that Morton poured down upon it.

Smith, licking his dry lips, said: "Suppose he'd got away, and dissolved into the nearest wall!"

Nobody said anything. They stood with intent eyes, staring into the vat. The eggs melted reluctantly, under the merciless fire of Morton's gun, and then burned with a queer, golden light.

"Ah," said Dr. Eggert; and attention turned to him, and the body of von Grossen, over which he was bending. "His muscles are beginning to relax, and his eyes are open and alive. I imagine he knows what's going on. It was a form of paralysis induced by the egg, and fading now that the egg is no longer present. Nothing fundamentally wrong. They'll all be O. K. shortly. What about the big fellow?"

Morton replied: "Zeller swears he saw a flash of red emerge from the main lock just as we swept the ship with uncontrolled energization. It must have been, because we haven't found his body. However, Pennons is out with half the men, taking pictures with fluorite cameras; and we'll know for certain in a few hours. Here he is now. Well, Pennons?"

The engineer strode in briskly, and placed a misshapen thing of metal on one of the tables. "Nothing definite to report yet—but I found this in the main physics laboratory. What do you make of it?"

Morton frowned down at the fragile-looking object with its intricate network of wires. There were three distinct tubes that might have been muzzles running into and through three small, round balls, that shone with a queer, silvery light. The light penetrated the table, making it as transparent as glassite. And, strangest of all, the balls radiated, not heat, but cold.

Morton put his hands near, but the cold was of a mild, water-freezing variety, apparently harmless. He touched the metal ball. It felt as chilled metal might feel.

"I think we'd better leave this for our chief physicist to examine. Von Grossen ought to be up and around soon. You say you found it in the laboratory?"

Pennons nodded; and Morton carried on his thought: "Obviously, the creature was working on it, when he suspected that something was amiss—he must have suspected the truth, for he left the ship. That seems to discount your theory, Korita. You said that, as a true peasant, he couldn't even imagine what we were going to do."

The Japanese historian smiled faintly through the fatigue that paled his face. "Honorable commander," he said politely, "a peasant can realize destructive intentions as easily as you or I. What he cannot do is bring himself to destroy his own property, or imagine others destroying theirs. We have no such limitations."

Pennons groaned: "I wish we had. Do you know that it will take us three months at least to get this ship properly repaired after thirty seconds of uncontrolled energization. For those thirty seconds, the ship created a field in space millions of times more intense than the energization output. I was afraid that—"

He stopped with a guilty look. Morton grinned: "Go ahead and finish what you were going to say. You were afraid the ship would be completely destroyed. Don't worry, Pennons, your previous statements as to the danger involved made us realize the risks we were taking; and we knew that our lifeboats could only be given partial anti-acceleration; so we'd have been stranded here a million years from home."

A man said, thoughtfully: "Well, personally, I think there was nothing actually to fear. After all, he did belong to another universe, and there is a special rhythm to our present state of existence to which man is probably attuned. We have the advantage in this universe of momentum, which, I doubt a creature from any other universe could hope to overcome. And in the world of man there is no just place for a creature that can even consider laying its eggs in the living flesh of other sensitive beings. All other intelligent life would unite against such a distinctly personal menace."

Smith shook his head: "There is no biological basis for your opinion, and therefore it falls in the category of 'things darkly spoken are darkly seen.' It dominated once, and it could dominate again. You assume far too readily that man is a paragon of justice, forgetting apparently that he lives on meat, enslaves his neighbors, murders his opponents, and obtains the most unholy sadistical joy from the agony of others. It is not impossible that we shall, in the course of our travels, meet other intelligent creatures far more worthy than man to rule the universe."

"By Heaven!" replied the other, "no creature is ever getting on board this ship again, no matter how harmless he looks. My nerves are all shot; and I'm not so good a man as I was when I first came aboard the *Beagle* two long years ago."

"You speak for us all!" said Morton.

AFTERWORD

A. E. van Vogt was always a favorite of mine. Joe Rico has already done most of the hard work in selecting the stories.

Hopefully you have read the stories before reading this. Van Vogt's first story, "Black Destroyer" leads off this collection. "Discord in Scarlet", written shortly thereafter, ends the collection. Those two, along with "War of Nerves" (also in this volume), were incorporated into the novel *Voyage of the Space Beagle*. Bob Eggleton's cover illustrates the former story. "The Monster" has been reprinted as "Resurrection" in some later publications. I think that "Resurrection" is more suggestive of where the story is progressing, and thus felt that "The Monster" was the better title to use. Due to space limitations, while "Asylum" was included, "The Proxy Intelligence", its sequel, was unfortunately not. "The Ghost" comes from *Unknown* and is a good example of van Vogt's fantasy stories. Finally, in reading "The Search" (most likely written in 1942 since it was published in January 1943) did you notice what was a very good description of a "Polaroid Camera"?

I could go on, but the rest of the space properly belongs to those people who helped make this book exist.

Priscilla Olson chose not to be listed as one of the "Editors," but she is in fact an editor in everything but name. Mark Olson and Sharon Sbarsky provided critical help in proofreading. Ann Broomhead, Tim Szczesuil, Dave Anderson, David Grubbs, Tony Lewis and Gay Ellen Dennett also provided special assistance in my time of need. George Flynn proofread many but unfortunately not all of the stories. I therefore plead guilty for the typos still remaining in the book.

Rick Katze
12/10/02

SOURCES

"The Man in the Labyrinth" by Joe Rico is original to this volume.
"Alfred E. van Vogt" by Hal Clement is original to this volume.
"Asylum" *Astounding Science Fiction*, May 1942.
"Black Destroyer" *Astounding Science Fiction*, July 1939.
"A Can of Paint" *Astounding Science Fiction*, September 1944.
"Dear Pen Pal" *Arkham Sampler*, 1949.
"Discord in Scarlet" *Astounding Science Fiction*, December 1939.
"Don't Hold Your Breath" *Savings Worlds*, 1973.
"Dormant" *Startling Stories*, November 1948.
"The Enchanted Village" *Other Worlds*, July 1950.
"Far Centaurus" *Astounding Science Fiction*, November 1944.
"Film Library" *Astounding Science Fiction*, July 1946.
"Final Command" *Astounding Science Fiction*, November 1949.
"Future Perfect" *Vertex*, August 1973.
"The Ghost" *Unknown Worlds*, August 1942.
"The Great Engine" *Astounding Science Fiction*, July 1943.
"The Great Judge" *Fantasy Book* V1 #3, 1948.
"The Harmonizer" *Astounding Science Fiction*, November 1944.
"The Monster" *Astounding Science Fiction*, August 1948.
"Recruiting Station" *Astounding Science Fiction*, March 1942.
"The Rulers" *Astounding Science Fiction*, January 1944.
"The Rull" *Astounding Science Fiction*, May 1948.
"The Search" *Astounding Science Fiction*, January 1943.
"Secret Unattainable" *Astounding Science Fiction*, July 1942.
"The Sound" Astounding *Science Fiction, February* 1950.
"Vault of the Beast" *Astounding Science Fiction*, August 1940.
"War of Nerves" *Other Worlds*, May 1950.
"Afterword" by Rick Katze is original to this volume.

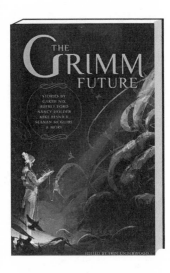

EBOOKS

The Halcyon Fairy Book
by T. Kingfisher

The Halcyon Fairy Book is a delightful collection of wry and insightful comments on traditional fairy tales, originally presented in her blog, along with her first collection of fairy-tale-inspired original work, *Toad Words,* previously only available as a self-published ebook.

$6.95 ebook

Making Conversation
by Teresa Nielsen Hayden

Twenty-two years ago, there was *Making Book.* It was a finalist for the 1995 Hugo Award for Best Nonfiction Book, but lost out to the dead guy. It's been through three printings and is still available from NESFA Press.

Making Conversation is available from NESFA Press in softcover and ebook form. 222 pages, 59 essays (long and short) about time, space, genre, editing, gardening, saints, libraries, food, democracy, drink, insanity, fear, hamsters, chaos, moderation, palimpsests, fanfic, clichés, books, slush, spelling, scams, sleep, fantasy, policing, infundibula, trolls, writing, knitting, fandom, habaneros, exposition, management, Selectrics, Brooklyn, literary agents, pygmy mammoths, and the true cure for scurvy.

$6.95 ebook

www.nesfapress.org

EBOOKS

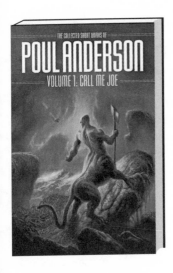

Call Me Joe: Volume 1 of the Collected Short Works of Poul Anderson

This first in a series presents the very best of the short works of fantasy and science fiction produced over Poul Anderson's 50-year writing career. The full series of seven volumes includes all of Anderson's Hugo- and Nebula-nominated and winning short stories.

Poul Anderson won seven Hugos and three Nebulas over his career. He was named a Grand Master by the Science Fiction and Fantasy Writers of America in 1998.

$6.95 ebook

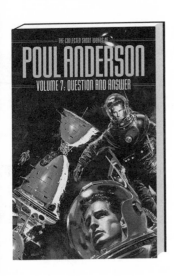

Question and Answer: Volume 7 of the Collected Short Works of Poul Anderson

This seventh in a series presents more of the very best of the short works of fantasy and science fiction produced over Poul Anderson's 50-year writing career. The full series of seven volumes includes all of Anderson's Hugo- and Nebula-nominated and winning short stories.

Poul Anderson won seven Hugos and three Nebulas for his writing. He was named a Grand Master by the Science Fiction and Fantasy Writers of America in 1998.

$6.95 ebook

NESFA
PRESS

www.nesfapress.org

HARDCOVER BOOKS

The Queen of Air and Darkness: Volume 2 of the Short Fiction of Poul Anderson

This multi-volume series includes the very best of the short works by Poul Anderson, including all of his Hugo- and Nebula-nominated and winning short stories. Volume 2 includes two of Anderson's Hugo and Nebula award-winning stories, "The Queen of Air and Darkness", and "The Longest Voyage".

Poul Anderson won seven Hugos and three Nebulas over his career. He was named a Grand Master by the Science Fiction and Fantasy Writers of America in 1998.

$29 hardcover | $6.95 ebook

The Saturn Game: Volume 3 the Short Fiction of Poul Anderson

The Saturn Game is the third in a multi-volume series including the very best of the short works by Poul Anderson. Volume 3 includes three of Anderson's Hugo and Nebula award-winning stories, "The Saturn Game", "No Truce with Kings", and "Hunter's Moon".

Poul Anderson won seven Hugos and three Nebulas over his career. He was named a Grand Master by the Science Fiction and Fantasy Writers of America in 1998.

$29 hardcover | ebook forthcoming

NESFA
PRESS

www.nesfapress.org

HARDCOVER BOOKS

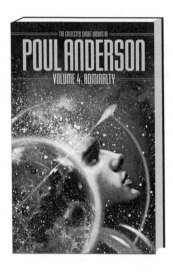

Admiralty: Volume 4 of the Collected Short Works of Poul Anderson

Admiralty: The Collected Short Works of Poul Anderson (volume 4) includes "Admiralty", a story of colonies on other planets in conflict with an alien empire, "Goat Song", the Hugo- and Nebula-award-winning story about a man's determination to bring his lost love back to life, "Operation Changeling", a world where magic and demons co-exist, "Delenda Est", a story of the Time Patrol and the choices that must be made to keep our existence intact, "The Adventure of the Misplaced Hound", co-written with Gordon R. Dickson, where aliens have recreated a portion of their planet as Victorian England with Scotland Yard and Sherlock Holmes, "Marius", which shows that the only thing we learn from history is history, and the delightful "Inside Straight", in which an understanding of poker defeats an invasion.

$29 hardcover | ebook forthcoming

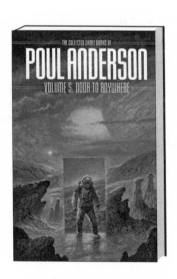

Door to Anywhere: Volume 5 of the Collected Short Works of Poul Anderson

Door to Anywhere is the fifth in a multi-volume compendium of Poul Anderson's best works from a writing career that spanned more than 50 years. This volume contains stories about Manse Everard and Wanda Tamberly, Dominic Flandry, the Hokas, Nicholas van Rijn, and Stephen Matuchek and Virginia Graylock.

$29 hardcover | ebook forthcoming

NESFA
PRESS

www.nesfapress.org

HARDCOVER BOOKS

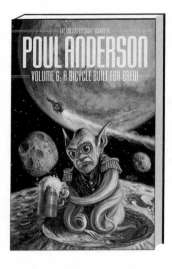

A Bicycle Built for Brew: Volume 6 of the Collected Short Works of Poul Anderson

A Bicycle Built for Brew mixes beer, a talking parrot guaranteed to repeat phrases laced with 4-letter indignities, a romance between an English lass and a Scottish soldier, and the need to communicate the fact of the invasion to authorities on a nearby asteroid in a very humorous tale. The original version of *Three Hearts and Three Lions,* long unavailable except in the 1953 magazines, in which Holger Carlsen, fighting the Nazis, is transported to a world where magic works and a growing battle between good and evil is raging. *Silent Victory* in which Mars has defeated Earth in a war but things are never that simple. "Territory" features Nicholas van Rijn, *A Plague of Masters* features Dominic Flandry, and *The Snows of Ganymede.*

$29 hardcover | ebook forthcoming

A Lit Fuse: The Provocative Life of Harlan Ellison

In late 2011 Harlan Ellison—the multi-award-winning writer of speculative fiction and famously litigious personality—did two uncharacteristic things. First, he asked biographer Nat Segaloff if he'd be interested in writing his life story. Second, he gave Segaloff full control. The result is the long-anticipated *A Lit Fuse: The Provocative Life of Harlan Ellison.* The expansive biography, which is the first such project in which Ellison has permitted large portions of his varied works to appear, is published by NESFA Press.

$29 hardcover

NESFA
PRESS

www.nesfapress.org